Oh, Promised Land

Oh, Promised Land

* *

BY JAMES STREET

THE DIAL PRESS · NEW YORK

DESIGNED BY PETER DÖBLIN
COPYRIGHT, 1940, BY JAMES STREET
PRINTED IN THE UNITED STATES OF AMERICA
BY THE HADDON CRAFTSMEN, INC.
SCRANTON, PA.
FOURTEENTH PRINTING

To my family including
Harold Matson

I wish to express my gratitude to my publishers for their faith and patience, to my secretary, Miss Alice Post, for her patience, and, above all, to Lucy Nash, who took the book apart several times but always helped me put it back together again.

JAMES STREET

*The Barricades
Old Lyme, Conn.
February, 1940*

Oh, Promised Land

1

SAM DABNEY leaned his spade against a tree and was careful with the hickory handle, for a good spade was a valuable implement and must be protected. His father had
worked five days shaping the handle, after waiting a
season for it to cure. The iron head of the spade had out-
lasted four handles. It had come from a hunk of good
ore up in the hills and had been fetched from Virginia.
So had Sam. The iron had done its job well, digging the
earth into furrows, graves, ditches and other things that
men needed, or thought they needed. The metal was of
good temper and had been in the Dabney family for
twenty-four years, two years longer than Sam.

Sam wiped his wide brow with the back of his hand
and flipped the sweat away. Some of it sprinkled the
earth he had turned, red earth from a wound in the virgin
land of the Chattahoochee country. He towered over
Honoria, his sister, who was smoothing the earth with a
leafless bough.

"I'm of a mind," he said, "to leave a marked stone here
so we'll know where our father and mother are buried."

Honoria got to her feet and sighed, then grunted
"Ummmm" and clasped her hands behind her neck, to
stretch the kinks in her muscles. Sweat was on her upper
lip and on her neck, and it rolled down her back and
between her breasts. She held her bodice from her flesh

and let the breeze cool her. Her back hurt but she did not complain. It was natural for her back to hurt because she had been working. When she used her muscles she expected them to ache, and there was no need to say anything about it. Fatigue was the natural consequence of hard work, she knew.

At sixteen, Honoria Dabney knew many important things. She knew why the travelers who passed by the Dabney homestead always stared at her when she stooped over the well to lift out the bucket. And she enjoyed stooping over the well just a bit lower than was necessary. When men looked at her, her flesh tingled and her breasts felt full and tight. She couldn't explain it but she enjoyed it, and surely men could do her no harm simply by looking at her. If they enjoyed staring at her and she enjoyed being stared at, then there was a pleasure that could be had without paying a price. Once Sam had knocked a man down because he had stared at her too long. It pleased her that her brother would fight for her and there was as much thrill in watching Sam fight as in having men look at her.

She liked the way he threw back his head and shook his long hair from around his ears when he was angry. She had tried to imitate the gesture, but her hair wouldn't fall free as Sam's did. It would form into curly knots about her shoulders and when it was sticky with sweat or wet with rain, as it often was, the curls became tighter. Her hair was so black that it looked almost blue, and her eyes were as blue as her hair sometimes appeared. Sam's hair was just as black, and his eyes were just as blue, but sometimes there was a hardness about Sam's eyes. Honoria never allowed her eyes to seem hard. She was wise enough to know that a woman can do more with her eyes than with her hips.

12

Her calicut dress with the tight bodice clung to her body, and again she pulled the heavy damp cloth from her flesh. She wiped her bare feet on the grass and lifted her dress and wiped her hands on the hem, to dry them well before she untied her bodice and exposed her breasts to the cooling air. Then she tied her bodice again and walked to her brother. Her head scarcely reached to his chest, but she looked up and smiled at him, a quick smile of confidence, understanding and sympathy. Sam smiled, too, a slow, warm smile that changed his whole face from somber bitterness and dread to determination and pride. He seldom smiled, and when he did it usually was for Honoria.

"Shouldn't we leave a head-stone?" he repeated.

"This thing," she said, "has upset you and dulled your wits. Don't be a sentimental loony. The Creeks will find the grave if we mark it. Our father and mother died with their scalps and it would be a prime shame if they lost them now. And you know how it is with the red 'uns."

"But the grass will take this place and we'll not know where our people are buried," said Sam.

"Ay. But it is wise. Have you forgotten so soon what our father always said? 'Of what use is a grave to the living; only a place to weep.' We must let the grass have the grave, Sam'l, or our people's scalps will hang from some Red Stick's belt." She jerked a tuft of saw-grass from the earth, scooped a hole in the grave and planted it, to help the land hide the scar quickly before the Creeks came again. "We'll never be this way, Sam'l. We're alone, and we have our plans."

He got on his knees and helped her plant grass on the grave. "You're a sharp girl, Hon; sharp as a meat ax." They worked in silence until Sam patted the grass with

13

his foot and said, "Maybe I should say something, or do something."

"We've done all we can do." Honoria leaned against the tree, near the spade. "But it might be fitting for you to say something. You remember how our mother was about praying."

"But our father didn't believe in God."

"And I wonder who was right." Honoria stared at the grass they had set out. The grave was almost hidden. The vines should be there soon, then the saplings. The trees would shield the grave from the Indians.

Honoria put her hand on her brother's arm, and when he looked at her she said, "Do you believe in God, Sam'l?"

"I do when I'm scared," he whispered, as though he were afraid godless old man Dabney would hear him and fling back the dirt and grass, and climb out of his grave and jeer his only son. Then Sam tilted his head until his long hair fell between his shoulder blades, closed his eyes and said, "Never has the iron entered so deeply into my heart." He reckoned it was a fitting prayer. He had heard his schoolmaster up in Virginia say the words. They were pretty words and must mean something.

He handed the spade to Honoria and lifted his father's Tower musket from the ground, glancing expertly at the powder in the pan. He looked around quickly, but not at the grave, and nodded to his sister, and they walked out of the woods and across a clearing to the Dabney homestead where they would gather their housen goods and move on. They had a plan. . . .

Sam walked five paces behind his sister. If Indians were ahead, he would see them, and if they attacked from the rear, they must pass him to reach Honoria. He bit his lower lip as his eyes moved from left to right, scouting the woods. He always bit his lower lip when he was worried. He walked on the balls of his feet, so quietly that Honoria could not hear him. Frequently he cocked his huge head to one side to distinguish sounds. His long hair dangled to his shoulders and was tied loosely behind his neck with a bit of rawhide. Often his hair slipped over his ears and he would toss his head to keep his big ears free. A man was a fool to let his hair cover his ears in the Indian country. His father used to say that if Sam had grown another inch he would have forked again. He stood six feet two, and weighed two hundred pounds. His mouth was broad and firm, sensuous but never generous. There was a brutal hardness about his mouth, too, when he clamped his teeth together and buttoned his lips into a thin line. The only things about him that seemed tender were his eyes when he smiled, and his hands at all times.

They were huge hands, but the fingers were long and tapering. They were good hands. He had a way of twisting his hair around his left index finger while in thought. Sometimes he ran his right hand across his forehead and sometimes he tapped a tune on the butt of his musket with his left fingers. His hands were never still. His shoulders were massive and his muscles rippled under his shirt of homespun—stringy muscles, never knotty. His legs were so long and his hips so narrow that he looked somewhat like an oaken beam supported by a lithe sapling. His easy swinging gait gave him the appearance of walking a bit sideways, his left shoulder forward.

Honoria, without slackening her pace, looked back at her brother and nodded quickly toward the woods ahead. Sam let his musket slide out of the crook of his arm and rested the butt lightly in his right hand. He focused his eyes on the woods and studied every tree, every bush.

"A doe," he spoke softly to his sister.

"Ay," she said without looking back. "I see her now."

"Are you tired?"

She glanced over her shoulder again and smiled. "A bit. Burying the dead is hard work."

"If you're tired, Hon, we can rest awhile."

"I'm not that tired," she said. "We'd better go on now that we've started. We have many things to do."

He caught up with her and put his arm around her and she lay her head against his chest. Sam stroked her hair gently. "Everything will be all right," he said.

"I know it will." She grasped his right arm with both of hers and clung to him. "We're all by ourselves now, Sam'l. But I have you and you have me. It will always be that way."

"Ay, it will always be that way." He patted her shoulder and they walked away again, Honoria five paces ahead of her brother, so that he could protect her if need be.

The settlers in the disputed Chattahoochee country always spoke of Sam and Honoria as "old man Dabney's brats" and believed that any issue of the Irish infidel was bound, by the laws of heredity, to be without merit. Old man Dabney and his bride had migrated to Virginia from Loughbricklin, Ireland, and had settled in the hills. He had no business grudge against England, and the Tidewater patriots called him a Tory because he wouldn't fight the King's troops and because he laughed at the Sons of Liberty. The Liberty boys, full of rum and patriotism, rode to his house one night and called him from his bed and demanded that he take a stand.

Old man Dabney had defied them mockingly. "I'm taking a stand, 'ygod. I'm standing right here and you leave me be or I'll blow you off of my land. Sons of

Liberty! Pups without your eyes open, that's what you be! Go out and die for those thieves and money-changers down at Tidewater. Be fools, but leave me be. I'd as leave serve a king in England as a king in America, because the king in England is not so nigh."

His barn had been burned the next night.

Sam and Honoria were born in Virginia and there Sam had studied with a schoolmaster, a hill Virginian, profound in his prejudices. He said that all Tories, lobster-backs and blue-noses were the scum of hell and, when it came to money matters, would steal a bit off a dead man's eye and kick him because it wasn't a sovereign. He knew that Sam's father had been branded a Tory, but uttered the insult deliberately, and before all the school children.

Sam had kicked the master in the groin and old man Dabney, unable to buy or sell in Virginia, moved his sickly wife and their two children to Georgia where even a King's man and a non-conformist Irishman might live and let live, cultivate his own land, earn his salt and rear his brood which, after all, was the maximum any man could expect from life. The Dabneys settled along the Chattahoochee, on land that belonged to the Creek Nation by the law of the tomahawk, but to old man Dabney by the law of his Tower musket.

He was there when the British finally struck at Georgia and he had walked to western North Carolina where the mountaineers were mustering in.

"La," the recruiting officer had said. "A Tory! Damme, Dabney. Reckoned you were for the British."

"I am, but they are too dom'd nigh," old man Dabney said. "I had them for neighbors and creditors in Ireland and I won't have them here. The Methodists and mouthing loonies, such as you, are all a body can suffer. I'll have no lobster-backs marching over my land and quartering in my house, 'ygod. I am offering you my gun shoulder, which you need. And my brains, which you need more. But hear this. After I drive the British out of these hills, I'm going home. I won't stay in your army, and you can report that to Elijah Clarke or Gen'l Dan'l 'ygod Morgan. What is your say?"

"Sign here," said the recruiting officer. "And if you don't hit your man between the eyes, it's a miss."

At King's Mountain he killed his quota of British soldiers and robbed them of twenty pieces of gold. Then he walked away, back to Georgia, and worked his land while other men gathered along the seaboard and founded a republic, about which old man Dabney knew little and cared less.

He had mapped his son's course of life early, but hadn't wasted time planning for his daughter. He reckoned Sam could shoot his way to prosperity, then trade himself to leadership among the Scots and Irish and Jews who were swarming into West Georgia and spilling over the Chattahoochee, settling as far south and west as the Alabamu tribe. The settlers needed scouts, for the Alabamu were the craftiest and bloodiest Muscogees of the Creek Confederacy.

Sam had agreed with his father's plans. A boy planned his life early on the Southwestern frontier in 1795, for there always was the probability that he wouldn't live long. He would scout the settlers as far west as they wanted to go, to the Alabama River, perhaps, and, if any were loonies enough to venture into the Choctaw domains he would lead them there. The fees for scouting were high, as high as $30 a month and keep if a scout could furnish fresh meat to boot. Some settlers, particularly the Scots and Jews, would accept venison as good meat. Immigrants from Sligo and Mayo, and the poor

18

hills of Scotia, even would eat wild duck and turkey every day without complaint. God's navel! They were poor folks, eating duck and turkey without bread. Why, even slaves objected to such fare and the law saw that slaves were not fed duck but thrice weekly. Beef—that was the food! A scout who could furnish beef was a bargain at $50 monthly, payable in hard money, of course, for goods were dear. And if a scout stood up for his just dues, he could get transportation for his swapping goods and smuggle in a bit of rum and powder to the Creeks. If the red 'uns got out of hand, it was easy enough to scalp them and take back the powder and the remainder of the rum. Scalps fetched bounties. If the red 'uns didn't get noisy, who was to say they hadn't? Who would believe an Indian? It was a simple way to make money. You traded rum for hides and beeswax, then killed the Indians, salvaged what goods you could, and collected for the scalps.

There was a factory just beyond the Chattahoochee that handled the red 'uns properly. A Scot was the factor at the trading post and he, by choosing the time and event, could get a Creek drunk on a pint of rum, mixed, of course. For three pints of rum he once got a hundred pounds of beeswax, a horse and a fresh maiden, but only got one scalp. He confessed later that he had nipped with his customers and his aim was bad. Another time he miscalculated and used a quart of rum to get a red 'un drunk and got only two beeves for the deal. Whereupon he wrote a letter to the Indian agent that the Creeks were bankrupting him and demanded that militia be sent to punish the thieves.

Sam knew he could steal beef from the Creeks and furnish his settlers with good meat. Then he could kill the Creeks. Scalps of marauding red 'uns were fetching ready money in Georgia. It was paper money, for sure, but paper money could be traded for hard money or tobacco. Old man Dabney told his son, "To hell with paper money. It's of no account even if the United States of North America is behind it. You notice the government agents pay themselves in gold. If paper money is of any account, why don't they pay themselves with it?"

He told Sam to get goods and trade them for tobacco, for tobacco always would be legal tender and the settlers always would be willing to pay a long hunter for scalps of marauding Indians, and every Indian was a marauder. Perhaps the settlers would pay a bounty for other varmints. God's jawbone! Up in Tidewater, the Virginians were paying a bounty for bears, and the hunter could keep the hides. But Tidewater folks were loony, anyhow. Old man Dabney swore he had seen a Virginian bathe all over in an iron tub. And he had seen another man, or so he vowed, clean his teeth with salt and a sweet-gum brush. His neighbors said you couldn't find the truth in old man Dabney if you cut him open and looked for it. You couldn't believe a man who didn't believe in God. What could he swear by?

Sam reckoned he could earn $50 a month scouting settlers, a goodly sum as bounties for his scalps and a neat profit on his own goods, rum and powder. Georgia had repealed its prohibition law, passed by Oglethorpe, but rum still was dear in the new West, dearer than along the seaboard, for Wesley had preached in Georgia and people were beginning to think as much of their souls as of their bellies and money belts. Well, almost as much, anyhow.

A trace of gold had been found in Georgia and the Georgians, who had not been very enthusiastic about the rebellion against the king, had become loud and belligerent in their demands of the United States, of which the state was a member, of a sort. Didn't Georgia's charter state that Georgia extended from sea to sea? Of course, no Georgian had seen the other sea, but he knew it was there. The mere fact that five independent nations, Spain, Creeks, Choctaws, Chickasaws and Cherokees lay between Georgia and New Spain, sometimes called Mexico, had nothing to do with the matter. The royal charter had assured Georgia that it owned land from the Atlantic to the Pacific and it was the duty of the Congress of the United States of North America to take the land and hold it.

Many of the settlers scoffed at the idea and said, "How can we take all that land, and hold it? It must be a thousand miles to the Pacific. We can't defeat the world."

Old man Dabney said, "We did. We beat England."

The frontier had changed since old man Dabney had made his plans for his son. Methodist melting meetings and whip cracking contests took the place of rifle shoots, for powder was dear and the king no longer furnished it. The southerners were breaking away from the Church of England, methodizing and modernizing it in keeping with the reckless tempo of the new land. A few, favored of God, had developed the use of unknown tongues and the holy barks, and would climb trees and bark and talk with God in yelps and growls. Sam's father said he reckoned God was the greatest understander in creation. He understood everything, even the barks of the Methodists, and the rolling Gaelic of the Scotch Highlanders. The Scots had ruined good Gaelic, old man Dabney said. They had been flocking to the South since Culleden, fifty years gone, and were bringing to the country their bloody customs, including feuds. The Scots shunned riotous living and had more time to improve

their habits of sharp practices in trading rice, rum, tobacco, slaves and other things essential to the well-being
of man.

Old man Dabney left Sam twenty pieces of gold when
he died. The father dared not use his gold or have it
changed into American currency. The traders might ask
questions because the gold coins bore the image of old
George, may his neck stretch in hell! Authorities had
confiscated much gold from American soldiers who had
got it as Dabney had, in honest body-looting of dead
Englishmen. There were many prosperous houses in
Tidewater and, too, in far-away Philadelphia and Boston
that had their beginning with gold paid to Hessians, taken
from them by Americans and confiscated by officers in
the name of wisdom and justice, and the Congress.

Sam and his father had gone out at dawn to beat the
brush for two Creeks who had been moseying around.
The Dabney larder was low and the scalps would come
in handy. Sam saw the Creeks drinking at a spring and
shot one of them before his father could get his Tower
to his shoulder. The second Creek, instead of running as
a sensible Indian should, heaved his tomahawk and opened
a gashing wound in old man Dabney's side.

The boy took his father to the corn patch back of the
cabin and called his mother. Carrie Dabney ran down
the path and was leaning over her husband when the
Indian, who had doubled his trail, leveled on Sam. Carrie
screamed and Sam dropped prone. The ball ripped
through the corn and tore into the woman's back.

Sam and Honoria put their parents on the same bed.
Old man Dabney died that night, cursing God. Carrie
Dabney died the next morning. Maybe she was batty. She
said she saw a vision before she died: a white ship sailing
out of a cloud and passing by her bed. She whispered to

22

Sam and Honoria that it looked like the ship that had brought her from Ireland, except that its masts were gold and its sails were lace.

Sam put coins on his mother's eyes to keep them closed. Then he sprinkled a bit of salt on his mother's and father's chests and placed there little crumbs of bread, seven crumbs on each chest. And while Honoria watched, he ate the bread and salt, and said, " 'Tis a bitter morsel. I've eaten the sins of my parents and may the first seven winds that blow over me, blow the sins away from me."

He and Honoria washed the bodies and dressed them, Carrie in her wedding dress, and old man Dabney in buckskin. Sam dug the grave and Honoria helped him lower the bodies into the earth.

Now, the burial completed, they returned to the cabin and made a list of their housen goods. Sam propped his musket against the door as they took inventory. Honoria told Sam the names of the articles and he made a list. He listed each article separately: ". . . four pewter plates; two iron pots; six earthenware cups, one cracked; six quilts . . ."

Finally, the inventory was finished. Sam took the twenty pieces of gold, the Tower musket, a tomahawk, a scalping knife, and then he and Honoria closed the door to the cabin, nailed it, and walked toward the village, to the home of Benjamin Frome and his wife, Edna.

Frome was a Jew whose family had arrived in Georgia during the great immigration of 1733. He was in his saddlery, and when he saw Sam he said, "I'm offering nothing for hides now, mind you."

"I have nothing to sell," Sam replied. "Mother and father are dead and buried."

"You should have told me," Frome said more kindly. "I could have helped."

"It would have hurt your trade. It's bad enough to be a Jew, but if you had helped bury my father, people would have shunned you."

Frome, the peddler and trader who made saddles with indentured servants and paupers, was silent, knowing Sam spoke wisely. He was opposed to slavery and owned no Negroes. It was not good business, slavery. A Negro ate more than a white person and didn't have the spirit. If you didn't feed a Negro, he wouldn't work, but would sulk instead. Pride drove white persons, so Frome used bound employes in his saddlery and paupers in his factory at the cross roads. He didn't have to pay the paupers. Once a year he got word that the Yankees were auctioning off paupers to any man who would feed them, and then he would drive North in his wagon and buy the services of every pauper under sixty.

He had one prerequisite for his paupers; they must be illiterate. He homesteaded land in their names and never told them that they, in spite of their rags and sores, were landholders in a land of the free. When they died, the land reverted to him, for his paupers always owed him money, often as much as eight bits, which some folks were calling a dollar.

But Frome was kind to his workers, his bound 'uns and his paupers. There was a distinct social difference among the three groups, and one group wouldn't live in the same quarters as another. In the new order of things in a new land, paupers were the lowest of the castes. Slaves were only a notch ahead of them. Then came the bound 'uns. Of course, the loony ones didn't count, or the felons. But there weren't many felons, for the theft of a bit was a capital offense and the hangman kept the criminals pretty well thinned out.

Frome never beat his employes. Once, a pauper had tried to run away and Frome had proclaimed her a loony and chained her in a cabin, with a ring of iron around her neck and a chain to a bolt. He was genuinely sorry when she strangled herself, but she wasn't. The only punishment he ever inflicted on his bound servants was to make them bend over and put the tip of their right fore finger on the head of a nail in the floor. They must bend over for hours, their legs rigid. If they moved, Frome didn't thrash them; he starved them for two days.

Sam told Frome, "My sister wants to bound out to you. She has nowhere to go."

Frome puckered his lips and looked away for a minute. He was wondering if it would hurt his business if he bound one of the Dabney brats. But he made up his mind quickly and said, "Come into the house and we'll talk."

"You've a good business here," Sam said as they walked out of the saddlery. "I like to smell leather."

"It's a terrible business," Frome complained, but he was proud of his trade. His saddles were known from Virginia to the border of Spanish Florida. His factory, in which he kept his trading goods, was on a creek. His saddlery was next to his factory and behind his saddlery was his foundry, made of oaken timbers and boasting a chimney of hand-pressed red clay bricks. His workers lived in cabins around the factory, but his house was more than half a mile away, so that the odors of the hides could be smelled only when the wind blew from the south. His house had many things in it that the Dabney brats had never seen before, brass candlesticks and rugs and fine furniture. It was a small house, for Frome was a simple man. Sam wondered why he didn't build a mansion. A man in Frome's position should have a mansion. The Fromes had only white servants, who glanced furtively at Sam and Honoria. One of the bound girls opened her eyes wide and stared at Sam. Another giggled. Honoria looked at them quickly, then at her brother. Sam paid them no heed and Honoria stared them down. The shameless wenches! Panting for her brother like fresh colts for a stallion. But the stares and giggles did not impress Sam. He was not even aware of them. All his life women would stare at him and always he would be unaware of their glances.

Frome called his wife and presented the Dabneys to her. Mrs. Frome had heavy black eyelashes and sensitive lips. She gasped when she saw Sam, then dropped her eyes quickly. Sam bowed politely. Frome explained that Honoria wanted to bound out. Mrs. Frome was disappointed; she had hoped Sam was entering their service. She said, without enthusiasm, that Honoria looked fitting. She envied Honoria her carriage, her small high breasts and her poise. Once she, too, had had small high breasts, but that had been long ago. She instinctively feared Honoria, but she dared not object to her husband's bounding her. And, too, maybe Sam would call often to see his sister. There was something hard and untamable about him that attracted Mrs. Frome. It was not merely his magnificent body; it was something less tangible yet more vital. He had the look of a man who would never be completely satisfied. She had once seen a picture of David holding Goliath's head. David had had that same look in his eyes.

Frome examined Honoria's face and hands and told his wife to take the girl into a room and strip her, to see if she had lice or running sores. Frome was very careful

26

about such things—lice and sores and naked women. He never would feel them. He was a rich man, but, after all, he was a Jew and the frontiersmen would rise to the defense even of a bound 'un if her seducer were a Jew.

Alone with Mrs. Frome, Honoria untied her bodice, slipped her dress down and stepped out of it. She stood triumphantly before the older woman and turned slowly so that Mrs. Frome could examine her. There was not a blemish on her body and she knew it. Her arms were brown to her shoulders and her legs were brown to her thighs, but the rest of her skin was pink.

"You're very beautiful," Mrs. Frome remarked without thinking.

Honoria smiled. "I'm healthy and I can work."

"You'll have to work here," snapped Mrs. Frome. She was annoyed that the girl was so beautiful. "And mind you, use that body only for work and not for pleasure. I'd as leave have a keg of powder near the foundry fires as have you here."

"I don't know what you mean," Honoria lied. Her eyes were unwavering. "I want to work and look after myself until my brother is able to come back for me. Then my brother and I are going away together and build a mansion, and have brass candlesticks such as you have. And rugs, too . . . And slaves."

"That's all you want of life?"

"Ay," Honoria answered. "Slaves—many slaves of all kinds."

Mrs. Frome glanced at her sharply, but she did not know the kinds of slaves Honoria wanted, or that they were white slaves—and that all of them would be men.

Mrs. Frome returned Honoria to her husband and nodded. Frome, understanding the nod, told Sam, "I'll take her, Sam'l boy." He drew up the papers. Honoria

Dabney, aged sixteen, was bounded to Benjamin Frome for five years to learn the art of housekeeping. She was to honor her master, "his secrets keep and his lawful commands obey." Frome was to give her keep, and at the end of her indenture he must give her two dresses, "one whereof to be new."

"Why don't you bound out, Sam'l?" Frome asked, "and learn a trade. You're a good lad, and strong. I've known you since childhood, egg and bird."

"I'm going away," Sam answered. "I'll be back for Honoria, and I'll buy her freedom. I ask you, Mr. Frome, not to teach my sister your ways. My father would have it so."

Frome shook his head. "That I vow, Sam'l. My ways and my beliefs are humble. Gentiles fester and die if they believe as I believe."

"Why don't you hitch on to the Methodists? Then they wouldn't call you a Christ-killer, and you could trade more and make more money."

The trader smiled, first at his wife, then at Sam. "My people didn't kill Christ, Sam'l. As you grow older, study as your father did and you'll understand. Christ preached a revolution, and the government killed him, just as England would have killed Washington had he been captured. I can't join the Methodists. A basin of water will never change a Jew. Now, away with you. I'm a slave to my household."

He and Mrs. Frome left Sam and Honoria to themselves.

"I'll be back for you," Sam told her.

"Fetch me something pretty," she said, taking his hand.

"It's a vow."

She put her arms around him and kissed him, first on the cheek, then on the lips. Sam and her father were the only men she had ever kissed. There were tears in Sam's eyes, but none in Honoria's. Oh, no—never in Honoria's!

He took the musket, a bag of dried victuals and the gold, and walked toward Frome's store. "I am away," he told Frome. "Our housen goods are still in our cabin. You may keep half of all they fetch. There's an ox, middling good. There's a good spade, hickory handle. Save it for me. It was my father's favorite tool."

He struck out across a field, then followed a sheep trail over the ridge until he came to the high road that led east to Twigg County, and west to the Chattahoochee. He was wearing his coonskin cap, homespun trousers and deerskin leggin's. He threw his head back as he walked and pumped the pine-scented air into his lungs.

Indian guides and troopers were loafing around the log cabin that served as headquarters for the Twigg County Dragoons when Sam arrived there. He asked for the leader.

"Cap'n Chadbourne is to home," said one of the soldiers who sprawled in a chair behind a table. "Want to muster in and shoot red 'uns?"

"I want to see the captain." Sam propped his musket against the wall and looked around. "I'll wait for him."

"Be mite of a spell," the soldier volunteered. "The agent is visiting with him. We can sign you, or mebbe you don't like our looks."

"I don't."

The other soldiers guffawed. "He got you there, Ab. The bucko's got spirit. Mebbe we better fetch him to the cap'n."

The man behind the table arose and seemed to unbend himself by sections, a bit at a time. But when he finally straightened up he was as tall as Sam, although not as broad or as heavy. He grinned at Sam and then began laughing. His laugh was infectious and soon Sam was laughing too.

"I'm the sergeant," the man said and offered his hand. "Call me Ab."

Sam judged the sergeant's age as about his own and could not help but admire the careless indifference of his bearing. He himself usually was tense.

"Ab what?" Sam asked.

The sergeant looked at him quickly and said tersely, "Just Ab." Then he grinned again and asked, "Can you sing? We got enough fighters in this army. What we need is a first-class singing man."

"I can call up a tune," Sam said.

"Do you know the 'Frozen Girl'?" Ab asked eagerly.

"Ay. And 'Little Scotch-ee', 'Barbra Allen' . . ."

"I'm on your side, brother," Ab interrupted. "I'll take you to the cap'n. But heed me, you must furnish your own equipment, except powder and lead. The scalps you take will be your bounty and the state will pay you $10 a month, hard money."

"How comes it that we can't cross the river and search for Creeks? They're plentiful there."

"That's no business of ours. Our government's at peace with the Creeks. Of course," Ab winked, "if you catch a red 'un marauding, he's fair game. Our business is to get settlers to the river. If they're going through the Creeks, God'll have to scout 'em. For sure, if a man's of a mind to, he can slip off at nights and cross the river and bag a few red 'uns. One of the boys tried it on our last go-out."

"How many did he get?" Sam asked with interest.

"We haven't seen him since."

"Do the regulars take the settlers through the Creeks?"

"There ain't no regulars in these parts, brother, 'course

30

they don't scout for settlers. We can't send soldiers into the Creek country. It's an independent nation. Be like us sending soldiers into Florida, where the Spaniards are. Damme, it would mean war. The people know nothing about this country. Georgia's claiming all the land to the Mississippi, and on to the Pacific, for that matter. But the Chocks and Chicks and Creeks own part of it. Spain has got a paw on it. Ever'body's claiming the land, and the devil really owns it. It's hell, brother."

Sam walked with the sergeant up the village street, to the end of town, thence up a ridge until they came to the house of Captain Pierce Chadbourne. Sam had never seen a house such as the Chadbourne place. There was a lawn where sheep kept the grass cropped. The house was made of white-washed bricks and had an upper gallery and a verandah. The mansion looked cool. A slave answered the sergeant's knock and when Ab announced his business, the man-servant disappeared and returned with his mistress.

Sam snatched his cap from his head so quickly that his hair slipped from the knot and tumbled over his face. He did not know whether to bow or to salute. So he did neither, but just stood there and stared at her. She had hazel eyes and they were frank. She was tall, too, and when she spoke she had to raise her eyes only a mite to look directly into his. Her eyes were very bright and her skin was as soft as old silk. She smelled good, not like sweat, but like fresh rain water and rose petals. She stood very erect, so erect that she seemed to force herself to stand so. Sam felt that her erectness reflected strength of body and that her firm red lips showed strength of character.

"Please come in," she said politely. "I'm Donna Chadbourne. My brother's busy." She looked closely at Sam

31

and laughed. "Hoity Toity! You're the biggest man I ever saw. My brother could split you up and have a regiment."

Sam grinned. "My father always said that when I stood still I looked like a pine tree, and my sister said that I often acted as though I had a wooden head."

The sergeant, Ab, put his hand over his mouth and stifled a laugh. Donna made no effort to hide her mirth. She dismissed Ab and showed Sam into the parlor. He sat on the edge of his chair, fumbling with the coon tail on his cap. He looked at the floor. "I'm Sam'l Dabney. I came to join up." When he raised his eyes she was looking at him and smiling.

Sam thought, "She's well taken up, and there's iron in her blood and salt in her craw."

He realized she was watching him. This woman was something for a man to think about. Sam had known women in his life. A full-bodied animal, his appetite for life was enormous. He was a man who usually satisfied his cravings, be they for food, sleep or women. If he were hungry for fresh venison, he would kill a deer. If he were hungry for a woman, he always had gone out and found one among the settlers' daughters and widows. It was all right for a man to take any willing women until he made his troth. He had never given women more than a passing thought. They apparently never expected any more from him, but were happy to have been with him. He was the kind of man to whom women would always be good. Sam believed that women were pleasant to have when a man needed them. There were many things in life that a man had to have to live: a gun, a knife, fresh meat, salt and a woman when his blood got hot. The women of the frontier always smelled sweaty and gave themselves in the same spirit

32

that Sam accepted them—a thing to be done, a yearning to be satisfied, an appetite to be filled.

But Donna Chadbourne was different. Instinctively, Sam felt it. She was quality and she had a mansion and slaves. A mansion with high ceilings and brass candlesticks. And she wore a clean white dress, tight around her breast and full around her hips. She wore slippers, too, and there was a comb in her hair. She had grace and dignity. She knew how to fold her hands in her lap when she talked and her finger nails were clean. She belonged in a mansion. Well, so would he some day. Old man Dabney's cabin down by the Chattahoochee suddenly seemed far away.

2

✩ ✩

SAM and Donna Chadbourne talked of many things, he mostly of Honoria. "I'm going to buy her freedom with my scalp bounties," he said simply. "Then I'll fetch her here and we'll set up housen goods together."

Donna nodded. She could sense his love for his sister. Sam arose when Captain Chadbourne and a florid man entered the room. The captain wore new boots and carried a cockade hat under his arm. He was a slender man and there were a few wrinkles around his eyes. He looked too young to have wrinkles, but there they were, evidence that Pierce Chadbourne had found life hard and that life had marked him. His smile was quick and nervous, and seemed to be mechanical. He shook hands with Sam. The Chadbournes were from Tidewater originally, but smallpox had taken their parents, and the factors their fortune, or most of it. The brother and sister had not moped about it, but had loaded their possessions into a wagon and headed southwest, eventually settling in the village.

After Donna had introduced the captain, he presented Sam to the other visitor, Mr. Dan'l Harkins, the Indian agent at Milledgeville. Harkins was the most elegant nabob Sam ever had seen. He wore his hair in a queue and had a white beaver hat in his hand. His

coat was green with wide skirts and a velvet collar and cuffs, and his riding breeches were of blue leather.

Donna excused herself and the men took seats.

"What service can I perform, Mr. Dabney?" Captain Chadbourne asked.

"I came to join you," Sam said.

Pierce Chadbourne glanced at the agent, then studied Sam. Sam resented the close scrutiny, but kept his peace. It was obvious that Captain Chadbourne was thinking of important things. "God's knees," the officer finally said, "but you're a giant. Did you ever scout, or hunt Indians?"

"I'm of a mind to scout later. Among the Creeks. I've hunted Indians, ay, since I was twelve. I'm a good man in the woods."

Harkins cleared his throat and put his white beaver on the floor near his chair. "I can pick men," he boasted. "I can pick a good man a mile away. I've never been wrong on a man yet. And when I make up my mind I make it up quickly. This is our man, Chadbourne. I know of his father."

There was no malice or haste in Sam's tone, but it was firm. "My father is dead, and buried beside my mother. He was not a Tory and I'll have no trifling with his memory. I know not what you mean, sir," he nodded toward Harkins, "but if you have work for me it must be honorable work. I've heard intelligence of plots against this government, of the Trans-Oconee Republic which would be independent of our country, and I will have naught to do with it, or with traitors——"

"Hold your tongue!" Captain Chadbourne stood up. "You must learn never to talk until you hear the other man's statement. If your tongue is always so active, the Creeks will cut it out for you. Perhaps that would be

35

a favor to your fellow man," he added sarcastically. Then his face relaxed and he laughed. "Damme, you have spirit. We're not traitors, Dabney. And the Trans-Oconee is dead. You are afar from the times if you didn't know that, and the republic's flag, the bonnie flag with the crossed bars, has been lowered at Milledgeville. It was such a pretty flag, too. But our offer is honorable, to serve your country."

"I like this wildcat," Harkins slapped his knees. "Iron in his guts, by God. Dabney, what know you of Natchez?"

"It is beyond the Choctaw Nation and a pesthole of Spaniards."

"The man is right," nodded Chadbourne.

"Natchez belongs to Georgia," Harkins said testily. "Always remember that. And Georgia belongs to the United States." He unfolded a crude map and motioned Sam to his side. "A lesson in geography and history, Mr. Dabney." With his finger he pointed out Natchez and New Orleans. "Mind you, Georgia's charter provides that our land stretches to the other sea. But common sense tells us that's too far away, and the land is of no account. But the Mississippi River is the natural permanent boundary of this country. Natchez is ours by right, and we'll have it, with steel if our diplomats can't settle with Spain."

Sam said, "But Natchez was settled by the French and belongs to Spain."

"Quebec was settled by the French, but England owns it. New York was settled by the Dutch, but we own it. We are extending Georgia to the Mississippi River and Natchez is the capital of the new county, the county of Bourbon. We flatter the French with the name. Of course, Spain doesn't recognize our rights.

36

Now see this." He referred to the map again. "New Orleans controls trading on the Mississippi and Spain will fight for New Orleans. But Natchez controls New Orleans, and we do not believe Spain will fight for Natchez. It's as a game of chess, Mr. Dabney. If we own Natchez, we can checkmate New Orleans. For sure, we cannot get an outlet to the sea without Spain's permission, but we can make New Orleans so poor that the damn'd dons will beg us to take the city as a pauper. If we control Natchez, it's simply a question of time before New Orleans is ours, and all the land between the Atlantic and the Mississippi."

"And what's this to me?" asked Sam.

"We need communications with Natchez. We need forts and roads, as far west in the Creek and Choctaw lands as our treaties will allow. I must go there soon, and Miss Donna and Mrs. Harkins are planning an early journey to Natchez. We want you to scout them through."

"Through the Creek Nation?" Sam stared at him. "With ladies? Why don't they go by water to New Orleans and up to Natchez? Or to Pensacola, and from there by keel boat over the lake route and up the Amite and Manchac?"

"Those damn'd foreigners in Pensacola and New Orleans—" Harkins spat and rubbed the spittle with his boot.

"There are sufficient reasons why the party must go overland," Chadbourne said. "There are many reasons why I'm offering you the opportunity to scout it."

Harkins added, "A good scout never asks too many questions, if he wants to live. Question the enemy, but never your friends. Keep your tomahawk and wits sharp, your mouth closed and your bowels open, and you'll be a good scout."

"If you choose this task," continued Chadbourne, "your pay will be $40 a month, hard money, Spanish silver. I'll take you in the Dragoons and train you. I'm confident you'll protect my sister and Mrs. Harkins. It's coming green-up time now, and you should be ready by summer, after the floods have passed."

Sam remembered Donna Chadbourne. "It's a vow," he said.

"How much Indian do you know?"

"Only Creek, but they are Muscogees, and one dialect is as another, even Choctaw."

"And what know you of Choctaw?" Chadbourne demanded quickly.

"Naught."

"You're our man, we'll drink to it."

He called his body servant and gave his order. Harkins leaned back in his chair and patted his boot with his crop. "Nice place here," he said. "Cotton?"

"Not much," Chadbourne answered. "The cleaning of cotton is too dear. We raise stock mostly. We tried to operate a saddlery, but Ben Frome has all the leather business in these parts. We also tried beeswax, but we can't compete with the Natchez country."

"Ay? And why?" Harkins asked.

"The land there is better. And the settlers have credit. Getting our goods to market is an expensive job, but in the Natchez district it's no problem. Man alive, they grow everything out there—tobacco, cotton, ginger, pimento, madder, saffron, hops, opium poppies, buckwheat, clover. Not to mention beef and pork and poultry. It's a land of milk and honey."

"It must be the promised land," Sam suggested.

"It is," said Chadbourne. "The planters do business with Panton & Co., or McMin, Miller & Co., of Pensacola. Trust the British to be on the ground when a shilling is to be made—or stolen."

"The bloody butchers!" Sam exclaimed.

"And all that," Chadbourne laughed. "But they're traders. The Spaniards haven't brains enough to trade. They plunder. So the British own the big houses in Pensacola. McMin, you recollect, is a branch of the great house of Swanson and Miller of London. Many of the Natchez planters order direct from the London houses, and the goods are sent to the Pensacola houses, thence up the lake route in keel boats. Some years the planters spend two thousand pounds with London firms, mostly for wines and perfumes and cloth goods. They also send their produce to England, either by way of New Orleans or down to Pensacola. It is business Georgia and the United States needs."

"And you can't compete?" Harkins asked.

"No. But we manage. Donna runs the place while I soldier. Capable lady, my sister."

"Ay, sir," said Sam enthusiastically. "She is that. I was sizing her up and thinking how well taken up she is. She's got salt in her craw, I'll vow."

Harkins' face dropped at the uncouth words of the backwoodsman. Sizing up a lady, a Chadbourne, as though she were a mare. The lad should be rebuked and taught a mite of manners. But Pierce Chadbourne laughed, and shouted for his sister. "Donna," he greeted her as she swept into the room, "Mr. Dabney here has a compliment for you. He says you've salt in your craw." Pierce's shoulders shook.

Donna's face tightened, then relaxed and she smiled at Sam. "It is a pretty compliment, sir," she said, for she knew, even as Pierce, that Sam had said a proud thing, and that he meant it. "For that flattery I'll give you the best drink."

She sat with the men. Sam never had seen a lady sit with men while they drank. He looked at the clear drink the slave gave him, and watched the other men out of the corners of his eyes. They sipped their liquor. Sam sipped his and it bit his tongue. He smiled at Donna, almost ashamedly. "My father always said never to try to be what you're not, and I vow this is the first fancy drink I ever tasted."

"That is naught to be ashamed of," Donna said. "And as our guest you need not drink it to be polite."

"By no means," Pierce laughed, and winked at Sam. "But you had best drink while you can, for after you join up you cannot drink with your officer. It's the way of the army." He held up his glass to Sam. "This drink is a Fish-house. An old drink back at Tidewater. Like it, Harkins?"

"Ay," Harkins smacked his lips. "A cocktail. My father, in Maryland, used to make this cocktail back in '40, long before the war."

"It's really a punch," said Donna, "although some people call it a cocktail. It's quite proper in Tidewater now to call all mixed drinks cocktails. It's very American, you know. I'll give you the recipe. Mrs. Harkins will be pleased."

She went to her writing desk, selected a quill and wrote, in a strong hand:

"Fish-house Punch Sometimes Call'd Cocktail.

"Slack three quarters of a pound of sugar (cane) in punch bowl. Add one quart lemon juice, of rum two quarters, of Cognac one quart, of Peach Brandy one wine

40

glass. Allow the spirits to brew for two hours. Stir occasionally."

Donna handed the recipe to Harkins and was returning to her chair when one of the housemaids caught her attention and nodded toward the slave quarters, a row of shacks behind the house. Donna excused herself.

Pierce ordered another serving of Fish-house. "One of our wenches is ready to foal. She's only twelve and Donna's worried a mite. I hope the little darkey slips a man-child as her first."

Harkins said, "But a woman-child is worth more, sir. Lor! You do strange things here. Miss Donna pestering her head with a Nigra that's foaling. Incredible."

"Our darkeys are Gullahs and their ways are strange," Pierce answered. "Donna understands them. The child is too young to bear. She'll need help. Dom' her, I was going to breed her two years hence to a Geiche buck of mine, but she came in fresh before her time and bred in the bushes."

"Indian?" Harkins arched his eyebrows.

"God forbid," Pierce frowned. "Gullahs are proud. If one of their families bred to a red 'un, her life wouldn't be of much account. If the Gullahs didn't kill the mother and child, the Indians would, if the father were a Creek. You know how it is with the Creeks. They won't have their blood mixed with negroid."

Sam heeded the conversation. He knew nothing of slaves or their problems. Old man Dabney never owned a Negro and out on the frontier the poor settlers hated darkeys and nabobs who owned them. Sam got up to take his leave. "When do I sign up?"

"Tomorrow," said Pierce.

"I'll wait and tell Miss Donna goodbye," Sam said, "if you'll allow me."

"Why, for certain," Pierce chuckled. Chuckles were rare with Chadbourne. There were no social barriers between the Chadbournes and the Dabneys. The Chadbournes were Scots, the Dabneys were Irish, and they were equal in the newest section of a new land. Sam didn't know there was such a thing as social barriers, and neither Donna nor Pierce ever would have told him.

When Donna returned, her face flushed from walking so fast, she asked Sam where he was going. "To the ordinary, ma'm," he said. "I sign tomorrow and will be at camp. I'm going to buy a fine horse when I kill some red 'uns, and it would be a superfine honor if I could see you around when you have to go anywhere. A lady needs a guard."

Donna turned to Pierce. "I'll not have Mr. Dabney going to the tavern. It's buggy, and the men have to sleep three abed. If Mr. Dabney is kind enough to consent to scout us through the Creeks, he must stay right here. For supper," she wiped her cheeks with a fluff of linen, "we're going to have victuals that all men like, roast pig."

"A whole pig at one bait?" Sam said.

They all laughed, Sam the loudest. "I'd be pleased to eat some of it. I'd even be pleased to see it cooked, ma'm. I have a curiosity. My father always said my curiosity was bigger than my appetite, and that my appetite was bigger than a German priest's."

"Then you shall see it cooked." She shooed her brother and Harkins toward the door. "You two men go talk, on the verandah. I'll show Mr. Dabney our kitchen. Maybe he'll learn something and some day be of real use to a woman."

Sam felt his ears burn. He was blushing when she

42

looked at him, and she blushed, too. She led him to the kitchen which stood apart from the house. The kitchen was larger than old man Dabney's entire cabin. Two black wenches tended the fire on the hob and another was peeling onions, while a fourth was soaking bread in milk. Donna took in the situation at a glance and the slaves began to work faster. She didn't upbraid them, but just looked at them. There was no singing, only the shuffling of bare feet. It struck Sam that the slaves were sulky, spoiled. It took him many years to learn what many persons never learned, that the Negro is not always a happy creature, but sensitive and easy to bruise, and ready to brood.

He leaned against the huge fireplace and watched, entranced. He never had seen so much food. He could make burgoo and cockie-leckie, the famous stew and soup of poor Scots and Irish. Wouldn't he cut a shine later teaching Honoria how to roast a whole pig? He would buy her a whole pig, too. She would have a kitchen as large as this, and slaves to tend it. Nothing was too good for his sister, nothing was good enough.

"There we are," said Donna finally. "And now, do you want to change clothes and wash up?"

"These are all the clothes I own," said Sam without embarrassment. "But I want to wash up. Is there a branch around? I need an all-over."

Donna blushed again. An all-over was a bath a gentleman never mentioned to a lady. But she really didn't mind.

"It will take a river for you," she said and called a servant, and told him, "See that Mr. Dabney has soap and towels. Be sure it's soft soap and not the kitchen ash soap. The last soap we made would take the bark off a tree. You go with Mr. Dabney and attend him."

43

Sam said, "Thank you, ma'm. But ash and lye soap won't hurt me. My skin's tougher than bark. We always used hard soap at our house, except my sister. She took her all-overs with suds made from ferns. How much soap do you use?"

Even the slaves stared at him, and Sam said quickly, "I mean for the plantation, not for yourself."

Donna swallowed her laugh. The servants must never see her laugh at a white man. "We use about twenty pounds a week," she said. "We make our soap in the fall. Why do you ask?"

"A thought came to me. I can make soap as my father made it, and Honoria knows the secret. Maybe we could make soap here in the village and sell it."

Donna was impressed. "It's an idea. I would buy from you, so would the other planters. Pierce would buy from you for his militia. You could turn a profit in the summer time. We never use so much soap in the winter time."

"I must remember that," he said. "There's much for me to remember. I'll buy paper and ink and keep a record of things I should remember. It was my father's way. First I'll write down the manner in which you prepared that Fish-house, then the pig. I'll make a notation about soap. And I also will put down that for the first time in his life, Sam'l Dabney took an all-over while a slave attended him."

The Negro followed Sam to the creek and tried to help him with his clothes, but Sam pushed him away. The slave stood on the bank, grinning, while Sam washed himself. When he came out, the Negro began rubbing him and Sam allowed it. "Jasper wash you in the hous'," the Negro said. "Jasper yo' man, now. Jasper good man. Christian. Jasper bo'n in Car'lina and

44

fetched a sack of money at the auction when Cap'n bought him. Jasper can do many things with his han's, and pray with his tongue. I'm Jasper."

Knowing it would take several hours for the pig to cook, Sam walked around the plantation, inspecting it. He impressed certain details on his mind—the size of the slave cabins, the length of the furrows, the depth of the well—and when he returned to the big house the pig was ready.

A kitchen slave cut off the pig's head before it was drawn from the spit, then she cut it down the back. She sliced the ears from the head, cracked the bone and removed the brains, which she put in a stewpan with stuffing, poured gravy over it and stirred it. She put the gravy in a boat, with the ears at each end, and put the pig in a dish, back outside. A man-servant carried it to the table.

Sam ate more than he needed and belched. After supper, he drank his first port and didn't like it. He sat with Donna and Harkins and Pierce in the parlor, but was silent, content to watch Donna. She realized his gaze was on her, but didn't mind. She liked it, and was glad to admit it to herself, and was glad, too, that intimate little female feelings ran through her when Sam looked at her. She had waited a long time, as time was measured on the frontier, for a man who could make her breasts tingle only by looking at her.

Sam didn't understand the things Harkins and Pierce discussed, trails and trade. He was determined to borrow Harkins' map and copy it. "I've a question," he said when the two men paused for breath. "There are things I want to know before I take commands from you, Captain Chadbourne. Will you heed me?"

Pierce nodded and Sam said, "Why do you pick me

as a scout when you know naught of me? Why are you glad I know naught of Choctaws and their tongue?"

Harkins said, "If you would be rich, you must learn to hold your tongue."

But Pierce interrupted, "The questions are well put, and proper. He's a cautious man, Harkins, and all the more valuable." A slave put an ember on Pierce's tobacco bowl and he sucked the smoke deeply into his lungs. "We chose you, Mr. Dabney, because you're strong, young and a stranger to the Choctaws. You're out to make your fortune, and will take chances with your hide. Our other scouts are known to the Chocks and Creeks. The government has a treaty with the red 'uns, but settlers pushing west will heed no treaty. That country is the promised land, and no barrier will hold back the people."

Harkins said, "Ay, those fools in Philadelphia think a man will be bound by agreements with Indians. Refiddlesticks! When there's land for the taking, men will take it. And there is land, black land, good land, from Georgia to the Mississippi. It belongs to us and we'll have it. There are a dozen schemes afoot to take it from Spain. For a vow, it's the promised land."

Sam held his peace. Pierce said, "There'll be a day when this country will be settled with forts and farms to the Mississippi. The Choctaws hold the keys to the program. The Creeks! Nay, Mr. Dabney, they'll be scattered. They're butchers and will be butchered. But the Chocks till their land and build towns. They'll be hard to uproot. They're between us and the river, the Canaanites between us and the promised land. Our government heeds their pleas. They're peaceful and have been friends to the United States. If you know their tongue and their history, you might give them your

46

sympathy. La! I do! Before God, they're right. But our mission is not to think of their cause, but of ours. The Choctaws must be our allies for the trial with Spain, then they must be uprooted. We'll need you among them. If they know our plans, they'll ally themselves with the Creeks and exterminate us. They might join with the Cherokees and Chickasaws. If that should come to pass, and the red 'uns ally with Spain, and Spain with England, we'd be wiped out. There would not be a white man's house south of Virginia. If we send a sea-soned scout to the Choctaws, they'll suspect trickery. But if we send you, a stranger, they'll believe us."

"Then I'm to live among them, smoke their pipes and eat their meat, and, when the hour is ripe, deliver them to the hangman?"

"Ay, and share their secrets and study their ways."

"There is a good word for it," said Sam. "I am to be a spy."

Pierce shrugged his shoulders. "Call it what you will. My sister and Mrs. Harkins will go with you on the western journey. The Chocks will be pleased that we trust our women in their land and will believe we're their friends. And because you're a stranger, they'll take you in. It is their religion that a stranger must be protected and honored until he gets Choctaw blood on his hands."

"What happens if he has Choctaw blood on his hands?" Sam asked.

Pierce said, "If he is condemned by their council, every hair on his body is plucked out. Then a master whipman—and the Chocks are experts with the bull whip—lashes the prisoner until his body is cut to rib-bons. Salt is poured into the wounds, then a mixture of pine sap, and clay is molded around the body. It helps cure the wounds. but it's torture. The prisoner is locked

47

in a room and steamed until his flesh peels. He is tied to a stake and around the stake is a trench filled with water, into which hot rocks are dropped until the steam parboils the man. If he lives, he next is locked in another room. Water is placed at one end of the room, but a nest of snakes is between the prisoner and the water. It's not a nice thought."

Sam said, "I'm to see that the Choctaws never join forces with the Creeks. Is that the plan?"

"Yes. You must be a man they trust, but a man who is loyal to his own people."

"I'm to be Cain and Abel."

"Someone must do this thing. We believe we can extend our frontier to the Mississippi without war if we can conquer the Chocks with friendship. They must never join forces with the Creeks and Spaniards. I'm a soldier, Dabney, and not a man of vengeance. But remember, the red 'uns killed your parents. True, they were Creeks, but the Creeks and Chocks are kinsmen, Muscogees. They believe in the same god, Aba Inki, the Father above. They believe they came from the same soil, Nanih Waiya, the Great Mother." Pierce crossed his legs and leaned back and watched Sam.

"It's a goodly mission for a man," Sam said. He knew the first settlers in the wilderness would reap the riches. He would be among them. "I'm your servant, sir."

3

To Sam, it seemed he scarcely had relaxed in the huge four-poster rosewood bed before his belly, trained to the harsh victuals of the frontier, rebelled against the rich food he had eaten. When he woke up, his stomach was cramping and he crawled from the bed and sought a candle. He had no taper and was too ill to call a servant to fetch a light. He opened the door quietly and almost stumbled over Jasper, squatting on the threshold, grinning.

"Too much pig," the slave said.

Sam did not reply, but brushed by the Negro, who followed him. The slaves had seen Sam stuff himself at supper, and knew he would be ill. Good slaves knew such things. The word had been passed to Jasper and he had posted himself at Sam's door, ready for duty.

Jasper held a torch as Sam walked down the path past the slave quarters. Returning to the house, Sam stopped and listened. From the slave quarters came a low wail, then a frenzied pounding of feet. Sam looked at Jasper for an explanation and the Negro grinned again.

"Gullah batty. Jasper Geiche."

"What's that noise?" Sam demanded. A scream echoed through the quarters, then was muffled.

"Gullah," Jasper said. "The child is coming."

Sam remembered what Harkins and Pierce had said

and the worried expression on Donna's face when she had gone to the quarters. The slave girl was foaling. And she was only twelve. She was a valuable wench and might die. Sam had seen a mare drop a colt and die. He knew much of such things, the foaling of colts, the whelping of hounds. Now he turned toward the quarters. Perhaps he could help the girl and save Donna and Pierce their investment in the wench.

Jasper dared not lay hands on Sam, but he was bold enough to say, "That is woman's business. Gullah not like my people. The girl is dirty and conjured. Jasper afraid."

Sam ignored him and trotted toward the cabin, whence the moans came. Jasper faded into the shadows and ran to the big house.

The slave girl was on the cabin floor and two old women were squatting by her. One held a rock on the child's stomach. The other was rocking on her haunches and wailing. The girl rolled her eyes when she saw Sam. The women looked up, fear crawling over their ebony faces as they slunk into a corner and stared at Sam. One covered her face as she leaned over the girl. Sam didn't know that a Gullah woman was believed to be in the power of witches when she bore her young, and that, had he been in Africa, he would have been drawn and quartered for looking at a woman during childbirth. But to him, the girl represented money. She must have cost $500, as much as the finest stallions. She mustn't die. He called one of the women.

"Water. Get water. Then take her outside." The floor was crawling with vermin and Sam felt the lice on his bare hands. The two women obeyed and under his direction they sponged the girl with water and took her outside where the earth, at least, was clean. Sam knelt beside the girl and pressed her belly gently, then stronger. Often, he and Honoria had pressed a cow's belly while old man Dabney had instructed them.

He didn't see Donna until she leaned over him and handed her torch to one of the women. "You're a strange man, Mr. Dabney," she said. "Now, please, leave this to us."

Sam returned to the house where Jasper gave him milk and rum. Back in the quarters, a fire was built and Donna and the girl and the two old women worked until dawn. The cocks were crowing when the woman-child was born. The mother rolled her eyes at Donna. There was gratitude and fear and hope in her eyes. Donna held the baby before the mother and smiled. The baby was wrapped in cotton sacks and placed on the ground beside the mother. The land gave it strength. The old women cowed in the shadows that the dawn was brushing away and watched Donna. She seemed to ignore them. They swayed and shuffled their feet. One chanted, the other took up the chant. Down the row of shacks, another woman answered, a low mournful chant. They were back in Africa. A woman-child had been born and they were singing the lamentations, for her soul was doomed. A man had touched her mother while she labored.

Donna felt sick inside and was weak, but the slaves mustn't know it. Her back was tired. She hated to be tired and sweaty. She called one of the old women. "I'm weary," she said. It was not a complaint, but a statement of fact. Donna spoke softly but authoritatively to the old woman. "Be quiet. The child is well. See." Out of the corners of her eyes she watched the women as she turned back the cotton sacks. The slave women stared at the baby. Donna threw a handful of pine needles on the fire and when the flames shot up, the old women drew back. The baby was copper-colored.

"Leave the two alone," Donna ordered. "Go clean the cabin and when the sun is high take them inside. The mother can get up this afternoon. I'll send food from the kitchen. And hear me. The child is fair. But if hurt comes to her or to her mother, I'll take you from my kitchen and send you to the fields. And tell the other women that if harm comes to this mother or child, they'll be punished."

Donna did not rebuke Sam and neither was she embarrassed when she faced him after breakfast.

"Did I do foolishness?" he asked.

"Yes," she said. "Our Gullahs have not been long out of Africa. The custom is for only women to be present at births. The presence of a man is considered an ill omen. But you didn't know. And you saved the mother."

"How is the child?"

"Well. Her father is an Indian."

"Will your slaves harm her, or the mother?"

"I don't know. But it is bad. If her father is Creek, which is likely, the Creeks will seek the child's life. The Creeks are very proud and their nation's law is that a black-and-red baby must not live. The Gullahs will believe the child is evil. Her life will not be easy." She smiled wearily. "We've named the baby Deborah, but we'll call her Dabby, in your honor. The mother is very grateful and she's proud to call her first-born Dabby as a tribute to the strange man who saved her."

Sam went with Pierce to the Dragoons' headquarters before noon and signed the articles of enlistment. Harkins returned to Milledgeville.

Sam easily learned the routine of the company. Pierce

52

spoke to him only with orders, but he saw Donna as often as his duty would permit. Sometimes she came to head-quarters for escorts when she rode the trails. She never had thought an escort necessary before Sam joined the Dragoons. Pierce always granted him the favor. Sam didn't know, or suspect, that his officer's sister had arranged that he always be her guard, but assumed that he got the assignment because he was a good soldier, alert and cautious. He and Donna had little to say to each other as they rode. He was content simply to be in her presence and protect her.

He stood his muster without complaint and got his share of marauding Creeks and saved his scalp bounties. His money belt was quite heavy one day when the Dragoons, led by Ab, marched away with a string of settlers, headed for the Chattahoochee.

"Might get a pas'l of red 'uns on this march," Angus McLeod, an old campaigner, told Sam as they walked behind a light Jersey wagon, one keeping his eyes to the right, the other to the left. "They been helling on that trail, stealing and burning."

"Settlers have no business in the Creek country," Sam said. "Why do the fools go there?"

"Law, brother, you can't keep white men from going where there's land and trade. Government's got a treaty with the Creeks, but it don't mean nothing. Treaties ain't no 'count. All they do is give each side a mite of time to catch their breaths. You heed my vow, and I'll vow that some day we'll jam the Chock treaty down their gullets and go in there."

"Why not?"

"Them Chocks are smart, sharp as meat axes. They know if we get a toe-hold, they are licked, and up the creek without a paddle. Best way to do it is to send some friendly scout among 'em, and don't tell 'em nothing, but keep 'em from j'ining the Creeks. Then we can take 'em one at a time. Yep, son, them Chocks are bright, and when two real bright men get together there ain't no fight. More deals are won with peace pipes and silver than with muskets and lead. We got to outwit them Chocks. Here, hold my rifle-gun. My nose is wet."

Sam balanced his comrade's long Kaintuck in his left hand. "Powerful pert weapon," he said. "Better than my old Tower. How does it come that your rifle-gun is called a Kaintuck? It was made in Pennsylvania."

" 'Tis a riddle, for fair. Some say old Dan'l Boone was the first rifle-gun man and being from Pennsylvania to begin with he hired some Dutch smiths to make his guns. Called 'em Kaintucks, 'cause old Dan'l took 'em there. For a Shadbelly, old Dan'l sure could cut a lick against the red 'uns."

"But he left Kaintuck and went among the Spaniards."

Old Angus accepted his rifle from Sam, looked at the priming powder and adjusted the weapon over his shoulder, on his gun-corn, a callus caused by the heavy piece. "I have my own ideas about that, and they likely ain't worth the breath I spend to tell 'em. Old Dan'l was empire-building, a double-jointed name for land-grabbing. We're going to see a heap of such expeditions, Americans setting up on Spanish land and brewing trouble against Spain."

"That's rebellion."

"That's another word that don't always mean what it sounds like. It's rebellion if you get caught. It's revolution if you win. I see it this way, Sam'l. Spain is fool enough to let Americans in, to trade horses and such. A man goes in with a heap of settlers, declares his land

54

an independent country. He gets money and help from the big-mouths up at Philadelphia. He revolts against Spain and forms a little sapling country, sells land to more settlers, divvies with the big mouths who backed him, j'ines his country to the United States and moves on to do it again."

"That would mean war with Spain."

"Mebbe, but the West wants war with Spain. Up in Kaintuck and Tennessee they're hossin' for a war and sayin' if the United States don't fight Spain they're going to quit the United States and strike out for themselves. But as I see it, Spain won't fight. Let's say you and your folks move into Spanish territory. You ain't Americans then, you're Spaniards. You revolt. Hell, man, the United States government ain't involved. Nobody can prove some of the nabobs who run this country were backing you. Then if you want to j'ine your country to the United States, it ain't none of Spain's business. For sure, if you get caught, you get shot, and a hundred years from now they'll say you were a traitor. But if you win, you're a hero and a rich man. As I see it, Sam'l, the Lord put this land here and said, 'Come and get it, there ain't no rules.' Best way for us to get it, is to get the Spaniards and red 'uns fighting among themselves, then move in. Once a white man gets on the land it takes a heap to get him off. I just happen to know that right now a heap of men are planning expeditions into Spanish and Indian lands. It's land-grabbing, Sam'l."

Sam didn't question the old man, but changed the subject. "We're drawing nigh the Creek country. Wish I could get more than one red 'un at a shot. My only sister is bound out and I want her release. I need money."

"Your sister's release ain't all you want money for, is it? I've seen you riding around with a pow'ful pert

55

gal. 'Pears to me you're hankering to buy your sister's freedom and hossin' to lose your own. She's a fit'n lady, that Miss Donna."

Sam flared with sudden anger. "If you were younger I might take offense."

"Or if I was a lying man, you would take offense. No harm intended, Sam'l. My only sister is dead. Creeks killed her. My wife's gone, too. Smallpox, but it's better'n Creeks."

"Is that why you hunt Creeks?" asked Sam more gently.

"Hunting Creeks is the only pleasure I know of that a man gets silver for doing. The Creeks are getting smart. All they do is jump us from the bushes and we can't get in mor'n one lick before they high-tail it."

"If I had two barrels on my gun, I could get two Creeks without reloading."

"Mebbe."

The column halted at a signal from Ab. "Resting," Sam thought. They were nearing the Chattahoochee, as far west as the wagon trail ran. Beyond the river, the settlers who were venturing into the heart of the Creek nation must go horseback and carry their goods in saddle bags. The oxen of the settlers who would stop at the Chattahoochee were outspanned, and the soldiers flopped on the side of the trail. Sentries were posted quickly. Sam examined his musket which was leaded badly. He could see the lead clinging to the barrel. The coating was smooth. He decided he would scrape the barrel that night when he would have time to heat his ram-rod. He stuck his ram-rod into the ground to clean it, and lay flat on his back, at ease with the world.

A scattered volley near the head of the column brought the Dragoons to their feet. Sam deployed noiselessly to

56

the right. No word was spoken. The Dragoons were trained for wilderness fights. Sam knew the Creeks had ambushed the advance guard and he was anxious to get a scalp before the Indians melted into the forests and crossed back into their own country.

"Damme," he muttered as he hurried through the woods. He had left his ram-rod poked in the ground back near the wagon train. Oh, well, he had a charge in his Tower. He dropped on his belly and lay still. He reckoned the Creeks would flee in his direction after scalping the advance guard.

The first Indian slid from behind a tree and was ready to dash to the shelter of another when Sam fired. The Creek gripped the tree for support, then slipped slowly to the ground.

Sam began counting as he waited to see if the buck had a comrade. "Eighteen, nineteen." If a second Indian did not appear before he counted a hundred, he should be safe to scalp his victim without fear of ambush. Creeks, accustomed to fighting impatient Spaniards, had discovered that most white men would not lie still with their nerves taut. The Creeks were trained to watch the movement of a fluttering leaf, and when it had rustled for sixty seconds or so without a white man showing himself, it meant the woods were clear.

Foreign regulars, disciplined for mass fighting, never learned the trick of outsmarting Indians and would charge recklessly into an opening after a few seconds' wait in the bush, only to meet the Indians' concealed fire. But wilderness scouts outwitted the Creeks by outwaiting them. "Twenty-five, twenty-six," Sam counted slowly. His musket was empty. He looked around for a stick to use as a ram-rod, still counting under his breath. A cane brake was near, and quickly, silently, he selected a cane and cut it near its roots, watching the jerking, wounded Indian the while. He poured powder into his musket, measuring the charge with his eye, and pulled a wadding from his pouch. With his thumb, he poked it into the maw of his gun and tried to force the wadding down the barrel with the cane, but the stick was too large. Cursing to himself, he split the cane and, bracing it against the butt of his palm, forced it into the barrel. The cane twisted. Its edges, sharp as steel, turned in the barrel, but it worked. Sam shoved the ball down the barrel, and more wadding. "Ninety-two, ninety-three, ninety-four —"

The second Indian slipped from behind a water oak. He wore a single feather in his scalp-lock and his chest was streaked with vermilion. A Red Stick, the highest order of Creek warriors. The Indian backed against the tree, hugging the shadow, and looking around. Sam marked the oak in his mind, for later he might have to prove that the Indians were marauding and trespassing. The Red Stick saw his companion on the ground, glanced only casually at him to see if his scalp were intact. It was. It meant the white man was hiding, impatient to collect the trophy. The Creek scouted the wilderness quickly with his eyes, his head cocked slightly to one side, his eyes roving. Sam pushed aside a low limb, waited ten seconds, then raised his gun. He squinted his left eye and focussed the Red Stick's mouth with his right, and when the gun's sight came into the focus, he held the bead for a moment and squeezed the trigger. The buck spread-eagled. Sam counted to one hundred again and when no Indian appeared, he walked to the first victim.

The Creek was still alive. There was no hate in his

eyes, or plea for mercy, only curiosity. Sam put his musket down carefully and withdrew his knife. With his left hand, he grasped the scalp-lock, entwined one finger in the oily hair and held the scalp with the other four fingers. Gently, he pulled the scalp until the skin was taut, then he punctured the skin with his knife's tip and ran the blade around the scalp. He tied the gory trophy to his belt. There was no regret in his heart. He was neither proud nor ashamed. He was a deft scalper. Old man Dabney had taught him the trick and the operation was neater than the scalping jobs of the Creeks. The Red Sticks always were impatient for scalps and took no pride in their work.

Only now did he glance down at the Indian. The muscles in the face were twitching, and the skin, released when the scalp was removed, began sliding over the high cheek bones. The Indian's mouth sagged as the skin crawled and the eyes opened. The Red Stick was breathing heavily. Sam had heard of men living after they had lost their scalps. He stood up, lifted his musket and pounded out the man's brains, wiped his gun stock with leaves and walked to his second prize.

The scalp was bloody. Sam grumbled. It was a messy operation. The Indian had been shot in the mouth. "Law," Sam muttered. "I missed." He had allowed for the drop of the ball and the Creek should have been struck in the throat. Sam examined his musket, holding it to the sun and peering down the barrel. The barrel was grooved tightly. "Hell!" Sam swore. "Riflings." The cane rod had twisted and its hard edges had cut grooves into the coated barrel. Sam twisted the split cane down the barrel again and examined his gun. "If I had a rifle-gun with borings that tight I could pick off red 'uns plumb across the Chattahoochee. And if it had two barrels, I could get two red 'uns without reloading."

He kept his secret and after he collected his bounty for the scalps, he went to Pierce. "It's green-up time, Cap'n," he said. "And there's a thing I would do. Soon it will be summer and time for me to ride to the Mississippi. But I have a plan. My enlistment is up and I'm riding East."

Pierce said, "Have you any spondulix?"

"Ay. Sovereigns and Spanish silver."

"You'll need a good horse. Buy a mare, Sam. And you had best tell Donna goodbye. She'll be mooning for you."

He told Donna where he was going and why. "It's my secret, but you may know. I'm going to the Dutch gunsmiths in Pennsylvania. I need a rifle of a kind."

She was happy that he had thought fit to tell her his secret, but all she said was, "When you return, I'll be glad."

He wrote Ben Frome and called him "Honor'd Sir and Benefactor" and said, "A post goes to You tomorrow and I Hasten this Intelligence. I Ride to Va. on Business." He requested Ben to take studied care of Honoria and added, "I will Secure Her Release when I return."

He traded the Dabney homestead and his half of the housen goods to a Scot for a mare and paid $85, hard money, to boot.

"Her name is Claymore," the trader said. "Named for the great sword my people carried in the Highlands, for the good cause."

"At Culloden?" asked Sam, fully aware he was on safe ground, for a great majority of Southern Scots were sons of Highlanders who fled Cumberland's brutality after the collapse of the Stuart cause.

"Ay, lad. And because you say Culloden and not Culloden Moor and prove yourself not to be English, I will stand you to a taste of grog."

"My people were Irish," said Sam, "and we, too, suffered at England's hands."

"But not at her knee," the Scot said. "We were never bent to her knees, ay, lad? The thieving bastards!"

"The bloody buggers."

They drank at the ordinary. The trader, mouthing in his grog, stood for two drinks, one to bless Scotland and one to damn England. "A mean land, lad, tight as a cat's tit and not much bigger."

Sam bought a drink and cursed England. The trader was so pleased that he relaxed his vigilance and Sam bought a fancy saddle for a bargain, the only man in the village who ever had bested the Scot in a trade.

He packed dried victuals and at dawn the next day was in the saddle, heading for Lancaster, Pennsylvania, where the great gunsmiths lived.

4

✫ ✫

SAM, following the best roads, traveled northeast to
Philadelphia, thence west to the Dutch country. He ob-
served everything on his journey and wrote down the
facts that impressed him most. He learned early, and to
his misfortune, the difference in currency between the
states, and the knowledge cost him a bit, or twelve and
one-half cents. A Pennsylvania tavern keeper, who sold
raw whiskey for three cents a glass, asked two levies for
a bed and, seeing Sam didn't understand, upped his price
to three bits. Learning he had been outwitted, Sam wrote
down in his record the value of coins and their names.
The coin he called a "bit" was called the "Spanish real"
by some travelers. New Englanders called it a "nine-
pence," New Yorkers called it a "shilling", and Pennsyl-
vanians called it an "elevenpenny bit", or "levy".

He learned that a Yankee was any shrewd, unscrupu-
lous trader, be he a New Englander or a Southerner. But
gradually the insult was being reserved only for New
Englanders who traded as far south as the trails ran. Sam
met a Yankee in Virginia, a man who peddled cooking
and eating utensils from a Jersey wagon. The man had
a supply of printed signs which stated that smallpox had
broken out and that all old cooking vessels were unsafe.
In each village, the trader posted the sign and sold his

62

stock to frantic housewives. Then he collected the discarded utensils and sold them in the next village.

In Tidewater, Sam saw women rub perfume under their arms. He wrote down how to make the perfume. He and Honoria would make some, and sell it. *Bouquet de Flora*, they called it.

The things he saw! Honoria and Donna—yes, and Pierce, too, and perhaps Mr. Frome—would be perted to hear his tales. Well, maybe not Mr. Frome. He had seen so much himself. But Jews wanted news. Perhaps Mr. Frome would pay him for his news. "News is money," Frome once had said. Sam thought, "I won't charge him. He's been kind to us. I'll report my intelligence—not all of it, but enough to stir talk and interest."

He got into several drunken brawls on the trip and in one village he and several other revelers almost wrecked a tavern. The other culprits paid the bill, including Sam's share, for he wouldn't part with his gold. Several times tavern wenches went to his room without invitation. Sometimes he lay with them, but more often he ordered them to leave him be. He never sat in the card games at the various taverns. Playing cards for money, hard-earned money, seemed stupid to Sam. He would gamble his life on his gun trigger, but he would not stake a bit on a card. In every village he visited, the tavern keepers drank with him and always remembered that he had been that way. Men liked to drink with Sam. He often sang when he drank, but when he drank too much he talked too much, and boasted in loud tones of his prowess and of his sister. He confided in strangers when he was drunk, but when he was sober he lived alone with himself, ashamed to ask any man's counsel, fearing he would be considered weak.

He never had seen such a city as Lancaster. Conestoga

wagons streamed over the sixty miles between Philadelphia and the Dutch country. Sam's horse was frightened by the wagons, miles of them, each carrying from three to five tons. They were built like boats, with canoe bottoms, rounded and smooth. The running gear and bodies were blue, and the sideboards were bright red. Each wagon was pulled by six horses and the horses' gear was heavy. Lor! The backbands were fifteen inches wide and the straps ten inches! The traces were made of iron chains. The harness was gay with brass plates and studs, and the head-stalls were decorated with bright bits of ribbon or ivory rings. The driver rode the near wheeler, working the six horses with a long whip. The rims of the wagons were eight inches wide. All the wagons were pushing toward the West. Sam had a yearning to follow them, but he remembered that the Ohio country wasn't the promised land, the promised land was back where the earth was black and the rivers big.

Brightly painted stagecoaches sped by the Conestogas. They were drawn by four horses, and hauled twelve passengers. Mail coaches made the best time, however, and Sam learned a man could send intelligence from Philadelphia to the far end of Pennsylvania for a fat fee. It should be remembered, he thought, and wrote it down.

He paid two levies a night for a bed at a second-rate tavern in Lancaster. Of course, he shared the bed with two men and never the same two. He asked questions and drank rum at the bar and learned the name of the best gunsmith. The smith shook his head when Sam showed him the specifications for his rifle-gun.

"I am proud of my work," the Dutchman said. "I do not make useless guns. This gun would be useless. Only a giant could balance it with two such long barrels and such a short stock."

64

"I can handle it," Sam said. "I have my own idea what a rifle-gun should be and, by the hinges of hell, I'll have it my way! Lead and brass the stock." He began stacking gold coins in little piles before the gunsmith's eyes. "You'll take English gold?" Sam said.

The smithy nodded. He had ways of using it. He never would question whence it came. "Here are five pieces of gold," Sam said. "There will be more gold pieces when the rifle-gun is finished."

The smithy agreed. Sam watched him put the English gold away. Old man Dabney had earned that gold, killing Englishmen for "God and Morgan's Men." And he had robbed them, too! Ay, of all they had. The butchers!

Sam made friends easily in Lancaster and at the Valley Forge Inn where he lodged. His best friend was a teamster who was waiting for his Conestoga to arrive in the Conestoga Valley where the wagons were made. Sam talked with him about the wagons. Maybe, he said, the wagons could be used in the South, if wider rims were forged.

" 'Stogas will serve your needs," the teamster said. "Ay, make their tires wider to take the mud, and their wheels smaller. Use horses in dry weather and over good roads, and mules in the woods. They're the best wagons ever made. I can drive one through a needle's eye, give me a big enough needle."

It was the teamster who taught Sam to smoke cigars. He noticed one day that his friend smoked light weed tobacco after rolling it between his palms. "Have one," said the guide. "They're stogies. If you ever snake a Conestoga you'll have to smoke stogies. The Dutchmen named 'em stogies because us 'stogas smoke 'em."

He entered into the sports of Lancaster and neighboring villages, wrestling and shooting and cracking bull

65

whips. The Pennsylvania teamsters used long stock whips and tipped the plaited rawhide with a single short strip of frayed green hide. They gripped their stocks in both hands and waved them around their heads and cracked them with sheer strength of shoulder muscle. The stogas could flick out a lighted torch at thirty feet, and their whips cracked like musket fire.

Sam made his own whip. He used the short stock of Southern teamsters, carving it from good hickory. He tipped his whip with a black-runner skin and practiced for hours, perfecting the wrist snap he had learned as a boy. Instead of whirling the whip around his head, he folded it against the stock and with one movement released it and with a quick snap of his wrist, a swinging underhand movement, he flicked it. Its crack was as loud as two muskets. Not only could he extinguish a torch at twenty feet, but he could uncork a bottle.

And Sam learned other things: that beer made him sleepy and that brandy awakened his senses and keened them and that when his belly sloshed with whiskey, all women were beautiful, even tavern wenches.

The gunsmith fulfilled his agreement to the day and Big Sam went with the Dutchman to prove the rifle before the final settlement was made. Sam chiseled a square hole in a board and stuffed the hole with beeswax. He scratched an "X" in the wax, painted the "X" white. He embedded a sharp blade in the wax. The blade cut the "X" exactly in half, lengthwise. The board was tacked to a tree and Sam began proving his gun at sixty yards. He leaned backwards to bring the long barrel to his shoulder and keep his balance. He looked only at the target, the center of the "X", and raised his gun until the silver sight blotted out the heart of the target. He touched the trigger. Then he examined the target. The blade had

66

cut the soft ball in half, and each half was buried in the wax.

The gunsmith gawked at him and ran to the tavern to fetch spectators. Sam shot from sixty-five yards, then seventy and split a bullet. At one hundred and ten yards, the bullet dropped a fraction. Sam measured the drop, allowed for it on the next shot, and split the "X" again.

"The deal is closed," he told the gunsmith, and paid him. He called on his friends and bade them goodbye. Then he mounted Claymore and rode away, singing the song of the 'stogas:

> "As I was going down the road, tired team
> and heavy load,
> "I cracked my whip and the leader sprung.
> I said day-day to the wagon tongue."

He traveled light, down the stage road to the Potomac, taking with him a supply of fine priming powder and a pouch of burgoo, dried oatmeal such as Scotch sailors had lived on for weeks by mixing it with water and cooking it into a gruel. He crossed the Mason-Dixon survey line and took the back trails to Maryland and came at last to the Blue Hills and followed the cuts until he reached the mountain passes of North Carolina's Great Smokies, named by the Indians who believed the haze over the hills was the smoke of the sun's peace pipe.

One night he stopped at Sergeant MacTavish's tavern on the high road to Salisbury. Traders, a lawyer, teamsters and a preacher, following the road back to Sevierville and the Tennessee frontier, studied him and his riflegun, carefully and respectfully, while he sat near the bar and stuffed himself with beef and beer.

67

"Ay," said the sergeant, lifting the gun. "It's a prime superfine rifle-gun, fitting for a giant."

"And a giant uses it," said the lawyer, smiling at Sam.

" 'Twould be a pleasure to see Andy handle this weapon," said the sergeant. "Maybe he couldn't lift it, he being such a mite of a fellow, but he could rest it in a fork, and blow off the ears of a bedbug."

"Who is Andy?" Sam asked.

"Andy Jackson," said the tavern keeper. "Over in Tennessee a'lawin' now. He's a heller with firearms. And sharp as a meat ax."

"He never took any shines to John Sevier and that State o' Franklin thing," volunteered the lawyer who wore a black coat and propped both elbows on the bar. "Andy's got a long head."

Sam accepted drinks from willing buyers and leaned against the bar and drank as became a gentleman.

"How goes politics in the Dutch country?" the lawyer asked.

"All they want up there is sound money," Sam said.

"Hamilton is a sound-money man," the lawyer said. "But Jefferson is stronger with the poor people and there are more poor people than chiggers. But mind me, only the popularity of General Washington is holding this country together."

"Jefferson's a fool," cut in the barman. "He talks about equality. How can we have equality with Indians and Niggahs ever'where? Either they are, or they ain't our equals. Burr is my man. There's a soldier for you. Burr would take a few swipes at the red 'uns out here and give us a chance to get some of that land that the good Lord intended us to have."

Sam felt grown-up, talking politics and drinking with important folks. He drank too much. His tongue was

68

loose. "I'll get my bait of red 'uns," he laughed. "I'll get 'em with my rifle-gun. I won't scalp 'em unless I shoot 'em in the eye, the right eye, by God!"

The preacher shook his head sadly at the group, gulped his last drink of rum and honey and wiped his mouth with the back of his hand. "Killing! That's all I hear," he said. "Hate. Indians, Nigras, British. We are sowing hate, and there will be a harvest."

"Reckon the rev is going out to save some red souls unless I shoot 'em first," said Sam impudently.

"Your gun will never disturb souls, son," the minister said.

The inn-keeper objected. "Now, look here, rev. You know as good as me that Indians and Niggahs ain't got souls. If they have, they is as good as us."

The lawyer coughed. "Oh, my! They have souls, yes, bob. Even the pope says so now. For years it was fit and proper to slaughter Indians and bond Niggahs because they were animals in God's eyes. The preachers and the pope said so, and took some of the money that God's children stole from the red 'uns. But finally the revs changed their minds and said the Indians and Niggahs had souls all the time. Of course, the idea of collecting money and sending missionaries out to build churches and control the country had naught to do with the sudden decision that the Gospel must be preached to Indians. Lor, bob, no!" The lawyer was drunk.

Sam smiled down at him. The lawyer was a chubby man with a little pot belly and a bald spot. When he talked and realized people were looking at him, he from time to time held his right hand over the bald spot. He carried two pistols in the tail of his frock coat. And as the discussion progressed, he withdrew the pistols and laid them on the bar. Sam noticed his hands then. They were

69

pudgy and the wrists were hairy. The lawyer removed the pistols from his coat only because they bothered him. His shoulders swayed while he talked and the pistols bumped against his legs and annoyed him. So he reached both hands behind him, flipped aside his coat tail and jerked the weapons out. Everybody jumped except Sam, and he looked down at the little man and laughed loudly. The little fellow reminded him of a bantam rooster stuffed too full of corn meal.

"I'll take the law to the Indians and let the revs take religion!" the lawyer shouted. "One is of no account without the other!"

"That's blasphemy," said the minister.

"Folderol," said the lawyer. "It's git as git can."

The preacher added, "We are digging our graves with slave labor and Indian bones. Oglethorpe was a wise man when he forbade the importation of slaves into Georgia. Shame on the slavers who cast aside that law! And what hear we now? A machine has been invented to clean cotton! The machine can do the work of twelve slaves! Slavery is doomed!"

The lawyer shouted, "What know you of the cotton machine? I know the snot-nose Yankee who made it. Old Eli. Down in Georgia, he made it. The Whitney gin. Look, you fools!"

He fumbled in his pocket until he found a sheet of paper and unfolded it. It was a drawing of the Whitney gin as it had been patented. "This was drawn from the patent," the lawyer laughed drunkenly. "The machine will gin fifty pounds of cotton a day! Old Eli thinks he is protected. Any blacksmith can make this machine. See how simple it is." He passed it around. Sam studied it, and while the crowd listened to the mouthing of the

70

lawyer, he wrote down the dimensions. That was a thing worth knowing.

"I've been traveling." The lawyer ordered more grog. "I know things. That machine will be king!"

He paused to watch the effect he made. "Ruin slavery? Ay, you buckoes, it will make slavery profitable. It will take a hundred slaves in the field to feed cotton for that machine. That machine will make cotton princes out of paupers. That machine will make England bow to us. That machine will build fleets and conquer new land. That machine is king! Cotton, men! The day will come when your indigo, your tobacco, your hemp, your rice— all away with it. You'll plant cotton to your verandahs, and that machine will gin it, and the Medes and Persians will wear cloth made in the shadows of these glorious and free hills!"

The lawyer weaved for a minute, then fell against the bar. The sergeant propped him up, shoved another drink toward him. "Go on! Go on! Hear him, men!"

The orator reached for the paper, a duplicate of Eli Whitney's patent. "This machine," the lawyer's voice was low and thick, "means that the boundary lines of the United States will extend from the North Pole to Mexico. Canada we will take! Old Eli thinks the law will protect his patent. There is no law out here and it will take weeks for him to hear that every blacksmith in the South is making his machine. A friend gave me this piece of paper. I'd rather own it than the jewels of England. This machine is king! It will build cities and roads. This young man," he tapped Sam's chest, "will see the day when cotton is planted to the eddies of the Mississippi River, and beyond. In the Louisiana country, on the Rio Grande. They will all be states some day. America! Plum' slap-dab to the Pacific! Indians! This young man," he pounded

Sam's back, "and his kind will take care of the red 'uns! This machine, my friends, is a machine of the inquisition. It will stretch the hides of Indians and will wipe out the only pure blood this nation will ever have, our noble red man—Goddom their stinking hides!" He gripped the bar for support and said, "Give me another brandy sling. Then I'm going to bed."

Sam, awed by the man's eloquence, asked, "What's your name, sir? Mine is Sam Dabney, of Georgia."

"Sam?" The lawyer put his hand on Sam's arm to steady himself. "It's a good name. My name is Thomas. Hosea Cincinnatus Thomas. Remember that name."

"I'll never forget it," vowed Sam. "And you remember mine. You'll hear of me. I'm going to the new land. I'm going to take my sister with me. We're going to have a mansion. We're ——"

"You talk too damned much!" Thomas interrupted him. "That's the difference in a good drinking man and a bad drinking man. A good drinking man talks when he's drunk but never says anything."

The rebuke sobered Sam somewhat. Most men would have been afraid to rebuke Sam Dabney, but not Lawyer Thomas.

"You're right, Mr. Thomas," Sam said quietly. "I do talk too much when I drink." And he went back into his shell.

"I like your name and I like your looks," Thomas added kindly. "Hope I see you again some time. I've been up in Virginia to see my kinsmen. Folks name of Houston. My cousin has a little bucko named Sam. Just like you. Sam Houston, 'ygod! He's not knee-high to a squatting bedbug, but 'ygod he can make himself heard already. Good night, you merry buckoes!"

The crowd raised their glasses as they shouted good-night to the staggering, swaggering lawyer. Sam lowered his drink when the Indian girl walked timidly into the tavern, her head bowed. Sergeant MacTavish stumbled to the end of the bar and growled, "Get out." The girl turned and, without a word, vanished into the darkness.

She was unlike any Indian girl Sam had ever seen. She was clean and there was no odor of fat or grease about her. Sam watched her out of the door. "Law," Mac-Tavish laughed. "She would have me sell her rum for her father even with guests at my bar. It's contrary to law. It would mean the irons for me."

"Who is she?" asked Sam.

"Mind that you be careful," the sergeant warned. "She's not fresh yet."

"Not fresh," a teamster bawled. "Ay, Georgian, if you would be a man, kink your backbone on an Indian virgin! It will make your beard black, and your hair wavy!"

"A kink in the back is not worth a knife in your back," MacTavish said. "She is a maiden and lives with her father in the first cabin down the trail."

"Trail her," the teamster pounded Sam's back. " 'Tis a dare!"

"It's folly," said the inn-keeper. "It's dangerous."

Sam said boastfully, "I fear naught of danger." He walked to the door. "I'll be spending the night here, but not *all* the night." He saddled his horse and trotted down the trail, peering through the darkness for a cabin. It was easy to find. A fire glowed near the door and the girl was there, scrubbing pots with sand.

She glanced up when Sam alighted. He spoke to her in Creek and she dropped her eyes. Sam misunderstood the gesture, not knowing she was Cherokee and that Chero-kee maidens never looked a man in the eye until they were squaws. She understood his desires and ignored him.

73

Enraged at her aloofness, he grabbed her shoulders and pushed her toward the shadows of the fire. She didn't scream, but made a whining cry, as a colt makes when it has wandered from its mother.

Sam's back was to the fire and the cabin when her father shot. He felt the ball rip into his shoulder and spread. He wheeled to face his assailant. The Indian stared at him for a moment, then vanished. The girl vanished, too, as a quail vanishes in the brush.

The wound wasn't painful at first. Sam mounted Claymore and was of a mind to return to the tavern and allow the sergeant to cut out the ball. Then he remembered the crowd. They would laugh at him. He could find some settlers down the trail and a white man would remove the ball. Foolishly, he headed his horse away from the inn and traveled all night.

He rested for several hours after sun-up and collected his wits. By cutting southeast through the valleys, he should strike the South Carolina military road that led to Hamburg. If he went southwest, he would follow the war path of the Cherokees. He might even have to cross the Smokies and find the Indian trail between the Hiwasse and Crow Town, past The Suck.

From The Suck, he could enter Georgia through a pass in the Cumberland foothills. But he would be foolish to travel the Indian trails with a wounded gun shoulder. So he headed southeast.

By nightfall, his shoulder was throbbing and he couldn't sleep. He began cursing himself. He was ashamed, too. Ashamed that he had wanted the Indian girl. True, he had not taken her, but an evil thought was as wicked as an evil act. It was evil to try to take a woman against her will. His father had said so. And Donna? He could never have faced her if he had gone into the bushes with an Indian. Ordinarily, Sam's conscience never bothered him. But now it did. Perhaps that was because he was in pain. Or perhaps it was because of Donna.

The pain became so intense the next day that he could see it, a wave of crimson, then a ball of agony.

"I've outwitted myself," mumbled Sam. "Are there no settlers in this valley? Damme, that's soft lead."

It suddenly occurred to him that the pistol ball in his right shoulder might kill him. He knew the wound was nasty and serious and that it was imperative to reach a settler's cabin before gangrene caused his flesh to slough. Surely, the South Carolina military road couldn't be far away.

He felt scorching stabs of pain dart down his side every time Claymore took a step and, by twisting his head over his shoulder, he saw livid streaks spreading fanwise across his back and under his arm pits. The flesh around his shoulder blade was yellowish-brown and stunk. The ball crunched against the bone. He knew exactly when, and how, the pain would attack and retreat. When his horse lifted her left foreleg, Sam closed his eyes and braced himself and, as the hoof descended, streaks of crimson flashed across his brain and rolled themselves into a ball and crashed against his nerves at the same instant the hoof touched the ground.

God's blood! Was his horse conspiring with the devil to torture him? How like an Indian to shoot him in the back. And over a wench. Perhaps she was a virgin. That was why he had wanted her. He had left home a boy and must return a man. A man wasn't a man until he had taken an Indian virgin. Everybody knew that. The soldiers and teamsters had told him so. For sure, some of the Dragoons had argued that a slave girl could take a yearling across that mysterious span that bridges the gulf between boyhood and manhood. But Sam didn't hold with that school. The men he admired had told him that only an Indian girl could make his beard black and wavy.

Then he thought of Donna and was ashamed.

He wondered again if he could gouge out the pistol ball by using his skinning knife with his left hand. Impossible. And if he attempted to cut a cross in his flesh and squeeze out the bullet by pressing the wound against a sapling he was almost certain to slash his tendons and perhaps disable his right arm for life.

Thoughts came to him easily in spite of his pain, or, perhaps, because of it. He wished he were left-handed. Or that he could use either arm dexterously. What was the word his Virginia schoolmaster had taught him, meaning a person who could use both hands equally? An ambidexter? He remembered the master's lecture. An ambidexter also was a bribe taker, a man who let not his left hand know what his right hand was doing.

He remembered many things. He had noticed often that men thought quicker and clearer when in danger. He had naught to do but think and keep his horse at a gentle walk to lessen the shocks to his injury. Riding alone through the Carolina wilderness a man could get in some licks at thinking.

Law! But that pistol ball hurt! Worse than breeching twins on a bed of splinters. His mother used to say that, and she should know about borning twins. There had been Molly and Dave. If they had lived, perhaps Honoria wouldn't have been so spoiled. His mother had said that, too. But his father had said she was batty and Honoria had laughed at her own mother and had caressed her father's face. Sam had wanted to caress his mother and to take her part, but he never had. He had never known his father to speak gently to his mother. But he didn't believe his mother was batty, even if she had wailed and clawed her breast and lain on the ground and kicked that day at the Methodist melting meeting. Everybody else was doing the same thing. Sam had hidden behind a log and watched them. And now that his mother was dead, he was sorry he had told his father about the incident. He used to hurt 'way down inside when his father abused his mother. Honoria would spy on her father and mother during their quarrels, and even at other times. She would try to tell Sam what she had seen and heard, but he wouldn't listen. He couldn't understand how his mother had disgraced her husband because she had professed God. At times, Sam wondered if his father didn't believe in a Methodist God, but was ashamed to admit it. There had been the time Sam had used God's name in vain and his father had told him, "Don't be a fool, Sam'l. If there is a God, you'll only make Him mad and if there ain't a God, you're wasting breath."

Sam reined his horse and swayed in his saddle. The lead in his back must have been mighty soft to have spread against his bone like a burgoo fritter. Never heard of anybody using such pure lead for ammunition except the British his father had told him about. But the British had been rich and had never worried about the waste of lead. British lead? Sam rested his bridle arm on the pommel of his Spanish saddle. "Damme," he muttered, "maybe that was British lead."

He was positive the pistol's charge had carried two buckshots behind the ball. He had felt them scatter when the charge tore into his flesh. Only the British used buckshots with pistol balls. Their smooth-bore guns were not true enough to risk only one ball with one charge. The British, extravagant butchers, had used soft lead with two loads even in pistols at King's Mountain. But there were no British pistols, or combat practices, among Carolina Indians in 1795. Or were there? After all, the Indian who had shot him was different from any Indian Sam had ever seen. The Indian wench was different, too. She was clean and smelled good. That's why he knew she was a virgin. Squaws smelled sour and would leave a man itching and scratching so he could hardly sit his saddle without squirming, even in the presence of ladies.

Well, Sam blessed heaven, he wasn't going back to Georgia with squaw-saddle. Honoria would know of his adventure if the evidence were on him, and she would pester him. Donna might hear, too. He was gripped with nausea when he thought of the possibility of Donna discovering his transgression. And Pierce? Pierce would never allow him in his home again and would forbid him to see Donna. Who would believe his story, that he hadn't taken the Indian wench?

Why hadn't he returned to the Ox Head tavern and let Sergeant MacTavish cut the ball out of his shoulder? The jeers of the sergeant wouldn't have hurt as badly as his wound. Why had he allowed his pride to warp his judgment? Why? Why? A hundred whys peppered his brain. He had been a fool to make the trip. He squeezed his legs against his horse's sides and Claymore resumed her leisured walk, perhaps wondering why Sam allowed her to mosey along so early in the day when she was fresh and should be making tracks.

"But I've not outwitted myself," Sam muttered. "I'm not batty." He looked lovingly at the long rifle tied to his saddle with rawhide. He was proud of it, with its silver sight, a radical rifle-gun that would explode if a whisker brushed its trigger. Its borings were tight and Sam could lay the seam of a bullet on a scratch at sixty yards, and splatter a gobbler's head at one hundred and fifty.

What if he had journeyed to the Pennsylvania Dutch country to have the gun made, and had spent his inheritance! The rifle was worth it.

Sam reined his horse again and tried to straighten in his saddle, but the pain was too intense. He remembered what his mother had told him, "When you can't go no more, call on God."

He braced his left hand on his pommel and pushed back his body and tilted his head, but the words wouldn't come. He remembered his father's admonition, "If God is all they say He is, He'll get you out of a tight place if He's of a mind to. But if His mind ain't made up by that time, ain't no use of begging."

Sam wondered if he were becoming delirious. His mother had been delirious just before she died and her mind had raced and skipped as his was doing. His vision was hazy. He centered his attention on a fat frog that sat, panting, by the trail. Then he closed his eyes tightly, and opened them quickly to clear his vision. The frog was gone. And Sam wondered if it had ever been there at all. He wondered if there was anything in the world except the things he could see, heat waves dancing over the parched earth, palmetto leaves caked with dust, splotched where dew had stood; and stillness, intense gripping stillness and bigness; and crows flying to the windward over the Carolina wilderness.

5

THE pain grew beyond endurance and Sam dismounted stiffly, determined to take the risk of cutting out the ball with his left hand. Claymore lifted her head and tossed her mane, and her ears quivered and stood erect. Sam watched the trail over which he had traveled. Everything meant something to the Georgian, and his horse's behavior might mean danger, but there should be no hostile Indians between him and Georgia.

The trail was deserted. Claymore wandered off the trail and poked her nose among the palmetto shoots. Sam swayed. "Maybe I'm dying," he muttered. "Or else I'm just scared, so scared the soldier in my knees has melted." Perhaps he never would see Georgia again, or Donna, or Honoria. He tried to think, if he had his choice of persons to see, would he rather see Donna or Honoria? Donna might caress him and calm him, then prod for the bullet; Honoria wouldn't waste time on caresses, but would rip away his shirt and dig for the ball.

Claymore cocked her ears again. Sam leaned against a tree and studied the trail, squinting one eye.

Two horsemen appeared simultaneously on a ridge to his left. "Master and Niggah," Sam mumbled. "Glory be!" One of the horsemen lifted his right arm, with two fingers extending. It was the sign of peace. The riders galloped down the ridge, the Negro, a huge grinning buck, slightly in arrear of his master. The master's hair was oily black, and when Sam first saw his face through the haze of his pain he instinctively reached for his knife. Never before had he seen such a face. It looked as though it were carved out of granite, tanned with hickory bark and polished with beeswax. The cheeks were high and the man wore two turkey feathers in his hair. Half-breed. Sam watched him curiously.

The pair slowed their horses to a walk as they approached the wounded man, and the master spoke. His words were soft, not guttural. "I am Tishomingo. This is my slave, Caesar, a Krooman."

"I'm Sam Dabney of Georgia and I've been shot."

The Indian dismounted and handed his gun to the Krooman. "It would have been wise to cut your jacket from the wound." He examined Sam's shoulder. "A Cherokee wound, it is. A ball and two buckshots."

"Are you Cherokee?" Sam demanded.

"Nay. I'm Choctaw. My father was white. I learned from him about white men. Sometimes, my friend, white men are foolish, ay?"

"Ay," said Sam. He studied Tishomingo. Choctaw. The first he had ever seen. Half white and educated. He was not as tall as Sam. His eyes were brown and were the saddest eyes Sam had ever seen. They were a white man's eyes, but Tishomingo's cheek bones and nose testified to his Indian blood. The eyes were never still. At first Sam thought they were cunning eyes and then he realized that only a man with a great hurt in his heart could have such sad eyes. Tishomingo's mouth was small and he often compressed his lips tightly. When he smiled, he smiled with only the left side of his lips. Even the smile was sad and bitter. A tired smile. Sam formed his opinion of men quickly. This man was brutal and shrewd.

A fire was burning inside of him. Only his eyes were kind. Sam had seen deer with eyes like that, soft and questioning. But the man's mouth reminded him of a catamount's mouth, a sharp line that never opened completely even when he spoke.

"The Cherokees are jealous of their maidens," Tishomingo said. He pressed the flesh around the wound. Sam winced, but the Indian ignored the evidence of pain. "Cherokee maidens wash themselves every new moon with ferns. 'A clean maiden gets a fine man.' That is a Cherokee proverb."

"Is my wound serious?"

"The flesh stinks. You could not have lived until you reached the settlements. There are no settlers in this valley." He cut the leather jacket from Sam's shoulder.

"It's soft lead," Sam said.

"British lead."

"Why have the Cherokees British lead?"

"The Cherokees were soldiers of the king during the war. They were allies of the British for many years. The British gave them powder and lead and rum in payment for scalps, first French scalps and later American scalps. They do not understand that the war is over."

He motioned to the slave and spoke in Choctaw. Sam said, "I do not understand Choctaw. Are you allies of the Creeks?"

"No. Our tribe is near the big water."

"Mississippi?"

The Indian nodded. "I told Caesar to fetch water. There's water over the ridge. I also have need of a deer. He'll seek one, if a lick is near and the sun isn't too high."

Sam watched the Negro disappear over the ridge. "I've water in my canteen," he said.

82

"It's not fresh. I need much water. I brought some too. I knew I would find a wounded white man."

"How?"

"I have been to the war councils of the Cherokees. I heard about the giant with the strange gun who spoke the hated Creek language to a maiden, and who sought her even under the eyes of her father."

"Why are the Cherokees in council?"

"Because they're fools." Tishomingo rinsed the wound with water. Then he cut ferns, rubbed them between his palms until they lathered and scrubbed the wound. "I knew I'd find you soon. Your trail showed your horse was walking slowly. Men don't travel so slowly unless there is trouble. I and my slave left the trail and cut over the ridge and found you." He pointed to a tree. "Stand against it and press your belly and chest against it. If you lie down, the blood will gush to your wound."

Sam felt the Indian's knife rip his flesh, and sweat popped from his skin and rolled down his back. Tishomingo worked rapidly. He cut a cross in the flesh, folded back the flesh, wiping away the pus with damp ferns as he worked. The knife scraped against the bone and the world swam before Sam's eyes. He gripped the tree trunk with both arms and hugged it while Tishomingo probed.

"Push harder," the Indian commanded. "The ball is ready." Sam strained his muscles and pushed until his chest ached and his wind was short. "It is out," Tishomingo said. "But you must stand straight. The blood will gush if you lie down."

Sam stood, breathing deeply but not gasping. "The buckshots?"

"One is out. The other must stay there. It will do you no hurt."

He sponged the wound again and was bathing it with

83

salt water when Caesar returned with more water. "No deer," he told his master. "Sun too high." His English was good.

"Will you pay me for my horse?" Tishomingo asked.

"It is a vow," Sam said.

The Negro unsaddled the beast he had ridden and led him to his master. With one hand, Tishomingo held the horse's head high, and with the other cut his throat. The Negro ripped open the belly and carved out huge hunks of the animal's liver. Tishomingo held the warm, quivering flesh to the open wound.

"Does it draw?"

"Ay," said Sam.

The liver turned green as it drew the poison from the wound. "It is done," said the Indian. "You may rest."

The slave pulled the carcass of the horse to one side of the trail and built a fire, heating water. Sam sat in the shade, his head drooped, his back throbbing. "I have burgoo in my pouch," he said weakly.

"You need meat. We will have meat when the animals walk at sun-down."

He left Caesar with Sam and took his gun and walked over the ridge to the stream and shot a doe and squirrels when they came for water at twilight. He pointed to the kill and the Negro began preparing food. The meat was mixed with the burgoo and a stew was made. Sam could feel his strength returning when he ate. The pain had settled to a slow throbbing. He would be ready to travel in a few days. He and the Indian sat by the fire while Caesar gathered pine boughs for beds.

"Are you a Christian?" Sam asked.

"Nay. My father was. But I am the nephew of Pushmataha, the Choctaw chieftain, and I hold with his people

84

that the Choctaws came from the Holy Mound, the great Choctaw mound near Locha Poka."

"Locha Poka?" Sam repeated it slowly.

"Ay. It means 'Here we rest' or 'promised land.' Some say Locha Poka, others Loachapoha. In our own language we say Lau-a-chih-fo-hah, and it means 'making many to rest in the good lands.' To the Choctaw, it is the promised land, the land set aside for my people by Aba Inki, the God of the Muscogees."

Sam stared into the darkness and remembered all that Harkins and Pierce had said. Oh, promised land, the blood you must drink, the feet you must feel—men and oxen, British feet, Indian feet, Spaniards, Texans, Tennesseans. And the hope and triumph that you will nourish, Locha Poka.

"Your father taught you English?" Sam asked Tishomingo.

Tishomingo nodded. "My father taught me much." He didn't tell that he had studied in New Orleans or that his father had been a British agent, sent first to the Choctaws to arouse them against the French. He had failed, but he had stayed with the tribe and married. Later, he had tried to ally the Choctaws with the Chickasaws against the Colonists, but failed again. Then the crown had recalled him, and he never returned. He had introduced slavery to the Choctaws. The Indians had loved him.

Sam was thoughtful, gazing into the fire. "Where did the Cherokee council sit?"

"In the Great Smokies. There will be trouble. Tribesmen from Ken-tah-teh gathered with the Cherokees. They sicken of losing their lands."

"Ken-tah-teh?" Sam was puzzled. "Kentucky? The dark land?"

"Ken-tuck-e," Tishomingo smiled sadly. "Ay, but it is not the dark ground. Ken-tah-teh! It's Wyandot tongue. It's mother is Iroquoian. It means 'land of tomorrow.' White men called it dark land because they feared it would be bloody and dark tomorrow. And it will be unless your people and my people agree on lands and rivers."

"Ay?"

"Ay. Even now Tecumseh, the Shawnee, is going about the land preaching war to the Indians. He's seeking an alliance between all nations."

"Ay?"

"Ay."

Sam selected a pine needle and chewed it thoughtfully. The wind rustled the palmetto leaves. He watched the fire leap and play. "Was Tecumseh with the Cherokees?"

Tishomingo's face did not change expression as he lied. "No. He wasn't there. But he'll come to them, and to us. He'll want us in his Confederacy. The Choctaws are rich."

"Will you join?"

"The white men must say. We know your people are going west. Our land is between you and the river. We must have a sign of peace. You're a Georgian. Do you know Mr. Harkins, the agent?"

Sam said, "I've heard of him, and goodly things."

"I have done you a favor," Tishomingo said.

"I am in your debt," Sam replied. "And I will repay. I will take you to Mr. Harkins."

The Indian called Caesar to the shadows and instructed him. "Go to my uncle," he said softly. "Tell him I ride to Milledgeville and that I will see and listen and heed and learn. Tell him a white man, a big man, is in my debt. I will know soon what the white men

86

scheme." The Negro grasped his master's hand, pressed it to his forehead and disappeared.

Back at the fire, Tishomingo said, "I've sent my slave to my people. He'll get a horse on the trail. He's like a black bear in the woods. I've sent word to my uncle that I'm with a big man, Big Sam Dabney, the scout."

Sam said, "I will repay your goodness."

"There is a way. Already your people are driving out the Creeks. Our lands are in your path. We'll need all the white friends we can make, and you'll need Indian friends. There's no war between your people and my people, Big Sam, but there will be if we listen to the old hungry people and to the toothless squaws and to the warriors who live by their guns. And there will be blood on the moon and in the river and in the fields. You and I may sow in peace, but the harvest will be hate unless there is council between your people and my people."

6

✶ ✶

TISHOMINGO made their camp beside a creek where a fast head of water broke out of the side of the ridge. He surveyed the creek quickly, marked the watering place of animals and made camp upstream, behind a bend. He chose a course where the water flowed rapidly and scooped a hole in the bank. Then he threw stones into the bottom of the hole and watched clear, pure water creep through the rocks until it reached the level of the creek. He made a lean-to of saplings, and roofed it with palmetto leaves. He sought the tender fronds of large ferns, twisted them into a string, slipped the string into Sam's wound, and was satisfied with the drainage.

And while he rested and regained his strength, Big Sam talked of his life and learned much of the south-western Indians. Tishomingo told him of the proud Natchez nation that had scattered rather than submit to assimilation by the conquering Choctaws, and of the Pascagoulas who had committed wholesale suicide rather than suffer slavery in the hands of the Spanish and French. Sam learned of a trail that led west from Georgia to the Mississippi, and of another that meandered north-east from Natchez to Tennessee, through the wild Chickasaw domains.

The Chickasaws guarded the trace and collected tolls. If a traveler wouldn't pay, the Indians disemboweled him, filled the cavity with rocks and threw the body in one of the rivers that criss-crossed the wilderness. It was a trick they had learned from white men.

Even then, the trading path between the Natchez country and Tennessee was being called the Natchez Trace. Sam asked many questions about Natchez. Its status was confused. France had ceded Louisiana to Spain rather than allow England to claim it as spoils of the Seven Years' War. Natchez, the oldest settlement on the Mississippi, was a part of British West Florida during the Revolution and was loyal to the crown. However, Spain, with France's silent approval, took the Natchez district from England by force of arms and opened the territory to Americans in 1781. But in order to reach Natchez overland, settlers had to cross the Choctaw and Creek nations. At the second treaty of Paris, in 1783, England recognized the United States' claim to the Natchez district. But Spain didn't. To complicate matters further, Georgia claimed the region and had organized it into the county of Bourbon.

"Well, who owns the blamed land now?" Sam asked as Tishomingo finished a lesson in the history of the Southwest.

"My people believe your people will keep it. Your people are there. The Spaniards and even the French sit around council fires and swap land. But your people take land with their rifles and keep it with their tomahawks. England has no claim in the South now. Only America and Spain, with France toying with Spain as a muskrat plays with a crawfish."

"How is it that you know so much?" Sam was ashamed of his ignorance, but he wasn't ashamed to ask questions.

"My father taught me. And I've traveled to Mexico and to Martinique."

"I never heard of Martinique," said Sam.

"It's an island, lush and heavy with trees. It is a beautiful land, but it is cursed. There is fever and pox and snakes, and strange things in the land. Lake Flournoy took me there. He bought slaves there for a pittance and sold them for much gold."

Sam said, "I know naught of all of this. Tell me more."

Tishomingo told him of Martinique and of other isles of the Indies. And of the great Flournoy who lived among the Choctaws. His mother was a Choctaw princess and his father was a Martinique Creole who had fetched slaves to Louisiana and had founded the family fortune. Lake Flournoy was a proud, boastful man, a kinsman of Marie Rose Tascher de la Pager's (a Creole who had gone to France and had become the bride of the Vicomte de Beauharnais). Flournoy would allow no man to forget that he was a kinsman by blood to Marie, and by marriage to one of the great gentlemen of France.

Tishomingo smiled as he told Sam the story. "If you would be Lake Flournoy's friend," he said, "tell him you have heard how beautiful his kinswoman is."

Sam said, "I'm not interested in Lake Flournoy's Frenchy kinsmen. But I am interested in his slaves he fetched from the isle. Are slaves cheap there?"

"Ay. They've married into the Caribs and they breed like flies and die as flies, of pox and fever and snake bites."

"Snakes?"

"The fer-de-lance. It's the best slave guard a man can find. A dainty snake that prowls at night. In the Indies, the jungles are so thick it was easy for slaves to run away. But the masters took the fer-de-lance there, and freed them in the jungles. If a slave runs away, the snakes may strike him. They kill as lightning kills and the slaves fear to run away. Lake Flournoy sends to Martinique for snakes and keeps them in a box and each day he fetches his slaves from the barricoons and parades them by the box. He tells them if they run away, the snakes will follow." Tishomingo smiled, rather sadly. "Lake Flournoy is a wise man, and rich. But he is also cruel. He breeds his slave girls too young. Once, he tried to breed a Chickasaw maiden, a prize of war, to a black. My uncle, Pushmataha, forbade it. Lake Flournoy said he could get good slave stock from Chickasaw and black. He lays with his own fresh slave girls. He says he is a noble man and that it is his privilege to take virgins before they mate. My father said such was the practice of noblemen many years ago in France and Spain. But most Choctaws hold to no such cruelty, even to slaves. Some day I will kill Lake Flournoy."

It was upon Sam's tongue to ask why, but he didn't. If this strange man wanted to tell him why, he would. It was Tishomingo's business and Sam was too wise a man to pry into it.

The Indian lit his pipe with a coal from the fire. Sam rested against the lean-to and paid apt attention to his friend, to every word. Tishomingo said, "Soon we can travel into Georgia. Your sister is weary of servitude."

Sam said, "In all my days, I've never heard an Indian talk as you. You speak wiser and better than Pierce Chadbourne."

"Wait until you hear Tecumseh, the Shawnee," Tishomingo said. "He's the greatest orator of all time, excepting Pushmataha."

"Where did you hear him?" Sam demanded. "You said he was not at the Cherokee council!"

Tishomingo drew slowly on his pipe. "My friend has a quick mind." He didn't answer the question and Sam reserved it. "Tell me more of Miss Chadbourne," the Choctaw said. "Does her brother approve of you?"

Sam said, "It is not for him to say. It is for Donna to say. And I have not the gift of words you have and cannot tell you of her. But she must never know why I was wounded."

"Ay, that is love. My new friend carries a long rifle and is strong, but he fears his woman will learn he was foolish with an Indian girl. It's our secret, I'll vow."

Big Sam closed his eyes and was thoughtful. "Will you teach me Choctaw?" he asked suddenly.

"Ay. It is not a difficult tongue if you know Creek. We're all Muscogees or Muskhogeans, all from Nanih Waiya."

"Nanih Waiya?" He remembered Pierce had mentioned it.

"The Bending Hill, or the Great Earth. The Muscogees lived in a far country, what is now New Spain. There were two brothers, Chahta and Chickasa and the Muscogees were the chosen people of Aba Inki."

"Ay?"

"Ay. Aba Inki is the Master of Life and we are his chosen people. Our prophets told us of a promised land and Chahta and Chickasa led my people through the wilderness, until we came to the great river, and it opened and we came to the land that Aba Inki had said was to be ours. Why do you smile, Big Sam?"

"Damme, man. I'll vow you've been heeding the teachings of missionaries."

"My people, my friend, should have sent missionaries to you. We believed in one God many years before your people came. You smile because our history seems as your history of the Jews. All religions are kin, Big Sam. But hear me out. Each night Chahta and Chickasa planted

92

a stick in the ground and the next morning the wanderers followed the direction in which the stick pointed. Then came a dispute. Chickasa said one day the stick pointed north, and some of his family followed him. But Chahta vowed the stick was straight and that our people had reached the promised land. A city was built, a great city, walled and beset with towers. And the Bending Hill, Nanih Waiya, was built. And thereafter, all the Choctaw great were born, not of woman, but of Nanih Waiya. Aba Inki is the Father of the Choctaw great and Nanih Waiya is the mother, God and Earth."

Sam asked, "Whence came the Creeks?"

"From the Chickasaws. A Chickasaw mingo, or leader, parted from his nation because of a dispute over the true religion, and founded the Creek nation."

"Does Mingo mean leader?"

"Ay," Tishomingo said. "My real name is Tishu Mingo, or Tisku Miko. *Mingo, micco* and *miko* all mean leader or prince. I was named for a Chickasaw friend of my father's."

"It's beyond my understanding," said Sam. "I'll call you Chock. I want to be your friend."

Tishomingo handed Sam his pipe, and Sam puffed it and passed it back. "You are my friend and I am your friend. I will teach you our language and our ways."

"Now let us talk of other things," Sam said. "What of your love, Tishomingo?" He spoke quietly as men do when they speak of love in the presence only of other men, and of the woods.

Tishomingo's mouth tightened, and an expression of bitterness and hatred spread over his face. But the expression passed quickly and his face was sad. "Already I think of you as a brother, Big Sam. The wilderness and danger make brothers of men, or beasts of them. Yes, I

93

had a love once. She was white. It was in New Orleans where my father sent me to study. I was of a mind to leave my people and go her way. I took her to our village to see my father and mother. She saw Lake Flournoy and went to him. I put on these," he motioned to his turkey feathers. "And I will always wear them."

Within a week, Sam was able to use his right shoulder. Tishomingo released the fronds, and the flesh healed on the outside. But the scar was jagged, a big cross. Sam still was weak, but they were resolved to travel the next day. Tishomingo awoke before dawn, stirred the fire into being and heated burgoo. Sam arose stiffly, flexed his muscles and exercised his shoulder. They were eating their food, squatting by the fire. The horses were ready. Claymore tipped her ears and shied. Tishomingo cocked his head, then looked quickly at Sam. Big Sam looked at the sky. Far away, he heard it, a low hum as the wind makes when it rushes into a shallow cave.

"Law!" he got to his feet. "The sun is up, but a storm is coming."

Tishomingo grabbed his left arm and shoved him toward his horse. "It is death from the sky!" He fumbled with his bridle, never taking his eyes from the southwest, whence came the hum. They mounted and dashed away, seeking shelter under a ledge.

"You're as pale as an old woman," Sam laughed. "Have you never seen a storm before?" Sam protested as Tishomingo pushed him under the ledge.

"Listen," the Indian whispered, lest his voice be heard by some terrible Unknown.

The hum graduated into a whine, then into a roar. The sky grew dark. A great cloud, a mile long and half a mile wide, swept up from the southwest, sucking leaves

94

in its wake. The sun was blotted out and the cloud seemed to shriek and wave.

"Birds!" Sam stared in awe.

"Pigeons," Tishomingo shouted. "The great migration. An ill omen. They are far to the east of their usual flight."

"What does it mean?"

"Death if the leaders light here. Take your blanket. If the leaders dart down, jump in front of them and wave your blanket!"

The passenger pigeons swept like locusts over the ridge, the leaders circling, dipping and soaring. The flight, to Sam, looked like a huge black sea monster weaving and diving. The birds swept over the ledge and the wind from their wings rustled Sam's hair. The scouting pigeons circled a forest beyond the ridge, then darted into the woods. A strange cry arose as the millions of birds plunged in, following their leaders blindly. A few stragglers passed over, and then the sky was clear.

Sam and Chock ran to the tip of the ridge and looked into the woods. It seemed alive and crawling but while they looked the green forest became bare. Every leaf vanished. Huge trees were denuded. Thousands of birds were smothered. Deer and coons ran from the forests. Others were caught in the crush and were smothered. The pigeons hopped across the ground, fighting for mast and insects. The leaders skimmed across the forest, herding the birds into the woods. Then the leaders took off, and the cloud arose and followed, leaving behind a pile of birds that stretched more than two hundred yards into the naked forest. Vultures appeared and began circling, taking up their sentry duty until the sun would begin the work they must finish.

"We must ride," Chock said. "The streams will be

stinking. And I must think of my people. They may be suffering."

Sam asked, "How do you know such things?"

"Everything means something. The pigeons came from the southwest. They have passed my people and I hear our maize is gone. The pigeons leave nothing."

They rode rapidly toward the Piedmont country, pausing only long enough at the cabins to get fresh victuals and water. Sam's wound had healed completely and his spirits had returned. He often sang as he rode. His music amused Tishomingo who tried to imitate him. "Ay, Chock," Sam said, "You sing like a frog with a cowhorn in his gullet." Big Sam sang the drover's song and Chock slapped his left palm against his saddle, keeping time. The horses stepped gayly. The roads were good. The weather was good, for summer time had reached the Piedmont.

Sam tilted his head as he sang:

"Now pretty Molly's daughter did keep the
   turnpike gate,
And all the travelers vowed she was prettiest
   in the state.
Old Johnny for a living did follow the drover's
   life,
And be Johned if Molly's daughter didn't up
   and be his wife."

They came at last to the plantation of Mr. Dohrman whose tobacco fields lay like crazy-quilts on the brown earth. Huge Krooman slaves stooped as they tended the plants. An overseer sat his horse near the field, his head drooped, his eyes closed. The chant of the male slaves, the hum of the women and the heat made all the world

96

seem drowsy. Sam reined his horse and heeded the slaves' song, impressing the melody and words on his brain. It was a sing-song melody about a man named Dixye, "a fine old man."

The negro pace-maker sang the words as he walked his furrow, "Ol' man Dixye was a fine ol' man."

The other slaves echoed, "I wish I was back on Dixye's lan'."

The overseer yawned and rubbed his eyes when he saw the pair. "What kind of red 'un are you?" he gawked at Tishomingo.

Sam said quickly, "My friend is a Choctaw. Mind your manners or I'll unwrap your navel and jerk your legs off."

Sam's haughty words belied his manner and dress, but not his gun. The overseer stared at the rifle, at Sam's tomahawk and said meekly, "I meant no offense, stranger. If your friend is a Choctaw, I can help you and you can help this place."

"How?"

"At the big house," the overseer dismounted and stood respectfully by Sam, "is the family of André Duportail. They're Frenchies, running to save their hides from the Revolution. They're going to the Choctaw nation if they can get through."

Tishomingo said, "Why?"

"They're looking for a man, a Chock bastard named Lake something."

The Indian's face was calm. "Lake Flournoy is a gentleman," he said quietly, "and my friend." Sam wondered why Tishomingo lied. That was the second lie he knew his friend had said. He had lied to him about Tecumseh. But being a wise man, Big Sam kept his own council.

7

THEY galloped to the big house, up the lane and dismounted at the steps. A slave took their horses and
fetched his master, Mr. Dohrman, who was impressed
particularly with Tishomingo. He never had seen a
cultured half-breed before, but he never had been among
the Creeks or Choctaws, where many British and Scotch
gentlemen had settled and married Indian girls.

Dohrman was a friend of Lafayette's and had been
at the Huger place down near Charleston when the
marquis had first arrived in the United States, and had
spent a day or so with the Hugers.

Through Lafayette, he had met the Duportails in
Paris before the Revolution. André Duportail, fleeing the
Terror, had escaped to America with his wife, Anestasie.
His father had died on the guillotine. He was not a
nobleman, but a writer who had displeased Robespierre.
His son, André, was a merchant of sorts, a dealer mostly
in perfumes and silks. He and his family had made their
way to England, thence to Norfolk and eventually into
South Carolina, to the home of Lafayette's friend. Dohr-
man summoned André to the verandah and presented
him to Sam and Tishomingo. The Frenchman bowed.
Tishomingo nodded. But Sam offered his hand and
André smiled at the friendly gesture and accepted it.

Tishomingo said, "I hear you seek Lake Flournoy, the Choctaw. I am a Choctaw."

André's face lighted. "God's mercy. This is the first good fortune I have encountered in years. I want to reach M'sieur Flournoy. The widow of Vicomte de Beauharais ——"

"Widow?" Tishomingo interrupted. "Is the vicomte dead?"

"Yes. He was president of the National Assembly, but that couldn't save him when Robespierre's venom began spewing. My father was his friend. They died the same day. The vicomte's widow, Josephine, told me of her kinsman in the Choctaw country. Can you take us to him?"

Tishomingo said, "Ay. I will see you through the Creek Country."

"*We* will," said Big Sam.

"The one you call Josephine is the lady Lake Flournoy calls Marie, the beautiful Creole."

André said, "She is beautiful, and wise. Already she has aligned herself with the revolutionists and is seen with Bonaparte of Corsica, a little soldier who struts in public places, but who is shrewd and expedient."

Sam was thinking of his good fortune and of how pleased Pierce and Harkins would be when he returned to Georgia with a Choctaw leader and a Frenchman who had a claim of friendship with Lake Flournoy, the most powerful Indian half-breed of the Southwest. Already Sam was making his plans.

"You must rest here," André said. "It will be several days before my wife can travel."

Dohrman said, "I'll be honored to have you." Then he frowned. He could lodge Sam in the big house, but what of Tishomingo? He was too well-born for the

99

quarters, but not well-born enough for the manor. The democracy and informality of the frontier did not exist in the Carolinas. Tishomingo read Dohrman's thoughts and said, "I will ride on. My friend may remain."

"No," Sam said testily. "I ride with you. We must go to Hamburg. If Mr. Duportail would go with us through the Creeks, he can meet us in Hamburg. What manner of wagons have you, and stock?" he asked the Frenchman.

André, sensing tension he did not understand, asked Sam and Tishomingo to inspect his equipment. He had bought it in Virginia. Sam was pleased when he saw the two wagons, sturdy three-ton 'stogas. André had eight horses for his wagons, and good mounts for his party, which included four blue-gummed Gullahs. Sam explained that the wagons' wheels must be changed. On paper, he drew plans for smaller, wider wheels. He told André the work could be done in Hamburg. He also counseled that the wagons be geared for oxen.

"This man is right," Dohrman said. "I suggest you ride to Hamburg with them and have work begun on your gear. I'll escort your wife to Hamburg within two weeks. I must go to Charleston and I can see them on through to Hamburg."

Sam said, "It is a good plan. We can have your gear readied in Hamburg, then send it to Savannah, and have it billed to Panton & Co., in Pensacola. The British tradehouse will send it on keels to Natchez. There you can get it and snake it through to Lake Flournoy's."

André was surprised. "Can we not drive the equipment through from Georgia?"

Big Sam glanced at Chock and the Indian laughed. Sam laughed too. "God's navel, man, no! There are no roads. We can get through on horses, but never wagons. And by sending your equipment through Panton, it will be safe from the Spaniards and Creeks. The house pays tribute for protection."

André said, "But my wife? Will she be safe riding from Georgia to Natchez?"

"She'll be safe so long as we are," Sam said. "Safer than if they go by boat. Panton can guarantee safety of goods, but not the lives of Frenchmen, particularly ladies who are beautiful and men who have scalps as tempting as yours."

"We will ride with you then," André said. "I am in your hands. But what will be your fee for your service?"

"We'll fix that later," Sam said and Tishomingo nodded.

André sent a slave to fetch his wife and she curtsied to Sam and then looked up at him quickly and caught her breath. Sam started to speak, but swallowed his words. He was learning manners rapidly. Anestasie was a small woman, a bit larger than Honoria to be sure, but not as tall as Donna. Her auburn hair was done in a fashionable knot, and her eyes looked green to Sam, a hazy smoky green. He peered into them. They *were* green. She smiled and his pulse leaped. He wondered if André were looking at him. Or Tishomingo. But even if they were, he couldn't take his eyes from the woman. And she did not lower her eyes even though he stared. Her dress was of green silk and was cut so low at the neck that he could see the snug tiny valley between her breasts. Sam suddenly forgot about Donna, and even about Honoria. This woman was regal. She looked as though she never had stooped to any task.

Anestasie laughed and broke the spell. It was a husky throaty laugh. "Never," she said, "have I seen a giant before. I will feel safe on such a journey with *you*, Mr. Dabney." She laughed again.

Sam said, "Tishomingo and I will get you through the Creeks. And it will not be a lonely journey. Mrs. Harkins, the elegant wife of the Georgia Indian agent, is going. And Miss Donna Chadbourne, too. They go to Natchez."

"Hoity toity," laughed Anestasie. "It will be a lark."

Sam stared at her again. "Madam," he said quickly, "what do you know of these things?" He showed her the recipe for the perfume he had written down.

She studied it. "*Bouquet de Flora*," she said. "It is a very cheap perfume. These ingredients are not dear. I have some very good perfume."

Sam turned to André. "You asked me, sir, about my fee for scouting you. You will laugh, but here is my proposition."

"Yes?"

"Your wife is going to Charleston with Mr. Dohrman. I would that she buy these ingredients for me." He pointed to the recipe for perfume. "I also beg one of your wife's old dresses and some silk and lace."

Dohrman laughed. "Are you going into the dressmaking business?"

Tishomingo realized Sam was embarrassed by his odd request and said, "Do not laugh. My friend has done a good thing. He has a sister."

Anestasie said, "It is a generous thought. I'll give you one of my best dresses for your sister, also silk and lace as you ask. And I will purchase the things you want. And more, I'll give you a bottle of my choice perfume."

"Then your husband will owe me naught for my service," said Sam.

102

"Have you no sweetheart?" Anestasie Duportail asked boldly.

Tishomingo slapped Sam's back and teased, "Ay, madam. She is all he talks about on the trail. She is the Miss Chadbourne you will meet."

"Are you taking her a present?" she said slowly and Sam wondered if that look in her eyes was one of disappointment.

Sam went to his saddle bag and returned with a conch shell he had purchased. "This is for Donna. You can hear the sea roaring in the shell. She was born near the sea, in Tidewater country. She's a very elegant lady and will be happy with this."

Anestasie excused herself and went into the house and Sam watched her walk away. André had one of his Gullahs pack his saddle bags. Sam studied the Gullah. "He is a Virginia Niggah," Sam said. "Didn't you fetch slaves from France?"

"There are no slaves in France," said André. Then he laughed derisively. "At least, our slaves are not called slaves. We've had a revolution! In my land, we have *metayer*, the share-cropper. He's a free man in the sight of God, but never in the sight of his landlord. The *metayer* was to triumph in the Revolution. But he didn't. He never does! The *bourgeoisie* won, as they will win eventually in America."

Dohrman said, "Share-cropping? It is an accursed system. Some planters in America use it. It's cheaper than slavery. But, André! The rich *bourgeoisie* were wiped out by the Revolution!"

André said, "No! It's a common error, my friend. The guillotine has become the poor man's enemy. My father wrote of such things and it cost him his head. Your friend Lafayette spoke of such things and he is in prison. You

Americans believe France has killed only noblemen and rich men, but you're wrong. Almost 3,000 heads have been lost in Paris in a year, and less than one thousand of them belonged to noblemen or rich men. Most of the victims were paupers and people who cried out against the *bourgeoisie*."

Anestasie rejoined the group and handed Sam a beautiful comb. "Take this to your love," she touched his hand as she gave him the comb. "And this dress to your sister." She looked up at Sam again when he thanked her, then walked to the edge of the verandah with her husband and whispered goodbye to him.

As they rode away, Mr. Dohrman and Anestasie waved. André sat his horse well. He carried a brace of pistols and a sword. Sam told him the sword would be of no account on the frontier. "You'll never get close enough to an enemy to use it. This is the weapon for infighting." He patted his tomahawk.

"I would feel undressed without the sword," André smiled. "I'll learn to use the tomahawk, too." He was a gay fellow and Sam liked him instinctively. He even sang as he rode, but Sam knew none of the songs. As twilight approached, Sam cast about for a camp-site. André was surprised and asked why they didn't ride to a tavern, as they were among the settlements.

Sam said, "You should know now that there is a difference in this country and the frontier. My friend Chock wears the turkey feathers. And as long as he wears them he is a Chocktaw. He might not be welcomed to bed in a tavern."

"Oh," said André. "There are class differences even in America. Well, my friends, we'll camp. The earth will bed any man."

After supper, they propped against trees and stretched

their feet to the fire. They could hear the rumble of freight wagons rolling down from the Piedmont, and the cry of drovers herding their stock to market. With their bellies full of food and their hearts full of peace, the men drew closer to one another in spirit and understanding. "Are you going in trade in the new land?" Sam asked André.

"Yes. I'll settle there."

"What goods have you?"

"Rum and powder ——"

"Among Indians!" Sam said. "You and your wife will wake up some day with your throats cut. You are a likely man, André. Will you hear a plan?"

André said, "Yes. I go West to make my fortune."

"The Creeks are as good as dead 'uns," Sam said. "Their land will be opened to white men. Even now, there are land lotteries in Georgia. You have gold and goods, and I have an idea. Together, they will make us rich."

He told André about the cotton gin, but was careful not to reveal the plans he had copied. He quoted Lawyer Thomas' prophecy that cotton would be master. André listened attentively and understood the wisdom of Sam's words.

"Hear me through," Sam said, "and if I'm batty, you may laugh. With your gold we can have gins made by smithies on the frontier. And when the Creek land is opened, farmers will grow cotton. Ay, you may lay to that. The land is black and the water is deep. It's cotton land, eh, Chock?"

"It is," Tishomingo said. "The land is too black for tobacco, the rains are too heavy. It's cotton land. I see the wisdom of Sam's idea. The cotton can be ginned by you and shipped to Mobile; even to New Orleans."

"That's it!" Sam said. "We'll build gins and run them. We'll collect a toll from every farmer."

"But," said André, "how will you protect our investment? What will keep other men from doing what we plan? You say yourself Whitney cannot protect his patent."

Sam said, "Whitney is in Connecticut. I'll be here."

André understood. A rifle and tomahawk were insurance in the new land.

Chock lit a pipe and passed it around. Sam took two puffs, passed it back and said, "When farmers grow cotton, slaves are in demand. There's no profit in working slaves. They eat up their worth. Look at stockmen! Do they work their stock? Damme, no. They breed and sell. There's the money. And the same is true of slavery—breed and sell. We can get slaves from the isles as Lake Flournoy does, breed them young and sell them in the new land and before they eat up their worth. A man's a fool to gamble on land and with cotton. Weather and wars are too dom'd uncertain. But breeding slaves and selling them to farmers is different. Ay?"

"Perhaps," said André. "But we must have a stock of slaves to breed. How will they earn their keep unless we farm?"

Sam stretched and kicked some wood on the fire. "The choice bucks we will work at the gins. The females too, when they are not bigged. The others we can lease for a season. At wages, mind you. We rent them to poor farmers and collect the wages."

"It's an ambitious scheme," said André. "And I'm your man. We'll have papers drawn in Hamburg."

"Some day," Sam said. "We will own a foundry and make our own gins. We'll build a settlement on the high

106

road between Georgia and the Mississippi. We'll have a ferry and a corn mill, a foundry and gins."

It was good to dream.

"You're married," Sam said, "and have need to settle down. I have a duty to do, and things to see. But some lay I'll settle down."

"In the Creek country?" asked André.

"Nay," said Sam "In Locha Poka, near the big river. We will build another settlement there and extend our business."

With his tomahawk he chopped a shallow hole in the ground to fit his hips. He stretched his blanket over it and lay down, humming the while. "I heard Dohrman's Kroomen singing a melody," he said. "It was a new song."

André stood with his back to the fire. The night was cool. "The song about old man Dixye?" he said. "I learned it. Listen." Then he sang, "Ol' man Dixye was a fine ol' man, I wish I was back on Dixye's lan'."

"Who is Dixye?" Sam asked.

"Dohrman told me the story. Dixye was a Dutchman in New Amsterdam before the English made it New York. He tried to grow tobacco there, but the weather was wrong. He fetched his slaves down here and sold them to Dohrman's father. The slaves still sing about old man Dixye because they had an easy time on his place."

Sam learned the song. He would teach it to Donna. He settled on his blanket and closed his eyes. André said, "Shouldn't we scatter the fire? It might blaze up."

Chock walked to the fire to scatter it, but Sam checked him. "Wait up, Chock. I'll show you a trick." He walked to his pack and picked up his bull whip. He stood ten paces from the blaze and flicked his whip. The wood was scattered, smoking.

André examined the whip. "What a weapon! You could peel a man's hide with this!"

Chock said, "That was a good trick, Big Sam. But the wood still is smoking. A breeze might blow it back into a flame. See this." He took the whip and snapped it. The tip was wrapped around a stick of the smoking wood and Chock dragged the stick back to the bed of the fire. He flipped the whip around another piece, and dragged it into place. Soon the fire wood was stacked neatly on its old bed. Chock lifted his blanket, fanned the smoldering wood and the fire blazed again.

Sam watched his friend admiringly. "Lor!" he said. "I'm glad I'm your friend and not your enemy."

8

✱ ✱

HAMBURG, an important trading post between Charleston and Augusta, lay panting and sweating on the South Carolina savanna. It was a motley town, a conglomeration of log cabins, taverns and blacksmiths' shops. There were a few brick houses along the main thoroughfare that led from the high road to the river. The street was knee-deep in mud. Sam studied the houses as he and his two friends rode into town at dawn. Most of the cabins were twenty by sixteen feet with puncheon floors. The roofs were of bark slabs and the windows were made of paper, coated with hog lard or bear grease.

On Sam's advice, they first sought a smithy and laid before him the plans for the wide-rimmed wagon wheels. The smithy said he could make the wheels in his own shop as he had apprenticed to him a debtor who had been a wheel-maker in Philadelphia. The deal was struck and Sam and his companions sought out a tavern.

They agreed to pay $2 a week each and share the same bed at the Liberty Inn. The inn-keeper's price included board and lodging. He was an unpleasant fellow, sour and evil-odored. He studied Tishomingo and was on the verge of refusing lodging to the Indian until he heard André speak, and noticed his French accent. The inn-keeper's face beamed when he heard it. He pounded the surprised André on the back and shouted, "Citizen

Friend! Only the best for you! And for your companions."

André asked, "Are you French?"

"No. But we are your friends. Ca Ira! After breakfast, we must drink to France, the savior of America."

André bowed. "I am grateful. But I never drink until the sun has crossed the halyards."

The travelers went outside to wash and to give orders for care of their horses. Sam said, "What does it mean, André? Citizen Friend, and all those Frenchy doings."

"I'm in the shadows as much as you," André said. "In France, during the Revolution, everybody who believed in the new order was called 'Citizen.' But Americans have been citizens for a long time now."

A flame of pro-French sentiment was sweeping the country and the frontiersmen, who wanted land, and the traders, who wanted business, were bitter against England whose ships were hampering American trade. France's actions against the new republic were even worse than England's, but the backwoodsmen gladly forgave France her transgressions, believing France was democratic and that she had saved the nation during the Revolution. France saw to it that the American masses believed she was the savior of America and for that salvation France wanted her pound of flesh.

Citizen Genêt had been to America, had snubbed President Washington and had sought to ally the frontiersmen against England. He had even commissioned American skippers to turn privateers and harass England. The American government was weak and willy-nilly. Washington had the support of the people, but other Federalists were hated. The reason was simple. Law and order were coming out of the new government, and law and order meant the frontiersmen must subscribe to a code written in the populous states. They must respect treaties and pay taxes. They didn't want any kind of reins on them. They had welcomed Genêt, but the government was sorely embarrassed by his presence and finally demanded that France recall him. In any other era, his incredible behavior would have caused war.

A French Party had been organized and wild-eyed Republicans (later Democrats) of the frontier wanted to march into Spanish Louisiana and take the land. John Jay had concluded his treaty with Britain and had got the worst of the deal. The pioneers believed he had sold his nation to the highest bidder. From New York to Spanish Florida, the masses were inflamed against England and no banquet was complete without a toast to France and a pledge of hatred to England and John Jay.

At breakfast, the travelers ate beefsteak, bacon, eggs, butter, coffee and johnny-cake. The price, usually one shilling, was included in their weekly lodging and feed bill. André never had eaten johnny-cake, and the inn-keeper took him to the kitchen to see the slaves prepare it. On the way to the kitchen, a loghouse set apart from the tavern, the keeper said, "Ay, Citizen, if you come this-here way again you will rest at the Liberty *Hotel*. Is Hotel not French? Is tavern not English?" He spat. "Mark you well, all the inn-keepers will change the names of their lodging houses to hotels. It is the spirit of the times."

At André's request the inn-keeper told him how to make various corn cakes, including johnny-cakes, hoe-cakes, and dodgers. "And I know something else about corn that only a few people know," he added. "Corn will make good heady whiskey. I've made some and we'll drink to France when the sun starts down."

After breakfast, the comrades went to the trading post and began buying supplies. Sam priced the goods and, with André's money, bought wisely. Salt was seven shillings and sixpence a bushel. On the frontier, it fetched forty shillings in bear or deer hides, beeswax, tallow, and hog lard in white walnut kegs.

Cotton was fetching thirty-eight cents a pound in Savannah. He could buy horses for $50, slaves for less than $1,000 each, for the slave market was unsteady, and land for two cents an acre. Sam jotted down all he learned. Slaves who knew a trade were worth $1,000. They could be bought in Martinique for less than $500 and if a man watched his cargo, he needn't lose more than five per cent of his slaves. For sure, some of the bloody Yankee skippers lost as high as 30 per cent, but they were butchers.

Sam bought calicut, slyders, barnies, beams, bodkins and many luxuries, including a charcoal foot warmer.

He knew André's wife would buy the supplies he had requested in Charleston, so he and André bought carefully. They priced a forge, but Sam refused to bargain. He told André, "I have other plans to get a forge. Also a slave to work it. I will not spend your money recklessly."

"I trust you," André said.

"That is well."

When his supplies were stored to await arrival of the wagons, Sam went to the public room of the tavern and wrote a letter to Mr. Frome.

"Dear Sir and Benefact'r:

"I have Intelligence that will serve you in Excellent Use. Meet Me in Milledgeville. I Will Ride From This

Town of Hamburg, Car'lina in two Weeks. I aim to Buy my Sister's freedom of you. Tell her That.

"Yr. Servant

"Sam'l Dabney."

Sam instructed André in the purchase of a rifle, a lighter gun than Sam's. They consumed most of the afternoon in selecting the gun, then Sam led André to the edge of town and taught him how to prove the gun and how to draw a bead properly.

Back at the tavern, they accepted the inn-keeper's hospitality and went to the tap-room where they were served corn whiskey from the keeper's private stock. Sam smacked his lips over the drink, asked questions and wrote down what he learned. André didn't like the drink, but was too polite to say so. Tishomingo scorned spirits, one of the few Indians who did. The tap-room was filled with travelers, traders from New England, mostly Connecticut, and Westerners going home. A little man stood at the end of the bar, gesticulating wildly and talking to all who would listen. He wore a shadbelly coat.

"Monarchists!" he shouted. "That's what the bubbers are. Even Washington is tainted. They wanted to put his image on a coin up in Philadelphia. We put an end to such nonsense. Washington vows he didn't want to be president this second time. Re-fiddlesticks! He's been president long enough. He'll reckon he has a claim on the office. He'll want to be king. One term is enough for any man. If Washington is such a great American, why does he live in a house that honors an English admiral?"

Sam said, "Pardon, mister. What is this thing you say?"

"That Washington honors an Englishman in the name of his home, Mount Vernon. 'Twas named for Admiral Vernon, old Grog Vernon."

Sam said, "La! Mister, I know not these things."

"Don't call me 'mister!'" the little man shouted. "It comes from 'master' and it's British. Call me 'Citizen.' I'm a member of the French Party. Let us drink, sir, to France and to the damnation of England and John Jay." He saw Tishomingo for the first time. "Oh, a Choctaw, men! We'll drink to the Choctaw Nation, the only civilized red nation in Creation. They are our friends! To hell with the Cherokees, the Shawnees, with England and John Jay, and old Knox and Hamilton."

They drank. "And Spain," the little man said as an afterthought.

André sipped his whiskey distastefully. Tishomingo acknowledged the toast with a bow, but wouldn't drink.

"Ay!" the politician smacked his lips. "I'm heading for the Natchez Country."

Tishomingo smiled at him. He didn't like the little man and spoke for the first time. "The Creeks will eat you."

"Creeks," the man laughed. "Don't you know there is peace with the Creeks! We've signed a new treaty with them. The Congress thinks all will be well now, but there will always be war between the Georgians and the Creeks. The treaty is all the land companies wanted. They're doing business already, several companies. Selling lands to settlers. Do you think the settlers will know a treaty when they see one? That's why I go to Natchez. The damn Congress can't reach there."

André asked, "Why are you opposed to the Congress?"

"Our leaders are loons! The Congress has gone batty. It has granted a franchise to a bank. It's unconstitutional! Show me where the Constitution gives Congress such power. Why, they've even voted a salary to the vice president. The Constitution doesn't provide any such

114

blamed salary. Spendthrifts! The Constitution says the states are supreme. But Congress is taking power. The president is taking power. And those damn justices of the Supreme Court are taking what's left. Mark my words, the day will come when Congress will be a privy council and the president will be king! Not in name, no! But it's just the same."

The little man was enjoying himself and the attention he had commanded. "Even Jefferson, God bless him, said the Constitution is an experiment. They're just trying it out on us common folks. Well, men, if the Congress is going to put images of men on money, charter banks and make fool treaties, I'm against it. Let's drink to the French Party, the Republic of France and to the health and success of Citizen Genêt."

André turned down his glass. "I won't drink to murderers."

"What is this?" demanded the inn-keeper. "Are you a Frenchman?"

"Yes," said André. "I'm a better Frenchman than Genêt and the Jacobins!" The fiery whiskey had made him reckless. He jumped on the bar and demanded attention.

"Hear him," the crowd roared. "He's a Frenchman."

"Don't be tricked by France," André shouted. "Genêt came here to stir up trouble, to make a cat's-paw of you. He came demanding money, payment of your debt to France. But America is repaying her debt to France faster than she agreed. It will be wiped out in six years. France today is not your friend. Lafayette was, yes, but even with Lafayette's influence France wouldn't recognize your independence until she was forced to save her face. Hear me! I know Europe. You have no friends in

Europe. I wonder if you ever will have? France, England and Spain are using you as a puppet."

"A French royalist," the little man shouted. "Have at him, men."

André leaped from the bar, backed against it and withdrew his sword. Tishomingo stepped to his side, fingering his tomahawk. Sam clinched his fists and spoke to the rabble-rouser.

"Shut up, you bantam cockerel. If you were a mite larger, I would pull your teeth, you bellowing tiny-mite."

The crowd, in too good a mood to fight, laughed. Even the little man smiled. "Tiny-mite, am I? 'Tis a good name. But my real name is Thomas, sir."

"Ay?" said Sam. "I met a Lawyer Thomas on the road to Tennessee. Hosea Cincinnatus Thomas, Esquire."

The little man bowed, "My beloved brother. I, too, am a lawyer. We're friends of Andy Jackson, the smartest man in the West. I have told my brother to join me in Natchez. The land companies will need lawyers." He dropped his voice. "Here, take this." He handed Sam a newspaper. "Read it later, and if you know the West, it will tell you much."

More drinks were ordered and Tiny-mite faced the crowd again. "I've come through from Philadelphia. They're building fast at Washington City. 'Twill be a city some day. Already they have laid the cornerstone for the president's mansion, with fitting Masonic ceremonies, of course."

André laughed. "What strange people you are. You object to being called 'Mister' because it springs from 'Master.' But, as Masons, you call men 'Most Worshipful Master.' "

"O! A French Papist," Tiny-mite said.

116

"Nay. An agnostic," said André.

Tiny-mite winked at him. "The Methodists will draw and quarter you." He turned to the crowd. "I have with me some lottery tickets. The money will be used to build our national capital ——"

"And line your pockets," said a heckler. "Lotteries everywhere. Land lotteries. Slave lotteries. We even build our capital with lotteries. But I'll take one of those tickets for the capital."

Tiny-mite sold his tickets for a profit and drank with André. "You have a glib tongue, Citizen. Will you live here?"

"In the new land, near the Mississippi," André said.

"Can you own land? Are you an American?"

André was puzzled. "Yes, I'm an American. I will fight for this country."

"Have you taken the oath? You have to take an oath to be an American. Am I right, men?"

"Ay," the crowd shouted.

Tiny-mite said, "I can give you the oath. I'm a lawyer. The fee will be two pounds."

André reached into his money belt. Tishomingo checked him and said to Tiny-mite. "You will do this favor free. You are going to Natchez. You will be near the Choctaws. You will need friends. You will not take my friend's money."

The lawyer understood. No oath was necessary, of course, but Tiny-mite had seen an opportunity for a fee. However, he felt he should administer an oath to satisfy the crowd. André was lifted to the bar. He held up his right hand and swore allegiance to the United States, the Declaration of Independence, the Congress, South Carolina and the Methodist Church.

"But," he protested, "I thought you had no faith in the Congress."

"Never you mind that," said Tiny-mite. "It's proper to swear to it. We have no flag for you to kiss, so we will dispense with that. Now, Citizen, sing us a song and you'll be an American, after you buy the drinks."

André sang the Dixye melody he had learned and the crowd joined in. The crowd demanded that Tishomingo take the oath, but he refused and they respected his stand. At the request of the revelers, André sang "Ca Ira!" first in French, then in English.

Sam sang the jug song:

> "Mush-a-ring-a-ring-a-rah!
> Whack fol'd the dady O!
> Whack fol'd the dady O!
> Thar's whiskey in the jug!"

The inn-keeper opened a barrel of new corn whiskey and many of the men tasted it for the first time. Fist fights began. Tiny-mite had taken a fancy to André. "Ay, Citizen, I'll show you some fun. Hear! Hear!" he shouted, above the din. "I have a slave outside, the best gouger in the West. Will anyone match him?"

"It's against the law," the inn-keeper protested. "Gouging is all right in the West, but here in Carolina it's illegal."

"To hell with the law," the crowd roared. "Fetch the gouger. We'll find a match."

The huge negro slave was brought in while other men hunted through the town until they found an opponent. One of the gougers had only one eye. He had lost the other in battles. One was without an ear. The gougers were trained for the sport. Their thumb nails were broad and long. A ring was formed, and the Negroes stood facing each other until the signal was given.

Then they lunged. One bit off the lobe of the other's ear.

"A cropper," the men shouted. "A score. Have at him! Lay on him. Pull out his tongue!"

One of the men tripped and sprawled. The other leaped upon him, gouging at his eyes. They were separated before either lost an eye. If an eye had been lost, the victorious gouger would have been lashed according to law, probably by a professional slave-whipper.

It was a new law to Sam, and he remembered it. He had learned most of the slave laws. A Negro could be whipped for owning a dog, a gun or hiring a horse; for attending a funeral, a merrymaking, riding along the highways or selling goods without the master's consent. Sam had never known of any of the laws being enforced except the one prohibiting slaves from selling his master's goods without consent. Slaves also were forbidden to learn to read or write. They couldn't travel in bands or testify against a white man. If a slave rode a horse without permission, he could be thrashed or suffer his ears to be cropped. A runaway slave could be killed on sight. Theft of a Negro was a felony, but if a slave were killed while being punished it was not a felony. A master's duty was to furnish his slaves with food, clothing and shelter and work him not longer than fifteen hours in summer, and fourteen in winter.

Sam and his friends left the revelry and retired to their room. Sam sat on the edge of the bed and made notes. "What are you writing?" André asked.

"Only notes to be remembered. I posted a letter today. It cost six cents to post a letter thirty miles and up to twenty-five cents for 450 miles. It's useful intelligence." He opened the newspaper Tiny-mite had given him. It was the *Knoxville Gazette* and was the first paper Sam had seen since he had left the Dutch country. He spread it on the bed. Tishomingo held the candle and Sam read aloud. The government was coining golden eagles. Tennessee was clamoring for statehood and Andy Jackson and William Cocke might stand for Congress when statehood was granted. Tennessee had a population of 35,000 in 1790 and the paper estimated the population had increased to 70,000. Kentucky's white population was estimated at 130,000 and Mississippi's at 3,000.

A list of proposed taxes for Tennessee was published, a twenty-five cent poll tax for males, a fifty cent tax for every slave, a tax of twenty-five cents per 100 acres of farm land and a $1 tax for town lots. Stud horses would be taxed $4 each.

"Going to tax men and studs," Sam grinned. "But I see nothing here of startling intelligence."

Then he read a public notice. Red Bird, a Cherokee chief, had written a talk to the other chiefs.

"I know Red Bird," said Tishomingo. "What is his talk?"

"He has written a talk warning the Indians of Upper Town to leave William Cocke alone. Red Bird writes that Cocke is 'The white man who lives among the mulberry trees and he talks very strong and runs very fast.' Red Bird paid two buckskins to write that talk in the paper. He says he wishes 'all the bad people on both sides were laid in the ground, for then there would not be so many mush men trying to make people think they were warriors.' What does it mean, Chock?"

Tishomingo stretched across the bed after handing the candle to André.

"Tecumseh has been to the Cherokees," he said simply. "I did not tell you so. Now I trust you."

"I knew," Sam said. "Tell us more."

"Red Bird is a friend of the white man. Tecumseh it was who tried to arouse the Upper Town against the white man who lives under the mulberry trees. Tecumseh knew that if the white man were killed, the settlers would attack the Cherokees and that they would join his Confederation. They haven't attacked the white man of the mulberry trees. He is a big man among his people. I made a big talk at the council and told the Cherokees that Tecumseh was a bad man."

"Is he?" Sam asked.

"No. But he's dangerous. His twin brother is the prophet of the Shawnees. The English bribe the Shawnees with rum and powder. The English trick the Shawnees and tell them Americans want their land. All white men are the same, Big Sam. The English want to dominate the big lakes, the fur trade there, so they play the Shawnees against the Americans."

"Ay," said Sam.

"Tecumseh is dreaming a great dream. He would unite the Shawnees, Cherokees, Creeks, Choctaws and Chickasaws into one Confederacy and make war on the settlers. He's a fool, a madman. He says his mission is from the Great Spirit. Many Indians believe him."

"You do not?"

"Nor my people. The Choctaws have the strongest nation among the Indians of the South. Tecumseh cannot be successful without us. It's my duty to prevent my people from joining him."

"But why, Chock? The white men haven't been kind to you."

"We're wise, Big Sam. We know that the white men

121

will control the land east of the sire of all rivers. If we befriend your nation, you will let us keep our lands. That is what I will tell Mr. Harkins, the Indian agent."

Sam returned to the paper. "Here is something more. A letter from a Chickasaw chief to the white settlers. It says, 'I hope you will exert yourselves and join us so that we might give the Creek lads a Drubben for they have encroached on us this great while not us alone you likewise for you have suffer'd a great dale by them I hope you will think of your wounds.'"

Tishomingo said, "That means trouble. The Chickasaws have many grievances against the Creeks. They want the settlers to help them against the Creeks. But now you have a treaty with the Creeks and the Chickasaws cannot get help from you. They cannot defeat the Creeks alone. That letter means the warriors are weary of peace. Their tomahawks are hungry."

"Will they go to war against the Creeks?"

"No. Your people will have to refuse them aid because of the treaty. It is the opportunity Tecumseh needs. He will tell the Chickasaws your people are not their friends. He will stir them against the settlers and will urge them to join hands with him to punish you."

"But if they join with Tecumseh, they will be joining with the Creeks. Tecumseh's mother was a Creek."

Tishomingo removed his leather jacket and turkey feathers and was ready for bed. "Tecumseh will tell the Chickasaws that the Creeks are their brothers and that the white men are the common enemies. He'll bribe them with British rum and powder. The Chickasaws are a foolish people. They may heed him. There'll be blood on the moon, Big Sam."

The three men spent every morning in the trading

posts and at the smithy's, but in the afternoons they joined in the sports of the town. Sam raced Claymore, but his mare was no match for the horses that were brought from Virginia for the races. Her wind was better, but her pace was slower. However, Sam won $50 for marksmanship. No other rifle was so true as his long gun. He and Tishomingo entered the whip-cracking contest. It was held on the bank of the Savannah River, where the freighters were camped.

The first test was to extinguish a candle at ten paces, but, gradually, the contest grew more difficult, until only Sam and Tishomingo were contestants. The judge stationed Sam twenty feet from the trapdoor of a box which held a rat. Sam was to kill the rat as it dashed from the box. The judge held up his hand as a signal, opened the box and the rat scooted away. Without haste, Sam flicked his whip, severed the rat's head and cracked his whip.

The crowd of teamsters shouted and passed drinks. "The Georgia Cracker! The Cracker!" They slapped backs and knees.

Sam smiled at Tishomingo and tossed his whip to him. The judge dropped another rat in the box and Tishomingo took his position. When the rat was freed, Tishomingo cut off its head as it ran, then flicked his whip and entwined it around the animal, and hurled the rat into the river. Then he cracked the whip, louder even than Sam had. The crowd went wild. Tishomingo accepted the prize without comment.

"You're better than I, Chock," Sam said.

"It's only fair," Tishomingo answered. "I'm the best with the whip, you're the best with the rifle. André is the best with the sword."

André's wagons arrived on schedule with Mr. Dohrman and Anestasie. Sam had thought about her often since he had left the plantation, but always he had forced her from his mind. She was the wife of his friend. And, too, there was Donna. Donna would be better for any man than Anestasie. Anestasie was wine but Donna was ale. Too much wine is not good for a man, but ale is good and comforting.

The new wheels were ready. The wagons were geared for oxen. They billed the equipment to Lake Flournoy, in care of Panton & Co., Pensacola, via Savannah, and soon were on the road to Milledgeville. Tishomingo paced the caravan, and Sam guarded the rear. Anestasie rode side-saddle and often came to the rear of the caravan to ride near Sam.

"I bought the goods," she told him. "Pretty silks. Hoity Toity! It is nice silk. Ruffles and laces." She was very gay.

Once Sam blurted out, "You're a pretty lady. Pretty as a little doe at green-up time."

"Is your love pretty, too?" Anestasie teased.

"Yes, she is pretty." He compressed his lips quickly and looked away.

He saw Anestasie at night when she entered André's lean-to, and his mind raced. He thought of Donna. He had been away a long time. He lay on his back and watched the stars. Donna's legs were longer than Anestasie's. He wondered which of them had the prettier legs. Well, he liked long legs. He had long legs, too. Donna's breasts were as high as Anestasie's but larger. For sure, he had never seen Donna's breasts, or touched them, but he knew they were firm. He had seen their shape. His body tingled as he thought of her and he drove his mind to think of other things.

In Milledgeville, Sam learned that Mr. Frome had ar-

124

rived. He sent word to the tavern that he would call in the afternoon, and went first to Harkins' office. The Indian agent grasped his hand, and offered rum. Sam wasted no words. He told all he had heard of Tecumseh. Harkins wasn't startled.

"I know these things, Sam'l."

"Does the new treaty with the Creeks change your plans? Do you still want me to scout your party to Natchez? There's no great danger now."

Harkins poured four fingers of rum, and lit a cigar. "Ay, Sam'l. We need you more than ever. Listen, carefully. The land companies are selling land in the Mississippi Territory. Settlers are swarming out there. These settlers will not respect Creek boundaries. There will be constant raiding. I'm one of the founders of the Land Company. We'll need you. So will Chadbourne."

"Ay?"

"The Choctaws must not be allowed to join Tecumseh's confederacy! It's your job to keep us posted. Make friends. Particularly with Chief Pushmataha and Lake Flournoy. The Land Company will send you word when a party of settlers are coming out. You must help them locate. The government expects you to report on the Indians. The company expects you to help our settlers. What else you do, is your affair."

Sam said, "I want land. The company will give it to me, ay?"

"Yes, five thousand acres. Where do you want it? We'll furnish you wagons and teams."

"There is land on the Halfway or Pearl River, on the fringe of the Choctaw Nation. I'll settle there, Mr. Harkins. I'll build a ferry."

Harkins was surprised. "What know you of that land?"

Sam told him of Tishomingo and Harkins jumped to his feet. "My God, Sam'l. Have you brought him here? He is favored of the Choctaws. Bring him to me. This is excellent work!"

Tishomingo was greeted warmly by the agent. He was invited to the Harkins' home. He was assured that the United States would remain friends of the Choctaws. "Our only desire," Harkins said, "is to be your friends. And you must be our friends. Heed not the Creeks, or the Shawnees. Our government will respect our treaties with you. And as long as the waters run to the sea and the sun warms the lands, your lands will be your own! Tell that to your uncle and to Flournoy. And take these to your uncle and to Flournoy." He handed cigars to Tishomingo.

"We saw the pigeons come from the southwest," Tishomingo said. "Have you any intelligence from my people? Did the pigeons eat our maize?"

"By God, I know not!" Harkins said. "But hear me, sir. I will send seeds to your people when you and Sam'l go West."

"It is a good token," said Tishomingo.

Harkins said, "And now, Sam'l, we must go see Mrs. Harkins. You've done well. And I have a gift for you."

Sam excused himself. Harkins protested. But Sam said, "My regards to Mrs. Harkins, sir. But I have an engagement I must keep at the tavern. I'll call later in the afternoon at your home."

"You're missing a treat," Harkins nudged Tishomingo. He and the Indian left Sam, who hurried to the tavern where Mr. Frome awaited him. They embraced and Sam heard news of Honoria. She was well and growing.

Frome said, "She's an impish one, Sam'l. She's a beauty.

Spirited. She'll drive a man mad. Now what want you of me?"

Sam opened the bottle of perfume that Anestasie had given him. "This is for my sister," he said. "Smell. It's Frenchy, and very fashionable. Tell me, Mr. Frome, are the people on the frontier as loony over France as they are back where I was?"

"And more so," said Frome, then frowned. "But Sam'l. You can't give this perfume to your sister. Law! It's dear, and if she has a bottle of French perfume every woman I know will want one. And, too, she is indentured to me. What's hers, is mine."

"You're right, Mr. Frome. Every woman who comes to your factory will want perfume if my sister has some. Or your wife. But never the mind of that. See this?"

He showed Frome the dress Anestasie had given him for Honoria. It was a muslin dress with a flowered skirt and a long-sleeved bodice. A kerchief was tucked into the dress at the front. He also had a large hat of blue silk faced with green and a soft fluffed crown. Such a dress was of absolutely no use on the frontier, and Sam knew that was what made it valuable.

"You're batty, Sam'l!" Frome gesticulated nervously. "If your sister has that, my wife will demand one."

"And other women, too, Mr. Frome. Mind you, I saw more money spent on such things in Tidewater country than on food. It's a way with women. And with the French spirit sweeping the frontier? Don't you see, man! Once a woman appears in such finery, every other woman will want such dresses."

Frome eyed Sam cagily and respectfully. "What is a deal for that perfume and dress?"

"My sister's freedom," said Sam quickly. "I'll give you silk and muslin and your wife can copy this dress. This dress is for my sister, but your wife can use it as a pattern. The perfume, I'll give you. It can be mixed with water."

"You're a wise trader, Sam'l. It's a deal. I'll go into the fine-dress business."

"That's not all, Mr. Frome." Sam handed him a cigar, a stogie. "Try it, man. They, too, will sell on the frontier." Then he told the merchant of the cotton gin. Frome's eyes blinked in excitement. Sam said, "You have a forge. You can make the gins. I'll give you the drawings."

"And what do you expect?"

"Three per cent of all the cotton you gin, Mr. Frome. I will run wagons and post from the Natchez country to Savannah some day, and I'll pick up the ginned cotton and freight it for you."

"Another deal," said Frome excitedly. Already, he was thinking it would be impossible for Sam to know how much cotton he ginned. Then Sam dashed his plans.

"I am going to buy slaves, train them and lease them. One of my slaves will supervise the gins. You'll pay his keep and pay me $5 a week for his services. I don't care how many gins you make and run, but you must not sell one. I'll know if you do," Sam smiled.

Frome shook his head. "Ay, you're a sharp lad. It's a deal." With cotton fetching almost forty cents a pound in Savannah, Frome knew he could clear a fortune. He could buy cotton in the fields for a few cents a pound, gin it and make a tremendous profit, despite the tariff he would have to pay to Sam.

"That's not all," Sam said.

Frome threw up his hands. "You've robbed me already."

128

"I want the loan of $2,000! Pierce Chadbourne has a slave I must buy."

"If you do not repay the $2,000 within a year, Sam'l, our arrangement for the cotton tariff will be forgotten, eh? And I will seize your property."

"Ay," said Sam. "A deal?"

They shook hands and Frome drew up the agreement. "I'll have the $2,000 when you reach the village where Chadbourne is. Your sister will be with me."

Sam bade Mr. Frome goodbye and hired a room in the tavern. He washed himself and dressed. He put on a short waisted coat, Nankeen breeches and a felt hat.

He shaved himself and combed his long hair, and tied it with ribbon. He went then to André's room and was surprised to find that his friend and Anestasie had gone to Harkins'. From the inn-keeper, he borrowed a light wagon. A man attired as he shouldn't ride a horse. Sweat would soil his pants.

Sam was very proud as he walked up the path to Harkins' mansion. He was a gentleman, a traveled gentleman. A slave opened the door for him. Tishomingo stared at his friend and muttered to Sam, "Mush man!" André saluted and Anestasie ran to him and curtsied. "You're elegant, Sam," she said.

Harkins slapped his back and Mrs. Harkins said, "We are honored, Mr. Dabney. Never have we seen such an elegant gentleman in these poor parts."

Tishomingo said, " 'Tis not the man I found in Carolina."

"Shame," said Anestasie. "Sam looks magnificent!"

Sam blushed. "I feel like a bullfrog wrapped in greased paper."

"Mr. and Mrs. Harkins asked us over," Anestasie changed the subject. "I'll fetch you some punch, Sam."

129

She disappeared into the dining room. Sam sat down, careful not to stretch his fine breeches. He was gulping uncomfortably and staring at Tishomingo when the voice behind him said, "Your punch, Mr. Dabney."

He turned and Donna was there, smiling at him. Sam got to his feet quickly and bowed. He fumbled for words and Donna laughed at him. He laughed, too.

"Aren't you surprised?" she said.

He forgot that anyone else was present and said softly, "Have you ever dreamed a vision and then had the vision come true?"

Her proud, lovely features glowed and he could sense that she was very happy to see him. His blood rushed to his head and her bright eyes caught his and they just looked at each other.

Harkins' words brought them back to earth. "That was our surprise for you, Sam'l. Your friend Mr. Frome told us you were expected at this time. Mrs. Harkins and I were visiting Pierce, so we fetched Miss Donna back with us."

He thanked Harkins and bowed awkwardly to Mrs. Harkins, forgetting for the moment the fine figure he had hoped to cut in his new clothes. Then his eyes returned to Donna's and he said, "You look well, Donna, and on your feed."

Donna laughed again and teased him. "One minute you call me a vision and the next you say that I am on my feed. You have strange compliments, Sam'l, but I like them. I've missed you a great deal."

Anestasie clapped her hands in delight and hugged Donna. "You're all he has talked about," she said. "You're as beautiful as he said you were. I must tell you before him how beautiful he said you are. I wish a man thought I was as beautiful ——"

130

André said, "Still your tongue, dear."

Sam's face was livid. Donna visibly was pleased.

They sat next to each other at supper. He had little to say. She, too, was silent. But after supper, Sam excused himself and returned to the tavern. He got out the comb Anestasie had given him. It was an intimate thing. He would not be so bold as to give it to Donna yet. He got the conch shell and returned to the Harkins' mansion.

Donna was expecting him. They sat on the verandah, and he could feel the warmth of her body next to his.

"I brought you this." He handed her the shell. "You can hear the sea roar."

Her fingers touched his as she accepted it. The touch of her hand was soothing. He remembered that Anestasie had once touched his hand and that her touch was hot. Then he was ashamed of his thoughts.

"It's very beautiful," Donna whispered, and put it to her ear. "When I was a little girl I had a conch shell like this. I will keep it always, Sam'l."

Sam turned and looked at her and was very proud. He wanted to hold her then, but he dared not, so he sat silently and stared, his mind jumping from one thought to another—Honoria, the Promised Land, Donna, trade, Indians, but always back to Donna. . . .

He heard her say, "You've been gone a long time, Sam'l, and you've changed."

"Very much?" he asked anxiously. His voice did not have its usual calm assurance.

"No, not very much," she smiled.

He wanted to boast, to tell her of the strange things he had seen and all his plans for the future. He wanted to tell her so much about the thoughts he had had of her on his journeys—yes, even of his desires during the lonely wilderness nights—but he said, "I'll not always be poor. Out in the Choctaw country, I'll have land. On the Halfway River. It's a quiet river, and there's good timber and good land. I'll have a ferry, a toll road. I'll have a foundry. I'll own freight wagons, and perhaps run a post. First, I'll build a cabin ——"

He paused a second and looked at her.

"Yes, Sam. Tell me more."

"And when I make more money I'll build a house. A big house with cypress shingles. I'll have sheep to tend my lawn. I'll name my house Locha Poka. It means 'Promised Land.'"

"It's a beautiful name," Donna said. "It's nice to dream, isn't it?"

Sam stood before her. "There's something I would say to you."

"Yes?" There was a catch in her breathing, but Sam did not notice it. He suddenly was embarrassed and he forgot the pretty words he had rehearsed so often. So he said simply, "You're a likely lady, Donna. You have salt in your craw. There are many things to be said when I have proved myself to you and to your brother."

Donna arose and walked to the door, but she was not disappointed. "Good night, Sam'l. We must be up early tomorrow, and travel to the village. I'm eager for Pierce to see you, and he's eager to see you. He's very proud of you. The horses are ready for our journey. I am waiting to see the land you speak of, Locha Poka."

9

★ ★

SAM got up before dawn and went to the tavern's kitchen to complete arrangements with the inn-keeper. He had planned a special breakfast in Mr. Frome's honor, for he would talk further with the prosperous Jewish merchant. He knew Mr. Frome had done some serious thinking and planning since their conference the day before and would be ready to talk trade. A good breakfast helped trade.

Sam sent a slave to Mr. Frome's room with a cup of hot coffee and a note asking him to be his guest at breakfast. Frome was delighted. It was the way they did business in Savannah. Ah, that Sam'l had learned a heap. He had gone away a boy and had returned a man. He was no longer the huge, rough backwoodsman, but was a man of parts and of knowledge. Frome tied his hair carefully at the nape of his neck. He would be glad to be rid of that Honoria. What a lass . . . a wench. Her blood was too hot. Frome blew his nose. Sam'l would have his hands full with his sister. He wondered whence she got such spirit. Her mother had been meek. From her father then: old man Dabney had been a wild one. Frome rinsed his mouth with salt water. Sam'l was like his mother in many ways.

Frome hoped that Sam, for his own good, was more like his mother than his father. Old man Dabney would never seek counsel, or take it. It was an axiom along the frontier that old man Dabney could be counted on to do the right thing at the wrong time. He always had piddled around with this and that, making a little money here and there, but when the test had come he had always been found wanting. The folks had been accustomed to say of old man Dabney, "In a deal, he's a sharp man for five times running, but on the sixth time he'll always act the fool."

Maybe Sam was different. But there was no indication to support that belief. He was stubborn as old man Dabney was stubborn. And he was super-sensitive, and arrogant. He made friends too easily. A man should work for his friends. Of course, he was a dreamer. He was Irish, and Frome knew the Irish. They were a gloomy people who tried to hide their gloom in loud noises. And they were always willing to go into strange lands and give their sweat and blood so that other men could come later and collect the rewards. Well, somebody had to take the chances. Frome had known Irishmen and Scotchmen, Englishmen and Germans—all manners of men in other lands. He wondered why an Irishman in New York was different from an Irishman in Georgia, why a Scotchman in Hampshire was so different from a Scotchman in the Carolinas. Up there, they were calm men, down here they became hot-tempered. Up there, they were Irish and Scots, down here they were Georgians. The land changed them. The land changed everything. The land made their skins thin and their blood hot. The land bred arrogance in them and a fierce brutal pride, a sensitivity, a childish sensitivity. They carried their honor on their sleeve. Ay, they were a strange people.

Sam was a strange man. He tried so hard to be impersonal and unemotional, but Frome knew that his friend's emotions always were at boiling. A man less intelligent than Frome might have misunderstood Sam's love for his sister. But Frome understood it. They had been lonely children and now they clung to each other because they thought that they were alone in the world and that all the world was against old man Dabney's brats.

Should he tell Sam'l his sister had run away to a Methodist meeting? And that he had heard her singing Methodist songs? And that she prayed every night on her knees and talked to God as though He were a merchant in heaven who delivered blessings at her requests. He had heard her say aloud many times, "Lord, give me this and give me that." Always, when she prayed she asked for things. But she never thanked God.

At the breakfast, Sam was dressed in his traveling clothes, leather breeches and doeskin jacket. André was attired as a French merchant and Anestasie wore pretty, flimsy things. Tishomingo never changed. He wore buckskin breeches, a doeskin vest and buckskin leggin's. Frome was introduced and bowed.

"This is my partner's wife." Sam presented Anestasie, who sat next to the Jewish merchant. She poured his coffee and saw that his plate was heaped with fish and eggs.

Frome was impressed. He was particularly impressed with André, with his careless manner. The Frenchman had a way about him, a nonchalance that the serious Jew envied. André could smile with his lips while his brown eyes never changed. Then his eyes would laugh, but his face would be serious. And he seemed always to be laughing inside of himself, laughing at men and at their stupidity. In a way, Anestasie reminded him of Honoria—of a polished Honoria.

Anestasie paid particular attention to his needs and Frome sensed a plot. Men didn't entertain at breakfast for nothing, but he was anxious to talk trade with Sam. He had made many plans during the night. He looked at Anestasie as closely as good manners would allow. Already, he had pictured the settlers' wives buying silks and perfumes. One thing troubled him, and he said to Sam, "Even with water, Sam'l, the perfume you sold me will not last forever. How can I get more when my business demands it?"

"I have thought of that," Sam said, and told him of *Bouquet de Flora*. Frome toyed with his coffee cup and Sam talked, and finally the merchant offered Sam money for the recipe and a supply of the ingredients. "I don't need money, Mr. Frome. Money is of no account on the frontier where there is naught to buy. But, my partner and I need a forge. When you pass through the village going to your home, buy a forge as I have described on this paper and leave it at the smithy's for me. Because you are a merchant, you can get one cheaper than I. I'll give you in swap a supply of the ingredients for perfume and the recipe. I can get the forge through on pack horses."

"It's a deal," said Frome. "But I ask you now, how many copies of that cotton engine's plan have you made?"

"I have two more," Sam said. "I gave you one. I will keep two. I promise you I'll not sell or barter the plans in the Georgia country. André and I will work only in the Mississippi Territory."

"But the law?" Frome said. "What am I to do if I am accused of stealing this patent?"

Sam winked. "By the time Whitney hears that we're ginning cotton, there'll be gins to the Mississippi River.

136

He can't sue everybody! And, too, our machines are not exactly like the one he invented. Our machines will have more teeth on the big drum. But I must caution you, Mr. Frome, if you manufacture the gins and sell them, I'll know."

Frome shook his head, "I would have to stay up all night to beat you. Well, I must take hooves. I'll do as you say, Sam'l. And for old times' sake, if you do any trading in this territory, remember me."

"'Tis a vow," Sam said. "And I would save you bother. My friend, Tishomingo, will ride with you. He knows the kind of forge I require and will help you select it in the village. He'll go to your home, too, and will fetch my sister back to the village. It will save you the journey. You can send the $2,000 by him."

Frome and Tishomingo departed. Sam went to Harkins' house and told him goodbye. Donna rode beside Sam.

He was glad to be back in Georgia. The red hills seemed home to him. He entertained Donna with stories of the marvels he had seen, but avoided any mention of his wound, fearing she might suspect him of wrongdoing. She never interrupted him. She seldom spoke unless she had something worth-while to say. Sam watched her out of the corners of his eyes. She was supple and seemed a part of her horse. Her long riding dress rustled against her legs as her horse loped. They reached the village three days later. The Dragoons saw them approaching and rode out and greeted them, firing salutes to Big Sam. They examined his rifle in awe.

At the Chadbourne mansion, Pierce met them on the path and embraced him. "You're welcome, Sam'l."

"It is good to be back, Captain," Sam said.

"Your sister is in the house."

In long strides, Sam walked into the mansion. He hadn't seen Honoria since the day they had buried their parents in one grave and he had bound her to Frome. She met him at the door. She was beautiful, as beautiful as Donna, but in a different way. There was the look of the hell-cat in her. Sam just stared at her, ill at ease.

"Aren't you going to kiss me?" She walked to him and threw her arms around his neck and kissed him. Her lips were moist and warm. Sam held her at arm's length. "You're a pretty mite," he said. "Blamed if you're not."

She sniffled and Sam wiped her nose on his sleeve. "My heart is light," she said. "But I want to weep. I've waited a long time, Sam'l, to see you. Kiss me again."

"Shame," he said and then kissed her. "You'd think I was a sweetheart instead of your brother. You're a minx, Honoria. Your lips are too soft."

"What know you of lips?" She patted his face with both hands.

Sam said, "I hope you have salt in your craw. Did you have a good journey? Was Frome a kind master?"

"Ay, Sam'l, he was kind. But Mrs. Frome. Ugh! She slapped me. She said I flirted with her husband. She's a cold-butted woman, I'll vow. She thinks every woman who sees her husband is envious of her bed. Re-fiddle-sticks! I'd leave sleep in the woods! With a bear!"

"Honoria! Mind your tongue! Is that the language our mother taught you?" Sam was shocked. But, then, he reasoned, how could he expect Honoria to be otherwise. She had been indentured on the frontier. The words were rough out there. He looked at her closely. Her hands were coarse and circles of dirt showed under her nails. Donna would teach her to care for her hands. He had a pair of chicken-skin gloves. She could wear them at night and her hands would be soft. She wore a linsey-

138

woolsey dress, open at the throat. Her throat was brown. Her breasts were not much larger than a peach. She smelled womanly, the good smell of earth, the sharp, salty smell of a woman who has ridden fast on a sweating horse, of leather saddles and pine trees. "What of the journey?" he asked again. "Was it pleasant?"

"Butter on bread." She ran her fingers through his long hair. "It was pleasant. I like Tishomingo. Is he the present you brought me, Sam'l? He said you had a present for me. He told me many things, how noble you are, and how strong."

"You're a vixen," Sam laughed. He liked his sister's spirit. She was gay, and he was proud to present her to Donna and Anestasie. Donna kissed her cheek. Anestasie studied her carefully and then called her "cutie bird". Honoria stiffened. She instinctively disliked Anestasie and her intuition told her immediately that Anestasie returned the feeling.

"What is a 'cutie bird'?" Honoria snapped.

Anestasie's green eyes seemed to shoot sparks as she snapped back, "*You* are a 'cutie bird'."

Honoria looked at Sam as though she expected help, but he had not understood the exchange of words; he was thinking of how much Anestasie reminded him of Honoria.

Honoria walked with the ease and grace of a cat. She had no stays and she moved with a swaying of hips that caused even gentlemanly Pierce to arch his brows and watch her. And André said of her, "What grace! Ay, Sam'l, you've got a parcel on your hands."

Only Tishomingo was aloof.

Honoria clapped her hands and hugged Sam again when he gave her the presents, the dress, a hat and a small bottle of perfume. Donna and Anestasie showed her to her room and helped dress her. A slave girl trimmed her nails and washed her. Neither of the women looked down on her just because she had been a bounded servant girl. Anestasie knew nothing of such things, and Donna was of the New West and a person was accepted for face value. The South was young and stretching. It hadn't become aristocratic, not in West Georgia. In Tidewater, of course, Honoria would have been scorned, but the West was different. It was poor and willing to work. Time enough for it to become cultured. Time enough for it to become a land that bloomed at the hands of slaves. And time enough for it to weaken and then crumble of its own weakness. . . .

In his room, Sam removed his jacket and washed himself. Jasper came to him. Sam was glad to see the slave who had served him the first time he had visited the Chadbournes. Jasper grinned when Sam gave him a cigar. The Negro chewed it. Sam had heard that Jasper was a trained craftsman with iron and he was determined to bargain with Pierce for the Negro.

The slave took the sheep's wool from Sam's hand, and washed the white man's back. Seeing the jagged scar, he ran his fingers over it and said, "A bullet here. Cut out."

"Say nothing of that," Sam ordered. Jasper grinned again. From the Negro, Sam learned that Deborah, the slave baby he and Donna had delivered, was well. Sam had wondered about her safety.

"Jasper watch her," the slave said. "Jasper know Massa Sam like. Jasper know heap. Baby's mammy is Sukey. Sukey has been brought to house to tend Mis' Donna."

Sam understood. Sukey's life was in danger from the slaves and Creeks because she had borne a half-Indian child. He sent Jasper away and was tying his hair when Honoria entered his room, without knocking. He reached

140

for a jacket to throw over his bare shoulders, but he dropped it in amazement as he saw her, dressed in the finery he had brought.

"You're a lady, Honoria," he said. "Our mother and father would be proud of you."

Honoria smiled happily. "I'm grateful for all you've done, Sam'l." She curtsied and he took her hand and bowed. "Oh!" She gasped. "Your shoulder!" She had seen the scar and she examined it.

"It's naught to bother of," he said. "I was hurt accidentally." But he was blushing. A sixth sense told Honoria he was lying. She could see it in his eyes. Why should he lie about a wound?

She said quickly, "I heard about the accident, but I didn't know the wound was so bad."

Sam's face drained. "He told you! Chock told you! Hear me, Honoria! I didn't lay a finger on that Indian wench! Her father shot. I did wrong! I'll see Chock about this."

Honoria laughed. "You're a wise man in the woods, but you're simple in many ways, Sam'l. Tishomingo told me naught. You told me. You cannot lie, Sam'l. A lie is not in you." She walked to the window, turned and faced him again. "I believe you. And it's our secret. I know your thoughts. They are of Donna. A woman can see things. I'll not tell her. If she loves you, she wouldn't believe you. She would choose to believe you lay with an Indian wench and were shot for your pleasure. Women always believe the worst about the men they love."

"You mustn't tell her anything," Sam said. "You tricked me, Honoria. It was a wily trick. You think very quickly. But I'm glad Chock didn't betray me. There's a thing you should know. I love Donna and I want her to be your sister. I haven't told her yet."

"Ay, Sam'l, but she knows it. Women feel such things. They can see love in a man's eyes."

"I'll tell her in due time. She's of the manor born, Honoria, and I dread to ask her to live in the wilderness. See this." He showed her the comb Anestasie had given him. Honoria's eyes danced. She took the comb and tried it in her hair and was pleased. Sam said, "It's for Donna. Should I give it to her? Is it too intimate a gift? Should I wait?"

Honoria preened herself. "It is. She would think you bold." Honoria knew Donna would love the gift, but said simply and with confidence, "I want this."

"It's for Donna," said Sam. "Damme, Honoria, I fetched you gifts."

"I want this comb. You'll give it to me."

She smiled at Sam. He read her thoughts and was frightened. She held the lash. Sam's temper surged and he grabbed her arm. "I should thrash you! Because you know I was a fool, you have a power over me! You'd betray me to Donna. If you do, I'll ——"

Honoria said, "If you thrash me, she'll hate you for beating your sister. She'll hate you more for that than for laying with a red wench. The comb is mine, Sam'l."

"Keep it! And every time you wear it, remember you tricked your brother who has been kind to you." He mulled the situation in his mind and his anger boiled. It would never do to give his sister any power over a man. He thought clearly. Taking her by the shoulder, he slapped her face and left his finger marks on her cheeks. "That's your punishment! You may have the comb. It's of no great worth! But my belly sickens at you. I'll tell Donna of my wound! I'll tell her of your trick. She'll hate you, and rightly so. And if you annoy me, I'll send you back to Frome!"

142

"You won't," she said defiantly. "You have big plans. You cannot have your sister in servitude! Men would have no respect for you!"

"Be that as it will," he said, "you can't hold a check rein on me. I'll be master of my family and you're my ward!"

Honoria bowed her head. "Yes, Sam'l," she said meekly. "Take the comb back. I wouldn't hurt you. You've been good to me. I was wrong. But, Sam'l, I've been in the service of Mr. Frome so long that I learned to be wily. I had to be! To save my few possessions, and my virtue! For the time, I had forgot I was safe again with you!"

He believed her and was sorry for her. "You keep the comb," he said tenderly. "Let's not have any ill-will between us. We're all who are left of our people."

She walked to a window and stared thoughtfully at the green lawns of the Chadbourne place. Then she turned quickly to Sam. "What I say is going to offend you."

"Why say it?"

"It is my duty," she answered. "When Donna gets away from all of this, will you love her then?"

"I'm quite capable, Hon, of making my own decisions about such matters."

"I wonder if you are," she sighed. "Mind you, I like Donna, but I wonder if she has iron in her blood. You're a strong man, Sam'l, and your wife must be a strong woman. Our mother was not a strong woman and our father crushed her—first her body, then her spirit. I ask you to think a long time before you wed."

"You're a child and you speak as a child," said Sam.

She left him and he finished dressing. He did not condemn her. She would learn to trust and to be trustworthy. She hadn't had a fair chance, he thought. Never-

143

theless, his mind was made up. He would tell Pierce of his wound and lay his case before him. It would not be wise to let Honoria think she shared a secret that Donna didn't know.

He went to Pierce and told him the story. He told Pierce many of his plans, and that he loved Donna. Pierce listened, then smiled.

"Have you spoken to my sister of these things?"

"Nay," said Sam. "I wanted you to know."

"Sam, no man, save a fool, would advise another about such things. My sister's a woman. You're my friend. I'd like you to wait until some of your plans take shape before you seek her hand. The wilderness is hard and life there for a woman is difficult. However, that is for my sister to decide. As for the story of the Indian wench, I believe you. You should tell Donna. She will hear of the wound and the story will be whispered around. Such a story in the hands of women can be made into a mountain. It's no account now. Tell Donna, and trust her wisdom."

"You're wise, Pierce."

"I'm a bachelor, and I hope to remain one," he laughed. "But I know my sister. She'd be hurt if you didn't trust her. She'd be angry if other women, even Honoria, knew of the wound and she didn't. And, too, Sam, if she accepts you, she'll see the wound. Ay, get it off your mind. Then no man, or woman, will have a cudgel over you."

The talk drifted to Sam's plans in the wilderness and he bargained for Jasper. Pierce was willing to sell the Negro for $1,000. "You need a body slave," he said. "And he works well at the forge. Donna may take Sukey on the journey, and if she goes Sukey will take her baby. Did you hear? We call the pickaninny 'Dabby' because you saved her life. Watch her, Sam. The Creeks know of her curse and she'll be a valuable wench some day, too valuable to lose to the red ones."

Pierce led him back to the slave quarters. He passed Sukey's cabin, and peeped in. Dabby was on the floor. Her mother was at the mansion. Sam examined the slave baby. She was copper-colored, bright copper. Her hair was straight and her nose was long. He felt her legs and arms to see if she were strong, and waved his hand before her eyes, testing her sight. The baby grabbed his finger and stuck it into her mouth. Sam laughed. "A likely young 'un—eh, Pierce?" He withdrew his finger. "She'll be a valuable property, right enough."

As they walked through the quarters, Pierce said, "Harkins told you of the land companies. There are several selling lands in the West. Their agents are here. Your company's agent has saddle and pack horses for you, and oxen. And a deed to 5,000 acres on the Pearl River. I saw the forge Frome selected for you. It's a good forge. I wish I were going on the journey. It's tiresome here, drilling my Dragoons and protecting the town. There's a secret I would show you."

His secret was a pigeon cote. Sam laughed as he saw it. "La! Pierce. Do you feed pigeons? There are millions of them in the woods."

Pierce caught one of the birds. "Not such fowls as these. I bought these of an Englishman. They cannot be lost. They always fly back here."

"What is this thing you say?"

"It's true. I've taken this very bird to Savannah and released him and he was back here in two days! You'll take some of these birds with you. If all is well in the Creek country, release this bird and I'll know. If there is conspiracy, free this one." He lifted a second bird.

145

Sam said, "This is a marvel I cannot believe. I would buy some of these birds, Pierce. Think of their value in trade. I can send and receive intelligence. Can they fly with a message tied to their legs?"

"Nay. Paper is too heavy. The only way is to have a code, or tie a splinter to their legs. Each splinter could mean something. But I am thinking of their use for the army, Sam. I'm not a trader. Business annoys me. All of these land companies, I'll have nothing to do with them. For my part, you're going to the new lands as a soldier, a scout. Your work with your company is none of my affair."

"I say this," Sam patted one of the pigeons. "There is much talk of war. What is your judgment?"

"We'll have no war with Washington as president, not with England, anyway. England doesn't want to fight us. What could she gain? And France? The people wouldn't fight France, even though she robs us in our own country. Spain is our real enemy, Sam'l. The Spanish in Florida and Mississippi! Watch 'em, lad. And the Creeks. If Tecumseh forms his confederacy, there'll be an Indian war, but it's years away and we'll be ready."

Sam said, "Why do the politicians preach hatred of England and love of France?"

Pierce shook his head. "I know nothing of politics. I'm a soldier. But I judge the politicians would have us hate some foreign country for fear if we do not, we would hate our own government."

The men gave the afternoon to sorting the goods. The agent for Sam's company helped him. It was the longest pack-horse train ever assembled in the village. The oxen were kept in a compound and slaves fed them and bedded them down. Jasper was at Sam's side and he supervised the work. The Geiche was proud of his new master. He

146

kept the cigar Sam had given him in a pocket of his cotton pants and showed it to the other slaves, now and then taking a bite from it to impress them. He listened to Sam's talk and tried to imitate him. He realized that as a Geiche he was unpopular with the Gullahs and Kroomen. His language and customs were different, but he was learning.

After supper, Sam set Honoria to the task of mixing perfume and bottling it in gaudy little bottles with colored stoppers. He was pleased when he learned she could keep a ledger, work she had been taught by Frome. She didn't wear the comb, but put it in her box and it was stored on a wagon.

Sam was proud of the train. He was proud that he would be a commander of such a caravan. After coffee and brandy, he took Donna to the outskirts of the village and showed her the horses, all ready to begin their journey the next sun-up. By the time they reached Natchez, the wagons would be there from Pensacola.

"It's a good job well done," she said. "You're a competent man, Sam."

"There's something you must know, Donna. I have a wound—" He leaned against a tree and stared at the ground. His face was burning and he was glad Donna couldn't see it. Then impetuously, he told the story. "It is my vow," he swore, "I had naught to do with that Indian."

Donna really was surprised. "You're a strange man. Why do you tell me this thing? Have you no respect for me, to tell me such!"

"Ay, Donna," Sam said. "I wanted you to know the story because I love you."

"Are you batty?" she laughed. "Do you have to tell me a story before you can say you love me?"

"I'm ashamed that I thought evil when I saw the maiden. I'm ashamed that I was shot. I knew you would hear the story some time. I wanted you to know the truth! It's because I love you."

"You speak quickly of love, Sam. You've been home only a short time." She wished he would take her hands, or her lips.

"I know I'm bold."

"I have no reply for you now," said Donna. "This thing must wait." In her mind she was counting the proper number of days a lady should wait before accepting a gentleman's proposal. Her mother had told her, but she had forgotten. She had forgotten everything except that in all the world there were only two persons, she and Sam.

"I will wait," he said simply, and took her hand.

She allowed him to hold it for a minute and then, reluctantly, withdrew it. Damn customs, she was thinking. Why didn't Sam hold her? What did she care about his silly story of the Indian? But she said, "I'm glad now that you told me of your adventure. Was it a pleasing adventure?" she teased.

"Don't ridicule me."

"Was she a pretty Indian?" Then she saw that he was hurt. "It was a jest. I believe you. And it's of no account. Think of it no more. My only fright is that you might have been killed."

"We should go back now," he said. At the door to her room, he said, "Good night, Donna. I love you."

She dropped her eyes. But alone in her room, she took the conch shell from her dresser and held it. She looked at herself in her mirror and preened. She disrobed and stretched. It was good to be loved. Anestasie came to her room. She looked only once at Donna and laughed, "Your skin is blooming. Your breasts are heaving."

"Oh!" Donna turned crimson, then she laughed. "He told me, Anestasie. He told me he loved me."

"Did he kiss you?"

"No. But he held my hand."

Anestasie kissed her cheek. "I'm so happy for you. I'll not tell even André. Next he'll kiss you. Tell me," she sat on the bed, "what did he say?"

"That I will not tell," Donna said. " 'Tis my secret."

"He's a good man, a good protector in the wilderness."

"He's a good man anywhere," Donna said. "He's my man."

"Does Honoria know?" Anestasie asked.

"No."

"She's a testy bit of baggage, Donna. She'll bear watching."

"She's only a child," Donna answered. "She has much to learn, but her heart is good. It's bound to be. I'll love her, Anestasie."

"Did he talk of marriage?"

"For sure, not! It's too soon. Why, he only told me he loved me."

"Hadn't you known he loved you?"

Donna sat on the bed and stretched her long legs and ran her hands through her hair. "Ay," she whispered. "I knew the day I saw him first. I've thought of nothing but him since that day."

10

SAM set his mind to arouse himself two hours before sun-up and he woke at the appointed time. He blinked his eyes rapidly to clear them, sat on the edge of the bed and stretched until the weariness of sleep flowed out of his muscles. This was the day, he thought. It was just like any other day to most men, but to him it was the day. He was going to shake the red dust of Georgia from his feet, leave the land where he had been old man Dabney's brat and go into a new land where he would be Mr. Samuel Dabney, or, perhaps, Samuel Dabney, Esquire, a man of property, a gentleman of affairs. Men would ask his counsel and women would point him out. Perhaps he would be Sam'l Dabney, Factor and Merchant, with the rank of Colonel; Colonel Samuel Dabney of Locha Poka—Promised Land. Donna would be the mistress of Locha Poka and they would have children. They would call him papa, not father as he had called old man Dabney. It was good to dream early in the morning when the body was awake. It was better than dreaming while the body slept. Big Sam was a young man and his dreams were of tomorrow. Only old men, tired old men, took time to dream of yesterday. But old men never suffered the strange fear that ate at Sam'l's mind now that the day had come at last. For old men, having tasted life, knew that the taste could be bitter and

sweet, but a young man, having smacked his lips in antici-
pation of tasting life, feared only that the taste would
disappoint him.

The young Georgian wondered if he could chew the
bite he had taken. He wanted to talk to someone, to tell
of his feelings. He was not afraid of the unknown or of
the wilderness or of responsibility. He feared only failure and the scorn that comes with failure. He knew he
could not seek counsel of any man, for a confident leader
never did. No man ever before had taken such a train
into the new land as he was taking.

He heard the horses crunching oats in the stable below.
The sound drove his dreams away and he was reminded
that there were many things to be done. He wondered if
Jasper had remembered to give Claymore a few licks of
salt. He smelled burning resin as sap oozed from the pine
kindling in the kitchen. He heard the scraping of the
coffee grinder and smelled the sharp, interesting odor of
the roasted beans. Coffee was a good thing, a luxury.
Strange how men paid fancy prices for luxuries and
haggled over the prices of necessities. Coffee would make
a good side-line to trade. Indians never drank coffee, but
they could be taught the habit as they had been taught
to drink rum. If the Indians could be convinced that coffee was a luxury that only the great white men enjoyed,
it would be simple to trade a handful of the beans for
hickory-nut oil, pelts and other things that the great
white men wanted. There were many things to be traded
in the new land—horses and cattle and slaves; perfume
and rum. A pair of tin shoe buckles for a hundred acres
of bottom land, a beaker of rum for the ferry rights on a
river. Damme! a man was a fool to be poor.

The eastern sky was a sickly gray. The western sky
was black. A few impudent stars were blinking as though

the coming sun hurt their eyes. A rooster crowed to the south and a calf bellowed. Then a dog barked and the earth seemed to stretch and yawn, too, and get up and be about its business.

Sam slept naked in the summer time. He would have to have night shirts if Donna married him. The thought tingled his blood. Honoria would make his first night shirt. After all, a man needed only one night shirt at a time. Then Donna would make them. It would be a task too delicate for the slaves. He never had owned a night shirt. Honoria had one, a bed gown she called it, and had made it out of an old petticoat. But she wouldn't wear it. She had said she was saving it for her wedding night. Old man Dabney had laughed in his coarse way and said he wondered why women saved pretty gowns for their wedding nights because they only put them on and took them right off. He remembered his mother had cringed at his father's crudeness, that Honoria had tittered.

For a few minutes, Sam forgot this was the day and began thinking about his sister. There were many things she must learn. She must have a corset. She must learn not to goggle-eye at any man, but to drop her eyes when men stared at her. He had seen her swish so closely to Tishomingo that her dress had touched his trousers. He had even seen her flip her head and smile at Ab, the big sergeant of the Dragoons. Such actions didn't become the sister of Mr. Samuel Dabney. They would reflect on him. For sure, Tishomingo ignored the girl, but that made it worse. Some day, some man wouldn't ignore her. She was a wood sprite, all right. He smiled as he thought about her. Old man Dabney's brat. Just like him, egg and bird, tooth and toe-nail. But Donna would take her in tow. He was afraid to put a check-rein on her. Only a loon handled a filly with a check-rein, for the minute the pressure slackened the filly was off. Ay! she would settle down. She would be busy with the perfume and her many other chores. A busy woman was a good woman. His mother had said that. His father had teased her by saying it depended on what the woman was busy doing.

Sam pulled his doeskin jacket over his head and tied his hair at the nape of his neck. Then he walked across the room and opened the shutter. Fresh air rushed in and drove away the smell of sleep. Law! He had seen fools sleep with shutters open. Small wonder mankind was cursed with pox and fevers. Even a loon knew that night air brought sickness. He never gave thought to the fact that he always felt better after sleeping outdoors. If the shutters were not to be closed, then why had the tavern-keeper paid to have them built?

Jasper fetched razors and hot water. He didn't look at his master or bid him good morning. A body slave, if properly trained, never spoke to his master until the morning toilet was done. Jasper put the blades and water on the dresser and peeped under the bed at the chamber, then walked to the door and shook his head at the tavern slave who was waiting there. Sam pulled on his breeches and tied his gaiters below his knees. Jasper stooped to help him, but Sam brushed him away. The slave's attention embarrassed Sam. He wished he knew how to accept attention from his slave, but he didn't, and he felt that Jasper was laughing at him.

The Negro began honing the razors, sharpening them first on a leather strop, then polishing them on a strip of hide taken from an Indian's back. He waited for his master to sit down and tilt his head, but Sam selected a razor and began scraping his own jowls. He did not use water to soften his beard.

"I'm neither an old man nor a child," Sam said gruffly. Jasper thought he was displeased, but because the master had spoken he must be answered.

"A good day, massa," Jasper said.

"It is not day yet, you blackamoor."

"A good night then, massa," Jasper said.

Sam laughed. Jasper grinned and his heart was happy. A man who could laugh before he broke his fast was a good master, a kind man. The Negro bustled around, trying to appear busy. Sam said, "You're a good slave, Jasper. Now fetch me coffee." He was drinking coffee and eating johnny-cakes with honey when Pierce arrived.

"We'll be away at sun-up," Sam said after greeting him.

"I dropped in for a few farewell words." Pierce poured coffee for himself and didn't trouble to remove his hat. "My sister is taking her slave Sukey and that Creek bastard child along."

"And why not?"

Pierce said, "It's like taking gun powder through hell to take that Indian niggah baby and her mother through the Creeks."

"Then why must Donna take them?" Sam asked.

Pierce glanced up, humor in his eyes. "A person always takes his property when he moves. Those are Donna's slaves and my sister is not the kind of woman who would leave her slaves behind. They're her responsibility and, too, should they stay here our Gullahs would torment Sukey." He looked away and ran his tongue inside his cheek. "Of course, Sam, if you cannot protect my sister and her property ——"

Sam said sharply, "I'm in no mood for jest. Your words

154

are lightly spoken and I take no offense. I can protect your sister." The words were haughty.

"You're a proud man," Pierce said, "watch that your pride doesn't trip you up. Many men stumble over their pride."

Sam said, "If Donna elects to take the couple with her, then her wish is my command."

Pierce clapped him on the shoulder. "That's the way to speak. Donna is taking many things that she prizes, things that women take when they do not expect to come back." He winked at Sam and his smile was friendly.

"I've made my troth," Sam said. "She will reply in fittin' time."

"Ay, she will that. When you get to the Choctaws seek out Pushmataha, a noble man, and Lake Flournoy, a rich man. You can trust Pushmataha, but never Flournoy. But he must never know you do not trust him. The nabobs in Philadelphia think he's our friend, but he's the friend of the side that can help him most."

"I've never heard good spoken of the man," Sam remarked. "Tishomingo will kill him some day. I wonder why he hasn't killed him already?"

"Because our mingo friend is more red than white in spite of his courtly manners and speech. He'll kill Flournoy in due time. His hate is so deep that it will simmer in his innards for years before it boils over."

"A white man would have killed Flournoy the day he betrayed the girl, eh?"

"Perhaps. But Tishomingo doesn't hate Flournoy only because he took his woman, but because he cast the woman aside for a slave wench. That made Tishomingo small in the eyes of his people. It's an Indian feud and it must be kept among the red 'uns."

Sam nodded, understanding. "There are white men who would like to see Flournoy dead? I've heard so."

"Many of them. But as our agent among the Chocks you must help protect him from white men. If a white man kills him, the white man will be tried and judged by Choctaw law. He'll be skinned with a bull whip and steamed. The United States would not suffer one of its citizens to undergo such punishment. We'd try to avenge him, and that would mean war."

"I am glad I am not Lake Flournoy. You should see Chock handle a bull whip."

"Flournoy knows that some day Tishomingo will try to kill him."

"Then why in God's name doesn't Flournoy kill Chock?" Sam put his coffee saucer down and stared at Pierce.

"You've much to learn. Tishomingo is the nephew of Pushmataha, the great mingo of the nation. There is intrigue there, Sam'l. Mind that you stay out of it, or get in on the right side, the winning side."

Sam said, "You are beating the bush. There's something you would tell me. Out with it."

Pierce toyed with his pipe before he replied. "You're ambitious, Sam'l. I feel already as though you were a member of our family. Donna's well-being and happiness are in your hands. I care naught that you were born poor, but in your desire to be rich you'll be tempted to take the short cut. I'll tell you quickly a way in which you can be one of the richest men in the new land."

"Eh?"

"Take Tishomingo's scalp to Flournoy."

Sam got to his feet. "If I did not know you were jesting I'd beat you."

"You're a good man. You'll see many plots in the new

156

land. You'll meet men who will try to buy you. There are many schemes afoot to divide our nation. There are plans a-borning to create new nations in the Southwest. Some of our big wigs are fathers of the plans. Have naught to do with them. Your duty is to fight, or to die, to see that every tree and hill between here and the Mississippi River belongs to the United States."

Sam said, "I'll try never to do anything that will shame you or Donna. Or my country. I know naught of the intrigues along the river. I'll seek to protect Lake Flournoy from white men only because we want no war. But Chock's grudge is his own. I know how he feels. A white man kills quickly, for hate and revenge. But to an Indian it is foolish to kill a man because you hate him. Death ends suffering. If a wise man hates deeply enough, he will allow his enemy to live and will play with him. That's Chock's game. And I pray he wins it."

Pierce said, "The sun is up."

Jasper brought Claymore to the turn-in and Sam rode to the edge of the village where the horse train was waiting. The dung of the animals smoked in the first light of the sun. There was an odor of hot tar which had been used on the wounds of many animals, the mules that had been de-horned because they were vicious.

All night the slaves had worked, slaughtering beeves. The hides had been packed green and now they stunk. The meat had been coated with salt and packed on mules. The weight of the packs and the motion of the animals would tear down the tissues of the tough meat and make it palatable. It could even be eaten raw.

Sam, Chock and André checked the train. Every hoof was examined. A smithy had filed too deeply into one horse's hoof and Sam ordered the beast to be unloaded and left behind. He might go cripple. Every slave, man

157

and woman, was made to strip and Sam and Jasper went over them carefully, looking for running sores. They smelled the breaths of the Negroes, studied their tongues, their eyes. He made the slaves run around for several minutes and then called them to him. They were sweating and panting. A slave taster, a big burly Negro, stepped from the crowd. He licked the sweating slaves on their chest and tasted their sweat. If there were illness in the blood, he could taste it in their sweat. He reported all the slaves sound.

Satisfied at last, Sam wrote in his ledger:

"Journey to the Choctaw nation, 18 August 1795."

He listed all the equipment, even the few iron nails in the packs. In his careful, studied handwriting he wrote:

"Of prime oxen, 146; of milch cows (2 with heifers), 16; of bulls, 4; of horses, 96 (80 of which have packs)."

He called Chock and André into counsel and instructed the Indian to pace the caravan one hundred and fifty yards ahead of the first pack train. The women would ride in the center of the line, protected by André on the right and Jasper on the left. Sukey and Dabby would travel near Donna. No slaves except Jasper would be allowed a gun. No horse must be allowed to get out of line. The oxen would trail in the wake of the train to prevent the dust from rolling back on the ladies. Sam said, "I'll guard the rear."

Tishomingo eyed him closely. "But you're the leader, Big Sam."

Sam knew his decision would impress the men. He really wanted to ride the advance but fearing the men would think he chose for himself the easiest task he elected to trail the drovers of oxen, protecting the rear from surprise. It was the place for a good shot and he was a good shot, but it was not the position of honor.

But by humbling himself he sought to convince his followers that he would never expect them to do a chore that he wouldn't do.

Donna and the other women arrived at the appointed time. She glanced at Sam and blushed. His face reddened. Anestasie saw them exchange glances and winked, brazenly, at Sam. He tried to hide his confusion by bawling orders. Also, he thought to impress Donna with his efficiency.

"Stop shouting," Honoria demanded of her brother. "You make more noise than one of the bulls." The Dragoons who had come to see the departure guffawed. Ab, the sergeant, laughed loudest.

"Ay," he shouted, "that Sam'l man is a stallion, all right, but that filly sister of his can handle him."

"She can handle you, too, Ab," a soldier said.

"For a fact," Ab laughed. "She could break me to a plow, buckoes."

Sam wondered if the levity embarrassed Donna. But she was laughing. Mrs. Harkins looked stern, but Donna and Anestasie seemed to enjoy the scene. He must not rebuke Honoria now. The party should be allowed to partake of all the gayety possible at the beginning of the journey. There would be many days without laughter. And he was rather proud of Honoria. She could take care of herself.

One of the Dragoons stepped to help Honoria mount, but she kicked him away. "You'll frighten my horse," she laughed, "even though you can't frighten me. Goodbye, Ab." She waved to the sergeant, who was sitting his horse near her.

"Why don't you go along, Ab?" someone yelled. "Ain't nothing tying you here. Dare you to go. And if you'll take a dare you'll sleep with a nanny."

"Don't dare me too hard," Ab said. "I'm half hoss and half alligator and I don't take no dares."

Honoria said, "Come along, Ab. I'd enjoy some pleasant company." She hoped Chock heard her.

"What you say, Cap'n?" Ab turned to Pierce. "I can't take no dare. Let me go. You can get another sergeant. Besides I want to plant myself a crop."

"Crop of what? Young'uns?" a Dragoon demanded.

Honoria tossed her head. "What ever kind of crop it is, I'll vow Ab will work it." She cut her eyes to see if Chock were watching her. He was busy with his horse.

Pierce said, "It's up to Sam. Ab is a good man, Sam'l. I can spare him."

Sam was delighted. He liked Ab. He had liked him the day the sergeant had greeted him when he first arrived at the village. "It's a go," Sam said. "Get down, Ab, and come over here."

The gangling sergeant dismounted and followed Sam to the edge of the clearing where the slaves were rounding up the oxen. "I reckon you think I'm loony, Sam'l boy," Ab said. "Just making up my mind like that to go along. But I been thinking 'bout it. An' when I saw ever'body all excited and the fun startin', well, I just up and decided that I better go with that train. I don't want to miss nothing."

Sam took out his journal. "I didn't want to ask any embarrassing questions back there by the ladies. You told me once just to call you Ab. I must keep a record. What's your whole name? Just Ab?"

"That's good enough," Ab grinned. "But being it's you, I'll let you write it down as it really is—Adam Bascomb. I'm from Kaintuck. I can't write my whole name but I can put down my initials. They are just A. B. and that spells Ab, leastwise back where I come from."

160

"Have you any folks?"

"None to brag about," Ab's jaw tightened. "Paw and Maw died up in Kaintuck during the big freeze. Saved me and my sister by cutting the guts out of two oxen and poking us in the holes. Damme, man, I can tell you a thing or two."

"Never the mind now. Is there any message you want to send to your sister? I'll write it for you and Captain Chadbourne will see that it reaches her."

Ab fingered his nose nervously. "There's no word for her. Don't know where she is. She went down the Mississip to get some schooling and the keelboat boys fetched word back to home that she wasn't a moderate girl, or fittin'. She shamed me, Sam'l. She dirtied the Bascomb name. That's why I just use the name of Ab."

Sam, sensing the man's hurt, changed the subject. "I'll pay you twenty dollars a month, hard money. You'll be paid off in Natchez, if we get there. You ride dog-trail on the wagon, from the advance to the rear. Keep the train in line. Chock will cover our advance. You'll like him."

"As much as I like any red 'un," Ab spat. "I rent you my gun and brains for twenty dollars, payable in Natchez. No sense of paying me now, 'cause we might not reach Natchez, eh, Sam'l boy?"

Sam nudged him playfully. "We'll get through. As you ride the train, make some fun, Ab. Try to keep the women gay. Sing and josh."

Back at the train, Sam announced, "Ab will go with us." He bowed to the ladies. "We must travel light. Have you anything in your saddle bags you don't need?"

"No," said Honoria.

"I must look," said Sam.

Anestasie laughed and Donna blushed again. "I'll vow

you will see things you've never seen before," Anestasie said.

"You don't know the things I've seen," said Sam cheerfully.

The crowd laughed, even Tishomingo. Donna laughed too, but Mrs. Harkins snickered, then her face was stern and she said, "You cannot search my saddle bags, young man."

"I am sorry, ma'm," Sam said. "But it must be done. We must take nothing that can be of value to the Creeks if we have to lighten our loads and run. Many articles of a lady's wardrobe are unnecessary on this journey, but to the red 'uns they would be of value, for trade." He tried to keep a straight face and watched Donna out of the corners of his eyes. "A pair of beams, for a case ——"

"What know you of beams, young man?" Mrs. Harkins said.

"They're only padding for a ladies' hips and such a charming lady as you, I'll vow, would never need them. But for a pair of beams a Creek could get two guns in Pensacola. Donna, your first task is to search the ladies' bags."

Donna found a bosom bottle in Anestasie's luggage, a tiny bottle that slipped between the breasts and was a receptacle for a fresh flower. "It's of no use," Sam said. "Leave it behind."

André protested. "It's a gift from our friend, the widow of Vicomte de Beauharais, the Creole Josephine. Please let my wife take it."

Sam agreed. After all, it was a tiny bottle and André not only was his financial sponsor, but he was Sam's contact with the powerful Flournoy. In Honoria's bags they found two pairs of slyders, overalls she would wear on

162

the trail. They also found a comb. Anestasie recognized it, looked quickly at Sam, and wondered.

In Donna's luggage, they found a conch shell, wrapped in a petticoat. Sam's heart leapt when he saw it. Donna looked full into his eyes as the gift he had brought her was unwrapped and exposed to the curious glances of the crowd. Then she re-wrapped it and put it away.

"It's a useless thing," Sam whispered to her. "Why do you take it?"

She didn't reply, but mounted her horse and galloped to her place in the line.

"All the plunder has been searched," Sam said. "We'll be away." He glanced at the sun. "I'll say it is a quarter hour before six. Is that right, Pierce?"

Chadbourne extracted his heavy watch. "It's ten minutes before the hour," he said. Sam entered the time in his journal. The men removed their coonskin caps. The slaves lowered their eyes. Only Tishomingo held his head erect. The Choctaws never bowed their heads to pray, but held up their heads to face God. The village minister, a Methodist, stood on a stump, held out his hands and petitioned God to bless the journey. "And may the Lord of Hosts go with you. May the Lord God Jehovah sharpen your eyes and keen your ears and damn you if you waste lead on a red 'un! God bless President Washington and the Congress and put some sense in their heads, not President Washington, Lord, because he's a fitting man, and moderate, but Congress' head. And bless Thomas Jefferson and Aaron Burr and the Jeffersonian Republican Party. And strike down England, oh, Lord. Bless these horse beasts that tote your children and these cow beasts that will feed them. Bless these slaves because we're slaves of Thine. And steady these men's arms, Lord, so they will never miss a red 'un. And in the end, gather us to Thy bosom and take us to the land where the woodbine twineth, and deliver us from the mountains of Hepsidam where the lion roareth and the wang-doodle mourneth not for his first born. Amen."

Tishomingo slapped his pony across the neck and the train moved, the first great caravan to the new land. The Dragoons fired their muskets. A cannon boomed. Sam doffed his cap and bowed. He was very proud. He wished old man Dabney could see him, and his mother. His good saddle creaked and his long stirrups were pushed forward. He rode that way, rearing back in his saddle. The reins lay loose on the withers of Claymore. His long rifle-gun lay across his saddle, balanced with his right hand.

The horse train spread almost a mile along the road. The children of the village ran along beside the train and shouted good cheer. Some threw rocks at the horses and laughed when they shied. One urchin saw Sam's long bull whip and pleaded, "Crack it, Mr. Dabney, let's hear you crack it."

Sam unwound the whip and snapped it. Claymore skitted at the noise. The oxen raised their heads and looked around. The children shouted, "Look at that cracker; he's the best cracker on the frontier. Sam Dabney, the Georgia Cracker."

Sam stood in his stirrups and watched the village disappear around a turn in the road. The red hills soon would pass away and the black lands would come. He looked longingly at the land. Man already had worked the land until it had wrinkled in protest. Man had taken the earth's virginity, had stolen its sweet richness, and had given the earth nothing except man's sweat. And the land cannot live upon the sweat of man. It can grow rich upon the waste of animals and of trees, but man can give it naught for its own good. The land had been cut into deep gullies, sickening red wounds that never would heal.

The trees trooped down from the hills and seemed to stand at attention as he passed. The branches waving in the early morning breeze seemed to salute him. The oak trees, the scaly barks and the slender little pines seemed to wave farewell to old man Dabney's brat going to the promised land commander of the greatest caravan that ever moved from Georgia. Sam wondered if there were friendly little pine trees in the new land. He wondered how the land would look. Would pine trees mat the earth with their needles? Would the scaly barks be brown and golden in the fall? He had heard that in the new land the trees were always green. That would be monotonous, he thought. He did not like unchanging things. The sound of the village died away and Sam Dabney seemed alone. Natchez was the next town, Natchez and old Fort Rosalie, more than five hundred miles due west. Much of the land was uncharted. A few horse paths criss-crossed the Creek and Choctaw nations. But Sam knew he would have to cut and pick his trail through a wilderness that white men had shunned for two hundred years. Until the United States had made a precarious and willy-nilly peace with the Creeks, the underwriters at Philadelphia had given odds of ten to one against the life of any white man who tried to ride from Georgia to Natchez.

He wished he could order one of the men to come back and ride beside him, so he could talk to him and make merry with him, but he banished the thought. He was the leader and he must ride alone.

The horse train moved down the road to the Chatta-

hoochee, the road Sam had taken to the village. To the
south was Frome's factory and the Dabney homestead.
Grass had grown over the graves of his parents. Surely,
a tree had seeded there by now. Soon the earth would
hide the place, and men would come and dig again; then
die, and the earth would hide them, as the earth was hiding old man Dabney and his loony wife while the Dabney brats rode forth to conquer the earth. As though any
man could.

11

THE plodding oxen smelled good to Sam. The sweat of his horse, of his saddle smelled good. He didn't mind the dust of the train because it was his train. The dust drifted into his nostrils and tickled his nose and made him sneeze. The sensation of sneezing was pleasant. Often he blew his nose loudly, holding one finger over a nostril and blowing the other. He could inhale dust and blow it out again. The dust seemed to give him strength. It was a good earth, he thought. It would give a man all he wanted; shade and heat and food. That's all a man really needed; shade and heat and food, and gladly would the earth give that without man turning his hand for the privilege of living.

But man must torture the earth and break it up and make it grow things it didn't want to grow. And earth and man must fight. Why? Sam wondered. Man came from the earth, from dust. Or so his mother had said. And he went back to dust, back to earth. So the earth always won. He watched the dust, the powder on earth's face, whirl up from the oxen's feet and scatter to the side of the road, then settle on the leaves. The leaves drooped. They were old leaves. A few months ago they were young leaves. But now they were wrinkled and weary. The dust was old, too. Soon the leaves would fall and would become earth again and change. But the dust wouldn't change. It would always be earth. It was a disturbing thought. Sam let his mind wander to his problems. He would put Honoria to making perfume as soon as they reached the new land. He must keep her busy, else she might go the way of Ab's sister. He must set up his foundry as soon as he stepped off the boundaries of his new home. He would sleep under the stars until his foundry was running. Then he would make gins. Maybe rifle-guns. And nails. Nails were worth their weight in silver. La! There were many ways to make money. And many new acres to own, miles of virgin earth, earth that had never been raped by a plow or beaten with a hoe. For sure, if you beat the earth, the earth died, too, and became dust. But what cared he of dust? Dust meant death and he was alive. He would make the earth work for him. Out of her womb he would drag ore. With her heat he would make things of iron and sell them so men could dig into the earth and stomp her and make her do their bidding. He would wed her to husbandry. He would run plows across her belly and sweep across her breasts with sickles and comb her hair with rakes. He would tap her veins and use her blood to turn his wheels.

He laughed as a young Negro ran into the herd to separate a bullock that had dashed for a heifer. He watched the hounds run to the bitches, lower their heads and smell. The slave girls who had been given permission to walk with the men, wiggled as they walked, enticingly, deliberately. Even Claymore cocked her ears and trembled with excitement every time she got down-wind from the stallions.

He wondered if Donna were comfortable. He couldn't see her for the dust. He wished Ab would ride back and relieve him. Then he could gallop up the train. Donna would think he had business there. But he only wanted

168

to see her. To pass by her. He could wave his hand and she would wave back. He could see her sleeves tight around her arms. There would be drops of sweat on her lips and her dress would be wet under her arms. Maybe he could smell her.

He studied the sun. It was an hour before noon. They would make only ten miles that day. It was better to make only ten miles the first day. Give the oxen and pack horses time to get hardened. Give the packs time to set. Then he could step the pace up to twelve a day, then to fifteen. And keep it at fifteen.

He forgot about the dust, even when he sneezed it out of his nose. The young will never think seriously for long. He took his right foot out of the stirrup and sat side-saddle. Claymore walked slowly. Sam felt drowsy and contented, and very proud. Afraid of drowsiness, he sang to sharpen his senses.

> "Light, light, light my little Scotch-ee
>   And stay all night with me;
>   I have a bed of the very, very best,
>   I'll give it up to thee."

The dust boiled to the right of the drove and Ab checked his horse. "Eh, Sam'l boy. So you know that song, for fair. I'll give you the next verse.

> "I cannot light, and I will not light,
>   And stay all night with thee;
>   For there's a girl in the old Scotch Yard,
>   This night a-waiting for me."

Sam interrupted him before he began the third verse of

the ballad. "What brings you back here? Is all well with the advance?"

"Ay. But your Injun friend wants to see you."

"Can you guard this rear while I'm away? We are only a few miles out of the village, but the red 'uns might be about."

Ab spat out the dust. "If I couldn't guard the arse end of oxen, I'd go back to Kaintuck."

"I heard that in Kaintuck that's all they had—oxen arses." He dashed away before Ab could reply. Claymore enjoyed the run and galloped around the herd and alongside the train. Sam started a song as he passed the negro drovers. He wanted them to sing.

> "Went out to milk and didn't know how,
> I milked a goat instead of a cow.
> A monkey sitting on a pile of straw
> A'winking at his mother-in-law."

The tired slaves grinned at him and took up the melody. Their feet seemed lighter. He dashed by Donna and waved. Honoria heard him singing as he passed by her and she joined in.

> "As I came down the new cut road
> Met Mr. Bullfrog, met Miss Toad
> And every time Miss Toad would sing
> Ol' Bullfrog cut a pigeon wing."

He held his rifle aloft in greeting to André and hurried along. Chock was one hundred and fifty yards ahead of the train, sitting his pony easily. He didn't turn when he heard Claymore's hoof-beats but shouted so

170

Sam could hear, "All is well. There's no need of sweating your horse."

"How did you know it was I?" Sam demanded as he reined Claymore to a walk beside the Indian.

Chock kept scouting the land, his eyes roving and taking in every movement in the woods, the flutter of leaves, the scurrying of squirrels. "The hawk can tell when the eagle comes, my friend. I had a thought that perhaps you would want to leave your dusty task and ride up the train. And, too, I wanted to talk."

"It's as lonely up here as it is back there. We've made a good start, Chock. Not a pack has slipped. What are the miles you would say we've come?"

"Eight. We will go twelve?"

Sam said, "Ten. A half of another on the morrow. Within a week we can be traveling fifteen miles a day."

Tishomingo glanced into the bushes, uncoiled his whip in one motion and flicked it, cutting off the head of a lizard.

"It might have frightened one of the ladies' horses. I wouldn't like to see Mrs. Harkins on a frightened horse, eh, Big Sam?"

"Has Ab been dog-trailing the train?"

"Ay, and well, too. He's a gay man. He and your sister sing on the trail. All the women are glad when he rides by. He's so cheerful. Whence came he?"

"Kaintuck."

Chock asked as though he really were not interested, "And his name?"

"He told me to call him Ab. If he has any reason to forget his whole name that's his business."

"I thought I had seen him somewhere, that I had heard his voice. In the Great Smokies perhaps? But if you trust him, I do. But many strangers are traveling to these parts, seeking to create strife. No man trusts another. It would not be impossible for Ab to be here to watch you. I'd vow I had seen his face and heard his voice."

"Was he at the council of the Cherokees?" Sam asked.

"No. There was no white man there."

Sam said, "Many men look alike. Your eyes and ears trick you."

The road to the Chattahoochee twisted through the shallow valleys. A few travelers, mostly traders from the Creeks, passed by, gaped at the long train and waved greetings. The sun still was high and the day was sultry but the birds began quickening their flights. The crows swooped overhead in haphazard formations and, following the leader, dropped into a thicket, cawing. The dust began forming little circular dunes as the breeze stirred it and lifted it to the side of the trail. The breeze felt cool to Sam, seeping through his moist jacket.

Chock sniffed the air and said, "Hashi illi."

"What?" Sam demanded.

"The weather god is angry and filled with tears. It will rain tonight."

Sam said, "Smells like rain. Maybe just a Scotch mist."

"It will be more than a shower."

"A bad sign," Sam said. "Rain our first day out. Rain is the only thing I fear. There are a hundred creeks and rivers between us and the Nation. High water would block us."

"There will not be high water. The season is not ripe. This will be a good rain, a south rain. Gentle as a mother's caress. It will bathe the earth and make her smell sweet, Big Sam."

Sam said, "We must be ready. We'll camp here."

"Ay, it's a good place. There's a fast creek and cha-hah-nu-chi."

172

Sam pronounced it *chatta-nooga.* "It means wild flax," Chock said. "It will make good beds."

The Indian wheeled his horse and trotted to the north of the trail, selected a site about fifty yards from the creek and dismounted. He measured the slope with his eyes. It was a good drainage.

Sam dismounted too, and went carefully over the ground. He noted that there was plenty of firewood handy, and that the ground was soft. He didn't want his company to sleep on rocky ground the first night. He tasted the creek water and then nodded approval. It was a good place. He would have the men build a stockade of dead logs and green brush. They must learn to build fortifications every evening. He knew Chock had thought already of all the things he was thinking, but a leader must decide for himself.

Satisfied with the site Sam mounted and trotted his horse back to the train.

"Making camp," he shouted to André who relayed the order. There was no confusion. The drovers herded the cattle into a circle and posted guards. Ab galloped from the rear and took up post at the advance. Sam bawled orders, but Honoria gave orders quietly.

She said to Sam, "Remember you have women with you, women who are not used to rough life. There are things to be done. Jasper!" Her voice brought the Negro running. "Have a darkey dig a privy just over that knoll. For the ladies. Have another fetch water to be heated, for washing purposes. You, Sukey!" She called Donna's maid. The Negroes ran to Honoria. "String up a parcel of cloth between those saplings as a screen for the ladies."

Sam watched the slaves do her bidding. He wished he could give orders that way. The Negroes seemed to obey her, not because they liked her as they did him, but because her voice commanded.

"You've made yourself a task," he said. "You'll handle the chores of making the ladies comfortable on the trip. I'll see only to the men." He strolled toward the drovers.

Donna dismounted stiffly and walked to the fire a slave had kindled. It was a small fire, built only to heat water. "You are a very efficient mistress, Honoria," Donna said.

"I'm used to work."

"I, too, can work," Donna said.

"But my brother would not have it. Men are that way, Donna. He would not want his love to do these tasks."

"How know you so much of men?" Donna said in jest.

"There are some women born with knowledge."

Honoria stepped behind the shelter and slipped off her slyders, unaware that Donna was staring at her. Honoria rubbed cold water on her body until her skin blushed. She rubbed ferns between her hands and then rubbed the lather under her arms, between her breasts and then all over her body. She chattered while she cleansed herself, and then asked Donna to dash water upon her. Donna envied Honoria's body. She wished she were small. She poured water on Honoria's body, carefully sparing her hair.

"Pour it on my head, too," Honoria said. "Water doesn't hurt my hair."

Donna toyed with her dress as she began disrobing and then suddenly, her mind made up, she took her clothes off quickly. She was embarrassed. Her skin felt hot and Honoria laughed at her. Honoria seemed like a child, at times, and again like a very old woman. But old man Dabney's brat was not embarrassed. She looked Donna over. "You're a pretty lady, Donna," she said. "You'll marry my brother, eh?"

174

Donna bridled. "This is not the time or place for such talk."

"What else can women talk about? Oxen and red 'uns? Land? Re-fiddlesticks! We can talk of nothing but men. They're all that really interests us." She laughed at Donna's confusion. "You had best put on a pair of slyders. They'll show the shape of your body, but you'll feel better."

"I'm weary," said Donna, and stretched her long arms.

"Of course, you're weary," answered Honoria quickly. "What else do you expect?"

Anestasie joined them, and Honoria turned to her, "I suppose you are tired, too."

"What if I am?" Anestasie said. "A body cannot expect never to be tired." She did not fumble with her dress as Donna had done but unbuttoned it quickly and pulled it over her head. Then she washed herself with good soap and daintily applied perfume to her body, under her arms and on the lobes of her ears.

"Hoity Toity!" Honoria exclaimed. "That's a trick. That's good bait. Please, may I use some? And you, Donna, try it. It makes your flesh feel cold for a minute, then sweet. I'll vow my brother will jump over those trees there if he gets down-wind from you now."

Donna and Anestasie laughed. Honoria helped them with their slyders. Anestasie looked down at herself. "I feel indecent in these trousers."

"That's a good way to feel," Honoria teased. "If I had a man as handsome as yours I would always feel indecent." She tickled Donna under the chin. "I know you'll marry my brother."

"Will you be glad if I do?" Donna asked.

"I don't know. I think I will. I measure all men by my brother's standard, and find them wanting. He and my

175

father were the only men I ever knew until I bound out to old Jew Frome. When I was a little girl I used to make play that a man drcve over the ridge to our house and took me away. He rode a great horse and wore a green jacket. He looked like my brother. Maybe that was because my brother was the only young man J had ever seen. And he was always good to me."

Donna put her arm around the girl. "He loves you very much and is proud of you. You must never hurt him."

"He loves you, too," Honoria said. "I've done a mean thing, Donna. I have a pretty comb that he brought for you, but I got it by a trick. Will you take it?"

"You keep it. He brought me a present. And I know he was thinking about me. That is gift enough. But I want you to know that he told me about the Indian wench."

Honoria said, "He really did nothing wrong. He only thought he did. A man's conscience is his master. My father said that. A woman can use a man's conscience and rule him. My father said that, too. He was a very wise man. He said marriage was made on a woman's back and kept in working order by a man's conscience." She stood on her tiptoes and kissed Donna, then ran from the shelter to complete her chores.

Anestasie shook her head slowly. "She's a minx, Donna. But a strange girl. A Jezebel one day, a Ruth the next."

"I like her," Donna said. "She reminds me of a beautiful little child whose mind grew older than her body. And, too, she's my Sam'l's sister."

The camp soon was organized. Sam ordered that no beeves be killed and that the travelers be fed game. He sent Chock with a party to find squirrels and other small game which were cooked with oatmeal into a burgoo.

He watched Chock as he rode away, for a great change had come over his friend. The look of cunning that had worried Sam had disappeared and Tishomingo's face was calm and almost happy. Back in Carolina, he had seemed as a savage to Sam, a brutal, calculating half-breed. But now he seemed different. Sam had often wished that he had had a brother. A man could tie to his brother. A man could go to his brother and talk to him. Well, Tishomingo would be his brother.

As he rode into the woods, Tishomingo was thinking as Sam thought. Sam would be his brother. He had planned to use Dabney and had known that Sam had planned to use him. But that was before he had learned to know Sam. Ay, a Choctaw could love as well as hate. He would always hate Lake Flournoy and would always love Sam Dabney.

At the camp, Sam directed that colcannon be cooked. It was a sustaining dish of potatoes and maize. Tafula was prepared for Tishomingo. A small ration of rum weakened with water was issued to the slaves. Honoria and Donna supervised the cooking. The cattle was driven into a clearing down-wind from the camp. Small fires were laid at regular intervals around the herd. The fires would be lighted when darkness came as protection for the cattle. One fire was worth five guards. Sam saw that every horse was rubbed down and that the packs were covered with oak branches and canvas. The slaves were told to prepare their beds close by the stream. The men made their beds in a big circle around the ladies' beds. The earth was scooped out so the hips could rest comfortably.

Sam almost laughed aloud as he supervised the preparation of Mrs. Harkins' bed. Honoria noticed his mirth. "You're thinking as I am," she said. "A gully is needed for Mrs. Harkins' hips." Sam frowned at his sister and tried to appear stern but he couldn't. Damme! Honoria was always thinking of hips. Hips and loins and bellies. But, after all, they were all that mattered. They and land. Land where man could lie down. Land where man could build a house. Land that would grow trees, that would shield a man in summer, and warm him in winter. Land that would give things: grass for the deer, pine needles for a man's bed. Land that would grow maize for a man's belly, tobacco for his pipe, flax for his clothes. Yes, that was all that mattered—hips and loins, bellies and land. Old man Dabney had said so.

Cloth was strung over the ladies' beds, the men would burrow their heads under their saddles when it rained. The sun went down behind a bank of heavy clouds and the cattle became restless, knowing that rain was coming. Two huge green logs were dragged to the fire and the blaze was kept between them.

They ate the meat with their fingers and licked their fingers clean. The smoking stew was poured into saucers and they drank it. Sam saw to it that the slaves were fed hot food and after supper he rationed tobacco to the Negroes and gave the men and women leave to mingle. He kept Sukey and Dabby close by the fire and told Jasper, "Guard them."

The travelers sat around the fire and relaxed, the men smoking pipes and the women doing chores, plaiting rawhide, measuring powder. A brooding silence fell over the assembly and each man had his own thoughts.

Anestasie broke the silence. "Who would have thought I would have been here in this wilderness, eating with my hands, sleeping on the naked earth."

Her husband said, "We're lucky to have our heads.

178

Were it not for our friend Josephine we'd be with her husband, in heaven."

"Or hell," suggested Anestasie.

"But Josephine did not say it would be this way," André said.

Tishomingo said, "The one you call Josephine never was here. In Martinique it is not this way. Lake Flournoy will be happy to serve friends of his noble kinswoman. What manner of lady is she?"

"She's not a lady," Anestasie answered. "She's a strumpet. Even before her husband's body was cold she was flirting with M'sieur Bonaparte."

"I would not speak so to Lake Flournoy," Tishomingo said. "He's very proud of his kin."

"I'll speak as I please," said Anestasie. Silence dropped over the group again. The wind rustled the leaves and darkness seemed everywhere except within the few feet where the fire spluttered. The crowd was getting moody. Sam felt it and winked at Ab.

Ab stretched. Then he sat upright suddenly. He had been whittling an ax handle and he laid it aside. "Well, hone my backbone with a meat ax. Tomorrow is Friday."

"Of what difference is that?" Sam asked.

"I can't talk on Friday. Can't say a word from sun-up to noon-out." He glanced around and saw that he had attention. "It's because of a sin I done. It's punishment. When I was a shaver of about three up in Kaintuck my maw sent me out one day to kill a mess of fe'larks. I took my paw's rifle-gun. Got a bead on a fe'lark only about three hundred yards away. And I missed him." He shook his head sadly and picked up the ax handle and resumed his whittling.

André waited for someone to ask a question, but when

no one did, he ventured one. "What has that to do with your penance of silence on Fridays?"

"I missed that fe'lark, I said," Ab looked ashamed. "And that bird was only three hundred yards off and I was three years old. And with my paw's own rifle-gun. And me from Kaintuck! My paw was so put out with me for missing such an easy shot that he told me never to talk no more on Fridays."

André glanced from one face to another. Sam bit his lip to suppress his laughter.

"You must have been a superfine shot, Ab," Sam said.

"I was better than middling. Every deer in Kaintuck knew me by sight. I was out one day to get me a buck and saw one grazing on the ridge. I got dead aim and just as I was fixing to knock him over that old buck turned his head and saw me."

"So you missed another shot, eh?" Sam said.

"Well, not exactly. When that old buck saw me he just gave up and whooped across at me, 'Is that you, Ab?' I said, 'This is me.' That old deer said, 'Hell, Ab, you ain't going to shoot me in the mating season, are you?'"

Sam could hold his mirth no longer. André tilted his head and laughed. But Tishomingo stared at Ab, at his deep blue eyes that danced in the firelight. He didn't take his eyes off of the Kentuckian even when Ab held up his ax handle for examination. "It's a prime ax handle," Ab passed it to André. The Frenchman studied it. It was curved.

"Why do you not use a straight handle?" André asked. "We use a straight handle on axes in Europe."

"Ay," cut in Sam. "So you do. My father told me about it. But with a curved handle a woodsman can clear four times as much land as with a straight handle. I remember as a boy my father held a curved ax handle in his hand and said, 'Boy, the man who first curved an ax handle did more to make this country than all the dom'd soldiers and politicians put together.' And it's true, eh, Chock?"

The Indian still was staring at Ab. But Sam's words aroused him and brought his thoughts back. "Ay, it's as you say."

Sam nodded to Ab. "Give us a song, Ab, before we go to bed. We'll all join in."

Chock said, "Do you know the ballad of Charlotte who lived on a mountain top?"

The Kentuckian's face lighted and he smiled at the Indian. "That is the ballad of 'The Frozen Girl.' Ay, I know it. My maw used to sing it to us before she died in the great freeze. It's a sad song." He looked into the fire as though to recall the words, then sang softly:

"Charlottie lived on a mountain top in a bleak and lonely spot.
There were no other houses there except her father's cot,
And yet, on many a wintry night, young swains were gathered there,
For her father set a social board and she was very fair."

Tishomingo's eyes never left Ab's face while he sang verse after verse. And when the song was finished, the travelers went to the shallow holes they had dug for their beds. But the Indian sat by the fire. He would take the first watch. He looked at the sky and knew it soon would rain. He tossed green boughs on the fire to help protect it. He pulled his rifle to his side and let it rest on the log. Then he stared again at the fire, and murmured. There was none to hear him. The wind could hear him but the wind would keep secrets. "Amelia," he whispered. "I should have known he was your brother. By his eyes and his voice. And his music and stories. I vow I'll guard him. And I'll avenge you, and avenge my name. Great will be the revenge of Tishomingo, my darling."

He heard Sam walking down the slope, although Sam stepped softly. "I was taking a last look," Sam said. "All is well." Tishomingo lighted his pipe and passed it to his friend. "You're different, Chock, than when I first saw you," Sam remarked as he passed the pipe back.

"I'm nearing home after a long absence." Tishomingo's sad eyes seemed to brighten in the firelight, and he looked at Sam and smiled.

"It will be good to be home," Sam said.

"Ay, it will be good. But the lodge of Tishomingo is empty. The heart of Tishomingo is empty of love. There's only hate in my heart. It is not good for a man to hate too much. . . ."

Sam put his hand on his friend's shoulder. "You're a good man, Chock."

"I'm not the man you are, Big Sam. I know my weakness. You are my brother and I will tell you that I am not the man my people think I am. You will hear the Choctaws say noble things of me. But a man cannot deceive his own soul." He stared into the fire as though recollecting his thoughts. Then he stood up. "It's a curse, Big Sam, to be half Indian and half white. My mind is Indian, but my heart is the heart of my white father. Never wait for love, my brother, but seek it and find it. Never worry about God or the Great Spirit, but find love and there God will be. Watch the birds and the beasts. They know God and they live only to love and be loved, because God wills it. Man is the only creature that abuses love or God. Man is not the most intelligent creature God made, but he is the loneliest because he tries to walk alone. There is a big tree up the slope. I can see its top even in the darkness. Go there now."

Tishomingo took his rifle in the crook of his arm and walked away. Sam went to the tree and Donna was waiting.

"It is I," Sam said.

She was leaning with her back to the tree, her head slightly thrown back as she watched the sky. She lowered her head and looked at him standing before her. "I know it's you," she said softly.

He took one step to her, put his arms around her waist and kissed her. Her body curved into his, and his kiss, which began tenderly, became hard and almost violent. "I knew you'd come." She pulled her lips from his to speak. "There's a thing I would tell you."

Sam pulled her to him again and felt her breasts pushing against him. She shivered slightly and moved until she seemed to melt into him. Her mouth was tense, and then it relaxed and opened as his caresses sent the blood rushing to her brain and then back again into her veins where it burned her body into a tantalizing numbness.

"This is your answer," he whispered.

"One moment, Sam," she begged, pushing him back reluctantly, "I had a speech, but I can't remember it. I want you to know that I'll marry you whenever and wherever you say."

"We'll be married at Natchez." His arms were still around her. He told himself that he should release her, but he could think only of the weeks of waiting before they would reach Natchez. "It will be such a long time, Donna. It's only because I love you so much that I'll wait so long."

She ran her fingers over his face, then through his hair and pulled him to her. They kissed again and both were trembling. Donna said, "There's no need to wait so long. In my dreams you've rested in my arms since the first day I saw you. I'm weary of dreams, Sam'l." In the darkness, Sam could not see her blushing as she added, "I'm without modesty now. I'm glad to be so. I couldn't have said such things, even to you, 'back there.' But 'back there' seems far away. We're going to a new land, to a new life, and I'm a woman in love ——"

Sam interrupted her. "What are you saying to me, Donna?"

"What else must I say?" She heard him gasp and then they clung to each other fiercely, panting, and neither was ashamed as they lay down on the soft earth.

The rains began gently and the grass where they had lain sprang up again and drank the rain. The cow beasts felt it run down their faces and they licked it with their long tongues. The trees curled their leaves so the rain could run off quickly and reach the earth. Sam Dabney pulled his saddle over his head and felt the rain seeping through his moccasins. It felt good to his feet.

The rain would settle the dust, he thought.

12

* * * * * * * * * * * * * * * * * * *

THE caravan moved in steady, easy stages to the Chattahoochee, one of the disputed boundaries between the United States and the Creek Nation. The Nation, under leadership of its wise micco, the half-breed McGillivray, had declared a perpetual peace with the United States. But McGillivray was dead and petty leaders, mostly the sons of Scotch and Indian marriages, were squabbling for power, all seeking to breed nationalism among the democratic and loosely organized Creeks, blaming them for all the ills of the red men.

The train passed through several Indian towns near the river and found the Creeks apparently friendly. The maize harvest had come and the Muscogees celebrated their feasts. They asked the white man to enjoy the hospitality of the towns and to participate in the games, Indian ball and *chunkey*, the bowling game. It was in these towns that André learned the Creeks were a confederation of many clans and that in their leaders flowed some of the best blood of England and Scotland, blood of the MacIntoshs, the Weatherfords, the McQueens and the Baileys. Only then did he understand why the Creeks condemned to death any person of negroid and Creek blood. To them, the Negro was an inferior person and the proud blood of the Creeks must not be contaminated. Only the blood of whites and of the other Muscogees would not contaminate the blood of the Creeks. If they married Indians who were not Muscogees they must suffer banishment from their clans, but if they married Negroes they must die. To them, a Negro meant servitude, and no Creek must suffer bondage. The Nation was divided into two states, the upper and lower state. The Muscogees ruled because they were in the majority, but the nation was called Creek by the white men because of the numerous streams in the territory.

It was impossible to conceal Dabby from the prying eyes of the Indians who always requested to see the young of visitors, but Honoria disguised the child by rubbing bear grease and soot on her body. Even Tishomingo was impressed with Honoria's strategy and said, "You're a wise woman." It was the first compliment he had ever paid her and Honoria was very happy.

Sukey, however, was so proud of her baby's Indian blood that she rubbed the blackening off at every opportunity until Donna threatened to slap her and Honoria to beat her with a willow cane.

A Creek Red Stick, a warrior of the first class, visited the train to barter for Sam's cheap perfume and saw Dabby's streaked face. He gave no indication that he recognized the bastard as such, but while the travelers camped by the Chattahoochee, a Creek runner sped into the Nation and reported to the micco that a red slave was with the train.

It took half a day to ferry the train across the river and, in the Creek Nation proper for the first time, Sam called a conference of the men. He showed them his map and the route. They would head almost due west for the Tombigbee, thence into the Choctaw Nation. There the party would split and most of the travelers, under Tishomingo's leadership, would go to Lake Flournoy's plantation near the Yazoo River. Sam's party would pause at the Halfway, or Pearl River, until he could mark the boundary of his new land. Then they would go to Natchez and later join their comrades at Flournoy's.

Sam assigned a slave to ride the advance with Chock and armed the Negro only with an ax. As they followed the old Indian horse paths or blazed new trails, the Negro notched trees that Chock pointed out. "Notch each tree three times," Sam ordered, "so those who come this way later will have an easier journey."

Before they were a week in the Creek country they were calling their trail the Three-Chop Way, the first trace to the promised land.

Donna and Sam met at tryst as often as discretion would allow and even in the presence of the party each tried to walk as closely to the other as possible, each to brush against the other. Donna could not think of the dangers. It is difficult to think of danger when the heart is singing. Often around the camp fire, Donna dropped her hand behind the log on which they sat and Sam held her hand, squeezing her fingers. Once he playfully slapped her bottom as she sat by him. "Sir!" she whispered, "that is a gesture that does not become a gentleman!" She looked full into his eyes and smiled. "You're a rake, my darling, and I love you."

"I'll buy you a ring in Natchez," he said. "A gold band like my mother wore."

"How much farther is Natchez? I'm weary of this hide and seek. I do not like to spend my honeymoon in secret rendezvous."

He said, "We have not yet reached the Choctaws. Natchez is many weeks away."

The travelers hardened to the trail and took their hardships without complaint. The land had changed. The earth had become black, a sticky black earth that clung to the oxen's feet. The slender, friendly pines had gone and huge, fat, virgin pines had taken their places. The land became gloomy, the waters deep and black. They saw gars in the creeks and wondered what they were until Tishomingo explained.

Bay trees paraded up the slopes. Their leaves turned their white sides to the sun and glistened. Some of the forests looked like fields of very tall cotton. The oak trees had larger leaves than Sam had ever seen. The ferns grew close to the trail. The land seemed brooding and melancholy. It seemed to be too rich—too luxurious, like a voluptuous, heartless woman, enticing but dangerous.

They were nearing the Tombigbee and the western end of the Creek Nation when Ab rode furiously from the advance to the rear, shouting for the train to halt. He told Sam, "Chock wants you."

Tishomingo was standing by his pony, staring into the woods ahead. In his left hand he held a bundle of small cane sticks, painted red and tied with rawhide. In his right hand, he held his rifle. "They have come," he said, and handed the sticks to Sam. "I found the bundle on the trail. It is the way of the Red Stick warriors to leave such a warning. They are in the woods ahead. These sticks mean they will not fire unless we do. They want to make talk."

Sam called André to guard the advance and, with Tishomingo, walked toward the woods, holding his rifle above his head. A Creek, unarmed, stepped from the forest and walked to meet the men. His head was shaved except for a crest of hair, two inches wide at the top of the forehead. The crest, short and frizzled, widened as it covered the crown of the head and the nape of the neck. The hair was decorated with silver quills and heron feathers. Sam knew he was a minor micco. He wore brass earrings and a band of wampum circled his temples. His shirt was of linen and he wore a wide kilt of blue around his thighs. His cloak was scarlet, the sacred color of the Creeks. A sunset was painted on his breast with vermilion. It was his holiday dress, for it was the season of the busk, the holy harvest season.

Sam bowed to the Creek and said, "I come."

"You do," the Indian said politely.

"I am Big Sam Dabney of Georgia. I'm taking a horse train to Natchez."

"I am Big Jack, a micco. We would buy from you a slave wench and her child."

Sam said, "Perhaps she is not for sale."

"Then many lives will be lost for a black wench and her bastard baby."

Sam made no attempt to deceive the Creek. It would have been foolish and dangerous. Tishomingo stood rigid and silent. The Creek ignored him, recognizing him as a Choctaw, the ancient enemies of his Nation. Chock said, as though he were honoring the Creek even to speak, "The bastard child does honor to your nation. Do you kill children during the busk? Is that the manner in which your people thank the Great One for His blessings? Is that your tribute to the Prophet?"

The micco did not lose his temper, but said firmly. "Well and with knowledge can the Choctaw mingo speak of bastards. But we will not kill the mother or child during the busk."

"Why do you not catch the Creek who sired the child? It is your law that father and mother must die with the child. Where is the father who has visited this sin upon his people?"

"Can the wise Choctaw catch the buck that mates

with the doe? Or the gobbler that takes the hen to mate?"

"Nay," said Tishomingo. "Not always."

The Creek said proudly, "The Creek can." He cupped his hands and grunted a signal. From out of the forest stepped two Creeks, dragging a third between them. The third man was naked. The skin around his shoulders and buttocks was in folds, hideous red folds. He had been steamed. It was the law, a punishment the Creek must suffer if he lay with a Negress. The judges who executed the council's orders steamed a man only enough to torture him, but never to kill him. He must die by stoning. So must the woman die and her children.

Sam remembered how Pierce had told him the Creeks steamed prisoners. Each prisoner was tied to a stake in a small grass hut. A ditch of water surrounded the stake and hot rocks were dropped into the water until the steam peeled the victim's skin.

The Creek turned to the prisoner. "Did you mate with a slave at the home of Captain Pierce Chadbourne in Georgia?"

The prisoner nodded.

"Was a child born?"

Another nod. Then the Creek told Sam, "We'll pay you a fair price for the woman and child. We want no war, for it is the time of the busk. But we are very strong. You may see our strength and judge for yourself."

He shouted a sharp command and fifty warriors walked from their hiding and stood a few hundred feet behind their leader.

Sam knew that the Creek was not showing all of his strength, so he said casually, "I will not be threatened into any decision. I must talk with my party. My advance party is with me, but the main body of my company is a few hours behind us."

He didn't know if the Creek believed his lie. He and Tishomingo studied the warriors and Sam looked each man over carefully and wondered if Chock saw what he saw. He dared not look at his friend. Two of the warriors wore black paint on their chests—black, the sacred color of the Shawnees, the tribal color of Tecumseh. Perhaps it only meant that some Shawnees were visiting their Muscogee kinsmen for the busk.

"Sa kullo. I am strong," the Creek said.

Sam said, "Ay, you are strong. But I am doubly strong because I am a white man. I must have time to make talk with my friends. The slave is not mine to sell."

"I will wait until the moon can be seen above the tallest trees in those woods."

Sam picked up the rifle he had propped against a tree and watched the Creek's eyes sparkle as he saw the fine piece. "It's a superfine gun," Sam said, and offered it to the Indian to examine. "It uses a superfine powder." He lifted his powder horn and handed it to the Creek. "I will give you the powder horn. It is a gift. Your Nation has been kind and has given us passage through your lands. I wish you happiness in this season of the busk and give you my powder as a token of the friendship my country has for yours."

The Creek could not refuse Sam a gift in the name of the busk and the gift must be as valuable as the one he had received. He slipped off his powder horn and presented it to the Georgian.

"You will have my answer by moon-up," Sam said. "I go."

"You do," the Creek replied politely.

Chock said, "Ea li. I go."

"Omih," said the micco. "Very well."

Sam did not turn his head to speak to Chock as they walked unhurriedly back to the train. "Did you see all that I saw?" he asked, looking straight ahead.

Chock said, "I saw two Shawnee warriors. I saw that the Creek micco was armed with a British musket, probably brought here by the Shawnees from the Ohio country. And I learned something."

"Ay?"

"The fox is crafty, Big Sam, but not as crafty as my friend. They cannot see us now. Open the powder horn."

They stopped beside the path and Sam poured the powder into his palm. It was Spanish powder. "It means," Sam said, "that the Red Sticks are buying powder in Pensacola."

"And the Shawnees are trading for British guns. British guns and Spanish powder are dangerous to the frontier. Tecumseh's agents have been here, preaching the holy war against the United States. Those Shawnees are not with the Creeks to celebrate the busk, but to see to it that the spark of the holy war is kept kindled."

Sam said, "This intelligence must get to Pierce. I'll find a way."

"What are your plans for the slave and her child?"

"I have my own plans," said Sam quickly, but his doubts assailed him. He wished he dared seek Chock's advice. If he should lose his train because of the slaves he would be scorned, but if he met the demands of the Creeks he would be laughed at. He tried to conceal his doubts with words.

"Never in my life," he said boastfully, "will I meet

the demands of a Red Stick if he is carrying his tomahawk. That I vow."

Under commands of Ab and Honoria the train had
prepared for defense and Sam and Chock found a stockade erected beside the trail. The cattle had been driven
into a gully a half mile behind the fortifications. Dead
logs and brush had been piled in a circle and the company was waiting behind the barricades. Guards had
been posted. Buckets of water were handy. Powder
kegs had been opened and placed in the center of the
circle and protected with dampened cloths.

As he entered the camp Sam noticed that Sukey was
close by Donna. The Negress rolled her eyes at him
until her eyes seemed to be all white. The company
watched him and none spoke. He ordered Jasper to take
Sukey and Dabby away and then he called the little
band around him. They sat upon the ground and Sam
spoke slowly.

"You know what they want. They're willing to pay
for Sukey and the baby. If we surrender them we'll not
be molested. If we don't give them up, we'll be attacked
tonight. I have no right to risk your lives without your
permission. I'll hear your expressions."

Donna said, "The slaves are mine, but I'll abide by
your judgment, Sam'l. I cannot bring myself to think
of selling a mother and baby to their deaths. But my
sentiment is foolish and I'll not ask this company to
suffer for my principles.

"Then why delay?" Honoria said. "They'll pay for
the slaves. Only a loon would risk his life for a slave.
Those red 'uns want the wench and baby badly. They'll
pay a fancy price—far more, I'll vow, than the slaves
would fetch on the block. Let us sell the slaves and be
on our way."

Anestasie seemed to recoil from Honoria's words. Sam spoke quickly in defense of his sister. "Honoria's words seem heartless, but she speaks with her mind and not with her heart. What say you, Chock?"

"I'll influence no man. You're fools to risk your lives when it isn't necessary. But I'm a mingo of the Choctaws. The Red Sticks do not make demands of a Choctaw mingo. If you meet their demands, then say to them that you surrender the slaves over the protests of Tishomingo, the nephew of Pushmataha. The Creeks have never seen the back of a Choctaw. I'll sell them naught but my life and my price will be dear."

Ab leaped to his feet. "There's a man to hitch to! Give up anything to a red 'un! God damme, no! I'll give them nothing save a dose of lead and a parcel of hell!"

"What do you say, André?" Sam asked.

The Frenchman glanced at his wife. "If I had a beast that a man sought to buy only to torture, I would refuse."

Anestasie patted his hand and said, "My husband speaks for me."

Sam said, "There is a thing you must know. The Red Sticks killed my father and mother. I have a grudge. I'll not take orders from a Creek. I plan to live in this country and if I bow to the red 'uns now, never will I be able to hold up my head again. This is my first command. If I surrender, I'll never have another command. It is better to die than to walk among men with your head bowed."

"But it isn't surrender," protested Honoria. "They'll pay."

"There is a principle to be remembered," said Anestasie. "If you know what a principle is."

194

Honoria laughed. "You cannot solve our problem with mean words. You're very brave now, but you have never seen an Indian fight. If you live, you'll sleep in a stinking red 'un's lodge. They'll take your husband's scalp and tie it to a pole so you can see it every day. They'll knock out the brains of your mother-in-law, thinking she is too old for the bed. And they'll get the slaves anyway. We're fools to fight them." She got up and walked over to the powder kegs and lifted the cloth. "This cloth is too damp. It will cause the powder to get damp." She spread the cloth in the sun to dry it.

Sam smiled at his sister and she smiled at him. Old man Dabney's brat.

"What is your say, Mrs. Harkins?" Sam asked.

"There is naught for me to say," she answered. "My husband is the Indian agent. The wife of the Indian agent scorns demands from Indians." She faced Honoria. "I, too, have seen Indian fights before."

Sam said, "My answer to the Red Sticks is no. If they want the slaves, they may come and get them. We will not send a reply. They'll know our decision when we do not make talk with them by moon-up. The ladies will go to the rear and if we are beaten here they will ride for the settlements. Jasper will guard them."

Honoria tied her hair tightly behind her head and walked to the stack of arms. She lifted several guns and, finding the lightest, loaded and primed it. The company watched her. She stacked the gun against the brush and took up her post.

"I said the ladies would go to the rear," Sam said.

"But I'm no lady. I do not even know what principle is. I'm old man Dabney's brat."

Sam walked to her and she put her hand on his arm. "Do you think I'd leave you, Sam? Let the other women go. You know that you and I stay together. We have a plan. Remember? We're going to be somebody, somebody big. Or we'll die together."

"But I have no right to ask these people to risk their lives this way."

"You have every right," she said. "You're the leader."

"It isn't a pleasant task," Sam said.

"Sometimes you act like an addle-pated fool. You would like to have the glories of achievement without carrying the burden of responsibilities. You may deceive many men but you do not deceive me. You cannot, for we are cut from the same mould. You ofttimes doubt your own judgment, not knowing, as I do, that your judgment usually is right. Remember what our father said, 'A really wise man sometimes doubts his wisdom, only a fool thinks he can do no wrong.' You wished that the company had agreed to surrender. You think that would have vindicated you. Well, it would not have. The well-being of this company is in your hands. Be not afraid of your own judgment."

Sam said, "There is nothing of which I am afraid."

"Oh, yes, there is. You're afraid of failure. You're afraid that men will laugh at you. Men are fools, Sam'l, and reckless; only women have real wisdom and real courage."

Tishomingo joined them and said to Sam, "Your sister is a brave lady."

Honoria looked away so they could not see her tears. That was twice Chock had complimented her. When she faced him she was smiling. "I'll fight next to you, Chock. I can shoot, can't I, Sam? I can shoot better than Ab. My father never imposed silence on me for missing a shot, because I never missed."

196

Anestasie told Honoria, "You're a strange woman. I regret I spoke hastily."

"Never the mind of that," said Honoria. "I still think we are fools but if my brother says this is right, then it is right. But instead of making pretty words, Anestasie, you should be making musket charges. Look at Donna. Already she's working while we talk."

Donna was measuring powder and Anestasie joined her. Honoria called Jasper and put him to strengthening the barriers of brush and logs. Sukey, realizing they would try to save her, began ripping strips of cloth for wadding. She greased the cloth with lard. They ate in mid-afternoon, then built a huge fire and heated ramrods and cleaned their arms. Chock sharpened his tomahawk on a whetstone. Ab honed his dirk, and sang while he worked. Donna, her work done, stayed close to Sam, but neither had much to say. There was nothing to be said. As darkness closed in, they put the fire out. Let the Creeks show a light. A light was a good target.

Sam instructed the company, "When the moon comes up, the men will crawl over the walls and take up posts fifty yards in the woods. Chock will go to the east. I'll go to the west. Jasper will go to the south and André and Ab to the north. I'm sending you two together because André has never fought in the woods and will need Ab's counsel. The red 'uns will attack in a body. When you see them, fire one round at them and return to the camp. We'll know then in what direction they come and can join here and beat them off. Don't attempt to attack them. Let them attack us. There are Shawnees among them. The man who kills a Shawnee will be rewarded. I want a Shawnee scalp as a present to Captain Pierce Chadbourne as proof that Tecumseh's men are with the Red Sticks."

Ab said, "Your plan is a superfine one, Sam. But how know you they'll attack in a body? We're splitting our forces to scout. Those devils may surround us and get to the camp before we can slip back from the woods."

"They'll attack in one body. I'll show you why. André! Sing a song. Sing it loudly. In French. Sing 'Ca Ira.' First in your natural voice. Anestasie will join you. Sing into your cupped hands, Anestasie. It will make your voice sound deep. Then sing into an empty powder keg. Sing anyway, but change your voices. They'll think we have a dozen Frenchmen with us."

The plan delighted André. "Mon dieu, a general! A general you are, Sam," he said enthusiastically. "That is strategy. Strategy. Strategy, first used by the marching Jews. It was my favorite Bible story."

Sam said, "Ay, the Jews conquered a nation by that trick."

André said, "Each day I learn something new about you. How know you of the Bible? I thought your father was a disbeliever and that you were raised to believe that God is a myth."

"Our father was not a disbeliever," Honoria said quickly. "He was an agnostic, but he knew the Bible far better than most craw-thumping preachers. And he taught it to us. Sam's plan will deceive the red 'uns."

Ab said, "God's hind leg. That's a scheme for you. I'll sing, too."

"And loud," Sam said. "Stand first at one side of the stockade, then run to the other and sing. Chock! Chant the war songs of the Cherokees. They'll think we've got an army here. That's why they'll come in one body. They will dare not split their forces."

Ab slapped his thigh in glee. "That is a better plan than Old Dan'l Boone ever used in Kaintuck. That'll fool the red 'uns, I'll vow."

He strolled to the barricade, tilted his head and bellowed the old ballad of the hills.

> "Lord Lovel, he stood at his castle gate
> A' combing his mild white steed,
> When along came a lady, Nancy Bell
> A' wishing her lover good speed."

Sam took up the chorus and Jasper joined in. André waited until the echoes of the song had rolled through the woods, then he began "Ca Ira." Soon all the party was singing. The woods rang with their music and their shouts. They sang until the moon meandered in the sky and, reaching the tops of the brooding pine trees, seemed to stop and hang there, as though suspended on a string.

André said quietly, "It is time."

Sam said, "Ay, the time is come. Go with Ab into the woods. And mind you, André, heed Ab's counsel. I don't question your courage or your judgment, but in these woods men must fight as the red 'uns fight."

Ab crawled noiselessly over the stockade and vanished into the shadows. André was at his heels. They walked for fifty yards and Ab put his hand on André to check him. "Hide behind that big tree," he whispered. "Get on the north side, so your shadow will not be seen." André obeyed, and Ab took his position in the shelter of another huge tree. The wilderness seemed to be sleeping until the moon crawled above the trees and sprinkled its brilliance upon the earth. Then the night things set up their cries. The cicadas fiddles, rasping their wings; the frogs took up the chants, bellowing defiance to the night. A low eerie call sounded to the north, a plaintive call.

André looked at Ab and the Kentuckian stared in the direction whence the cry had come. André opened his mouth to speak, but Ab shook his head for silence. The call was repeated, a long low cre-o-o-ooooooo. "A catamount," whispered André, unable to hold his silence.

"Catamount, hell!" said Ab. "It's a red catamount with a greasy scalp. Them's injuns, you merry bucko! Get set, because here comes hell!"

Ab saw the first Indian slip from behind a clump of huckleberry bushes and fall on his hands and knees. The red man began inching his way toward the stockade.

Ab raised his gun slowly. "I'll get this one. Then stay low until I count one hundred. Then cut and run for camp."

The Frenchman did not wait for the backwoodsman to fire, but leveled his pistol and squeezed the trigger. The sound roared through the woods, and the Indian clasped his belly, stood as though to run and fell on his side.

"You damned fool!" Ab said. "Now stay still." Ab began counting, "One, two, three—" André, not knowing the backwoodsman's method of war, jumped from behind his shelter and ran toward the man he had shot. Ab sprang after him. They had taken only a few steps when a party of Creeks slipped between them and the fort and cut off their retreat.

When Sam heard the thunder of André's pistol, he ran back into the barricade and found Chock already there. "That was a pistol shot," Sam said hoarsely. "Only André had a pistol and the Creeks never carry them."

He turned quickly to Anestasie. "You're husband had the trigger itch. They probably are prisoners by now. But don't be alarmed. The Creeks will not kill them. Alive they're hostages. Dead they're no good to the Creeks."

He didn't wait for the women to ask questions, but plunged into the woods where he thought Ab and André should be. He and Chock cast around the woods for a few minutes and Chock said, "They have taken them."

"Ay," said Sam, "that damned-fool Frenchman tried to charge the red 'uns, I'll warrant."

They found no signs of their comrades or of the Creeks, even the dead Creek was gone, for the Muscogees always remove the bodies of their dead. It was impossible to find tracks in the moonlight.

"They have outwitted us," Sam said. He shouted loudly enough for the company at camp to hear him. "Build up a fire." He knew the Creeks would hear him but he wanted them to. The barricade would not be attacked again.

No one spoke to Sam and Chock as they entered the camp. Sam's look at Anestasie told her that André had been captured, but she accepted his word that her husband and Ab would not be killed. Sam sat on a log away from the company, staring at the ground. Chock walked to him and said, "We can tempt the fates and go and seek our friends."

"Nay," said Sam, "it is done now."

Anestasie, with no visible show of emotion in her voice, asked, "What will they do to my husband?"

Sam said, "They'll hold him until we deliver the slave and her baby. And my name will be a case for laughter over all of this frontier, for the Creeks have outwitted me."

Sukey, knowing that the capture of Ab and André had sealed her doom, ran to Donna and fell at her mistress' knees. She did not whimper, but knelt there imploring mercy. Donna stooped and lifted the girl to her feet. She told Jasper, "Give her brandy and take her away behind the camp." She put her hand on Sam's arm. "You'll want to surrender Sukey and Dabby tonight?" she asked.

"I know not," said Sam. "We must wait. The Creeks will not suffer any torments to our friends without warning to us." He directed that they pile logs on the fire until the flames lighted the woods. It was a signal to the Creeks that the company would not attack. The lonely cry of the catamount sounded again and Chock said to Sam, "There they are, to the north of us. We'll have their demands soon."

Sam faced the company, "Stay close to the fire. There's no danger now to us. A Creek runner soon will appear with a message from the micco. Above all, do not fire again. If you do it will be a death warrant to our friends. Pay no heed to the runner."

The messenger walked boldly to the barricades and flung a small bundle of red canes at Sam's feet. Sam did not stoop to pick them up while the Indian was there, but kicked them aside contemptuously and deliberately turned his back on the runner and held his hands out to the fire. When the messenger had vanished, Sam picked up the bundle of three sticks. He tossed them to Tishomingo and said to Anestasie, "This means we have three days to deliver the wench and her baby to the Creeks. When this is done André and Ab will be free. They will be treated as guests. Do not worry."

He told Donna, "Go and call Sukey. I'll not burden you with the task of telling her. I will tell her." He wished it were a task he could designate to another man. His heart was sick and he felt nauseated. He must lose two valuable properties and much prestige. It was a blow to him. Pierce would have his doubts. Mr. Harkins would shake his head. Natchez would hear and wonder if he were capable of leadership.

Honoria fetched him a cup of the black brew, a potent drink of holly berries. "This will warm your innards," she said and watched him drink. "There is a favor I would ask," she said as he handed her the empty cup. "Let me tell Sukey. It will be easier for Sukey if a woman tells her."

"I am the leader here," said Sam, knowing she sought to free him of an unpleasant duty. "It is my chore."

Sukey and Donna advanced from the shadows and stood in front of Sam. Donna swallowed to gain time to control her feelings. She spoke softly, but firmly. The slaves must not know her emotions. Jasper was eyeing Sam, and the other slaves huddled around the fire, not daring to speak, but rolling their eyes in fear.

"Sukey," Donna said, "will go. I did not have to tell her. She told me she would go. She wanted me to be spared the ordeal. She would speak with you, Sam'l."

The Negress raised her eyes and spoke clearly. "Sukey knows. Sukey is not afraid of the red 'uns. Sukey will walk alone to the red 'uns, but my young 'un should live. You were with Sukey when my young 'un was breeched. A wise master would not give up a young 'un."

Sam put his hand on the girl's head. "You're a good girl, Sukey." Anestasie put her arm around the girl.

"You're a brave woman and a good mother." To Donna, she said, "See. Courage is a thing which all women share, and color becomes suddenly of no value."

Sam forsook the company and stood by himself at the far side of the barricade. The fire shadows danced over the walls and leaped and spread among the trees. For a minute, he wished that his father were there to help him. His father would have found a way out without giving in to the red 'uns. It would take him years to live down the disgrace, for on the frontier a man was measured by his wits as much as by his courage. Anybody could kill, but only a real leader could win by his wits. Hell's hinges! He had got himself into a hole for fair, and pulled the hole closed. And all over a bronzed bastard, a snotty-nosed bumbo. There were thousands of babies just like Dabby, but he had to have the one baby the Creeks wanted in his care. Well, damme! he was in a hole all right. It would take a wiser man than Solomon to beat this game. Solomon! A baby almost tripped him, too. But he had figured a way out. Sam rubbed his hand across his chin, then pulled at the lobe of his ear. He wheeled and walked to the fire, his eyes blazing. He commanded Jasper to fetch razors and shave him. Close. The company stared at him as though he were batty, but asked no questions and he volunteered no information. His face shaved, he took one of the razors, called Chock and walked from the camp.

Beyond earshot of the train, he told Tishomingo to shave his scalp as a Shawnee's is shaved. "Fix my hair," he said. "Get me a band of wampum for my forehead. Within an hour I must look so much like a Shawnee that even you would not know me. I'm bronzed. My nose is long."

He removed his jacket and gaiters and borrowed a pair

204

of Chock's doeskins. He mixed a bit of tar with hickory-nut oil, then poured off the black oil and with it Chock painted weird designs on his chest. He didn't have time to make butter-nut dye. The tar oil would do. Chock stuck two feathers in Sam's scalp and stepped back and surveyed his work. "Even your father wouldn't know you. Tecumseh would call you his brother."

"Now get me a bottle of rum, another of brandy and another of sweet, heavy wine. It is almost midnight. If I am not back within two days, take Sukey and Dabby to the Creeks, then move on without me, and I will join you later at the Tombigbee. Tell Donna I'll be safe. Watch over Honoria."

He mounted Claymore, guided the horse to the thickets where pine needles would deaden her hoof sounds and headed hard east, back toward Georgia and the Creek villages through which they had passed.

At camp, Donna asked nervously, "Where has he gone?"

Honoria said triumphantly, "To teach the Red Sticks a lesson, I'll vow. They cannot outsmart my brother. He knows a thing or two, eh, Chock?"

Tishomingo smiled and Donna accepted the smile as reassurance. Anestasie's heart thrilled at Sam's courage and at Honoria's confidence. She was sorely afraid but none knew it.

Sam rode until after dawn. He skirted the villages, seeking lonely lodges away from the council hall and the center of the towns. He stopped often at Indian huts, drank the black drink in honor of the busk, spoke to the Indians in Creek and praised Tecumseh. The Creeks welcomed him, and because they welcomed him so warmly Sam knew they were accustomed to Shawnee visitors. He spoke to them of the holy war against the United States and they all agreed that the war would begin when Tecumseh and his twin brother, the prophet of the Shawnees, gave the sign. They were waiting only for a sign, the Creeks said, and the sign would come from heaven. Tecumseh had said so. There would be a flaming comet and the stars would fall, the earth tremble when Tecumseh stomped his feet. That would be the sign. Then let the white man beware.

Sam stayed only a few minutes in each lodge until, toward high noon, he found the lodge he was seeking. It was more than a mile from the village micco's house and no other house was near. The Red Stick husband was an Alabamu, the chosen clan of the Nation. He was a young warrior, a member of the village council. His squaw was heavy with child. A son also blessed the home, a slender youth in his teens. And in a crib was a baby about the age of Dabby.

Sam was greeted at the house in the name of the prophet. He asked to see his host's young. That was good manners. The Red Stick protested, in keeping with good manners, and insisted they were ugly children and unworthy of the attention of the noble Shawnee. But Sam said no Creek ever sired an ugly child and the father, beaming, called his son and fetched his little daughter, holding her in his arms. She was the same color as Dabby. All colored children look alike, Sam thought. Even Solomon could not have decided which of the babies was Sukey's.

The squaw, keeping her eyes to the ground as a modest pregnant woman should, brought tafula, but Sam refused it politely and fetched the rum. The Red Stick looked longingly at the rum and said, "It is against the teachings of my people to drink rum. And, too, only a fool drinks rum before he has put food in his belly."

Sam said, "It is the busk. I thought the Creeks were men. You speak as a child. May I drink my rum with your son? Perhaps he is the warrior in this lodge."

The father sent his squaw for two cups and Sam filled them. He drank only rum, but he gave wine and brandy and more rum to the Indian until the father's head wagged and his tongue rolled. When the Creek had drunk himself insensible, Sam lifted him and got him on a bench. He walked to the door, lifted his rifle and held it just above the heart of the squaw. The woman looked at her husband, then at the stranger.

"I am with child," she said humbly.

The son stood with his hands on the table and watched Sam. Sweat had smeared the black oil on Sam's chest. The boy said, "He is not Shawnee."

"I am Big Sam Dabney of Georgia. If you obey me, you will suffer no hurt. If you don't, I'll kill you both."

The boy said proudly, "You are a white man. Only a white man would foul the spirit of the busk and the name of the Prophet. You come as a weasel. What would you have us do?"

Sam directed the boy and the mother to mount their pony. He took the baby in his arm, in his left arm for he held his rifle in his right. "Your father will wake up tonight. He will be all right and so will you, if you do as you are told."

They rode due east for several miles, leaving a broad trail. The Indians made no attempt to escape. They would not forsake the baby and, too, it would have been suicidal. At a creek, they turned downstream and waded their horses until Sam was convinced they had covered their trail. Then they turned west and, traveling through the pine forest so the needles covered their trail, reached the Three-Chop Way by evening. Sam knew the Red Stick father would sleep until dark when it would be impossible for his Alabamu kinsmen to trail him. They would take up the trail at dawn, but would go east. It would take them hours to discover his strategy, and if his luck held he should have at least a two-day start.

He reached the camp early the next morning. He hadn't slept for forty-eight hours and he was hungry and weak. He shook his head at the band as they opened their mouths in astonishment to ask questions. "Pay no heed to me," he said. "Do not make a commotion. The Creeks must not know that anything has changed in the camp. Feed these people."

They fetched food to him, but he did not take time to change his clothes. He summoned Sukey and, between mouthfuls of tafula, spoke slowly to her, so his words would impress themselves upon the slave's mind. "Take this baby," he handed the Indian child to the Negress. "She is yours. I gave the mother chance to suckle her. But she is hungry again. Hold her to your breast. The child must learn to reach for your breasts as your own child did." He washed his words down with a swallow of weakened rum. "I will take you, and this baby to the Red Sticks. Dabby will stay with us. The father of your child will not know this is not his daughter. Watch the sun. Watch the moon. Count them. The busk lasts so long as the moon is full. They will do you no harm during the busk. Three suns from this day, send for the micco and tell him this is not your child. Understand?"

Sukey nodded her head. Sam continued, "They will leave the child in your care. Do not give the child to the micco, or to anybody. When you tell them it is not your child, hold your hand over the baby's gullet and

208

tell them that if they harm you, you will pull the gullet out of the child's throat. Tell them they must deliver you, without hurt, to our camp on the Tombigbee. They will know where it is. Do you understand?"

Sukey took the child and fondled it. Sam explained to the company. "This child's father is an Alabamu and his voice carries authority. Right now he and his kinsmen are seeking these people. Soon he will hear that a strange child is held with her slave mother. They will see the child and know it. We will take the mother and son with us as hostages. The Red Sticks will not dare to harm Sukey for fear of the child's life and the lives of these prisoners. At the Tombigbee, we will send the son back here with word where we are, and with a message that unless Sukey is delivered to us we will take this woman into slavery, and mate her with Negroes. Unless they meet our demands, we will sell her baby, too, when it is born. They will ransom this woman. A big'd woman is sacred to the Creeks."

Honoria's admiration of her brother showed in her eyes. Donna said, "It's a desperate chance. If you're caught, Sam'l, you'll be tortured."

Mrs. Harkins said, "The Alabamu are fast trailers." The father will be at the micco's camp tomorrow, and they'll send a war party after us. They can travel fast. We cannot. Our oxen and pack horses cannot travel fast in this heat. They will die like flies."

"It is better that they die than us," Sam said. "The Red Sticks cannot boast that they outwitted Sam Dabney for the sake of our horses and oxen. If I have to drive every horse and every oxen to death I'll reach the Choctaw Nation as I vowed. What think you of the plan, Chock?"

"Sometimes the fox outsmarts himself."

The Georgian laughed. His confidence had returned. He lost no time in completing his plans. He ordered that the train be made ready for the trail. He would send Chock with Sukey and the Indian child to the micco and ransom Ab and André. He could not go, for his scalp was the scalp of a Shawnee. Tishomingo was pleased with the chore. It would insult the dignity of the Creeks for a Choctaw mingo to act as intermediary between them and a white man. He took Sukey by the hand, and led her boldly out of the barricade without giving her a chance to say goodbye. He wanted no lamentations. Up the trail they walked. Sukey fell three steps behind him, as a slave should. She held the Indian baby to her breast. The micco walked out to meet them and Chock said, "I come."

"You do."

"I would save my friends," Chock said. "The white leader would not stoop to make talk with you, and I do so only to save my friends."

The Indian did not look at Sukey, but grunted a call and the Creek prisoner was dragged from the woods. Sukey glanced at the Indian, then turned her head. The prisoner said, "That's the woman."

The micco asked, "Is this the child?"

The prisoner said, "Yes, that is the child, a girl child."

Two warriors stepped to Sukey's side and laid their hands on her. Chock jerked their hands off and said harshly, "You do not own this woman and her child until my friends are free. And what is the payment for these slaves?"

"The only payment we make is your friends' freedom," the micco said. He shouted another command and Ab and André were marched from the forest.

Neither spoke to Tishomingo. His presence instead of Sam's suggested that a plot had been agreed upon.

Tishomingo said to the micco, "You're stealing these slaves. A man is entitled to payment for his slaves. You do not outwit Big Sam Dabney so easily. He is a young man and will see many moons, and will count them until he can repay you for this insult. I go."

The micco bowed and said, "I, too, am a young man, but the Creek Nation is an old nation. We were here before the white man came, and we will be here when he is gone. There will always be Creeks to meet your friend." He and his party faded into the woods with Sukey and the Creek prisoner marching before them. Tishomingo and his comrades walked slowly to the camp. They must not let the Creeks know that they were in a hurry.

"We will move as soon as we reach camp." Chock said. "Hold your heads high. Never bend your necks if a Creek can see you."

André said, "I was a fool. Ab tried to save me."

Tishomingo said, "A man who thinks he is a fool really is not a fool. You will be a fool if you make the same mistake again."

The train got under way a few minutes after the men returned. Chock was assigned to the advance again and one hundred and fifty yards behind him came the first pack horses. A slave on foot ran beside the tenth horse. Then came the women and their horses, flanked by Jasper and André. Strung out behind the women was the remainder of the train, protected and driven by foot slaves. The herd followed the train, the first oxen almost at the pack horses' hooves. The company was ordered to travel at its usual pace until the train passed over the next ridge, beyond view of the Creeks.

Then the pace was increased. "Drive 'em," Sam ordered. He rode alongside the train, shouting to the slaves, "Drive them until they drop." He rode to the advance and had Chock set a fast pace. He stayed with his friend for a few minutes to see that all was well. Chock was silent as they rode. Sam said, "What meant you when you said, 'The fox sometimes outsmarts himself'?"

Tishomingo answered, "This day you have made more enemies than one man should have. The Creeks and their kinsmen will never forgive you for this day's work. There are five thousand Red Sticks between my nation and the Chattahoochee. You have made five thousand enemies to save your own vanity and a negro slave, and a bastard baby. There are ten thousand Shawnees beyond the Ohio. You have made ten thousand enemies. There are two thousand Seminoles. You have made two thousand enemies, Big Sam. I do not envy you, but I am proud to be your friend."

"I saved the child," Sam said. "Some day that child will be valuable. She will make a good brood wench in my slave quarters. When she comes in fresh she will be worth two thousand dollars. And too, Chock, she has my name."

Beyond the ridge and into the wilderness again, Sam rode back to the rear and as he passed the foot slaves, he shouted, "Drive 'em! Drive those horses." He saw that his prisoners were guarded in the center of the train. He saw to it that the slaves had sticks with which to beat the horses. "Push on," he said. "The Tombigbee is ahead, and we will reach there, by God, or Sam Dabney will spend eternity in hell, if there be a hell."

Drive them! Drive them until they drop. Lay on the whip! Cut canes and sharpen them, and prod the oxen. Flay the pack horses with rawhide whip. Push on! There will be no rest this day. Eat in the saddles. If you are not beyond the Tombigbee within two days, your scalps will dangle from an elm pole in Old Town, and your women will warm the beds of the greasy Creeks. The packhorses, laden heavily, soon were in a lather. The milch cows dropped their heads almost to the ground and hurried along bellowing in pain as the whips cut into their flesh. God, Sam thought, if cattle could only sweat. Sweat was good for an animal. But the heat that the cattle generated went back into their bodies and burned their strength away. Sam uncoiled his whip and cracked it over the heads of the oxen. He cut their skin with its sharp tip. The beasts walked faster, then began to jog. "Keep them jogging," Sam shouted. His whip nicked the bottom of a slave drover. "Drive them, you shining bumbo. Beat their hides, or your hide will rot here." The slave turned to stare at Sam. The tar paint streaked Sam's chest, and dust caked on his face, except where the sweat ran down. The feathers, which he still wore, were wet and soggy. To the slave, he looked like a loon bewitched, his frizzled hair, his streaked sweaty torso. The slave was struck with awesome fear of Sam for the first time. He was no longer the kind master who gave his slaves rum and tobacco. He was old man Dabney's brat again, driving ahead, driving himself and his slaves and his oxen. Even the woman he loved, he was driving. And his sister. Drive on! Keep jogging! To hell with the heat! To hell with the sun! To hell with thirst! And with dust, and with sweat.

The sun climbed to the peak of the blue, cloudless sky and spread its August wrath upon the train. It seemed to stop in the sky and to wait there, grinning and blazing. It poured its heat upon the earth and even the earth cracked and gasped. The pine needles drooped, and the leaves of the great oak trees sagged. Nothing moved in all the land except the train. There were no birds on the wing. The lizards lay in the shade of the rocks, panting for breath. But the train moved. The oxen jogged. The slaves ran alongside the pack horses, prodding them. Dust rolled in layers and heat danced on the trail. The oxen's tongues rolled and their eyes became glazed. But when they slackened their pace Sam cut their rumps with his whip. Drive on! Two milch cows with heifers foundered first. They fell on their knees, then on their sides. Their tongues slipped between their cracked lips and rolled in the dust. Flies swarmed their tongues and clustered around their eyes. Sam cut their throats, then the throats of their heifers. A pack horse fell on one knee, struggled to his feet again and collapsed. Ab drove his tomahawk into the beast's head. The most valuable goods in the pack were distributed to the other packs. Sam threw away the goods they couldn't carry. He threw them in a brook. Be damned if the Creeks would get them. One of the slave women running beside the train pitched forward and fell upon her side and lay there twitching, and frothing at the mouth. Sam took her on his horse. She was a good slave, worth seven hundred and fifty dollars hard money. Maybe one thousand dollars in Natchez. Drive on!

Two more pack horses went down. Ab was the first to protest. "We won't have a train to cross the Tombigbee," he said. "No animal can keep this pace and loaded. Those horses are totin' iron. It's hard work for them to walk. They can't live, man. And those oxen are burning up inside. Look at them heave. Look at their tongues and their eyes. It's too hot, Sam'l boy. Too hot for me even. I'm sizzling like fresh cow piss splattering on a hot rock."

"You'll sizzle in hell if those Creeks catch us. Drive 'em!"

They made no camp but drove on until moon-up. Then they rubbed the horses and oxen, and gave them drink when they were cool. The pack horses were set to graze with their packs on. The company lay beside the trail and slept, the women, like the men, on their saddles. Even the slaves slept near their masters. They all slept except Sam, and he posted himself to the east of his camp, watching the trail. Chock tried to relieve him but Sam pushed him away. Donna begged him to rest, but he ignored her. Then she kissed him and he tasted sweat and dust on her lips. The dust was gritty. He hated dust.

"I'm tired," she said. "But I'll go on."

"I'm sorry that you're tired," Sam said testily. "It does no good to mention it. Everybody is tired."

Honoria fetched him food and Anestasie brought him drink. The Frenchwoman held the dipper while he drank and said softly, "You're a great leader, Sam." Sam looked at her over the rim of the dipper and she smiled. Honoria glanced at Anestasie, then at her brother, but said nothing.

Sam aroused the company two hours before dawn. They ate dried raw beef. He rationed a bit of rum to the slaves to quicken their muscles. And now drive on.

The more Sam thought about it the more he realized the gravity of his situation. He had defied and scorned the foundation of the Creek civilization. He was saving a child the Creeks would give a thousand warriors, nay, five thousand warriors, to kill. So long as Dabby lived there was a blotch upon the Creek nation. The minute his prisoners' Alabamu kinsmen found his trail they would ride west. They would take him and kill him

215

and his company if it meant war with the United States, And they could travel fast. They would have no oxen or pack horses to slow them up. He had kidnapped a Creek woman in the season of the busk. He had kidnapped the only son of an Alabamu. He had tricked Big Jack, the petty micco. Only the Tombigbee could save him. He must get across. Quickly. Two days might be too long. Chock was right. Every Shawnee would seek him, for he had worn their sacred colors and defiled them. The Seminoles, the Creeks, maybe the Chickasaws, every Muscogee from the Great Lakes to the Great Gulf, would curse his name. Every Muscogee save the Choctaws, and they would honor him for his wisdom. If he lived to be honored. If he reached the Tombigbee. He would reach it. By God! he would reach it. If the Creeks overtook him he would abandon the train and the slaves. He and the other white people could outride the Creeks. If they were shed of those jogging, bellowing oxen, and those weary pack horses. No, he would not surrender his train. He would throw up a barricade and fight. The women could push on. The men could stay and fight. Never would he surrender a bit of goods to a Creek. Not even a bodkin. He would give them only lead, lead and fire, and the earth would give them a place to rest. The earth cared not who rested beneath its grass. The earth knew not the difference in men, red men and white men and black men. Push on! Drive on! To the Tombigbee! Move, you lead-butted bumboes. Beyond the Tombigbee is the promised land—Locha Poka. There they could rest.

All that day they jogged along. Sam searched the sky for a cloud to hide the sun, but there were no clouds. The sun was merciless and bitter. On into the night they went. The women rode with their heads bowed. All

216

except Honoria and Anestasie. Honoria rode the train with Ab, hurrying the slaves, kicking them as she rode by, cursing them as she had heard old man Dabney curse, calling down the wrath of God, if there be a God, upon their kinky, greasy heads. Anestasie rode with her head high. Her whole body hurt but she held her shoulders back.

Chock never left the advance. He sat his pony easily and showed no fatigue. He cut his eyes to the right, then to the left. Nothing escaped him. He inhaled deeply of the night air. That towering tree to his right was a magnolia. That stark lonely sentinel dead ahead was a cypress. He studied the ferns by the trail. They were greener and their ends curled. He listened to the night life. The minx and the muskrat were abroad. And the whippoorwill was crying. It seemed to be saying, "These old hills, these old hills." His pony raised his head and sniffed the night. The mistletoe bunched in the tops of the cypress. Chock could see it, a blob against the moon. Mistletoe and cypress and green fern and a sniffing horse. It meant water. Big water.

The busk moon was waning when Chock sent for Sam. "We're there," he said. "The Tombigbee is beyond that ridge, and beyond the Tombigbee are my people."

"We'll cross tonight," Sam said.

Tishomingo said, "You gamble with fate, but you're right. We must cross tonight. For the Red Sticks surely are on our trail."

Sam sought no counsel. He wanted none now. He gave orders, quickly, surely. When Honoria sought to speak with him he said, "Shut up, and do as you are told." The slaves looked at the lazy yellow waters of the river and were afraid. Even Ab shook his head. To drive the hot oxen and horses into the water was courting disaster. Sam called the band around him. He commanded Ab to take two pack horses into the river. "And leave their packs on. See if they can make it across."

"God damme, he is crazy," muttered the Kentuckian. But he drove the horses into the river and plunged in after them. The horses disappeared beneath the tepid waters. Ab swam back to camp. "We'll never make it that way," he said.

Sam directed the slaves to build fires along the bank. He sent Ab across the river to kindle fires on the other side to guide them. He put the slaves gathering logs, "Don't cut them down. Find dry logs in the woods. Light torches and run through the woods until you find logs."

He used the saddle horses to pull the logs to the water's edge. They tied the logs with ropes. The white women made the first trip. Sam steered them across, heading for the lights that Ab had kindled. Fires sprang up all along the bank, and the slaves heaped pine knots upon them so they could see their way in the woods. Their torches looked like huge fireflies darting in the forest. The woods rang with cries of, "Log here." Tishomingo supervised construction of more rafts. André saw that they were loaded, and as soon as one raft was ready, it was poled into the river and was steered for the beacons. Chock guarded the Indian mother and her son across. The horses, free of their packs, were driven into the river. Ab and the women on the other side ran along the bank with torches and as the horses scrambled up the sides of the Tombigbee they herded them into a clearing. Mrs. Harkins waded in water up to her hips to save the horses. Anestasie floundered in the mud. But they all worked. The women with the slaves. Sam thanked his luck that the river was low. The last horse 'was driven into the water. The last raft was sent across. Then he and Chock lashed the oxen until the beasts plunged into the river, and lowing and splashing, struck for the other side.

Sam told Tishomingo, "It is done. Now you cross." Chock held the pommel of his saddle and swam beside his pony. Sam turned back to one of the fires and stooped and lifted a bundle. Dabby looked at him and whimpered. He had not trusted her with any of the slaves, and would not burden the white women with her. He mounted Claymore and, holding the child in his left arm, drove his horse into the river. He looked back only once. The fires were dying down. The moon had gone. A few sparks rose from the spluttering logs and darted above the tree tops.

Claymore swam strongly, breasting the current, her head high. Sam slipped out of the saddle as they neared the west bank, and waded ashore. Tishomingo reported their losses. Sam handed Dabby to Honoria and unsaddled Claymore and hobbled her. He looked around at his muddy, bedraggled company. He ordered rum rations for the slaves, and tobacco. He told the slaves to go to bed. They would rest on the morrow. He kindled a small fire there on the banks of the Tombigbee, and took out his journal and wrote down his losses: "of oxen, 18; of horses, 24." All of the milch cows were dead, of the heat or of drowning. The slave he had helped was sick of the fever. Other slaves would be sick on the morrow. But he was across. The price had been high, but the red 'uns would know that they could not outwit old man Dabney's brat.

No one thought of scooping out a bed. They lay on the slope back from the river and slept. Chock and Ab took the first watch. Sam was busy with his journal when Tishomingo walked to the water's edge and said, "Listen!" He stared across the river. The plaintive cry of the catamount sounded to the east, then to the south. "They've come again," Chock said. "Soon the sun will come. The Red Sticks are over there. They'll wait for the sun and then will make talk with us. They will not come over here. The Creeks do not tread the land of the Choctaws. I'll keep guard while you sleep."

Sam thanked him and in his journal he entered, "Arriv'd in Choctaw Nation September—" He had forgotten the day. He must remember to ask Donna or Honoria on the morrow. But now he would sleep. He didn't seek a dry slope or the comfort of pine needles. He sat there on the bank of the river where the cat-tails waved and rustled, and the frogs cried. He watched his little fire die out. He must go and see if the company was bedded down. He must tell Donna good night. It would be good to kiss her good night. Perhaps he could lay by her. A man got strength from a woman. He would kiss her eyes and her ears, and feel her heart pounding. He must go tell her good night. But no, he was too tired. He folded his arm under his head and slept in the black, sticky mud of the Promised Land.

13

★ ★

THE lush, brooding valley of the Tombigbee woke up slowly and lazily. The night things ran and hid themselves, leaving the valley to itself for a few peaceful minutes before the dawn aroused the day things. The muskrat, the coons, the owls, the catamounts scurried to their homes, their bellies full, their eyes heavy for sleep. The fireflies put out their lights and flew away. The wind ran away. The land seemed to hold its breath, awaiting the command to be up and about the chores of another day.

Nothing moved in all the valley except the river, and it slapped playfully at the banks and crept among the cat-tails and willows. Mast fell from the trees and into the river and made little ripples that lived for a few moments on the river's bosom, then died away. Slowly the valley seemed to breathe. A fish leaped from the river and made big ripples. A kingfish dived for the fish, clutched it, and skimmed the water, making ripples larger than the fish had made. Blue jays darted into the magnolias, fighting for the juicy red seeds of the flower. Their chattering aroused the valley.

Tishomingo leaned over and touched Sam's shoulder. "It's dawn," he said, and handed his friend a gourd of *ussayoholo*, the bitter black drink. "The Creeks will be here soon to make talk."

Sam rested his head in his hands for a minute, then drank the black drink, and shook his head to clear it of sleep. Jasper, knowing his master's habits, fetched salt and Sam rubbed the salt on his teeth and gums and washed his mouth until it tasted clean. He instructed Jasper to prepare drink and food for the Creeks and to protect the Indian mother and son. He saw the Creeks' camp fire spring up across the river and a party of Red Sticks walked to the water's edge and waited there. Two war canoes soon appeared around a bend of the river. The Indians got into them and paddled toward Sam. In one of the canoes sat an old man. Sam had never seen such an old man. His face was as wrinkled as dried holly berries and his long white hair reached to his shoulders. Tishomingo stared at the old man, scarcely believing his eyes and said to Sam, "It is he." There was awe and reverence in the Choctaw's tone.

"Who?" demanded Sam.

"It is Jim McQueen, the great white leader of the Creeks."

Sam had heard of the great McQueen but had thought he was dead many years gone. The Creeks had said he would never die and Sam wondered if perhaps they were not right. He must be at least one hundred and ten years old, Sam thought. Colonel Harkins had told him about McQueen. He was a Scotchman, born about 1683, and had deserted a British ship at Saint Augustine in 1716. They had tried to whip McQueen to death for striking a British officer, but the Scotchman had escaped and fled to the Creeks. He had led the Creeks through many wars and long periods of peace, and it was he who joined with McGillivray in persuading the Creeks to make peace with the United States.

The Red Sticks beached their canoes and one of the

222

warriors turned to help McQueen from a canoe, but the old Scotchman scorned his hand and came ashore without aid. His blue eyes twinkled when he saw Sam and he walked to the fire and warmed himself. The Creeks followed him. Sam offered them the black drink but McQueen shook his head.

"Get me rum, you wildcat Irishman. *Ussayoholo* is good for young men and nursing mothers but my bones are old and my blood is thin. I need rum."

Sam saw to it that his guests were comfortable and waited for the talk to begin. After they had eaten and drunk, the Alabamu Indian whom Sam had tricked got to his feet.

"I have come for my wife and son."

Sam said, "You may have them when the negro wench is brought here."

"She will be brought here," the Creek said. "We met Big Jack on the trail. He told us my daughter was at his camp, and he told us how the white man had outwitted him. We rode on, hoping to catch you in the Creek country and kill you. But we will not invade the Choctaw nation, because there is a truce between my people and the Choctaws."

Sukey had not been harmed. The Creeks had spared her because it was the holy season and, too, they feared she would harm the Indian baby if she were seized. Sam explained that he had intended freeing the Indian boy so he could take his message to Big Jack, but now it was not necessary. Old McQueen listened to the talk for several minutes, then got slowly to his feet and said, "I'm a very old man. I've seen many things. Everything changes except the white man. You've done a vile thing, Mr. Dabney. You crossed the Creek nation. They let you cross in peace. You blazed their trees, marking a trail.

222

Some day more men will follow your trail. You chopped your trail to the Alabama River. Men will come and chop the trail to the Tombigbee, then to the Halfway River, then to the Mississippi and the Creek Nation will vanish. The Creeks sought only to buy slaves from you in honest barter. You defied their laws. You scorned them. For many years I've worked for peace between your nation and the Creeks. It's hard to keep the peace with young men like you. Give the Indian mother and her son to this man. I'll stay here as hostage until the slave wench is delivered here safely. And always remember that old Jim McQueen was a hostage to you for a negro slut."

Sam looked at Tishomingo expecting guidance. Tishomingo looked away. Sam studied the ground, mulling the problem. He dared not defy McQueen, but he knew if he held the old leader as a hostage for a slave it would be an insult. "I must think over this thing you have said," he told McQueen.

"It's no problem," the Scotchman answered. "If you must ponder such a small matter as this, you'll not live long on the frontier. What's your verdict? Quickly."

His taunt angered Sam. He sent Tishomingo for the prisoners and delivered them to the Alabamu. "You'll stay with us," he said to McQueen, "until the slave is brought here. The talk is over."

The Indians took the woman and the son and crossed the river. McQueen rested by the fire drinking his rum and watching Sam. At one minute there was mirth in the old man's eyes, then pity. He got up and walked around the camp. He studied Honoria and Anestasie as a horse trader studies a team of fillies. Anestasie stood very straight and returned his stares. The old man said to her, "There's hope for this land with such stock as you to settle it."

He bowed when he saw Donna. She was the first person to whom old Jim McQueen had bowed his neck in a long time. But Donna was the kind of woman men bowed to. The old man didn't study her as he had the others, but said to her, "Ma'am, sometimes the body has more courage than strength."

"You speak in riddles, sir," Donna said.

"I never thought I would live to see the day when a lady such as you would come to this land. Mind your health, ma'am. This land is like the she-wolf, sometimes it kills the thing it nourishes."

Honoria prepared him a pallet and the old man thanked her. He watched her as she bustled around the camp getting it in order. "Ay," he mumbled, "there's a parcel for a man. If I were seventy years younger I'd fight every man between here and Tidewater for that lass."

Honoria heard him and replied, "If you were seventy years younger you wouldn't have to fight any man for me, for I would come to you." McQueen laughed, a high cackling laugh.

He talked of Europe to André and Anestasie. He had heard nothing of the French Revolution and seemed to like André.

"Heed me, Frenchy lad, if you plan to settle in this land and trade, then settle here. Some day the road from Georgia to the Mississippi will pass here, and a mill and ferry and factory will net a man a fancy profit."

Sam asked, "But would he be safe here? What of the Creeks?"

"He's done the Creeks no harm," McQueen said. "You would not be safe here. You will not be safe anywhere."

Sam said, "My brother and I will be safe. I have a large family. We'll be safe." He lifted his rifle. "This is my brother." He fingered his tomahawk. "This is my uncle. Here is my father." He balanced his bull whip in his hand.

"Pride and ignorance are man's greatest sins," McQueen said.

Sam left the old man with André and took up his chores around the camp. There were many things to be done, harness to be repaired, gear to be mended. Three of the slaves had developed chills and one had a high fever. The Negroes already were turning to their voodoo gods for cures and were worshiping tobies, the sacred charms of the Africans. The tobies were made of chicken gizzards, rooster spurs and ashes. Sam let them keep their tobies but he gave them medicines too, a syrup made of mullen leaves, sugar and vinegar. He gave them tar, honey and a tonic made of yellow river water mixed with the bark of the red oak tree. He rationed rum to the sick and fed them a gruel made of corn meal. While he was administering his duties as leader, old McQueen drank himself into a loquacious mood. He was the first white man André had seen who knew the history of the Indians, but he did not want to talk about his red friends until André happened to remark that the Indians had many practices similar to the ancient Jews.

"Many people think the Indians came from Israel," McQueen growled. "It's a silly notion. If some Indian words sound like Hebrew words, it's because white men have made them so. White men already have confounded the Indian tongue, trying to pronounce their words. Some day man will invent an Indian alphabet and then the language, or what is left of it, can be preserved. But until then the world will know nothing of the Indians except what white men write and say. It's a damned shame, for the white man has given the red man nothing except horses and wheels, hogs, bloodhounds, guns, rum and the cross. The Indians need the guns and hogs."

"But what has the Indian given the white man?" asked Anestasie innocently.

"What, indeed!" stormed the old man. "Corn, potatoes, tomatoes, cotton, gold, silver, tobacco, squash, beans, chicle, cocoa and a way of life that the white man will never understand."

"But they have slaughtered white men," Anestasie said.

McQueen snorted, "What know you of slaughter? More Indians have died of the fevers and pox and running sores of white men than in all their wars or of the lung sickness."

André learned much from the old man: that Maubile once was a great Indian city, that *walla* means roll, that *hog walla* is a place where a hog rolls, and that *thlea* means bullet or arrow.

"There are many things you should know," McQueen said, "if you hope to prosper in this land. Most of the leaders of the Creek Nation are of mixed blood. The children usually take their mother's name. A woman, because she can breed, is more important in the nation than a man. The tribes are divided into clans, the people of the Wolf Clan are the favorites of the nation, and have privileges no other clan enjoys. Visit me sometime and I'll tell you more of the Indians."

The old man stretched upon the pallet and snored.

Sam posted Ab to watch him and called André aside. "That old man is right," Sam said. "This is a good place to build a ferry and a mill. When your goods arrive in

Natchez we'll bring them here and set up your factory. This is halfway between Georgia and Natchez. All the trade will pass this way." Sam got out his map and drew a straight line from Georgia to Natchez. "Frome will be at the eastern end. You'll be here. I'll be on the Half-way River and every pound of goods that goes from the new land into Georgia will mean money for us."

"It's an ambitious plan," André said. "I'm anxious to begin our work. When can we leave here?"

"Within three or four days. We must rest the stock and cure the slaves."

Sukey reached camp late that afternoon. Big Jack surrendered her. "My people," he said, "will remember this day." He looked around at the party that had accompanied him. Old Jim McQueen examined Sukey. "So this is the slave for whom I was hostage. She's a likely-looking wench. I'll give you good silver for her. I need a fresh slave and she is ripe again."

"The old man's smart," Sam said, "but Sam Dabney isn't sleeping. You'd give the slave to the Creeks. She is not for sale to any man. The Creeks can have her and the child only if they conquer my family."

McQueen cackled again and pointed to Sam's weapons. "Those are his family," he told the Creeks. Then he turned to Sam. "These are my friends, Billy Weatherford, Far Off Warrior, Josiah Francis, Paddy Welch, High Head Jim, called Jim Boy, Mad Dog, and Davy Cornels who is called Dog Warrior. I wish for you to know them. You will meet them again." He bowed to André and Anestasie. "See that you come to see me," he told the Frenchman. "It is good to make talk with you."

"I hope to build a factory here and be friends with your people," André said, "but there is a thing that I would ask."

228

"Ay?"

"I have heard much of Simon Girty. Did you know him?"

"He was a half-breed renegade," Sam broke in.

"He was not a half-breed," McQueen said. "His father was John Hague who was taken as a lad by the Ulgees in Pennsylvania. Old John married an Indian woman but he also mated with a white woman named Girty and Simon was his son. Why do you ask?"

"Because I had heard that Girty had kinsmen among the Creeks."

"You have big ears for a Frenchman," one of the Creek warriors said. "Big ears are better than a long tongue. Girty lived among the Shawnees and the Shawnees are our fireside kin. Some of his kinsmen may be among us."

McQueen looked at André approvingly. "You have made a wise question. You are seeking to learn if there are many Shawnees among the Creeks. I will not lie to you, there are many and more will come. The Shawnees want war, the Creeks want peace. The white man wants land. Now I go."

They rowed the old man back across the river and Sam set his company to work preparing the camp for the night. The women's beds were scooped out of the sandy soil and lined with oak leaves, then with pine needles. A trench was dug around the women's camp. At Honoria's suggestion, the women bathed in the river. She made the slave women bathe, too. Jasper took a company to the stream and they caught fish with their hands, wading in the water up to their waists and feeling along the bank until they found fish holes. They wrapped the fish in wet ferns, then in clay and baked them. Ab and Tishomingo went down the river to a watering place and using torches to blind the deer, killed five of them.

The animals were skinned and the skin was stretched on the ground and pegged to the earth. The meat was jerked and was hung to dry. It would be pounded into pemmican and, mixed with corn, would make a good dish. Every bone of the animals was cleaned and the marrow was stuffed into the bladders. The women scraped the flesh from the hides and rubbed fat and brains into the hides until they were soft.

There was no singing in camp that night for the company was too tired and everybody except the watch was asleep by moon-up.

The Choctaws from the neighboring villages arrived the next morning to welcome Tishomingo home and to trade with the white men. The Choctaws' land had escaped the great pigeon migration. There had been a dispute with the Chickasaws but instead of going to war to settle the controversy the Indians had played a ball game. The Choctaws had won the game and the dispute.

There were many other bits of news. Many white men were coming down the Mississippi in keel boats. Outlaws were raiding the Natchez Trace. There was war talk of a treaty between Spain and the United States.

Sam traded his cheap perfume for hides and horses and hired one of the Choctaws as a runner, and sent him to Georgia with dispatches for Harkins and Pierce. In his letters, Sam explained that they had blazed a trail from the Chattahoochee to the Alabama, that he had marked the trees with three niches. He suggested that scouts be sent to mark the trail from the Alabama to the Tombigbee. He told of the Shawnees being with the Creeks, and to Pierce he wrote, "Donna has agreed to accept my hand. We will be wed in Natchez."

He had sent the runner on his way when Donna reminded him of the homing pigeons. Sam had forgotten about the pigeons. Jasper had seen to their well-being and at Sam's order fetched one of the birds. From Honoria Sam got a bit of silk and wrote a message to Pierce. "If what Pierce said is true," Sam said, "this bird will arrive in Georgia long before the runner. The runner will bring us back news of its arrival."

"What did you tell my brother?" Donna asked.

"I repeated that we would be married."

He tied the silk around the bird's leg and released it. The pigeon circled the camp for a minute and headed east.

The great Pushmataha visited the camp that afternoon and brought Caesar, Tishomingo's slave, with him. The Indian embraced his nephew and welcomed him. Caesar knelt at Tishomingo's feet until Chock touched his shoulder and told him to get up.

Pushmataha wore a beaver hat and epaulets. The hat had been sent by General Washington and the epaulets were a gift from the Congress. He wore a blue jacket with brass buttons, and bowed gravely to Sam when he was introduced. Sam gave him presents and a seat of honor at the council fire and told Pushmataha his plans to settle in the nation.

The wise old Indian agreed to sell the land on which they rested to André and the deal was struck. The Frenchman gave Pushmataha a bottle of wine, a handful of buttons, a brass cross and a pistol for seven hundred acres of land on the Tombigbee. Pushmataha agreed to furnish slaves to help André build the ferry and factory. When he heard Sam's plan to split the party he said,

"There is no need of your staying here until the slaves are well. We will look after them and my nephew can guide your friends northwest of here to the home of Lake Flournoy. You and your party can be on the way tomorrow. You are in a hurry to reach Natchez. Eh?"

"Ay," said Sam, "and there is a reason." He took Donna's hand in his.

"I am not old or blind," said the chief. "The heart of my nephew's brother is light. Only man's first love can make the heart so light. It is a good season to wed, for soon the winter will come. But a man should marry his woman at his home."

"I have no home," said Sam. "I'll build one. And, too, there's no one nearer than Natchez to marry us."

"I'll get someone," said Pushmataha. "I'll have a party meet you at the Halfway River and there you can be married where you will live." He turned and grunted an order to a warrior.

Tishomingo whispered to Sam, "My uncle is sending to Natchez for a company of soldiers. He thinks soldiers can do anything."

The Choctaw warrior smiled at Sam and Donna, lifted his musket and began running toward the west. "He'll soon reach Natchez," Tishomingo said. "He is a flathead. Did you notice? As a child he was put in a cradle and a bag of sand was laid on his forehead. It made his forehead tall and sloping. It is a mark of beauty with many warriors. The flathead warriors are like foxes in the wood. Excepting the Chickasaws, they are the best woodsmen of all the Muscogees. The Red Stick warriors are the tallest. The Chickasaws are the most ferocious. The Choctaws are the most peaceful, but the bravest and the wisest."

Another Choctaw walked into the camp with a long

retinue of slaves behind him and a company of warriors before him. He did not speak even to Pushmataha but took a seat by the fire. Tishomingo bowed politely to him and held a gourd of the black drink to his lips. Then Tishomingo summoned a slave woman and gave her food. She chewed the food, then took it from her mouth and put it into the mouth of the stranger. The man held his hands before him as he ate. His finger nails were more than an inch long.

"My God!" André whispered to Tishomingo. "Who is he?"

Chock took André aside, beyond hearing of the stranger. "He is a bone picker and his presence is sacred. He will not speak until he has eaten. He cannot feed himself because of his nails, and he is so old that a slave must chew his food. His name is Hottak Fullih Nipi Fani and means 'One Who Picks Flesh.' His nails are sacred. He is the elder son of another bone picker. It is a position of honor, handed down from father to eldest son. The Choctaws always take the bones of their dead to Nanih Waiya, the Sacred Mound. When a Choctaw dies his body is mounted on a scaffold until the flesh falls from the bones, then the bone picker cleans the bones and takes them to the mound."

The bone picker finished his meal and said to Sam, "Sa Mintih. I have come. Welcome to our land."

"I have no chore for you," Sam said.

"I am glad," said the old man. Sam gave him trinkets of tin and a cupful of coffee berries.

"Roast these berries," Sam said, "and drink the brew. They will put life in your bones." Sam knew that if the bone picker drank coffee, the other Indians would want it. Ay, he would build up a coffee trade too.

They feasted that night and the Indians ate all the

233

food that was given them. When they were filled they went into the woods and vomited and returned to the board and ate more. They drank Sam's rum and sang the war song.

Sam was very attentive to Pushmataha. The great chief was pure Muscogee. He was not as tall as Sam and his eyes were black. His cheek bones were not as high as those of the Cherokees, but he was the haughtiest man Sam had ever met. The Choctaws believed that Pushmataha had been created by a bolt of lightning when it struck the Great Sacred Mound.

Sam offered drink to Pushmataha and said, "I have heard great stories of your origin, great mingo of the Choctaws. Will you tell us whence you came?" He sought to flatter the old man and his words pleased the chief and Tishomingo. Pushmataha told his story and when he had finished, without another word, he arose and walked to his bed, a couch of oak leaves and wild flax. He called Tishomingo to him, "My son, who is the tall man, the one called Ab?"

"He is her brother. The eyes of the eagle still are sharp."

"Why did you bring him here?" the chief asked.

Tishomingo explained and when he had finished his uncle said, "You must tell Big Sam of this." Then the old man, wearing his blue jacket with the brass buttons and the epaulets that the Congress had presented him, said good night. In his hand he still held the tall hat, the gift from George Washington.

Tishomingo touched Sam's shoulder and motioned for him to follow. Beyond the shadows of the fire, Chock whispered, "Are you taking Ab to Natchez? Or does he go with me to Flournoy's?"

234

"I'm taking him to Natchez, but why do you ask?"

"There's something you must know," Tishomingo said. "Ab's real name is Adam Bascomb, and he is the brother of Amelia Bascomb, the woman I loved, and the woman whose life was ruined by Lake Flournoy."

"When did you learn this?" Sam demanded angrily. "Why didn't you tell me? I knew his name was Bas· comb and I knew he had a sister, but why didn't you tell me that his sister was the woman you took to the Choctaw Nation?"

"This matter," Chock said, "is my concern. I did not tell you for I did not want you to send Ab back to Georgia."

"But his life is in danger, you fool! Flournoy will kill him. Or he'll kill Flournoy. Then he'll be tried by the Choctaws for murder and my nation will not suffer one of its citizens to be tortured by the Choctaws. It would break the friendship between our peoples."

Tishomingo said, "Sometimes, my friend, your tongue is quicker than your brain. Ab does not know the story and will not know it until we tell him. He will be told when the time is right. Flournoy will do him no hurt. Flournoy knows that if he kills a white man the American soldiers will come and hang him. I'll tell Flournoy that her brother is with you. I'll tell him that if harm comes to her brother he'll be held responsible. Flournoy will be frightened as the rabbit is frightened. He'll dream of death, fearing that I will tell Ab the truth, and that Ab will leave his dirk in his back. At the proper time I'll kill Flournoy, but he must suffer. The revenge of Tishomingo must be complete."

"My God, man," Sam said, "you're cold-blooded."

"I have never taken an Indian baby from her mother,"

235

Chock said. "I have call for revenge. I'll make Flournoy suffer because he did hurt to my woman."

"But Ab will hear his sister's name mentioned. He'll find out."

"My people did not call Amelia by her American name. To us she was Ta-lo-wah, the songstress."

14

✩ ✩ ✩ ✩ ✩ ✩ ✩ ✩ ✩ ✩ ✩ ✩ ✩ ✩ ✩ ✩ ✩ ✩ ✩ ✩

THE trail to the Halfway River lay entirely within the Choctaw Nation and was easy to follow. There were no dangers, save the rivers they must ford and the fevers they must risk, so Sam's party set off in high spirits, with Sam leading his train and Ab guarding the rear. Tishomingo bade Sam a friendly farewell, but his farewell to Ab was tender.

Donna rode by Sam as the caravan moved from the Tombigbee across the low hills and into the piney woods. Sam noticed everything as they traveled and entered his discoveries in his journal. He noticed there was gravel in much of the land, but that the land along the creeks was black and rich. They rode almost due west, through Indian villages where Sam paused to trade, and after seven days' journey they reached the Halfway River, the sluggish, yellow Pearl, halfway between the Tombigbee and the Mississippi. Sam left Jasper and Ab to arrange the camp and he and Donna rode down the river seeking his land. "I have my choice of five thousand acres," Sam said. "And I know the kind of land I want. I'll search until I find it."

He found the land he wanted near a bend in the river. The water was deep at the north end of the bend but spread into shallow shoals. Sam pointed to the river. "Where the water is deep I will build a ferry. My factory will be up the slope from the ferry. There I'll keep my goods for trade. My foundry will be just east of the factory. I'll build my slave quarters near my foundry. I'll make my slave houses of cypress so that they will last forever. My foundry will be built of oak. In dry weather we can ford the river south of the bend there. It's a likely place, Donna."

"Ay, it is that, Sam'l," she said. "But where will we build our house?"

"We'll find a spot. Our house must be on a ridge but my foundry must be near the water."

They rode east again until they came to a ridge that sloped to the river on the west and to a creek on the south. Black willows and water maple were along the creek. Cypress and swamp oak grew near the river. Slaves could log it and oxen could dray it up the ridge for the big house, the mansion of Locha Poka. "We will cut down many of these pine trees on the slope," Sam said, "and build our lawn. I will get sheep to keep the grass cropped. We will plant China trees for shade."

"I have never seen so many trees," Donna said.

"Nor I," said Sam. And as they rode over the land he listed the trees in his journal—pecans, willows, ash, maple, bays, cypress, papaws, magnolias, catalpa, persimmons, dogwood, locust, white oak, black oak, swamp oak, red oak, plum, chestnut, cedars, yellow pine, broom pine, buck eyes, wild cherry, palmettos. There was mistletoe in the cypress and sumac and polk near the swamp. There were trumpet flowers and violets, wild jasmines and water dock.

Donna counted a score or more kinds of flowers, Virginia creepers, dandelions, black-eyed susans, cinnamon ferns and Cherokee roses. There were signs of bisons and bear, catamounts, wolves and cougars. Beaver and musk-

238

rat lodges were along the creek and Sam saw evidence of mink and otter. In his journal he listed the birds that he saw, thrushes and warblers and a few egrets, the pine warbler, the brown-headed nuthatch and the woodpecker. There were mockingbirds and jays, ducks and turkey. The birds were almost tame. Most of them had never seen a man before and were not afraid.

Sam and Donna dismounted and sat under a huge hickory tree on the top of the ridge.

"It is a beautiful land, for fair," he said, "a fitting land for a man to settle in. Look at those bottoms, Donna, black as tar. Cotton will grow there. It's a rich land."

"Perhaps it is too rich, Sam'l," Donna said. "It seems so to me. It seems that things grow too easily here. It is not good for things to grow too easily. The land seems too lush, the foliage too heavy. I fear there is fever in that river, and chills. You see only the fish in the river and the silt that it spreads on the land. But I see the alligators and the snakes. You see only the timber in these trees, but I see the land, dank and moulding when the leaves have fallen. You see cotton in the bottom lands, I see weeds choking the cotton. But never will I complain; this will be our home."

"Do not worry about the fevers. I'll build my road down this ridge and across that little valley to my foundry. I'll have a toll gate and will charge every traveler a fee. I'll run a post from Natchez to Milledgeville."

Donna wished he could cease saying "I" and "my." How like a man. *My* land, *my* factory, *my* world—but *our* children.

Sam took his dirk and in the great hickory under which they rested he carved, "Here on 28th September, 1795, Sam'l Dabney selected site for his home. This land is the

239

homestead of Sam'l Dabney and belongs to him and to his wife, Donna, and to their children."

"But I am not your wife," Donna said.

"You soon will be," Sam laughed and hugged her.

"And we have no children," Donna continued.

"But we will have," Sam teased her. "I'll send a surveyor and he'll mark this land, five thousand acres with this tree as the center."

"We'll not cut down this tree," Donna whispered. "We'll let it stand forever."

"Ay," said Sam. "It's a big tree and a strong tree."

He stretched out on the ground and she lay beside him, resting her head on his right arm. Neither spoke for several minutes and each just rested there, staring through the branches of the tree at the blue sky beyond. Finally, she said, "You remind me of a big tree, Sam'l. A strong tree. You're putting your roots in this ground and nothing will ever uproot you."

He turned on his side and caressed her face with his left hand. He kissed her tenderly, and then quickly his emotions burned within him and he kissed her fiercely.

She pulled herself from his embrace and whispered, "Not now, Sam'l. Please."

He looked at her and for the first time he felt ashamed, as though he had done something wrong.

"Do not look at me so," she begged. "We soon will be married. I'm rather tired now. My body aches."

"I understand," he said. "Of course you're tired. This journey has been a terrible strain on you. I was thoughtless."

He sat up and she leaned against him and they looked again at the tree. Thereafter they called that tree the "Big Tree." This day they sat under it and dreamed and made plans until Sam, glancing up at the sun, said, "We've been here too long. Let's go back to camp."

Sam heard the shouts from the camp before he reached it. He heard strange voices. Glancing apprehensively at Donna, he kicked Claymore's flank and hurried to his friends. Ab was sitting on a log, a tankard of rum beside him, and around him were soldiers drinking rum and making merry. Honoria was in their midst; even Mrs. Harkins was laughing with the visitors.

"What is this?" Sam demanded.

"Soldiers," Ab said. "Good old 'yGod American soldiers, from Natchez, Sam'l boy."

A young man arose and walked to Sam. "I'm Lieutenant Abernathy. A Choctaw runner brought us news from Pushmataha to meet you at the Halfway River. The courier said you had a task for us." Sam looked at Donna and laughed loudly.

"What's so funny?" demanded the lieutenant. He held his cocked hat in his hand. Sam noticed the union cockade on his breast, the red and blue cockade, the French influence. His coat was blue with the lapels fastened back.

"I beg your pardon," Sam said. "I was not laughing at you or your men. This young lady," he presented Donna, "and I are to be married in Natchez. Pushmataha thought that we should be married here where we'll live and so sent for you. I had thought you would fetch a magistrate from Natchez."

The soldier laughed too, and turned to his men, "Damme, men, I have had to do many things for this army but never before have I been expected to act as a parson." To Sam he said, "The runner did not tell me my duty. I thought perhaps you were in danger. Had I known you and this young lady— Damme, are you Pierce Chadbourne's sister, ma'am?"

"Ay," said Donna.

"One of my best friends, he is. It's a shame that damned Choctaw did not tell me you wanted to be married here. I could have fetched a magistrate."

"We'll be married in Natchez," Donna said.

"And a big wedding it will be," Lieutenant Abernathy said. "Pierce Chadbourne's sister must have an elegant wedding. We'll see to that. The last fashionable wedding we had in Natchez was four years ago, when Colonel Green married Andy Jackson and Mrs. Donaldson in Natchez."

"We heard of that wedding," said Mrs. Harkins. "There's been ugly talk about it. Mrs. Jackson had not divorced her first husband."

Lieutenant Abernathy said quickly, "Yes, there's talk, but 'tis only in whispers, for no man dares gossip aloud about Rachael Jackson. Andy would shoot the fellow's teeth out. And as for the divorce, ma'am, I don't know. I've heard that Mrs. Donaldson was granted a divorce last year. If that be true, then he married Mrs. Donaldson before she was legally free of her first husband."

"Yes, that's true," said Mrs. Harkins. "Her formal decree was granted by the Kentucky Supreme Court last year, and Mr. Jackson and Rachael went through another marriage ceremony."

Lieutenant Abernathy said, "We've ridden out here for naught. I regret I don't have the authority to marry you, Mr. Dabney. It would be nice for you and Miss Chadbourne to wed where you'll live."

Mrs. Harkins laughed gayly. "Huh, young man, you do not know your own authority. As an officer of the

United States army in a foreign nation you can perform a marriage between two Americans."

"Ay?" the lieutenant asked. He began repeating to himself his articles of enlistment and commission. "I'm charged to keep the peace and to protect American lives and obey the laws of the Congress of the United States and the commands of the president and my other superior officers. Perhaps I do have the authority to perform marriages. After all, I'm supposed to keep the peace. And ofttimes it takes a wedding to keep the peace."

"Or to start a feud," said Ab. "Captain Chadbourne married a couple in the Creek Nation. I was with him. Do you remember, Donna?"

"Yes, I remember."

"If you choose to be married here," the lieutenant said, "I'll do the chore and when you get to Natchez you can have the knot tied again, if you're not satisfied that I tied it all right."

Donna said, "I'd be honored to be married by an officer of the United States army, and I'm sure you have the authority." She looked at Sam expecting him to settle the question.

"It's a superfine plan," Sam said enthusiastically. "We'll be married tomorrow under the Big Tree, where I marked my land. We'll send word to the Choctaw villagers near by and invite the Indians to the wedding and to our feast. It will please them. It will be a good stroke of diplomacy. They'll bring many presents. We can trade with them. Ay, it's a great plan. I'll buy you a ring in Natchez, Donna."

"Re-fiddlesticks," Honoria said. "I have the ring, the ring my mother wore. I was going to give it to Donna for her wedding ring."

"You can stand with me," Donna told Honoria.

"And I'll stand with you, Sam'l," Ab said. "I'll see that you're married as tight as hickory bark."

It was all arranged. They sent soldiers to the Choctaw towns to spread the word. Ab and Sam went into the woods and killed game for the feast. Jasper caught fish. Sukey prepared a pudding with honey. Mrs. Harkins supervised the preparation while Honoria and Donna rode to the Big Tree and Donna pointed out the spot where she would be married. "I'll have the slaves cut down the brush and the Indians can sit on the ground. Sam'l and I will stand by the tree. I had wanted to have a big wedding and wear a pretty dress, but if Sam'l wants to be married here, we'll do so. It will be nice to be the first white people to marry in the new land."

"I have a night gown you may have," Honoria said.

"Nay, but thank you. I have a gown, too, and I have a banian made of brocaded silk, but I cannot be married in a banian. I also have a sacque of white dimity. It's cut very low with ruffles around the neck. I have another sacque made of muslin with chintz border. I could wear that with my best petticoat."

"You must not be married in a sacque," Honoria said. "It's bad luck. My father said so. He called a sacque a slamkin and said it meant slattern."

"I have a perriot," Donna said. "It has tight sleeves, and flares open over a petticoat. I have a pair of prunella shoes I can wear, but I have no wig."

"You don't need a wig," Honoria said. "We'll wash your hair with fern soap and do it in a small roll over your forehead and let the curls hang around your ears and neck."

"But that isn't fashionable," said Donna. "Anestasie told me a woman should powder her hair, and wear it very tall, macaroni style. If her hair is too scant, she should have a wig. Personally, I don't like the macaroni style; it's very awkward."

"It's a silly style," Honoria agreed. "The style of yankee doodle. He stuck a feather in his hat and called it macaroni. Eh? I saw men and women in Georgia wearing the style. I thought it was horrid. Your perriot will be very pretty. We'll put a flower in your hair as the Indian brides do. Sam'l will wear his green jacket, but what will Ab wear?"

"We'll never get Ab out of buckskins," said Donna. "But wait. Perhaps he has his Dragoon uniform in his pack. It's a pretty suit. But what will you put on?"

"I'll wear the dress that Sam'l brought me," Honoria said. "It will be a pretty wedding, Donna."

She hugged Donna around the waist and they both laughed. "This will be your bridal chamber," Honoria said. "Here under this tree. I'll have the slaves build a soft bed for you."

Donna blushed, then laughed again. "I'll stand with you when you are wed," she said. "And I'll tease you as you have teased me. Is it a vow? Do I stand with you?"

"It is a vow," Honoria said. "I hope you don't have to wait long."

"I have seen your eyes follow Tishomingo. A woman always watches the man she loves."

"But he ignores me," Honoria said. "I'd wed with him this night. I'd go to him without a wedding," she said brazenly. "Yes, I love him. He knows it, and sometimes he looks at me as though he wanted me, but then again his looks are cold. I wonder, Donna, if it's because he is half Indian. That is of no matter to me. Should I tell him?"

"I would not tell him; I would wait."

"Maybe there's some Indian maid he loves. Ask Sam'l if that is true. Sam'l will tell you and you can tell me."

Donna promised, "I will ask him. After tomorrow he'll be my husband and I can ask him anything."

Sam and Ab walked up the river's east bank scouting the land and hunting game. The woods rang with their laughter and shouts and they were quiet only when they stalked deer. Eventually, however, Sam became somber. He asked Ab, "Have you ever thought that in Natchez you may get word of your sister?"

"I've thought naught of it," said Ab. "She went to New Orleans, not to Natchez. There was a story that she followed a man into Mexico. There was another story that she went to the Spanish Isles. I heard too, that she went away with an Indian. I hope she's dead."

"Would you rather your sister be dead than to live with an Indian?" Sam asked.

Ab looked at him quickly. "I know what you're thinking, Sam'l boy. I, too, have noticed Honoria. I have seen that look in her eyes as she watched Tishomingo. I had hoped I could make her look at me that way. But Tishomingo is a good man. I would not mind my sister marrying an Indian if the Indian was as good a man as Tishomingo."

Sam said, "Ay, Chock is a good man. My sister's life is her own. She must choose her man for herself. But you said your sister might have gone away with an Indian. What of this?"

"Why do you ask me so much of my sister? If a man betrayed my sister I'd kill him, but if my sister went willingly with any man I would not hold him to blame, would you?"

"I don't know. I don't know what I'd do."

The women retired early that night, but the men stayed up late, drinking and telling stories. Abernathy was a North Carolinian. He had been in the Natchez country

246

for five years and knew much. A survey line was being run between the United States and the Spanish possessions. Andrew Ellicott, a blue-nose yankee, an astronomer of sorts, was running the line. He would reach Natchez in a couple of years if the Indians didn't kill him in the Creek Country. The Virginia Company, the Georgia Company, the Tennessee Company, and other concerns had bought huge tracts of land, believing that Spain soon would be driven from the Mississippi. The South Carolina Yazoo Company had purchased more than fifteen thousand square miles for four dollars and a half per square mile. The company was selling the land very cheaply and was raffling it off at lotteries. Thomas Pinckney was in Spain arranging for the transfer of Natchez to the United States.

Spain's claim to the Natchez district was just. Galvez had conquered the land from England, but England had given the land, which it did not own, to the United States. Georgia claimed the land under its old charter and the Georgia land companies had sold huge parcels of the territory to speculators. They had even sold the very land on which the Spanish garrisons slept. They had sold the land of the Choctaws and had ignored the Indian nation.

"There'll be a stink about the land companies," Lieutenant Abernathy said. "The Spaniards were in a mood to vacate the land peacefully until they got word that the Americans would try to force them out. Now they have a strong garrison at Natchez, and up at Fort Nogales. They also have fortified New Madrid and Baton Rouge. There's hope that Pinckney will settle the problem. If he doesn't there'll be trouble. The port of New Orleans is closed to the United States and the western Americans will see that it is opened if we have to blow it open."

247

Settlers were pouring into the lower Mississippi valley. They came from Kentucky and Tennessee, and some from Massachusetts and Connecticut. The British still owned most of the factories in Natchez, and near by the settlement of New Scotland was thriving. The Scots had settled there after Culloden. They had fought the English crown in Scotland, and in America they wanted peace. The Sons of Liberty had given them their choice, either fight for the United States or get out. Many of them had gone to the river believing they were beyond reach of the new republic.

The last census of Natchez, taken in 1788, showed that the town had two thousand, six hundred seventy-nine persons. New Orleans had about five thousand residents. But both towns had tripled their population within the past six years. The frontiersmen were in an ugly mood because Spain had closed the port of New Orleans. The port was essential to the prosperity of the West. It was expensive and slow to get goods to the eastern seaports, and the West insisted upon shipping its goods down the Ohio and Mississippi, thence to Europe. Roads were being built, westward from Virginia and Pennsylvania. But the river was the natural outlet for commerce. The Natchez Trace, from Tennessee to Natchez, was open to horse travel and was being widened into a wagon road. But travel overland was slow and dangerous and the West was calling the Mississippi its own. Politicians, factors and soldiers were saying that the Mississippi was more important to the West than the half-hearted protection of the Philadelphia government.

Spain had protested the presence of American troops in Natchez, but the troops were there and Spain could do nothing about it, except shut up or fight. Spain didn't want to fight. The Westerners, however, strained the patience of Spain and threatened to secede from the United States because the Congress would not give them permission to take the land from the Spaniards.

All of this and more Lieutenant Abernathy told Sam. "We don't quarter in Natchez, but outside the city. We have orders not to antagonize the Spaniards. Those damned big-wigs at Philadelphia are afraid of Spain but we're not."

"Suppose Spain doesn't open the river or surrender Natchez to America's claims?" Sam asked. "What then?"

Lieutenant Abernathy looked at his men and smiled. "Then we will take the damned country. We'll organize our own nation."

"It's strange to hear an American officer speak in such a manner," said Sam.

"Ay, strange it is. The people in the East do not know this country. Already England has suggested to certain big men in Kentucky, that Kentucky withdraw from the United States, throw itself under protection of England, and take New Orleans—even Louisiana. If the United States doesn't take this land quickly there'll be a new republic down here. Have you heard of Philip Nolan? Well, you will. He's in Natchez now, forming an expedition to go into Mexico. He's going to trade horses he says." Abernathy slapped his thighs and guffawed. His men laughed too. "Trading horses! He's taking guns to trade for horses. If I weren't an American soldier I'd go with him. He's going land-grabbing, you buckoes! He's going to carve a new country over in Texas. There are many plans afoot but all of them concern land-grabbing. It's get as get can now. We're going to run all the damn Spaniards off of the land. If United States will not help us, England will. If England won't help us, we'll do it alone. We'll build our capital in Kentucky. I say we

249

should make Andy Jackson our president or perhaps Aaron Burr."

It was wild talk to Sam. But if land-grabbing was the thing, then he, too, would grab land. But he must protect his company's land. To hell with the other companies! He struck a deal with Abernathy to protect all lands which his company had bought. "Sure, I'll do it. I don't mind turning an honest penny," said the lieutenant. "I'll announce it in Natchez and send word to Georgia that any man who settles on your company's land without paying you a fair price will be punished. And I'll survey your five thousand acres. I can run a line better than that old Quaker Ellicott. I'll survey your land as a wedding present, and I'll guard your company's land for ten dollars a month. Other soldiers are selling their arms to private businesses. Now to bed with you. A bridegroom needs sleep, for I'll warrant you'll get none tomorrow night."

The Indian guests began arriving early the next morning and many were drunk before the sun had driven the dampness from the land. They brought blankets, hides, beeswax, honey and corn for the bride.

The young bucks played ball and *chunkey*. Sam never had seen an Indian ball game before. It was the national sport of the Muscogees, and often the nations settled disputes by playing ball instead of fighting. Sometimes, however, the ball games wound up in wars. Each player was equipped with a ball stick, a club with a cup on the end. The ball was made of buckskin, and the object of the game was for one side to get the ball between the goal posts of the other side. They played on a field three hundred yards long. As many Indians could play as the chiefs decided, but each side must have an equal number of players. When a player was injured an opponent

250

must drop out of the game. The players could run with the ball or throw it. The runner's favorite method of advancing the ball was to put it in his mouth and run down the field. His opponents beat him with clubs, gouged out his eyes and choked him, anything to make him surrender the ball. The judges carried cudgels and often beat the players if the game became too rough. Two Indians were killed in the day's game and several suffered broken bones.

After the game the Choctaws took Sam to the river and purified him by bathing him in the yellow water. The Choctaws all wore their best clothes, long-skirted coats of blue and buff; capots, red cuffs and capes. Some wore white waistcoats and white shirts, with scarlet leggin's. But none of them wore pants. Even in their full regalia they wore loin cloths. High hats were marks of distinction, and the higher the hat the greater the personage. The women took Donna into the woods, disrobed her and chanted the wedding songs of the Choctaws. One Indian woman pricked Donna's flesh with a deer horn. "Your first son will be fleet as the deer," she said. Another tied a catamount claw around Donna's waist. "He'll be as wily as the catamount." They bathed her and rubbed her body again until it glowed.

The bucks sang their love song and invoked the blessings of the Great Spirit upon the union. Sam was very serious as he accepted the tributes and homage. To have done otherwise, would have been to commit a sacrilege almost as great as mentioning the names of the Choctaw dead.

Jasper and Mrs. Harkins saw to the feast. Huge trenches were dug and meat was barbecued over hickory logs. Three beeves were killed and there were deer and birds. Some of the Indians had sought a buffalo, but the big beasts were becoming scarce. The Indians apologized for not fetching a buffalo. "But the buffalo are going away," one Indian said. "They cannot live near the white man. No animals can live near the white animals."

In mid-afternoon, Honoria and Mrs. Harkins began dressing Donna. First they put on her chemisette and then her corset, lacing the stays until Donna grunted. "Your husband will have to get you out of this," Mrs. Harkins tittered. "But I'll vow he won't mind."

They rolled Donna's hair above her forehead and it hung in curls around her ears and neck. The Indians put yellow jasmines in her hair. Her perriot swept the ground and hid her fine prunellas.

Honoria's hair was fluffed around her ears and hung loosely over her shoulders. She wore the fine dress that Sam had brought her, but she had no stockings.

Sam donned his fine coat, but Ab would not change his buckskins.

Honoria led Donna up the ridge to the Big Tree where Ab and Sam and Lieutenant Abernathy were waiting. The Indians sat in a semi-circle, swaying and pounding the ground with their open palms. Mrs. Harkins stood by, beaming proudly. Jasper and Sukey were grinning. Dabby was sleeping. A blue jay sat in the Big Tree and scolded the company. A thrush called and a mocking bird tried to imitate the sound.

Lieutenant Abernathy told the couple, "Now stand there at attention. Look smart. You're a mighty pretty bride, Donna." He seemed in no hurry to get along with the ceremony. He examined the ring that Sam held and reckoned it was almost pure gold. He turned to his company of soldiers and commanded, "Keep order while I do this." He took Donna's hand and put it in Sam's, then intoned solemnly, "By the power invested in me as an officer of the United States army, I pronounce you husband and wife. Now go your way and behave yourselves."

Sam slipped his mother's ring on Donna's finger and they stood there holding hands, wondering what to do next. "That's all," said the lieutenant. "Kiss her, you ninny. If you don't, I will." Sam kissed his bride on the cheek.

"That was just a peck," Ab said, and kissed Donna full on the mouth. "How's that for a kiss, Mrs. Dabney? And there's more where that one came from."

Honoria ran to Sam and threw her arms around him and sobbed. "I can't help it," she said.

Lieutenant Abernathy commanded his company, "Fire a salute, you hellers! Haven't you got any manners?"

The salute was fired and Donna took Sam's arm and they walked down the ridge and back to the camp. The guests sang and drank and ate far into the night.

Ab and Honoria drank with them and once Ab playfully leaned over her and begged, "Give me a buss. Everybody else has been kissing."

She stood on her tiptoes and threw her arms around him and kissed him. The soldiers cheered. They liked Honoria. She didn't know it, but throughout the ceremony all the men had watched her and not Donna.

Sam and Donna returned to the Big Tree and sat there until the moon came up and turned the yellow Pearl River into gold. Neither spoke much. There was nothing to be said. Sam was glad that Donna did not talk when she had nothing to say. He was content to sit there with his arm around her, listening to the night things and thinking of his plans. He felt her shiver. She coughed softly, holding her hand over her mouth.

"It's chilly," she remarked, "and damp."

"I'm not chilly," Sam said. "Maybe the excitement has made you ill."

"But I'm not ill. My head is light, but my skin is dry and I feel strange. Perhaps it is love."

"Ay," he said. "Perhaps it is love." He fingered her dress and teased. "Are you still weary?"

"No," she smiled. "I'm not weary." But she was. Her body ached and, although she gave herself to him with wild abandon, the love that she had for him could not soothe the pains in her body. Sam was reluctant to free her, but realizing her passion had burned out, he pulled her head to his shoulder and stroked her hair. The fireflies lighted their couch and whippoorwills sang them to sleep.

15

✮ ✮

SAM rested his caravan on the outskirts of Natchez and made ready for a grand entrance into the city. The women preened themselves. Jasper sleeked up Claymore, and Sam shaved. He told Ab to shave, but the big Kentuckian refused.

"God's eye-teeth, Sam'l," he grinned, "I'm proud of these whiskers! Besides, I've got a couple of pet lice that have mated in my beard and I'll be damned if I'll drive them from home. How would you like to be driven from your home just when you got mated and all set to put up housen goods and raise a crop of young 'uns?" He laughed uproariously.

Honoria laughed, too, but she scolded him. "If you're buggy, I'll have naught to do with you."

"You ain't had a heap to do with me anyway," Ab said.

"Now you go shave," Honoria cajoled him. "Sleek up your hair."

"Yas'um," Ab laughed, and winked at Sam. But he shaved and sleeked up.

Sam tried not to appear impressed, but to act impressively, when they rode into town. Donna acted naturally, but Ab and Honoria gaped at the wonders of the city.

Natchez, named for the sun-worshiping Indians who were scattered by the French, first masters of the valley, sprawled on a bluff that guarded a big bend of the

Mississippi. Below the town the river banks were lined with orange groves and *bois d'arc* that bore a yellow fruit. The Indians called the tree the yellow dyewood and extracted from it the yellow dye that was prized so highly by the Choctaws.

Sam, his touch on Claymore's reins as light as a butterfly's, checked his horse and surveyed the scene. The Trace wound down from the north and the old Spanish road meandered from the south. The bluff stood more than two hundred feet above the river, and on a clay shelf between the river and the base of the bluff was Natchez-under-the-hill.

There were about three hundred houses in the town, mostly of frame and one story. The iron grillwork and high corridors of the public buildings testified to the Spanish influence. Most of the roofs were shallow and sloping, and extended beyond the walls and sheltered the piazzas. There were a few mansions in the town. Concord, the executive mansion of the gracious Spanish governor, his excellency Don Manuel Gayoso de Lemos, was two miles from the fort. The cornices and mantels of the mansion had been brought from Spain, and the house was the most elegant along the river.

The town's main street ran east from the bluff and was lined with bazaars and the trading factories of the Scotch merchants. Most of the men in the town were planters and wore white blanket coats and wide-brim white hats. Women, always with escort, walked along the main thoroughfare avoiding drunken Indians and keel-boat Kentuckians.

Donna had never seen such elegant ladies, even in Charleston and Norfolk. The women wore curled wigs and powdered wigs and silks from Cathay. They carried fans, ivory fans inlaid with gold. Slaves carried their

256

parasols. Honoria scrutinized the ladies, and would nudge Donna when she saw one who demanded particular attention.

One lady was riding a bay colt and was wearing a riding habit with hat and peruke. Other women riders wore velvet caps with white feathers and some wore brunswicks, tailored like a man's coat with collar and buttons. The women wore jewelry, and bracelets dangled on their arms. The bracelets were set with miniatures or locks of hair.

The Spanish gentlemen who promenaded the streets paid scant heed to Sam's train, but the Americans watched him closely. One man, a Kentuckian, stopped Sam and asked his name.

"What is my name to you?" demanded Sam heartily.

"I meant no offence," the stranger said. "But we've been expecting a long train from Kentucky. Do you know General Wilkinson, Mr. Blunt, or any of the honorable men who would help us kick the damned Spaniards into the river?"

"I'm from Georgia," Sam said, "and you speak in riddles to me."

Lieutenant Abernathy saw to their quarters, and made them comfortable. Donna lay down to rest as soon as their room was ready. She was running a slight fever and her cough persisted. Honoria gave her sassafras tea, and tucked her in. Sam kissed her goodbye and promised to return before dark. He took Mrs. Harkins to the home of her kinspeople, then saw to it that his goods were unpacked and stored. He went to the landing and learned that the goods he and André had shipped by water had not arrived, but keel boats of Panton & Company were pushing up toward Natchez and Sam knew

257

the goods were aboard. He left his address with Panton's agent and he and Ab began a tour of the town's taverns.

"You must be looking for someone," Ab said, as they walked from one ordinary to another, pausing only long enough for a drink at each bar.

"So I am," said Sam. "And if the man I want is in Natchez, I'll find him in a tavern."

As he opened the door to one tap room a blast of musty air welcomed him, and from the bar came a loud voice and the pounding of a fist upon the wood. "I'll tell you, buckoes," the voice said, "Andy Jackson is the smartest man between here and hell. If those loony nabobs in Congress won't give us permission to take this land for the United States, then we'll take it anyway, elect Andy as our president and form our own country. We don't need the seaboard. Those high-hatted bastards in Boston and Norfolk will do naught for us. We have everything in this country that a country needs. And this new cotton gin will make us the richest people on God's great green footstool."

Sam nudged Ab. "That's the man I'm seeking."

"He talks like a lawyer," said Ab.

"He is," said Sam. "He's Hosea Cincinnatus Thomas. I met him in North Carolina and his brother in South Carolina."

Sam walked to the lawyer and tapped him on the shoulder and said, "You remember me, eh? I would deem it a pleasure to buy you a drink, and we'll drink to the new lands."

The lawyer studied Sam for a moment, then offered his hand. "Why, hell's hinges, it's young Mr. Dabney of Georgia. The last time I saw you, you were snorting around and horsing for an Indian wench. I must buy you a drink and welcome you to Natchez. My brother is

258

in New Orleans. He tells me he met you, and a Frenchy friend of yours."

Sam and Ab drank with Thomas, and Sam learned much of the politics and intrigues in Natchez. He told Thomas a few of his plans and retained him to represent the land company for which he was the agent. He assured him a fee of three hundred dollars a year, for which amount he also would represent Sam'l Dabney, but the funds were to be paid out of the company's purse.

"Within a few days," Sam said, "I'm sending a rider to Georgia. If you know of anyone who wants intelligence sent to the East, my man will take the messages. My fee will be five dollars for each letter between Natchez and Milledgeville. But if you can collect more than five dollars you may keep the difference."

Thomas said, "You're a slick trader, for fair. You'll teach the Scotch factors a trick or two. I'm your man, Mr. Dabney. I'll check your contracts with Panton and will see that his agent doesn't rob you. You're entitled to a fee from your Frenchy friend for your work in seeing that his goods got safely to Natchez. Ten percent of them is a good fee and I'll charge you two percent of your fee for my advice."

"There's a thing you must know," Sam said. "André Duportail is my friend. I'll not charge him for this service, and I'll not pay you for your advice. When I want your advice I'll ask it and you'll furnish it to me for the fee my company pays you. I first want contracts drawn up and I'll call at your office tomorrow and tell you about them."

"But you're entitled to a fee from your friend."

"Sam Dabney will never grow rich by taking money from his friends."

Ab said, "Well spoken, Sam'l boy."

The lawyer laughed it off, and the three sat near the bar and drank until the supper hour. For the first time in his life Sam was unsteady on his feet. As he walked to the inn where Donna was waiting, he staggered. Donna was in bed when he arrived. He stooped over to kiss her and almost fell.

"You've been drinking too heavily," she said. There was no bitterness in her voice, but disappointment.

"Ay," he said. "I have that, and I'll do it no more, I vow. Do you feel better?"

"Yes," she lied. "I'll be able to travel to Lake Flournoy's when you're ready. I'm anxious to get back to Locha Poka and build our home."

Sam called upon the governor the next morning and found him a gracious host. Gayoso avoided the discussion of politics and only once did he mention governmental affairs. He said, "The western citizens of the United States are being swept off of their feet by their blind love for France." He spoke excellent English, having been educated in England. "You'll learn, Mr. Dabney, that the present government of France is not a friend of the United States."

"Is his Catholic majesty's government our friend?" Sam asked.

"That is for the United States to say," Gayoso parried the question.

Back at the tavern Sam posted his journal to date and went to the tap room and drank ale. He wanted to be alone to think. Finally, his mind made up, he sent a courier to Ab's lodging.

"Ab," he told his friend, "I'm sending you back to Georgia."

"But why?" said Ab. "I want to go to Flournoy's plantation."

"There's a thing you must do for me," Sam said. He was determined to keep Ab from Flournoy as long as possible. "You must ride dispatches to the East and fetch dispatches back here. I'll not be here when you return, but meet me at Locha Poka. The task of managing my post from Natchez to Georgia will be yours. We'll have three remount stations between the river and Milledgeville, one at Locha Poka, one at André's place on the Tombigbee, and the third at Chadbourne's home in the village. Soon we'll hire riders. The post will be a good business. I'll help you get it started, then I'll lease it to you, ay?"

"Nay," said Ab. "I'll ride the post for you until it is organized, but damme, Sam'l boy, I didn't come this far just to ride a horse through the Indian nations. I want a parcel of ground and a cabin somewhere near Locha Poka."

Sam understood his friend's desires. Perhaps Ab was thinking that if he had a home near Sam's he could see Honoria often and pay his court. Sam didn't argue with him, but gave him money and told him to frequent the taverns and coffee houses and seek information. He also collected information from Abernathy; from planters and merchants and from Thomas.

He disposed of the goods he had traded from the Indians and took two drafts in payment. One of the drafts he addressed to Frome to wipe out his indebtedness. He traded some of the horses in his train for steers, milch cows and other stock. Then he took a count of his status. He had very little cash. His personal assets included Jasper, Claymore, his gun and the profit from his journey. Of course, he had Donna's goods to trade with. These included twelve slaves, several horses and a small amount of gold. But he had made up his mind never to trade slaves except as a last resort, and under no condition would he trade female slaves. A slave woman, a cow, a jenny, a sow, an ewe represented potential wealth to him.

He determined to go into debt and bought all the supplies his credit would bear, pledging the slaves and his land against the debts. He did business only with the Spanish merchants, for he believed that soon the Spanish merchants would be driven from the territory and would liquidate their business for whatever they could get. He pledged an interest of five percent on all bills not paid within twelve months. His supplies included tools, particularly saws and farming implements and nails. He also bought salt and sugar. Most of the Indians used honey for sweetening and Sam reckoned they would pay fancy prices for sugar. He bought green coffee berries and rum, needles and spinning wheels. Sam knew the Indians did not want beads and trinkets. They made the best wampum in the world, so why should they want beads? They wanted needles and hoes and plows, and he would sell them to them.

His goods arrived from Pensacola and he haggled all day with the Panton agent over the fee. When Sam paid the bill he used André's money and kept a record of it. He would not make a profit on his friend. He would skin the Spanish until they screamed and the Scotch until they wept, but he would not play tricks with his friends. His wagons were assembled and geared. Natchez had never seen such wagons, long Conestogas with small wide-rimmed wheels. He allowed eight oxen for each wagon. The wagons were loaded, with his goods and André's goods.

Donna's fever subsided gradually and under Honoria's administerings she improved rapidly. The color returned to her cheeks and she was gay again. She had never been moody, but Sam knew she had been forcing her gayety. She tired easily, however, and usually was exhausted by mid-afternoon. Often she had chills and she coughed almost constantly. She would leave Sam's presence when the cough would not go away. Sam wanted a doctor to see her, but she insisted that nothing serious was the matter. They called upon William Dunbar, the leading planter of the district and then they called formally at the governor's house.

When his wagons were ready, Sam was anxious to be away, but delayed because of Donna's health. He wrote many dispatches, one to Frome telling him of the post and suggesting that he collect letters for Ab's return trip. He also suggested that in payment for ginning cotton Frome take receipts from the planters which would pledge the crops against the bill. "Mind you," Sam wrote, "these receipts some day will be legal tender. Give the planters three years to pay their bills. That is the way they do here. The planters are a stupid lot. They'll not pay their bills the first year and gladly will promise to pay an interest of ten percentum to carry their bills for two years. The longer they carry their bills, the harder it is to pay them. At the end of three years, you can take their crops and goods in payment for the bills. It's good business."

He wrote to Harkins and reported that he had hired soldiers to protect the company's interest, and told of hiring Lawyer Thomas. "The land companies are not popular," he wrote. "Many think they are swindles and some are calling them frauds."

He also reported in detail that Shawnees were with the Creeks and warned Harkins that trouble was brewing. "It's the British," he wrote. "The British in the Northwest. The Spaniards in the South are playing second fiddle to the British. Some of the people here hate Spain so greatly that they are ready to listen to England's suggestion, that the West unite under the protection of the king. These fools cannot see further than their noses. They've been blinded by their love for France and their desire to take this rich land from Spain. There's really naught to worry about from Spain. I have good intelligence. The Kentucky militia could drive Spain into the Gulf. We have two enemies, the English and the Indians."

He wrote a long letter to Pierce telling him first of the wedding and then of Donna's health. "I am not yet alarmed about her health. She has a cough. Many people here have the lung fever, but I do not believe Donna will suffer the ailment. She is weary from the long trip. Before we go to Flournoy's, I'll have a doctor cup her.

"This is indeed the promised land. The Spaniards are very tolerant of the Americans, really too tolerant, for you know if our people are given an inch they will take a mile."

Sam wrote in a large firm hand and put many curlicues at the end of his sentences. The curlicues looked impressive, he thought. Often he put the damp end of his quill in his mouth as he sought the proper word. And then he had to get a new quill. He did not like to write letters. It was hard work for him. Sometimes he wanted to put his own feelings in the letter, but he restrained the impulse. A good business man wrote impersonally.

"There is a conflict here between the planters and the merchants [he wrote]. Many of the planters began producing tobacco several years ago for which the king of Spain promised them ten silver dollars per hundred pounds. The planters bought their implements and other necessities from the factors at a usurious rate. The merchants sold iron implements for six reals a pound and salt for twenty dollars a barrel. Osanaburgs, needed in the shaping of the tobacco into carrots, were sold at one dollar per yard. The foolish planters, having visions of great prosperity, stopped raising corn, which sold for one dollar a bushel, and pork which sold for ten dollars per one hundred pounds, and beef which sold at six dollars and twenty-five cents, and devoted all of their time and land to tobacco.

"General James Wilkinson of Saratoga fame then fetched a cargo of Kentucky tobacco down the river. It was a better grade than the Natchez weed. The king of Spain stopped buying Natchez tobacco and the Spanish leaders began buying Kentucky tobacco and gave Wilkinson valuable concessions and many favors.

"The merchants then called their debts against the planters and there were riots and bloodshed. The planters petitioned for help. Now a lawful interest of five percentum has been set.

"With their tobacco markets ruined the planters turned to indigo and realized from one dollar to two dollars and fifty cents per pound. However, only this year a pest ruined the indigo and now the planters are turning to cotton. They will not learn to grow more than one crop. The time will come when the planters will either destroy the merchants or the merchants will destroy the planters. Some of the merchants have taken over the debtors' land and are working them with free labor on shares. It is a vicious system. The poor sharecroppers, mostly Scotch and Irish immigrants, are forced to buy all of their goods from their landlords, and pay an interest as high as twenty-five percentum. That is beyond the legal limit, but the authorities do naught about it. The merchants are able in that way to have their land worked without the responsibility of providing for their slaves. I believe slavery is a better system. But mind you, Pierce, we must do something to stop the importation of slaves from foreign lands. The market soon will be flooded with Jamaica fellows. I see another danger here, the mating of masters with their slave wenches. It's an all-too-common practice. Even the other slaves shun the yellow bastards, and of course, the white masters will not recognize them. The Creeks are right—one drop of negroid blood makes a blackamoor. Some of the masters free the yellow children. The yellow girls usually wind up under the hill or in New Orleans selling their beauty.

"There is much levity in this land and easy living. The land is so rich that it gives abundantly and the people seem to think the prosperity will last forever. But it will not. I believe that within a few years this will be the greatest cotton country in the world. But cotton ruins land, and the free land will not be here forever. I'm going to protect myself. I'll be both planter and merchant. I also will manufacture goods and run the post. I cannot fail.

"I'll not soil my hand with politics. But you can wager that I know on which side of the bread my butter is spread. The Americans here hold Thomas Jefferson, Andrew Jackson and Aaron Burr in great esteem. Of course, Washington is their idol, as he is everybody's idol. But these wild Kentuckians hate Hamilton and all that he stands for. I believe Andy Jackson will be in the national eye soon. He's a good man to watch. I only fear that his domestic situation will work against him.

"On Locha Poka I'll plant the same kind of cotton that grows so well here. The seed comes from Georgia and Jamaica. It is a black seed of fine fibre and good staple. This year's crop of Mr. William Vousden sold for 2s. 4d.

266

per pound. It was very clean and was equal in quality to the best Georgia sea island. The cotton is put up in long bags. Mr. William Dunbar and other planters have been using a small roller gin, but the gin that I will make is much superior. Word of Whitney's invention has reached here, and several men have planned to manufacture it. There is talk of a public gin. This will not hurt my business, for I will gin in the back country.

"Mr. Dunbar is a very intelligent man. The Spaniards and Scots call him Sir William Dunbar, but the Americans will not so honor him. Some Kentuckians call him Billy Dunbar. He has ordered from Philadelphia a screw press with which he plans to bale cotton. He hopes he can use the press to extract oil from the cotton seeds. He believes the oil will be of a grade between drying and fat oils, but he wonders where he can find a market for such a product. I wonder, too, but I will watch his experiment with much interest.

"The slave market here is booming and tradesmen are in great demand. Ordinary hands are worth five hundred dollars each, cash. The best time to fetch slaves is in the early spring. The sugar planters in Louisiana are paying as high as one thousand dollars for a prime fellow. A healthy ordinary slave of docile character will fetch easily six hundred dollars here at the February auctions. I believe the price of slaves will double within two years. The slaves here are treated better than in Tidewater. I do not attribute this to the goodness of the people, but a good man is so valuable here that he is almost pampered. The slaves are furnished clothing of good material and are given hats, shoes and heavy blankets. They are fed good beef and pork and often are allowed to raise hogs and poultry for themselves. They are furnished as much bread, milk and vegetables as they want and each family is given a garden plot. Damme, Pierce, I'll vow that many slaves live better than some of the whites. In picking season every slave who gathers more than eighty pounds of cotton a day is rewarded. They do not have to work at night and have all the fuel they need. In Louisiana their lot is not so happy. Because of their great number in the sugar country the discipline is very strict, and the Spanish masters are harsh. The Governor, however, protects them and Spanish laws provide they must be given holidays at regular intervals. Even here the slaves are released from work on feast days of the Catholic church.

"A great effort is being made to convert the bumboes to the Catholic faith, but the priests have not been very successful. Romanism, of course, is the established religion here, but the Spaniards are tolerant of Protestants. I find that the Catholics are more tolerant toward the Protestants than the Protestants are toward the Catholics. Most of the priests are Irish and a jolly lot. There are many Irish here. The Spaniards say they would need no jail here but for the Irish.

"I have seen Baptist, Congregational and Episcopal ministers here, but there is none of the shouting and hell-raising that we have back in Georgia at camp meetings. The Protestants are not allowed to perform weddings here. One preacher defied the law and the Spaniards were ready to send him as a prisoner to the mines in Mexico, but a lawyer friend of mine intervened.

"However, if a couple wants to get married in the Protestant faith, they can ride over to the Choctaw Nation where anybody can tie the knot. It is better that way and cheaper. Some of the American officials here assume a great deal of authority, although legally they have no authority. But the Spaniards do not molest them. Some

268

of the officials charge eight dollars for a marriage license and eight dollars for the privilege of a tavern license. They even charge four dollars for a passport into Spanish territory. It seems to me that the Spanish authorities are too lenient with the American settlers. The taxes are very low and the settlers are not forced to undergo military training of any kind.

"There are many intrigues aborning here. I can feel a definite move afoot to take this land from Spain by fair means or foul.

"I even hear rumors that perhaps it will become an independent republic. I have made a friend of Philip Nolan, a young hellion. He soon is going into Mexico apparently to trade horses but I believe there is more behind his expedition than horse-trading. I know he is in receipt of a letter from General Wilkinson in Frankfort, Kentucky, in which Wilkinson says that he has made expensive contracts for provisions, horses, etc. It sounds like more land-grabbing schemes to me. I have even heard the name of Andrew Jackson mentioned in this connection and the names of many other prominent men. I do not know what to believe. I have heard—but mind you, I cannot prove it —that Wilkinson is a pensioner of Spain. If that be true, it is treason.

"This is the same Wilkinson who helped General Gates kick the hell out of Burgoyne at Saratoga. My father told me of him. It was he who received from General Burgoyne the British 'convention,' as the British insisted upon calling their surrender. He stands high with General Washington and we hear here that he may become commander-in-chief of the army, but you know more of that than I do.

"Send me by return post a letter. I am this day releasing a homing pigeon with a band of silk on his leg. Tell me the exact time he arrives in your cot, if he arrives at all."

Sam wrote until his fingers ached and, finishing his correspondence, he called Ab and gave the letters into his safe-keeping. The Kentuckian collected mail from Donna and Mrs. Harkins and one letter from Honoria to Mrs. Frome. "I had to write that old hen," Honoria said, "and tell her about my new clothes and the wedding and my perfume business." Ab got a pack of letters from Thomas, and when he left Natchez the next morning his saddle bags were stuffed with mail. Sam made a profit of two hundred and fifty dollars on Ab's east-bound trip and expected to double the amount on the west-bound journey.

"I'm going to take our old trail," Ab said. "I can make fifty miles a day, I believe, and will be in Georgia before you can suck the suds off of your ale. Then I'm coming right back and will meet you in Locha Poka." He leaned from his horse and shook Sam's hand and patted Donna's cheek. But when Honoria walked to his horse to bid him goodbye, Ab leaned over and picked her up and kissed her.

"How's that for a buss?" he asked.

"It's the best kiss I've ever had," she said. "If you hurry back I'll have two more for you."

"I'll bring you something back," Ab said and whispered in her ear, "You're the prettiest thing I ever saw. My blood boils and I get dizzy when I look at you."

"You're like a fire to my blood, too," she said and smiled at him. She wondered why she lied. It was so easy to lie to men. She was thinking of Tishomingo and she wondered for the thousandth time how his lips would feel and how his hand would feel around her waist. But

270

it was a thrill to kiss Ab and pretend that he was Tishomingo.

Donna was up and about her chores but she was pallid
and her reserve strength was low. Over her protest Sam
called a doctor. The physician would not examine Donna
except in Sam's presence.

He advised her to stay in bed for several days and
wrote out prescriptions, including Seidlitz, Elizir, Vit-
riol, and a tonic powder. At Sam's suggestion he filled the
prescriptions too. Sam didn't trust the Spanish druggist.

He walked outside of the tavern with the doctor and
asked him bluntly, "What is the matter with my wife?"

The doctor said, "She has a touch of the swamp fever;
malaria it is called."

"Are there any signs of the lung sickness?" Sam asked.
"Her cough is a source of worry to me and of pain to
her."

"I don't believe she has the lung fever," the doctor said.
"If she rests she'll be all right within a few days and able
to travel. But she must not take too many tasks upon herself until she grows accustomed to this climate. She is a
strong, healthy woman, but the lung fever attacks the
strong."

"I'll see that she stays in bed until her good color returns," Sam said.

"There is a personal matter that I should discuss with
you," the doctor said.

"Ay?"

"Yes, you should see that your bride does not become
with child until all the signs of the swamp fever have
gone. The swamp fever is a treacherous thing. You may
think your wife is cured and she will not be so. If the
fever doesn't return within six months it is a good sign
that she is cured. But should she carry a child now, and

271

bear one, the ordeal would weaken her, and leave her so weak that the lung fever might develop."

"Do you mean that my wife must not have children?" Sam was dismayed.

"Good heavens, no, man," the doctor nudged him and laughed. "Nothing so serious as that. She was made to be a mother. She should be able to bear children easily. But wait awhile. Don't make a brood mare of her. Let her strength return. I doubt if she could carry a child now."

Donna was sitting up in bed when Sam went back to her. "What did he say?" she demanded.

"That you'll be all right after a rest. You must stay in bed. You mustn't get out of bed for anything. Sukey will sleep in this room with you. I don't like to leave my bride but it is necessary."

Donna lay back on the bed and told Sam to sit by her. Then she pulled his head on the pillow beside her and teased his ear. "I don't want you to be apart from me either. I pray that my strength will soon return. I want to give you a child, Sam'l, a son."

He said, "The doctor said we should wait."

"That is a matter which the doctors cannot control." She laughed at his visible embarrassment. "I'll be well and strong again within a few days. I know that I will. I'll bear you a son at Locha Poka."

Sam kissed her very tenderly. "I had rather have a daughter. Perhaps she would be like her mother, and we could name her Donna."

"A man's first-born should be a son."

"We'll not quarrel over the sex of our child," Sam said. "We're acting as children, planning for a child at this time."

"I like to act as a child," said Donna. "All my life I have acted as a lady. I never had much childhood, Sam'l.

272

It seems I've always been a lady. Sometimes I weary of being a lady. I had rather be a woman—your wife. It's good to be a man's wife."

"It's good to have you for a wife," he said reverently. "I must go now and call Sukey and she will stay with you."

"Don't go away. Don't call Sukey. Can't you stay with me? I cannot sleep unless you are by me. Should I wake up, I'd be frightened. I won't be any trouble."

"You could not be any trouble," he said softly. "You're so beautiful, Donna. Your eyes are so bright—perhaps it's the fever." Suddenly he was worried again.

"It's not the fever, darling. I have no fever now. It's love that makes my eyes shine so. It's love that makes my body warm. Don't leave me with a slave. I'll not sleep unless you are with me."

"All right," he said. "I'll sleep here by you and look after you. After all, I, too, am your slave."

16

LAKE FLOURNOY rode down the dusty pike from his mansion to greet his guests. Sam reined Claymore and rested his hands on his pommel as he watched the rider approach. Dabney was proud of his horsemanship but he realized that in watching Flournoy he was seeing a master. Flournoy sat his horse slightly forward. He was an Indian horseman, but was lighter in the saddle than any Indian Sam had ever seen.

He galloped up to the train, and checked his horse with a word. There was Arabian in that horse. Flournoy looked first at Sam and smiled. His teeth flashed under his thin lips. He dismounted and made an elegant leg to Donna and then to Honoria. His coat was of blue twilled cotton, his waistcoat of white silk, delicately embroidered, and his knee breeches of yellow satin.

Sam dismounted and offered his host his hand. There was strength in Flournoy's hands. They were not as large as Sam's, but the fingers were just as long and almost as strong. The two men stared boldly at each other, sizing each other up. Flournoy was almost olive-skinned, a more handsome man than Tishomingo, more graceful and gracious. The Latin and Indian mixture was apparent in his skin. But his eyes were blue, a frosty blue. They were big, inquisitive eyes, never friendly, but neither were they unfriendly. Flournoy used his eyes only to see with, never to express his feelings. To Sam, the eyes seemed sensitive, so sensitive that the things they saw seemed to hurt them. They were eyes that should have seen only beauty and they seemed to cringe and smart at the ugly things of life, and almost to rebel against their task, watching the world move by *Maison Blanche*, the mansion of Lake Flournoy, kinsman of Josephine, son of a Choctaw princess and a French trader.

Looking at the man, it was difficult for Sam to believe the things he had heard of him. Then he remembered that the most dangerous things often were the most beautiful. A panther was the most beautiful animal in the woods and the most dangerous. The moccasin was a beautiful thing, graceful, courageous and crafty. The hawk was a beautiful bird. . . .

Sam thought at first that Flournoy wore a powdered wig but soon discovered that his host's hair naturally was white, soft, thick and wavy. His hair had been white since his youth and now, at thirty-five, he was very proud of his hair. It was a mark of the white man. He was ashamed of his Indian blood and glad that he had none of the appearances of an Indian. He wore his hair with a puff on top and his queue was tied with gay ribbon. He was a tall man, not as tall as Sam or Ab, but tall, nevertheless. And he was proud. There was pride in his smile and in his haughty bearing, in his courtly manners and in his careless gestures. He wore tiny pearl earrings and a sword, the sign of the Frenchman. Sam felt shabby in his presence and glanced at his own moccasins, then at Flournoy's booted feet. Those boots must have cost two hundred dollars. Sam looked at his well-shaven chin, his aquiline nose.

Flournoy's eyes clouded slightly and narrowed a bit under Sam's gaze, and then he turned again to the ladies. "My friends and guests, the Duportails, did not deceive me," he said to Donna. "You're as beautiful as they led me to believe. And you," he smiled at Honoria, "are even more charming than André reported. And André is a good judge of beauty and charm."

Honoria gasped at the compliment and almost unseated herself in her anxiety to dismount and curtsy. She did not know she should not have dismounted without assistance, and almost tumbled from her horse and stood there in the dusty road and stared at the great Flournoy. "You're the first young man I have ever seen with white hair," she said. "It's very pretty." Sam blushed at her impudence, but Flournoy laughed and bowed again.

"Never have I had such a pretty compliment from such a pretty woman," he said and gazed full into Honoria's eyes. She returned his gaze and it was Flournoy who first turned his eyes away. He wondered if it had been proper for him to call her a woman instead of a lady. It seemed natural to call Honoria a woman and Donna a lady.

Donna did not dismount, but bowed her head in recognition of the introduction and Flournoy went to her and kissed her hand. He was standing by her horse when André and Anestasie arrived to welcome their friends.

"Where's Chock?" Sam asked quickly.

"Tishomingo, the one you call Chock, is at his lodge near the Sacred Mound," Flournoy said. "And where is the other member of your party, the one called Ab?"

Sam searched the man's eyes as he spoke. If Tishomingo had told him who Ab was, there was no evidence of it in Flournoy's eyes or voice.

276

"I've sent him back to Georgia on business," Sam explained. "I had hoped Chock would be here."

"Your friend has set himself to a very difficult task," Flournoy said. "He's trying to devise a Choctaw alphabet so the history of his people can be written." Even Donna noticed he said "his" people instead of "our" people, although they both were half Choctaw. "I had assumed he had told you about his work. He doesn't have much time to visit with me."

"Chock doesn't talk much of himself," Sam said pointedly. "I know little about him or his life." For the first time he noticed a change in Flournoy's eyes. They seemed to dart to a point and to pierce his brain, seeking there the lie that he had told. The eyes seemed to know that he had lied.

"Sometimes you must ask your friend about his life and his work. He's a very remarkable man to have had an Englishman for a father." Flournoy's tone was cold. "Was your journey from Natchez eventful?"

"No," said Sam. "It was a very dreary journey. My wife has been ailing but she stood the journey well."

They had traveled up the Trace from Natchez. The Trace ran between the upper reaches of the Halfway River and the Big Black River. They had crossed the Big Black at Flournoy's ferry, and then had journeyed toward the Yazoo and Flournoy's *Maison Blanche*, the largest plantation west of South Carolina..

Flournoy's home was on a hill above the Trace. It was a Greek revival structure, with fluted Doric columns two stories high, and was surrounded by water oaks and magnolias. Its roof was of cypress, hewn from the swamps, but the columns and the stones of the foundation had been brought from Europe by ships and ballast. Every nail in the house had been hand-wrought in

277

Spain. The grillwork of the small upper porch which extended out from a middle hall, had been purchased by Flournoy in Venice. The double drawing rooms were furnished in rosewood. Bronze sperm oil lamps with crystal pendants, two chandeliers, and a bronze candelabrum with cut-glass prisms, lighted the drawing rooms. The walls of the banquet hall were paneled with soft green felt and the furniture was made of hand-rubbed mahogany. There were fourteen rooms in the mansion. A set of slave bells was in the drawing room and another set was in the long lower hall. Each bell had a different tone and each house slave knew the tone of the bell that summoned him.

Flournoy owned a bathtub, the first Honoria had ever seen. It was made of lead and a slave filled it with warm water and emptied it by scooping out the water in a pail and drying the tub with sponges. The slave had no other chore.

Honoria was delighted with the tub and Flournoy exhibited it with much pride. Sam was embarrassed when Honoria asked permission to use it. A creek had always been good enough for old man Dabney's brats. But Flourney was pleased at her request.

"The ladies surely are tired," he said to Sam. "My slave will prepare their baths immediately."

When the men were gone Honoria said excitedly, "May I use it first, Donna?"

"Why, yes," said Donna.

She was very tired but she did not want Honoria to know she was tired. She did not want Honoria to know she was weak, either. Honoria was such a healthy sprite. Donna was ashamed of her fatigue. Honoria had been very solicitous of her—too solicitous of her, Donna thought. Perhaps it was just her imagination, but Honoria seemed to be scornful of her delicate health. Once she had said, "Perhaps marriage does not agree with you. I hope I will not be ill when I first wed."

Her tone had irked Donna and without thought Donna had said, "You'll never be ill, for you have no feeling. Your body and heart are trained to hardships. You were born to this life."

"So was your husband," Honoria had said quickly. "No, I'll never be ill, I'll be happy and gay and a comfort to my husband. Thank God, I know how to work as a wife should and I know other things, too. I'll give my husband a child before we've been married a year. I'll not be so puny that I cannot do the things a wife should do."

Then she had regretted her words and had thrown her arms around Donna and had begged her forgiveness.

Donna had kissed her. "You don't mean those things," she said. "I know you don't mean them. You're my Sam'l's sister, and my Sam'l's sister would not say mean things to me and mean them."

But Donna's illness made her very unhappy and she felt that Honoria thought she was not a good wife. She worried lest Sam would think so too. A man did not like a sickly wife. She'd always been healthy at home. "Well got up with salt in her craw," Sam had said. But that was back in Georgia, away from the fevers and dampness of the new land. She lied to Sam about her feelings. Her pride would not allow her to tell him the truth. She would work. She would make a home. She would bear his children, she would do anything to challenge those sly, searching looks that Honoria gave her.

It never entered Honoria's head to suggest that Donna bathe first. She never thought that Donna, too, was tired. Donna was her brother's wife. She was his sister, the sister of the master. There is a difference in being the sister of a master and in being his wife. She was a Dabney by heritage. Donna was a Dabney by law. Honoria had cooked for Sam and had made his bed for years. They had buried their parents. They had gone out alone to face the world. Donna had only known him for months. She didn't even make his bed but allowed Sukey to do it, until Honoria put a stop to such foolishness, and made the bed herself as she had always done, with no pillow for Sam and the covers tucked in tightly, so his feet would not poke out from under the ends of the covers. She never thought that she was making Donna's bed, too. It was not Donna's bed; it was Sam's bed. The slaves belonged to Sam, the horses, the oxen, Locha Poka belonged to Sam. Donna was Sam's wife, but she was Sam's sister.

Donna tolerated the situation only because she wanted peace. She understood how Honoria felt. She knew the girl loved Sam with a blind, senseless devotion. She had felt all along that Honoria would resent her. She mustn't let Sam know that a gulf was forming between her and his sister. He had worries enough, and perhaps it would pass. She believed Honoria would find a husband soon and would move away and leave her and Sam to their own lives. And until then she would say or do naught to provoke the situation. She had tried to forgive Honoria for taking the comb that Sam had brought her. She had tried to forgive Honoria for making her husband's bed and for telling the slaves the kind of food Sam liked and the way he liked it. She'd never thought to condemn Sam. Even Sukey had noticed that Honoria was assuming the station of mistress of the household and the slave had said tactfully, "Sukey belongs to you and to Massa

Sam." But she took orders from Honoria and obeyed them promptly.

Donna, knowing the slaves would gossip, had told Sukey, "Mr. Dabney's sister is to be obeyed. She's trying to relieve me because I'm ill." Sukey knew she was lying and Donna knew Sukey knew, and it hurt her to have the slave know she was lying to protect her dignity.

Honoria stayed in the bathtub until the warm water wrinkled the skin on her toes. The slave sponged her and rubbed her. Honoria was surprised but not shocked to learn that the slave wench who bathed her, also bathed Flournoy and his men guests. The toilet complete, the slave called an old black woman and they helped Honoria into her best dress and saw to her hair. The bath slave looked Honoria over critically and spoke rapidly in French to the older slave.

"What does she say?" Honoria demanded haughtily. She was displeased because the slaves spoke a language she did not understand.

"She meant no disrespect," the older slave said. "She's not long from Martinique and speaks no English. She said you were the first white woman she has bathed since Ta-lo-wah lived here."

"But that's an Indian name," Honoria said.

The old slave smiled tolerantly. "She was a white woman, a very beautiful white woman."

The younger slave spoke again in French and the older woman rebuked her. They knew something Honoria didn't know and it angered her.

"Tell this wench never to speak a tongue I don't understand when I'm in her presence," Honoria demanded. "And who was this white woman with an Indian name?"

The old slave shrugged her shoulders. "You should ask the master," she said. Honoria stamped her foot and slapped the old woman for her impudence. The old woman smiled again and opened the door so Honoria could go to the drawing room where Lake Flournoy was drinking madeira with his guests.

It did not take Donna so long to bathe. When the slave felt her skin she looked quickly at the white woman, then examined her eyes closely. She mumbled in French and went away and fetched the older woman again.

The old slave said to Donna, "The bath girl says you have fever."

"It's nothing," said Donna. "Only a touch of the swamp fever."

"I know things the white man does not know. I'm from Martinique as are most slaves in this household. We have much fever in Martinique and I have a remedy for you." She gave Donna a bitter concoction made from the bark of the cinchona tree. "It will make your ears ring, but it will make you well. Whenever you feel the fever coming on, take the remedy. You're a bride and a bride should not be ill."

"I'll take the medicine," Donna said. "And if it helps me I'll send you a gift, a bit of pretty calicut for your hair." Donna knew that many slaves from the island had remedies the white man did not understand.

The old slave rubbed her skin with a sweet oil, caressing it until Donna felt drowsy. "The lady who was just here—she is your kinswoman?"

"She is my husband's sister."

The old slave didn't reply for several minutes. "The fever is burning your skin, but something else is burning your heart." She spoke in correct, precise English. "Man is a strange thing. When a fox mates, or a monkey, or any animal, the animal will never bring one of his family to his nest or den. Only man is so foolish."

282

"You should not meddle in the business of white people," Donna said.

The slaves rubbed Donna until her skin glowed and they put a delicate perfume under her arms and a japonica in her hair. They let her hair fall in waves over her neck and rolled it in loose curly waves around her ears. They laced tightly her long stays which reached from her breast to below her thighs. Her petticoat was embroidered silk. They selected her prettiest dress, a sacque of fawn-colored silk, with short sleeves and a low square-cut neck. The young slave handed Donna a mirror and the old slave said, "You're the most noble lady we have seen at *Maison Blanche*."

The Martinique girl spoke rapidly in French and the old slave laughed and explained to Donna. "She said you're more beautiful than Ta-lo-wah, the lady who was mistress of this house."

"Where is she now?" Donna asked.

"She's dead."

Donna thanked the slaves and before she went to the drawing room she asked the old woman, "You know much of life. When will I be safe to have a child?"

"Wait until three moons have gone. Then the fever will go too, and you'll be strong enough to carry your son." She fumbled in her dress and found a tobie, a rooster spur, and gave it to Donna. "Keep it," she said. "It's a good tobie."

Donna laughed. "I don't believe in such charms, old woman." But she kept the tobie. It would have been ridiculous back in Georgia for Donna Chadbourne to have carried a charm. But it was different in the new land. She was afraid of the new land and a charm would do no harm.

It was late afternoon when Donna and Honoria joined

283

the company in the drawing room. Sam, Flournoy and André had been discussing business but suspended the talk when the ladies arrived. At André's suggestion, Flournoy agreed to show the ladies the plantation. Anestasie would not go on the tour. "I have seen the place," she said. "Show them your snakes, M'sieur Flournoy, the fer-de-lances. I'm sure Honoria would enjoy seeing them."

Honoria understood the sarcasm in the remark and laughed. Donna said, "I don't care to see snakes either. I'll stay here with Anestasie."

"I'm not afraid of snakes," Honoria said. "I want to see them. I want to see all of the plantation, Mr. Flournoy. It's the most beautiful place I've ever seen." He offered her his arm and they walked behind the big house to the snake shed.

"Perhaps I should explain," Flournoy said. "These snakes are very dangerous. In Martinique where I buy my slaves, the fer-de-lance is believed to be the devil. The slaves down there never run away. They had rather remain in bondage than face the swamps and the fer-de-lance. Every time I bring a cargo of slaves, I also bring a few snakes. I simply tell my slaves that I release the snakes and that the swamps here are filled with them. They will not run away. But to make sure they don't I send them by the snake house every day, so they may see the fate that awaits them if they desert me. They're deathly afraid. Of course, I never release the snakes." He laughed and opened the door to the shed. The snakes were sleeping in their pits which were protected by mesh. The snakes were brown, marked with black, and most of them were from five to six feet long.

"They look like copperheads," Sam said.

"They're closely akin to the copperhead," Flournoy

explained. "They're nocturnal in habit and I feed them rabbits and rats. Their tempers are not as vile as the copperheads. I've known people in Martinique to pet them. Some people call them rat-tailed vipers. They strike without warning and their bite is fatal. My slaves believe the snakes will trail them if I free them. The snakes, I mean, not the slaves. I never free slaves, and never allow them to buy their freedom."

"It's a good system," Sam remarked.

"It is a brutal system," André said.

Flournoy put his hand on André's shoulder. "Yes, my friend, it's a brutal system, but this is a brutal land. These snakes cost me nothing. Guards for my slaves would cost me much money. For sure, I have never released any snakes, but their presence is sufficient to keep my slaves subdued."

"How many slaves have you?" Sam asked.

"Six hundred. Most of them are in the cotton fields. But I also grow indigo and tobacco, cattle, sheep, and even bees."

"How often do you bring slaves from Martinique?" Sam watched Flournoy as he bolted the door to the snake shed.

"Usually a cargo a year. I sell them in Louisiana, at Barataria, at three hundred dollars a head. The dealer buys the entire cargo, sick and well ones. I realize a good profit."

"That is a thing I would talk to you about," Sam said as they walked toward the slave quarters. "The slave market is going up as soon as the United States takes the Natchez district. It wouldn't surprise me if this land soon became a territory of the United States."

"And very soon," said Flournoy. "The land is filling up rapidly."

"We would be wise to forbid the importation of slaves in this territory," Sam said.

"Yes, and why?"

Sam said, "I do not make my ideas known for naught. But I've been thinking about it. If I show you a way in which you can double the value of your slave cargoes, will you give me ten percentum of their price?"

"Of course." He said it casually.

"André will bear witness to this, and when we return to your house we can sign the contracts. I have them ready."

"Then you expected my answer to be yes?" Flournoy lit a long cigar from a taper that his body slave fetched.

"I knew a man of your wisdom would say yes." Sam outlined his plan briefly. He picked up a stick and drew a rough map on the hard bare earth. He had heard much of the organization of a Mississippi territory and knew it would come to pass when the Spaniards surrendered Natchez. The Americans had settled in the southern part of the new land. He drew a line from the mouth of the Yazoo River straight across to the Chattahoochee River, and Georgia. "The settlers are homesteading south of this line. The territory probably will include only this land. The land north of this boundary and to the Tennessee territory surely will not be included. It still will be Indian land. The independent nations are the Choctaws, Chickasaws, Creeks and Cherokees." He pointed the stick at Flournoy. "You'll notice that your home is north of this line, and will not be included in the territory. Legally you'll still be a citizen of the Choctaw Nation. My plan is that the importation of slaves from foreign lands will be forbidden in the new territory."

Sam believed it would be easy to forbid a traffic in

286

slaves between the territory and foreign nations. In Natchez, he had been surprised at the feeling against the institution of slavery. Many opposed it because they thought it was evil. Even some slave-holders opposed it because they thought slavery was economically unsound. The poor whites opposed it because it ruined their chances for profitable labor. And most of the settlers who were pouring in were poor whites, too poor to own slaves, and generally opposed to slavery for moral as well as economic reasons. Sam had employed Lawyer Thomas, not only as a counsel but as a rabble-rouser. He could send Thomas among the people and arouse them and lead them to oppose slavery. The advocates of slavery naturally would fight for unlimited traffic with bumboes. The solution would lie in a compromise, the privilege of trading in slaves between American states and territories, but a law against the foreign traffic of slaves.

"It can be done, I'm sure," Sam explained. "We can win such a compromise. And with the demand high and the supply limited the price will double. Ay?"

"It's a smart plan," Flournoy said. "It's too smart. If it's against the law to import slaves, how can I import them?"

"It will be against the law of the United States," Sam said. "Not against the laws of the Choctaw Nation. You're not an American. As a choctaw——"

"I am not a Choctaw," Flournoy said sternly. "I am a Frenchman."

"But as a French citizen of the Choctaw Nation, you can import slaves for your own country. And too, Louisiana is foreign territory and will be so until the union squeezes Spain out. The American laws will not apply there. You can still bring your slaves to Louisiana and

for a price we can find men who will run them into the
United States. Your home will even be outside of the
territory. You'll be a Choctaw—I mean a French citizen,
of an independent nation importing slaves to Spanish
territory from a French island. My government would
not dare molest you. The only risk you would take
would be in running the slaves from Louisiana into the
Mississippi territory."

Flournoy did not answer immediately but studied
Sam closely. Here, indeed, was an adversary. Here was
a man who could think. Here was a man who must be
watched. Mon Dieu, he was a big man, a strong man.
He would be a fine man for a friend and a dangerous
man for an enemy. And what a parcel his sister was.
André was a sentimental loony. His wife had more
courage and intelligence in one hair of her head than
André had in his whole head. He was a reckless man,
stupidly brave. But this Georgian was a bucko for fair.
A man who made up his mind without counsel. A good
man to tie to.

As Flournoy walked on without speaking, Sam's
doubts returned. Perhaps he had spoken too hastily,
perhaps he had offended Flournoy. He's a strange man,
Sam thought. Surely he's not as dangerous as Tishomingo
has said. No man with such skin and eyes can be so
dangerous.

Dabney is a wily man, Flournoy thought as he strolled
along, slightly in advance of his guests. How much does
he know? Has Tishomingo told him of Amelia? Has
he told Ab? Why has he sent Ab back to Georgia? What
is his weakness? He isn't conceited, but proud. He's
a cautious man, but quick to anger. Flournoy knew that
every man had a weakness. Where was Dabney's? Flournoy knew his life, knew that he was the son of a poor

288

Irish infidel, an Irish bucko who had married a Chad-bourne. Was his wife his weakness? His sister? He remembered how Sam had blushed at his sister's boldness. He recalled how he had looked at her, tenderly and proudly, when she had joined them after her toilet.

He turned suddenly to Sam and said, "Your plan is a superfine one. I'll do it. I'm getting a fair price for an ordinary slave, delivered to Barataria. The same slaves are worth much more in the sugar country, but I prefer to sell my slaves at Barataria and not bother with regulations at New Orleans. The day I can get double that price I'll give you ten percentum of the money, provided of course, you see that the importation of the slaves is forbidden."

Flournoy was suddenly pleased with himself. Dabney was an addle-pated fool after all. Smuggled slaves would net a fortune and Dabney would have no way to check the cargoes or their sales prices. He gladly would give the young Georgian ten percentum of the profit on some of the slaves. Dabney thought he was taking no chances but the young fool even had contracts. Dabney's name on such a contract would be a valuable weapon to use against the Georgian if he got out of hand. Dabney was an American citizen. If he violated the law he would go to prison. It was worth a goodly sum to have the young man scheme and work to have a compromise slavery law passed. And if he demanded too much, the contracts in the hands of the American authorities would put Mr. Dabney where he could do no hurt. Flournoy had to restrain himself, else he would have smiled. But his complacency vanished and his pride fell when Sam said:

"Of course, I'll have a man at Barataria to check the cargoes. It's business. This man also will deliver to me the sale's price of each slave, and will collect from you ten percentum of all monies over the current price of the bumboes. In other words, if your slaves are averaging three hundred dollars a head now, I'll get ten percentum of all monies above three hundred dollars."

"Then you don't trust me?" Flournoy said.

"That's beside the point, but I'm an Irishman, Mr. Flournoy, and I trust no man. The only man I ever trusted was my father and he's dead."

Sam's statement surprised André, for Sam had trusted him and other men. But he did not trust Flournoy and he was glad that Sam would not.

"Then what man will you trust to check the cargo? He must be a man that I trust, too. After all, I don't want my business known to every man."

"I've selected a man we both trust for the task," Sam said nonchalantly. "He is Tishomingo." He watched Flournoy's eyes, but the man did not show any emotions when the name was mentioned. Sam knew that Chock would relish the task for the opportunities it would present, the opportunities to harass Flournoy and to complete his vengeance.

"Tishomingo is satisfactory," Flournoy said. He couldn't have said otherwise. "It's a wise selection. He's not an American citizen and as a prince of the Choctaw Nation will be beyond reproach." He offered his hand to Sam and as they shook hands, Flournoy received another shock.

"Of course, the contracts that I sign will state only ten percentum of the monies agreed upon by you and Tishomingo. All contracts that mention slavery or the slave traffic will be signed by Tishomingo as my agent."

Flournoy threw away his cigar. "Tishomingo told me that you are a fox. He was wrong, for the fox sometimes

290

gets caught. But you're smarter than the fox. Never before did I know that Irish has such good heads for business. For wine and song, yes, but not for business."

"The French, my friend, as well as the English, have never understood the Irish."

Back at the mansion, Anestasie and Donna sat and talked. Donna was happy to make conversation again with a woman of Anestasie's breeding. It was the Frenchwoman who brought up the subject of Donna's health.

"I'm not really worried about my health, but my illness exhausts me," Donna said.

"Are you sure it's the fever?" Anestasie said slyly. "You're not the first bride to be ill so soon after wedlock."

"It's not what you think," said Donna. "I would that you were right. I want a child." All of the emotions that had been welling up within Donna burst their bounds, and for one of the few times in her life she wept. "I hate myself for weeping," she cried. "But I must talk to someone, someone who understands. I don't feel sorry for myself, only baffled."

"What is it that bothers you? Honoria?"

"Yes, I feel that she's jealous of me."

"You can keep her in her place," Anestasie said. "That bit of baggage is not your equal. Your wits are more than a match for her."

Donna wiped her eyes and tried to smile. "Have you ever wanted to tear a woman's hair out? To scratch her face? If Honoria weren't my Sam'l's sister, I'd cook her goose. But it isn't a fair fight. I have weapons that she doesn't have, but I cannot stoop to use them. And I have dignity. That is, I'm supposed to have, but at times I hate dignity. I cannot have a scene in my household with my sister-in-law. It would not injure her dignity, for she has none, but it would cheapen me in the eyes of my husband and my household."

"Dignity or no dignity, I'd put the girl in her place. I'd tell her that unless she ceases any annoyance you'll tell your husband and have her sent back to Georgia."

Donna shrugged. "But I cannot do that. There's a pact between Sam'l and Honoria, a pact that they would stick together. They worship each other. I'm sure if I insisted upon Sam's sending her away, he'd do so. But it would make him very unhappy. And I cannot stand to see him unhappy. Honoria seems to be ridiculing me all the time. She resents me. She seems to think I'm lazy, a sickly woman and already a burden to Sam."

"She'd have resented any woman who married her brother," Anestasie said. "She's a minx, Donna. I've told you so before. You mustn't humor her. If you do, she'll take advantage of your good nature. You should tell your husband your thoughts."

"But I don't want to tell Sam'l. He might laugh at my idea and that would pain me. I cannot put my finger on anything she has done. I can show him no proof. But even if he believed me, that she is a danger to our happiness, he couldn't send her away without breaking his heart. Where could she go? I'll not have Sam'l thinking that there is bitterness between me and his sister. He knows I'm a good wife. She cannot poison his mind. Mind you, Anestasie, I know she dare not speak ill of me to him. But it's just the way she does things. There are little things that I want to do for my husband, for his comfort, and when I start to do them Honoria always says, 'Let me do them, you're ill.' And Sam'l thinks she's being good to me. When I protest he agrees with her and tells me that I should rest and take care of myself."

"A man does not see such things," Anestasie said. "I know how you feel, and I see the danger. Honoria needs a husband. Has Tishomingo shown her any mind?"

"No. I don't think he cares for Honoria, except that she's Sam'l's sister. I don't believe that Tishomingo loves anybody, do you?"

"If I didn't have a husband, I'd see that he did." Anestasie laughed. "He's my choice of all the men I have seen in the new land, except of course, Sam'l."

"And Flournoy?"

"He's a fascinating man, isn't he?" Anestasie said. "Did you notice how Honoria ogled him?"

"He's not fascinating to me," said Donna. "I don't like anything about him—his house, his clothes, his manner. Ab is in love with Honoria. He's almost beside himself when she's around. There's a good match for her."

Anestasie patted her hand. "You're the most beautiful sick woman I've ever seen and soon you'll be well. You'll forget your illness when you begin building your home. Mind you, if you haven't a son within a year I'll give you a present. I'll wager it."

"I'll not wager, for I would win."

"You're silly to worry about such a thing," Anestasie said. "You're still a bride. It wouldn't be proper to be with child so soon."

"The doctor said I must not have a child so long as this fever persists. My fear is that the fever will sap my strength, and I can never have a child." A man's manliness was judged by his sons, and a woman's worth was measured by the sons she could produce. A man's wealth was judged by his horses, his cattle and his lands. But a man without a son was poor indeed. If a woman did not give her husband a son within a year or two after her wedding, people shook their heads and believed she was barren. Donna feared that the fever would defeat her greatest desire.

"You also fear Honoria's taunts," Anestasie said. "You think she's looking at you in ridicule because you're ill with fever and not with child. You're overly sensitive. This new land has upset you. You're nervous. It's proper for a bride to be upset. It will pass."

Donna thought once that she would tell Anestasie that her lungs hurt and that she feared she had the lung fever. The fever, she knew, was weakening her courage. She was losing her spirit and could do naught about it. She wanted to tell Anestasie that she was discouraged, but fearing Anestasie would think she wanted sympathy, she kept her thoughts to herself. She had come to the new land to live and to make her home. And fevers and Honoria would not defeat her. She remembered how proud Sam had been of her the night Dabby was born. She remembered how his eyes had sparkled as he watched her, the mistress of the Chadbourne place, directing the slaves about their duties and managing a plantation. But that was back there in the old land, land that she knew and understood, where the sharp air stirred the blood. This was a new land, dank and brooding. The air was sweet and burdened and crept through the lungs and made the eyes heavy and the muscles tired.

Donna had never seen such a board as was set at *Maison Blanche*. Even in Tidewater the planters did not set such a table. She was rather shocked, but nevertheless pleased, when Lake Fournoy offered his arm to Honoria as they went to the banquet room. It would have been proper for him to have offered his arm to Donna. He sat Honoria at his right and Sam at his left, and the first toast he drank was to the Dabneys but he looked at Honoria and her brother as he raised his glass. André, gallant as always, quickly raised his glass to Donna and toasted her. He cut his eyes quickly at Lake Flournoy, then at Sam. Sam had noticed nothing, but André, sensitive and alert, sensed a meaning in their host's actions. André's eyes narrowed and his brow furrowed. He did not like the man. He did not trust him.

A house slave stood between each couple and saw to their needs. First a light French soup was served and a light wine.

"It's a special feast," Honoria said gayly.

Flournoy said, "This is a wedding banquet for your brother and his bride."

When the chicken à la Malabar was fetched, Honoria remarked enthusiastically, "I must know how to make this. I'll make some for Sam'l."

"It's very good," Sam said. "Food fit for a king. But I like roast pig, too. My wife knows how to roast a pig. You must visit us sometime, Mr. Flournoy, and my wife will have the slaves prepare a pig for you that will melt in your mouth."

Donna could have kissed him then. She wanted to very badly. She slipped her hand under the table and patted his leg. Sam didn't realize he had said anything unusual or done anything worthy of a caress, but he was pleased at Donna's attention.

"You shall have the recipe," Flournoy said to Honoria.

They also ate pigeon stuffed with veal. Cheese and syllabub were served and the company went to the drawing room for coffee and brandy.

Flournoy was the perfect host, and again Sam felt ill at ease in his presence. Flournoy had a way of making light conversation that pleased the ladies.

295

"I have coffee among my goods," Sam said as he sipped his delicious brew. "I hope to trade it to the Indians."

"I had heard of that," said Flournoy. "André told me. Rum is better merchandise. But let's not talk of business. Tell us more about France, André—of the Revolution and this Bonaparte who is seeing so much of my kinswoman."

Anestasie said sharply, "This Bonaparte is a rogue. He struts like a little gamecock."

"Is he nobly born?" asked Flournoy.

"Heavens, no! He acts as though he were born in a stable," Anestasie snapped.

Flournoy frowned. "He must not be such a rogue or my kinswoman would not tolerate his company."

"He is a rogue," maintained Anestasie firmly, "and if your kinswoman doesn't know it, she's blind."

Lake Flournoy passed over the remark. "I'll not banter words with a lady," he said.

"Particularly a French lady with a sharp tongue," laughed Anestasie. "If you loved your kinswoman as you say you do, you'd be wise to bring her here, or have her return to Martinique. France is a boiling pot of intrigue and corruption."

Sam changed the subject and gave Flournoy the latest news from Natchez. "The landing there is jammed with keel boats. When New Orleans is opened to the United States—and, mind you, it will be or there will be war— a score of ships will leave this land every day for Europe. . . . Are they bringing many goods down the Natchez Trace from Tennessee?"

"You'll talk nothing but business," Flournoy chided him. "Yes, many trains are coming down the Trace."

"What are these outlaws and land pirates along the Trace? The terrible Harpes?"

"What know you of the Harpes?" asked Flournoy.

"Only what I heard in Natchez—that they were raiding along the Trace."

"They're very dangerous men," said Flournoy. "The Harpes, Micajah and Wiley, are brothers. They call Wiley, Little Harpe. There's a rumor that they are part Negro. I have heard much of them from my drovers who travel the Trace. Their father was a Tory. After the Revolution, the brothers were driven from North Carolina by the Americans because their father fought with the British. They went to Tennessee. They've been raiding along the Wilderness Trail, as well as on the Trace and along the river."

"Are they as bloody as I was told?"

"I don't like to tell such stories in the presence of ladies, but the Harpes are butchers. Little Harpe said, so I was told, that the only murder he ever regretted was when he brained his wife's child because it cried. Incidentally, it was not his child."

Honoria said, "What charming people they must be."

"Yes, they lure the keel boats to the banks and butcher the men and steal the goods. The bodies of the men are never found, for the Harpes cut out their stomachs, fill the cavities with rocks and sink the bodies. A lone traveler isn't safe on the Trace."

"Why don't the authorities do something about it?" André demanded.

"That's easier said than done," Flournoy continued. "Much of the Trace is in the Chickasaw Nation and Americans have no legal right to travel it without permission. The Spanish and American authorities would think twice before they sent an army into a friendly nation, even to capture the Harpes."

"That is where you're wrong," Sam said. "The Americans at Natchez are going to send an expedition against the Harpes unless the raiding ceases. My friend, Lieutenant Abernathy, told me so. Word has already been sent up the Trace that if one more American is molested the soldiers will hunt the Harpes and hang them, even if it means war with the Chickasaws. The Americans threaten to send troops with each train."

"That's an excellent idea," said Flournoy. "But what of the Spaniards? Will the United States protect the Spanish travelers, too?"

Sam shrugged his shoulders, "I suppose not. Why should we protect them?"

The ladies retired early and the men fell to discussing business and their plans. Flournoy signed the contracts to pay Sam a percentage of his slave profits if the territory, which everyone knew would be formed, forbade the importation of slaves and made the smuggling of bumboes profitable.

André had told Flournoy about the plans for the cotton gin and no talk was necessary to sell Flournoy on the idea of manufacturing them and operating them under lease from Dabney.

"It's the greatest plan I've ever heard," said Flournoy. "The gin will increase the price of slaves too. The opening of New Orleans will give us access to Europe. I'll gin the cotton of every planter along the Yazoo and Big Black. You'll take care of the Halfway River business and André will have the Tombigbee. It's a deal and we'll drink to it." He called for brandy and drank to their success.

"Ay," said Sam. "It's a superfine plan. I have grants from the Indian agent to open a factory. I also have a grant for André. The Choctaws are willing and anxious that we should trade with them. If you'll get me a grant from the Chickasaws to send a trader into their land,

I'll return the favor with a grant to you to trade south of here in the territory of the land company I represent."

"Who'll do your trading among the Chickasaws?" Flournoy asked.

"The one you spoke of—Ab. He's the fitting man for the job. He's not afraid of the devil. He's not even afraid of snakes. And he can blow a fly speck off of a horse's mane at a hundred yards."

Flournoy said, "I'm anxious to meet him. I've heard much of him."

Shortly after dawn the next morning, Sam and André and their wagon trains departed from *Maison Blanche*, heading southeast for Locha Poka. On the way they would stop at the lodge of Tishomingo, and from Locha Poka André and his company would go back to the Tombigbee, and build their home. Flournoy rode with them to the Big Black, waved them Godspeed and, when they were beyond sight, he rode up the Trace for forty miles, abandoned the road and went into the swamps to "The Nest," the haven of the terrible Harpes.

"Why do you come here?" Little Harpe demanded when he saw Flournoy. "It's dangerous. You might get us all drawn and quartered."

"Perhaps I came to make a check upon my lovely band of butchers. Perhaps you've been cheating me."

"Your talk is not witty. We've kept our promise; one quarter of all the goods we've taken has gone to you. You have no complaint, you're getting rich and taking no chances."

Flournoy said, "If you're not pleased with your position I'll engage another leader. After all, I give you protection from the Chickasaws and you would never capture a single keel boat or traveler without my intelligence."

Little Harpe grumbled, "I'm satisfied with the arrangement."

"Then mind your tongue, or some day your tongue will anger me and I'll cut it out and stuff it down your throat."

"Well, why are you here?" Little Harpe asked again. "Are you bringing us news of another horse train or a parcel of keel boats? And since when did the great Flournoy act as his own messenger?"

"I'm here to tell you not to molest any Americans until I give you the signal. I don't care if your neck is stretched, but I am very proud of my neck. It's the best neck I've ever had, and I believe that if a rope were around your neck you would tell more than you should and somebody might believe you."

"We'll do as you say," said Little Harpe. "But what of the Spaniards?"

Flournoy turned his horse back toward *Maison Blanche*. "Who cares for Spaniards?" he said. "And too, I need some more fine wines. Also a shawl, if you can get one—a pretty shawl for a pretty woman."

17

✬ ✬

TISHOMINGO's lodge was near a creek, almost in the shadows of Nanih Waiya, the sacred mound of his nation. It was a small lodge of only two rooms. Behind his house was the cabin of Caesar, and near by was a long, roomy lodge built of pine and roofed with broom sage. The train halted by the creek and camp was made while Sam went to the lodge of his friend. It was deserted, and Sam found Tishomingo in the long house, drawing rude characters on a smooth board and lecturing to a group of Choctaw children. None of the children was a flathead and each face was very clean.

Tishomingo put his arm around Sam and presented him to the children, who arose from their wooden benches and bowed very politely and solemnly. Then Tishomingo dismissed them and they bowed again, and each child said, "I go, good day."

"Where's your wife?" They were Tishomingo's first words. "I must go see her and wish her happiness and take her a wedding gift." He asked next of Ab, then of Honoria. Sam noticed that his question about Honoria was casual, as though he asked it only to be polite.

"We'll go to the camp, soon," Sam said. "But first I must know about you. Who are these children? And what of this alphabet?"

"The alphabet still is mostly a dream," Tishomingo

301

said. "In my spare time, I've been working for years trying to invent a Choctaw alphabet. I would that our history could be written in the Choctaw language, so posterity would not judge us by the word of the white man."

"It's a noble task," said Sam. "But what of the children?"

Chock looked at the empty benches and at his crude drawings. "It's a school, Big Sam. I told you naught of this for fear you might laugh at me. The children you saw are my students. I'm teaching them the history of their people. I'm trying to teach them dignity. I hope to teach them all of the virtues of the white man. That should not take long." He smiled at his friend. "The white man is here to stay and these children soon will be the leaders of our nation and I want them to know how to live in peace and happiness with the white man. I'll teach only children whose parents have not suffered them to be flatheads. I teach them personal health and the songs and stories of our people. If I can invent my alphabet I'll teach them to write in Choctaw."

"When do you find the time for such work?"

"I have naught else to do. I travel sometimes for my uncle but most of my time is my own. Some day I'll have a great school here. Perhaps you'll help me. I need more teachers, a white teacher or two, maybe a missionary who'll be willing to teach my children the story of Christ, but who must not insist that my children adopt Christianity. My greatest handicap, of course, is money, or the lack of it. I'm a prince of the Choctaws but I'm a poor man. Flournoy is the only rich man in our nation."

The news delighted Sam. He sat on a bench and motioned Tishomingo to sit by him and he recounted all that had happened at *Maison Blanche*. "I knew you'd help me. I knew you'd do anything to injure Flournoy. And now I'm doubly sure, for there's money in my plan and you can use the money for your school. I'll give you three percentum of all the monies you collect from Flournoy."

Tishomingo said, "I'm your man, but I see many hazards. I'll not live in Louisiana."

"No. Flournoy's slave cargoes will arrive four or five times a year and you'll only have to be there when the ships come in to see that our interests are protected. You'll not deliver to me my seven percentum but will use the money to buy slaves."

"Ay?"

"Ay. You'll pay Flournoy the same price that he has been realizing for slaves, about three hundred dollars each. We'll not pay the high price."

"But Flournoy's no fool," Chock said. "He'll charge you the top prices for his slaves."

"He will not. Flournoy will be engaged in slave-running. He'll not dare to cross us."

Tishomingo shook his head, "But we, too, will be engaged in smuggling and be as guilty as he."

"You're in error. My lawyer in Natchez showed me a way in which we'll not be involved. Our contracts show that I'll receive ten percentum of certain monies for certain merchandise disposed of by Flournoy. You simply are my agent to collect this money. It will not be against the law to bring slaves to Barataria and there you'll collect the money. The law will be broken when Flournoy runs the slaves from Louisiana into the United States, and we'll not be involved in that."

"Did you ever hear the story of how the fox outwitted himself?" Chock began.

303

Sam interrupted him. "Save your Choctaw stories for your students."

"I was only thinking of you," Chock said. "My hands will be clean and I have naught to fear from the white man's laws, for I'm a prince of a friendly nation. But if I'm to take your money and buy slaves in Louisiana from among Flournoy's cargo, how will you get them here without violating the law that you say the white man will pass?"

Sam got up and stretched. "That's the most beautiful part of my plan. Jasper and Caesar will bring them in. You will buy only females for me, young wenches. I'm deeding Jasper to you and will pay you one dollar a year for his services."

"Who knows of this?"

"It's a pact between us. No one knows my plan except you. Legally Jasper will belong to you, but he must not know it. You will agree, of course, that he will stay in my service as long as I want him and I may buy him back for one dollar at any time."

"You have plotted well," Tishomingo said. "You also know that if I own Jasper your government can levy no tax against him."

"Ay, I have thought of that. I might even deed many of my slaves to you and hire them for a pittance."

"I'll not do that," Tishomingo said. "I'll do anything to complete my vengeance upon Flournoy, but I'll not use my position to flaunt your nation's laws."

"Well spoken. Now when Jasper and Caesar cross the boundary from Louisiana with two or three women with them, no one will question them. In all appearances the wenches will be their wives or daughters. If they are questioned, then Jasper and Caesar are the slaves of a Choctaw prince and have a perfect right to bring their wives and daughters to you. But they'll not be questioned. From Barataria they'll bring the slaves in the lower route, across the Mississippi's nearest delta and up through the swamps on the east side. They'll see nothing on the journey except muskrats and birds. There will be none to question them."

"It's a dangerous plan," Chock insisted. "But I'm with you."

"Flournoy thinks the price of slaves will go to six hundred dollars. They'll go higher than that. When this land is open and the slave traffic is limited, a fine buck will be worth $1500 in the new territory. Mark my words. We'll pay only about $300 for each slave at Barataria. For every slave that Flournoy sells for $1500, our commission will be $150. When he sells two slaves our commission will be large enough to buy one slave. So every third slave that Flournoy brings in will be ours. Do you see the beauty of my plan?"

The cunning and hatred that Sam had first seen in Tishomingo's eyes reappeared now. Chock glanced into the woods, thinking of the pleasure he would derive in outwitting Flournoy. Any triumph over Flournoy was revenge. He could not stick a big knife into his enemy yet, but he could prick him with needles and thorns. He could not cut him to pieces with his bull whip now, but he could lash him with willow switches until his flesh cringed in agony. The mere thought of Flournoy suffering, even in a business deal, gave Tishomingo a glow of savage delight.

"It will be like gall to Flournoy," Tishomingo said. "Ay, I'll help you. But what assurance have we that Flournoy will keep importing slaves when he realizes that we are growing rich while he is taking the risk?"

"His greed and his pride are our assurances. He'll

305

never admit that we've beaten him. And, too, his profits will be great. There are contracts at his house that you must go and sign as my agent. Make sure they are witnessed by a man you trust. And when Flournoy signs his name, tell him then that we want slaves, and that unless he sells us slaves at the price he has been getting for them, we'll call the deal off and turn the contracts over to Lieutenant Abernathy, who is my friend, and who will believe me if I tell him that Flournoy tried to trick us. Flournoy will do anything to prevent a scandal."

Tishomingo lighted a pipe and passed it to Sam and they smoked on their new partnership and while they sat there smoking Tishomingo told Sam the news. The first pigeon that Sam had released had reached Chadbourne long before the Choctaw runner got there. More Shawnees were moving among the Creeks. Tecumseh's twin was preaching a crusade in the Ohio country.

"The white man knows naught of this," Tishomingo said. "Tecumseh's brother is calling himself 'The Open Door.' His following is small now, but soon it will be large and the white man will hear of the prophet and realize his power. His teachings are good. He tells his followers to shun whiskey and other of the white man's evils. He is denouncing witchcraft and tells his people to discard flint and steel of the invaders and return to the simple ways of their forefathers. The white men in the Northwest have made a treaty with the Indians. It is another treaty the white man will not keep, but it has opened many new lands to the white man. Lands around Fort Wayne and Detroit."

"When you took the train to Flournoy's, did you tell him about Ab?"

"Ay, he knows and he's afraid. He wonders how much

you know, and if I will tell Ab. Doubt and fear are twins and torture him."

Tishomingo took Donna a tiny gold cross and gifts of blankets and wampum. Honoria, seeing him walking through the woods with Sam, ran to him, and Tishomingo greeted her politely. She thought at least he could have kissed her hand and asked of her health. Spitefully she said, "We had a banquet at Mr. Flournoy's home. He's a great man, isn't he, and handsome and rich?"

"Yes," said Chock, "he's a very rich man."

Tishomingo took her arm to assist her over a log. It thrilled her, and when he released her arm she took his for support. Her touch warmed Tishomingo's flesh, but he looked straight ahead, affecting a nonchalance that infuriated and baffled Honoria. She felt his flesh tremble under her touch, but his eyes were cold and his lips were buttoned. He was not human. How could a man's flesh tremble when his eyes were cold? Sam walked ahead to tell the company that Tishomingo was coming.

"Tell me, Chock," Honoria asked, "who is Ta-lo-wah?"

Tishomingo stopped suddenly, gripped her shoulders and glared at her. "Did Flournoy mention her to you?"

"No, the slaves told me of her. My curiosity was aroused." Honoria was not afraid of Tishomingo's glare, and his grip on her shoulders delighted her.

The Indian released his grip and she took his arm again as they walked on. "Your curiosity is not becoming," he said. "She was Flournoy's mistress, a white woman who went to him because he was rich. She was a very beautiful woman, about your size with hair like yours."

Honoria held his arm tightly as he spoke. "Do you

think I am beautiful?" she asked, her lips parting and her eyes radiant.

"Yes, you're very beautiful. You're almost too beautiful. Ta-lo-wah was too beautiful. And she was a good woman in all ways except one. She was ambitious and proud. When she came to the nation she was poor and happy. But she went to Flournoy because he was rich. Flournoy tired of her and left her bed for the couch of a Martinique wench, the bath slave. Ta-lo-wah withered and died. She couldn't stand the disgrace."

"It's a sad story," Honoria said. "But I don't blame Flournoy. If his woman couldn't hold him, it was her fault and not his."

Donna was very grateful when Tishomingo gave her the cross and told her that it had belonged to his mother, a gift of his English father.

Honoria looked longingly at the cross. "Why do you give it to another man's wife?" she demanded of Tishomingo. "You should have saved it for your own bride."

Donna pressed her lips together to smother the bitter words that were in her throat. Tishomingo measured his words carefully. "My mother was a good woman and she would want her cross to go to a good woman."

The words had a double meaning and Sam could say naught. Anestasie looked gratefully at Tishomingo and there was admiration in her eyes for him, but her heart went out to Sam. If he condemned Tishomingo it would be a slur at his wife. Ay, Anestasie thought, Tishomingo was cruel, cruel even to his friend and to Honoria. She hated Honoria, but now she felt sorry for her.

Honoria's eyes filled with tears, but she blinked them away and said softly to Tishomingo, "There is no need to tell us your mother was a good woman. You are evidence of her goodness and kindness."

308

They, too, were bitter words and Sam turned on his sister. "Your tongue is forked. Mind your manners. If my friend elects to give my wife a beautiful present, it is no concern of yours."

His sister recoiled as though he had struck her and then she regained her poise and clenched her fists and stared at him. He would remember that insult.

Donna suddenly was glad. It was the first time she had heard Sam upbraid his sister, but she, too, had a measure of pity for Honoria and she told Tishomingo, "Honoria is right, you should save this token for your bride."

"I want you to have it," he said. "For you are the bride of my brother. The lodge of Tishomingo will always be empty."

Honoria felt that the words were cruel and unnecessary. Sam tried to pass it over; he slapped Chock's back and said, "You're a wise man, my friend. Look at me, I'm a foolish man; I've lost my liberty. But I'm happy to be without it." He put his arm around Donna and kissed her in front of everyone.

It was a hearty kiss, and its meaning made Donna blush, but she was very happy. She chided Sam to save her own dignity. However, that kiss was something she would always treasure. If husbands would just learn, she thought, to be attentive to their wives in the presence of other women. . . . If they would just flatter their wives in public. Law! the hurts that a few words of flattery and a few gestures of attention could heal.

"A beautiful gesture," said André. "Now put the cross around her neck and make a wish."

As Sam fastened the tiny chain, Donna turned her head slightly and whispered, "It's a beautiful gift and I'll always cherish it. At night I'll keep it by the conch shell that you brought me."

They feasted that night and made merry, for it was a parting of the ways for many of them. They exchanged stories and sang songs and at Sam's suggestion Tishomingo told them about the school. Honoria got to her feet when she heard the story and crossed near the fire and sat on a log beside Chock and Sam.

"There's a favor I would ask," she said. "Let me help you with the school. Sam'l can get along without me. Even though Donna is sick and puny, she can give orders to the slaves."

"I don't give orders to my slaves," Donna remarked quickly. "My slaves know my orders and obey them. A good mistress does not have to give orders. Running a household, Honoria, is an art. I believe I could spare you, if your brother is willing."

A torrent of abuse rushed to Honoria's tongue, but she swallowed it and smiled. She wanted something of Sam and she would be a fool to antagonize him by quarreling with Donna.

Sam had not understood Donna's sarcasm and he laughed. "There's a woman for you," he patted his sister's cheek and was ashamed that he had spoken so harshly to her. "She loves my wife so much that she wants to relieve her of the burdens of running a house. Ay, Honoria, Donna was managing a big plantation when you and I were running through the woods seeking hickory nuts and honey so there would be food upon our table. What could you do at the school?"

"You forget the things I learned when I was bound out to Mr. Frome. I could teach the children to sew and cook. I could keep them clean. It would be a noble task for a woman."

"What say you, Chock?" Sam asked. "My sister would become a school mar'm to the new land."

310

"I am not ready yet to bring in white teachers," Tishomingo said. "There's no place for her to live."

"I could live in the village at one of the lodges," Honoria protested. "Please, Chock, let me do it. I'd work only for my keep."

Tishomingo dared not refuse her. It would have been an insult to Sam and, too, Honoria could be a great help. She also was very beautiful and Tishomingo was often lonely.

Sam studied the ground for several minutes turning the idea over in his mind. His sister in a Choctaw school would be a good stroke of diplomacy. It would draw the Choctaws closer to him. It would strengthen the ties between his nation and Tishomingo's nation. He knew a time was coming when those ties would be strained. He knew his country would need the Choctaws in the inevitable struggle with the Creeks and perhaps with the Spaniards. Harkins would compliment him when he heard that he had placed his sister in a Choctaw school. Even the big-wigs at Philadelphia might hear of his wisdom. Yes, it would be a good stroke. The Indians would praise him for his charity and the white people of the territory would approve his actions. He would need all the white friends he could get, for there was certain to be an issue on slavery in the new territory.

"I must think about it," said Sam. But his mind was already settled on the problem. "Of course I would trust my sister with you, Chock. She could live in the village and go to your school each day. Your nation has been good to me and I am anxious to repay that goodness. Besides, it's a good business. Honoria can teach the children to drink coffee and can point out to them the evils of rum. I'm going to sell coffee, you know. I hope that the Indians will cease drinking rum and drink coffee. A drunkard Indian is a liability, an industrious Indian means prosperity for us all."

When they were alone that night, Donna told Sam that she hoped he would allow Honoria to take up the work. She explained that it would widen Honoria's horizon.

"You're right," Sam agreed. "There's only one thing I worry about. Honoria is my father's child and is like him in many ways. She's an impetuous girl. I believe she loves Tishomingo. I would not want my sister to throw herself at a man."

"I threw myself at you, but you didn't know it."

"That's prattle."

"It's the truth," she said without shame. "You could have had my hand or me the first night you saw me if you had been a bold man. But you weren't. You're a big timid Irishman." She rubbed his hair playfully. She was feeling much better.

"Nevertheless, I don't want my sister to be indiscreet."

Donna said, "I think Honoria is growing very fond of Tishomingo. Their association will be a source of joy to both. Tishomingo is a lonely man."

"Have you any other reason for wanting Honoria to take the work?" Sam asked.

"Yes, Sam'l, I have. I want you to myself. I am a selfish wife. I don't want to share your time with anyone. Not even your sister."

"If you wish it, I'll do it." He got up and dressed and walked noiselessly from camp, through the woods to Tishomingo's lodge, but he was not there. He called softly and Tishomingo answered him. He found his friend in the woods, sitting on the needles under a pine and beside a grave.

"Whose grave is this?" Sam asked.

"It is hers—Ta-lo-wah's, Amelia's. I brought her body here and it is a joy to me to come here at night and think."

"You're sentimental, Tishomingo," Sam said and sat beside his friend.

"Maybe I am. Maybe some day you'll understand. These woods are very lonely and I like to come here and speak aloud. Maybe she can hear me. Who knows? Who knows what the spirit is, Big Sam? Or where it is. I'm glad that I could bring her here. Only an Indian can be buried in the earth of Nanih Waiya, but my love is buried almost in the shadows of the sacred mound."

Sam told him that he would allow Honoria to work at the school.

"I'm glad," Tishomingo said, and he really was. He had sensed the strain between Donna and Honoria. He would do his friend a favor, and give Donna peace. "She can be of much help to me, and my people will not forget your kindness." Then he spoke of Donna's health to Sam.

"I doubt if she has the lung fever," Tishomingo said. "I have seen much of the lung fever. It's a gift to us from the white man. But if she has only the swamp fever, make her rest, Big Sam. I have seen strong men and women come to this land and waste away. If she doesn't improve you should send her back to Georgia."

"If it's necessary for her health, I'll move back to Georgia too," said Sam. "My wife means more to me than my ambition."

"That shouldn't be necessary. If the fever seems to have a grip on her, why not let her go back to the hills until she can break the grip?"

"We'll see."

They made arrangements the next morning for Honoria to stay in a village lodge and Sam left her goods and money, kissed her goodbye and walked away, leaving Donna and Honoria alone. Donna kissed her too, lightly on the cheek. But Honoria threw her arms around Donna. "You're a sweet woman, Donna," she said. "I know that you asked Sam'l to let me do this."

"You're right," said Donna. "I've a great desire to look after Sam'l without the interference of his sister."

Honoria's eyes flashed. "Sam'l would scold you if he knew you said that."

"Come with me," said Donna, "and I'll tell him I said it. There are many other things I'll tell him too. Shall we take our quarrel to him and let him settle it?"

"No," said Honoria, fearing the result. "I'll not burden my brother with such a chore. It would hurt him to know that his wife and his sister have quarreled. You don't love him as I do or you would think of such things."

"You don't know what love is."

"I know if I had a husband, I would not sicken so quickly after my wedding, and I would be strong enough to give him a child." Honoria's tone was brittle. Donna turned and left her and rejoined the train.

André and Anestasie headed their horses east for the Tombigbee, and Sam and Donna and all of their goods moved west for Locha Poka and the Halfway River, which some men called the Pearl and which the Indians called Hot-che-ah. Sam and Donna slept under the Big Tree until a cabin was built, a cabin with one room and no windows. He built a bed of green pine, and the sap oozed out and formed hard little blobs and turned brown. The bare earth was the floor. He and the slaves built a fireplace and a chimney of sticks and clay.

314

Next he built shelters for his goods. A permanent pen for his cattle and a stable for his horses.

Deep autumn came and Locha Poka began to take shape, a definite form, and no longer was just a cluster of cabins in the wilderness. A little ferry ran across the Halfway River. A rope was strung across the stream and the ferry was worked with two pulleys. Every day the men built at least one hundred feet of road. The foundation for the foundry was laid and a rude trading factory was built. On a pine board Sam wrote his name, "S. Dabney, Factor." He nailed the sign over the door to his post. Once a week he sent a teamster to Tishomingo's school and the teamster fetched perfume that Honoria had made. Sam sold it and kept track of his sister's profits. He also sold baskets and wampum made at the school and credited the earnings to Tishomingo. He traded needles for hides, rum for beeswax, soap, which Donna helped to make, for indigo, perfume for hickory-nut oil and once a week he sent his goods to Natchez to be sold.

Ab arrived from Georgia in record time and brought news from Pierce and Frome. Mr. Frome already was ginning cotton and Sam had accrued a profit. Many of the land deals in the West had been proved frauds and there was much agitation in Georgia. Some of the companies had ignored the Spanish and Indian rights in selling the land and the scandal echoed in Congress. But Sam's company, one of the smallest, had clear title to its land by right of treaty and purchase. The wave of pro-French feeling in the Southeast was running its course and the people were becoming disgusted with the leaders of the French republic. A treaty with the bey of Algiers soon would be signed, and the United States no longer would be molested by the pirates. The nation was building ships and keeping its skirts clear of the European

315

mess. Washington's Declaration of Neutrality was popular with the people. The name of John Adams was on many tongues and many of the southerners favored him as Washington's successor. But the westerners opposed him. He was a blue-nose, and the westerners wanted no blue-nose at the head of the State. They wanted a man who would fight Spain. There was talk that Washington would not stand for a third term. Such talk was silly. Washington would be president as long as he lived.

Sam realized a good profit on his first post. Donna wrote down all of the news that Ab had brought back and sent the intelligence to Lawyer Thomas. Thomas passed the message around in the taverns of Natchez and charged men a shilling to read it. Ab built his shack down the river from Locha Poka. He often rode over to see Tishomingo and to visit with Honoria and he always took her a gift. He was disappointed that Honoria was not living at Locha Poka, but he was happy because she was happy with her work. The friendship between Ab and Tishomingo grew until even Jasper remarked upon the beauty of it. The Choctaw mingo gave the Kentuckian new buckskins and taught him how to use the bull whip as a weapon. Ab helped with the school when he was not busy with Sam. He taught the little Indians many tunes and soon the village was ringing with the drover songs. Ab was very popular in the village. When the Choctaws saw him they always smiled, but none ever revealed to him that they had known his sister.

Once Ab said to Sam, "Ay, that Chock is a great man. Sharp as a meat ax and sentimental as a loon. He often goes at night and sits by a grave, his mother's grave I reckon. The Choctaws love their dead, you know. He just sits there for hours, staring into the night. He must have loved his mother very much."

316

Sam did not reply but turned away so Ab could not see the look in his eyes.

Flournoy kept in touch with Sam. He already was manufacturing gins and hoped to have them working the next year. If he was angry at Sam, there was no betrayal of it in his correspondence. He even flattered Sam and said it was an honor to work with such a wise man. Donna warned Sam of the flattery.

The terrible Harpes raided an American train, despite Flournoy's orders, and soldiers were sent after them. Flournoy joined the soldiers, determined to kill the Harpes himself. The brothers, however, escaped, and got word to Flournoy that they would raid when and where they pleased.

Flournoy was annoyed by their impudence. With other planters in Natchez he posted a reward for their heads. Then he made a deal with the Clewy brothers, Jacob and Esau. For Flournoy's protection and information about trains and boats, the Clewys agreed to give him one fourth of their loot, and they agreed to take orders. Flournoy instructed them to make "The Nest" the headquarters for their band, and to send word to the Harpes that so long as the Harpes raided only along the upper Trace there would be no conflict between the bands. But he personally promised a thousand dollars to the outlaw who would fetch him the scalps of the terrible Harpes. The Clewys did not molest American trains or the travelers who were moving down the Trace from Kentucky and Tennessee. They robbed only the Spaniards and Indians. The traders who went to *Maison Blanche* to buy and sell were waylaid by the Clewys after they had done business with Flournoy. The land pirates never bothered to conceal their faces, but always killed their victims and threw their bodies into the swamps. At

317

Flournoy's suggestion, the Clewys built cabins on the Trace and moved their families there and passed as respectable citizens. Once they even led a posse in search of themselves.

Honoria worked hard at the school, seeking to impress Tishomingo. She always hurried from the village to the school to be with him as quickly as possible, and she was reluctant to leave. Tishomingo scarcely noticed her presence, and once she asked, "Why do you shun me?"

"I do not shun you."

"You act as though I weren't here," she said. "Am I a knot on a log to be treated as such?"

Tishomingo said, "I'm sorry if I've been aloof. I didn't mean to be."

His calmness infuriated her. "Don't think that I've been lonely," she said. "Ab comes to see me and brings me presents."

"Ab is a good man," Tishomingo said.

"And Lake Flournoy has sent me a letter. He says he is sending me a beautiful shawl. 'A beautiful shawl for a beautiful lady'—those were his words."

"Flournoy is a very rich man. He can afford to buy you a shawl."

When the shawl arrived several days later, Honoria wore it to the school, hoping Tishomingo would be jealous. He complimented her. Then he examined the shawl closely and that night he sent Caesar to Lake Flournoy with a message.

"That shawl," he wrote, "might become a hangman's noose around your neck if Tishomingo were not determined to kill you some day with a bull whip."

He told Flournoy no more, but Tishomingo knew that the Harpes had raided a Spanish train several weeks before and had taken silks and madeira. What would the terrible Harpes want with fine shawls and fine wines?

The autumn brought rain. The curse of the season was upon the land and the rains fell day and night, a swishing rain that made the earth soggy. The supports of the foundry crumbled and the floor of the cabin was muddy until Sam cut pine boards and put them on the floor.

Sam and Donna had never seen such rain. It pounded the earth and then it swished and blew across the land, caressing it and cleansing it. The earth seemed to open its arms to the rain and to gulp it and to swell up. The earth seemed big'd, pregnant with rain. The earth was conceiving. It was the mating season for earth and sky and a billion seeds were in the earth's womb. The stars looked red and the moon was pallid and sought to hide its face, ashamed to watch the tryst between earth and sky. The old Indians said it was the season when the snakes left the swamps and crawled about the earth and led men and women into the ways of evil. The devil was abroad. The slaves wore their tobies around their necks and prayed to their voodoo gods.

And it kept raining. The bayous got full, and there was a rumbling in their bellies. The river got full and crept out of its banks exploring the swamps. The ferry was washed away. The rain washed up the logs in the road and the river carried the logs away. The cattle lowed all night and huddled under the dripping trees by day.

A slave died from a moccasin bite. Another bore twins. One of the mares foaled. Life moved on. The pine worms bored into the trees to escape the rain and their shavings and the dust of their work formed on the outsides of the trees until the wind blew the tree dust away. It scattered over the earth. Earthworms, the farmers of nature,

319

crawled to the surface and tilled the earth, crushing it. The wind blew seeds where the worms had worked and the tree dust covered the seeds. The rain beat the tree dust and the seeds into the ground, bigging the earth. Rain cannot stop life, Sam thought. Rain makes life. Only dust can stop life. Life thrives in dark gloomy places. It thrives as the ferns thrive, green and tender at first, then brittled and then withered.

Sam and his slaves worked despite the rain. They built a new ferry, new roads. He built another foundation for his foundry and moved in his forge. By God! he would make cotton gins. He would make cotton gins if he had to stand in a canoe and pump the bellows himself.

The rains went away and the winter came. It was a strange winter. Nothing seemed dead and the land still was lush. The leaves remained green. The holly trees put on their berries and the mistletoe grew. They broke the land. The oxen bogged while they worked but they broke up the land, ripped it, tore it, leaving great black wounds in the soft flesh of Locha Poka.

Sam began the big house that winter. The stones were fetched from Natchez. They had come from France in a ship in ballast. The first stone was laid on the brow of the slope, one hundred and fifty yards from the Big Tree. Workmen from Natchez pitched tents and built sheds on the slopes and lived there while they built Sam's mansion, a twelve-room mansion for old man Dabney's brat.

The post went to Georgia twice monthly. Ab hired a Choctaw and a Creek to help him. He always brought back news and Donna turned a penny distributing the news in Natchez through Lawyer Thomas. She was feeling better. The fever had gone away and there was color in her cheeks, a song in her heart, and hot blood in her veins. If the fevers did not come back she would have her child.

The high water had washed André's house away, but he had rebuilt it. André had sent to France for some of his kinsmen to settle in the new land.

Sam pledged his last acre, his post business and the twin slaves to get enough money to lay the foundation for Locha Poka. Next year he would build the first floor. His sweat would be on every board and shingle. Donna stayed by his side as he worked. She even helped measure the timber. Once when an ox team couldn't handle a big cypress, she brought up two more oxen and helped yoke them and cracked the whip over them until the job was done. Sukey worked in the kitchen and in the fields. Jasper toiled until his muscles became hard and stringy. Little Dabby played in the mud near the river and seemed to grow strong on it.

They celebrated Christmas in the trading post. Tishomingo and Honoria and Ab came, and Lawyer Thomas rode out from Natchez. It was he who brought the news.

"The treaty has been signed!" He shouted the words as he waddled into the house, his face flushed with rum and his little pot belly heaving with excitement.

Sam leaped to his feet and threw his arms around him. "Is this some of your drunken prattle—or is it the truth?"

"It's gospel truth," Thomas replied. "Treaty of San Lorenzo!"

Sam tossed his great head and pounded Thomas' back until the little lawyer coughed. Then Sam ordered rum. "And brandy, too," he shouted at Jasper. "And whiskey! Strong drink for the men and wine for the ladies. This is a day! Best news I've heard since Tyrone kicked the British."

Thomas chuckled. "Best news, Sam'l boy, since the

great Scipio salted Carthage and proclaimed forever the supremacy of the white race!" The little lawyer was working himself up to an oratorical outburst.

Sam handed him a drink. "Tell us about it!"

Thomas downed his drink, put his right hand under the breast of his frock tail coat and spoke eloquently. "Pinckney did it. Good old Pinckney. Pinckney for president, by God! If we had him in England instead of Jay we would have outwitted the damned British. New Orleans is open to us. We can trade to hell and back, from the Ohio country to the Gulf of Mexico. The Mississippi is open to us. It's our river now. Spain still claims it, and England thinks she owns its upper reaches, but, damme, give this country a toe-hold and we'll soon get our foot in. We can export from New Orleans without paying a duty, except a fair price for the hire of the stores. Spain cut her throat when she signed that treaty. She saved us the trouble of cutting it. Natchez is ours! Soon the Spanish troops will go and the United States will stretch from the Atlantic to the Mississippi. Tennessee is hossin' to become a state. Andy Jackson for Congress! We'll have a territory down here before you can skin a skunk. Europe is fixing to boil over again. Well, let her boil. While those fools are drowning in their own blood, we'll build this country. To the Mississippi? No river will stop us; it'll take an ocean! You'll see the day, Sam'l, when this country stretches to the Pacific. We'll drink to it, by God!"

"You're already drunk," Sam laughed. "Slow down and give me a chance to catch up with you."

Sam's words frightened Donna. She dreaded to see him drink. He got boastful and overconfident when he drank. But she kept her peace. A wife dared not criticize

322

her husband's drinking habits. However, she and Honoria stayed with the men only a short time and then retired.

It was the first time Tishomingo had ever seen his friend drink himself into a fit of loquacious stupidity. Liquor changed Dabney. His deep blue eyes became clouded and his black mane often fell over his face. He bragged loudly of the things he would do.

Thomas pointed an unsteady finger at him. "You can't drink, Sam'l boy. There never was a God damned Irishman who could drink!"

"What's this, Hosey—an insult?" Sam threw his head back and laughed uproariously.

"No one but my friends call me Hosey," Thomas growled.

"Am I not your friend?"

"Ay, Sam'l boy, you're my friend. You can call me Hosey. My father used to call me Hosey when I was a little boy."

"My father called me Sam. My mother called me Samuel."

Ab smiled tolerantly at the two men. He had spoken only a few words all evening and had devoted himself to the serious business of drinking. But he didn't drink as Sam drank. Liquor didn't change Ab much. He broke into the senseless conversation. "I was just thinking," he said. "You two men are worth more right now than you ever will be worth, for you've got a bait of expensive brandy in your bellies."

The men laughed again. Sam said, "You're way behind, Ab. Why don't you catch up?"

The Kentuckian got slowly to his feet. He knew that Sam would drink until he was unconscious. And Donna was unhappy. So was Tishomingo. Well, the best thing to do was to get it over with. "Tell you what, Sam'l,"

323

Ab drawled, "I'll lay you a little wager. I've been drinking while you've been talking and I worked myself up a thirst. Drink for drink I'll stretch you on the floor. But I warn you, up in Kaintuck they used to call me 'Hollow-leg Ab.' And you can't drink. The lawyer's right. An Irishman can't drink."

Sam called Jasper and instructed him to keep the glasses full. Sukey came with a sage-broom and swept away the ashes. Ab told her to clean one spot very well. "That's where your master is going to stretch out." Ab winked at Thomas, who grinned.

"Why can't an Irishman drink?" It had taken Sam several minutes to word the question.

"God knows," said Thomas. "I think it's because you're such a damned emotional people. A Scotchman drinks for pleasure, but an Irishman drinks because he wants to forget, or remember. Watch yourself, Sam'l boy. We're your friends. You're the kind of man who'll go along all right for a while. But you can be counted on to make big mistakes. Now, don't get riled. You'll go along all right for about eight or nine times in business, but the tenth time you'll blow up. That's the Irish in you, too."

Ab, fearing that Sam would take exception to the words, began singing, "Over the Hills and Far Away." Thomas joined in and so did Sam. They drank drink for drink for two hours, and then Sam's tongue became so thick that he scarcely could talk. Thomas was reciting the Constitution, and Ab was humming a melody. Finally, Sam staggered to his feet. "All right, I can't drink," he mumbled. "I'm an Irish brat and I can't drink." He stumbled over his own words and there were tears in his voice. "I was born in a cabin without a floor. The red 'uns killed my folks. But I'm going to be somebody. I

324

make mistakes but I pay for them. And I don't need your God damned help."

Thomas took another drink while Sam was talking and passed one to Ab. Tishomingo stared at the floor, thinking of Donna.

"I'm a fool in business," Sam muttered thickly, "but all of you work for me. Maybe I can't drink, but I can fight."

He reeled and fell. Tishomingo and Thomas jumped to help him, but Ab waved them aside. He rolled Sam on to the spot that he had selected. Then he turned to the men and said, "Now let's have a drink."

Thomas and Ab drank to Sam. Tishomingo sent for the black drink and joined in the toast. Jasper came to his master and looked down at him. There was compassion in the slave's eyes. He put his hands under Sam's shoulders and tried to lift him.

"I'll help," offered Tishomingo.

"Naw suh," said Jasper. "Jasper thanks you, but Jasper will look after Massa Sam. Massa Sam wouldn't want nobody to help him. He's a proud man." The Negro shook Sam gently and said softly, "Massa Sam, git up. Miss Donna wants you."

Sam opened his eyes slowly, struggled to his feet and lurched from the room.

18

TIME rolled by to keep its rendezvous with eternity. John Adams had been elected president and the nation had fought its undeclared naval war with France. The United States had come to hate France almost as much as she hated England and Spain, and she didn't have a friend in the world. Spain was in no hurry to evacuate Natchez, and the first mob in the history of the South stormed the Spanish governor's house and forced him to seek refuge in the fort.

Meanwhile, Sam, convinced that the time soon would come for the new land to be made a territory, went with Thomas among the people and exhorted them to be ready for the day. As a slave-holder, Sam advocated a free traffic in bumboes, but Thomas, his tongue in his cheek, pleaded for the abolition of slavery, posing as a friend of the poor whites. Before summer came to Locha Poka, the people were ready for a compromise.

Sam built slowly at Locha Poka but he built well. His architect, hired in New Orleans, had shuddered at some of Sam's ideas. Sam wanted a gaudy house. Donna was able to override some of his suggestions, but she dared not go too far. After all, Sam would be the master of Locha Poka.

His house must be white. The foundation would be made of white-washed stone, but the wood must be of pine, hand-hewn, and the roof of cypress. He would have four columns and a top gallery. There must be a wrought-iron balcony around the gallery. There must be colored glass over the front door. Sam liked to watch the sun play on colored glass. His front door must be made in New England and there would be a silver knocker on it. Donna wanted a brass knocker, but Sam insisted upon silver. There would be stone urns on his front lawn and roses by his front steps, red roses.

The furniture for their room would be rosewood. Each room must have a different kind of furniture, maple for the drawing room, oak for the dining room, and cherry, pine, cypress, walnut and mahogany for the bed chambers.

Much of the furniture could be hand-made, but for their room Sam wanted imported furniture.

The ceilings must be high and the windows tall. On the lower floor he wanted the French windows to be three feet from the ground and six feet high. Sam liked windows. There had been only two windows in his father's cabin.

He would import Bermuda grass for his lawn and his lawn must stretch five hundred yards down the slope from the hill where Locha Poka stood. There must be a formal garden for Donna.

He retired his debts as rapidly as his income from his factory and post permitted. His first gin was completed that summer and he leased it to a planter who had his place between him and Natchez. Others planters brought their cotton to him and he ginned it. When they could not pay cash, he took a mortgage against their cotton. Donna's fever returned with the summer and she lay abed during the scorching, sultry days.

Tishomingo went to the Cherokees and to the Ohio

327

country on a mission for his uncle. Before he left he told Sam, "There's talk of a war council and I must go and see what it is about. Your country is very foolish. It has made enemies of many nations; only the Choctaws are your friends."

"But what is your mission?"

"I must learn if Tecumseh is trying to arouse the mountain tribe."

"And if he is?" Sam asked.

"I'll notify my uncle and he'll go to the tribes and preach against Tecumseh. Tecumseh is a great orator. His voice is as the sounding of bells on a moonlit night. But Pushmataha is a greater orator. His voice is like the thunder rolling in the valley."

Honoria wanted to close the school and go to Locha Poka to live while Tishomingo was away, but he had only to request that she keep the school open and she agreed willingly.

The uncertain state of affairs at Natchez hampered Sam's business, but he turned a neat profit that year, largely through his agreements with Frome and Flournoy. He used his surplus money to buy new materials for his home. The skeleton of Locha Poka was completed and enough of the rooms were finished for Sam and Donna to move in. She almost was sad when she left their cabin and moved to the big house. She and Sam purchased the furniture for their room from a bankrupted planter. The kitchen and dining room were complete and they used the dining room as a sitting room while the workmen finished the other parts of the house.

Donna suffered attacks of fever monthly and each attack kept her abed for three days. The fever always broke with a chill. Her ears rang constantly and she was faint and dizzy. But when she felt strong she liked to sit with Sam on their verandah and look at their land. The house faced the west and the river. They couldn't see the river for the water oaks. The Big Tree was to the south of the house. The slave who had died during the winter was buried near the Big Tree and they called the earth there "the burying ground." Sam set the land apart as a place to bury his dead.

Donna had supervised the thinning of the trees on the lawn and had spared many of the oaks and magnolias. The kitchen with its huge oven was fifty paces behind the house and was connected to Locha Poka by a covered passageway, so the slaves could bring food to the big house in all weather. The floor of the kitchen was earth, and twice daily the kitchen slaves brushed it with bundles of broom sage. The pots and pans hung by the fireplace. A basket of pine and a basket of hickory chips were handy.

The slave quarters were behind the kitchen. The cabins were made of pine and stood in neat rows. A bell in the quarters sent the slaves to the fields and called them home again.

Sam worked his slaves from sun-up until twilight. Later he would give them opportunities to build their own gardens and pig-pens, but now they must clear the land of Locha Poka. There were a hundred tasks for every slave. When they were not working on the foundry they were building roads. When it was too wet to build roads they worked on the ferry or on the factory. Jasper saw to the foundry, for he was a trained slave and could handle the forge. On clear days they tore up the earth. First they burned and then they uprooted the brush. They cut away the small trees and left the big trees standing like charred sentinels in the fields. Some day they would cut away the big trees, but now they plowed around them and planted corn. Corn was the staff of life. With a handful of corn and a pinch of salt a man and his horse could live.

From the big house they could see the roof of the store and the side of the foundry. They could see the road running past it and down to the river, to the ferry.

Ab completed his cabin down the river and furnished it to his liking and needs. He was making monthly trips to Georgia and Sam had raised his pay to fifty dollars a month. Perhaps he would remind Sam some day that he had been promised a percentage of the post business, but now he didn't need the money and he wouldn't bother Sam'l about such trifles. He had his plans, too. He spent as much time as possible with Honoria, and one day she asked him, "What is your name, Ab? Here you are paying court to me and I don't even know your name."

"My whole name is Adam Bascomb. It's a good name but you are one of the few persons who knows it. There's a story about my name that I'll tell you some time."

Sam saw to it that Flournoy and Ab did not meet.

When dog days came and Donna's health did not improve, Sam insisted she return to Georgia until the fever broke.

"Who will take care of you?" she asked.

"I'll take care of myself," he said. "But if I need help there's always Honoria."

"It would not be right for Honoria to leave her school. She's very happy there."

Sam almost lost patience with Donna and to save his patience she agreed to go to her brother. Sam took her as far as André's place on the Tombigbee where she rested for two days and Ab took her through the Creek Nation. The clean, sharp air of the hills would break the fever.

330

When Sam returned to Locha Poka, Honoria was there. "I've left the school," she said. "You mustn't be alone."

"Chock will be disappointed when he returns."

"If your wife isn't able to care for you, I am. Your well-being is more important to me than all the Indian brats in the world."

"What do you mean?"

"A wife should never leave her husband, Sam."

Sam took Honoria by the shoulder, "I don't like the way you said that. There was gall in your words. Never again cast any barb at my wife. I've not been blind, Honoria. You've tried Donna's patience. This is her home ——"

"There was a time when you said that your home was my home." Honoria tossed her head angrily.

"But not for you to wreck." Sam's words cut her, but she returned his glare. He spoke quickly, for he wanted to be done with the things he had to say. "I'll give you my life, but I'll not let you wreck Donna's. She's sick. I've sent her to Georgia believing the fever will disappear. When she returns, if you trouble her in any way, you'll be accountable to me. You're a spiteful woman sometimes, Honoria, and my patience has been strained. I'm in no mood for trifles."

"Am I not welcome here?" Her words were almost a whisper.

"You're always welcome, Hon, but you must remember that Donna's to be respected."

"I don't have to stay here," she said bitterly.

"Where can you go?" Sam regretted his words as soon as he had said them. Honoria's eyes were misty for a second and her chin quivered. She turned pale and to Sam she seemed very small and alone and helpless. Then

331

her cheeks colored quickly and her eyes flashed. She squared her shoulders and her breasts heaved in indignation.

"So it has come to this—my brother wonders where I could go. My brother has become so high and mighty that he forgets the pledge he and his sister made. Well, Mr. Samuel Dabney, I have no brother in Georgia to whom I can run. I have no kinsmen anywhere except you. But I don't need you. I can take care of myself." Her words trailed into a sob and Sam put his arms around her.

"I'm sorry," he said impulsively. "I'm sorry I said it. I'm worried, Hon, and my temper is sharp. Please forgive me. Whatever I have is yours and you know I mean it."

She put her head against his chest and wept. She vowed she would forgive him his words, but she knew full well that she never would. She would never forget. Donna was the cause of it all. Donna had taken her brother from her.

Tishomingo understood why Honoria left the school, and on his return from the Cherokees he decided not to reopen it until Donna returned and Honoria was free again to help him.

"You see," he said, "I cannot run the school without you."

They were standing near his lodge when he spoke. Honoria had gone there to welcome him home and to invite him to Locha Poka. She had dressed in her best and when he complimented her on her beauty her restraint was unleashed. Only a small barrier held Honoria's restraint and Tishomingo's glances and his words tore away the barrier and without shame Honoria walked to him and put her arms around him. "I'm weary of waiting for your love," she murmured. "My brother is angry with me. He doesn't want me any more. I have no one except you."

The mingo put his hand under her chin and tilted her head. "You're lying, Honoria. I can see it in your eyes. You cannot lie to me. I'll vow to you that all the way back from the Cherokees I counted the hoofbeats of my horse, impatient to be here where you are. And then you come to me with a lie. I know your brother would never do anything to hurt you. You're seeking to arouse my sympathy and to turn me against your brother. It's a way of a white woman. I'm afraid to love you, for I have no faith in you."

"And who are you to scorn me?" Honoria barked the words. She suddenly was ashamed of her boldness and furious that she had been rebuked. "Oh, Chock, can't you understand what I'm trying to say? You say you can read a lie in my eyes. Can't you read love when you see it? What you say is true. My brother, of course, hasn't turned me away. He upbraided me, but he was sorry." Her anger passed and she clung to him. "I did lie to you. I lied to you because I wanted you to feel sorry for me and love me. I'll use any weapon to win your love. I'll go to your lodge tonight. I'll leave my people. I'll do anything. . . ."

Tishomingo said, "All white women are alike."

"And what know you of white women?" she demanded scornfully.

"I loved one, one time. Perhaps that is the reason why I don't trust myself with you. There are times, Honoria, when I'm very lonely and I want you, but it is a weakness. I could never love you. I, too, loved Ta-lo-wah. Flournoy took her from me. She was as you are in many

333

ways, beautiful. But never will Tishomingo give his troth to another woman."

She wanted to cry but she did not. She bit her lips until they were white. Her anger surged through her blood and turned to resentment and without another word she walked to her horse and rode away. In her room at Locha Poka she wrote a note to Lake Flournoy and told him that Tishomingo was bitter because he had lost Ta-lo-wah. She warned Flournoy of Tishomingo's wrath, not knowing that she wrote the truth, and never realizing that Flournoy knew all that she wrote and more. She told Flournoy she did not blame him and said boldly that a woman who could not hold a man was not worthy of a man's attention. She thanked him again for the shawl and the other presents he had sent her, and wrote that she wanted to see him, so he could see how beautiful his gifts really were.

It was twilight when she rode down to Ab's cabin. The big Kentuckian was sitting by his fire whittling a new ax handle. He went to the porch and stood there and talked to Honoria until she said, "Come inside, there is a thing I would ask you." She handed him the letter and asked him to deliver it.

"I'll leave in the morning," Ab said. "But first I must ask Sam'l about this. Perhaps he has another message to reach Flournoy."

"Please, Ab," Honoria said, "do not report to Sam'l that you're taking this message."

Ab looked at her quickly and she turned her eyes away. "What is it, Honoria? Something is eating you. I would not ask this if I didn't love you."

Honoria looked at the fire and was silent, then she looked at Ab. He stood over her, friendly and towering, a big man. She glanced around the room at his bed, at his

334

table, at his pipes. There was an odor of man about the place. Her blood tingled as she smelled it.

"Do you really love me, Ab?"

"God knows I do. I love you so much that it hurts way down in here." He tapped his chest. "You know I love you. Women can feel such things. Now tell me what is wrong."

"Sam'l and I have had words."

"But what is this message you would have me take to Flournoy? He's not a good man, Honoria. Don't do anything you'll regret."

She walked to the fire and threw her letter into the blaze, then faced him, her eyes smoldering. "I've changed my mind," she said huskily. "It was a silly letter. I was thanking him for the presents, but he might misunderstand and think I was a brazen woman."

Ab watched her and a great yearning came to his heart. "It's not Flournoy that I worry about, but Tishomingo. You love him, don't you?"

"No!" She said it quickly to get the lie out of her mouth before it burned her lips. She walked toward him. "Men are blind! And you are the blindest of the lot. Must I rip my modesty from my heart?"

Ab couldn't speak. His breath choked his words.

"Why do you think I came here?" She smiled as she moved toward him. "Why do you think I wrote Flournoy? I wanted you to be jealous. Of Flournoy. Of Tishomingo. Of everybody! That letter was only an excuse to come here."

She pushed the bench back and sat at his feet. The fire shadows danced in her hair and the heat of the fire and of her desire flushed her face. She put her hands on his knees and he stooped over, lifted her to her feet and held her to him.

"This is something I've dreamed about," he said softly.

His big hands fumbled with the strings of her bodice. She laughed and took his hands away, held them for a second, then kissed them. "Your hands are clumsy, but sweet." She began untying the strings.

"I can't believe ——"

"Don't talk," she whispered and let her dress fall in a heap on the floor. "Just hold me. Tight." She closed her eyes so she couldn't see him. Tishomingo was as tall as he. Tishomingo would smell as he did. This was not Ab holding her; it was Tishomingo. This was Tishomingo's bed and this was Tishomingo's lodge. And all the while she lay in his arms she was trying to pretend that he was Tishomingo.

The fire died to red coals that struggled to blaze into life again. Tiny blue flames spurted and vanished. The coals became ashes.

"Do you love me now?" Ab asked tenderly.

She turned her face to the wall, "Yes, I love you. I do, I do!" She would make herself love him. This was the answer. This was the solution to all the puzzles of life, to all the riddles.

"We'll go to Natchez and get married," Ab said.

She did not reply. She didn't want to think, but her mind was choking. This was not Tishomingo, this was Ab. Ab and his cabin. She didn't want a cabin. She had lived in a cabin all her life. She wanted a mansion—a mansion or the bare lodge of Tishomingo.

"Sam will wonder where I am," she said. "I must go."

He built up the fire and she dressed, unashamed of his presence.

"I'll go to your brother tomorrow and ask for your hand," he said. He kissed her good night and her lips were dry.

Sam asked her no questions, for when she returned to Locha Poka, Donna and Pierce were there. Honoria noticed first that Donna's eyes were bright and that her color was good. Damme, those hills of Georgia had broken the fever quickly. She went to her sister-in-law and kissed her on the cheek, and welcomed Pierce.

"We did not expect you back so soon, Donna. Are you well?"

"Ay, I'm well," Donna said. "Ay —"

"Say naught." Sam put his hand over Donna's mouth and ruffled her hair. "This isn't the time."

Donna removed her husband's hand. "But I will have my say. I can scarcely wait to tell Honoria. She'll be very happy to know that Pierce brought me back to my home before the appointed day, because I am with child." She said it proudly, but there was scorn in her eyes as she looked at Honoria.

"But the fever?" Honoria said. "You're too weak!"

"Does she look like a sick woman?" Pierce asked. "When she reached my house she was sick and melancholy. But when the doctor there told her the true nature of her illness, she got well. Never before have I seen a woman get well so quickly. She couldn't wait for us to pack."

Sam said, "I had wanted Donna to keep this secret from Honoria until we could drink to my wife."

Honoria kissed Donna again. "I'm so happy for you," she said. "I'll start tomorrow and make some clothes."

"I'll make my own child's clothes," Donna said sharply. Pierce glanced up at his sister, then at Sam, but held his peace. His sister had told him naught of her feud with Honoria.

Honoria ignored the remark. "Now mind you, Sam'l

337

Dabney," she said, "don't go strutting through this new land and brag that your wife is with child."

"But I've got to tell Chock. And Ab. And André. And Thomas. What is the purpose of a man's wife having a child if a man cannot boast of it?"

The women went early to bed, but Sam and Pierce sat up late discussing the affairs of the country. Pierce must begin the return trip to Georgia the next morning. He had left his command to accompany Donna and, too, he wanted to cross the Creek Nation to study the signs.

"There's trouble brewing among the Creeks, Sam'l," he said.

"And it's certain to flare into war," Sam added.

"But when?"

Jasper brought pipes to the men and Sam puffed his for several seconds before he replied. "The day this country is admitted in the union as a territory the war will have begun. Mind you, I don't say the action will start then. This territory will include lands that belong to the Creeks and Choctaws. We can get the lands from the Choctaws for a price and a treaty, but the Creeks won't give in."

"If I had my way," Pierce said, "we'd go among the Creeks now and disperse them."

"And the day we send an army against the Creeks, we'd have Spain on our backs. Maybe England would be at our throats. Even France might attack us. The Shawnees would be sure to go on the war-path. We haven't got an ally except the Choctaws. We must bide our time, Pierce, or have our throats cut."

While they were talking Donna came to the fireside. "When are you coming to bed, Sam'l?"

Sam and Pierce drank a good-night toast and in the

338

seclusion of their room Sam asked his wife, "Why did you come for me?"

"I had to talk to you. I've been talking to Honoria. She and Ab are planning to be married."

"What's that? What of Tishomingo?"

"They've quarreled."

"Ab is a good man, a fitting moderate man. He'll make Honoria a good husband."

"But that's not the point, Sam'l. I'm a woman and I know how a woman feels. Honoria doesn't love Ab. She's trying only to spite Tishomingo. And she's haughty enough to ruin her life to carry her point. Please don't tell her that I've talked with you. She probably regrets that she told me. Her pride made her do it. Her pride and her vanity. She wanted me to know a man wanted her. Ab is coming to you tomorrow."

"I'll do what I think best," Sam said. He kissed Donna good night but lay awake a long time, for there were many things to be decided. He knew Ab had not told Honoria about his sister. It was a thing Ab would have to do. And there was always Flournoy. Sam knew that Flournoy would not hesitate to kill Ab if the opportunity arose. Ab wouldn't have a chance. His ignorance might mean his doom. But if he told Ab the truth there would be trouble between the Kentuckian and Flournoy. There mustn't be any trouble. And yet, if Flournoy injured Ab, then Sam would have to take up the feud. One false move would ruin his chances of leadership in the new land. However, he was not a man to tamper with his sister's happiness.

He was at Ab's house before dawn and appeared surprised when Ab told him that he wanted to take Honoria to Natchez and marry her. Sam shook his hand.

"Ay, Ab, I'm pleased that you love my sister. I saw it

339

in your eyes. You're a good man. But I must have time to think this over."

"Don't take too long. You didn't wait forever for Donna and I won't wait for Honoria."

"I'll make up my mind before you return."

"Return? Where am I going?"

"Back to Georgia with Pierce. When I came here I overstocked on coffee. I want you to take some of my supply to Frome. The damned red 'uns won't buy it and maybe Frome can turn it over. When you come back, you'll have my answer." He nudged his friend in the stomach. "Maybe we can have a wedding at Locha Poka."

He wanted to give Honoria an opportunity to think over her decision. He would not meddle with his sister's affairs, but he did not want her to marry for spite. He would not even announce his sister's engagement. She must have a chance to change her mind if she cared to. Honoria kissed Ab goodbye in the presence of all and fled to her room to be alone. Sam found her there and sat beside her.

"You'll not find a better man than Ab in all of this land," he told her. "But do you love him, Honoria?"

"Yes, Sam'l, I love him."

"What of Tishomingo?"

"He doesn't love me," she said.

"I wish I could have spared you this. I knew Tishomingo would never love but one woman and she is dead. But because your heart hurts you must not hurry into marriage with another man. That will not soothe the hurt. And Ab is my friend. If you don't love him, you'll ruin his life and yours too. I will not have it so."

He got up and left her and went about his chores, hurrying his tasks so he could spend all of his leisure with

Donna. He had never seen Donna so happy. She often sang and her joy spread through the household and the household was happy, all except Honoria. Donna's songs were like brine to Honoria. She was restless and cross. Once she rebuked Donna because Donna stayed in bed until after sun-up.

"Is your child keeping you in bed?" Honoria said. "You let me get up and see to your husband's needs. I wish I could lie in bed."

Donna got up from bed and began to dress. But then, angry with herself because she let Honoria's words inflame her, she took off her clothes and went back to bed. "Sam'l wants me to stay in bed," she said simply. "You don't have to see to his needs. You do it only because you think it hurts me. But it doesn't, Honoria. Nothing you can do or say can turn Sam'l from me."

The winter rains had set in when Ab returned from Georgia. He reined up at Locha Poka and ran into the house. He patted Donna's cheek and congratulated her on her appearance, "I got that brother of yours through all right." He shook hands with Sam, "And I got your coffee delivered. Frome will sell it for you." He looked around the room and then back at Sam and grinned. "Where is she? Where's Honoria?"

"She's around somewhere."

"I'll go find her," Ab said. "And then I must go on through to Natchez. I have the post. What say you to my troth?"

"You have my blessing," Sam said. "I was waiting only to make sure that Honoria loves you. I think she does. She has pined and mooned while you were away."

Ab found Honoria near the river and not far from his cabin. She was leaning against a tree and staring at the river. Ab touched her and she was frightened until she turned and saw him. Then she threw her arms around him.

"Sam'l gave us his blessing," Ab said. "Let's go to Natchez now."

"Tonight?"

"Ay, and why not? We can be in Natchez tomorrow, and tomorrow night you'll be my bride."

"But it will rain tonight. We must wait till morning and, too, I'm already your bride, you big loony." She toyed with fringe on his buckskins. "It's damp here. Let us go to your cabin and I'll fix food for you. I want you to see how well I can cook."

He built a fire and she brewed coffee and cooked food for him. He put the betty lamp on the table he had built and they ate and laughed and made plans. The rains came again and swished around the cabin. They lay together and Ab held her in his arms and told her many things. He would take a percentage of the post business. He would buy a slave for her and homestead more land, and build her a mansion.

"Once you told me," she whispered, "that there is a story about your sister. You must not keep a secret from me."

Ab told her of Amelia. "She was a very beautiful girl, Honoria. She looked something like you. There's a tale that she went away with an Indian."

She stood up quickly and looked down at him. She put her hand across her mouth and bit her fingers nervously.

"What is wrong, darling?" he asked.

"Your sister looked like me and she went away with an Indian from New Orleans?"

"Ay, that's the story."

"Ta-lo-wah!" Honoria almost hissed the words.

342

Ab leaped from the bed too, and gripped her shoulder until she winced. "Ta-lo-wah! The woman Flournoy disgraced. My sister? How do you know this thing?"

"I know it. I know it! I feel it now. I should have known it all along. That's why Tishomingo loves you like a brother."

"Tishomingo?" Ab sat down to collect his thoughts.

"Yes, it was he who brought your sister to this nation. It was for him that she forsook her people. He told me that she looked like me. It's she who is buried near Tishomingo's lodge."

"Then Tishomingo loved my sister. I have seen him sit by that grave. He would not have harmed her. Why did she go to Flournoy?"

He did not wait for the reply, but pulled on his buckskins and put tafula in his pouch. He lifted his rifle and walked to the door. Honoria, dazed by the revelation, watched him, unable to speak for several seconds.

"Where are you going?" she asked quickly.

"To find the answer to this riddle."

"But our marriage."

"I'll be back soon. Tell Sam'l I've gone."

He went first to Tishomingo's lodge, and finding it empty rode furiously all that night and reached *Maison Blanche* the next morning. He did not sound the door knocker, but opened the door and went into the mansion, brushing past a slave. He did not even remove his coonskin cap or stack his rifle. Flournoy was in his drawing room and leaped to his feet when the gangling Kentuckian entered.

"Who are you?" Flournoy demanded, fingering the hilt of his sword.

Ab said coldly, "I'm Adam Bascomb." He held his gun

in the crook of his left arm and hooked his right thumb around the handle of his tomahawk.

Flournoy bowed. "Forgive my abruptness, but you startled me. I've heard much of you and am glad to know you. Sit down."

"Answer me quickly, man," Ab said. "Was Ta-lo-wah my sister?"

"God's name!" Flournoy rubbed his chin, and appeared surprised. "I don't know. Her real name was Amelia Bascomb. I don't know much about her. Was Amelia Bascomb your sister?"

"Yes. What was she doing here?"

"There's only one man who can answer that." Flournoy walked to Bascomb and put his hand on his shoulder. "I regret that I must tell you. I had hoped our first meeting would be under happier circumstances. I suggest you see Tishomingo. He brought her to this nation. She came to this house when she was heartbroken and sick. I know naught else about her."

"Where is Tishomingo?"

"He rode up the Trace to old Chicaco, yesterday. It's a capital of the Chickasaws, up near the Tennessee line. He went there on business for his uncle. You're welcome to wait here until he rides back this way."

"I'll go up the Trace to Chicaco."

Flournoy said, "You're a white man and it's dangerous for a white man to ride the Trace alone. I'll send escorts with you." He watched Ab closely as he made the offer. If he knew his man, Ab would refuse help.

"I'll go alone," Ab said simply.

"You're a brave man, but foolish. The responsibility of the trip is not mine. I call upon my slaves to witness that I offered you an escort."

Ab walked to the door, "I would trust the outlaws

344

quicker than your escort. If that be an insult make the most of it. I'm going to Tishomingo. I'll believe him. If you have lied to me, I'll come back here and kill you." His words were calm and deliberate.

Flournoy shook his head at the slave who moved as though to grab Ab. "You're excited," Flournoy said, "and I'll not hold you accountable for your words. That is because I respected your sister. No other man could insult me here."

He watched Ab ride toward the Trace. Then he called a runner and sent him up a back trail to "The Nest" with orders that Ab must not reach old Chicaco.

Tishomingo had not been to old Chicaco, but to André's house. Anestasie had given him presents for Donna and he arrived at Locha Poka about the time Ab left *Maison Blanche*. Sam told him of Honoria's approaching wedding and Tishomingo pretended gladness. He was wondering if Ab would be happy. He and Sam were smoking and talking when Honoria found them.

"What's the matter with you?" Sam asked his sister. "Your face is ashen. I've just told Tishomingo about you and Ab. Does the prospect of marriage frighten you so that your skin becomes gray?"

"Did you see Ab?" She looked steadily at Tishomingo.

He explained that he had not been at home. "You deceived him," Honoria said. "He went to see you. Now he has gone to Flournoy's. I know he has. He knows who Ta-lo-wah is."

"You little fool!" Sam shouted. "Why did you tell him?"

"I didn't know," Honoria pleaded. "I was so surprised when it dawned on me. I just told him that I was sure Ta-lo-wah was his sister."

"There's no need to rebuke the girl," Tishomingo said. "I'm going to Flournoy."

"I'll go with you," Sam said.

"This is a thing I will do alone."

He did not wait for a reply but rode rapidly to the river, swam his horse across it and turned north toward *Maison Blanche*. Near the Big Black he met a traveler who had seen Ab riding up the Trace. He did not go to Flournoy's house, but rode to the council town of the Chickasaws. There he went into the lodge of a mingo and took off his buckskins and painted his chest and his face. He wore only a loin cloth and when he called the Chickasaws into council he stood before them and held a peace pipe in his left hand, and a war club in the other.

"My brothers, the nephew of Pushmataha has come to make talk with you. The heart of Tishomingo is heavy. I bear the name of a Chickasaw mingo, the friend of my father. Many moons ago I loved a white maiden, but she withered and died. The maiden had a brother who was as a brother to me. He was an impetuous boy and he rode alone up the Trace. I must find him. I am an Indian and I care not if the white outlaws of the Trace kill white men. But this man was my brother. I have come to ask you for help. The Choctaws are brave and wise, but the Chickasaws are the favored woodsmen of all the Muscogees. The fox cannot hide from the Chickasaws. Search the Trace for me."

"Why do you hold the war club?"

"With this club I will avenge my brother, if harm has come to him. For my friends I hold this pipe." He puffed on the pipe and blew the smoke to the four winds, and passed the pipe to the old mingo.

"We will help our Choctaw brother," the old mingo said.

346

He called the deer clan of the Chickasaws, the best woodsmen of all the Indians. They divided into small war parties and began searching the Trace. For three days they stalked the woods beside the trail and on the fourth a Chickasaw brave halted his party and pointed to the ground. "A tall man wearing moccasins was killed here. He was a white man. See? When he walked the heels of his feet fell heavily upon the ground. He walked straight, not as an Indian who walks on the balls of his feet and never in a straight line. The man was a horseman. He rode much. The soles of his moccasins were worn where they fitted the stirrups. He was killed with a knife. His throat was cut. The blood spurted. If he had been shot, the blood would not have spurted, but would have gushed. His gun was propped against this tree. It was a long rifle and one screw was missing from the butt."

Tishomingo said, "It was my brother."

They searched the woods thereabouts and discovered "The Nest." It was deserted, but Tishomingo found evidence that led him to the cabin of Jacob Clewy. The Chickasaws surrounded the house and Chock walked in without knocking and seized Clewy as he sat at table with his family. He brushed aside the man's children and dragged him into the woods and tied him to a tree.

"In God's name," Clewy pleaded, "don't kill me. I've done nothing. I'm a family man and a respectable settler."

"A respectable settler doesn't keep a dead man's gun in his cabin. His son doesn't wear a dead man's cap. I saw them." Tishomingo ripped the man's shirt off and stepped back ten paces. He uncoiled his bull whip and cut a gash in Clewy's chest. "I'll ask you once," the Choctaw said. "Where is the white man?"

347

Clewy did not answer immediately and Tishomingo broke his arm with the war club. The white man fainted and Tishomingo revived him with water, then twisted his arm until his hand was against the trunk. He crushed the hand with the club. Even the Chickasaws cringed at the torture. "I will break every bone in your body," Tishomingo said. His words were almost soft. Finally the man mumbled that Ab had been killed and that his body had been thrown into a swamp.

Chock sent some Chickasaws to find the body and guard it.

"You cut his throat?" Tishomingo asked.

"No. It was my brother who cut his throat." In his torture Jacob Clewy did not realize that he had sealed his brother's doom. "Now let me go. For God's sake!"

"I will torture you no more. I had planned to kill you with the club. But I'll let you die as a white man should die." He borrowed a rifle from a warrior, placed it against the man's temple and pulled the trigger.

He wrote a message to Sam that Ab was dead and gave the message to an Indian runner. To the other Indians he said, "The nephew of Pushmataha is in your debt. I will find Esau Clewy." He left the warriors with the body of Jacob Clewy and disappeared into the woods.

Word that Ab had been killed by the outlaws spread like wildfire along the Trace, but at Locha Poka Sam kept the news from Honoria and Donna. He told them only that Ab was lost and that Tishomingo had sent for help. He rode to Natchez and rallied a posse. He announced publicly that Jacob and Esau Clewy had committed murder and that Jacob was dead. He offered a reward for the capture of Esau. He read Tishomingo's message to the men and said, "Tishomingo would not lie. The Clewy brothers killed Ab. Tishomingo is after Esau, but we must seek him too. The time has come to put a stop to the outlaws."

The American soldiers and men from the Spanish garrison took to the Trace. Flournoy organized another posse. He led his men first to Esau's house. He ordered Esau's wife whipped.

"She knows where he is," Flournoy said, as one of his slaves made ready to apply the lash.

Sam jerked the whip from the Negro's hand, "I don't care if she is his wife. I'll not allow a woman to be whipped."

The woman sobbed her thanks, "I don't know where he is. Before God, I don't. A man came here and told him that the Chickasaws had formed war parties and were seeking a white man. My husband left. Then that Choctaw devil came here. He took up my husband's trail and followed it to the west."

The men rode up the Trace, but Tishomingo long before had deserted the road and was following Esau's trail near the Mississippi. In every Chickasaw village he saw traces of the man. The tunica clans said he had passed that way. He followed the river to Chickasaw Bluff and beyond the bluff, in a half-breed's cabin, he found Esau Clewy. He would not allow the outlaw to speak but bound his arms with rawhide and started back with him toward Natchez. Only once did he release Clewy's hands.

"I'll show you no mercy," Tishomingo said. "But there is a thing you should know. Flournoy will not protect you. I know that Flournoy is your master. But even now I'll vow that he's seeking you. He'll never allow you to be taken alive."

Esau Clewy protested his innocence and begged for

349

mercy. "I may not kill you," Tishomingo said, "if you write a confession."

"I have nothing to confess."

Tishomingo lifted a twig and sharpened the end. He heated the twig and held it up. "Among my people there's a strange custom. When guilty men will not confess, we drive a sharpened peg under their finger nail."

"Great God, man!" Clewy trembled.

"But I'll not do that to you. In the white man's court a confession obtained while you were suffering would be of no use. I'll not make you confess unless you care to. But Flournoy is a rich man. If he's guilty and is tried with you his power naturally will help you. If you're a wise man you'll confess."

And there in the light of the fire, Esau Clewy wrote his confession that branded Flournoy. Tishomingo smiled as he put the confession away. The white man's court would never see it. The white man's court hanged men and death was quick and merciful. Flournoy must not die yet. He must suffer.

They traveled down the Trace for two days until they came to the country where Sam and Flournoy were hunting. Tishomingo sent word to the posses telling them where he was, and he and Clewy were sitting by the Trace when the hunters galloped into view, Flournoy leading them. Tishomingo had known Flournoy would lead them. He must reach Clewy first.

The Choctaw turned to the outlaw and said quietly, "You are about to die." He jerked Clewy to his feet and held up his hands, "Here is your man," he said, and stepped quickly to one side. "To you, Mr. Flournoy, goes the honor of killing him. Perhaps there's a reward on his head. Perhaps even you offered a reward for the head of the man who killed Adam Bascomb."

Clewy shrieked as Flournoy jumped from his horse and reached for his pistol. The outlaw blubbered incoherently and stared at Flournoy, who took careful aim and shot him through the head.

Abernathy rode up as Clewy fell. "He had the right of a trial. Maybe he wasn't guilty."

"Yes," one of the men grumbled. "You acted powerfully high-handed."

"He was guilty," Tishomingo said. "He confessed to me."

Flournoy rammed another charge into his pistol and faced the men. "Perhaps I was impetuous," he said, "but the sight of this bloody butcher angered me so that I shot him. In your land this man might have had a trial, but this is the Chickasaw nation. We'll cut off his head and post it on the Trace as an example and a warning to the other outlaws."

"I'll be damned if you will!" Sam pulled the body into the shade of a tree and threw a covering over it, for the flies were already gathering. "This man has a wife and children. They weren't outlaws. And I'll not let those children see their father's head on a pole."

Tishomingo did not look at Flournoy but said to Sam, "You should go tell his woman that he is dead. She will want to bury him. I'll be along later. There is a thing I will ask Flournoy in private."

Flournoy waited until the posses had ridden away and asked coolly, "What would you say to me?"

"You sent Ab up the Trace."

"That is not true. I have proof that I tried to keep him from going. I have proof that I offered him an escort."

"But you wanted him killed. You knew if he learned the truth, he would kill you."

Flournoy said, "I knew you would not tell him the

351

truth, because you want the pleasure of killing me, but I'm not afraid of the nephew of Pushmataha. I'm a man. If you were a man your woman would not have come to me."

"Your taunts will not provoke me to kill you now. My hate will never make a fool of me. The day I kill you I must leave this land. I'm not ready to go yet. I brought Clewy to you so you could kill him. He gave me his confession. I have it here." He held the letter up. "This letter is worth your life."

Flournoy moved back two steps and studied Chock. Tishomingo returned the letter to a place of safety and let his long arms hang loosely by his side. Flournoy dropped his hands, too. He saw that Tishomingo was armed only with his bull whip, but he knew the whip was like forked lightning. His one chance was to get to his pistol before Tishomingo could uncoil his whip. The letter was worth that chance. . . .

He saw Tishomingo flex the muscles of his right hand. His own pistol was primed and ready. He could extract it with one motion and fire at almost the same second. He wouldn't have to aim. The ball would strike Tishomingo in the belly.

He studied Tishomingo's eyes, but did not cringe from the look of cold brutality that he saw. His own eyes were open wide and they sparkled. Danger made his eyes sparkle. He held his right hand taut for a split second, then snatched for his pistol. Tishomingo's arm swept up and he uncoiled his whip on the upsweep, and wrapped it around Flournoy's wrist before the French half-breed could reach his gun. He jerked Flournoy to the ground and stooped over him, smiling for the first time. He withdrew the charge from the pistol and returned it to Flournoy. The sparkle had gone from Flournoy's eyes and they became as cold as Tishomingo's. But there was no fear on his face, and the master of *Maison Blanche* did not plead for mercy. He stood up and casually brushed the dirt from his clothes.

Then he folded his hands behind him and stood very erect, calmly awaiting the blow that he knew would come. He had wondered often how it would feel to face death, and his only concern was that he might show fear before his enemy. He thought quickly of many trivial details. What would happen to his snakes? Josephine would get his property. He hoped she would provide for his bath slave. . . .

Tishomingo flicked his whip behind him, then snapped his wrist and the tip of his whip opened a gash in Flournoy's cheek. Flournoy felt the blood pour down his face and trickle into his mouth, but he did not put his hand over the wound.

Tishomingo coiled his whip slowly and Flournoy's heart began beating loudly for the first time. Tishomingo was not ready for his revenge.

"You can tell your friends," Tishomingo said, "that you were injured by a fall. But every time you look at yourself, you'll see the mark of Tishomingo and know that some day I'll kill you with this whip. White men will never see this letter."

Flournoy put his handkerchief to his wound.

"There's blood on your chin," Tishomingo said. "Wipe it off. And come! We must not keep the white men waiting and they must not know that there has been a quarrel between the half-breed Tishomingo and the half-breed Lake Flournoy, the noble kinsman of Josephine."

The posses disbanded but Sam and Chock went to the swamp where the Chickasaws guarded Ab's body. The

353

Chickasaws revered the dead and would not leave the body alone in the woods. The outlaws had weighed the body with stone and the swamp things had ripped it. Sam wanted to bury Ab beside the swamp. To him the earth anywhere was good enough for a man's grave. A grave was not important to Sam Dabney, only life was important. A grave meant dust and he hated dust.

Tishomingo objected to leaving Ab in the earth by the swamp, "I'll stay here by him, and when you return to Locha Poka send word to my uncle. Tell him that Il-le-hi-ah, the death messenger, has called. Tell him where I am and that I have need for the bone picker. I'm an Indian, Big Sam, and I'll not suffer the bones of one I love to be buried so far from those who loved him. I'll bury his bones by his sister. It is the end of the family of Ta-lo-wah."

Sam bowed his head, "It is well. But I thought a white man could not be buried near the sacred grounds of the Choctaws."

"Ay, that is so. But I will not bury the bones of Adam Bascomb. I will bury the bones of Hush-a-lah, the Burning Sun, the kind brother. Now you go. There is a vigil I must keep."

Locha Poka knew that Sam brought tragic news when he rode Claymore to the stable and tossed the reins to Jasper. He walked into his house and sat down. "The iron has entered deeply into my heart again." He put his arm around Honoria. "Ab is dead."

"I felt that he was," Honoria said. "Last night I dreamed he was dead. What am I to do?" She looked first at Sam and then at Donna.

"You must go to bed now," Donna said. "I'll fix you some coffee. Time heals all wounds. We all loved Ab,

354

but something told me, Honoria, that you never would have been happy with him."

"Happy. You speak of happiness as though it were just a word. And of time as though it, too, were only a word." She put her hands by her side and stood very straight. "I am not ashamed. You think I did not love him, but I did. I loved him in a way you'll never understand. Ab was like a little boy to me. I held his head here on my breast. I saw him cry when he told me of his sister and I kissed away his tears. I did love him. Every woman loves two men. One man who quickens her blood and the other man who soothes her. He was a comfort to me. He was mine and I'm proud that I will bear him a child."

19

✦ ✦

HONORIA stood very still there in the center of the floor and stared defiantly at her brother and Donna, then walked to a chair and sat down and faced them again. Donna was the first to recover from the shock. She went over and sat on the arm of the chair and pulled Honoria's head against her. There was no need to say anything. Words were of no use. All of the color drained out of Sam's face and then his face flushed and drained again. It was on his tongue to ask, "What can we do?" but he swallowed the words and paced the floor for a minute.

"Say something," Honoria demanded. "Say something, quickly. Do not walk the floor as though you were passing judgment upon me. It was partly your fault."

"My fault?"

"Ay. If you had let Ab take me to Natchez instead of sending him to Georgia I would have been wed. And you, the mighty Sam Dabney, would not face disgrace because his sister carries a bastard in her belly."

"Honoria!" Donna was aghast. "Do not speak so."

But Honoria was old man Dabney's brat again. "I'll speak so! It is true. I'll have a nameless child and when people look at my brother they'll say, 'That's Sam'l Dabney whose sister had a woodscolt.'"

Sam walked to his sister and scowled down at her. "Be

356

quiet, you fool. The slaves will hear you. Did this thing happen the night Donna returned from Georgia?"

"Yes."

"And knowing this you let Ab go away?"

Donna got up and faced her husband, her chin quivering. Her eyes were blazing but her voice was firm. "Do not speak so to her. I'll not have it. This is no time for harsh words. Honoria is upset. She needs your love now."

"Sit down, Donna, and hold your tongue. Honoria and I have been in trouble before. We've had to make decisions together and we'll do it again. I'm not rebuking her, I want to get my bearings so we'll know what to do."

Honoria's eyes brimmed with tears as she looked at her brother. Old man Dabney's son. Trouble had come again and they would meet it again. Honoria felt then that Donna was outside of the family and Donna felt so too. There was an affinity between this man and his sister that Donna did not understand. Sometimes they closed themselves within a wall and Donna could not see through the wall. She could not understand that poverty and hardship and ridicule had bound them together. Sam called Sukey and directed her to fetch brandy and they drank. And when they were alone again Sam said, "Give me time and I'll think of something. The slaves must know naught of this."

"But how can I hide it?" Honoria asked. "I'm a month gone now."

"You'll stay in your room. If anyone asks where you are, we'll say that you are ill, that Ab's death made you ill. Above all, Tishomingo, or André, or Flournoy—none of them must know this."

"I'll never be able to marry now," Honoria said. "No man would have me."

357

"No man will know," Dabney said.

Donna said, "You speak as a child, Sam'l. You cannot hide a baby."

"Before Honoria's day arrives we'll send her to New Orleans, or maybe to Mobile. Her child can be born there. And when she comes back she can bring her baby with her. She loves children. She taught them at the Choctaw school. Is it so strange that a young woman should adopt a baby? It's a good Christian act. We can say the child's parents died of the yellow fever. Or even that the child's parents were my kinsmen. I have no kinsmen in the United States but who knows that or cares about that? Oh, there are ways, I tell you."

"I knew you would do something," Donna said. "Come, Honoria, I'll see you to your bed." Sam sat alone for a long time drinking brandy, and when he got to his feet he was unsteady. Donna came back to him and they sat together by the fire. Sam was a little drunk.

"That could have been me, you know," she said. "Who are we to cast stones?"

"I thought of that. But we loved each other."

"Perhaps they did too, and love will not wait for preachers."

Sam lit his pipe and inhaled the smoke to clear his head. "But they didn't love each other. Not that way. I know my sister. She loves only Tishomingo and she always will."

"Then why did she go to Ab?"

"I cannot explain why women do things. They're a mystery to me. She wanted to love Ab. Oh, well, it's done now. It's strange, Donna, but to me conception is like death. There's nothing to be done about it. Man

358

is helpless. Life and death are inevitable and there's naught that we can do."

The next day it was hard for Sam to realize that things were different now. Ab was gone and Honoria would have a baby. All morning, while he visited his factory and his foundry, he found himself stopping and staring into the distance to recollect his thoughts and to convince himself that things were different. He walked through the fields and saw to his slaves. He made a trade with a Choctaw buck, four needles for four hides. He collected a toll from his ferry, a horseman riding into the Creek Nation. A train passed and he sat in his factory and talked to the leader. The travelers had their possessions packed in hogsheads, and shafts were connected to the barrels. Mules pulled the hogsheads. Many planters sent their tobacco to market in the same manner.

The settlers were from North Carolina and were going to Natchez. They had heard that the Spaniards soon would leave. Sam sold them rum.

He walked through his slave quarters, inspecting the cabins. He made a slave woman scrub her floor. He ordered another to bury a tobie, for it was a deer heart and stunk. He clanged his bell and called the slaves from the fields. He directed a slave taster to lick the sweat of his Negroes. "There's yellow fever abroad," Sam said. "I hear it's in New Orleans and Mobile. You must be careful. My sister was planning to go to New Orleans but I have had to postpone her trip."

He stopped in at Sukey's cabin and played with Dabby. She was getting to be a big child and for the first time Sam noticed that she was a beautiful baby. There wasn't a kink in her hair, and it was long and glossy. It was tied with a red ribbon. She was the color of polished bronze. Her eyes were as black as midnight and her nose

359

was straight. Her teeth were like her mother's, white and flashing, but her lips were thin and red. Damme, she was a healthy child. What a brood wench she would make. Sam smiled at the child and Dabby laughed out loud at him. Sukey brought him a chair and insisted that he sit down.

"You're warm and dry here, ay, Sukey?"

"Yas, massa. Sukey and Dabby are warm and dry. Jasper fixes our house."

"Jasper, ay?" He looked closely at Sukey. She was about ripe again. Jasper, huh? Ummmmm. That would be a good match. Geiche and Gullah. Long limbs, big feet, flat nose, blue gums. Good field stock.

If Sukey was bigg'd, and he felt sure that she was, he hoped she would not slip her child until after his baby was born. He would want her with Donna. That doctor in Natchez would never get out to Locha Poka in time. He should take Donna to Natchez to see the doctor. No, he would have the doctor visit her, but he mustn't see Honoria. You couldn't trust a doctor's tongue. He would blab from Natchez to New Orleans and back again. He would go to Natchez on the morrow and fetch the doctor. He must hire another post rider.

Honoria came to supper that night, but she spoke crossly and snapped at Donna, but was sweet and gentle with Sam. The next morning Sam promised his wife and his sister that he would bring them presents.

"What do you want?" he asked.

"Anything you select," Donna said.

"There are several things I want," Honoria said. "I'll give you a list. If you do not care to buy them for me, then I have money, you know—money from my perfumes."

360

He kissed Donna goodbye and she clung to him for a moment. Honoria hugged him tightly and kissed him full on the lips and patted his cheeks playfully. Donna tried not to think so, but Honoria's gayety almost was revolting. But why should she be morose, Donna thought. She really was not gay, she was pretending. It was an act to lighten Sam's burden.

Sam had not crossed the river before Honoria wheeled on Donna and said, "I know what you're thinking. You're wondering how I can laugh. The prospect of having a child doesn't frighten me. In some ways I'm glad. And I'm almost glad he'll have no father. Do you know why?"

"You're mad."

"No, I'm not mad. But I saw something the other night you didn't see. Did you notice how my brother rallied to me and how he rebuked you? My brother will always care for me. He'll feel sorry for me. My child will give me a hold on my brother that you can never break."

"Come into the house, Honoria. You're beside yourself." They went to the drawing room and sat down. "I do not want my Sam'l —"

"Stop saying, 'my Sam'l'!" Honoria demanded.

Donna stood quickly and crossed the room to Honoria's chair. "Enough of your damned impudence! You can fool your brother but you can't fool me. I'm a woman, too. And because I'm a woman I took your part the other night. But don't misunderstand and think me weak, Honoria. Men are fools, we both know that. When women are as we are, men condemn themselves and feel sorry for us. This is our rule over men. But I really don't feel sorry for you. Yes, your brother does and he'll protect you. I'd hate him if he did otherwise."

Honoria sat back in her chair. "Don't be so haughty. We are both women, yes, but to a man there's a difference in his wife being with child and his sister being with child. He expects his wife to conceive, but he cringes from the thought of his sister doing the things his own wife has done."

"You're a cold-blooded creature."

"There's nothing cold-blooded about love, and there's another thing you must know. You don't fool me. I know why you took my part the other night."

"What do you mean?" Donna stood over Honoria. Honoria was sitting in a big chair, her legs crossed. She looked up at Donna and her lips scarcely moved as she spoke.

"Do you think I'm blind?" Honoria said. "The thing that has happened to me might have happened to you. I could even tell you some of the things you said to Sam. I could hear you panting from where I was. . . ."

Streaks of black and red danced before Donna's eyes and her blood seemed to freeze. She opened her mouth to catch her breath, but she was choking. The world reeled before her eyes. Honoria was just a blurred vision. If she only had a knife, a butcher knife; a pair of scissors, a knitting needle. . . .

"Yes, I watched you." Honoria laughed a bit hysterically. "That first night that Sam went to you. I knew you were waiting by the tree." Honoria's words pounded against Donna's brain. "You're no better than I am. *You* who are so high and mighty! I heard everything you said. I said some of the same things to Ab. I learned a lot from you. But at least I took my man in a bed and didn't roll bare-butted in the grass."

Donna tried to speak, to stop her, but words would not come.

Honoria laughed again and her words poured out. "You'll not tell my brother! you dare not! It would em-

362

barrass him. He'd never love you again. Every time he held you, he'd remember that I had seen you. He couldn't stand it. He'd never touch you. No, you won't tell him!"

The world stopped whirling before Donna's eyes. She closed her mouth and breathed deeply through her nose. The color returned to her face, and she slapped Honoria across the mouth.

Honoria uttered a little cry of amazement and kicked out. Her foot struck Donna in the stomach and Donna gasped with pain.

"You vile slut!" Donna clenched her fist and struck Honoria again. She clawed her and kicked her and bit her until Honoria cried out with pain. "That's right!" Donna screamed. "Beg!"

"For God's sakes," Honoria pleaded and covered her face with her arms, "you're killing me! For God's sakes, remember that I'm pregnant!"

Her plea caused Donna's temper and fury to boil over and she held Honoria in the chair and beat her until her own energy burned out. Honoria's face was streaked with blood and she was trembling with fright.

Donna crouched over her chair. "If ever you mention this to me again, I'll whip you as I would a negro wench. I'll whip you even if your brother leaves me. I, too, have a brother. If he thought I had suffered such indignation he'd come for me. I'll never tell your brother what you said, but not for the reason you think. You're foul, Honoria. I love your brother. He must never know this. It would break his heart. And if he knew that you had spied upon us, he'd half kill you. But he'd be ashamed, ashamed to face me. There's nothing good about you. You're old man Dabney's brat, all right!"

"Leave my father out of this," Honoria found her

voice and interrupted Donna. She jumped to her feet, but Donna pushed her back into the chair.

"Your mother must have been a marvelous woman and my Sam'l must have inherited all of her good traits and the few that your father had. He must have taken them all because there was none left for you. Now get up and go to your room. I'm mistress here. This is my home. You do as I say or I'll drive you out of here as I would any common slut!"

Honoria tossed her head and tried to stare Donna down. Then she spoke slowly. "Words do not come to me as easily as to you, Donna. My father is dead. He was a good man. If ever again you cast a barb at his memory I'll not beat you as you have me, but I'll beat you with a stick. And I'll not go to my room. You don't give orders to me as you do to a slave or to a child. I'll go to Tishomingo."

"You wouldn't dare!" The color drained from Donna's face again and she feared that Honoria would dare. It would ruin Sam. Of course, Tishomingo would keep the secret but someone else would find out, and Sam could never hold his head up in the new land. A man was judged by his family's behavior. If a man could not control his wife, or his children, or his sister, he was not worthy of leadership. She mustn't let her go. Sam would never understand. She loved him enough to make any sacrifice for him. She would swallow her pride, she would bury it. Sam had worked too hard to suffer a setback so early in life.

"I'll dare anything," Honoria said defiantly.

"You'd ruin your brother. You cannot go for his sake. You must think." It hurt her to speak so. She held to the chair for support and she suddenly was weak and her head swam. Her side hurt. There was a sharp pain and she was faint but she would not let Honoria know of her agony. Honoria would think she was weak or that she was seeking sympathy. "Don't you realize that if you leave your brother's house, you'll be branded as an outcast, and that he'll be branded too?"

"It's you who are driving me away. My brother will hold you accountable. If he's ruined, it will be you who ruined him by driving me out of his house."

"It's impossible to reason with you, Honoria. I'm sorry now I spoke to you as I did." There was nothing else for her to say. Her spirit revolted against seeking Honoria's forgiveness. But she must. The little hell-cat would ruin Sam. "But if you love your brother, please don't go."

Honoria smiled triumphantly. She had only contempt for Donna then, for Donna had allowed herself to be bluffed. Honoria never had any intention of leaving Locha Poka. "I'll stay for Sam's sake," she said.

Black spots leaped before Donna's eyes and darkness closed in upon her. She clutched at the chair but her knees buckled slowly and she collapsed. Honoria and Sukey were over her when she regained her senses. Honoria held a glass of brandy. Jasper took her to her room and Sukey tucked her in.

Honoria sent Sukey from the room. "What happened, Donna?" Honoria's voice trembled and she was really afraid to hear Donna's verdict.

"I don't know. I got sick and weak and there's a pain in my stomach."

"Maybe the baby moved," Honoria said hopefully. "They tell me a woman is ill the first time the baby moves."

"The baby didn't move."

Honoria sat on the bed and clutched Donna's hand. "My God, Donna, did I hit you there? I didn't know!

I swear I didn't! I just kicked out when you slapped me. Don't tell Sam'l. He'd beat me."

"I won't tell Sam'l and I don't know if you hurt me. Maybe the excitement and all made me sick. We've been fools, Honoria."

"Ay." She put her head beside Donna and cried. "I wonder why I do the things I do and say the things I say. I'm always sorry for them. I'm jealous of you, Donna. I knew I'd be. I know that Sam'l loves you more than anything in the world. I'm a wicked woman and God's judgment has been visited upon me."

Donna sat up in bed. "Don't feel sorry for yourself. I can't stand it. You're not even a woman. You're a child. A spying, prying girl with big ears and a forked tongue. We're all what we are, Honoria, and all of our tears won't change it."

"But you'll always hate me."

"Yes, I think I will. But sometimes I'm jealous of you, too. I'm envious of your shamelessness. You're a minx. Every woman, in her heart, envies a minx."

"May I sleep in here with you tonight?" Honoria pleaded like a child pleads. "I want to. You're not so much older than I am, but sometimes you seem old, Donna, and very wise. I can't blame Sam'l for loving you."

"Of course, you may stay here."

"And sleep right here where Sam'l always sleeps?"

"Why, yes. You can't sleep on the floor."

"When I was a very little girl I use to sleep with Sam'l." Honoria looked away as she spoke. Her voice was tender. "I would sleep in my dress in the winter time, and Sam'l would put his jacket over me to keep me warm. I'd snuggle up to him. And in the mornings he would wash my face. Mother was always abed and

366

Sam'l made me eat and nursed me when I was sick. He used to mumble in his sleep. About Indians. Does he still mumble, Donna?"

"Yes, he still does," Donna smiled at the recollection.

"Will he wear a night gown yet?"

"That's none of your business. I won't discuss my husband's night clothes—not even with his sister."

Sukey helped Honoria undress and bathed her with a warm cloth. Then she tucked her in and stood over the white women for a minute, awaiting further orders.

"Good night, Sukey," Donna said.

"Good night." The slave woman blew out the candle and closed the door.

Donna was up and about her tasks when Sam returned. He brought them presents and was in gay spirits. The doctor would call within a few days. There had been a yellow-fever epidemic in New Orleans and several ladies in Natchez had adopted children whose parents had died. Honoria would go to New Orleans and when she returned she would have an adopted child. No one would ever know the truth.

There was much excitement in Natchez. Spanish Governor Gayoso had taken refuge in the fort and the Americans were clamoring for war. Andrew Ellicott had arrived to mark the boundary line, but he was a high-handed man and demanded that a Mississippi Territory be formed. He and the committee he headed petitioned Congress that a government be established similar to that of the Northwest Territory. But the Northwest Territory had forbidden slavery. Lawyer Thomas had used all of his wiles—and some of Sam's and Flournoy's money—to reach a compromise on the slavery issue. They could not abolish slavery. Half the wealth of the new land was in slaves. But slavery was a damnable institution. It must be regulated. The poor Negroes must be protected. They had souls, hadn't they? And, too, the planters had a right to expect protection from the cheap island markets. Why not keep slavery, but forbid the importation of slaves from any foreign land? Hurray for the new territory! Hip, hip, hurray for Thomas Jefferson!

Spain protested to the United States concerning the action of the Americans in Natchez. The federal government in Philadelphia expressed its regrets and did nothing; but over in Natchez, Captain Guion arrived with his regulars. Spain protested again, but Guion said simply that he would stay there. Then the western Americans took matters into their own hands and told Spain that if she did not surrender Natchez by March 31, 1798, they would throw the garrison into the river and poke them under the water with the staffs of the Spanish flags.

Sam's eyes danced as he told the news to Honoria and Donna. He paced the floor in his excitement, pausing frequently at the sideboard for a drink of brandy. Jasper ran to him to light his pipe and Sam clapped his slave on the shoulder and handed him a silver dollar. When Jasper thanked him, Sam laughed loudly and said that every slave should have a silver dollar. And a drink of rum. Ration rum to the bumboes! Let 'em sing! Light a fire in the quarters and let 'em dance!

Even Donna, despite a pain which she concealed, joined in the merry-making. The slaves danced and sang until Sam ordered them to bed. They must work tomorrow. There was land to be cleared, gins to be made. Get to bed you bumboes. You've funned enough. You must be up with the sun. You must work. That is your mission in life. Work! Sweat! Eat and sleep! Copulate and die! And go back to dust. You'll lose your color in the dust. It will not be black dust. It will be gray dust. A king's dust is gray. All dust is alike. . . .

Sam slept late the next morning and had a big head. He was grumpy all day and his good spirits did not return until after dinner.

The doctor arrived three days later and, after examining Donna, called Sam to the verandah.

"All is well, isn't it?" Sam asked anxiously, noticing the doctor's serious expression. "She looks well; she hasn't had a touch of the fever in a long time."

"No, all is not well. She's having trouble carrying her child. She must stay in bed. She's been injured in some way. A blow or something. Surely she hasn't been riding?"

"She has not been injured."

"Nevertheless," the doctor cautioned, "she must be very careful."

Sam went first to Honoria and told her what the doctor had said and instructed her to see that Donna stayed in bed. "She mustn't get up for anything. You stay right by her."

They went to Donna's room and Sam passed the instructions to her. "The doctor said you had injured yourself somehow. You haven't had a fall, have you?"

"No, but there was a slight injury, Sam'l. I said naught to you about it at the time. I was drawing water one day and the windlass slipped and struck me in the stomach."

"Drawing water! What are the slaves for? You might have hurt the baby." Her carelessness angered him.

The weeks sped by to Sam and Honoria but they crept by to Donna. She never left her bed and her fever returned. She often was in pain.

Word came from Natchez that yellow fever was rag-

369

ing in New Orleans and that the town was quarantined. Honoria was ready to go to New Orleans.

"We'll send you to Mobile," Sam decided. "I cannot take you. I'll not leave Donna. But Jasper can take you. He'll keep our secret."

But Mobile was quarantined, too. Sam became alarmed. Honoria's baby would have to be born at Locha Poka. He must take Sukey into his confidence. Honoria could not be seen much longer without all of the slaves knowing her condition.

He called Sukey to his bedroom and while he sat at Donna's side, he talked to the slave and told her that Honoria would have a child. "I saved your life once, and your baby's life twice. You must be with my sister when her time comes. You'll tell the other slaves that my sister is sick. You must never tell that she has had a child. You and Jasper are the only house slaves. The others must not know."

Sukey promised and when she was gone, Donna asked, "But what will you do with her baby, Sam'l? We can't keep such a thing a secret. The other slaves will hear the child. What will we do?"

"I'll cross that bridge when I reach it." Sam could not bring himself to tell Donna that he didn't know what he would do.

Honoria stayed in her room and Donna in hers. Sam busied himself at his factory, trying to forget his dilemma. He made a hundred plans, then tore them down. He could trust Tishomingo. Tishomingo could say it was a Choctaw baby. No, he couldn't do that. There was a chance that Tishomingo might love Honoria and the information would shatter the romance.

He was at his foundry when the runner arrived at Locha Poka from Lake Flournoy with a letter for Hon-

370

oria and a gift. Jasper took the letter and present to Honoria's door. Honoria opened the present first. It was a golden chain for her neck. Then she read the letter.

"I had wanted to write you sooner [the letter said] but good taste would not permit. I heard of your betrothal to Mr. Bascomb and my heart is heavy with yours. I trust this little gift will express my esteem and lighten your burden."

Honoria stared at the next line and sat on the side of her bed and read it again. Then she shrieked, a hysterical shriek of amazement. Donna heard and leaped from her bed and ran bare-footed down the hall. Sukey called for her to stop and ran after her.

Donna opened the door and hurried to Honoria's side. "What is it? What is it, Honoria?"

Honoria looked up at her. "I didn't realize I screamed. I reckon I was excited. He's coming to see me. Lake Flournoy wants to call on me and pay me court." She stared wild-eyed at Donna. "Why are you so pale, Donna?"

Donna held the bedpost and sat down weakly on the bed. "You frightened me. I thought something had happened to you."

"Merciful God! Why did you leave your bed? Sam'l will be furious with me. Sukey, help me take your mistress to her room. Quick! She is faint."

They lay Donna upon her bed and she was limp. Honoria rubbed her wrists and gave her water.

Sukey peered into Donna's eyes. "Better git Massa Dabney," she said.

"I can't go," Honoria answered. "Send Jasper."

"You stay here." Sukey took command. "I'll send Jasper and I'll get water. Rub her hands."

Donna regained consciousness soon after Sam arrived.

371

She clutched his hand. "Don't leave me," she whispered. "My time has come."

"It can't be."

"But it has, I know."

"Jasper will ride for the doctor."

"That will be useless," Donna said calmly. "He can't get here in time. I'm stronger now, Sam'l. Please go away. I don't want you to see me."

Sam walked to the drawing room and sat down. Jasper fetched his pipe, but Sam brushed it aside. He paced the floor noiselessly. He knew full well that the chances were against his child's survival. And that Donna would need all of her strength and will to survive the shock. He wished his wife had Honoria's strength. Such a thing would never happen to Honoria. Never! She would have her child easily and soon would be up again and about her work. Honoria's child would be healthy, tough. Like Ab and Honoria. A fitting child for the new land. He paused suddenly and sat down. Damme! If his baby died, who must know it? Honoria's baby could be his. It would solve all the problems. He walked to the sideboard and reached for a drink, but changed his mind. Donna wouldn't want him to drink on this night. If his baby died—! Honoria's baby could be substituted and who would know!

All night Sukey and Honoria worked over Donna. They took turns massaging her stomach and often Honoria pushed back Donna's eyelids and glanced into the pupils. Donna's life ebbed and Honoria and the slave worked frantically. They worked until their muscles ached and the sweat popped out of their skin and dropped on Donna.

"It's no use," Honoria said. "The baby won't come." She straightened up and stretched her tired back muscles.

Then she stared at Sukey for several seconds. "Sukey, you're a woman, too. We've got to take this baby."

The slave rolled her eyes in fear. "But Miss Donna might die!"

"If we don't take the baby, she'll die anyway." Honoria was surprised at the calmness of her own voice. "Go get your master."

Sam tiptoed into the room and in low, tense words Honoria told him the situation. Sam studied his wife's pupils and looked up at his sister. "She's going fast, Hon. Take the baby. Do you need any help?"

Honoria squeezed his arm. "No, Sam'l. I'll call you if I need you."

She washed her hands and arms and told Sukey to hold the candle above her. She bit her lip until it hurt. Thank God, old man Dabney had told her about such things! Sukey mumbled a weird prayer while Honoria worked. But Honoria didn't pray. Once she glanced up at Sukey and commanded, "Hold the candle closer, you damned fool!"

The dead child was delivered shortly before dawn. Honoria handed the little body to Sukey and devoted her attention to Donna. She rubbed Donna's hands and chest and held her face close to Donna's mouth.

"Great God! I can't feel her breath."

Honoria gulped air into her own lungs and stooped over and put her mouth over Donna's and breathed into her lungs. She breathed until her own lungs tortured her, then without taking her mouth from Donna she reached up and grabbed Sukey's shoulder and pulled her beside her. The slave got on her knees and when Honoria took her mouth from Donna's, Sukey, in turn, pumped fresh air into her mistress' lungs.

"Get Sam!" Honoria commanded when she again relieved Sukey.

Sam did not speak when he entered the room, but put his hands under Honoria's arms, pulled her gently away, and then stooped over and began breathing into his wife. Honoria lay on the floor beside the bed, exhausted.

Sam was on his knees, his left hand under Donna's head. He breathed slowly and regularly, inhaling through his nose and exhaling through his mouth. He closed his eyes. His wife's flesh was cold to his lips. Sweat rolled off his forehead and ran down the sides of his face and into his mouth. It got into Donna's mouth, too.

His throat hurt and his lungs ached, and his body felt dead. First his feet seemed to tingle and then go to sleep and gradually the numbness spread through his body. Honoria tried to relieve him, but he shook his head. He felt Donna breathe slightly and her body trembled. He felt for her pulse and found it.

"Brandy!" he ordered. "Rub her legs! Her arms! Rub them hard!" Sukey put her hands over Donna's lungs and worked. Honoria rubbed her arms and Sam fed her sips of brandy. They worked until Donna's pulse grew stronger and her eyelids fluttered.

Only then Sam straightened up. "The child was dead, of course?" he asked, but he already knew the answer.

"Yes, he was dead, Sam'l," Honoria replied sadly.

"Then he was a son?"

"Ay." Honoria nodded toward the cradle that Jasper had made. Sukey had wrapped the dead baby in a quilt and laid him there.

Sam stroked Donna's forehead. "Poor Donna. I believe she knew our baby would not live. I've reconciled myself to this tragedy. I realized last night that my child probably would be born dead." He turned to Sukey. "Go

374

fetch Jasper, but mind you, not a word to him or to a soul about my baby."

He went to the cradle and looked at his son. "Donna will not want to see her child. I know she won't." He wrapped the quilt tightly around the body and lifted it and handed it to Jasper. "I want you all to listen to what I have to say. Jasper, my child was born dead. Bury him under the Big Tree. But leave no sign where you bury him. No one but ourselves knows that this child was ever born. No one must ever know. Do you understand?"

The slaves nodded. Honoria started to speak but changed her mind.

"Sukey, you and Jasper must swear before God that you will never tell. If you talk, I'll sell you in the sugar country."

"Jasper will not tell. Massa knows Jasper. Massa can trust Jasper. Jasper will bury your baby now before the other slaves get up."

"Sukey will not tell," promised the Negress.

"I'll explain later to you, Honoria," Sam added quietly. "Now go to your room and rest. We must not have this happen to you. Sukey and I will stay with Donna."

"I'll stay with you," Honoria whispered. "The iron has entered deeply into our hearts again."

Donna did not ask about the baby when she opened her eyes. She simply said, "I'm sorry, Sam'l."

He leaned over and kissed her. "He was dead, you know. And I feared I had lost you."

"I knew he was dead." She turned her face to the wall.

Sam got on his knees beside the bed and reached for her hand and held it. "I prayed for you last night, Donna. It was the first time I ever prayed. And you got well."

"But you don't believe in God. You told me you didn't. Your father didn't."

"But I believe now."

"Where is Honoria?"

Sam looked around. "She was here a minute ago. Maybe she went to her room. She stayed with you all night. She breathed into your lungs. She and Sukey saved your life. You must sleep now."

"I'm glad I did not see the baby. You understand."

"Yes, I understand."

"But there will be a child in our house," she smiled weakly. "Honoria's baby. Because we lost our baby we'll love hers all the more."

Sam thought then that he would tell her his plan. But she was too weak. He must wait. He walked out of the house and across his fields. It was good to walk across his fields. The earth was soft and spongy. His fields were rich and the furrows were open, waiting for the seed. Soon the earth would take the seeds and warm them until they swelled and burst. Then the earth would nourish them into life, and at the appointed time life would go away and there would be brown leaves and rotting wood and dust. It was all arranged, life and death.

Sam walked along the river and back up to the Big Tree. The sun had dried the earth that Jasper had turned and no one would have known that a child was buried there. Perhaps Tishomingo was right: the dead should be revered. Old man Dabney had once told him that all old civilizations revered the dead. The dead should not be allowed to sleep alone. He wished he could put a marker over the grave. He could use one of the stones that had been fetched from France for Locha Poka. The dead were entitled to a stone. The stone would be there a long time and men would pass by it and know that a baby was buried there. They would ride by in wagons, coming to the new land, over the road that he had helped build, by the house that he had built. They would see the stone and know that the first white child born in the Promised Land slept there.

Sam banished the thought. The grave must remain un-marked forever. The world must never know that Sam Dabney's son was born dead. Honoria's child would be his child. Donna would agree and Honoria would be willing. It would solve the problem. There would be only five persons who would know that Honoria had a child. The child was due soon and Donna would stay in her room. No one would ask questions. When Honoria's child was born he would take it to Donna and the child would be named Dabney.

He laid his plan first before Honoria. "You're mad!" she exclaimed.

"It's a wise plan," Sam argued. "We can trust Sukey and Jasper. Do you want to rear the child? If you want it, I will not take your child from you."

"I don't mind giving the child to you, Sam'l. It would be better for all of us. But can this thing be done?"

"You leave it to me," he said and patted her cheek. "Do not leave your room. No one has seen you except Sukey and Jasper."

She reached under her pillow and handed Sam the let-ter from Lake Flournoy. His eyebrows arched as he read it. "So he wants to see you. We'll talk about this later."

Donna agreed willingly to Sam's plan. "I did not ex-pect to go to such a limit," she said, "but I had hoped that we could keep the child. We could say that our baby died and that we adopted the child, that it was an orphan."

"My plan is better."

"But will Honoria give up her child?"

"Yes. She's wise enough to see that this is the best way.

If we say the child is an orphan, somebody will become suspicious. People don't adopt a child so soon after losing their own. Honoria knows that the child would ruin her life and that it would be branded a bastard if the world knew the truth. You stay here in bed. Only Sukey will see you and Honoria. I'll send word to the doctor that you're doing well and that we have a negro midwife with you. I can say that your child is expected soon. And when Honoria's baby is born, we'll leave it with her for a few days and then bring it to you and announce that our baby has arrived."

"Can you trust Sukey and Jasper?"

"Ay, with my life. You mustn't even tell your brother, Donna. The child will be our heir, remember."

Sam sent for Jasper and Sukey and outlined the plan to them. Unless the body slaves told, there would be no chance for the other slaves to know. The two Negroes took an oath of secrecy and Sam trusted them.

Donna improved rapidly but stayed in bed and Honoria never left her room. Sam stayed in his fields most of the day and trusted the store and foundry to Jasper. They had two gins in the foundry and his bottomland was planted with cotton and his rolling land with corn. He sent a runner to Tishomingo with a message that his child was expected. He allowed Honoria to answer Flournoy's letter and give him permission to call. Sam, however, also wrote to Flournoy and told him he would be pleased to have his sister receive him, but suggested that Flournoy wait a bit.

"We're expecting an heir at Locha Poka," Sam wrote. Donna was able to sit up in bed and Honoria was counting the days, when a runner arrived from Natchez with news that the Congress had voted Mississippi into the union as a territory. That was April the 7th, 1798. The

378

northern boundary of the territory reached from the mouth of the Yazoo River, due east to the Chattahoochee River. The Chattahoochee River was the eastern boundary and Georgia was just across the stream. The thirty-first degree of north latitude was the southern boundary, and the territory extended west to the Mississippi. Lawyer Thomas had done his job well. *Maison Blanche* was just outside the northern boundary! Spanish West Florida was to the south and New Orleans was open to the slave trade.

Sam studied the slavery law carefully: ". . . It shall not be lawful for any person or persons to import or bring into the said Mississippi Territory from any port or place within the limits of the United States, or to cause or procure to be so imported or brought, or knowingly to assist in so importing or bringing any slave or slaves."

Sam smiled at the wording. He and Flournoy would be guilty of smuggling all right. But the penalty was ridiculous: a person, if convicted, must ". . . Forfeit and pay for each and every slave so imported or brought, the sum of $300; one moiety for the use of the United States and the other moiety for the use for any person or persons who shall sue for the same; and every slave so imported or brought shall hereupon become entitled to and receive his or her freedom."

So that was the law. It was legal to trade in slaves between states but unlawful to import them. The hypocritical old New England blue-noses! Where was their rum trade to the islands? Many a bottom would rot at the wharves of Boston. But many a sanctimonious Puritan would laugh at the law. Slaves for molasses, molasses for rum. New England was built upon that trade. The triangle from Boston to Africa, Africa to the islands, the islands to Boston was the keystone in the temple of the blue-noses. A $300 penalty! Damme! Each slave would net a profit of one thousand dollars. There was no prison term. The slaves would be freed if the smugglers were caught. Then what would happen? Run them over the line to another state and sell them again. Didn't the fools know that the way to make slavery profitable was to try to curtail it? Either abolish it or let it thrive. There was no middle ground. Sam laughed out loud. The law had passed by only a few votes. The Congress almost had prohibited slavery!

Sam took the runner to the factory and gave him rum and they drank to the new territory. "But what of the Spaniards?" Sam asked.

"They've gone," the runner said. "I thought you had heard. They picked up and left, bag and baggage, without firing a shot. And Winthrop Sargent has been appointed governor."

"Who is he?" Sam demanded.

"He is from Massachusetts."

"A damned blue-nose. I'd as leave have the Spaniards."

"He's a fitting man, I hear. And moderate." The runner held up his mug. "We'll drink to him too."

"Ay, and to Thomas Jefferson." Sam drank deeply.

"And to Andy Jackson."

"And to old George Washington. To our Choctow friends. To the damned nation of the Creeks and the British. To my friend Thomas."

"And to you, by God!" The runner drained his mug and refilled it.

Sam tilted his head and laughed.

The runner slapped him on the back, "I'm not being personal but I hear you are soon to become a father. We'll drink to your son."

"To my son," Sam shouted. "May he never miss a red 'un!"

He was groggy with drink that night when Sukey aroused him. "Come, massa. Her time is here."

Sam shook his head to clear it. Jasper brought him cold water and Sam dashed it against his face and then went to Honoria's room.

Honoria smiled up at him.

"Are you all right?" Sam asked.

"Ay," she said calmly, "I'm all right. My pains began yesterday, but I said naught of them, fearing it would alarm you. My baby should be here soon. Now go out and leave Sukey with me. And don't drink too much."

He was proud of his sister—old man Dabney's brat having a baby. She would have no trouble.

Sukey gave Honoria a drink of brandy and a pillow to clutch while she labored. The slave sat by the bed and waited. Honoria looked up at the ceiling and counted between pains. When the pains became intense, she clutched the pillow. But she didn't cry out. Women were supposed to labor. Her body hurt, but her spirit was strong. She even prayed a bit. She asked God that her child be a son, and strong.

Honoria's son was born shortly before noon. She watched Sukey slap the baby on his rump, and smiled when he cried. "Now bathe him," Honoria instructed, "and go fetch my brother."

Sukey bathed the child and gave him to his mother.

"He's a beautiful baby," Honoria said, and gave her breast to him. "I'll nurse him for a few days and then we'll take him to Donna. I will get up then."

Sam kissed his sister when he came into the room to look at the baby. Then he laughed. "Damme, Hon. He's

381

big as I am. He's big enough to handle my rifle-gun right now."

"He looks like Ab, doesn't he, Sam'l?" Honoria whispered. "And I'm glad."

"I'll take him to Donna, now, so that she may see him. Then I'll bring him back. Don't worry, I won't drop him."

He took the child to his wife and laid him by her. "Here is our son," he said proudly.

She lifted the covers and looked at the child and pulled him close to her. "Is Honoria all right?"

"Ay," he said, "she's a Dabney. And having a baby is no job for a Dabney."

He didn't mean his words to sound as they did. Donna knew he had not meant to hurt her. She studied the baby for a long time. "He looks like Honoria."

"He looks like Ab," Sam insisted. "Even Honoria said so. A man-child always looks like his father."

"He looks like both of them," she smiled sadly. "He is both of them, but he will have your name."

"No, he will not have my name. We will name him Hoab—Honoria and Ab."

Sukey watched over the child day and night. Jasper hung around Honoria's door waiting for orders and happy to do any little service. Three days later Honoria got up and went with Sam to Donna's room and put the baby by her sister-in-law.

"And now," Honoria said, "there's a tie between us that must never break."

"He's a strong baby," Donna said. "He takes after you and his father."

Honoria smiled and kissed her. "Always remember that you're his mother. I hope he takes after you and Sam'l."

That day Sam sent out runners announcing that his son was born. He sent them to Tishomingo and to André. He issued rum to his slaves and gave them a holiday. They danced in the quarters and sang. All except Jasper and Sukey; they stayed near Hoab.

20

＊ ＊ ＊ ＊ ＊ ＊ ＊ ＊ ＊ ＊ ＊ ＊ ＊ ＊ ＊ ＊ ＊ ＊ ＊

Tishomingo arrived at Locha Poka two days after Hoab's birth was announced and brought presents. There was a gift from Pushmataha for the baby and presents for every member of the family. He brought an umbrella, imported from India, to Donna, and an oiled linen cape to Honoria. They would turn the rain, he explained. He had purchased them in Pensacola.

An eel-skin, decorated with beads, was Sam's present. Sam should use the skin to tie his hair. It was very fashionable, more fashionable than wearing the queue in a black bag. He also fetched Sam a supply of Kit-foot tobacco, a product of Philadelphia and a sweeter tobacco than the rough burley of the Southwest. For Hoab he had a pair of doeskin breeches.

The breeches brought an exclamation of surprise from Honoria and peals of laughter from Donna.

"The baby can't wear breeches yet," Donna said.

"He needs pants," Tishomingo answered. "I made them myself. They will not leak. Every boy needs doeskin breeches—ay, Big Sam?"

"For sure," Sam agreed. "It's a rightful heritage of every boy. But how will he hold them up, Chock?"

"That's his problem, not mine. How does any man hold up his breeches? The Indian makes his breeches tight enough around the waist to stay up. But the white man makes his breeches loose around the waist and they are everlastingly slipping down."

Donna measured the doeskin on the baby and shook her head. "He'll have to wear dresses for a while."

Sam chuckled. "Ay, he won't have trouble keeping his dresses up, for they fit over his shoulder. I wonder why grown men don't rig some sort of gear that will hold their pants up. A piece of cloth over the shoulders and connected to the top of the breeches would do the trick. I think I'll make them."

"You're always thinking of turning a penny," Chock laughed.

"I must think so." Sam walked out of the room with his friend. "I have a family now."

Jasper fetched their pipes to the drawing room and they talked long and earnestly of their problems. Now that the slave laws were passed Tishomingo should go to Barataria and meet a cargo of Flournoy's slaves. Sam was anxious to turn a quick profit on the bumboes. He needed money badly. He had been able to settle with the Spanish merchants for fifty cents on the dollar because their businesses were ruined when the Americans took over Natchez, but it had taken all of his cash to settle up. His land still was heavily mortgaged for the material and labor that had been put in Locha Poka, and his place was not half completed.

He had realized virtually no profit from his gins. The cotton market was depressed, due to wars in Europe and the dangers of sea travel. And, too, hundreds of planters were making their own gins. Crossroads blacksmiths had lifted Whitney's invention without permission, and gins were being turned out like spinning wheels. Of course, Whitney had sued, but it was impossible for him to protect his rights.

Frome had seen that a monopoly on the gin was impossible and had offered Sam $3,000 cash for his percentage of the Georgia business. Frome had sent word to Sam that he no longer cared to gin cotton on a percentage basis. He was being paid in cotton and he had cotton stacked on the wharves of Savannah, but could not ship it to Europe. If the French or Spanish didn't seize it, the British did. Frome was willing to manufacture gins and sell them directly to the planters, but he would not pay Sam more than $3,000 for his rights.

"After all," he had written, "you had no legal right to the gin. The patent belonged to poor old Whitney. It is true that you improved the gin. I am willing to pay you for this improvement. If you do not care to accept my proposition, then I will manufacture gins without your permission. No court of law would recognize your claim against me, because you violated the law in pirating the plans. The only reason I offer you any money at all is because of the love I bear you and your sister."

Sam had guffawed at the letter. It was the first good laugh he had had in a long time. The idea of Frome surrendering $3,000 for love amused him. Frome was afraid that Sam would divert all the horse-train business from the new land to Savannah by another route and leave Frome on a dead trail.

He had written the cagey trader that he would accept $5,000, hard money, for his interest in the business. "If you do not care to accept my terms," Sam had written, "I will divert all business from the Choctaw Nation to Pensacola or to Savannah by the lower route. Cobwebs will gather in your factory. I will have my friend André increase his tolls on the Tombigbee ferry, and hides from the Choctaw Nation will become so expensive to you that your saddlery will fail. My friend André has much influence among the Creeks and I will see that he limits your supply of hides from the nation. I also will bring a lawsuit against you for manufacturing perfumes from a formula that my sister owns. I counsel you to send me $5,000. The only reason I will sell to you for this small sum is because of the love I bear you."

Frome had screamed blackmail but had paid the $5,000. He insisted upon a release from Sam for any claim Dabney might have against him for the manufacture of cheap perfume. But Sam refused a release. The perfume business belonged to Honoria and she had written Frome that she would not give him anything.

Sam had sold his interest in Flournoy's ginning enterprises for $2,000. It was better than nothing, and Flournoy had threatened to suspend the business altogether unless he had the right to manufacture, sell and lease the gins without paying a percentage to Sam. Too late, Sam had realized that there was no profit in leasing gins. But he would continue to manufacture them and to sell them on long terms.

The trade route from Natchez to Georgia had not proved profitable. With New Orleans open, most of the goods cleared for Europe from that port. They had cut a canal to Lake Pontchartrain, and small boats took produce from the city to the big ships, anchored in the lake. In that way, many ships avoided the long voyage up to New Orleans from the Gulf.

Traders would not risk the hazards and expenses of sending goods on horse trains through the Creek country to ship them from the American port to Savannah. They needed a wagon road to Georgia but the Creeks forbade it.

Sam's post was netting a good profit, but with the territory part of the union, the government might take it over any time. Sam must see that Thomas looked after that. If the government did take over the post, he must retain the right to operate it. All of the profits from his trading post were eaten up by Locha Poka.

"So you see, Chock," he told his friend, "I've got many irons in the fire but most of them are cold. I'm a poor man. I will use the cash from my deals with Flournoy and Frome to liquidate my debts. Then I'll mortgage my land again and finish my house. I really am not making any money except from the post and the ferry. My cotton has netted me nothing because of the situation in Europe."

"Then it seems to me," Chock advised him, "that you should take cash from Flournoy instead of slaves."

Sam shook his head violently. "I will not. Slaves will be a gold mine in this territory. A slave wench can produce two children every three years. That is where I'll make my money. Then I have other plans. . . . But there is a personal matter I must speak of."

"Ay?"

"You're my best friend. I have an heir now and I'm having Lawyer Thomas draw my will. If I should die, Pierce Chadbourne will execute my estate. But if Donna and I both should die ——"

Tishomingo interrupted. "You shouldn't speak of death."

"I walk with death every day, and you know it. And Donna's health is poor. It's a thing we must face. If we both should die, I want you to rear my son."

"But what of Honoria? It seems a man would want his sister to care for his child." Chock was openly surprised.

"I want you to do this for me. It is a responsibility I will not pass to my sister."

388

Tishomingo agreed and they shook hands before the Choctaw took his departure for Louisiana.

André and Anestasie arrived. The Frenchman was in gay spirits, for his trading post was booming. True, the business that he and Sam had expected from the Natchez-Georgia trail had not materialized, but André had devoted all of his time to building trade with the Creeks. He had called on old Jim McQueen, and most of the business along the Tombigbee went to his factory. He had made only two gins in his foundry and couldn't lease them.

"Every planter is making his own gin," André said. "Nails! That's the thing. I make nails in my foundry. And wheels. Is it not strange to you, Sam'l, that the Indians never thought of a wheel? They didn't even have a pottery wheel until the white man came. The wheel will be the salvation of the Indian."

"And his ruin," Sam said. "My father always said that the wheel was the greatest curse and the greatest blessing of mankind. It is not strange that the Indian never thought of it, for he had no beast of burden until the white man came. Why did he need a wagon if he had no horse to pull it? For that matter, the Indian never thought of putting a sail on his canoe."

Sam was surprised when he realized that André was not a citizen of the territory. John Adams' harsh naturalization laws had barred the Frenchman. Of course, the ceremony back in South Carolina when André had been sworn in as a citizen had been a farce. "So I have no voice in the government," André declared bitterly. "But you have much influence. Our plans to grow rich on the trade from the Mississippi to the Chattahoochee will never bear fruit until we get a wagon road. It is too expensive and uncertain to ship by horse train. I send my

389

goods to Mobile and Pensacola. In a few years I am going to build a mansion."

The Frenchman had built his barn before he built his cabin. He and Anestasie still were living in their cabin and would not build a big house until the stock and slaves were housed and comfortable. He would not go into debt as Sam had done.

Because of his friendship with McQueen and the Creeks, André was a fountain of information. The Spaniards had allied themselves with the Creeks, Chickasaws and Cherokees, and were determined to protect their western lands from the United States even if they had to foment rebellion among the Indians. Spain was not nearly so interested in holding Louisiana and West Florida as most Americans thought. The Spanish didn't want American soldiers in Louisiana, because Louisiana bordered Texas and Texas was the key to Mexico. Spain wanted American settlers in Louisiana, however, but never soldiers. There was always a possibility that the dream of Spain, and even France, might materialize—that the West would leave the United States and set up its own republic. England, too, was playing for such a republic. It would be a buffer between the valley and the ambitious republic along the seaboard.

Gayoso, the ex-governor of Natchez, had been made governor of Louisiana. There was a man to watch. He had friends among the Americans. His leniency at Natchez had made him popular. Why had he been so kind and tolerant in Natchez? A fool could see it. He wanted support from the westerners. Spain would never give up the idea of a weak American republic in the Southwest.

Sam tapped André on the knee. "And what of Ellicott; what have you heard of him?"

"He's honest, but he is too high-handed. The Creeks hate him. He has included much Creek land in the Mississippi Territory. You will have to fight to hold it. He has insulted Gayoso. He has intercepted Gayoso's mail and opened it. You do not know Europeans, Sam'l, as I do, but Spain would never tolerate such a situation if it did not believe that the West will leave the United States."

"And what else know you?"

"There's talk that France will get Louisiana. The Duke of Orleans has been in New Orleans and to Natchez. If the monarchy ever is reëstablished, he may be king of France," André said prophetically.

"What does it mean?" Sam asked.

"Never be foolish enough to think that Spain really is your friend. Spain's at the mercy of France. And neither country can see England at the mouth of the Mississippi. I wouldn't be surprised at all if Spain gave Louisiana back to France. Most of the people there still are loyal to their first allegiance."

New Orleans had become the city of sin, André explained, and was filled with pirates and smugglers, spies and revolutionists, pimps and whores. In far-away Boston, the ministers thundered against the wickedness of the city, while many of their devout worshipers visited the Sodom at every opportunity. Every Sunday was a feast day. The quadroon girls, always chaperoned, strolled the streets in their gay finery. Young Creole blades, the proud sons of French and Spanish unions, eyed the quadroons. The quadroons never lifted their eyes to return the stares. Natchez was as wicked as New Orleans. The favorite sport in both cities was animal baiting. In one event, six dogs fought a bull. A fight between a Canadian bear and four dogs was considered a sport worthy of the keel-boat men. Tigers were matched against bears. The main event usually was a fight between a bear and a bull. The judges then tied fireworks to the back of the grand champion and shot them off. The explosions drove the animal mad. The price of admission to the circus was one dollar for adults and fifty cents for children. There was no charge for babes in arms.

"There are still not enough women to go around in New Orleans," André remarked. "Many white men have taken up with squaws and Negroes. There's talk that another cargo of young women will be shipped to the planters. *Filles à la Cassette* they are called—the casket girls. We need some of them in this territory."

"Why do they call them casket girls?" Sam asked, amused. "Because they are coming to their deaths?"

"Oh, no," André laughed. "Because they bring their clothes in small trunks shaped like caskets. And here is the most important news of all. Bonaparte has married Josephine. Our friend Flournoy will be prouder than ever now. Napoleon bids fair to become a most important man in France. He already is a hero. His campaigns in Italy and against Austria made him the public idol. There's danger of war between him and Spain. If it comes to pass, he will snatch Louisiana, maybe West Florida. Do you know what that would mean?"

"Ay, the end of Spain."

"But more," André said earnestly. "England will never allow France to control the Mississippi River."

They talked far into the night and Sam gathered much intelligence to send to Harkins. He told André of Flournoy's request to visit Honoria and asked his counsel. The Frenchman advised against it. He suggested politely that Honoria be sent to Natchez or New Orleans. At

Locha Poka there was no opportunity to meet any eligible men except Tishomingo and Flournoy.

"I have thought of that," Sam considered. "My wife has mentioned it to me. She, too, suggested that I send Honoria to Natchez."

André glanced up quickly and Sam continued. "My wife is very interested in my sister's well-being, of course. We naturally are anxious to see her happily married. I can send her to visit Mrs. Harkins' kinspeople in Natchez. I'll do that soon, but first there's some business I would talk with you. I need cash."

"What is your plan?" André asked. "Your plans for the trade between Natchez and Georgia and for the gins didn't work out so well, you know."

"But this is a better plan." Sam put down his pipe and faced André. "Sargent is very unpopular. That damned Adams has sent three judges to the territory and only two of them are lawyers. They work hand and glove with Sargent. They have levied all kinds of taxes against the people and are lining their pockets with the fees. Sargent has even proclaimed that treason shall be punished by death and that a man's land can be taken if he is judged a traitor."

"A traitor should die," André said with finality.

"Perhaps, but Adams' judges have the right to say who is a traitor. Why, man, according to Adams' idea, half the people in this land are traitors, for they are opposed to him. Only the Congress really has the right to declare the punishment for treason. The Constitution says that excessive fines and punishment shall not be imposed, but Sargent's code holds that a man convicted of arson must be whipped, pilloried, imprisoned for three years and his estates forfeited. The people won't stand for it. He's driving this territory into rebellion. Either he'll be driven out or the people will rise up."

"But why does that concern us?"

"There's talk of a great change, even of a new capital. Many of us want to move the seat of government from Natchez."

"But where would it go?" André demanded with interest.

"It's up to us to see that it goes where we own land. My man, Thomas, is a good man for such a task. He can work miracles with cash. If you'll put up the money, I will see that we get land where the new capital is built. I cannot secure my loan from you. I'm mortgaged to my neck."

"Your word is good, Sam'l. I'll put up the money. I'm not a citizen and cannot buy land. You buy the land in your name and we will turn a neat penny. You're one of the few men in the territory I will trust. It is a deal and we will drink to it, but there is a thing I would say."

"Speak," said Sam.

"We're friends, Sam'l, and I feel that I have the right to talk to you. If I were you, I'd beware of debt. You've got too many irons in the coals. Get some of them out. You've a good location here and can make a fortune with your factory and land. I know the Creeks won't trade with you. They hate you. But the Choctaws' trade is ample. I advise you to cease going off on these wild schemes. A fortune cannot be made in a day."

"I think you're right," Sam answered gravely.

André took back with him a cote of Sam's homing pigeons. He planned to use them for quick communication between his place and Locha Poka. Sam had tried to interest other traders in the pigeons but they had

394

laughed at him. He had used them a few times himself but they were not the asset Sam had hoped they would be.

He sent money to Thomas and instructed him to use it to buy options on land and to see that if and when the capital would move, it was located to their advantage. Then he devoted his time to Locha Poka. He hired two post riders and pushed the traffic for all it was worth. He sent traders among the Chickasaws with needles and perfume. Honoria was kept busy mixing the perfume.

The child Hoab soon was able to suck a sugar tit that Sukey made. Jasper kept bacon rinds and ham skins within reach, and Donna divided her time between the baby and her household. Despite Sam's protest she worked until her low reserve was exhausted. The fever, however, did not return. But she constantly was tired.

Often Honoria in fits of temper and irritation intimated that Donna enjoyed her own illness. Honoria was so healthy that she could not understand sickness. Donna remained aloof from her sister-in-law and ignored her taunts, determined that if a break must come, Honoria must make it in the presence of her brother. Donna's complacency infuriated Honoria and once Donna told her, "I sicken of your outbursts of temper, of your malicious behavior and of the tears of regret that always follow. But they have no effect on me. I'll not subject my household to a common family brawl."

Honoria tossed her head and laughed mockingly. "You speak of brawls. You seem to forget ——"

"Shut up!" As weak as she was, Donna opened her hand to strike Honoria, but managed to regain her temper.

"I wonder what people would think if they knew that Hoab was my baby?" Honoria taunted her.

Donna laughed at the idea. "Who would believe you? I wish you would state publicly that Hoab is your child."

"Why?" Honoria was surprised and baffled.

"Because people would say you were a loony. And I could send you to a mad-house."

Honoria trembled. She had bluffed Donna, but she knew that Donna wasn't bluffing.

"My brother wouldn't allow it."

"Just dare and say that Hoab is your child and see what your brother will do. You gave Hoab to us, and even he will never know that you're his mother."

Honoria cocked her head slightly and looked quizzically at Donna, trying to read her mind. She was puzzled, but she dared not force the issue. Donna held the trump hand and Honoria boiled inside of herself. She turned and left Donna. Donna smiled to herself and wondered what Sam really would do in such a crisis. Anyway, the word "mad-house" had frightened Honoria.

They built two new rooms at Locha Poka and Sam gave much of his time to his land, and to the land company that had retained him. He sent regular dispatches to the company, reporting the news of the Territory. He sold land to three families and located two more families on places that the company had sold.

By midsummer, the mansion virtually was complete, but many of the rooms were not furnished and others contained only the bare necessities. There were rugs in the drawing room, two of the guest rooms and the master room. Sam's office was off from the drawing room. There was a library with a few books. They were Donna's books, but she never found time to read them. Sam never read many books; however, he often studied the Bible and read it aloud to Donna and Honoria. Once, to Honoria's amazement, he entertained a traveling evangelist at Locha Poka and plied him with questions about God which the evangelist could not answer. The Baptists, Methodists and Presbyterians were sending missionaries to the new land. Over at New Scotland a kirk had been built, but the members spoke only Gaelic, and Sam could not understand them. There was a report, the evangelist said, that Lorenzo Dow was coming to the Territory. Dow was a Methodist from Massachusetts and considered the world his circuit. He often rode horseback from Massachusetts to Georgia to conduct a revival meeting. He mapped his engagements two and three years ahead and never failed to meet them.

There was no school for white children in the district, but plans were afoot to organize a Society for the Diffusion of Useful Knowledge. The evangelist left some religious literature with Honoria, but she never read it. She had never read a book in her life.

The slave ship arrived on schedule and Sam got five handsome wenches as his commission. A new process for refining sugar, invented by Etienne Bore, had increased the price for slaves twofold in Louisiana, and Flournoy disposed of his cargo at a fat profit. He didn't have to run the slaves into Mississippi, but Sam's five were smuggled in and were fetched to him at night by Tishomingo and Caesar.

Sam had expected a good assortment of slaves. He knew that the traders expected to lose thirty percent of their cargo on each voyage, but the losses on Flournoy's ship appalled him. He also had expected to get mixed-breeds, some Wolofs and Fulans from Senegambia, some Yorubams and perhaps some Ewes and other Soudanese. Maybe he would get some bumboes of Moorish blood.

397

But Flournoy's cargo was made up of Bantu Negroes. Sam did not want to have many of his slaves of the same tribe. It was too dangerous. So long as the Negroes could not speak among themselves and so long as their customs were different there was small chance of an uprising. The South Carolinians had made the mistake of buying many slaves of the same blood and had paid for their stupidity with a rebellion in which twenty-one whites were killed. New York had forbidden slavery partly because the state feared an uprising. And twice in New York City the people, apparently fearing a rebellion, had burned Negroes. All of the North was turning against slavery. Vermont slaves, the first to be freed, had been emancipated for twenty years. The Northwest Territory was forbidden slaves, and although the people petitioned twice that slavery be permitted, the Congress had refused the request. The Constitution sanctioned the slave trade but the politicians in Philadelphia were doing strange things with the Constitution.

Sam had never seen such slaves as the ones he got from Flournoy. Their ears were notched and they crawled with lice. Jasper rubbed their heads with oil and made them wear dresses. But they would wear nothing under their dresses and were filthy. Sam wanted to breed them immediately but the other slaves shunned them. They were surly and savage. He put them in a barricoon, afraid to trust them in the quarters. They spoke no English and had not the vaguest notion where they were. Sam was frightened when Tishomingo explained that the reason he received only five slaves was because the black vomit had decimated the cargo.

"Then why did you bring them here?" Sam demanded. "The black vomit is a sign of yellow fever and it spreads like wildfire."

"That's not true," Tishomingo answered. "I have seen men sleep with other men who had yellow fever and they did not catch it. At this season there's little danger of the yellow fever here. We're too far from the sticky swamps. That's where the fever breeds."

Flournoy had sent the ship back to Martinique in ballast and it soon would return with more bumboes.

"I only saw Flournoy once," Tishomingo volunteered. "We did not speak except of business. I expect to reopen my school this fall. Will Honoria help me?"

"No," said Sam, "I'm sending her to Natchez."

Flournoy arrived at Locha Poka after he disposed of his slaves. Sam purposely had not set a date for the visit and had hoped Flournoy would not come. He would not offend the man, however, and made elaborate preparation to entertain him. Donna had a pig roasted and Sukey prepared her famous dish of corn roasted in the shuck. Sam opened a new cask of madeira.

Flournoy's eyes sparkled when he saw Honoria and he bowed gallantly. The scar which Tishomingo's bull whip had penciled on his cheek gave his face a sardonic, yet somehow attractive, cast. She took him to see Hoab and he had a present for the baby and one for Donna.

"You look tired, Mrs. Dabney."

"She's always ailing," Honoria cut in before Donna could speak. "The new land doesn't agree with her."

Donna bridled. "I'm stronger than you think."

"The fever and childbirth will leave any woman weak," Flournoy said soothingly. He realized his remark had started friction. "Be careful that the fever doesn't reach your lungs. The best preventive is lots of rest."

"She rests enough," Honoria laughed bitterly. Her

sarcasm startled Flournoy. He liked spirit, but he didn't like to hear women squabble.

"Ay," Donna smiled. "I get lots of rest. That is, my body rests. Honoria is such a competent and cheerful housekeeper that I turn my duties over to her. I dislike to impose upon her goodness, but she is such a sweet girl that she insists upon trying to take my place as mistress of this house."

Honoria smiled too, a quick fleeting smile, but her eyes burned into Donna.

Flournoy went with Sam to the barricoons and examined the five new slaves. He took one of them by the arm and pulled her into the sunlight and spoke to her in French.

The Negress rolled her eyes in fright and Flournoy turned to Sam. "I told her that the fer-de-lance was in the swamps hereabouts. You may let them out. They'll not run away. Send them down to the river and make them wash."

"My other slaves will have naught to do with them. I want a buck among them."

Flournoy said, "Your bumboes are afraid of these, but I have a buck I'll trade you. What will you give me?"

"I'll give you the choice of any of my bucks, except Jasper."

Flournoy watched Jasper as he marched the slaves to the river. "I don't want him. But I'll give you a prime buck and three hundred dollars for that house slave of yours."

"Sukey?" Sam shook his head quickly. "Oh, no. Damme, man, I'd as leave trade my right arm as Sukey. What else have I got for the bargain?"

"I'll not rob you. I'll take one of your field slaves and send you a Martinique buck."

"You're very kind," Sam thanked him, "and generous."

Flournoy smiled his charming smile. "I am your friend."

He rode with Honoria that afternoon and she showed him all of the land. He spoke to her of his family and of his childhood. He complimented her upon her energies and her ambition. "You're a very clever woman. Let me buy perfumes from you. I can get them at a good price."

Honoria was flattered but she set a high price on her perfumes. He didn't tell her that he was a lonely man and he made no effort to arouse her sympathies. "I was quite surprised," he said, "when you told me that you bore me no malice because of Ta-lo-wah. Most women are rather silly about such things. Believe me, my dear, I'm not responsible for the tragedy."

"I know that Tishomingo brought her here," Honoria said.

"It would not be becoming for me to discuss my friend's personal matters, but the girl was ill when she came to my house, I did the best I could for her. She was not as pretty as you are. Perhaps if she had been, I could not have been so impersonal."

Honoria tossed her head. "You embroider your words. You don't have to explain to me about Ta-lo-wah. I'm not jealous."

"I wish you were," he replied, glancing at her with interest.

"Why should I be jealous of a dead person?" Honoria asked boldly. "I'm afraid only of the living."

He leaned from his horse and patted her arm as she spoke and then reined his horse closer to hers.

Honoria checked her horse, too, and looked over at him and said, "You're the best horseman I've ever seen."

"I have other accomplishments, too." He reached for her hand and she allowed him to hold it for a second or so; then she withdrew it.

"Such as?" Honoria smiled suggestively.

"I know good perfume when I smell it. I know your perfume is not really good perfume. It might be good enough for many ladies, but not for you."

"What kind of perfume should I have?"

Flournoy reached for her hand again but she refused him the privilege of holding it. "Your perfume should be lily of the valley. A bit for your hair and perhaps a drop on your breast. That is enough. Just a trace. . . ." Flournoy's eyes danced and he gesticulated with his strong hands as he talked.

Honoria was enraptured. A man talking of perfumes. Ab had spoken to her of lice in his beard, but this man spoke of perfumes.

"Yes, go on."

"And you should have a black dress." Flournoy drank in her youth and freshness as he talked. "Black velvet. With a brooch at your throat. It should be simple but made of old, old gold."

"And I need rings on my fingers," Honoria laughed excitedly.

"No! Good God, no, Honoria! Perhaps one gold ring but no more. You yourself are a jewel. . . ."

She allowed him to hold her hand again, and to kiss her fingers, each finger separately, and then he kissed the palm of her hand.

After supper Sam and Flournoy sat in his office and drank brandy, and Flournoy boasted of the marriage of Josephine to Bonaparte. "It's lucky for me," he said, "for mind you, Dabney, France will own Louisiana some day and because Bonaparte is my kinsman by marriage I will have influence there."

"Then perhaps we can strike a trade," Sam said. "I may want to do business in the sugar country. And I'll need friends."

"I think you can count on me. And, by the way, I would be honored if you and your family would visit me."

"I cannot get away now," Sam replied, "and my wife is not well."

"Perhaps your sister could visit *Maison Blanche*."

Sam got up slowly and looked coldly at Flournoy, "I hope I do not misunderstand you, sir."

Flournoy waved his hand and smiled, "Great God, no, man! I don't even hint that she should come alone. I'm a gentleman. If your wife cannot be with her, I had planned to ask my friends, André and Anestasie."

"Oh," said Sam, and sat down. He felt very foolish. "Of course if my sister wants to be your guest, I'll be happy to give her my permission. Now about this sugar country. My friend, Philip Nolan, over in Natchez, plans a trip to Texas to hunt wild horses. I may help back him. If I do, I'll want to trade some of my horses in the sugar country."

Flournoy took a pinch of snuff and glanced up at Sam and smiled slowly. His teeth flashed and he burst into a loud laugh. "I admire you, Dabney. I admired you when you drove such a hard bargain with me about the slaves. I admire you now because you're a man who will take a chance ——"

"By God, what do you mean?"

"Don't excite yourself. I know you have no money. Yet you talk of backing Philip Nolan as though you were a rich man. I know that Nolan says he is going after horses but I also know the real purpose of his expedition and so do you. If the Spaniards don't kill him, then there will be American settlers west of the Sabine. It's another land-grabbing plot, Dabney. Let me in on it and I'll back you up to $10,000."

"I know naught of what you speak. My lawyer is giving Nolan money to catch horses; that is all I know. I ask you to introduce me to your friends in Louisiana so I can sell my horses. I'm bringing some of the horses here and hope soon to get some jacks from Tennessee and raise mules."

Flournoy slapped his thigh. "You've got your fingers in a hundred pies, Dabney. People are saying you're going to get burnt, but I don't think so. You'll stumble into a gold mine some day. You'll keep on dabbling around until you make a lucky strike and then you'll buy us all out. But why, in the name of God, do you want mules? This is ox country."

Sam filled their glasses. "Never you mind that, I have my reasons." He drew deeply on his pipe and boasted for one of the few times in his life, when he was sober. "You're partly right, Flournoy, I cannot put my hands on a lot of money now. But a few years ago I was a ragged-arsed, snotty-nosed brat with only a Tower musket and a bound-out sister. Now I've got five thousand acres of good land. Locha Poka soon will be finished. I own slaves, a post, a ferry, a factory, a foundry and I have friends ——"

"And enemies," interrupted Flournoy.

"Only the Creeks, and to hell with them! I have a beautiful wife and a healthy son. I own the best rifle in the United States."

"Yes, you've done well—much better than I have. I

404

envy you. I envy you your home and your son." Flournoy's tone was smooth as glass—and as brittle.

"You should have no trouble getting a wife," Sam said. "And I'll give you a recipe for a son."

They both laughed. "I've a lot of faith in you," Flournoy continued, "and I know you don't owe much money and that you'd like to get your hands on some cash. I'll always buy that Sukey of yours and any time you want to talk business I will take over your mortgage and advance you $10,000, hard money, for a second mortgage."

"God's navel!" Sam stretched in his chair and stared at his guest. "Are you jesting with me? Those outlaws up on the Trace would not hold a man up in that manner. My land alone is worth $20,000."

"Maybe it is worth that much to you, but not to anybody else. You're squatting too near the Creeks and Choctaws. You couldn't sell your land for a bit an acre. It's too close to the powder barrel. But we won't haggle. If ever you need any cash, just come to me."

Flournoy slept late the next morning but Sam was at his factory when Tishomingo rode up. "Where's Flournoy?" Tishomingo demanded.

"He's sleeping it off," said Sam. "What's up?"

"The Spaniards threaten to close New Orleans to the Americans again. Three regiments of the regular army are forming along the Ohio. Kentucky and Tennessee are up in arms. If the Spaniards cock a trigger there'll be war."

They aroused Flournoy and he sat on the side of his bed while his body slave removed his fine gown and sponged his body with warm water. "It looks like war," Tishomingo told him.

Flournoy yawned and tilted his head so his slave could shave him. "What do you want of me, Tishomingo?" he asked suspiciously, and walked to a mirror and ran his finger across the scar that Tishomingo's whip had left.

Tishomingo looked into the mirror at Flournoy's eyes and Flournoy returned the look of burning hatred.

"The minute the Americans march, the Creeks will go to arms and they'll call upon us to help them," Tishomingo said. "My uncle sent me to you. For no other reason would I come. He says you must speak to the Chickasaws and to the Choctaws near *Maison Blanche*. If the Spaniards demand that the Chickasaws fulfill their alliance, you must tell the Chickasaws not to heed the Spaniards. If they do, they'll be scattered."

"You're insane," Flournoy flared. "The Muscogees will help the Spaniards."

"You don't know your own people, Flournoy," Tishomingo hissed. "The Choctaws are the greatest of the Muscogees, and if the Americans march, the Choctaws will march with them. It is a pledge of Pushmataha." To Sam he added, "If war comes, you must abandon Locha Poka. You're too close to West Florida and the Creeks for safety."

Sam assembled his household around him and told them the news. He paced the floor to give the import of his words time to register with his people. He hoped that Donna, someone, would make a suggestion. He wanted to go off with Tishomingo and Flournoy and talk it over. But his wife was watching him. Tishomingo, standing by the door to the drawing room, was watching him, and Flournoy, lolling insolently in a big chair, was staring at him through a haze of smoke.

"I came here to live and I'm not going to run away." The words sounded hollow even to him. "If there's war we'll be in danger, but Sam Dabney will never run from

406

a Red Stick or a greasy Spaniard. I'll not leave Locha Poka. Donna, you and Honoria will take the baby to Natchez. Sukey and Jasper will go too."

Donna spoke calmly, "You forget yourself, Sam'l. I, too, came here to live and I will not go away. And, too, who will look after you?"

"Sukey and Jasper will have to stay to look after the little massa," Jasper said.

"I will not make anyone leave this house," Sam said. "But if the Red Sticks go on the war-path, they'll strike this place first to get Sukey and Dabby."

"But first," declared Tishomingo, "they must cross the Choctaw Nation. We're the allies of the United States, Big Sam, and so long as one Choctaw brave is alive, the Red Sticks will never reach Locha Poka."

"Then it's settled," said Sam. "We stay—except you, Honoria. I want you to go to Natchez. It was my plan anyway."

Honoria shook her head. "I'll stay here too." There was an air of finality about her voice, as though none should doubt that she would stay.

"You'll go to Natchez," Sam said firmly. His sister gasped, then glared at Donna. Donna ignored the stare.

"But, Sam'l," Honoria cajoled, "I've always ——"

"Enough of this mouthing," Sam said. "I have no time for your whimpering. My wife and I have decided that you should go to Natchez. We will not change our plans."

Honoria sat down on her chair quickly, as though she had lost her support, but she soon regained her composure. Donna must not enjoy her triumph. "Hoity Toity," said Honoria gayly, "I'm glad. Natchez will be interesting and filled with soldiers. I'll leave tomorrow." She looked boldly at Flournoy. "And, too," she said, "I want to purchase some things in Natchez. A black velvet dress, some lily of the valley perfume and perhaps a beautiful brooch. . . ."

"I'll see that you get there," offered Tishomingo.

"That is kind of you," said Flournoy. "But I'm going that way. There's no need for both of us to go."

"No, there's no need for both of us to go." Tishomingo's voice was as sharp and stinging as his whip lash. "I'll be ready tomorrow, Honoria."

"Don't bother," Honoria looked at him coldly and haughtily. "I will go with Mr. Flournoy."

Ah, that should hurt him. That would be a lesson to him, the high and mighty half-breed. But there was only pity in the mingo's eyes. Flournoy smiled his triumph, but Tishomingo looked at Honoria and then away.

"I hope you're safe," he said, and turned his back to them.

"Where are you going, Chock?" Sam asked.

"To warn our friends, André and Anestasie."

Sam walked to the porch with him and put his arms on his friend's shoulder, "Honoria is a spit-fire. She has a grudge against you."

"I'm not offended," said Tishomingo evenly. "The only reason I volunteered to escort Honoria was because she's your sister and I love you. But if she were my sister, Big Sam'l, I'd rather leave her here exposed to the dangers of the Red Sticks than to trust her beyond that river with Lake Flournoy."

"You overstep yourself, Chock," Sam said quickly. "I'm capable of running the affairs of my family."

"Your words do not hurt me. Nothing you can ever say or do will offend me, for I pledged to you that I would be your friend as long as the waters run to the sea. But mind you, Big Sam, you'll regret this day. And

408

your sister will regret it. This day will leave a wound in your heart that time can never heal. Flournoy is playing with you as a cat plays with a mouse. Be on your guard lest he take your sister, your home and all of your friends, except me."

21

SAM watched his sister and Flournoy ride toward the
west, and a few minutes later Tishomingo rode away
toward the east. Sam ran his long fingers through his
thick hair and went to his office to think. He glanced up
into the mirror above his desk and his own appearance
surprised him. There were tiny wrinkles around his eyes.
He was too young a man to have wrinkles, but men wrinkled early in the new land. A man was full-grown at
eighteen. Sam ran his tongue over his teeth and examined
them in the mirror. That was the best way to tell a man's
age—look at his teeth. His teeth were even, hard and
bright. Not as sparkling as Flournoy's teeth, but good
teeth. The rough coarse food was good for his teeth.

He tossed his head and let his mane fall to his shoulders. There were a few gray hairs in his head, mostly
around his temples. Old man Dabney's black hair had
been shot with gray before he was thirty, and Sam realized that soon his hair would be sprinkled with white.
But he felt strong and young. His blood was rich and his
lust for life was richer. Donna was sick . . .

He had denied himself the joy of his wife's bed, for he
was a tender man. But the abstinence had caused his
temper to sharpen, his nerves to become taut and his
emotions to well up. Of course, a man could always
satisfy his lust with a slave wench. But not Sam Dabney.

Donna understood his torture long before he did, and her heart hurt for him. It was she who suggested that they use separate bedrooms. She knew that it was mental agony for Sam to sleep beside her. So she had told him, "It would be best if you slept in one of the guest rooms, Sam'l. My coughing keeps you awake."

"But you might need me during the night," he said.

She had wanted so badly to caress his face then and to run her hands through his hair. But she lowered her eyes so he could not tell that she was lying. "Your presence disturbs me, Sam'l. I believe I can rest better alone."

Sam had looked into her eyes. "Look at me and say that, Donna."

"I can't," she said. "I can't lie to you about such a thing. But you know I'm right. This way is torture for you and agony for me. Some day I'll be well and strong again. . . ."

Sam had moved into a guest room.

He sat now in his study and thought of many things. Donna would never be well again. He knew it. Had he done wrong in allowing Honoria to go with Flournoy? Nay. Honoria could take care of herself. And if he had forbidden her to go with Flournoy, she might have gone anyway.

He wrote a few words to Pierce concerning the things Tishomingo had told him, and sent the news by pigeon. He asked Pierce for all the information he had. He sent word to Thomas for news.

The intelligence that he wanted began trickling into Locha Poka less than a week later. Old John Adams finally had got his Yankee dander up and was horsing for a fight. France still was looking down its long bloody nose at the United States, and diplomatic relations between the two nations were at a stand-still. Napoleon was standing on the parapets of Paris and crowing like a game-cock. Thomas Jefferson saw his beloved France sweeping toward a dictatorship and wrung his hands. He always was helpless in a fight.

Haughtily, France rejected an American minister. Proudly, Spain told the westerners they could no longer use New Orleans. Boldly, the Creeks said, "Drive the white man into the sea!" . . . "Let's fight France!" the seaboard shouted. "Let's fight Spain!" the Kentuckians demanded. "Let's fight anybody!" the Southwest cried. A war with France would be popular to the seafaring East. It would give the merchants a chance to seize rich prizes. A war with Spain would be popular in the West, and God knows old John Adams needed a bit of popularity.

Erroneously, the populace thought that he was the head of the war party, but even then he was planning a truce with France. France, knowing that a war with England was inevitable, suddenly began patting the United States on the back and tickling the Federalists under the chin. Of course, they would accept an American minister. Weren't the United States and France bound by hoops of steel? France needed a friend very badly, so why not reach across the sea and take one? Even a weak friend was better than no friend at all.

Washington's popularity returned and he overworked his tired old brain in a futile effort to organize an army. He was willing to forget all of the bitterness of his administration. His reputation had been slandered and his enemies had called him the stepfather of his country. However, when the dangers of war quickened the nation's temper, people turned again to their old leader.

In every village of the West militia gathered. "We're going to fight Spain," the soldiers shouted. "We're going to New Orleans." The bands played "The World Turned Upside Down" and the melody reminded many veterans of the surrender at Yorktown when the British had marched out, its band blaring that the world had turned upside down. Indeed it had and it still hadn't righted itself.

All along the frontier, the people made ready for an invasion of Louisiana. The Creeks poured into Pensacola and bought arms. The Shawnees began chanting their war-cries. It was time for the holy crusade. Drive the white infidels from the Promised Land! The Creeks went into council and their warriors streaked their chests with vermilion. Sam sent word to Harkins that a Creek invasion was imminent. Old Jim McQueen called his warriors together and pleaded with them to preserve the peace, but many of the young bucks scorned the old white man and heeded the words of the Shawnee prophets—"Drive the white man into the sea!"

André would not leave his land. He was in no danger. He was a friend of the Creeks. Old Jim McQueen was his friend. He laughed at Tishomingo and at the suggestion that he leave his home.

"I beg of you to go," pleaded Tishomingo. "McQueen won't be able to hold his Red Sticks in check. It will be a holy war against all white men."

"I'll not go," André answered stubbornly.

"Then send your wife away. Send her to Natchez. Honoria Dabney is there."

André saw the wisdom of Chock's advice and Anestasie packed and went with the mingo to the safety of Natchez. André refused Pushmataha's offer of a company of Choctaw braves to guard his land.

"I tell you I'm in no danger," André insisted. "The Creeks won't bother me."

413

Old Pushmataha shook his head. "But there are Shaw-nees among the Creeks. They will arouse the Red Sticks. No white man will be safe."

The Frenchman tried to calm Pushmataha's fears. "I doubt," he said, "if there will be war. France and the United States will never fight. Spain will not fight, and if the Creeks go on the war-path they won't molest me."

News that John Adams had patched up America's feud with France trickled in over the Natchez Trace and the people were confused. America had preserved her honor, the Federalists said.

"Honor, hell!" the seaboard sneered. The traders wanted war, not honor. You couldn't enrich colleges at Cambridge and build warehouses at Charleston with honor. The seaboard wanted money, prize money. There were a thousand French ships out there waiting for cap-ture. If America didn't take them, England soon would. So there would be no war with France. Peace with honor. Folderol.

The Southwest at first was jubilant over the news. Maybe old John Adams was cagey. Maybe he was mak-ing peace with France so he could devote his time to Spain.

"It's wishful thinking," said Lawyer Thomas over in Natchez. "Spain is taking orders from France. She won't fight. If we march over there and take Louisiana, the Federalists will make us give it back."

And he was right. Spain backed down again, reopened New Orleans to American traffic and the cause of war was removed. The militia disbanded and the backwoods-men hung their muskets over the mantels and went back to their fields. It was good to be at peace. It was good to stay home and make a crop and watch the children grow up.

414

The Creeks were disgusted with their ally's timidity and Spain was condemned at a Red Stick council held at the Holy Grounds. Old Jim McQueen tried to use the discord in an effort to drive a wedge between the Creeks and Spain, and all of the Creek war-parties rubbed off their vermilion war-paint, except one group, a party of fanatical young bloods headed by Big Jack, who still was smarting over his defeat at Sam Dabney's hand.

It was Sam's post rider, racing from Georgia, who brought the news that electrified the frontier, and dismayed every settler between the Chattahoochee and the Halfway River.

The rider swam his horse across the Tombigbee before André's ferry could cross the stream, and spurred his dripping, sweating pony by the Frenchman's factory, pausing only long enough to shout, "The Red Sticks are moving."

André waved him on. The Red Sticks would not bother him. He was not Sam Dabney. Had he not sat in council with the great miccos? Had he not smoked their pipes?

Sam's field slaves, hoeing the tender cotton more than a mile from Locha Poka, heard the rider shouting the alarm long before he was visible. They saw the powdered dust churning behind his pony and heard his hoarse cry, "The Red Sticks are moving. Get to the house. Old Jim McQueen can't hold them. Big Jack is on the war-path! The Choctaws are rallying. The Chickasaws are dancing. Drums are rolling from the Chattahoochee to the Tombigbee, from Fort Stoddard to the mountains. To the house, you bumboes! To arms!"

Jasper grasped the horse's reins as the rider pulled up at the factory, and Sam helped the man from the saddle. "I saw them," the rider panted. "The war-party. At the

415

Alabama crossing. They chased me across the Tom-bigbee."

"Great God!" Sam hurried the man into his factory beyond earshot of the slaves. "Did you see André? He's alone."

"I saw him and warned him but he wouldn't leave. He thinks he is safe."

"At that, he's probably safer there by himself than here with me." Sam handed the rider a beaker of rum. "The Creeks like him. Now to Natchez with you!" Sam slapped the man's back as he mounted his horse. "Inform the garrison that the Creeks are marching."

The rider galloped away and Sam ran to his house. There were no doubts to bother him now. Tersely he broke the news to Donna. He sent Jasper to Tishomingo's lodge and ordered other slaves to arouse all settlers along the river and escort them to Locha Poka.

"Will the Red Sticks come here, Sam'l?" Donna asked. "This is the Choctaw Nation."

"I don't know, but we'll be ready," Sam announced reassuringly. "Those Red Sticks have been hynotized by the Shawnees; they may dare anything, even an invasion on the Choctaw Nation. They'll want Dabby and Sukey. And me."

"Shall we leave Locha Poka?"

"Never. We'll fortify here."

The settlers began arriving by noon and Sam built a stockade around his factory and quartered the families there. It would have taken too long to convert the big house into a fort. He drove his cattle and his sheep into the stockade and posted guards, and then nervously awaited developments. The rider returned from Natchez and reported that the garrison would not march against the Creeks without orders from Philadelphia.

"But why?" Sam demanded in anger. "Now's the time to teach those Red Sticks a lesson."

"The army says that the Creeks mustn't be attacked," the courier explained. "They say only a small band of Creeks are marauding, that there's no cause for a war."

"They'd leave us at the mercy of the Red Sticks, would they?" Sam cursed softly. "The dirty yellow bastards!"

All the settlers grumbled against the government for not sending the soldiers. Sam was baffled. He couldn't understand why the government would leave its citizens exposed. He fumed and raged. "They want us to leave our homes," he said. "They want us to go to Natchez and beg protection from those damn regulars. Well, I won't do it! I'm staying here. What's the use of living if you can't sleep in peace?"

He posted scouts in the woods and prepared his stockade for the first shock of assault. He wrote a letter to Pierce and reported all the news. He would get a Choctaw to run the message through. "The damned soldiers won't come to help us," Sam wrote. "They think we should flee to Natchez. But we're going to defend Locha Poka."

He believed the war-party would cross the Tombigbee near André's place and then attempt to slip through the Choctaw Nation and strike at him. If André saw them he would spread the alarm some way. Sam allowed only small fires within the stockade, for the danger of a conflagration was great. He made all the settlers stand a health inspection and separated the women and children from the men. Some child was sure to have a disease and it mustn't spread to the fighters. He rationed the food and was writing a dispatch to Harkins when a scout slipped in from the woods and reported that Indians were coming.

Sam gathered his force around him and spoke slowly. "They're coming. You know what to do. Shoot for their bellies. Big Jack is mine. Remember—if they take this fort, your children's brains will be beaten out and your wives will warm the beds of the bloody Red Sticks."

Quickly and quietly the men manned their guns. The children were sent to the rear of the factory and were put under guard of Sukey. There was a door near by through which they could flee if a flaming arrow set fire to the factory. Sukey knew her orders. If the Indians carried the stockade she was to cut Dabby's throat. Above all, the Creeks must not get the baby. The white children were to race for the woods and scatter, and head for the Choctaw villages. The women must try to follow. The men must stay there. One blast from Jasper's cow-horn would be the signal for the women and children to flee. If a woman or a child disobeyed orders, a beating would be the punishment.

"And mind you," Sam's face was stern, "if a man, woman or child, including my own family, makes a dash for the gate without orders, I'll shoot."

Sam's eyes burned with a fanatical luster as he worked and gave orders. This was the kind of business he knew best. Maybe he wasn't a trader, but he was a fighter. The settlers looked at him in awe and their wives and daughters looked at him with admiration. Danger, perhaps death was at hand, but many women there in the stockade washed their hair in rain water and put on their best dresses, hoping to impress Sam.

He sent to his kitchen and had Jasper fetch and sharpen every butcher knife.

Powder kegs were broken open and the fires were extinguished. Sam stationed himself near the gate and watched the trail. Heat waves danced before his eyes and

418

he closed his eyes tightly, then opened them quickly to clear his vision. There was no sound from the woods except the scoldings of some jay birds and the tapping of a woodpecker. He heard the low muffled roll of a drum and cocked his head. He could not believe his ears.

"Do you hear what I hear?" a settler whispered in awe.

"Shut up, you fool!" Sam whispered hoarsely. "Of course, I hear it." He wanted .to ask the settler what he thought the meaning of the drum was, but he mustn't let the man know that he was not sure of himself. The drum rolled slowly, a sad, eerie pounding, a measured boom-boom-boom—like a cannon firing in a deep cave.

"Death drums!" There was dread in the settler's voice. "Great God Almighty!"

"Keep quiet," Sam repeated. He judged the drum to be several miles away. The rolling ceased and then grew louder. They must be marching through the ravine about four miles east of Locha Poka. Yes, he was sure they were. Now they were marching over the far ridge. Another drum joined in. They were on the top of the ridge, the rolling was louder, clearer. Sam watched the sun and knew the Indians would not arrive at Locha Poka before the sun went away.

"They're moving at a snail's pace." The nervous settler shivered. "They're up to something. It's spooky, I tell you. I don't mind shooting Red Sticks, but when it comes to spirits I ain't got no solder in my knee-joints."

Sam did not reply. The Creeks wouldn't roll drums. They would attack without notice.

Jasper stepped closer to Sam and whispered. He was a wise Negro. Sam was very proud of him. Most Negroes would have shouted, but Jasper whispered so the others couldn't hear him, "They are drums of the dead, massa.

419

I have heard them before. They are beating the drums to drive the evil spirits away from the dead. Look!"

A procession wound slowly down the trail, lighting its way with torches. A tall Indian, naked except for his feathers and loin cloth, preceded the marchers and carried a big drum. A few steps behind him two other Indians carried smaller drums and behind the leaders marched the old bone picker. The settler at Sam's right raised his musket.

Sam knocked the gun from his hand, "Hold your fire." Sam sent the order down the line. "They're Choctaws." He jumped to the ground from the stockade wall and opened the big gate. "Now close it behind me," he said quickly, and ran up the trail. He half stumbled as he ran. The bone picker carried a small box and Sam knew that it contained the bleached remains of somebody he loved. But he mustn't ask. It would be an insult to the dead. Old Pushmataha stepped from behind the bone picker and bowed. No word was spoken. The torch bearers stood in a circle and Pushmataha and the bone picker sat down. The drums ceased. Sam must have a gift of food for the bone picker before he could speak. He cursed himself under his breath for his negligence and was standing there, embarrassed and baffled, when Jasper whispered from behind him, "I am here, massa. I followed you. Here is meat."

Sam took the meat and handed it to the bone picker's chewer and stood rigidly while the toothless old man broke his fast. The first bite of food transformed him from the agent of the Great Spirit into a mortal and he could be approached and spoken to by any man. Sam stared at the box while the old man ate.

He knew then that the box contained the bones of

420

André Duportail! He felt it. Something kept saying to him, "André is dead; his bones are there."

What would become of Anestasie? Or of André's property? It was good property; it was the key to the trade route from Natchez to Georgia. He must get the property. Strange how a man thought of property even in the presence of death, but property represented tomorrow and death meant yesterday. The bone picker chewed slowly and a thousand thoughts crammed themselves into Sam's brain, each thought trying to elbow the other one out. André was dead. He would have to be avenged. But first Sam must make arrangements about the property. Anestasie could not be trusted with such a valuable possession. She might sell it and return to France. It might fall into the wrong hands. The Creeks had killed André. His friend had thought he would be safe. He must get word to Anestasie. He must go after the Creeks. He must see that Locha Poka was defended. Great God, would that old man eat forever?

The bone picker spat the last mouthful upon the ground and turned his sunken old eyes upon Sam. "I come," he said.

"You do," Sam answered.

Old Pushmataha stepped forward. "My heart is heavy," he said gravely. "We bring you the bones of your friend, the Frenchman who lived near the Tombigbee."

"Who killed him?" Sam asked impatiently.

The old chief sat down and motioned Sam to sit by him. The bone picker came forward and placed the box at Sam's feet. The Choctaw warriors crossed their arms and stood very still and erect. Sam had never seen such warriors—their foreheads sloped and they were stark naked, save for loin cloth and moccasins. No warrior wore paint, but each had a scar either on his face or chest.

421

They were veterans of a hundred Indian campaigns, the flatheads of the Choctaws. No Choctaw with a scar on his back was permitted to fight with them. Each warrior carried a tomahawk, a knife and a blow-gun. Their blow-guns were painted red and tipped with feathers. They could wing a sparrow at a hundred yards with their darts and could knock out a Creek's eye and puncture his brain at seventy-five yards.

Old Pushmataha wore his tall beaver hat and his epaulets were tied to his bare shoulders with rawhide. There were two scars on his chest.

He spoke slowly, weighing his words, "Your friend was killed by a small war party of the Creeks. They were led by Big Jack. The Shawnee prophets told them that they would receive the reward of the Great Spirit if they killed a white man. Do not blame the Creek Nation. The great miccos of the Creeks have sworn to avenge your friend because he was their friend, too. Old Jim McQueen would make talk with you."

"Your words are good," Sam replied thoughtfully. "But the time for talk is past." He nodded toward the warriors. "Why did you rally your warriors, O chief, O beloved of the Great Spirit, O Flaming Arrow?"

"It was reported to me that the Red Sticks might march against the white settlements. I called my warriors to protect our white brothers. We marched to the Tombigbee and there we found your friend. His home has not been destroyed, but his slaves have been stolen."

"But why did they kill him?" Sam demanded. "He was their friend."

The old chief's voice was sad. "Your friend was killed because he was your friend and now you have a blood feud to settle."

"Ay," said Sam very softly. "I will settle it."

"My nephew will go with you. You know the laws of the Choctaws. Your friend can be avenged only by you and Tishomingo. He was a stranger in a far land and there are no kinsmen on whom his spirit can call for revenge."

Sam knew well the laws of the Choctaw. Ordinarily a member of the widow's clan must avenge the murder of a man. Only blood could wipe out blood. The avengers were given one year to do their task, and during that time the widow must remain single and in quarantine. The murderer or murderers must satisfy the widow's kinsmen. Some Indians would accept a fine as satisfaction for the crime. In some nations, a murderer could buy a sacrifice. The sacrifice might be a young brave, willing to die, to pay the debt so the real murderer could go free. Some nations did not insist that the blood of the murderer be spilled. The blood of any of the murderer's kinsmen would pay the debt. But to the Choctaws no blood was acceptable save the blood of the man or men who had murdered.

"Where is your nephew?" Sam asked.

"He went into the Creek Nation alone," Pushmataha replied. "He said tell you to meet him at your friend's house."

"I will go," said Sam.

"Alone?" asked the old Indian.

"Sam Dabney never goes alone. He always travels with his kinsmen—his gun and his tomahawk. There's a task I will do."

Pushmataha stood up. "Then we will stay here and guard your home and your family."

"I thank you," said Sam. "Watch well my wife and baby, and the slaves Sukey and Dabby."

The bone picker lifted his box but did not speak. Sam

told him, "Guard his bones. His wife will want to dispose of them."

While Jasper saddled Claymore, Sam took Donna and Hoab into the shadow of the stockade to tell them goodbye. He bent over and lifted the child in his arms, and Hoab played with the fringe on his jacket. "I'm going away," he told Donna. "You'll be safe here." He set Hoab down and put his right arm around his wife.

"But where are you going?" she asked, a trace of alarm in her voice.

"First to meet Tishomingo. There's a thing I must do."

She was almost afraid of Sam then. His mouth was tight and there were lines in his face, lines that his hate had etched. Donna stroked his head a moment, then ran her fingers over the lines. "I know you want to avenge André's death. I'm not one to question your decision, but you must think of us."

Sam glanced down at Hoab and tightened his grip on his wife's shoulder. "I never think of anything else, Donna. But this is a thing I must do. Tishomingo and I were his friends. The Creeks have put a blood feud upon us, and Anestasie must have satisfaction."

"That is Indian law ——"

"We must live among the Indians. If I did not do this thing, I would be despised by the Choctaws. And, too, if the Creeks go unpunished for the death of one white man, then none of us will be safe. I want you to write Anestasie. Break the news gently to her. Tell her that I will avenge her. And tell her, too, Donna, not to make any decision about her property until I see her."

"I cannot mention business in such a letter." Donna was astonished. "It would be too crude."

"Crude or no," Sam muttered sternly, "it must be done! That property must not fall into the wrong hands.

424

It's the key to the Georgia route." He saw the look of injury in Donna's eyes and regretted that he had spoken so sharply. "You can do it in a nice way, darling."

"All right," she said, "I'll do it." But there were tears in her eyes. It was one of the few times Sam had ever seen her cry. He kissed the tears away and held her head against his chest. She got as close to him as she could. The tomahawk and knife in his belt pressed into her flesh and hurt her, but she did not mind.

"I am afraid," she whispered. "I am afraid for you."

Sam tried to calm her, and she beat back her tears.

"That's better," Sam said.

"My man mustn't see me crying when he goes away," Donna smiled.

"It's not fitting." Sam patted her cheek, then stooped and kissed her tenderly. "Dear Donna. I love you so very much. I will be back soon. Goodbye." He bent on one knee and kissed Hoab again. "Goodbye, son."

The boy grinned up at Sam, but did not speak. God, Sam thought, how like Ab he was. Ab's smile and Honoria's eyes.

He swung into his saddle. A guard opened the stockade gate and he galloped up the trail, heading for the Tombigbee. A mile from André's house, he turned Claymore into the woods, dismounted, and led his horse noiselessly to the top of the ridge that sloped down to the Frenchman's cabin. Sam lay upon the ground and scouted the land, fastening his eyes first to the south, then to the north. Not a thing seemed to move except the river. He got to his feet and walked about fifty yards and hid his horse in a clump of underbrush, then crawled down the slope until he reached the outbuildings of the plantation and lay flat on his belly, scarcely breathing, attuning his senses to the silence. His nervous system became so accustomed to the silence that he knew the slightest sound would warn him.

He heard the sound back up the slope, down which he had crawled. He heard the footfalls of moccasins and counted them. It was only one man and he was making no effort to conceal his presence. Sam primed his rifle and waited, his eyes focused on the woods where Claymore was hidden. He heard the low call of the bobwhite and knew it was Tishomingo's signal. He lowered his gun and Tishomingo stepped from the underbrush and surveyed the scene. Then he joined Sam near the barn and said simply, "We're alone except for the spirit of our friend."

Sam propped his rifle-gun against the barn and opened his tafula pouch and ate the food raw. "Tell me about it," he said. "What did you learn?"

"There's trouble among the Creeks," Tishomingo answered. "When the great miccos heard that your country and Spain would fight, they called their warriors. But when the war-clouds passed, all of the warriors listened to old Jim McQueen and disbanded, except one party, led by Wild Dog and Big Jack. They crossed the river here and André gave them food. When he had fed them he asked them why they were in the Choctaw Nation wearing war-paint. One of the young bucks said they were going after you. André tried to get to his horse to warn you. A Shawnee shot him, but Big Jack would not let the party scalp him. Big Jack was ashamed. He reported the tragedy to Jim McQueen and McQueen told me. McQueen has ordered their deaths and there is threat of a revolt among the Creeks. The younger miccos will no longer listen to old McQueen and civil war is imminent within the nation. Old McQueen would see you and make talk."

"Why did they take his slaves?"

Tishomingo shrugged his shoulders. "I do not know. My uncle and his party of flatheads arrived that night, but the Red Sticks had gone back across the Tombigbee. The bone picker burned André's body and cleaned the bones. That is all. Will you see McQueen?"

"Ay," Sam said. "But how many Red Sticks were in the party?"

"There were twelve," Tishomingo replied. "I trailed them to the Alabama River. Eleven are still alive. I found their camp near the lodge of Dirty Horse. Their guard was asleep. I gave his scalp to McQueen with my promise that André's death would be avenged."

"You should have told McQueen that it was *our pledge* —yours and mine."

"I did," said Chock simply.

Sam smiled at his friend and laid his hand upon his arm. It was good to have a comrade like Tishomingo. Tishomingo clasped his hand over Sam's and they looked into each other's eyes and then away. Neither spoke. Some friends are like that and between them words are not necessary. Tishomingo and Sam were both lonely men and their friendship was more than a mutual admiration. It was a trust, a bond. They often were so close in mind that each could anticipate the other's thoughts and actions. They both were happy now for the first time in many months. They were together. They were taking up a blood trail together. They would fight together and eat together. They both examined their weapons carefully. Sam hummed while he worked—"Over the Hills and Far Away."

They went to the bank of the river and Tishomingo cut an armful of cat-tails while Sam went into André's cabin and found lard and tallow. They rubbed the grease

427

on the cat-tails and went back to the brow of the ridge and lighted them. Black smoke rolled skyward and Tishomingo and Sam waited near the barn until their signal was answered. A spiral of black smoke arose to the north and Chock said, "A band of flatheads will be here soon."

"Don't you trust McQueen and his Creeks?" Sam asked.

"Ay, I trust them," Chock grinned. "But I will trust them more if we have a band of good Choctaw warriors behind us."

When the warriors arrived Tishomingo told them, "We will have a talk with the Creeks, there on the river bank. Protect us."

The warriors disappeared into the woods, and each cut brush and stuck the brush in the soft mud along the river. A warrior hid behind each bush and aimed his blow-gun at the spot that Tishomingo had designed as a council ground.

Satisfied that he was ready, Tishomingo tilted his head and screamed the cry of the catamount. The cry was answered from beyond the river and soon Jim McQueen and two canoes full of warriors were crossing the Tombigbee. Sam folded his arms and waited until the old Scotchman approached. McQueen stepped from his canoe and walked to Sam. His long soft white hair rustled in the breeze, and his tired, old, weather-beaten face was creased with wrinkles, but his eyes were bright and undaunted. "It is a sad mission," the old man said. "André was my friend ——"

"Then why did the Creeks kill him?" Sam demanded savagely.

"The white man does not blame all white men because there is a murderer in their midst. The Creek Nation is not responsible for this outrage. I give you my word. If

428

the white settlers do not take up arms to avenge this man, we will punish the murderers of the Frenchman."

Sam answered more quietly, "I believe you. But you are getting old, McQueen, and your grip on the Creeks is slipping. The young bloods are scorning your counsel. Your nation is threatened with civil war. What proof have I that you are powerful enough to punish the men who killed André?"

"You have my word. If a white army marches against the Creeks, it will mean the beginning of a war that will burst into flame from the Great Smokies to the Mississippi. I pray of you, do not ask your government to avenge this wrong."

"The United States will not avenge the death of my friend. He was not a citizen of this country. Eleven men are alive in your nation who must die for this crime. André's slaves have been stolen. What of them?"

"I have them. I will send them to his widow."

"Send them to my house and I will give you twenty-four hours to bring me the scalps of his murderers."

The old Scotchman looked at his Creek warriors, then back at Sam. "You talk very high and mighty, Mr. Dabney," he snapped. "You do not give orders to Jim McQueen like that. I gave you my word that we would punish these men, but I cannot promise you that their scalps will be brought to you so quickly."

Sam lifted his rifle from the crook of his arm and examined it carefully. "Then I will go after them," he said slowly.

"You're a fool Irishman," McQueen stormed. "There's a price on your head in the nation. I don't care if you are killed, but you're an American citizen and my only fear is that your death might cause war. For God's sake, be reasonable!"

429

"I've given you my answer. Eleven scalps here by tomorrow night or I go into the nation. Alone."

"Very well." McQueen nodded sadly. "We go." He and his warriors turned to reënter their canoe and the old Scotchman hesitated and looked at Sam. He walked slowly back to the council ground and offered his hand. "I don't like you, but I want to shake hands with a brave man. I'm from Scotland and we always avenge the deaths of our friends. I'm sorry you do not trust me."

"But I *do* trust you," said Sam.

"Then you may tell your flathead warriors to come from behind those bushes." There was no anger in the old man's voice. "Son, I am more than a hundred years old. I saw flatheads hiding behind bushes with their blow-guns aimed at my heart when your grandfather was hunting wild pigs in Ireland."

He turned and walked slowly to his canoe, waved farewell to Sam and Tishomingo, and was paddled back across the Tombigbee.

Tishomingo shook his head. "He is a wise man. I believe, Sam'l, that so long as Jim McQueen lives there will be no war with the Creeks. His people love him better than any micco. He has more influence with the Creeks than Tecumseh. But his end is almost near. When he dies no one will be able to hold the Creeks in check and his grave will be drenched in blood."

True to his word McQueen sent André's slaves across the river, and Sam sent them under Choctaw escort to Locha Poka. He wrote to Donna to inform her he was well and he wrote long dispatches to Harkins and Pierce, reporting that civil war threatened among the Creeks. The young miccos, he explained, had long been waiting an opportunity to challenge old McQueen's authority and André's death had presented the young leaders with

430

the chance they wanted. The old peace faction of the Creeks was in disrepute.

Sam knew that Georgia authorities would not send an expedition against the Creeks because of the murder of one Frenchman in the new land. Georgia had no authority to avenge the crime. Only the United States army had such authority and the government refused to fight a war over one Frenchman's death.

Sam sent his messages to Georgia by a Choctaw runner, and he and Tishomingo kept only one flathead with them while they camped by the river and awaited the expiration of their ultimatum to McQueen. Sam waited until the sun began hiding behind the horizon the next day and then told Tishomingo, "We go among the Creeks tonight. I knew old McQueen could not deliver those scalps."

He instructed the flathead to deliver their horses at Locha Poka and when darkness fell he and Tishomingo walked down the river for several miles and swam across.

"You have the names of the men we seek?" Sam asked.

"Ay. Big Jack, Wild Dog, Dirty Horse, Fat Father of Many Sons," Tishomingo called them off. "But they have been warned, Big Sam. They'll be together. They'll be near the Alabama River."

"It's to our advantage that they have been warned." Sam laughed mirthlessly. "They will not dare go farther east for fear of McQueen's men. They must avoid us, as well as McQueen, and a hunted man is a nervous man."

He walked ahead of Tishomingo, keeping to the woods where his footsteps would make neither sound nor trace. All night they marched and rested the next day, hiding in the deep swamps. The third dawn they arrived at the

431

lodge of Dirty Horse, on the west bank of the Alabama River, and Sam hid near the north side of the house. Tishomingo slipped past the lodge and into the woods to the south. They both watched the sun and as soon as the day was full-born, Sam sounded his signal, three quick calls of the whippoorwill. Tishomingo fired his gun, reloaded quickly, ran about fifty yards and fired again. Sam fired one barrel, ran several yards and discharged the other barrel. To anyone in the house it would have seemed that the place was surrounded.

Tishomingo circled and hurried back to the north side of the house and he and Sam crouched in the woods and waited. There was no sound from the lodge. Sam counted up to one hundred to give any Creek warrior a chance and then they walked boldly to the house.

Dirty Horse's wife and his brood of children were cringing in a corner. Sam assured them that they would not be molested. Tishomingo stood guard at the door while Sam searched the cabin. He found nothing to interest him and walked to the Indian woman and ordered, "Feed us."

She fetched tafula and Sam watched her while he ate. He complimented her on her food and walked to the pot in which she had prepared it. There was enough tafula in the pot for a large company of men. Sam gave her a bit of silver and prepared to depart.

"Aren't you going to burn the house?" Tishomingo was surprised.

"Nay, the house is shelter for this woman and her children. I will not make war on women and children." As they walked toward the river Sam whispered to Tishomongo, "Now prime your ears. If old Dirty Horse's wife doesn't follow us, then I'm a fool. That's why I didn't burn her house. I wanted to give her a chance to follow us."

They went deeply into the woods and sat down as though to make their plans. "We have been followed," Tishomingo whispered. "The squaw is in the bushes behind you."

Sam picked up a stick and made marks upon the ground. "We will go to the river and get Dirty Horse's canoe," he said loud enough for his voice to carry. "Then we will go down the river to the ford. Perhaps we will find them there."

"Ay," said Chock. "That is what we will do." He winked at Sam. "She has gone now."

"Yes," Sam chuckled. "She has gone to report to her man. She has been feeding them. No squaw cooks more food than she needs for one meal. She knows where they are hiding and will tell them that we are going to the ford. I have a plan. I will tell you later."

They poked along the bank until they found Dirty Horse's canoe and poled it out of the rushes and paddled to midstream. They made no effort to hide their movements but turned downstream and rode the current, Tishomingo watching the west bank and Sam the east. They floated around a bend and Sam turned the canoe toward the east bank. They were out of the sight of the lodge when they pulled the canoe into the mud and walked along the bank studying the ground. The bank was bare of trees but was thick with cat-tails. A screen of trees stood about twenty yards back from the river.

"This is the spot," Sam decided. "We'll let them come to us."

"Ay," said Chock. "Now I see your plan. If the hound cannot find the wolf, he lets the wolf find him."

Sam said, "There's a price on my head and the Creeks

433

will be anxious to take me. When the squaw reports that we're headed for the ford, they will come after us in a canoe."

"Why are you so sure?" Tishomingo asked.

"Do you follow men in water on foot? Big Jack is no fool. The men are staying together for safety. Jack will think that eleven men in a big canoe can overtake and capture two men in a little canoe. They will be paddling fast when they round this bend. You will stay here on the east bank. I'll take the canoe and cross to the west bank. They'll make a perfect target, Chock. When they round the bend I'll fire first and take the first man in the canoe. They'll, of course, head for the east bank and expose themselves to your fire. Fire from this screen of trees and they cannot see you. The minute you fire run twenty steps, load and be ready to fire again. I'll take the third man. You take the fourth. But be sure, Chock, that you pick the men off from the bow toward the stern. Do not shoot the men in the boat's stern until we first have killed the men in the bow. If they continue downstream, we'll slip along the bank and pick them off. If they turn around, the current will slow them down and it will be easy to kill them."

Tishomingo shook his head. "It would be a superfine plan if the Creeks were fools. You can get the first man and I can get the second before the Red Sticks collect their wits. But then they'll either fall to the bottom of the canoe or jump overboard."

Sam said, "While you're firing one shot I can fire two, because my rifle has two barrels. The Red Sticks will think I am two men and if they jump overboard they'll swim toward you. That is your problem. If they fall to the bottom of their canoe I'm going out after them. There will be several dead men in the canoe and the

Creeks will not be able to fight because the bodies of their comrades will be in their way."

Sam began taking off his clothes. Tishomingo slapped his friend on the shoulder. "The very boldness of your plan is its strength."

"A man's plan is only as good as the man," Sam laughed. "My father used to say that. He also taught me that it is hard for several men to attack one man in a small space."

They both stripped, and Sam tied a rawhide thong around his waist. He took his tomahawk, his knife, his rifle and powder horn, and got into the canoe and crossed the river. He hid the canoe and took up his post on a bluff near the bend where he could watch the stream. He checked the sun and studied the shadows. It was mid-morning. Mosquitoes swarmed about his face, but he dared not slap at them. His movements would disturb the squirrels and birds. He peered across the river but could see no sign of Tishomingo. Wood ants crawled across his bare feet and tickled them, but he was afraid to stoop to scratch his flesh. He attuned his hearing to all of the usual sounds of the swamp—the chattering of squirrels, the drumming of woodpeckers. He tapped his fingers on his gun stock and tried to keep time with the wood-peckers, and as he tapped he sang very softly, "Over the Hills ——"

He stared at the bend of the river until the sun's reflection hurt his eyes. Up the river, beyond his view, a king-fisher darted up from the water and whipped around the bend. An alligator slapped the bank with a heavy thud. Something had disturbed the animal.

Then Sam heard it: the even swish of paddles. He lifted his rifle, glanced at the priming and measured his distance again. The big canoe swept into view, the pad-

435

dles flashing as it shot around the bend. Quickly Sam counted the Indians: ". . . nine, ten, eleven."

They were all there. Sweat glistened on their bodies; their torsos were streaked with red paint. They bent to their task. Sam could see their muscles rippling. He smiled to himself and began humming again.

He waited until the craft cleared the bend. When it swung into the fast channel, he drew a bead on the first man, squeezed the trigger and, while the smoke still enveloped him, ran several yards down the bank and slipped behind a tree. When the smoke cleared he saw the man's body hanging over the bow of the canoe. Tishomingo's shot thundered from the west woods, and the second Indian toppled. A salvo from the canoe swept the spot where Sam had stood. Sam almost laughed out loud. Just like the ninnies to fire all together. Now they must reload. Sam fired at the third man and saw him sprawl to the bottom of the canoe. Tishomingo fired again, and the Creeks turned their muskets toward the west bank and shot at the ground where Chock had been. Then he and Tishomingo fired simultaneously.

Smoke rolled over the river and Sam could not tell how many of the Creeks were down. The canoe swung with the current, and its occupants could be seen huddled in the rear, trying to peer through the smoke for a target.

Big Jack stood in the stern of the boat and shouted, "*Yos-ta-hah!* They're spoiling us." His comrades ducked to the bottom of the canoe among the bodies there, but Big Jack dived overboard and began swimming toward the west bank. Sam, concealed by the rushes, hurried along the bank, watching the canoe drift toward still water, but the Indians did not show their heads. Big Jack was nearing the west bank when Tishomingo shrieked

436

the war-cry of the Choctaws, sped from the woods and dived into the water.

Sam waited only long enough to see Big Jack brandish his knife and swim rapidly toward the mingo. The scream caused the Creeks in the canoe to jump to their feet and stare toward the west bank. Sam picked off another and waded into the rushes where his canoe was hidden. He shoved the canoe into the stream, leaped into it and shouted to the Creeks, "I am Big Sam Dabney! I am coming!"

Their leader gone, the Red Sticks were bewildered. Sam's shout sent chills to the marrow of their bones and they stared at him as though he were the avenging angel of Aba Inki. They were too surprised to shoot; they just huddled there in their canoe, their eyes frozen upon Big Sam Dabney, a bronzed naked giant with long black hair.

One Red Stick recovered quickly from his surprise, however, and leveled his gun. Sam dropped to the bottom of his canoe. He rested his rifle on the side of his craft and discharged both barrels into the Red Sticks. The blast threw the Indians into confusion again and Sam used the precious moments to paddle swiftly nearer the big boat.

Two of the Creeks fired into Sam's canoe, ripping big holes in its frail sides. Water poured in and dampened his powder. He peered over the side. The Indians were still crowded together and were getting into one another's way. Two or three were watching the fight between Tishomingo and Big Jack, which was raging in deep water near the west bank. The others had their eyes toward Sam. Their canoe rocked and almost overturned as one of the Red Sticks fought for room to shove his ram-rod down his musket barrel. But the Indians were so close together that none could load.

Sam's canoe was sinking rapidly as he swung alongside the Creeks'. The instant his craft ground against the other boat, he leaped to his feet, balanced himself in the bow, and jumped among his enemies.

Only five men were on their feet and they crouched in the rear of the canoe, too amazed for immediate action. Sam hurled his tomahawk at the nearest man. The hatchet head was buried in the side of a Red Stick, and the handle protruded grotesquely. The Indian's mouth flew open and he stared down at his side. Then he screamed, not in agony, but in rage. He grasped the handle with both hands and pulled out the tomahawk, ripping his flesh as he collapsed. His blood spurted on to his comrades, and his death added to the Creeks' confusion. They tried to balance themselves, each to get by the other and reach Sam. They clawed at one another and fell in a heap when Sam rocked the boat quickly.

Two wounded Creeks squirmed at his feet. Sam heard them groan and glanced down at them. He put his right foot on the throat of one of the men and pressed down savagely until he felt the man's breath die away. He smashed the other Creek's head with the butt of his gun.

One warrior managed to get past his comrades and bore down upon Sam, waving his knife. Sam drove the end of his rifle into the man's stomach, bowled him over against his fellows and crushed his head with the stock of his gun.

He grasped his rifle tightly by the barrel and swung again, breaking the back of a Creek who had stooped over to attack him in a crouch. Suddenly Sam began humming again, "Over the Hills and Far Away . . ." A look of dread spread over the faces of the Creeks, and even the dying Indians looked up at him and mumbled, "Big Sam. Il-le-hi-ah!"

438

Big Sam Dabney, the messenger of death!

What manner of man was this who sang while he killed, whose flesh oozed sweat and whose hair was matted with the blood and brains of his enemies? The Creeks shuddered and mumbled their prayers to Aba Inki, but did not ask mercy of man.

Dirty Horse pushed one of his comrades aside and rushed at Sam, but he tripped over the body of another Creek and sprawled at Sam's feet. Sam lay his gun down and took out his knife. He held Dirty Horse by his scalp lock and calmly cut his throat. He pushed the man from him, so his blood would not drench him, and straightened up, then laughed at the last Creek, cowering in the stern of the boat, half hidden by the bodies of his friends.

"I am Big Sam Dabney!" Sam yelled. "I am a man!"

The taunt enraged the Red Stick so he forgot his fear. He stood up. "Our powder was wet or you would not have lived to boast."

"My powder's wet, too," Sam mocked him. "You're a Creek, but you're not a man. Why don't you rush me?"

"And slip over the bodies of my comrades?" the Red Stick muttered. "That's what the others did."

Sam straddled one of the bodies, "Then come on. We'll fight man to man with our knives."

"I'll fight you alone," the leader shouted. "In the middle of the boat where there's room. I am Tar-cha-chee!" He slipped past his comrades and advanced upon Sam, waving his knife. Sam braced himself and waited until he could smell the sweet odor of the Red Stick. He shifted quickly to the left, kicked the man viciously in the groin and, as the Red Stick bent doubled in pain, Sam drove his big knife into his enemy's stomach. He clung to his knife as the Indian stumbled. Then he yanked it to the right, laying open the man's belly. He pulled his knife

439

out as the Red Stick fell, and wiped it on the side of the boat.

He recovered a paddle and, humming again, sat in the rear of the canoe and maneuvered it toward the still water of the west bank. As he neared the shore, he jumped overboard and grounded the canoe and ran along the bank seeking Tishomingo. He found him near the bend, wiping his scalping knife. "Did you get him?" Sam asked.

"Why do you think I'm wiping my knife? Do you think I scalped myself?" Tishomingo threw his arms around his friend and they both laughed.

"I got the rest. The devils were so crowded that they couldn't fight. Come on, I need your help."

Tishomingo tied Big Jack's scalp to his waist and he and Sam trotted down the bank to the canoe. It took them only a few minutes to scalp the party and while Tishomingo went for their clothes Sam piled the bodies into the boat, set it afire and shoved it into the stream.

"I'll vow there never has been such a fight as this," Tishomingo exulted. "Who was the man who stood at the bridge in Rome and killed so many of his enemies?"

"I don't know and don't care," said Sam. "But let us get away from here. Those shots will bring a thousand Creeks to this river."

He wrote a note to Jim McQueen, tied it to Big Jack's scalp and fastened the scalp to a pole that he stuck in the bank of the Alabama.

"This is the revenge of Big Sam Dabney and Tishomingo for the death of André Duportail," the note said. "We have paid our debt to our friend's widow."

They dressed, then tied the other scalps to their belts and trotted down the river, sloshing in water to hide their tracks. They turned west. All afternoon and all night

440

they jogged, neither speaking. They hid in the woods the next day and dared not build a fire to cook food. Tishomingo killed a rabbit with a club and they drank the blood to sustain them. Toward high noon the next day they stole two horses from a Creek farm and shortly after twilight they crossed the Tombigbee. There they rested until midnight. They cooked hot food and brewed sassafras tea, and journeyed to André's place where they would part.

"It was a task well done," said Tishomingo.

"Ay," Sam answered, and gripped Chock's arm. "I must write the details to Georgia. How large would you judge their canoe was?"

"About thirty feet long and four feet deep. The Creeks make them out of cypress logs. They are used to haul corn. You may write the story down, Big Sam, but no one will ever believe you.* Only I will know and believe you." He laughed.

They shook hands and Tishomingo rode off toward his lodge and Sam headed his horse toward Locha Poka.

* According to the biographer of Sam Dale, the great Mississippi scout, a similar fight occurred on November 13, 1813, at Randons Landing, in what is now Alabama. In this fight Dale and two friends are credited with killing eleven Creeks. Dale killed seven with his gun butt and a bayonet.

22

* *

Sam dismantled the stockade at Locha Poka and used the posts for fences. The settlers returned to their homes, and the camp fires of the Creeks turned to ashes and their war-chants to songs of the busk. The government, through Harkins, officially reprimanded Sam for his adventure in the Creek Nation, but in a second letter Harkins congratulated him.

That was the way it was: the government officially could not sanction expeditions against the enemy but privately the big-wigs encouraged them. Although Sam could not prove it, he knew that some of the most powerful men in the country were behind Philip Nolan's contemplated expedition into Texas. Sam was not sure what Nolan's purpose was, but he was confident that it was a land-grabbing scheme. He wished he could get in on the plan, but neither he nor Thomas could locate the sponsor. Nolan would not reveal the name of the man who was behind him. To all appearances he was going to Texas to catch mustangs and he would bring some back to Sam according to their agreement.

Honoria's report from Natchez was that she was having a dreary time because of André's death. And, too, there were no soldiers in town and she would not associate with the wild Kentucky keel-boat men. Anestasie also was at the home of the Harkins' kinspeople.

She was taking her loss heroically, Honoria wrote. Almost too heroically . . .

"At times she actually is gay [Honoria stated]. Mr. Flournoy has been here to see me twice and he says Anestasie is acting and trying to hide her sorrow. I do not believe it. It seems to me that it would be fitting for her to appear sorrowful whether she is or not. But maybe it is the way with French people. I think it is disgraceful the way she traipses around Natchez. She is very pretty, however, in black, but she thinks she is prettier than she really is. It is well known that Mr. Flournoy comes to Natchez to see me, but this French widow was brazen enough to suggest that Mr. Flournoy came to see her."

Donna had written Anestasie concerning her property, and Sam counted the days until he, without violating conventions, could call upon the widow of his friend and discuss business. He wrote his sister to be kind to Anestasie.

The story of Sam's canoe fight grew out of all proportions to the truth. It was natural that the frontiersmen would exaggerate the story. They exaggerated everything else, their dangers, their hardships and their adventures. Exaggeration was a way of humor. It was a big land and the stories were big. Northern peddlers, working the territory and selling clocks and cooking utensils, wondered if the truth was in the southwestern pioneers. They never understood the nature of the backwoodsmen, mostly Irishmen with a gift of tongue and an overly developed sense of drama. They never knew that many of the tall tales told them by the pioneers were told simply to josh the blue-noses. The Westerners didn't expect anyone to believe the stories. When they told stories about their land, the trees, the rivers and the animals, they were not satisfied with telling only about ordinary rivers and trees. All the rivers were huge, the animals ferocious, the trees giants. It was a blustering, swashbuckling era, and the man who could outtalk his comrades was a somebody. A man never shot a small deer in the side at forty paces, but always a big deer in the eye at one hundred paces. Exaggeration was an art and tall tales became ballads.

So Sam's adventure, incredible enough in reality, was stretched into a saga. The Creeks whispered his name in awe and all the other Muscogees sang of his prowess. Up in Tennessee, Andy Jackson heard his story and sent congratulations. Keel-boat men, working their way down the river and walking back to Kentucky, went out of their way to pass by Locha Poka just to shake hands with Big Sam.

Sam had watched the keel-boat men since he first arrived in the new land and believed that some day they would make his fortune. Reluctantly, he had admitted to himself that his cotton gins were not a good investment, and his plan to trade goods between Natchez and Georgia would never be of any account until a wagon road was built. There could be no wagon road until the Creek Nation was scattered. But some day it would come and he would be ready. He must have André's ferry and control the route. But meanwhile the Natchez Trace was carrying all the northbound commerce and a wagon road had been built from Nashville to the Chickasaw Nation. A road was going north from Natchez to the nation and soon the Chickasaws would grant a right of way through their own land. And then his chance would come. Hundreds of keel boats were crawling down the river to Natchez and New Orleans, but only a few boats were going back. It was too great a task to

444

pole or pull the great boats up the stream. There were goods in the Southwest that Kentucky and Tennessee would buy if they could get them. There was no reason why the West should buy its goods from the East, Philadelphia to Pittsburgh, Pittsburgh to the West.

But it was too expensive to send pack horses from Natchez up the Trace, and most of the keel-boat men walked home from New Orleans. They could carry no goods. They usually carried nothing, for they left their money with the gamblers and prostitutes. If they had teams to drive home, they gladly would handle the teams for their transportation. It was a superfine plan, wide-rimmed conestogas lumbering up the Trace, handled by boatmen who would work for keep.

Sam long had been thinking of the plan. That was why he wanted mustangs from Texas. Mustangs from Texas and jacks from Tennessee. He would breed mules and build his own wagons. He would hire an agent in Nashville and the agent would dispose of the cargoes and then of the wagons and mules. The keel-boat men would come back down the river and he would have more trains waiting for them. Ay, it was a superfine plan.

He talked much of the Trace with the keel-boat men who dropped by Locha Poka. The outlaws were riding the Trace again and the keel-boat men usually traveled in bands for protection. And they traveled fast, even on foot. They had been known to beat the post from Natchez to Nashville. But they would welcome a chance to drive teams back to Tennessee. The trains would be safe from the outlaws. Sam did not reveal his plan, but made friends among the boatmen and bided his time.

All of the keel-boat men were cut from the same pattern, loud talkers, heavy drinkers and reckless cut-throats. Most of them floated down the river in flatboats and Kentucky arks. The men demanded double pay to get their keel boats back up the river and the task took months. They called their favorite method of working their boats up-stream "bushwacking." They would steer their boats near the bank and would pull on the bushes growing from the bottom of the river. Some of the people in Natchez even called the boatmen "bushwhackers," but the term soon fell into disrepute and a man never applied it to another man unless he wanted to fight. A man had to be careful when he talked with the keel boat men for fear he would use any of the many expressions that were considered fighting words. It was all right to call a man a rascal, or even a dirty dog. But the expression "son of a bitch" meant a fight, unless it was used in a joking manner. If you called a man a son of a bitch, he would ask you immediately, "Do you mean it?" If you told him you were joking, it was all right, but if you told him you meant it, the first blow of the fight was considered struck. It was never safe to call a man a liar, even though the man probably was one. The Kentuckians and Tennesseans liked Sam, for he spoke their language.

The months slipped by and Sam decided to leave Honoria in Natchez until she asked to come home. He and Donna hoped she would meet some of the young planters along the river, but all reports indicated that the only man who attracted her was Lake Flournoy.

"I don't like it," Sam remarked anxiously.

"Maybe we have misjudged Flournoy," Donna suggested. "After all, there's no reason we should distrust him simply because Tishomingo does. Perhaps there's another side to that story. Don't judge Honoria harshly. She hasn't had a happy life and it's perfectly natural that

446

she should be fascinated by Flournoy. He's handsome and rich and attentive. And I'll warrant you that Honoria can take care of herself."

"I believe she can, too," Sam nodded, and then frowned slightly. "But sometimes I don't understand her. She loves Tishomingo, yet she is seen constantly with Lake Flournoy."

Donna laughed at him for his naïveté, his unaffected simplicity about women. "Women are the greatest hunters in the world, Sam'l. Maybe Honoria's trying to make Tishomingo jealous. Maybe her plan is to lure Tishomingo to her. Tishomingo is very gallant. If he thinks Honoria plans to throw her life away on Flournoy, he may try to save her from herself."

"The game is too complicated for me," Sam shrugged. Women were still a mystery to him.

"And, furthermore," Donna continued, "being a woman, Honoria will never sit idly by and see Anestasie win Flournoy, if that's Anestasie's intent. Maybe Honoria doesn't want Flournoy, but she doesn't want anybody else to have him. In many ways Honoria and Anestasie are alike. They both have spirit."

It was a good season at Locha Poka, but Sam made no cash crop. The cotton market was so depressed that he ginned his cotton and stored it. The plantation needed all the corn he grew, and his tobacco was so inferior to the Kentucky weed that he did not even bother to take it to Natchez. Donna seemed gayer, but Sam worried more than ever about her health. Her cheek bones showed too prominently and he noticed that the skin on the back of her hands was dry. Her teeth bothered her, too. Sukey's second child was a son, and when he was born she moved into the cabin with Jasper. Sam baptized the baby and christened him. Dabby was shooting up like

447

a swamp sprout and was with Hoab from the time Donna dressed him until he was put to bed. Hoab was shooting up, too, and was permitted to visit daily in Sukey's cabin. When he said his first word, which was "Da," Sam vowed that he was trying to pronounce his name, but Donna laughed.

"He's trying to say Dabby," she said.

He was a sturdy child, with Ab's long legs and twinkling, mischievous smile. Sam often took him with him on Claymore when he rode across his acres. All the slaves called him "Little massa."

It was a good life. The slaves were docile and the land was fruitful. But the land was never docile. It was sly. A man could beat the land and rip it open and tear out the grass, but while the man slept, the land would open its bounty to the grass and would shield it and try to hide it from man. The land was never the same and would not surrender its freedom without a fight. It welcomed all the seeds except the seeds Sam wanted it to have. It was kind to the roots that Sam tried to dig out, but it was harsh to the roots that Sam wanted it to adopt and nourish. It famished the roots of the peach trees and the fig trees and bestowed its kindness upon the orphan roots of the hickory trees and the pine trees. It would never give up to the will of man. Man might work it and beat it. But even then the land would not be subdued. It would never be a slave to man. Man could put irons on other men, but he could not put irons on the land. If man punished the land too much, it would die and turn to dust. It would let the rains wash its richness into the rivers and then man would starve and turn to dust. The land had to be pampered and would not be driven. It was like a fickle woman and must be allowed to have its way sometimes. After being preg-

448

nant with cotton and weary with the travail of producing, it wanted to rest. It wanted to take the wild grass to its bosom and suck nourishment from the grass. The land grew weak when it was made to grow cotton and corn. It cried out for rest. Man could kill his wives with young and his slaves with work, and he could kill his land too, by pouring seeds into its womb year after year. Sam thought that it was strange how the seeds of man produced and then killed.

Sam was good to his land. He gave it rest. When one field was exhausted with the task of bearing cotton, he let it lay fallow for a year. Sometimes the land became sour and Sam sprinkled it with lime to sweeten it. And he gave it plenty to drink. He was even glad when the river crept out of its banks and covered parts of his land. The silt was sinews for the land and the water was blood. Often after supper Sam took Hoab by the hand and they walked to the fields and just sat there, Sam watching his land and Hoab watching his father. Once Sam struck a slave because the bumbo threw a clod from a furrow.

"Never throw the land away," Sam cautioned the Negro. "If you find a clod that the plow has left, hold it in your hands and crumble it, but don't throw it away. This is land, you fool. This is my land. You would not waste your master's food, or your master's money. Then don't waste your master's land. This is money. This is food. This is shelter. This is everything that man wants and needs. This is land."

Donna had a small chapel built down by the scuppernong arbor and circuit riders passing that way held services. The settlers always came and stayed for days, camping near the river. They brought their slaves and many of their goods and traded with Sam.

449

Sam subscribed to the *Knoxville Gazette* and, although it was weeks late, he was the best-informed man along the Halfway River. It was through the *Gazette* that he learned of Washington's death. He also learned that Adams had taken up his residence in Washington City and that the new capitol would soon be ready for occupancy. The East was seething with politics. Adams would attempt to succeed himself but Jefferson and Burr also were in the running, and Hamilton, too. There was a report that Hamilton was scheming against Adams, and their political feud had reverberations all over the country. The Federalist Party had been split wide open over the French issue, and on the frontier the odds were two to one that Jefferson and his Republicans would be elected.

Lawyer Thomas explained the situation in a letter to Sam.

"Talk to the keel-boat men who stop by your place. [Thomas wrote] Impress upon them the necessity of voting for Jefferson. We want Jefferson for president and Burr for vice president.

"Governor Sargent is more unpopular than ever. We are going to petition the Congress for relief against his obnoxious laws. It will be another Declaration of Independence. We have no representation, so we will pay no taxes. We plan to send Norsworthy Hunter to present our declaration to the Congress. If they will not heed our request, then we may consider that we have the same right to leave the union that the colonies had to withdraw from the Crown. After all, the situation is similar. We are being treated as a colony without the right to elect our own officers or levy our own taxes. While it is true that our population is not large enough, legally, to permit us to be a territory of the second rank, we are going to demand that we be given such a rank. We are taking a census. A preliminary survey shows that our population is about 8600. Almost 4000 of these are slaves. We need 5000 free male inhabitants of full age to be a second-grade territory. If we haven't got them soon, we will demand that the Congress overlook the law and give us the right of a legislative assembly.

"I am working hard to have the capital moved from Natchez to a location about six miles away. I have much support in this. My argument is that Natchez is vulnerable to attack from the river. I have purchased land for you at the proposed site. We should turn a neat penny in this.

"I have information that the transfer of Louisiana to France is imminent. This Bonaparte, who is kin by marriage to Flournoy, has got France under his thumb. Perhaps Flournoy knows something of the plans for Louisiana. I fear two things. If Louisiana becomes French, it might prove difficult for us to take it. Also, France might close New Orleans to us and that would mean war. You may be sure if France takes the land the importation of slaves will be forbidden there. There have been slave revolts in the French islands and whites have been massacred. France will not relish too many slaves in Louisiana. And, too, many of the French people do not believe in slavery.

"There are many rumblings of dissatisfaction here. The Spanish province of Baton Rouge—that is, West Florida—is almost ripe for a rebellion. We need that land for our territory. It will give us a sea coast. I hear much talk of some of the settlers down there around Baton Rouge and east at Biloxi and Paseagoula, striking a blow for independence. They are Americans and do not like

451

the Spaniards. They reason the time is ripe to over-
throw the Spanish régime from Baton Rouge to Mobile
and establish a *de facto* government. The plan is to make
West Florida independent and then apply for admission
into the United States. I have heard some of the government officials talk about it. For public consumption they
are opposed to the plan and yet they say in whispers that
if the settlers rebel against Spain it is of no concern to
the United States and that Spain could not hold the
United States responsible if the independent nation of
West Florida asked to become one of the United States.
Arms for the settlers are being run from Natchez. If
they are going to strike they had better strike quickly.
It will be too late if France gets the territory. Make
friends with the Kemper brothers over in your part of
the territory. They are ring-tailed hellers and love liberty. A word to the wise, etc. Also many Acadians who
were exiled to Louisiana by the English are moving over
near the mouth of the Halfway River. Make friends
with them.

"Philip Nolan soon will leave for the West. To save
my life I cannot discover his mission. Reuben Kemper,
one of the boys I spoke about, believes that Nolan plans
to put settlers in Texas. Kemper thinks that a revolt in
Texas against Spain is possible. If we have American
settlers there, they might rise up and establish a *de facto*
government. It is a desperate plan. If we can free West
Florida and Texas, and then have them join the union, we
will have New Orleans between the pinchers and, re-
gardless of who owns it, it will have to be surrendered
to the United States. If we play our cards right, we can
own the entire Mississippi Valley without fighting a war.
Nolan is taking nineteen men with him and plans to
build a blockhouse between the Trinity and Brazos

Rivers. He will use the blockhouse as a base for his hunting expeditions. But I hear that the Spaniards in San Antonio are waiting for him.

"I see your sister often. She is well. That damned half-breed, Flournoy, is hanging around her, however. He also is seen with Duportail's widow. I caution you to watch this man. We hear lively stories about your adventures among the Creeks.

"You recall that I once mentioned to you my kinspeople, the Houstons of Virginia. They have moved to Tennessee. The boy I mentioned, young Sam, is quite a heller I understand.

"I will keep you posted, etc."

Sam left for Natchez the day he received Thomas' letter. He would talk to Honoria about Flournoy. Perhaps he should speak to Anestasie, too. She was the widow of his friend. In his heart, however, Sam knew that was not the reason he yearned to speak to Anestasie. He liked her more than he would admit to himself, and he believed she was fond of him. He remembered how she had looked the first time he saw her, her gay dress, her daring green eyes and the outlines of her breasts. His mind dwelt upon her beauty until his blood raced through his veins. But it was not right for him to think of such things. There was Donna. What if she was sick and unable to share herself with him—she was still his wife. If a man made a troth, he stuck to it. A pledge was a pledge and a debt was a debt, and the most sacred pledge of all was a man's vow to his wife.

He arranged accommodations at the best tavern in Natchez, then went that evening to visit his sister and Anestasie at the home of Harkins' relatives. Honoria plied him with questions about Locha Poka, but asked only casually of Donna and not at all of Tishomingo.

Honoria was wearing a black velvet dress and a simple brooch of very old gold. Anestasie wore black silk and there was a cameo at her throat. The dainty odor of lily of the valley was noticeable about each woman.

Anestasie offered her hand to Sam. She wished Honoria wasn't present. It was impossible for her to be in a good humor in Honoria's presence, and she wanted to be kind to Sam for a while, anyhow. This probably would be their last meeting and she wanted very much to say some nice things to him before she said the cruel things that she also must say. She liked Sam better than any man she had met in the new land, even Flournoy. But Sam was beyond reach and Flournoy was within reach. Men were as necessary to Anestasie as breath and bread. She steeled herself for the ordeal. Flournoy had told her what to do and she would do it. . . .

"I suppose," she said, and her voice was unnatural, "that I should be impressed by your exploits among the Creeks, and grateful to you for avenging my husband's death. But I don't believe in an eye for an eye. I wish you had consulted me before you took the law into your own hands." Her voice was cold, and Sam was amazed, but perhaps she was just upset.

"After all, Anestasie," he said, "I don't seek advice from women. I make my own decisions. Tishomingo and I were your husband's friends and we settled his debt."

Then he regretted his words. He saw that Anestasie was angry. "It seems to me," she said, "that you should first think of settling your own debts."

"What do you mean?" Sam demanded, his face flushing. Honoria, who had sat by calmly during the conver-

454

sation, started to speak, but Sam motioned her to be quiet.

Anestasie said it slowly. "I mean that you owed my husband money."

"Is that a disgrace?" Sam was bewildered. "Your husband and I entered a business deal together."

"I'm a bit weary of your business deals," she said slowly and coldly, weighing her words so neither Sam nor Honoria would know that she was playing the rôle that Flournoy had assigned her. "You're always dreaming great visions, but none of them ever come to pass. You think you have done me a favor, but you haven't. My house is close to the Creek Nation and I must do business with the Creeks, but because of your vengeance I may be unsafe on my own plantation."

"That is a thing I would talk to you about," said Sam paternally. "I have sent your slaves back to your plantation in command of one of my post riders. I knew that was the way you wanted it. Your husband and I were business partners in a way. We had a great plan."

Anestasie nodded, but her voice still was cold. "I knew of your great plan but so far it has been a failure."

Her tone infuriated Honoria. No woman should speak so to her brother, and she broke into the conversation. "You would be wise to hear my brother," she said testily.

"This is a business talk between your brother and me."

"My brother's business is my business." Honoria warmed to her task. "He will not talk up to you because you're a woman and the widow of his friend. But I will not suffer him to be insulted at your hands." Sam rebuked his sister gently and cautioned her to silence.

"Forgive my sister," he said. "But she thinks I can do no wrong. It is true that our plan for a great road between

455

Natchez and Georgia has not come to pass. For that reason the value of your land and ferry is slight. I know you do not want to go back there ——"

"How do you know such a thing?" Anestasie demanded.

"But the dangers?" Sam uncrossed his legs uneasily.

Anestasie's laugh was shrill and forced. "There would have been no danger if you hadn't butchered the Creeks."

Sam got up from his chair and walked across the room and then turned suddenly upon Anestasie and asked angrily, "Who filled your head with such foolishness?"

"Lake Flournoy told her," Honoria sneered.

"That's true," agreed Anestasie. "And why shouldn't he? He's my friend. He says I should hold the land because it will be valuable when the road is built."

"He is right," Sam said quickly. "I would not try to do the widow of my friend out of her property. But it will be many years before the road will be built, Anestasie. I'll pay you a fair price for your land. Think it over."

"I will."

"Now enough of this bickering," Sam said. "What are your plans?"

Anestasie sent for wine. She wanted Sam to have as pleasant a memory of her as possible. André had had a great deal of faith in Sam. For sure, Flournoy had told her that Sam was a wild dreamer—a man who could be counted upon eventually to make a fool of himself. But Flournoy had cautioned her to speak naught to Sam of his feelings. She had confidence in Flournoy and his prosperity warranted her confidence. After all, none of Sam Dabney's schemes had made him rich. It was reasonable to assume that Flournoy's advice was better than Sam's.

"My plans are indefinite," she remarked after a moment. "I may liquidate my husband's property and move to New Orleans. I have friends there, refugees from the Revolution. However, first I will visit *Maison Blanche*."

"Alone?" asked Sam and looked at her quickly.

His glance angered her. She knew what he was thinking. "And why not?" she demanded. "Mr. Flournoy's a gentleman. I don't like the way you looked at me, Mr. Dabney."

"How did you expect him to look at you?" Honoria laughed.

Sam placed his glass on the table and rose. "Enough of this damned nonsense from both of you. Sam Dabney is too busy to listen to the cackling of two pullets."

"You mean hens," said Anestasie, and laughed too. She was ashamed of herself. "I am sorry, Sam. But your sister and I squabble every time we're together. Mr. Flournoy was kind enough to ask me to his home. I care nothing for the conventions of this land. I certainly would be as safe there as I am in this town, which is filled with drunken keel-boat men. But Mr. Flournoy has asked your sister to accompany me to *Maison Blanche*."

"It seems to me that I should have the right to tell that news to my brother," Honoria snapped. "But never the mind." She turned to Sam. "I was going to tell you about it as soon as I had an opportunity. Mr. Flournoy did ask me to *Maison Blanche*, but not as a chaperon for the widow Duportail. The widow is to be *my* chaperon."

Sam sensed another argument and shook his head. "You two fight like two tabbies. I don't care why Flournoy asked you to his place."

"Then you'll let me go?" Honoria asked quickly.

"I must think about it."

"Why do you hesitate?" Anestasie was amused.

Honoria jumped to her feet and snapped at Anestasie.

457

"Stop baiting my brother! He's too much of a gentleman to put you in your place, but I'll handle you. You're a damned shameless hussy! Your husband's body scarcely is cold and you're swishing around here in silks and primping before the garrison at the fort."

"Honoria, be quiet!" Sam took his sister's arm.

She jerked away from him. "I will not be quiet. She can't treat you this way. I'm a grown woman. I'm going to Lake Flournoy's too. He asked her only because he wanted me there. I know Mr. Flournoy quite well. When he buys goods, he insists that they be brand-new goods."

Sam caught his breath at Honoria's insult. Anestasie turned white, then crimson. She got slowly from her chair and stood before Honoria. Sam started to speak but Anestasie cut him short. "I am sorry for this scene, Mr. Dabney, but it was inevitable. This woman tried to break up your home. She has driven your wife to the brink of insanity. She ——"

"Shut up!" Sam took one step toward Anestasie and she stepped back quickly, stifling a scream. "Your husband and I were friends but that does not mean I will take such talk from you." He took Honoria's arm. "Let us go, Honoria. I might lose my temper if I stay here."

Anestasie watched them to the door. "If you have any business to transact with me," she said bitterly, "please speak to Mr. Flournoy. I'm turning my affairs over to him."

"He's welcome to them," Sam muttered.

Anestasie frowned slightly. Perhaps she had been a fool. And, moreover, she was sincerely sorry she had hurt Sam. "I do not see," she remarked, "why this rather unfortunate scene should be related to Mr. Flournoy. I'm sure he is not interested in the squabbles of women. If Honoria and I are to be guests in his home, we at least should try to make our visit a pleasure to Mr. Flournoy."

Honoria turned to Anestasie for one last fling. "I'm quite sure, Anestasie, that it isn't necessary for me to tell Mr. Flournoy that you are a slut in silks. If he hasn't found it out, then he is entitled to the pleasure of making the discovery for himself."

Anestasie was speechless and Honoria took her brother's arm and they walked away.

Back at the tavern Sam had brandy sent to his room and drank in silence. Once Honoria started to speak but he told her to keep quiet. Finally he said, "I will not rebuke you for the way you have acted. We are what we are, Honoria, and words cannot change us. You're sorry now that you spoke so quickly. Your words were harsh and unladylike but they have been said."

"I want to go to Lake Flournoy's," she said with determination. "I will not let that woman best me. She's playing a game, Sam'l. She deliberately baited you, knowing there would be a scene. She reasons that you'll not let me go to *Maison Blanche*. And that's what she wants. She's setting her cap for Lake Flournoy already."

"And you?" Sam looked his sister fully in the eye.

"No," she said. "Not I. But I cannot let that woman win." She walked to her brother and put her arms around him. "You know my heart, Sam'l. And you know where it belongs."

"Then your actions belie your love," he replied. "You know that Tishomingo hates Flournoy."

"If I go there, maybe he'll be jealous. Do you think so?" she asked eagerly.

Sam drained his brandy glass, tilted his sister's chin and kissed her on the cheek. "You're entitled to the truth,

459

Honoria. I don't think Tishomingo would be jealous of anything you did. He doesn't love you."

"Has he said so?"

"Is it necessary for him to say so?" Sam asked. "There, there, now, don't look that way. You look as though the world has fallen from beneath your feet and that you are alone. You're not alone, Honoria."

"I know, Sam'l; I'll always have you," she said gratefully, and then added, "What is your verdict? Do I go to Flournoy's?"

"Yes, if you want to."

"Is it so necessary that you have André's land?" she asked.

"The land is of no great value. But the ferry is very valuable. It is the key to my scheme of running wagon trains from the Mississippi River to Benjamin Frome's, and thence to Savannah. Flournoy knows that. That is the reason he influenced Anestasie. He wants the land and crossing himself. In his heart he has never forgiven me because I outwitted him on the slave deal. Why do you ask?"

She ruffled his hair and poured him another glass of brandy. "Are you blind, Sam'l? I have influence with Lake Flournoy."

Sam pushed the glass aside. "Sit down over there, Honoria, and listen to me. I will never use my sister to better myself in a business deal. If ever you give Flournoy or any man the impression that Sam Dabney is using his sister's beauty to improve his lot, I'll rawhide you until you can't sit down."

"I meant nothing wrong," she said, and her eyes filled with tears. But her mind was racing. Hadn't Flournoy told her that the only reason he was asking Anestasie to his plantation was so she could visit him too? He had

460

held her hand and had whispered, "I want you to visit my home and be my guest. If I ask Duportail's widow, your brother will allow you to go."

Honoria had asked him, "Are you sure that is the only reason you asked her?"

He had whispered, "Yes. And why do you ask? Are you jealous?"

"Yes, I am jealous," Honoria had allowed him to fondle her but not to kiss her. His hands had felt hard, not kind as Ab's hands had felt.

Now Sam watched his sister and tried to read her thoughts. "Yes," he repeated finally, "you may go to Flournoy's and I hope you enjoy yourself. I care naught for this silly feud between you and Anestasie, but I do ask you to keep your eyes open. Flournoy and I are in several business deals together, but I don't trust him too far and he doesn't trust me as far as I trust him."

He kissed his sister goodbye, and went to see Lawyer Thomas and they talked business for several hours. Then Sam mounted Claymore and hurried up the Trace to *Maison Blanche.* Flournoy greeted him warmly and had good wine brought. They wasted several minutes on formalities and then Sam asked of the news. Flournoy had no word from France concerning the plans to acquire Louisiana, but he had heard that such a move was afoot.

"That will mean we cannot import any more slaves," he frowned. "It's a shame, too, for the market is improving. A prime fellow is worth almost a thousand dollars in the sugar country, and nearly as much in Natchez. I'll have another cargo in next week, you know."

Sam knew quite well when the cargo would arrive. He also knew that the price of slaves was going up. One of the slaves he had got from Flournoy already had breeched a son and he soon would be ready for market. If worst came to worst Sam could unload some of the females, but he would never do it unless necessity drove him to it. He learned that the Chickasaws had granted rights for a wagon road through their nation. He and Flournoy talked of crops and business and finally Sam got around to the purpose of his visit. "I understand my sister is to be your guest," he remarked.

"I hope so," said Flournoy. "I told her to ask your permission. I'm bringing Duportail's widow here. Perhaps I can help her forget her sorrow. I wanted your sister to accompany her. You will let her come?"

"Ay, and we are honored that you should ask her."

"Then I will send my coach for them tomorrow."

"There is another matter about which I would speak," Sam began. "Mrs. Duportail tells me that you're taking over her business affairs."

"I volunteered to help her, yes."

"What is your price for her property?"

Flournoy tilted his head and laughed uproariously. "There you go again, Dabney. You're the damnedest fellow I ever saw. You ask what we would take for the property. Just like that. Poooooff! You haven't got enough cash to buy ten acres of that Duportail land and you know it. Give me credit for a little intelligence. I know how valuable that ferry crossing is to you and it's not for sale."

Sam laughed. This half-breed was no fool. "All right, Flournoy. Have it your way. But remember—a Frenchman never outsmarted an Irishman."

Flournoy studied Sam closely for the hundredth time, trying again to evaluate him. He thought he knew his

462

weakness—give Dabney enough rope and he would hang himself. He was a man who could be depended upon to succeed eight or nine times and then stake all on the tenth throw. He was an intelligent man, but not a clever man. And he was a gambler. He wouldn't gamble for small stakes, but he would gamble his whole kingdom and his own life. He was a man who would play his luck until it ran out.

"Perhaps a Frenchman never outsmarted an Irishman," Flournoy said, and motioned to his slave to refill their glasses, "but I took the liberty of looking over Duportail's books. I reasoned that Anestasie would let me handle her business. I notice there is a little matter of some cash you borrowed from Duportail recently. Of course, I will have to ask payment."

"Of course," said Sam smoothly. "The amount is $3,000, but you may be assured that when André let me have the money he did not intend that I should be pressed for it so quickly."

"I do not know Duportail's intentions."

"I didn't intend to charge André for a service I did him," Sam added, "although at the time my lawyer said I should. When André's goods were brought around from the seaboard, I didn't collect my commission for the work. I've taken the liberty of having my lawyer draw up the papers. Amazingly enough, the bill comes to $3,000."

"That's ridiculous!" Flournoy flared. "Those goods were brought around several years ago, and you've no legal right to demand a fee at this late date."

Sam tapped Flournoy on the knee. "I don't intend to collect the fee unless you drive me to it. I always pay my debts and if you'll give me a decent length of time I'll

463

repay the $3,000. André and I had a plan for that money, but if you insist upon immediate payment then so will I. My bill is several years old and the interest will be considerable."

"No court would support you."

Sam grinned. "You forget that when those goods were brought to Natchez this land was under Spanish jurisdiction. There's no such thing as a statute of limitations among the Spaniards. And all debts contracted in those days still are valid under American law. For sure, if you want to contest the amount you can go to court in Natchez."

Flournoy scowled and his eyes narrowed. "I'm no fool. Those damned American judges would hold for you." Then he leaned back in his chair and laughed again. "Damme, Dabney, you're a fast thinker. I respect you—really I do. I like to do business with you, for you keep my wits sharp."

Sam thanked him. "I like to do business with you, too," he said. "I like a man who does not let business interfere with his friendships. And we are still friends, aren't we?"

"I'll vow to it," said Flournoy. "I had thought I could demand that $3,000 and persuade you to give me those slaves, Sukey and Dabby, as payment. But I'll tell you what I'll do. I'll give you perpetual rights to use the Duportail ferry if you'll deed that negro wench and her baby to me."

Sam accepted a pipe from a slave, crossed his legs and puffed in silence for several minutes. "Why do you want those slaves so badly?"

"Why? For breeding stock, of course."

"I've told you before," Sam watched him closely, "that they're not for sale. Sukey is my wife's favorite and my son is fond of both Sukey and Dabby. Dabby will make

464

the finest house slave in the new land. Perhaps she'll be my wedding present to my sister."

"But you need the Duportail ferry very badly," Flournoy insisted.

"Ay, but I don't worry about it. If you try to hold me up there when I send my goods to Georgia, I'll have the territory take over the damned ferry and operate it as a public service. If they won't do that, I'll have the Choctaws sell me the right to build my own ferry a few miles up the river from the Duportail crossing. And I'll have the road built that way. I can do that you know."

"You wouldn't dare," remarked Flournoy coldly. "For the sake of your friend's memory you wouldn't dare. It would pauperize his widow."

"Just try to hold me up and see what I'll do," said Sam. "André Duportail was my friend but when his widow got into trouble she went to you and not to me. All right, let her take the consequences. If either of you try to block my plan, I'll make that Duportail property useless to anyone except the Choctaws for a burying ground. May I have another drink?"

"Help yourself," said Flournoy. "I think I'll have one, too. I need it. I thought I had you out on a limb, but now you've got me out on one." He clapped Sam on the shoulder and had his slave take the wine away and bring brandy. He flattered Sam and even toasted him. "You've outwitted me again. But every man has a weak spot. Where's yours?"

"This," said Sam and held up his brandy. "But don't tell anybody." He laughed.

"It is my weakness, too," chuckled Flournoy, "and I feel that the time has come for us to satisfy our weakness."

465

"Then why the delay?" said Sam. "Send these little glasses away and have tumblers fetched."

They drank until the dinner hour and at the meal they toasted each other in drunken revelry.

"To my noble kinswoman, Josephine," Flournoy said. "And to her illustrious husband. To all the French!"

"To all the Irish," Sam roared. "And God-damn the English. To the United States!"

They drank to the Choctaws, to the departed spirits of the Choctaws, to all of the women they knew, and finally even to their horses.

As the evening waned Flournoy said more soberly, "I want to talk to you about those slaves."

"God's jaw bone, man!" Sam hurled his glass into the fireplace. "You were getting me drunk to talk business. Not I, you merry bucko! Sam Dabney never talks business when he's drinking. There's a time for drinking and a time for making love and a time for fighting and a time for business. This is the time for drinking. But soon I'm going to bed. I've got to travel tomorrow. I think I'll have a bath before I go. Is that comely bath wench of yours still up?"

"I have no bath wench," Flournoy answered. "I sent her to the kitchen. It was your sister's idea. In Natchez she chided me because I had a woman bathe me. Rather than take a chance on offending your beautiful sister, I sent the wench to the kitchen."

" 'Tis a shame," said Sam.

Flournoy smiled. "Of course, for you I can send her to the bath."

"Hell's hinges! Not for Sam Dabney. I wash myself at home and what I do at home is good enough for me when I'm away. The reason I asked about her is because I didn't want her around me when I bathed. Women are

466

not among my vices, Lake. This is my only vice." He drained his glass and staggered off to prepare for bed.

He departed for Locha Poka the next morning and Flournoy sent his coach to Natchez to fetch the ladies. To all appearances, the feud between Honoria and Anestasie had ended in an armistice. Anestasie feared Flournoy's displeasure if she quarreled, and Honoria endured the peace, for she felt that she held the winning weapons anyway. Flournoy sensed the hatred between the two women and enjoyed it. It pleased him to think that the two women might fight over him. He bestowed his attentions equally between them. One night he sat Honoria at his right and the next night Anestasie occupied the position of honor. At Anestasie's request he put a special steel screen around his snakes. She would not even pass by the snake den and one day when he and the two women were walking on the lawn Honoria, for sheer devilment, pointed to an exposed root and shrieked. "Look out!"

Anestasie fainted and remained in bed all day. Flournoy scolded Honoria for her prank and Honoria said she was sorry. But she really was glad, for it gave her an opportunity to be alone with her host. They rode together that afternoon, over the banks to Big Black, and there they dismounted and walked along the river. Again she allowed Flournoy to fondle her but when he sought to kiss her she turned her head away modestly.

"You're overly bold," she said softly.

"I cannot help but be bold around you. You're like fine wine in my blood. You go to my head."

"Be careful that you don't lose your head," she smiled at him, then slowly stooped over to pick a flower, confident that her breasts would be visible. They were.

467

Flournoy put his hands on her shoulders and tried to pull her to him. She made as if to struggle and then surrendered to his arms as though he had overpowered her.

"I've already lost my head," he said, and kissed her. His lips were hard, not warm and moist as Ab's had been. There was no tingling in her spine when he kissed her. She did not feel as though she were floating away as she had felt in Ab's arms, and as she felt when Tishomingo even brushed by her. She allowed Flournoy to kiss her until his breath came quickly and his eyes blazed.

"You'll think I'm an abandoned woman," she whispered. "And you're not being true to Anestasie."

"I care naught for Anestasie." He breathed deeply and quickly and pulled her to him. She writhed in his embrace for only a second or so to tantalize him, and then curved her body close to his and kissed him. After a moment she pushed him away. Flournoy's breath came in gasps. "It's *you* I want. You! Please, Honoria, I want you so much. I need you so . . ."

Honoria interrupted him curtly. "I'm not for sale, Mr. Flournoy. You speak tenderly of your needs but lightly of your love."

"But I *do* love you," he replied earnestly. "I swear I do. I swear by God. Is there anything else I can say?" She was the first woman Flournoy had ever said he loved.

She kissed him again, quickly, but full on the lips. Then she turned her head pertly and smiled at him. He tightened his arms around her waist and her lips parted as he stooped over. "Yes," she said, while her lips were free, "there are other things you must say and do before you can have me. I think you understand. I'll give myself to no man except my husband. Now let us return.

468

I'm beside myself. I'm so excited by your caresses that I'm giddy."

He kissed her on the neck and ears, and she allowed his passion to boil. She even provoked it—and then she tore herself from his embrace. "I cannot stand it," she gasped. "You set me on fire." She turned and walked up the path toward the house and he followed her, his brain still reeling and his temples throbbing.

Anestasie was in a pout when they returned, but soon her good spirits returned because, when Honoria was looking the other way, Flournoy patted Anestasie's cheek, and at dinner that evening he playfully pinched her knee.

He left the women in charge at *Maison Blanche* while he went to Barataria to receive his new cargo of slaves. Tishomingo, Jasper and Caesar were at Barataria, and Tishomingo took twelve of the slaves as Sam's commission.

Sam was highly pleased with the blacks when Tishomingo delivered them at Locha Poka. They all were females, ten Senegals and two Aradas. Sam knew he had two Aradas in the bunch before he saw them. He could smell them. Of all the Negroes in the world, the Aradas stank the worst. A white man gagged if he got downwind from the Negroes. Soap and water would not take the smell away. Nothing would remove it. It was their natural odor. Sam ordered that special barracoons be erected for them northeast of the house. The winds usually blew from the southwest. Donna urged him to get rid of them and he agreed to put them on the block as soon as he could get them to Natchez. Tishomingo apologized for bringing them, but explained that since Sam had demanded all females it was necessary for him to take two Aradas.

Sam and Jasper braved the odor and examined the Negroes. The slaves were very frightened of their white master and Sam was baffled until Jasper explained their fears. In the French isles the white man told the blacks that they were drinking the blood of slaves when they drank claret. The Negroes were in mortal fear of their lives. Sam had never attempted to breed fear in his Negroes. He believed that a frightened man is not a good workman.

The Aradas called their tobies *gris-gris*. Sam held one of the women and examined her teeth, then called Jasper and had him look at her teeth. Jasper said, "Bad."

Sam made the women strip and examined them from head to feet. He looked between their toes but made Jasper do the chore of examining them minutely.

Jasper pointed to a yaw on one of the women.

"I feared as much," Sam shrugged. "This wench has got the yaws!"

He sent Jasper to the foundry and the slave returned with a cup of iron rust which he pounded into a powder. Sam mixed the powder with citron juice and spread the ointment on a cloth greased with lard. He laid the plaster upon the yaw and explained to the woman in sign language that if she removed the plaster he would beat her.

He instructed Jasper to change the plaster morning and night. The yaw would open in about three days and then he would dress the Negress' sore with a mixture of lard, terebinthine, verdigris and vinegar. Then the Negress would be sweated. If the treatment didn't cure her, she would live only a few weeks. One of the Senegals had a touch of the scurvy. Sam treated her by making her wash her gums six times daily with a mixture of scurvy grass, ground ivy, watercress and citron juice. She was allowed to drink no water, only a mixture of scurvy grass, ground ivy, watercress, citron juice, salt-peter, all steeped in water. Sam added sugar to the medicine to improve the taste and made the slave drink four pints a day. He ordered that both of the sick Negroes be given special food from the kitchen and a liberal quota of brandy.

Sam had decided to allow Honoria to spend a month at *Maison Blanche*, and was planning to send for her when smallpox was reported in the neighboring Choctaw village. He and Tishomingo went immediately to the village in an effort to check the epidemic. They isolated all the cases and treated the patients with poultices and herbs. Only two of their patients survived, but Sam considered that a triumph.

He and Tishomingo were together day and night and the Choctaw Nation was very grateful to Sam. Push-mataha sent him gifts. Tishomingo, however, was rather aloof and finally, at insistence of Sam, explained that he was rather disappointed in his friend for allowing Honoria to visit Flournoy.

"So that is what's eating you," Sam said.

"Ay," Tishomingo replied. "Since you have asked I say, ay. I'm surprised at you, Big Sam."

Sam explained, "Honoria is not the kind of woman who will take orders. She's too much like my father for that. If I had forbidden her to visit Flournoy's, it perhaps would have made her determined to do so anyway. By forbidding her to see Flournoy I might make Flournoy attractive to her. It's human nature to want the thing that we are told we cannot have. It's my hope that my sister will see Flournoy as he really is. I believe I have acted wisely." He wondered why he bothered to explain to

471

Tishomingo. After all, it was his own business. But down inside he felt that he had committed an error and it helped his conscience to try to explain away his error.

Tishomingo wasn't satisfied and he rebuked Sam until Sam said angrily, "Damme, Chock, if you're so interested in my sister, why don't you show her some attention? I know of but one man in the world who can handle her. And you're that man."

Tishomingo was impressed. "Perhaps I'll ask her to return to the school, Big Sam, I need her badly."

"Then why in God's name didn't you ask her?"

"Because I'm afraid."

"Afraid of what?"

"Afraid that I'll forget my vow. My vow to Ta-lo-wah. We'll speak no more about it."

"I've been thinking," Sam remarked casually after a moment, "and the more I think the more I wonder why Lake Flournoy is so anxious to own Sukey and Dabby."

"Has the fox been so busy that he has not had time to think?"

"What do you mean?" Sam demanded.

"Sukey and Dabby are worth a fortune to Flournoy. The Creeks would pay him any price he asked. And the deal would make the Creeks his debtors. They'd trade with him, they'd consider him their friend. Particularly now that he intends to manage the Duportail place he needs friends among the Creeks."

"The cold-blooded bastard!" Sam cursed. "I never thought of that."

He told Tishomingo about his debt to the Duportail estate and of how he had outwitted Flournoy.

"But you'll repay the money?" Tishomingo asked anxiously.

"Yes, as soon as I get it."

472

"I have it, Big Sam," said Tishomingo. "I have that much money for my school. You're welcome to it. André was our friend. We would not charge him a commission for the service we did for him."

"I will not charge him. When I sell the land that Thomas purchased with money André let me have, I'll repay the loan."

Despite their efforts, the pox spread to Locha Poka and seven of Sam's slaves were stricken. He isolated them in Ab's cabin. Three of them died the first week.

It was time for Honoria to come home but Sam sent her word that she must remain at *Maison Blanche* until the epidemic was spent. Honoria was very happy to get the message, for it saved her the trouble of writing Sam and telling him that she expected to remain at Flournoy's house for another month. She had noticed a strange light in Anestasie's eyes, a light of conquest.

One afternoon after she allowed Flournoy to caress her, and then pushed him away again, Honoria saw him whispering to Anestasie in the drawing room. At dinner Anestasie laughed in emotional drunkenness. And that night Honoria discovered that Anestasie had the bath slave rub her body with perfume. After Honoria retired she heard the master of *Maison Blanche* tap gently on the door of Anestasie's bedroom. Honoria waited several minutes and then tip-toed to the door and listened. The sounds she heard did not offend her, nor did they particularly upset her. They only increased her determination.

She knew then that some day *Maison Blanche* and its master must be hers. She almost sickened at the thought of bedding with Flournoy, but the dividends would be worth the investment. So Tishomingo had scorned her . . . She would win the richest man in the Choctaw Nation. Then she could call Tishomingo by the familiar Tisku. She could sponsor his school; he would be in her debt. She could help her brother. She would be a great lady. Old man Dabney's brat, the mistress of *Maison Blanche*, the kinslady of Josephine! Ay, the dividends would be worth the investment.

23

HONORIA made no effort to disrupt the relations between Anestasie and Flournoy; neither did she allow either to think that she even suspected the affair. She knew that love is like a burning candle and that it is foolish to attempt to extinguish it while it burns brightly. She would wait until it spluttered, until its wick was burned black and the strength was out of its tallow—then she would snuff it out. If she snuffed it out now it could be rekindled again. It rather pleased her vanity to watch Lake Flournoy try to deceive her, and Anestasie try to convey the impression that Flournoy was paying her proper court without conveying the truth. At times, however, Honoria suspected that perhaps Anestasie wished she could know the truth. Anestasie had triumphed, but a triumph is not a victory unless the vanquished knows she has been defeated.

Honoria often absented herself from the house to give them opportunities to be alone. The candle was burning brightest now and Honoria felt that soon the flame would flicker desperately for life and then drown itself in its own refuse. Old man Dabney used to say, "If you go to the well too often, you'll soon get tired of water."

She was very sure of herself. She knew that Lake Flournoy was not a man to marry unless it was necessary. Anestasie was a fool. She should know that men never valued anything that was given to them without a struggle. Man loved his land because he worked for it, and the same was true of his women. If a woman put no value upon herself, she could not expect a man to. Honoria smiled to herself. Anestasie had run to Flournoy's arms the first time he had opened them. She had even turned the covers back for him. Of course, Honoria admitted to herself, she would go to Tishomingo the same way, but Tishomingo was different. Tishomingo was like fox fire dancing in the swamp, always just beyond reach. Tishomingo was unattainable. And yet, he was a man, too. She had felt him staring at her, she had heard him breathe deeply when she had swished by him, flaunting her grace and beauty. But he wouldn't surrender. Well, she couldn't wait always.

Anestasie was overbearing to Honoria, and Honoria patronized Anestasie. Only once was there any hint of a quarrel. That was the time Flournoy, usually meticulously proper about such things, forgot his routine and gave Honoria the seat of honor at the banquet table two nights in succession. Anestasie wept at the table and Flournoy demanded, "What's the matter with you?"

His tone was harsh. A man does not speak harshly to his love. Honoria sensed that his ardor for Anestasie was cooling. God's earmuffs! what a fool she was. A widow— and she didn't know how to keep a man's desire at fever heat. Sniffling and whimpering like a spoiled child. Even a maiden should know that she could drown a man's love in her tears quicker than in her venom. That a widow should act so—re-fiddlesticks! Perhaps in France a woman could use her tears for persuasion but never in the new land. Men didn't have time to pacify weeping women, and Flournoy was a man who hated tears. Teary women disgusted him.

476

"It was my night to sit at your right," Anestasie said childishly, and pouted.

"Oh, nonsense," said Flournoy. "Such a slight mistake isn't worth your tears."

Honoria got up quickly. "But it is, Mr. Flournoy," she said graciously. "And you should be ashamed of yourself. I don't want to be selfish. It's Anestasie's night to sit here."

Her action pleased Flournoy and after dinner he complimented her.

"I haven't seen very much of you recently," he said when they were alone.

"But you've not been lonely," she teased and saw to it that a slave prepared his brandy as he liked it. She also saw to his coffee and his pipe. Flournoy reached for her hand when she served him his coffee. She allowed him to hold it, but withdrew it quickly when she heard Anestasie approaching.

Honoria thought there might be an open break between Flournoy and Anestasie the day some Chickasaw chiefs came to *Maison Blanche* to make talk. Flournoy presented Honoria to the chiefs first. A man always presents his favorite first, and thereafter the chiefs addressed her as the most important woman on the plantation. Anestasie ran to her room and lay on the bed and wept. Honoria saw to the Chickasaws' comfort and was an impressive hostess. It was important that Flournoy impress the Indians and he was very proud when they complimented him upon his selection of a hostess. After they had been served and had gone away Flournoy told Honoria that she had done him a great favor.

"If I have, I'm happy," she said. "It pleases me to be of service to you."

"Then why do you avoid me?" he asked.

She said, "I haven't avoided you. You've avoided me. I've been lonely and you are never lonely."

He said, "I'm always lonely when I'm out of your sight."

Honoria patted his cheek playfully, "Anestasie has retired and she'll wonder what is keeping you."

Flournoy's chin quivered and a look of annoyance flashed across his face, but he regained his composure quickly. He was too wise a man to try to lie to so wise a woman, and it thrilled him to think that she would tolerate his attentions to Anestasie. It was thrilling to have two beautiful women in his house, one a riddle and the other a puzzle that he had solved easily. His admiration for Honoria's intelligence increased twofold. Damme, here was a riddle to test a man's wits, here was a parcel of flesh and hair to stir a man's strength. "You know everything, don't you?" he said. "Nothing escapes you."

"I know naught," she said, and turned her eyes from him. "Except that I'm willing to wait for the man I want. Good night, Lake."

He caught her in his arms as she turned. "Not now," she said.

"But I have a right to know what you meant by that remark."

"About waiting for the man I want?" She allowed him to put his arms around her waist. "I think I make myself clear. There are only a few really worth-while men in the world. Every girl, Lake, picks out her man and says to her heart, 'That is my man.' A wise woman is willing to wait for her man. She's a fool to run to him. He must come to her and it is well if he has drunk deeply of love before he comes to her, for then he will be satisfied with

478

his true love. And he will really know what love is and can teach his bride its ecstasy, and teach her its mystery."

He buried his face in her neck and whispered, "You're wonderful. So wise, but so young and tender. I love you."

Honoria's lips parted and she whispered, "When you say that I become giddy and am not sure of myself."

"You're always sure of yourself, Honoria," he said.

"Maybe, and maybe not. I've been unhappy of late. I have been puzzled by your attentions to Anestasie, but I have not been mortified or angry with you. I've been thinking of going away. I cannot return now to Locha Poka because of the pox that is there, but I can go to Natchez."

"You cannot leave me," he said. "I don't know what I will do if you leave me."

Honoria sat down and invited Flournoy to sit by her. "Yours words drip like honey. I'm quite aware of the relation between you and Anestasie. I know, also, that you don't want to be left alone in this house with her. She's not like Ta-lo-wah. She cannot be loved and then thrown away. She has powerful friends in France. If I should go away and she should stay here you might have to marry her to save your reputation and hers. I'm quite aware that as long as I am here the world will think no evil of her. It's nice to have a chaperon who will close her ears."

Flournoy attempted to interrupt her but she silenced him. "Yes, it's very convenient to have me here," she continued. "But, after all, I'm a woman, too. It is not a happy thought to lie awake at night and know that the man you love is in the arms of another woman. No, wait! Don't interrupt me now."

"But I must tell you something," he said.

"There's nothing you can tell me that I don't know. I don't blame you. I blame no man for taking a woman

479

who throws herself at his feet. A man is entitled to enjoy his youth. You don't love Anestasie."

"No, I do not. I love only you. Ay ——"

"You mean that you want me," she said, "and I am flattered."

Flournoy said, "What a remarkable woman you are! You know about Anestasie and yet you don't shun me."

"No, I don't shun you. I had a very wise father, Lake. My father used to say that a man's mission on earth is to take all the women who will give themselves, and that a woman's mission is to hold her man with bonds of passion and sympathy so he will not wander far from the hearth. My father said that the covenant of marriage is a woman's institution through which she tries to protect herself and her security by conventions. I know you want me. But I won't throw myself away. My heart urges me to, but my brain is a check-rein on my emotions. I'm not a harlot and I'll go to no man's bed until he is my husband."

Flournoy said, "Marriage is impossible now."

"I'm quite aware of that. You allowed yourself to get involved with that woman upstairs. Understand—I don't condemn you, but I'm disappointed in your lack of wisdom. You misjudged me completely. No man ever has been able to keep two women under his roof and deceive them."

She put her hand on his shoulder and looked deeply into his eyes, then she slipped her arms around his neck, parting her lips and closing her eyes. Flournoy almost smothered her. She lay in his arms and counted under her breath, counted the wild beats of his heart and when she knew that his emotions had reached the point where they might drive him to violence, she whispered, "But I can wait."

480

"But I cannot," he said. "Will you marry me?"

"Not as long as Anestasie is here."

"I'll send her away."

"Don't be a fool again," she said. "Anestasie's tongue is loaded with poison."

"But what can I do?" he said. "I'll do anything for you."

"Then take a drink of brandy and go to bed—alone." She kissed him lightly on the cheek and got up.

Anestasie came to her bedroom that night, and Honoria saw that she had been weeping again, and that her nerves were on edge. Honoria could not help but admire her beauty although she was disgusted with her tears. Anestasie had drunk deeply of the cup of life. She had been intoxicated with love many times, but her body still was young and firm. For the first time in her life she was tasting the dregs in the bottom of the cup, and although her pride was cut there was no evidence of it in her eyes or around her mouth. Honoria tried to put herself in Anestasie's position and wondered what she would do. Suppose she had come three thousand miles to a strange land, from Paris to the wilderness. Suppose she had suffered the shocks that had come to Anestasie, could she still be proud? Would her eyes still flash as Anestasie's flashed? Would her body still be young and supple?

Anestasie primped before Honoria's mirror. "I look like a vagabond," Anestasie said. "I couldn't sleep. I've been thinking about André."

"Great God!" Honoria lay on the bed and rolled with laughter. "I'd forgotten about André and I thought you had. I hope his ghost is not following you, Anestasie."

"What do you mean?" Anestasie ceased combing her hair and glared at Honoria.

481

"Hoity Toity," said Honoria. "I wonder how the ghost of a man would feel if he could see his widow. Everything she does."

"Your insinuations are intolerable," Anestasie said. "You have a filthy mind."

"But a clean body. My body is new, Anestasie, and I'm not insinuating anything. When are you going away?"

"I? I came to ask you the same thing. I'm not going away."

Honoria laughed again. "Oh, I thought you'd be going to New Orleans to buy your wedding clothes. You cannot be married in black. And will you keep the snakes here when you are mistress of *Maison Blanche*?"

"You're jealous of me," Anestasie said fiercely. "You're envious because he loves me."

"For a widow you're very stupid, Anestasie. Mr. Flournoy loves, for a while, any woman who smells sweet and whose flesh is firm."

"You're disgusting!" Anestasie said, and left the room.

Flournoy's weariness of Anestasie soon became evident to everybody at *Maison Blanche* except Anestasie, and she no longer was wholly confident of her position. The idea, and it persisted, that he was tiring of her, kept her emotions frazzled and her temper frayed. She wept often. Once she pretended illness in an effort to attract his sympathy, but he ignored her.

Honoria rarely allowed herself to be seen alone with the rich half-breed. She would not give Anestasie any excuse to carry tales to Sam. She knew Flournoy was scheming to himself in an effort to make Anestasie leave *Maison Blanche*. But she must leave of her own accord, and willingly. A man could not drive away the widow of

André Duportail. It would be an insult that too many men would avenge. Sam Dabney would be the first to take up arms to avenge such an insult, not for Anestasie's sake but for the sake of the memory of his friend. Nay, Lake Flournoy could not drive her away. Once he suggested to her that he would take her to France to see Josephine, but Anestasie's intuition warned her. Something told her that if she ever left *Maison Blanche* she never would return and be its mistress. Flournoy had never really proposed marriage to her, but she certainly had every reason to believe that they would be married after an appropriate period of mourning had passed for her. She had suggested that he let it be known that Honoria's welcome was worn thin. Flournoy rebuked her severely for her suggestion.

"Don't be a fool," he said. "I dare not offend her because of her brother. And, too, so long as she is here, it's quite respectable for you to be here."

She asked Flournoy to get rid of his snakes and was afraid even to walk by the den.

"I often dream about them," she said. "They terrify me. Please get rid of them, darling."

"I'll do nothing of the sort," he said impatiently. "They're the best slave guards a man can have. And I'll not suffer interference in my business. I have no patience, Anestasie, with frightened women."

Honoria gave Flournoy no apparent help in his schemes to rid himself of Anestasie. She saw him no more often than discretion would allow. She tormented him with her looks and her suggestive gestures. She kept his emotions as taut as rawhide and laughed at him. She teased him and left him weak and angry at his own weakness.

One night she told him, "Why, darling, you have a fever. Your eyes are bright and your skin is hot."

"I'm burning up inside," he said. "As soon as I can get Anestasie off my hands, I'm going to your brother and state my troth."

"Will you, Lake?"

"Ay, and I'll send you to New Orleans to buy your trousseau. We'll be married here. I'll invite every important man in the territory to be our guest. There will be a week of celebration."

"And may I ask all of my friends?"

"Of course."

Honoria toyed with the buttonhole on his silken coat. "And you'll ask Tishomingo?"

"No. Good God, no!" He took Honoria by the shoulders. "Why do you ask that? Has there been anything between you and Tishomingo? What does he mean to you?"

"I thought you knew," Honoria said softly. "Everybody else knew. Tishomingo tried to make love to me. I scorned him. I hate him. I hate him because he hates you. He called me 'old man Dabney's brat,' one time. And that's why I want him at my wedding. I want him to be present when I marry the most important man in the new land."

She felt his eyes burning into her. "Are you sure he means nothing to you?"

"He means as much to me as he does to you," Honoria said. "We have much in common. We both hate him. I hate him for the way he treated me in Georgia. He fetched me from Benjamin Frome's to my brother. Because I was a bound girl and an orphan he tried to make love to me. I've never told my brother. My brother would kill him. When I spurned him he called me a

484

brat. And I'm woman enough to want him to see me marry his enemy."

"That's a good revenge," Flournoy smiled. "It will make him the laughing-stock of his nation. His first love left his barren lodge and sought a haven here. I was kind to her. I didn't love her. But Tishomingo has never forgiven me. And now I take you from him."

"He's a dangerous man, Lake."

"I'm not helpless, Honoria. You should know that he has sworn to kill me. He'll try some day. Perhaps he'll try when he hears I will marry you."

"Aren't you afraid?"

Flournoy said, "I'm afraid of only one thing in the world and that is that you might not love me forever."

She kissed him until his brain whirled. "Then you have nothing in the world to be afraid of."

Honoria eventually grew impatient of Flournoy's unsuccessful efforts to get Anestasie away, and decided to take matters into her own hands. Flournoy had dillydallied long enough. Now she would get results. It should be very simple to get the temperamental widow away from *Maison Blanche*. Honoria had thought about it often. The snakes would do it! The dread fer-de-lances which Anestasie feared more than death.

Maison Blanche lay still and brooding in the late afternoon sun. Anestasie was sleeping, Flournoy was in his study and the slaves were about their appointed tasks. Honoria walked out of the front door, circled the lawn and paused at the rear of the house, near the snake den. She glanced around to make sure she was not watched. She took a long forked stick and lifted one of the smaller vipers from the pit. She pinned its head down and glanced around for a stone to crush it. The snake, however, slipped its head from under the fork and wriggled into the grass before Honoria could kill it. Her first impulse was to scream for help, but, fearing Flournoy would never forgive her, she ran back to the front of the house and into the mansion. She had meant only to frighten Anestasie with a dead snake; now there was a live one loose! No one had seen her. She went to her room and undressed and lay down. For the first time in her life she was frightened. Flournoy might stumble on the snake. The snake might get into the house or into her bed. She took a deep breath to regain her poise. Surely the snake could not live long in the swamps. If it survived the other snakes and wild animals, it could not survive the climate.

She was nervous as she dressed and went to the drawing room. Anestasie and Flournoy were there. They were drinking wine when a field slave ran in, his eyes rolling in fear and his mouth drooling. One of the house slaves attempted to stop him but he fought his way to Flournoy and fell on the rug, babbling incoherently.

"What is it?" Flournoy leaned over the man. Anestasie and Honoria stared in horror at the fear-stricken Negro. The slave's tongue clung to the roof of his mouth and Flournoy slapped him. "Speak, you fool!"

"The snake," the slave said in French. "The jungle devil!"

"He is crazed with fear," Flournoy said. "Sometimes they go mad like this when they are marched by the snake pit. It is naught. I'll have him sent away."

He called a house slave and had the crazed man removed, and went to the quarters to speak to the other slaves. He knew that fear was contagious.

Honoria, ill with a sinking feeling in the pit of her stomach, sat on the edge of a chair and stared into space. She was sitting there when Flournoy walked back into the house, visibly struggling to maintain his aplomb. He went to the slave bells and sounded them and spoke rapidly in French to his house servants.

Anestasie understood his words and there was a gurgling sound in her throat as she watched him. He bowed to the ladies and said, "It is best that you know so you can defend yourselves. One of the snakes is loose." Even his steel nerves could not control his voice, and it trembled slightly.

Anestasie still could not find her voice and Honoria swallowed the scream that was in her throat. "It has killed one of the field slaves," Flournoy said. "It is one of the smaller snakes. Go to your rooms. We'll find it and kill it."

He left them and went to the spot where the snake had been seen. Many of the Negroes would not hunt the snake, even after they were beaten. Flournoy armed himself and several of his stauncher bumboes with sticks and they began the search.

Anestasie pleaded with Honoria to go with her and they went to Anestasie's room. It was Anestasie who bolted the door.

"I'm faint," she said, "and weak. I feel sick."

"This is no time to faint." Honoria's heart was pounding in her throat.

"But it might get in here. It might be in this house, this very minute! In this room! Please, Honoria, take the candle and look for it. It's so gloomy and dark in here. You're brave, Honoria. Please look for it."

Honoria walked first to the windows and saw that they were bolted. The twilight had come. "Ay, it's gloomy in here. But I'll search. I won't use a candle though. If the snake is here, the fire might excite it."

"Merciful God! What can we do?"

487

"Be still! Sit there on the bed. The fer-de-lance does not always strike. It probably wouldn't bother us unless we angered it."

She saw that Anestasie was half blind and almost senseless with fear. "Just to comfort you, I'll look for it." She peered first under the bed and then in a clothes chest. She looked under Anestasie's bureau and in the bureau drawers, among Anestasie's clothes. She rummaged through the chemises and ribbons, then stopped suddenly and stared at something in the drawer, her mind racing. She glanced quickly at Anestasie and, realizing that the other woman could not see her clearly, her hand moved stealthily from the drawer to her bodice.

"There!" said Honoria. "It isn't in the room."

"But take a candle and look closer," Anestasie begged. "You can't see without a candle."

Honoria lit a candle and examined the bed again. Then she walked slowly around the room, holding the candle high. By the door she stopped and glanced again at Anestasie. She reached into her bodice, then held her hand over her mouth and screamed. Still screaming, she leaped back, flinging the candle at the door sill as she ran to the bed.

"It's there!" Honoria put her face close to Anestasie's and cried again, "It's there!"

"Oh, God! Oh, my God!" Anestasie shrieked. "I saw it too! There by the door!" She gripped Honoria. Her nails dug into Honoria's flesh.

Honoria whispered, "Be still. Be very still."

"But we must attract attention," Anestasie mumbled in terror. "We can't get out. It's by the door!"

"And nobody can get in," Honoria said.

Anestasie's body convulsed and her lips trembled. "We're trapped! They'll have to break the door down!"

488

"And even then," said Honoria, "no man will dare cross that threshold."

"But Lake will save me. He loves me. He'll save me."

Honoria said coldly, "How can he? If they cut into the door the snake will be angered and will be waiting for them."

"He'll think of a way. We must scream."

"Your scream will attract the snake. Sit here and wait. Maybe all night, until the light comes again and we can see it."

"Why did you throw the candle at it, you fool?"

Honoria did not reply. Anestasie sobbed and bit the back of her hand. "If I ever get out of here I'll make Lake get rid of those things. Or I'll go away. Will it stay by the door, Honoria?"

"I doubt it. When darkness comes it will seek a warmer place."

Anestasie moaned at first and clutched Honoria. Then she held her hands to her mouth and screamed. She crawled to the head of the bed and screamed again. Honoria made no effort to calm her. She heard Flournoy run to the door and try to open it.

"What's wrong in there?" Flournoy shouted. "Why did you bolt this door?"

Anestasie shrieked again and blubbered. "The snake!" Her voice was shrill and piercing.

Flournoy shouted again. "Shut that hysterical woman up. She'll have every slave on the place half dead of fright. Anestasie! Shut up, you little fool!"

Flournoy's words rang in Anestasie's ears and she screamed again. "Fool, am I? You're the fool! You murderous half-breed!" She buried her head in a pillow and kicked and screamed. Honoria shook her to bring her to

489

her senses and she gripped Honoria and clung to her as a drowning person clings to a rescuer.

Flournoy ordered Honoria to open the door, but Honoria shouted, "I can't. Anestasie's holding me. She's beside herself with fear."

"Then we'll break the door down," Flournoy said. "That fool woman might go mad."

"Yes, hurry," Honoria shouted. "She's choking me." She tried to push Anestasie away, tried to free herself, but Anestasie locked her arms around Honoria's neck.

"The snake!" Anestasie cried. "Tell him about the snake!" Her words trailed off into wild blabbering.

The first blow of the ax against the door caused Anestasie to sit up quickly. "They're coming," she said. "The Indians are coming. The Indians who killed André."

Honoria wrenched herself free and leaped from the bed. Her first impulse was to open the door but she caught herself in time. Her foot touched the candle and she lighted it. She called to Flournoy to hurry and ran to the bed and stood over Anestasie. "Stop blabbering, you fool! It's all right. They're not Indians. It's Flournoy. I have the candle. We're all right."

"They're coming."

Honoria scarcely could hear her above the biting of the ax and Flournoy's orders to his slaves.

"It's only your imagination," said Honoria frantically. She stared at Anestasie. Anestasie's hair had fallen over her face and there was a wild look in her eyes as she focused them on the door. She was slobbering and had ripped away part of her dress.

"They're coming," she mumbled over and over. "The snake will get them. The snake will get them when they come through the door."

The successive shocks that had pounded against

Anestasie's brain had caused something to snap. Even a courageous woman could not stand the things she had suffered. Uprooted from her home! The journey to the new land! André's death! Her scene with Sam! Her affair with Flournoy! And now this! . . .

Honoria trembled too. What had she done? This woman was mad. She must open the door. No, if she did that, Flournoy would know. He would wonder why she dared open the door. She went across the room to the bed. She couldn't look at Anestasie as she sat there on the bed, rocking and mumbling. She, too, was frightened. The devil was in mad persons. She clutched the candle and looked for a weapon with which to defend herself if Anestasie attempted to attack her.

"Are you all right?" Flournoy shouted. The silence in the room alarmed him.

"Hurry!" Honoria called hoarsely. "Anestasie's mad, stark mad! She's raving. I'm afraid to be in the room with a crazy woman."

They cut a hole in the big door and Flournoy reached his hand through and pulled the bolt. Then he and the slaves crowded into the room. He went to Honoria, to the corner in which she had slumped, and lifted her up.

"I'm all right," said Honoria, "but look at Anestasie."

Flournoy took one look at his mistress. "Great God!" His heart seemed to sink to the pit of his stomach and his nerves trembled. Flournoy was not a man to be frightened by man or devil, but this . . .

Anestasie was sitting rigidly near the head of the bed. Her own head was thrown back and the muscles in her neck were contorted. Her green eyes were opened wide and seemed to be staring at something that no man could see. There were flecks of foam at the corners of her

491

mouth. She had ripped her bodice open and her flesh was bloody where her nails had clawed it.

Flournoy mumbled a prayer in French and turned his eyes from her. He ordered a slave to take her to Honoria's room, but the slave protested. He would not touch a mad woman. The devil was in her. Flournoy struck him across the mouth and, whining with fear, the Negro lifted Anestasie and took her away.

"The snake!" Honoria feigned fright. "The snake's in here. We saw it, by the door."

"You're mad too!" Flournoy whispered, for he still was awed. "The snake was killed almost an hour ago!"

He lifted his candle and began searching the room. He paused by the door, stepped back quickly and then advanced slowly. He stooped over and lifted a piece of twisted brown ribbon and held it up.

"This is your snake," he said to Honoria. "A bit of ribbon. Anestasie's ribbon."

Honoria buried her face in his chest and sobbed, quietly but not hysterically. "She must have dropped it herself. Poor Anestasie."

The enormity of her crime almost overwhelmed her. She wanted to run away, to run home to her brother and seek refuge in his arms and tell him she was sorry. But she couldn't tell anyone. Not even Sam. And she had thought Anestasie would faint with fright and that Flournoy would be disgusted with her. She had wanted only to cause an argument between them, only for Anestasie to go away. She had never dreamed that the silly little fool would go mad from shock.

But that ribbon did look like a snake. Her own heart had almost stopped when she had seen it in Anestasie's drawer. It had been easy, in the dimness of the room, to drop the ribbon by the door. But she didn't know what it would do to Anestasie. If she had known she wouldn't have done it. It was worse than murder, killing a woman's mind.

Maybe Anestasie would never recover. Maybe they would put an iron ring around her neck as Benjamin Frome used to put iron rings on his loonies. Maybe they would send her to a pest-house and chain her to the floor. And nobody would touch her or go near her. They would throw food to her and put water in a bucket and shove it close to her with a stick. She would wallow in her own filth. Her finger nails would grow as long as an Indian bone picker's. Vermin would crawl on her. Even if she regained her senses no one would ever believe her sane again, once she was condemned as a loony. Honoria knew that all of her life her own heart would cry out against what she had done. And she was sorry. God knew that she was sorry! But she must suffer because that damned spineless slut had allowed her imagination to drive her mad. Honoria felt very sorry for herself.

The doctor from Natchez said that Anestasie must be sent to an asylum in New Orleans. Flournoy ordered the doctor to see that she had the best attention possible and instructed that she not be sent to a pest-house or to a poor-farm. He would pay the expense. He would take it out of the profits from her plantation and ferry. Honoria did not know then that Anestasie, confident that she would marry Flournoy, had given him the right to manage her business and his extravagance irked Honoria. After all, if Anestasie were mad there was no reason why he should spend money to keep her in luxury. A loony didn't appreciate luxury. She would be no expense at a pest-house. But she held her counsel, knowing that she had no right to influence Flournoy now.

She wrote Sam a long letter and told him that Anestasie

had lost her mind from fright. And she expressed sympathy for Flournoy.

"The poor man is so shaken," she wrote. "It was a terrible thing to happen in his house. But Anestasie was always flighty, you know. She had never seemed very stable to me since the death of André. I hate to leave Lake at such a time. He really needs me now, but I realize I cannot stay here without a chaperon. If the danger of smallpox has not passed at Locha Poka I will go to Natchez. When the shock of this terrible tragedy has passed I will talk to you about my plans."

It was safe for her to return to Locha Poka, however, and Sam sent Jasper to escort her home. Flournoy, still shaken from the ordeal, was reluctant to let her go, but realized it was for the best.

"I soon will go to your brother," he said.

"I'll be waiting for you," said Honoria. "We can still be married here. I'll be very lonely without you." She held his head against her breast and comforted him.

"You're a strong woman, Honoria, and brave. I find refuge in your strength."

She smiled to herself. Ab had been like that. All men were little boys, seeking strength in women, first in their mothers and then in their wives. All men were weak. Even Tishomingo. Had he not shown himself weak in his love for Ta-lo-wah? Her heart leaped when she thought about him. He was a fool, a fool to love the memory of a dead woman when a live woman was waiting for his call. Honoria knew then that she would always be waiting. She hated herself for it. She hated herself because she knew that if ever the call should come, she would go to him. She could close her eyes and pretend that Flournoy was Tishomingo. It was sweet to pretend that he was hers.

494

24

HONORIA's report that she would marry Flournoy did not surprise Sam as much as she had thought it would. If it did, he did not show it. Her long stay at *Maison Blanche* had prepared him for the news. The fact that she had remained there so long was evidence that she was enjoying herself and Sam had known all along that Flournoy's wealth had impressed his sister.

His first reaction to her report was one of indignation but he never allowed her to see the reaction. He realized it would be foolish to forbid his sister the thing she was determined to do. Perhaps, Flournoy would make her a good husband. Surely, she never would have another care and he couldn't help but think of the personal advantages. Flournoy would be his kinsman and Flournoy was the most important man between Milledgeville and New Orleans. Maybe Flournoy would back him in his freight enterprise without demanding too much toll. All he needed was backing. All he needed was cash. He had a hundred schemes and a thousand dreams, but no money.

He was standing by the window in the drawing room at Locha Poka, gazing at his fields while Honoria talked. He did not answer her immediately, being so engrossed in his own thoughts. She talked quickly, jerkily trying to get her story out without catching her breath.

She had returned home that morning and had been

welcomed by Hoab and Donna. She had expressed amazement at Hoab's growth and had kissed his cheek. She was a stranger to him and the boy paid her no attention, even when Donna explained that she was his Aunt Honoria. Hoab tried to say "Aunt Honoria" and it came out "An' Oria." It was hard to realize that this was her son and she made no effort to realize it. There was no pang in her heart when she saw him, no yearning to fondle him. Even mother love, she realized, is a fruit of association. To her, Hoab was a stranger, and she was too interested in her own affairs to pay him more attention than any aunt would pay a nephew. She would not allow herself to think that he was her son. She must never allow herself to love him yearningly. She couldn't have him and she would not covet a thing that she knew she couldn't have. It might make her unhappy. She could not help but notice, however, that the boy had Ab's long legs and her eyes. It really was Dabby who impressed her. The child was growing beautiful, sleek as a young mink and as graceful as an eel.

She gasped when she saw Donna. Donna's high cheek bones seemed higher than they really were because they protruded over her hollow cheeks. Her neck and hands were bony and a hacking cough often shook her frame. Only her eyes hadn't changed. They still were bright.

And Donna was as proud as ever. Hard work and hardships could not take the pride out of a Chadbourne. Honoria noticed that she frequently moistened her dry lips to make them red and that her nails were well-tended and her hair was beautifully combed. Her clothes were cut loosely to hide her gaunt frame and Honoria suspected that she wore a beam to make her hips look rounded.

The scourge of the pox had struck Locha Poka like a

496

hurricane of death. Sam had lost eight slaves and because of the shortage of labor he had not been able to harvest all of his crops. There was grass in his fields and weeds on his lawns. She could not help but compare the shoddiness of Locha Poka to the beauty of *Maison Blanche*. Her brother was not doing well. There were a few tiny wrinkles just above his nose, and his head seemed to sit rather wearily on his shoulders. These days he did not carry his head in that jaunty confident manner that used to set him apart from his fellows. There were no signs of defeat at Locha Poka, only signs of a setback. Sam's eyes still were calm and determined. He also was well-tended. That was Donna's influence. Neither of them had compromised with hard times. After all, he had pulled Locha Poka out of the new land in a few years. He never had had much money, but he had much to show for his effort.

She could help him. With Flournoy's wealth she could do wonders. Perhaps Sam was thinking about that.

He turned from the window and asked Honoria, "But do you love this man?"

"Ay, I love him." It was one of the few lies of her life that was hard to tell. It was hard to lie to Sam. But was she lying? Perhaps she did love Lake Flournoy. She tried to convince herself that she did.

"Do you remember, Hon, what our father used to say?" Sam smiled at her. "He used to say, never tamper with a person's heart."

"Ay," she said, "I remember. We've come a long way, Sam'l."

"A long way together. It gives me cause for thought. Now we must separate and you'll establish your home."

"Then I have your blessing?"

"Ay. God bless you. I want you to tell Donna."

Honoria said, "Her health is not good."

"Nay, I wanted her to return to Georgia but she wouldn't go. The swamp fever persists. She's ailing all of the time."

"And your business, Sam'l?"

"It will be all right soon. The pox did me much harm. We've not been able to give the land our attention. Land is like human beings, Hon. If you don't primp it and dress it, it soon will become shoddy. But I'll be all right next season. I have plans."

"As Lake Flournoy's wife I can help you, you know."

"I had not thought of that and I will not. But I have thought of one thing—Tishomingo."

Honoria asked quickly, "And what of him?"

"He has vowed to kill Flournoy," Sam said.

"Flournoy isn't afraid."

"There's only a fine line between hate and love," Sam said. "The longer love is still, the weaker it becomes. The same is true of hate. Tishomingo has waited a long time for his revenge."

"Why?" asked Honoria. "Why has he waited so long?"

"Because he wants his revenge to be complete. He wants to play with Flournoy. Also, he knows that when he kills Flournoy he'll become an outcast. His own nation will cast him out. He'll have to leave. Times are too crucial with his people for him to leave now. Maybe I can influence him. I'll try. Maybe he'll not want to kill my brother-in-law."

They talked long of Anestasie and Sam resolved to keep in touch with the asylum where she was quartered. Even if her mind improved, the chances of her surviving the diseases of the asylum were slight. There might even be a leper among the pests. Leprosy had been discovered in Louisiana. The quarters of the outcasts had been

498

burned and they were left to wander aimlessly about the city. Some had found refuge in asylums. Anestasie might be exposed to the disease. Sam would write to her people in France. He felt that he owed that to André.

"It was a strange fate," Sam said. "The new land wiped out a whole family. There's one thing I wish you'd keep in mind. I need André's place. Perhaps you can persuade Flournoy to sell it to me."

Honoria said, "I doubt if Flournoy will sell the property. It's a rule with him that he'll never sell property. But I'll see that he does not block your plans for a road to Georgia."

"I cannot give you a great wedding present," Sam said, "but I'll give you Dabby. You can train her as you want her. My son," he glanced at his sister as he said it, "is very fond of her. But I want you to have her. It will please your husband. However, there is one thing that you must swear to me."

"Ay?"

"That you'll never sell her. To anyone. Your husband may want to sell her to the Creeks but you must swear that you will not allow him to. She means something in my life. Will you swear?"

"I swear it," promised Honoria. "And you needn't be bothered because you cannot give me a fine present and a dowry. I have my own dowry. I've made money from my perfume. Of course, I'll leave the business with you."

Donna congratulated Honoria when she heard the news. It was a relief to know that Honoria was to be married. It was a relief to know that she would not live at Locha Poka. Donna did not want her there and she made no pretense of wanting her there. She did not put it beyond Honoria to attempt to recover Hoab if she took a fancy to him. She knew Honoria never could get the child but the thought of a scandal frightened her.

She no longer expected to recover from the fevers. The attacks came regularly now, and each attack left her weaker than the other. It probably would do no good to return to Georgia, but even if there were any hope, she would not return because she could not leave Sam when he needed her most. And for no consideration, even for her health, would she go away from him. She had come to the new land to make a home and she would make it. Even if she could not survive the hardships of the new land, she could leave her influence upon it. It could not drive her away. It had taken Ab and André and Anestasie. It had taken her son. It had left her body weak with fevers but she would not run away from it.

She was too proud to write her brother for money and Sam would be furious if she did. He long since had spent her inheritance. It hurt her heart to see grass in Sam's fields. She often lay awake far into the night and worried about her husband while he sat in his study scrawling figures. He was always exhausted when he went to bed, but even if he had not been exhausted she could have offered him no passion, no forgetfulness. Much as she desired it, it was not in her to give him forgetfulness. That hurt her most of all. Sam was very tender about it all and never mentioned it.

And every morning he was gay again. His eyes danced with hope and he always told her his plans. But as the day wore on the luster disappeared from his eyes and by mid-afternoon he was weary and discontent. But things would be all right next season and she would be able to rest.

Hoab was getting large enough to look after himself. Some of the slaves' children soon would be old enough

500

to take the places of those that the pox had destroyed. Sam'l had so many irons in the fire that one of them was certain to make him rich. He had got nineteen slaves in all through his dealings with Flournoy. If he would only sell some of them. But he wouldn't. He wouldn't sell a female slave or an ewe or a mare. He had bred the slaves as rapidly as possible.

His foundry was cold and cobwebs hung on his forge. Iron was too expensive for him to obtain. Iron was coming down the river to Natchez but he couldn't afford to buy it. He had made many wheel rims and had stored them in his foundry. Some day he would use them. They would have been worth a small fortune in Natchez. But he wouldn't sell. Some day he would put them on wagons and his wagons would rumble from Natchez to Nashville, from the river to Georgia.

The cotton in his fields hardly was worth picking. Europe was in turmoil and only a rich man, or a man with lots of backing, could risk his cotton through the English and French fleets. Strange stories were seeping into the new land. There was a story that the English farmers were leaving their lands and moving into the cities. Who ever heard of such a silly thing? Leaving land to move to town. The stories said that a few men were getting control of the looms in England and that they were hiring people on the farms to run them. The workmen lived in quarters like slaves. They bought even their milk, when they had milk, from merchants. The men were away at war, and women and children were running the looms. Soon, the story said, there would be a great demand for cotton. Ay, things would be better next year. A few cotton factories were springing up in New England and up there the people also were beating their plows into spindles.

Maybe Sam'l would strike it rich with his land over near Natchez where the new capitol might be built. The Natchez district had been divided into Adams and Pickering counties, honoring the president and the secretary of state. The other district of the territory, the area above Mobile and around the lower Alabama and Tombigbee rivers had been named the Bigbee District and had been organized into Washington County. Fort Adams had been built on the Spanish border, south of Natchez, and Fort Stoddard had been built north of Mobile, on the river of the same name. Some of the pioneers were making money by supplying fodder and food to the forts. Many of the other pioneers were getting rich. Frome was very rich because he had stuck to saddles. She noticed that the frontiersmen who were giving their time to one enterprise were prospering.

There was money in cotton if a man gave all of his time to cotton. There was money in slaves, in beeswax, in transportation. And there was money in land. She had heard that the territory probably would build a new capitol the next year and if Sam's land was at the site, he surely would make a good profit. If he would only put some of the money aside for a rainy day and invest the balance in real estate near the new capitol. If he only would hoard some of his money. She could understand money that she could see and feel. If he would only stick to the business of land—planting land, trading land. Land was a thing anybody could understand. First you cut down its trees and sold the trees or made them into houses. And then you worked the land. You had something, something you could always sell. A pox on all the plans to breed mules and run wagon trains. Perhaps if Sam would concentrate on one business. . . . But she wouldn't suggest it to him. He had always been a man who made his own decisions without help.

She wondered how he really felt about his sister's marrying Lake Flournoy. She never discussed Honoria with him. She didn't trust herself to do so. Her tongue might get ahead of her brain and she might say something she would regret. She didn't care if Honoria married Lake Flournoy, or Tishomingo, or Lawyer Thomas, or even old Jim McQueen. She didn't care whom she married so long as she married somebody and stayed out of her sight.

Sam's promise to give Dabby to his sister for a wedding present infuriated her. Honoria did not need the slave. She would have a hundred slaves to choose from at *Maison Blanche*. And Dabby meant something to their family. The child had been with them since the first day she had seen Sam. He had risked his life to save her and it was not fair for him to give her up. She had a sentimental attachment for the girl, an attachment almost as strong as her love for the conch shell Sam had brought her. The slave child meant much to Hoab too. It would be wrong to separate the child from her mother. And what assurance did she have that Flournoy would not sell Dabby to the Creeks? Honoria's word? Re-fiddlesticks! Sukey and Dabby really belonged to her. Of course, the law said that a wife's property belonged to her husband and legally Sam could do with her property what he saw fit, but he had no moral right to give Dabby away. She thought of a hundred reasons why she disapproved of his promise, but the strongest reason was because she simply did not want Honoria to possess the slave who had helped bring her and Sam together.

Sam was taken aback at the temper Donna showed when she expressed her disapproval. "You should have consulted me," she said. "I'm not willing to part with Dabby."

"But, darling," he said, "I promised."

"Then you can un-promise. You can explain to Honoria that we'll keep Dabby for Hoab. You can break your promise for many reasons. It's not often that I make demands, but I ask you not to give the child away."

"I must give my sister a fitting present."

"You have given your sister many fitting presents. My suggestion is that we buy her trousseau."

Sam would not argue with Donna. She was ill. If she wanted to keep Dabby, she should. But Honoria, learning that Donna really wanted the slave, pouted when Sam told her he had changed his mind.

"I really wanted Dabby," she said, "but if your wife wants her I'll not take her away. After all, I'll have a hundred slaves. As for buying my trousseau, I'll not allow Donna to do that. It will be necessary for me to look very stylish at my wedding and I don't believe Donna's the proper person to select my clothes."

"What do you mean by that?" Sam demanded.

"Oh, Sam'l, you wouldn't understand. Donna hasn't seen the latest fashions. And she's getting middle-aged. She wouldn't know what a young girl wants."

"Very well," said Sam. Was Donna really getting middle-aged? he wondered. "But I'll give you the money for your trousseau."

"And where will you get it?"

"That's none of your damned business, Honoria." He knew he could raise money from Frome by pledging Jasper. He would borrow the money through Tishomingo who still held title to the big slave.

He dared not tell Donna what Honoria had said, particularly that Honoria had said she was getting middle-aged. Sam was too wise a man to carry tales between women. Honoria, however, was not so peace-loving. She was angry because Donna had refused to surrender Dabby. Not that she needed Dabby, but the knowledge of Donna's influence on Sam angered her. She went to Donna and thanked her for the offer of buying the trousseau.

"But I cannot allow you to do this," Honoria said. "You're ill and I'll not burden you with such troubles. Besides styles have changed since you were a bride."

"Styles have changed since you were a bride, too," Donna remarked quietly. "I have a letter from some kinspeople in Tidewater that tells of the newest styles. You're welcome to it. But don't be haughty, Honoria. Your first bridal gown was a bit of calicut and your bridal bed was made of corn shucks. In the eyes of God you're a widow."

Honoria framed a biting retort but did not utter it. She must not offend Donna. One word from her sister-in-law and there would be no wedding at *Maison Blanche*. Honoria had learned to hold her tongue when silence was to her advantage. As she looked at Donna, hate smoldering in her eyes, she remembered that, after all, Donna was only five years older than she. But she looked twenty years older. The years had not changed Honoria much. If anything, her body was harder. Surely her spirit was harder. Lotions and good living had softened her skin and she was no longer the brown wood sprite who had left Georgia. She now used a bit of coloring on her cheeks. She had learned the art from Anestasie. She did her hair in a graceful roll at the back of her neck and allowed a curl to dangle over each ear. Her clothes were immaculate—silks, satins, velvets and organdies. She usually wore a comb in her hair or a flower, a cape jasmine or a red rose-bud. She wore no jewelry except two tiny pearl earrings and a wide bracelet made of beaten gold. In the evenings she always had a brooch or a cameo at her throat, suspended on black silk ribbon. And she was the only woman in the new land who wore silk next to her skin all of the time. She painted her lips slightly and the coloring made her sensuous lips the most impressive part of her face, excepting those blue-black eyes.

"Tell me, Donna," she crossed her legs properly, and smoothed her dress, "do you think Flournoy will know that I'm not a maiden? You know what I mean. You're wise about such things."

Donna laughed. "I think you can deceive Lake Flournoy. You've deceived everybody else. Yes, I know what you mean. I'm glad you think I'm wise about such things, but, really, I'm not as wise as you."

Honoria turned on her heel and swept out of the room.

Sam rode over to Tishomingo's lodge to take the news and to talk business. Tishomingo heard Sam's story without interrupting and sat silently for several minutes when the story was finished. Finally he said, "I don't blame you for this, but you'll regret it. After all, Sam'l, she's your sister and I have no right to criticize you for your decisions."

"That's right," said Sam'l. "It's my business. We can't explain some things, Chock."

"Your sister doesn't love him." Tishomingo got to his feet and stared down at Sam.

"She says she does." Sam got to his feet, too, his face tense, his words biting. "My sister's not one to marry a man she doesn't love."

506

"She is lying to you and to herself." The stoical calm vanished, and Tishomingo's words rolled out in a torrent of emotion. Then, suddenly, he checked himself and sat down and put his head in his hands. Sam waited for his friend to speak. Tishomingo sighed and ran his hand over his hair. "I regret that some day I'll have to kill your brother-in-law."

"Damme, Chock," Sam said impatiently. "For years you've been talking about killing Flournoy. If a man has murder in his heart he doesn't wait so long. I'd hoped that you would be willing to forget your revenge."

"You're not an Indian, Big Sam. My revenge is only partly complete. When the time comes for me to complete my revenge I'll skin Lake Flournoy alive."

"You believe the Choctaw law?" Sam spat out the words.

Tishomingo arched his eyebrows and said slowly, "I believe the law and I know what you're thinking—that if I spill the blood of your kinsman, you must spill my blood; that there will be a feud between you and me."

"Won't that deter you?"

"I'll skin Lake Flournoy alive with my bull whip. I'd do it, Big Sam, if he were your real brother or even your father." Tishomingo arose again and folded his arms and looked at his friend. There was not a flicker of emotion in Tishomingo's eyes. They were as hard as steel and as cold. Then his expression softened and he said, "Sam, you cannot bluff me. You bluffed Lake Flournoy —"

"Ay —"

"Ay. When you told him you would take the Duportail property you were bluffing. You wouldn't rob Anestasie. You bluffed Flournoy and made him believe you. But I can read you, Big Sam. I can read you as I

507

can read the signs in the sky, and the tracks in the earth. You and I will never fight."

"There'll be no feud between you and me," said Sam quietly, and smiled at his friend. "You've called my bluff. A brother doesn't kill his brother. Nay, you're right, Chock; nothing will ever shatter the bond between us."

He was sure of that. He understood why Tishomingo delayed his revenge. Under the law he would be a fugitive if he killed Flournoy and he dared not leave the Choctaw Nation at such a time. If he should kill Flournoy, then only Flournoy's widow could demand his blood. Honoria would never demand the blood of Tishomingo.

What if Chock did kill Flournoy? Then all of Flournoy's property would be his sister's. And his sister surely would turn her affairs over to him. The Dabney brats would be the most powerful people in the West. Sam tried to banish the thought but it would not go away. Flournoy's death might make his sister unhappy. Or would it? She did not love Flournoy. She loved this big brooding Indian. Well, a man's fate was in the stars. If Tishomingo killed Flournoy, Sam Dabney would not take up the feud.

When Sam explained to Tishomingo his plan to borrow money from Frome, using Jasper as security, the Indian volunteered a loan to his friend. He had saved the money he had made in the slave deals and offered it willingly to Sam.

"I'll be glad to advance you the money," he said. "I'll not need it until plans for my school are complete."

"And the security?" Sam said.

"Your word is sufficient. However, I caution you not

to tell your sister that my money is purchasing her wedding clothes."

"And why do you say that?" Sam glanced at his friend.

"Oh, it was just an idea of mine. Perhaps Honoria would not like the idea of my money buying her clothes. I'm sure Flournoy would not like it. I'll write friends of mine in New Orleans that Honoria will be there. They can be of assistance to her."

Sam said, "You soon will be going to Louisiana to meet another slave ship. Honoria can go with you."

"You'd trust your sister with me?"

"Ay, of course."

"No," said Tishomingo. "I'll not do it. Flournoy wouldn't stand for it."

But he wanted very much to take Honoria with him. He knew that she would go. New Orleans and Honoria. He had brought Ta-lo-wah out of New Orleans and Flournoy had taken her. It would be revenge to take Honoria to New Orleans. Sam would trust his sister with him, but he wouldn't trust himself with the woman. It would be too obvious to Flournoy. He must do nothing to endanger the wedding. Flournoy must marry Honoria. Then there would be time for his revenge. Flournoy must suffer as he had suffered.

Sam accepted the money from Tishomingo and gave it to his sister. She went to Natchez, thence to New Orleans. Soon after her departure Flournoy arrived at Locha Poka and asked for her hand. Sam gave his blessing and they drank to the troth.

"I regret," said Sam, "that my sister's dowry will not be large."

"I'm not marrying a dowry," said Flournoy. "I'm happy that you give your sister's hand to me. That is suf-

509

ficient. There are a few details about the wedding we must settle."

"You'll be married at *Maison Blanche*?"

"Ay. First by a magistrate from Natchez. Then we'll have a Choctaw service. It is the law, you know, and I'm a citizen of the Choctaw Nation."

They planned the details of the wedding and then fell to discussing the news of the day. Flournoy believed that Louisiana soon would pass to France.

"My noble kinsman, Bonaparte, is France. My information is that France hopes to build a new colonial empire."

And he was right. The great slave rebellion of Santo Domingo had broken Europe's stranglehold in the Indies. If France could establish itself in the islands and hold Louisiana it would own a far more valuable territory than English Canada. Santo Domingo was the key. It would open Louisiana. Slavery had been abolished on the island. Napoleon would try to reëstablish it. Louisiana would soon pass to France by secret treaty. Flournoy knew more of the negotiations than he revealed. He was sure, however, that he and Sam should cease running slaves to Louisiana. It was getting too dangerous.

"Any day," Flournoy said, "Louisiana may come under French law. France will not tolerate the smuggling of slaves. I'll run no more slaves into Louisiana. If I should be caught there might be a scandal in a French court—the kinsman of Bonaparte breaking the law. I'll not do it."

Sam argued with him but it was to no avail. Flournoy would not take the chance.

Again he tried to persuade Sam to sell Sukey and Dabby, but Sam was adamant. He tried to pry from Sam the purpose of Philip Nolan's expedition, but Sam as-

510

sured him that, so far as he knew, Nolan's plan was to capture mustangs.

"I'll get some of the mustangs," Sam said. "I hope to sell some of them to the sugar planters to whom you have spoken about me. The others I'll use for breeding purposes."

"But they're no good," Flournoy said. "They're plain horses and are worth only about eight dollars a head. Why do you want them?"

"For mules," said Sam, and would not pursue the subject further.

Honoria's wedding was the biggest social event in the history of the territory, far surpassing in local importance Andrew Jackson's wedding in Natchez.

Every mingo of the Muscogees sent presents. Even Tecumseh sent a gift. He had lived many years among the Creeks and was anxious for Flournoy's friendship. Jim McQueen sent ten head of cattle. The Spanish governor in New Orleans sent wine. Andy Jackson gave Flournoy a brace of pistols and Honoria a fine lamp. Frome sent perfume and Pierce some fine old linen.

Even Josephine sent a gift. The drawing room of *Maison Blanche* was filled to overflowing with presents. The guests began arriving two days before the ceremony and there was feasting and drinking every night. Honoria stayed in her bed chamber with Donna while the men made merry. She was to have no attendant save Donna. She had promised years before that Donna would be in her wedding, and, too, there was the looks of the thing. Sam would give her away.

Donna had a new dress with a train of blue satin, bordered with white satin and embroidered with roses. The shoulder ruching was made of plaited white crêpe. The turban was blue satin. Her brother had sent her long gloves and a fan.

Sam would wear his wedding suit. Sukey had mended it and it looked as good as new.

The civil ceremony was said on the verandah of *Maison Blanche*. The guests stood on the lawn, Indians on the left and the white visitors on the right. It was necessary to have the first service in the morning, for the Choctaw ceremony would consume the remainder of the day. There was no music. Flournoy gave most of his slaves a holiday and they stood behind the white people, and craned their necks and watched the big door through which the bride would come. An altar had been built near the door, against a mass of wild ferns and orange blossoms. The magistrate stood near the steps.

Flournoy appeared first escorted by the great mingo of the Chickasaws. Even the governor of New Orleans arched his fashionable eyebrows when he saw the bridegroom. Flournoy wore a coat of blue cloth cut high at the back. His stock was of fine cambric and the ruffled shirt front showed above a white satin waistcoat. The trousers were of buff kerseymere and were fastened at the knees with small bows.

Sam's dress was shabby in comparison to Flournoy's elegant costume. But his appearance, as he walked out of the door and took his position, caused a ripple of excitement. Many of the ladies from New Orleans had never seen him before and they gasped in delight. He seemed to tower above Flournoy, to tower above everything there. He carried his head at that old jaunty angle and his eyes danced again. His hair fell below his shoulders and was tied in a careless knot. His shoulders seemed to be bursting through his coat. Here was a man who

512

wanted room to breathe in, and the world was not big enough to breathe in.

When the Creeks saw him they mumbled, "Big Sam."

The murmurs spread—Big Sam Dabney, the messenger of death, hero of the canoe fight, the man who had outwitted the Creeks, the giant from Georgia. He had the finest horse in the new land, the finest gun and the finest eye. Many of the women looked at him, then at their own husbands, and the comparisons were not flattering.

Inside the house, Donna gave her final instructions to Honoria. Honoria wet her lips so that they would be red and looked into the mirror that Sukey held. Her complexion was perfect. It should be, for she had slept with a mould of saccharine alum on her face. The paste had been made of egg whites, alum and rose water. Donna had put a trace of rouge on her cheeks, "You must look like a blushing maiden," Donna had whispered.

When Honoria stepped through the doorway a lady in the crowd whispered to her husband, "Why, she's just a girl."

Her gown was of India muslin, embroidered with silver thread. It was very high around the waist. Her slippers were white and her white gloves reached above the elbow. Her hair lay about her shoulders in curls and she wore the comb that Sam had given her, the comb that had once been intended for Donna.

Sam stepped forward and took his sister's arm, then turned to the magistrate and handed him the wedding contract which had been drawn and signed the night before. The magistrate scanned the document and said to the bridegroom, "Did you, Lake Flournoy of the Choctaw Nation, sign a contract of marriage with Honoria Dabney?"

"I did," said Flournoy.

513

"And you know its contents?" asked the magistrate.

"I do."

He asked the same questions of Honoria and received the same replies. He knew well what was in the contract for he had witnessed it. It provided that Honoria would share Flournoy's bed and board until death parted them and that in payment for her security she must give Flournoy all of her earthly possessions, her loyalty, her love, her obedience.

The magistrate gave the contract to Flournoy and he and Honoria stood by the altar and clasped hands while the magistrate intoned, "By the authority vested in me as an official of the Territory of Mississippi I pronounce you husband and wife."

Legally the marriage was not worth the words that were uttered, for the ceremony was performed in the Choctaw Nation, outside of the jurisdiction of the United States.

After the civil ceremony, Flournoy was not allowed even to kiss his bride. They were not married according to the laws of the Choctaws. Reluctantly, Flournoy dropped her hand, and the two walked into *Maison Blanche*, the groom to the drawing room and his bride to her bed chamber. There she took off her wedding finery, even her under things. She remained naked until an old Choctaw woman appeared and began rubbing her body with oil. It was the first step in the Choctaw ceremony.

"Has he come yet?" Honoria asked.

"Nay, but he'll be here soon," said the old squaw.

"Is Pushmataha coming to read the law to us?"

The old squaw looked up at Honoria and smiled. "Nay, my daughter, his nephew is coming."

514

"But Tishomingo was at the wedding," Honoria said. "I invited him. I saw him in the crowd."

"It was vain of you and impudent to look at another man while the contract was being read."

She put a simple gown on Honoria and led her to the drawing room where Flournoy was waiting, dressed as a Choctaw, with heron plumes in his hair. Tishomingo was there, too, and so were Sam and Donna. Tishomingo also wore heron feathers and on his left arm was a silver bracelet, his badge of authority.

Tishomingo said, "My uncle had hoped to come here and bless this union and explain the law to you, but today I received word that he was ill and the duty fell to me."

Flournoy bit his lip. Sam started to speak but changed his mind. He knew that Pushmataha was not ill. Honoria knew it too, as did Flournoy. But there was naught that Flournoy could say or do. He dared not defy the code of his nation. A member of the Great Family must bless the wedding and Tishomingo had taken the task upon himself. Flournoy wondered about his game. He clenched and unclenched his hands as he watched his enemy. He was sure that the mingo had asked permission of Pushmataha to officiate at the purification rites for the bride and groom.

Sam was alarmed. Tishomingo had not confided in him. Tishomingo had known all along that Pushmataha would not attend the ceremony. What was his plan? Great God! Sam suddenly remembered that Tishomingo and Flournoy would have to be alone in the wedding lodge. Was Tishomingo ready to strike? Had he selected this time to complete his revenge? Anyway, the contract was signed, and according to law his sister was the wife of Lake Flournoy.

Flournoy too, was thinking that he must be alone with

Tishomingo. He must be unarmed, even naked. Tishomingo could strike him down. Flournoy's lips parted and
he breathed heavily through his mouth.

Tishomingo glanced at him and said solemnly, "Your
fears are unfounded. You should not be thinking of
yourself ——"

"How do you know my thoughts?" Flournoy asked
sharply.

"There's worry in your eyes," said Tishomingo. "You
should be preparing yourself for the purification rites,
banishing all evil thoughts from your mind." He turned
to Honoria, "And you, Honoria, should be purging your
soul of all evil thoughts."

But Honoria was thinking that she, too, must be alone
with Tishomingo.

Tishomingo put Honoria's hand in Flournoy's and said,
"You know the law."

"Ay," said Flournoy. "I know the law. I'm taking my
mate from outside my nation. I'm wedding with a
stranger to our faith. For one year I must suffer banishment from the Choctaws. It will take me a year to purify
myself. During that time I am an outcast among my people. I cannot sit at the council fires. I cannot demand protection ——"

His voice suddenly stopped. "Cannot demand protection. . . ." The words stuck in his throat. So that was it.
No law could protect him. He was not an American
and now he was not a Choctaw. If Tishomingo wanted
to kill, now was the time.

"Finish it," said Tishomingo.

"I cannot demand protection of my nation's laws,"
Flournoy said. Sam could hear his own heart pounding.
What a fiendish revenge. Flournoy was helpless. Donna's
breath came hoarsely. Honoria buttoned her lips and

516

glared at Tishomingo. He smiled at her and her heart leaped again.

Flournoy was frightened. It was the first time anyone had ever seen fright on his face. And well might Flournoy be frightened. He must go to a lodge and wait there alone until Tishomingo arrived. There would be no one to hear what was said and no one to see what was done. If he were beaten there was no law to which he could turn. If he were killed there was no law. Sam watched Tishomingo, saw the savage joy in his eyes.

Tishomingo waited until the words of the law had impressed themselves upon the people and then he said, "You're wrong again, Flournoy. Only fear causes you to think what you are thinking. The nephew of Pushmataha would not violate a wedding lodge with blood. My revenge will wait. Have you a name for your bride?"

Flournoy said hoarsely, "Ay, we have chosen the name of Nadowah, the beautiful daughter."

"Nadowah," said Tishomingo. "It is a beautiful name and a fitting name." He took Honoria's hand. "To the Choctaws, you always will be Nadowah. My people now are your people. You know the law. Your life belongs to your husband. His will is your will. You can take no other husband unless you divorce this man. Should you weary of your man and your man weary of you, you may state publicly your desire for a bill of divorcement. If you have been a faithful wife, the divorce will be granted and then you may take another husband."

Honoria scarcely heard his words. She was thinking: "He is holding my hand. He must come to my lodge. It is the law. He must come to me and take me to Flournoy. There will be no one at the lodge except the old squaw."

Tishomingo droned on, reciting the law to her. "Your husband may have as many as six wives, but they cannot

517

live together. You may have only one husband. However, your husband has pledged himself to monogamy in the civil contract. Your marriage will be on trial from this day until the busk. If, when the busk comes, you decide your marriage was a mistake you and your husband may part without a formal divorce. If any children are born, they belong to the mother.

"If you are unfaithful, you will be whipped and your ears will be cut off, tied to the sticks with which you were whipped and set up in a town square for all to see. Your husband will be scorned because he was not able to hold you. Your seducer will suffer the same punishment as you. If he escapes, his nearest kinsman will be punished in his stead. If the woman be punished and the man be not punished, then the kinsmen of the woman may punish the leader of the party that punished the woman.

"Only the crime of murder can be held against you for more than a year. If you commit a crime against the nation, you must be punished between the time the crime is committed and the next busk, or green corn dance. All sins are forgiven during the busk, save the crime of murder.

"If you are unfaithful to your husband, he will suffer more than you, for he will be scorned as a weak man who could not hold his mate. That is all."

He released her hand. Flournoy stepped forward and gave her a bit of venison. She gave him an ear of corn. Had Honoria been a Choctaw the ceremony would have been complete, for a public expression of intent and an exchange of gifts sealed the wedding covenant. But because she was white, she must be purified.

Tishomingo motioned to the old squaw and she took Honoria by the hand and led her out of the door and

518

across the lawn, between the rows of staring people, and delivered her to the Indian maidens. The maidens took her into the woods and removed her dress and rent it. They chanted the love songs of the Choctaws, bathed her and rubbed her body with oils and finally surrendered her again to the old squaw, who took her to a bare lodge near the stream and dressed her in a wedding gown, a slip of linen. Then the old squaw sat with her, reciting the law. She must stay there until twilight when she would be taken to her husband.

Flournoy went to another lodge and waited there with Chock. The bridegroom sat on his wedding couch and waited. Tishomingo folded his arms and stood by the door, watching the sun. Flournoy's duty was to spend the hours in meditation. During the day he was bathed three times by a party of flatheads. Honoria was bathed five times.

Most of the Choctaws hated water on their bodies. They usually cleansed themselves with oils, but only water could purify. Not one word did Tishomingo utter as he stood by the door. He fastened his eyes on Flournoy and pinned them there for hours. Flournoy returned the stare.

It was twilight when the old squaw sent word to Tishomingo that the bride's purification rites almost were complete. As the agent of the Great Family, he must go to her, instruct her again in the law and bring her to her husband. He would leave her at the door of Flournoy's lodge and she must enter alone. The wedding must be consummated in the lodge of the Choctaws.

Tishomingo left the bridegroom's lodge and walked down the river to Honoria's lodge. The old squaw welcomed him.

519

"You may go." Tishomingo nodded to the squaw, and the old woman smiled at him and then at Honoria.

Tishomingo was very calm, and his mouth was a hard, cold line, but his eyes were soft and tender. Honoria had never seen his eyes so tender; her flesh tingled when he looked at her. Then suddenly the softness passed from his eyes and they, too, were hard. He made no movement toward her but stood staring at her and saying nothing. For a moment Honoria was frightened. She could not fathom his thoughts. Then her alarm passed. This was Tishomingo. She had seen him in a hundred moods, but this was a new mood and she was not afraid. She stared up into his eyes and said, "Is this part of the law, too?"

"What?" he asked, the word forcing itself between his compressed lips.

She could feel the suppressed excitement in his voice. "That a man should be alone with a bride before she goes to her husband."

"It is not the law." Tishomingo's voice was brittle. "But that squaw is a wise old woman. I am very dear to her. She knew I wanted to be alone with you."

Honoria started to say, "What do you mean?" but changed her mind. They were such silly words. Whatever Tishomingo intended to do, he would do. She was sure of that. Then a great fear rushed into her heart. The minute she had long dreamed of was approaching. She was not afraid of Tishomingo, but of Flournoy. He might know. On her wedding night! Could she fool Flournoy? Would he not know that her passion had burned to an ash before she went to his couch? She wanted to run to Tishomingo, but she dared not. She half dreaded and half anticipated his next move, but instead of demanding an explanation she said, "I had to be purified . . ."

Before she could finish the sentence, his arms were around her, crushing her to him, savagely, almost brutally. She felt the breath go out of her body and she gasped. Then he tilted her head and kissed her, sealing his lips to hers. She tried to cry out, but no words came. Suddenly, she was afraid.

His kisses were violent and he pressed her lips so fiercely that hers hurt. This was not love he was demanding, not the tender love that she would have given so freely and unstintingly. He was forcing her, bruising her, lashing her with the whip of his hatred. He was paying a debt to Flournoy. He was taking her in payment for the sufferings of Ta-lo-wah. This was not love; it was revenge. It was cruel and horrible and she forced herself to struggle against him. Her teeth sank into his lip and she clawed his face. She kicked wildly as he carried her to the couch, scratching him and calling him hateful names.

Then she was in his arms and suddenly she no longer had the strength or desire to fight. She forgot Flournoy. She forgot everything except that the man she loved was hers at last. Once she opened her eyes and saw that the hardness had gone from his eyes. They were soft and gentle, and his lips were sweet to her. She closed her eyes again.

Night had fallen over the swamps and the whippoorwills had begun their requiem when he finally released her. Her first words were, "You'll come to me again?"

"Ay, I'll come to you again." Tishomingo held her tenderly and stroked her hair. Honoria lay on his arm and a drowsiness spread through her body. It was good to be tired and drowsy. She wished Tishomingo would tell her he loved her now. He must love her. She knew he must. Only a man in love could be so tender. He kissed her eyes shut and whispered, "I should have gone to you before."

"I was waiting for you," she said simply.

He did not answer her but lifted her to her feet. "I'll take you to your husband." He felt her body shudder. "You don't love him," he said. It was a statement of fact.

"How could I love anybody now? Except you. All my love is gone to you. Please take me away, Tishomingo. I don't want to go to him. I'm not married to him in the sight of God. Please take me away. I'll be a good wife to you. I've loved you so long. I've lived for this hour. I've dreamed of it."

Tishomingo smiled at her and his eyes were kind. But he said, "I will not leave my people. Come, I'll take you to your husband."

Honoria cried almost hysterically, "But he might know. He might know that I'm not coming to him as a maiden. He may be able to tell I don't love him. How can I explain it? What can I tell him?"

"Tell him that the revenge of Tishomingo is almost complete."

Flournoy and Honoria spent their wedding night in the small lodge by the river. She went to a corner of the lodge and undressed quietly. Her flesh was clammy and there was a feeling of dread within her. Flournoy was very considerate of her, but she wept when she lay with him. He thought it was becoming of her to weep. It pleased his vanity to think that his wife was a maiden who wept on her wedding night.

His caresses could not drive away the weariness of her body. Flournoy was bewildered. Was this the woman who had tormented him, whose kisses had burned and whose eyes had spoken of the great mysteries of love? Was she frightened? He fondled her tenderly and because her lips still were cold and her breathing even, he caressed her fiercely, striving to awaken her spirit. Once she even turned her face away and stared into space. She gave him her body but none of her spirit, and when he turned from her he was miserable and baffled. She rested her head on her own arm and dozed off to sleep, but Flournoy lay awake a long time, an overwhelming yearning tantalizing him. And there was an ugly doubt in his mind.

Finally he awakened her. "How long was Tishomingo in your lodge?" he asked.

"It seemed forever and forever," she said sleepily. "It seemed that he would never let me come to you. Even the old squaw was surprised. She sat there by us while he talked to me of the law. I know he wanted to talk to me of love, though."

"If ever he looks at you again I'll kill him. Even if the Choctaws quarter me I'll kill him." He pulled her body to him again, but she was rigid under his caresses.

Finally, she put her mouth close to his ear and whispered, "Tishomingo said a strange thing. He said I should tell you his revenge is almost complete. What did he mean, my love?"

"He meant that he would try to take you from me. Perhaps that would complete his revenge. But no, only death can satisfy him. I wonder what he meant."

Honoria smiled and closed her eyes.

"If I thought you loved him," he said fiercely, "I'd know what he meant. I took Ta-lo-wah from him." He said it boastfully. "If he had taken you from me, or if he had held you as I now hold you, I'd know what he

523

meant." He gripped her shoulders. "Tell me," he demanded hoarsely. "Do you know what he meant?"

"Of course not. This is no time for questions. A man should not shower his bride with questions, but with love."

The doubt that was born in Flournoy's mind would not be banished. Surely he could teach her to love. That would come in time. All maidens were shy as she was shy. And yet there was something strange about her, something baffling. She took his love and gave him nothing in return.

25

SAM's luck turned when the century turned.

Lawyer Thomas, in as much a lather as his horse, rode out to Locha Poka with news that the territorial capital would be moved to a spot six miles east of Natchez and that he, as Sam's agent, had been offered a fancy price for the Dabney holdings. The territory's declaration of independence had been submitted to Congress and that august but slightly befuddled group of patriots, realizing the justice of the plea that the new land was entitled to govern itself, had decided to advance the territory to the second grade even though its population was not large enough legally to receive such a favor.

On May the 10th, 1800, the Mississippi Territory was given the right to run its own business to a degree, and to be represented in the national government to which it paid taxes and pledged allegiance.

"It's a great day," said Lawyer Thomas. "We've taught those Tidewater blue-bloods and those Yankee blue-noses a thing or two. The damned loonies! They fought a war against England so they could have the very things we wanted."

"But they don't like us," said Sam.

"Of course they don't like us. They never will like us. We might as well make up our minds to that. And I'll tell you why. An old man is always jealous of a young man. A Virginian will always boast that he's a Virginian. He never boasts that he's an American or a Southerner. Same is true of a New Englander. But this is the melting pot. A hundred different nationalities are being boiled together in this new land. God knows what's going to come out. But one thing, sure—they'll be Southerners. They'll never boast that they are Mississippians. Oh, no. Their boast will be that they are Southerners. And they're going to establish a new order in this country, the same as the boys up in the Illinois country are going to establish a new order. You mind my words—those old rascals along the coast never wanted the United States to extend beyond the mountains. Washington was the only man among them who had any sense. He and Jefferson. Washington knew this country was going west, and by God she is!"

Sam said, "I'm in no mood for oratory. What about my land?"

"I have the contracts here," Thomas said. "Unload it now, Sam'l. They soon will start building the new capitol and within two years the territorial flag of Mississippi will be pulled down at Natchez and we'll move away and leave the last stench of Spanish rule."

Sam signed the papers and instructed Thomas to complete the deal. With the money he realized, he first would pay himself out of debt. Some of the money must go to André's estate. He would invest the balance of it in iron, iron for wagons of the Natchez Trace.

Sam ran to Donna with the news. He hurried out of the study and upstairs to her room where she was resting. He stooped over and lifted her up and hugged her to him. Damme, but she was light. As light as a feather.

"What is it, Sam'l?" She gasped between his kisses. "Have you lost your mind?"

526

"No, I've just found it. I'm back in the game, darling. I have money. My land speculation has worked out."

"You'll save some of it?" she asked quickly.

"Save it? For what? Of what use is money? No, I'm going to invest it. But first we'll pay our debts."

She didn't argue with him but got up and dressed and they returned to his study where Thomas was waiting. Thomas was so surprised at Donna's appearance that he scarcely could mutter a greeting. She was naught but skin and bones. Swamp fever, hell! he thought—that woman has the lung fever. Look at those cheeks and that pallor. Look at those deep eyes and the fire that burns in them. Listen to that cough. Death was knocking at Locha Poka. Didn't Dabney know it? Didn't his wife know it? Well, be damned if he would tell them. But maybe he could help a bit.

He took the wine that Sam offered him and drank it and then crossed the room and addressed his friend. "There's a thing I would tell you, Sam'l. I'm more than your lawyer, I'm your friend. Save a bit of this money. Bury a few gold pieces. You may need them." He saw the gratitude in Donna's eyes.

Sam said, "My wife has said the same thing and I'll do it. Never again will Sam Dabney find himself where he cannot put his hands on a bit of money."

"What do you hear from your sister?" Thomas asked.

"She is well," Sam said.

Ay, she was well. Honoria would always be well. She had been to Nashville and to New Orleans. The social life of the territory had moved from Natchez to *Maison Blanche*. Flournoy gave her everything. She gave him naught. He had given her an allowance of a thousand dollars a year just for her pins, among the most important and expensive items of a woman's wardrobe. Honoria's pin money was the envy of the new land. She still was baffling Flournoy. Always dutiful, always passive. She sapped his vitality and left him frustrated and angry with himself because he could not conquer her.

As hostess of *Maison Blanche* she was the wife of Lake Flournoy, but at night in his bed she, in her imagination, was the bride of Tishomingo. Why didn't he come to her again? She had sent him word, but he had not replied. Sometimes she thought Flournoy was suspicious of her. He was, but he dared not express it. She was never out of his sight, so how could she have a lover? But the doubt was always there. Her eyes always danced when Tishomingo's name was mentioned. And Flournoy wondered what Tishomingo had meant by saying his revenge was almost complete.

There was a celebration at Locha Poka in honor of Thomas's visit and even the slaves joined in. After dinner, Sam outlined to Thomas his plans to run wagon trains up the Trace.

"The Trace will be open for wagons this year," said Sam. "I'm going to buy a few mules to begin my business. Soon I'll be breeding my own. That's why I want the mustangs from Philip Nolan."

"It's your best plan," said Thomas. "It's an amazing plan. You cannot fail. I'll select an agent for you in Nashville."

They drank to the plan. They both drank too much again and spent the evening toasting each other and the new land. They even toasted the mules that Sam would breed.

Sam took as many slaves out of his field as he dared and put them in his foundry, and all day they made wagon rims and assembled wagons. He got five fine jacks from Tennessee and twelve mules.

Over in Natchez, Philip Nolan and eighteen friends crossed the river and headed for Texas, ostensibly to hunt wild mustangs but actually to grab Spanish land. Nolan captured a few mustangs and sent them back. Sam sold some of them to the sugar planters and ran the others to Locha Poka and bred them to the Tennessee jacks.

But Nolan went on. Between the Trinity and the Brazos he built a blockhouse and was there when Lieutenant Musquez and a hundred Spaniards attacked him. Nolan was killed in the first volley and the survivors of the battle were sent to Mexican prisons.

News that Spain was after the Nolan party threw the frontier into an uproar and many Americans were for seizing Louisiana and West Florida. The Kemper boys, living near the border of West Florida and Mississippi, tried to persuade the Mississippians to sponsor a revolutionary government in West Florida. The movement probably would have come to a head then had the Mississippians known that Nolan's fate was sealed, but the only information they received was that Spanish troops were seeking Nolan. So the attempt to organize West Florida against Spain collapsed before it got under way. Sam was among the men who were for seizing the land.

The year 1800 was one of the most eventful in the history of the territory as well as within the nation. The seat of the federal government was moved to Washington City and in the national election Jefferson and Burr tied in the vote for president. The people obviously had voted with the intention of making Jefferson president and Burr vice-president, but the election was thrown into the House of Representatives. Burr surely would have been president had not Alexander Hamilton forsaken his party and thrown his weight behind Jefferson. And on the thirty-sixth ballot the Virginian was elected.

Sam's first wagon train moved north over the Trace a few days after Natchez received word that Jefferson would be inaugurated president. There were two wagons in the train, long Conestogas with wide wheels. The bodies were of good hickory and the iron of good temper. Each wagon was drawn by six mules and Natchez had never seen such a hitch. The mules were arranged in pairs, of course, but Sam used chain traces and full collars. The collars were made of good leather, soaked and molded to fit the animals' necks. They were stuffed with cotton and horsehair. None of those old-fashioned, uncomfortable breast traces for Sam Dabney! They threw a mule off balance and rubbed sores.

Sam loaded his trains in Natchez, partly with produce picked up in New Orleans and partly with local goods. The cargoes consisted of leather, which was plentiful, harness, spices from the Indies, coffee beans, Spanish powder, sugar, hickory-nut oil, mussel shells for buttons, and wine. Four Kentucky keel-boat men were with each wagon, two to tend the mules and two to tend the wagon. They had come south the week before and their transportation home was their wages.

Sam's agent in Nashville disposed of the goods, reloaded the wagons with goods for Louisville and sent the travelers on their way. In Kentucky the wagons and mules were sold just as they stood to a party of Connecticut folk who had brought their housen goods overland to Pittsburgh then down the river to Louisville. They even bought the bear grease that was used on the wagon's axles.

Sam's agent spent part of the profits for iron and sent it back down the river to Sam.

Ay, it was a superfine plan and it worked. Sam realized a profit of four thousand dollars on his first train.

He spent the money for equipment. He let contracts for cured hickory, for rims, for harness. Houses as far away as Pensacola supplied him with material. His horse collar was the talk of the new land and he sold the plan for a thousand dollars.

None of his wagons returned. That was the beauty of the plan. He got his drivers for nothing and along the Ohio and in Tennessee he was able to sell wagons, mules, harness—everything to the settlers who were coming down the Ohio and heading northwest. Many immigrants set out from New York with no supplies save gold and in Louisville purchased their housen goods, and a Dabney wagon and hitch and sought their homes.

Prosperity came at last to Locha Poka. Donna and Hoab went on a visit to Georgia but Donna's health did not improve. Pierce had a doctor from Charleston call on her and he cupped her and awaited results. After several days of examination he gave her the news she expected.

"You have the lung fever, Mrs. Dabney." The doctor had studied her carefully and knew that she was the kind of woman who would want the truth. To him, it seemed brutal to put it that way. But he might have been more brutal. He might have said, "You haven't long to live, Mrs. Dabney."

Donna took a deep breath when she heard the news and looked the doctor full in the face. She wanted to close her eyes and rest, but she wouldn't do that. She had known she had lung fever. But there had always been a chance that perhaps she was wrong. And now that she heard the sentence of death passed upon her, her first thoughts were of Sam. Sam knew she had the lung fever, too. She knew that he knew, but they had never mentioned it. She closed her eyes then. Death wouldn't be painful. She had suffered so much pain that death

531

would be a relief. She could rest. At Locha Poka. And she wouldn't worry any more about the grass in the crops, the sick slaves, the floods and the droughts. She could stretch out and rest and there would be no pain in her lungs. But she would be away from Sam. She wouldn't hear him humming to himself in his study. She wouldn't see him toss his mane of hair. She couldn't see him eat any more. She had loved to watch Sam eat. Breakfast was his big meal. She smiled as she thought about it. He liked sausage and corn cakes, butter and honey and coffee. He was always in a good humor at breakfast. Often he chided Sukey. And he teased Hoab. Sometimes he would take a big bite of food and dare Hoab to try to take one just as large. She thought about many of the little things that suddenly were very important—how her roses looked with dew on them, how the Bermuda grass waved in the spring, how good coffee smelled early in the morning, and how the black earth smelled at noontime when it lay panting and sweating, how the mist rolled from the river, how the river turned yellow when the sun struck it and how it changed to gold when the moon came up. . . .

She opened her eyes and said, "It has taken you a long time, doctor, to tell me the thing I already knew. Is there no cure?"

The doctor shook his head slowly.

"Then I pray you," said Donna, "not to tell my brother. He'll tell my husband and I don't want my husband to know yet."

"But why?" asked the doctor.

"Can my husband cure me?"

"Only God can cure you."

"Then why tell my husband? If he can do naught about it, why make him unhappy?"

532

The doctor's voice almost choked. "I don't quite understand, Mrs. Dabney. If it is any of my affair ——"

Donna laid her bony hand on his. "My Sam'l knows I have the lung fever. But he had hoped I might get better here. We have never mentioned the disease. It wasn't necessary. It has built a strange barrier between us, doctor. We both loathe it. We loathe it so much that we have never mentioned it."

"I think I understand," the doctor said softly. "You're a woman of courage."

"You should know my Sam'l. He has courage. A *big* kind of courage. Men will never understand just how brave my Sam'l is." She smiled again. "Oh, I don't mean physically. Physically he's reckless. But I mean spiritually. He's a good man, doctor, clean, gentle and forgiving. And he didn't believe in God until a few years ago." She choked up for the first time and the doctor patted her hand. "I want him to think I'm getting better."

"I'll respect your confidence." The doctor's voice was sad. "But you must stay here for a while. You couldn't live but a few months in the new land. Here you may live for several years. Promise me that you'll stay here for at least a year, and I'll promise not to tell anyone of your ailment."

"I promise," she said.

She wrote Sam that she would remain in Georgia for a year and said she was feeling much better. He was glad of her decision. He was too busy to be lonely.

Under Sam's direction Locha Poka became one of the show places of the new land. He poured his money into it. He was determined that when Donna returned she would find a place as beautiful as *Maison Blanche*. He imported more grass. He had stones sent down from the Tennessee Valley and paved the paths around his place.

533

He had the house painted and bought rugs and tapestries. He planted roses and jasmines. And for the first time all the rooms of the mansion were furnished. The only room he did not touch was Donna's bed chamber. But often he went there to be alone and to think. He got inspiration and comfort there, just by sitting in the rocker by the big window, by looking at her clothes, at the conch shell on the mantel.

He bought books and paintings. He knew nothing about paintings and decorations and Locha Poka resembled a museum. There was a heavy air about the place and the walls were decorated with an incongruous conglomeration of pictures, oils and sketches. There were knick-knacks everywhere. He even purchased a suit of armor and crowded it into the drawing room. He kept his long rifle-gun in the same room. Visitors from Natchez smiled behind their palms and dainty handkerchiefs at his taste. His banquets were too elaborate. It was a strange house, his rifle-gun by a suit of armor, a gaudy oil painting by a beautiful sketch, heavy rugs and fancy bric-à-brac. And rows of books, books that he would never open. They looked impressive, however.

Locha Poka was Sam Dabney, big and strange. After all, he was old man Dabney's brat and he didn't know how to decorate a house. He could rip the earth open and plant cotton. He could handle men. He could crack a whip and could scalp an Indian without wrinkling the forehead. He was a Georgia redneck with a pocket full of yellow gold. He was the New South, the get-rich-quick South. He drank too much and talked too much, ready to fight, hyper-sensitive, trying to hide his red neck under a fine collar.

The profits from his wagon trains were far beyond his wildest expectations. Soon Thomas was giving all of his time to Sam's business. They had an agent in Louisville and another in New Orleans and the Dabney wagons were daily sights on the road. Horsemen followed Sam's wagons because they afforded protection, and he organized a side-line business. He sold his protection to travelers for a small fee and even moved express goods. The West was living on wheels. Wheels were the greatest implements a man could make. Wheels could get you places. If you didn't like where you lived, you could roll on wheels to a new home. But a man had to settle down some time and open the earth. So perhaps the plow was the greatest implement of mankind. Well, Sam wouldn't bother about that. He was in the business of wheels.

Other traders began running freight north over the Trace but because Sam was a pioneer he had the cream of the business.

Even his cotton business boomed. The wheels of Manchester were turning and England was crying for cotton.

Sam bought more slaves and cleared more land and planted it to Sea Island. He encouraged other planters along the Halfway River to do the same. He ginned his own cotton and the cotton of all men who brought their staple to Locha Poka. He surrendered his post to the government willingly. After all, it was insurance against his brother-in-law's ever closing the Tombigbee ferry to him. Flournoy dared not put a high toll on his ferry with the government post using the route. To hell with the post! Sam was after bigger game.

The Three-Chopped Way had been surveyed far into the Creek Nation. It reached almost to the Alabama River. The wagon road was being built from Natchez to the Tombigbee. True, the Creeks along the Alabama had forbidden the white men to build a road between the Tombigbee and the Alabama, but it would come. The Creeks would be scattered some day. The road would be built and Sam's dream of a pike from Natchez to Georgia would be realized. And he was ready for the day. He had the wagons, the mules, the men. Not only would he send goods to Nashville, but also to Georgia, to old Ben Frome who would drive hard bargains for him. From Frome's factory the goods could move to Savannah. Then let them close New Orleans. What did he care? He could reach Tidewater in Georgia and get his cotton to England. And the cotton of all the men who would use his train.

He had trained his slaves not only to harvest cotton but to gin it and even to pack it in long bags. Lawyer Thomas had been right—the cotton gin was the most powerful machine of all time. Whitney had done something when he invented it, the addle-brained fool who was too weak to protect his own rights. By God, the cotton gin was more important than the curved ax handle. Or was it? Old man Dabney had said that the curved ax handle would make America. Well, maybe he was right. It took an ax to clear land and a plow to break it, but it took a gin to separate the milk and the honey that the land gave so bountifully.

Yes, cotton was the most powerful thing in the world. It was money. A man could take a sack of cotton to any merchant and say to the merchant, "Here's payment for my debt." England begged for cotton. The maws of Manchester gulped it and spat out cloth. The blue-nosed Yankees fumed because the Southwest sent its cotton to England. "Sell us your cotton," they demanded. "Our mills need it. We're Americans and you're Americans. Sell us your cotton."

"To hell with you!" the Southwest roared. "Pay us

the price England pays us and we'll send our cotton to your puny little mills. A tariff? You dare not. You dare not try to protect your mills at our expense. Cotton is the king and you are the jester."

Napoleon was cutting his swath through Europe and every time he hacked down a man he increased the cry for cotton. The men of England were in the fields, killing but not plowing, and their womenfolk flocked to the towns to run the mills. "Send us cotton," England begged. "We can beat Napoleon with money, and cotton means money to us. The civilization of England will never be built by a general or an admiral, but by the tired fingers of the women in Manchester who weave. For our cotton goods we can get gold and supplies. We will choke the damned Corsican with a bolt of cotton goods!"

Ay, cotton was sitting in the big chair. The territory's currency was the receipts given at the public gins for cotton deposited there. The planters hauled their cotton to the gins where it was weighed and receipted and the ginner was legally bound to deliver the cotton, baled and ready for market, to the holder of the receipt within four months. The toll for ginning was one twelfth of the value of the cotton and the ginners tacked on two dollars a bale to pay for packing and rope. The receipts that the ginners gave the planters were as good as gold.

They were good years for Locha Poka. Donna came home and she was happy because Sam was happy. She stayed in bed more than half of the time. She insisted to Sam that the doctor had diagnosed her case as malaria.

"Quinine will cure it," she said. "I'll be a new woman next year. You wait and see. My heart feels better. It laughs all the time. I'll be strong again. Maybe I'll fool you and bear you a son."

537

Sam held her in his arms when she said it. He wanted to crush her to him but he was afraid she would break. She seemed so thin, thin as a reed. He feared that if he held her tightly, something would snap. But he wanted to hold her. Great God, how he wanted to hold her! But there was no refuge for his loneliness in her arms. It would be inhuman, brutal, to seek refuge there.

Claymore had been retired to the stables and her colts were the pride of Locha Poka. Sam purchased a young Morgan saddle horse for his own use. He taught Hoab to ride and Tishomingo taught him to swim and to crack a bull whip. The boy shot up like a swamp sprout, lithe and strong. He went everywhere with the man he called his father. There was a strange affinity between him and Dabby. She was more than a slave child. She had the run of the house, and sometimes when the family was dining she would run out of the kitchen to the big table and ask for food. Sam always gave her tidbits and Hoab shared his possessions with her.

Hoab called Sam "Papa." It was the French influence in the new land. Sam had wanted his son to call him "father," but after he began calling him "papa," Sam decided he liked it better anyway. The word "father" was too cold, too British.

It was good to have a boy call him "papa." Sam tried to exile from his mind the knowledge that Hoab was not his son, but the boy would never allow Sam to forget it. His mannerisms, his mirth, his smile—he was Ab. Only his eyes were like Honoria's. The boy heard tall tales from the keel-boat men and repeated them to Sam. He told Sam about the Kentucky boat man who ran his ark on a turtle's back because he thought it was a sand bar.

"And, papa," Hoab said with a straight face, "that old Mississippi mud turtle just turned his head and looked at

538

the ark and said, 'The durned minnows in this river sure are pesty.' Then he went back to sleep."

Tears came to Sam's eyes when he heard the story. And then he told the boy another tall tale, but there was no sparkle to it. People must be made to think that Hoab got his story-telling talent from Sam.

Thomas was at the house one day when Hoab suddenly burst into a melody and in a sweet childish voice sang:

"And if a daring foe annoys,
 Whate'er his strength and forces,
We'll show him that Kentucky boys
 Are alligator horses.
Oh Kentucky—oh Kentucky ——"

Thomas looked up quickly, then laughed nervously. "Damme, that scared me for a minute. I thought it was Ab. Where did that little shaver learn to sing?"

"He comes by it naturally," said Donna quickly. "Sam'l is always singing around the house."

"I've never heard him sing much when he was sober."

Sam laughed, a hollow laugh. "Oh, I can whistle up a tune without wetting my own whistle."

A few minutes later he excused himself and went to his study, ostensibly to get some papers, but once within the room he took a deep breath and began singing so Thomas would surely hear him.

"We're a hardy, free-born race,
 Each man, he fears a stranger;
Whate'er the game, we join the chase,
 Despoiling time and danger.
Oh Kentucky—oh Kentucky ——"

539

Hoab cocked his ear and then went to his mother and whispered rather loudly, "Mother, papa ain't much shucks as a singing man, is he?"

Donna forced a laugh and a few seconds later she excused herself and went to her room where she fell across the bed and wept. Sam had tried so hard ——

Thomas called Hoab to him and held both the boy's hands. "Sonny," the little man said, "there are men who can sing and men who can't sing. Your father can't hold a candlelight to you. You'll be a singing man. But there's a way your father can sing, too. When your father sings one old song, there are ten thousand Indians who quake in their boots and whisper, 'Big Sam Dabney! Il-le-hi-ah, The Messenger of Death.'"

"What is the song?" Hoab asked.

"'Over the Hills and Far Away.' And I hope you never hear him sing it. I hope when you grow up, you'll be half the man your father is."

"That's what Mother says. And Dabby and Jasper. Everybody likes my papa, don't they?"

"Yes, son. All good men like your father. Now, get along with you."

The boy was singing, "Over the Hills" as he ran out of the house. Jasper had taught him the song.

Tishomingo visited Locha Poka frequently but he never mentioned Honoria. He had reorganized his school, and a Methodist missionary and his wife were teaching there. He still was working on his alphabet. He was happy over his friend's prosperity.

William Charles Cole Claiborne, of Nashville, was appointed governor of the new Mississippi Territory. Both Sam Dabney and Thomas were elected to the legislature and soon set up a cry for acquisition of the lands north of the territory. Georgia claimed it, and the Chickasaws and Choctaws held it. Sam knew the territory must exert jurisdiction over the land. The Trace ran through it and he was anxious to have his trains protected by American soldiers. The outlaws had returned to the lower Trace and although they had not molested the Dabney trains they had plundered many wagons and killed many traders and settlers.

Georgia did not want to surrender claim to the land. It already was jealous of the territory, jealous of its trade and its great cotton plantations. But the country was moving west and Georgia finally was persuaded to surrender all claim in the new land for the sum of $1,250,000 and soon the Mississippi Territory reached from the Chattahoochee to the Mississippi River, and from the Tennessee line to West Florida.

It was Sam Dabney who said in the legislature, "And now, gentlemen, we must acquire a seacoast. We must have the Gulf coast."

Thomas rebuked him and after rebuking him whispered in his ear, "Keep quiet, you fool. Every word you say here can be held against you. There's not a man here who's not willing to take West Florida, and the Louisiana Gulf ports from Spain, but we must not advertise our plan."

The status of Louisiana was a puzzle that even the inhabitants of New Orleans could not understand. The Spanish authorities were still in power but the rumor persisted that Spain had traded Louisiana to Napoleon in the secret treaty of San Ildefonso. The Mississippi Territory was growing by leaps and bounds and then the blow came. The port of New Orleans was closed again, and again the frontiersmen sprang to arms. Drums rolled and an American rabble, without orders and without authority, gathered in Mississippi, determined to settle the issue once and for all. The prosperity of every settler from the source of the Ohio to Natchez depended upon keeping New Orleans open. The new lands would never be safe so long as New Orleans was in the hands of a foreign power.

"Take New Orleans!" the backwoodsmen shouted. "Remember Philip Nolan! God damn Spain!"

But Spain no longer owned New Orleans. France owned it. The authorities, fearing that the Mississippians would march on the city, let the word leak out that Louisiana was the property of France and that one shot would mean a war with Napoleon.

"Then let's fight Napoleon," the Southwest said. "We'll teach him a thing or two. He may be the cock-of-the-walk in Europe but we'll cut his spurs if he comes over here."

Riders hurried frantically from Washington City, beseeching the settlers to lay down their arms and trust President Jefferson. He had friends in France. He would see that the port was reopened.

"But we don't trust Napoleon," the Southwest cried. "We don't trust a man who would make such a secret treaty as San Ildefonso. Secret treaties, be damned! We don't like secret treaties and we never will! Let's fight Napoleon now! Let's be stern with him. Let's fight and have done with it!"

"Don't fight France," the level heads begged. "If you fight France you become an ally of England. You'll be playing into England's hand. It's better for France to own Louisiana than England. Trust Jefferson."

The president succeeded in having the port reopened, but the settlers would not disarm. They must be ready if France closed New Orleans again. The tempers of the

542

people were short. Fist fights were frequent. If a man wanted a fight in Natchez or New Orleans he could get one simply by shouting, "Hurrah for Napoleon!"

Flournoy was very proud because France owned Louisiana, but he didn't boast openly. Several settlers went to him and demanded where he stood.

"What do you mean?" Flournoy asked.

They told him, "Napoleon is your kinsman. Are you for him? Or for us?"

"I'm for you," said Flournoy, but to his French friends he talked differently. "Any man with a long head can see my noble kinsman's game," he said. "He'll reëstablish a French empire in America. First he must take Santo Domingo. That island is the key to the Caribbean."

But Napoleon could not conquer Santo Domingo and so Louisiana was useless. Without Santo Domingo he couldn't hold it. Napoleon knew that the former slave, Toussaint L'Ouverture, had crushed his dreams of a great French empire in America. He must get rid of Louisiana. Why tempt England with it? Sell it to America, and good riddance.

The humbug and mumbo-jumbo of European diplomacy entered the picture. Jefferson wanted to buy merely the Isle of Orleans and West Florida. He was worried. If the Southwest couldn't get New Orleans and West Florida in honest trade then they would take them. But Jefferson must not let Napoleon know that he was trying to buy off a war.

"What will you take," the American minister asked Talleyrand, "for the Isle of Orleans?"

"What are we offered for Louisiana?" asked Talleyrand.

Louisiana! He was jesting. But the sly American minister appeared not to be surprised. He must let France

543

think that all the time America had intended to buy Louisiana. Surprise is seven tenths of a good bargain. Never let the other man know that you are surprised at any offer. And if he thinks you are not surprised then he will be surprised. The American minister stalled for time and sent word to Jefferson what was up. Obviously, Napoleon knew that Louisiana was worthless to him. And he must need money.

The day Louisiana went on the block the American minister and the French authorities argued from mid-afternoon until midnight about the affair. More than nine hours. It was a long time for such important men to argue. Nine hours to seal the fate of an empire. Nine hours to barter for the most valuable land in all the world. Millions of men had spilled their blood in a futile effort to say who would be master of the Nile's delta. But it took only hours to say who would be master of a land in which the Nile delta could be buried and never missed.

"What is your price?" the American minister asked.

"The price is sixty million francs."

"That's very high," said the American.

"It's very cheap. And you must assume claims of your fellow citizens against France for twenty million francs. That makes a total of eighty million francs."

"Eighty million francs! That's fifteen million dollars."

They haggled on and on, and finally the United States minister agreed to the price. Fifteen million dollars for a land so rich that its value could not be figured.

Then arose the question of boundaries. The treaty specified that the United States receive "the colony or province of Louisiana with the same extent that it has now in the hands of Spain, and that it had when France possessed it, and such that it would be after the treaties

544

subsequently entered into between France and Spain." But what did the words mean? Even the American minister didn't understand them. What had America bought? Did the land include Texas? West Florida?

The minister asked what the words meant and Talleyrand replied, "I do not know. You must take it as we received it."

"But what did you mean to take?" asked the American minister.

"I do not know," the Frenchman replied. "You have made a noble bargain for yourselves and I suppose you'll make the most of it."

Make the most of it! Ay! The United States would make the most of it.

Louisiana once extended to Pensacola and included Mobile. So Jefferson made the most of it and ordered that Mobile be annexed to the Mississippi Territory. At Natchez the Mississippians were delighted. They had a port. Mobile was their port. New Orleans belonged to the United States. Sam Dabney's dream for salt water washing the new land had been realized. But Spain wouldn't surrender Mobile or West Florida. She claimed that her lands extended west to Baton Rouge.

"Let's go fight for it," said Sam Dabney. "Let's take West Florida from the Spaniards and settle this question once and for all."

"Ay," said the firebrand, Reuben Kemper. "Who'll follow me into West Florida?"

They all would. But Thomas pacified them. "Trust Jefferson. Can't you see his plan? He has located a customs house near Mobile but just north of the Florida line. He'll play with Spain until the Spaniards get into another war. Then he'll seize Mobile. We can get it without shedding a drop of blood."

545

"Perhaps so," said Sam. "But Napoleon is master of Spain. France really owns West Florida. How can we get it unless we take it?"

"Trust Jefferson," pleaded Thomas.

They would. They would trust Jefferson. Jefferson and old Andy Jackson and their long rifles.

Sam and Tishomingo and Hoab went to New Orleans to witness the transfer of the city to American hands. Donna was unable to make the trip. Flournoy and Honoria were down for the celebration, too. They found that many of the people in the city had been apprehensive of French domination: France might free the slaves. But the old families didn't want the Americans either. New Orleans was a city of twelve thousand people. A motley money-mad citizenry. Here, indeed, was a melting pot, the first great melting pot of a nation that boasted it could pour a thousand different bloods into one pot, boil the bloods together and produce a new kind of man. Very well, this was the place to try it, New Orleans, with its thousand bloods.

Governor Claiborne and General Wilkinson marched down from Fort Adams to accept the city from the French. The ceremony was very brief. Claiborne presented his credentials and those of General Wilkinson. A salute was fired and the French commissioner delivered to Claiborne the province of Louisiana. The banner of France descended halfway down a mast in the Place of Arms. The American flag ascended halfway up the mast. Both flags were stopped for a minute and a gun was fired. Then the American flag was run up.

Sam Dabney was the first to shout, "Hurrah for the United States! God bless Jefferson!"

"Hurrah!" shouted Thomas.

546

A handful of Americans joined in. Kentuckians, Mississippians and Tennesseans shouted approval, and raised their bottles and drank to the occasion. But the French and Spaniards were strangely quiet.

Immediately after the ceremony Sam plunged into business. He made arrangements to run his wagon trains from New Orleans to Nashville. The wagons would pause at Natchez for all the business available there. He and Thomas took Hoab with them when they kept their business appointments. Tishomingo wanted to be alone.

"I have many friends here I would like to see," Tishomingo said, and they left him to his own devices.

Thomas caught Tishomingo's eye as the Choctaw turned to leave them, and for a few seconds the two men stared at each other. Tishomingo was the first to drop his eyes.

Sam put Hoab to bed. He and Thomas were in their hotel room when Flournoy arrived, his tongue thick with wine, his eyes rimmed with red and his brain spinning.

"Where's Tishomingo?" he demanded sullenly.

Sam saw that he was drunk and led him to a chair. "*You* of all men," he said, "don't want to see Tishomingo, and surely not alone."

"Where is he?" Flournoy's voice rose. "God damn it, Dabney, where is he?"

"I don't know, man," Sam tried to quiet him. "Why do you ask?"

"Where's my wife?" Flournoy chewed the words for a second and then spat them out.

Thomas started from his chair, but changed his mind and leaned back. He folded his hands across his pudgy little belly and wrinkled the bald spot on his head. Here comes trouble, he thought. Well, Sam didn't need him.

Sam's voice was low and even, without a trace of doubt

or bitterness. "I don't know where your wife is. Perhaps she went out to see the city."

"Good women do not go unescorted in New Orleans." Flournoy almost hissed the words.

"Careful, man!" Sam's voice suddenly was hard. "She's my sister."

"And she's my wife! She's with Tishomingo!"

Sam gripped Flournoy by the front of his waistcoat and slapped him with his open palm. Flournoy would have fallen, but Sam supported him and slapped him again. He didn't want to injure Flournoy, only to sober him. Sam wouldn't hurt a drunken man. Flournoy struck out blindly and Sam slapped him a third time and hurled him into a chair. Flournoy's face was bleeding.

Sam tossed him a handkerchief. "That will sober you and bring you to your senses. Do you realize what you're saying?"

"I know what I'm saying. There are some things a man can feel. Where's Tishomingo if he's not with her?"

Sam could not speak. He, too, had the same feeling that was overwhelming Flournoy. Thomas looked quickly at his friend, saw the anguish in his eyes and said calmly, "Tishomingo has returned home. I thought I told you, Dabney. He left this afternoon."

Flournoy got up from his chair, mumbled an apology to Sam, and staggered out of the room. Honoria was in the Flournoy apartment when he returned. "Where have you been?" he demanded.

She took a deep breath to regain her poise. She saw that his face was cut and bloody. She could feel the color mounting in her cheeks. Her heart still was pounding and she feared he could hear it. If he couldn't hear it pounding, perhaps he could hear it singing. Tishomingo

548

had left her heart singing and even her husband's anger could not still the song.

"I've been out walking," she said. "I was weary of staying here alone."

"A modest woman does not walk alone in New Orleans."

"The wife of Lake Flournoy can walk among any people with honor and dignity," she said. "Do you accuse me?"

"Where's Tishomingo?"

Honoria clenched her fists and stared him down. "The very tone of your voice is insulting. I will not even stoop to answer you. If you accuse me, you'll answer to my brother."

"I don't accuse anybody. I simply asked a question and as your husband I'm entitled to an answer."

Honoria laughed. It was a haughty laugh. "You're jealous, Lake."

"Of course, I'm jealous. I'm half insane with jealousy. There are things a man can sense. There's something eating at your heart. Don't you think I can tell?"

"Am I not a good wife? Am I not obedient to your wishes?"

"Ay, but there's something lacking. You're not responsive to my caresses."

"Then you must teach me to love." She moved close to him and put her arms around him.

"You're a damned hard pupil," he said, but he couldn't resist her presence. He didn't trust her any more. He really had never trusted her. Honoria always meant exactly the opposite of what she said. She had said she hated Tishomingo. Flournoy knew now that it was a lie. But he mustn't accuse her. Great God, no! Unless he had proof, Dabney would kill him. He feared Tishomingo's whip but he feared Sam Dabney's big hands more. Dabney would not wait to kill if he were angry. He would strangle a man and Flournoy knew it.

No, he couldn't accuse his wife. He must have proof. He would have her watched by one of his slaves. If he could only prove what he suspected. She would be punished and Dabney would be ruined. But, above all, Tishomingo would be punished as Honoria was punished. It was the law. He could demand her death, but he wouldn't do that. He would have her ears cut off and hung in the council town of the Choctaws. Then Tishomingo must suffer the same fate and Dabney could never hold up his head among his fellows. If he could only get proof. He rather hoped she was guilty of adultery. It would settle all scores. How simple it was. Why hadn't he thought of it before? For sure, he would be scorned because he couldn't hold his woman. He could not kill Tishomingo himself. He dared not do it. He dared not hire a man to do it. But the Choctaw law would settle his score. A woman, his own wife, was the answer to his problem. Yes, he would have her watched. She would go to Tishomingo or Tishomingo would go to her. It was very simple. His wife would be the bait and he would spring the trap, and Tishomingo's own uncle would have to pronounce sentence.

Sam did not speak to Thomas for several minutes after Flournoy had left their room. He sat in his chair, his great head in his hands. Finally he looked up at his friend and asked, "Why did you tell that lie? You know Tishomingo did not return to the Halfway River." He glared hard at the little lawyer.

"I wanted to avoid trouble," said Thomas.

"What should I do?" Sam asked, and then was sorry,

and before Thomas could reply he said, "Never mind answering that. I'll make my own decision."

"Are you suggesting," Thomas said, "that there's anything to Flournoy's insinuation?"

"I'm suggesting nothing," said Sam. "If he accuses my sister falsely I'll kill him. I have faith in Tishomingo. There is no need of hiding from you what every man can see. My sister loves him but he doesn't love her. He would do naught to injure me."

"Or himself," said Thomas.

"What does that mean?"

"Great God, man! I'm a lawyer and I'm simply stating a case. So hold your temper while I talk. We know that Tishomingo is determined to kill Flournoy. They're both half-breed Indians, absolutely without mercy. Revenge is the most important thing in Tishomingo's life. An Indian has no honor where revenge is concerned. Tishomingo would like nothing better than to take Flournoy's woman. Hold on, Sam'l—keep your tongue and your temper, and hear me out. He'd like to do everything to Flournoy that Flournoy did to him—and then kill him. But he dare not. Not even Tishomingo dares to take that chance. Should Flournoy ever be able to prove before the Choctaw council that his wife and Tishomingo were guilty of wrong-doing, then they both would be punished. Tishomingo would not be able to complete his revenge. I'm a man of logic. I claim that if Tishomingo could repay part of his debt to Flournoy by taking your sister, he'd do so. He's that much Indian. But it's too great a risk."

Thomas watched his friend closely as he talked, building up a case for Tishomingo and Honoria that he knew they did not deserve. Thomas was a good lawyer. He could argue a lie as well as the truth. There was a time

551

when a lie was useful. He wouldn't stand by and see his friend hurt. But sometimes Sam was a riddle to him. Surely, Sam must see through his sister. Perhaps he wanted to be fooled, to believe a lie. He had known men like that, men who loved a woman so much that they never wanted to know the truth. . . .

Sam let Thomas' argument roll over in his brain and then said, "I don't believe you." But he knew he would make himself believe.

"You're a fool about many things, Sam'l, and among them is women. Your mother must have been a remarkable woman. You inherited many noble traits from her. You're a strange man. You'll kill at the drop of a hat. You'll cut a man's throat in a business deal. You'll break the law in business. You'll smuggle slaves. You were neck deep in that illegal Nolan expedition. You'll give bribes and buy judges. And yet you're the man who would not do André Duportail out of a bit because he was your friend. You're the man who trusts me because I'm your friend and you trust Tishomingo for the same reason. You've put your sister on a pedestal and you'd kill the man who said she had feet of clay. Your wife has been sick for years, but not once have you forgotten your pledge that you would love only her. You have a dozen handsome slave wenches, but not once have you stooped to touch them, except with a gentle hand, to treat them for their ills, to give them rum as a reward for hard work. Ay, you're a strange man. It's an honor to be your friend, and I hope to God, for my own hide, I'm never your enemy. Let's have a drink."

They were drinking fine wine when Tishomingo arrived. Sam handed him a glass of wine, knowing he would refuse it. "But let's drink to Louisiana," he said. "This day our country —"

"Your country," said Tishomingo.

"This day our country has become an empire."

"I'll smoke a pipe for the prosperity of your country and for peace between your people and my people."

"Where have you been, Chock?" Sam asked, trying to appear casual. "We've missed you."

Tishomingo knew Thomas was watching him but he did not glance at the lawyer. He looked at Sam and said, "I've been to the asylum to see Anestasie. She's hopelessly mad. The poor woman even accuses Honoria of trying to frighten her to death."

"Do not tell Honoria that," Sam said as he got up from his chair. He believed Chock's story and was relieved. "It will worry her. I'm going outside to buy a stogie and I need air. That wine is going to my head."

When he was gone Thomas filled his tumbler, not with wine, but with rum. He gulped it down and smacked his lips. Then he reached into the tail of his long clawhammer coat, pulled out a pistol and began examining it. He blew down the barrel. Finally, he glanced up at Tishomingo, squinted his left eye and spoke slowly, "It has been my misfortune to kill a few men in my life. There are those who enjoy killing men and those who don't. I don't. . . ."

The little lawyer fascinated Tishomingo. He watched Thomas, making no attempt to interrupt him.

"I've never believed much in revenge. Revenge is the action of a savage. If a man kills in the heat of passion, I can forgive him. But when a man plots another man's death, broods over it, and then kills, it's murder. I've never committed murder in my life, but if you ever do hurt to Sam Dabney, I'll kill you. Kill you in premeditated murder. I mean I'll try to kill you. Perhaps I can't. They tell me you're like lightning with a bull whip and

553

almost as handy with your fists as Sam Dabney. But if I can't kill you, I'll pass the task along to my kinsman. Young Sam Houston, he is."

Tishomingo replied calmly. "A lawyer always uses too many words. I'm Sam Dabney's friend."

"But you're also an Indian. You think as an Indian. To you Honoria Flournoy is no longer Sam Dabney's sister but the property of your enemy. You're able to draw a line between your friend, Sam Dabney, and the wife of your enemy. A white man does not reason so."

The lawyer held the pistol up to the light and balanced it in his hand. Tishomingo smiled at him.

"You're a wise man, too," Thomas continued. "There's a strange thing about going to an asylum to see crazy people. Even if a woman's husband went to the asylum to get proof and a loony said you had not been there, who would believe her?"

"Then you don't believe me?"

"Ay, I believe you. And I'll not ask you where you were before you went to the asylum. Or whom you were with."

"It would be wise not to ask me," said Tishomingo, and stood very straight, watching Thomas's fingers and not the pistol.

"I believe you saw Mme. Duportail," Thomas said. "It would have been strange if Mme. Duportail had told you what you hoped she would tell you, that Flournoy had had her committed so he could get her property. But even loonies don't lie. It would have been strange if she had told you that Flournoy had frightened her into hysterics and then had had her sent here. It would have given you more cause to hate him. But I reckon Mme. Duportail surprised you. I think she's telling the truth about Honoria. And I believe you know what I've

554

known for a long time. She's not hopelessly insane, but she might as well be. She'll never be released. Only Lake Flournoy can get her release and Lake Flournoy's wife will see that he doesn't do that. Some damned fool might believe Anestasie Duportail's story."

"Once we had a lawyer among the Choctaws," Tishomingo began quietly, "but he grew wiser than the great mingo. He tried to take the great mingo's power. He understood the law too well. He could put things together and weave them into stories and the people believed him. He was a dangerous man."

"What happened to him?" asked Thomas.

"The mingo cut his throat."

Thomas poured himself another drink and his hand flicked out as he reached for his second pistol. Tishomingo's eyes, as quick as they were, could not follow the movement. He had never seen a man move so quickly. The lawyer's pudgy little hands seemed to caress his weapons as he rested them on his little pot belly. Once he scratched his bald spot with the butt of one of the guns. A fool might have laughed at Thomas, but Tishomingo was no fool. That was death sitting there in that chair. There was the lawyer, jury, judge and executioner. Thomas smiled and showed his teeth. It was the first time Tishomingo had ever seen his teeth. His teeth were stained with tobacco and were uneven.

"There's a strange thing about lawyers," Thomas drawled. "When you kill one, two spring up—one to prosecute you and one to defend you. I was born in Virginia, Tishomingo, and up where I was born there are two things we don't like. One is a God-damned stinking Indian. You can breed them to white men until their skin is white but they're still Indians. The other thing we don't like is a God-damned British lobster-back. Put them together and you've got the orneriest combination this side of hell. And you're British and Indian. Now, don't move! I'm a nervous man. I don't care what you do to Honoria Flournoy. I don't care what you do to Lake Flournoy. But if ever you do any hurt to Sam Dabney, I'll blow a hole in you, hang your scalp on a stink-weed rack and stretch your guts over a hickory pole. You're Dabney's friend. But you're living only to complete a bloody Indian's revenge. Mind you, if you must take another man's wife to complete your revenge, you be damned sure you don't get caught. What Sam doesn't know won't hurt him and if you want to live to kill Lake Flournoy you be sure that Dabney never suspects that his sister is a part of your scheme to pay off a debt. He's a big man, but if he knew his sister and his friend were doing what I *know* you're doing, it would break his heart."

Tishomingo stood very erect while the insults burned their way into his brain and imprinted themselves there. No other man had ever said such things to a mingo of the Choctaws. But Tishomingo felt humble, even meek, in the presence of this just man. And he liked Thomas. This little man was Sam's friend, too. They both loved Big Sam. His secret was safe with Thomas.

Tishomingo bowed his head and stared at the floor. Then he raised his head and said with feeling, "I fear no man. I'm afraid only of the truth. Your insults are harsh. Ay, perhaps I deserve them. The English in me makes me ashamed of my behavior, but the Indian in me rejoices."

Thomas got slowly to his feet and put his pistols away. "Only a brave man could speak so. Dammit, Tishomingo, you can't help being British and Indian and I can't help liking you."

"I would like to be your friend," said Tishomingo, smiling.

"My friendship is easy to get, but hard to keep. So is yours." He offered Chock his hand. "We understand each other."

"Ay," Tishomingo grasped the hand. "If ever you need me ——"

"That goes for me, too. And when you kill that half-breed Frenchman, make a first class job of it. I'll defend you and won't charge you a penny!"

26

* *

THE old squaw who had assisted Tishomingo at Honoria's purification ceremony brought him word that Honoria planned to visit him. Flournoy was in New Orleans on business and pleasure, pleasure he could not find at home. His wife was well aware of his intention to dip into the fleshpots of the city of sin. And she was glad. Perhaps he would satisfy his lust and cease annoying her, and, too, his absence would give her the opportunity for which she was waiting. Tishomingo would not come to her, so she would go to him.

She knew she was being watched and it amused her. Lake Flournoy had instructed the girl who had been the bath slave to watch her. Flournoy didn't know and apparently didn't care that his slaves hated him. Neither did he know that the bath slave had loved Ta-lo-wah and that she was anxious to see her master suffer as he had caused others to suffer. It was the bath slave who told Honoria she was being watched and who smiled knowingly at her mistress when she said it. Honoria rewarded her, one of the few slaves she ever rewarded, and sent her to fetch the old squaw.

Tishomingo brewed the black drink for the old woman and made her welcome at his lodge. She did not mention her mission at first. It would have been bad manners. She must say naught of her mission until she was asked and Tishomingo must not ask her until she had rested and refreshed herself.

But when the business of welcoming her was over, Tishomingo asked, "Why do you come to me?"

"To tell you that your woman is coming here. She sent me ahead. The man whose name she bears, but whom she hates, is away and her heart yearns to be with you."

"What shall I do, old woman?" Tishomingo asked.

"Do you want her here?"

"Ay. Sometimes I want her and sometimes I do not."

"Let her come here. You have much to forget and she'll help you to forget. It's not good for man to live alone. It's not good for a man to live as you live, close by the grave of his first love. If a man lives alone, he'll die inside and grow old before his appointed time. Do you still hear the voice of Ta-lo-wah crying and sighing in the night wind?"

Tishomingo did not reply and the old squaw continued, "You don't hear it as you used to, then? That is good. Man wearies of thinking of the dead and loves to think of the living. Ay, let her come here."

Honoria announced at *Maison Blanche* that she was going to Locha Poka. Ordinarily it would take her three days to reach there, but by riding rapidly she could have the nights to spend with Tishomingo, and still reach Locha Poka the day she was expected. She took the bath slave and one of the men slaves with her and rode to the Big Black where Tishomingo was waiting. She hurried ahead of her small party when she saw him and got down from her horse and went to him. He kissed her tenderly.

"Are you glad I came?" she asked when he released her.

"Why do women waste words to ask questions when they know what the answer will be?"

559

"I do not know that," she said. "I suppose it's because a woman never tires of sweet words. You know that Lake has set a slave to watch me."

"I knew he would."

"Then you would dare have me even though it's dangerous?"

"Sometimes I think I would dare anything for you. There's a thing I must tell you. I took you first from your husband because I hate your husband and wanted to hurt him as he has hurt me. But you have become a part of me now. It's a thing I cannot explain. It is as though there was a great hole in my heart and you have filled it. Ay, I would dare anything for you."

"There's naught to worry about," she said. She was intoxicated with joy. "The bath slave knows I'm going with you. We can trust her."

"There's a thing I must ask you," he said. "I visited Anestasie in New Orleans. She speaks evil of you. She blames you for her predicament."

"Would you believe a loony?" Honoria asked quickly, for her mind already was plotting. It would be easy to accuse her husband. Tishomingo might believe her. He hated Flournoy enough to believe anything against him. But then, on the other hand, he might not believe her.

"Anestasie is not wholly mad," continued Tishomingo. "At times she is rational. I believe if she could get away from that place she'd be all right again."

"I'll ask my husband to use his influence," Honoria said.

"You haven't answered my question."

Honoria said, "I wish I could lie to you. But I cannot. I'm afraid you'll hate me. I'm responsible for Anestasie's insanity." She said it slowly. "The thought has almost driven me mad. I'd do anything to undo the harm I did.

560

I, too, thought the bit of ribbon was a snake. I lost my head. I'll always believe that if I had kept my head Anestasie would have kept hers."

"Then the whole thing was an accident?"

"My stupidity was to blame. I don't know how the piece of ribbon got by the door. I might have dropped it myself. I should have remembered that Anestasie was nervous."

Tishomingo said, "Poor Honoria! You mustn't think too much about it."

"But I do. I can't help it." Her eyes filled and she rested her head on his chest.

He helped her to her horse and they rode together, several hundred yards ahead of the two slaves. The bath slave prepared their couch that night and they slept together under a tree and resumed their journey the next day. Neither spoke often. Honoria would not allow herself to think for fear her thoughts would drive her happiness away. But Tishomingo was thinking of many things. Their second night together he told her, "I have dedicated my life to avenging a wrong that Lake Flournoy did me."

She was resting in his arms, her head snuggling on his shoulder. There was no fire or candle in the room and the darkness was kind. The darkness was blind, too, and could keep a secret.

"I know that some day you'll kill my husband," she turned her face to his and whispered in his ear. "And I know that you'll never love me as you loved Ta-lo-wah." She felt his muscles jerk when she mentioned the name. "But I love you, Tishomingo. Please take me away. Let's go to Texas! Anywhere! You can pass for a white man or I'll be an Indian. It doesn't matter! Nothing will matter if we're together."

561

He propped himself on his elbow and tried to see her in the darkness. He stroked her face as he said, "Perhaps some day I'll take you away."

"If you love me, why don't you take me away now?"

"Because there's a thing I must do."

The night she spent with him in his lodge he did not go to the grave of Ta-lo-wah. After all, Ta-lo-wah was only a memory and Honoria was very real and very beautiful. She was new every time he went to her. She gave herself to him with an abandoned recklessness, as though their hours together were their last on earth. She sang for him and he laughed at her capers. Nor did she again mention her hopes that he would take her away, but was content to live out every minute they were together. She was determined not to be sad when the time came for her to travel on to Locha Poka.

She left Tishomingo standing by the door of his lodge. He watched her ride away and immediately a feeling of revulsion gripped him. He felt dirty inside. He swore to himself that he never again would allow her to come to him, knowing full well that he would violate the oath at the first opportunity. She made him forget the things he did not want to forget. She made him gay and he wanted to be morose. She got into his blood. He was never certain of himself when he was with her. He had always prided himself upon his strength, but he had no strength when she was within reach of his arms. He wanted to hate her. Perhaps he did. He thought of a hundred things about her—the tantalizing odor of her hair, the fresh salty smell of her sweat. But then, too, there was always the subtle, sweet odor of lily of the valley, and Tishomingo hated it. . . . His thought exhausted him and made him angry with himself. She was a minx and he despised her now that she was gone, but he knew she would be back and he would be glad.

Honoria did not look back as she rode away. She wanted to remember him as he had been up to the minute she had kissed him goodbye. She felt cleaner and better, and resolved that her life would be cleaner and better. She would try to make up to Donna some of the cruel things she had done. She would even send Anestasie a gift. But better still, she would work for Anestasie's release. After all, Anestasie was no longer a dangerous adversary . . . Well, she couldn't be certain of that. No, on second thought, she would just send her a present. That would be enough. . . .

All the way to Locha Poka she thought of the kind things she would do for people, but as she came down the pike to the factory she saw Hoab and Dabby and straightway forgot her good intentions. She wanted Dabby. She wanted Dabby because Donna owned her. And she would have her. Suddenly she wanted Hoab. Sam had brought a teacher to Locha Poka for the boy. They might have consulted her about it, Honoria thought. How like Donna to hire a Virginia schoolmaster. Yes, her opinion should have been sought. She didn't know, and didn't care, that Donna thought a tutor too expensive. It had been Sam, always grandiose, who had insisted upon a private instructor. He could well afford it. Nothing was too good, or good enough, for the son of Sam Dabney.

Honoria embraced the boy. He was shy in her presence, and treated her with the dignity and respect he would have accorded any stranger. She resolved to pay more attention to him. She would get him a present. She never had given Hoab a present, had never thought about it before. She admitted to herself that he looked

563

strong and was well-mannered. That was because he was her son and not because of Donna's training. She wanted him because Donna loved him. And when she realized that she dared not demand him, her temper shortened. She was irked and impatient because her brother had not come out to meet her. She kicked her horse and, commanding her slaves to follow, galloped past the factory and up the lane to Locha Poka.

Old Benjamin Frome was at the big house and his eyes bulged when he saw her.

"You don't look like the same lady who was bound to me," he said, and bowed to her.

"I'm not the same person," snapped Honoria. She did not ask of Mrs. Frome or of any of the Georgia people, but went to the room that Sam always kept ready for her, and changed her clothes. She waited until she was dressed before she went to Donna's sickroom and stooped over the bed and kissed her sister-in-law on the forehead.

"You look better, Donna," Honoria said condescendingly.

"You won't even tell the truth about my looks; will you, dear?" Donna smiled wanly.

"I was only trying to be nice," said Honoria haughtily.

"Don't try, Honoria," said Donna. "It doesn't become you. You're much more attractive as a minx than as a saint. But let's not quarrel. Did you have a good trip?"

"It was very slow."

"How is your husband?"

"He's in New Orleans."

"That's right," said Donna. "I had forgotten. Then how is Tishomingo?"

Honoria glanced around to make sure they were alone. The look of fear that spread across her face was evidence of guilt. "I don't understand you." Honoria said. "I demand an explanation. Why should you ask me about Tishomingo?"

Donna's laugh was drowned in a fit of coughing. "The guilty flee when no man pursueth."

"Does Sam'l know?"

"Know what?"

"You know what as well as I do." Honoria sat on the bed. "You can read me."

Donna said, "I knew naught, not till now. Once you trapped my husband the same way. Now I know that you've been with Tishomingo. I don't condemn you. Sam'l doesn't know. He must not."

"Thank you," said Honoria. "What should I do? I believe Tishomingo is beginning to love me."

"You can do naught. But if Sam'l knew he might forget himself and kill his best friend. Frankly, Honoria, your honor isn't worth a quarrel between Sam'l and his friend."

Honoria, enraged but afraid to start a quarrel, stalked out of the room.

Frome had come to Locha Poka with important news and a great plan. He brought intelligence that the English had conquered the French fleet at Trafalgar. It meant that England was mistress of the seas but that Napoleon still was master of continental Europe. It meant a struggle to the finish between the traders of England and the peasants of France. The United States, small as it was, was the only important neutral in the world.

"If we play our cards right," Frome said, "this nation can get rich. I've come to you because you're a rich man and influential in this part of the country."

"What is your plan?" Sam said.

"First we will build a store ——"

565

"A what?"

Frome said, "A store. Over in Georgia they are calling factories stores now, and calling mills factories. We must build a store up the river from Natchez. Some day there will be a city on the bluffs at Walnut Hills. The city will be more important than Natchez. You and I will be partners in the new store."

"Not I," said Sam. "I'm no merchant. My fortune is in my land and in my wagon trains. I want naught to do with any store."

"A wise man will spread his money over many investments," Frome replied sagely. "But I will not try to persuade you. If you'll not go into partnership with me in a store, then let me use your name. I'll pay you. I want to call the store, 'Dabney & Company'. I'll give you a small percentage of the profits. Your name is important here and will draw trade."

"What of your business in Georgia?"

"My wife's nephew has come to this country. He will run the business there. It will be many years yet, Sam'l, before our road to Georgia is opened. Meanwhile, I want to build a store on the river. Is it a deal?"

"Ay, it's a deal," said Sam. "I'll rent you my name. Of course, my lawyer will have to have the right to examine your books. Sam Dabney will not lend his name to any enterprise that is not honorable. Now, what is your other plan? You didn't come so far just to tell me about this store."

He was right. Benjamin Frome had a great plan. With England in control of the seas, the cotton market was certain to boom. England was sending agents to the United States to buy all the cotton available.

"We'll buy the cotton," Frome said.

"You're loony."

"I have a long head," said Frome. "Most of the cotton is being produced in Georgia and in the new land. I can handle the Georgia end. You and I will get together on a price so we will not be cutting each other's throats. We'll make the price slightly above the prevailing price and buy on long-term contracts. We'll control all of the cotton between the Sea Islands and New Orleans, and when the British agents arrive they'll have to do business with us and at our price."

"It will take a lot of money," said Sam.

"I can raise a lot of money," Frome stated.

"I can, too," said Sam boastfully. "My credit is good for any amount. But I must think on this thing. I'll admit your proposition is a superfine one, but something might go wrong."

"What can go wrong?" asked Frome. "We contract for all the cotton between the river and Georgia. The price is bound to skyrocket. England will give the crown jewels for cotton."

Sam said, "I know that, but we're gambling, Ben. We're gambling that England defeats Napoleon."

"She will."

"I think so, too," Sam agreed. "Napoleon has shot his wad. But still I must think about this. I'll give you my answer soon. I have many irons in the fire, you know."

And so he had. He had gambled $5,000 in the Kemper brothers' plot to wrest West Florida from Spain. The plot had fallen through, but Sam knew that some day West Florida would revolt and establish its independence. Then he would have his choice of land there. Thomas had supported him in the West Florida venture, but had turned thumbs down on Sam's proposal to back Aaron Burr.

"Burr's a fool," Thomas had said. "He's at rope's end.

Expediency now is his master. He doesn't know where he's going or what he's doing. He's neck-deep in a land-grabbing scheme, too, but you stay away from him. You've got enough projects afoot now."

Sam and Frome discussed Burr and the plan that was to collapse. Burr was in Natchez. Frome agreed with Thomas that Sam should avoid doing business with the disgraced New Yorker. The two friends talked long and earnestly about the old days in Georgia. Frome was proud of Sam and proud of Honoria.

"Back in Georgia," Frome said, "I often tell my friends that the wife of Lake Flournoy once was my bound 'un. You two have come a long way, Sam'l boy."

"Ay," said Sam. "If my wife were well I would have everything."

"How long have you known that she has the lung fever?"

"I have known it a long time. Strangely enough, we never discuss it. She has never told me, but she knows that I know. We try to act as though it isn't true."

"There are no hopes for her?" Frome asked.

"There's always hope, man. But I'll not discuss it further. It's a thing that is never mentioned in this household."

Frome returned to Georgia the next day and Sam took Honoria with him to Natchez. He could feel the tension between Donna and his sister, and decided to keep them apart as much as possible. Honoria would wait in Natchez until her husband returned from New Orleans.

Thomas' eyes sparkled as Sam unfolded his plan to buy as much cotton as possible and hold it until England was willing to pay his price.

"It's a bold plan," remarked Thomas, "but you're gambling a fortune."

"I have thought out every detail," said Sam, "and I cannot see how I can lose. England controls the seas. She must have cotton. All right, I'll buy every pound of cotton I can get my hands on and store it in New Orleans and tell England to come and get it at my price. They'll have to take title here. Can you arrange the contract?"

"Yes, that can be done," Thomas replied. "We'll contract for next year's crop. You'll agree to pay the planters three months after they deliver to you and at a price attractive enough to assure that they'll do business only with you."

"And Frome," said Sam.

"Why Frome?" asked Thomas.

"Because I promised. He'll buy in Georgia, and I'll buy here. He'll take his cotton to Savannah and I'll take mine to New Orleans."

Thomas clapped Sam on the shoulder. "All right, you bucko. Frome is in. You always honor your promise, Sam'l. A wiser man would play this game alone. You can cut Frome's throat."

"I'll not do it. But what think you of the store?"

"We'll rent him your name if that is what you wish."

"It sounds like a good plan," Sam said. "I would go into the store business, too, if I didn't have so many other things to do. Please get to work on those contracts and let's get them out."

He and Thomas traveled over all the new land, signing contracts with the planters who would deliver him their next year's cotton. It was a busy year for Sam. In most instances he was forced to contract for the cotton at higher prices than he had anticipated, for the market was booming.

Sam attended the territory's legislative sessions, but spent most of the time in the taverns, pulling strings to protect his wagon trains and other investments.

He made an attempt to see Anestasie in New Orleans only because he wanted to help her, but her doctor told him, "You're a Dabney and my patient has a grievance against the Dabneys. If you see her you'll upset her and I forbid it."

Sam thought Anestasie's grudge dated from the scene he had had with her over disposition of her property, and he never knew that André's widow held his sister responsible for her plight. It was a thing no man would tell him.

His wife and his friends tried to keep from him the scandal that was on every tongue in the new land, and Sam knew they were trying to shield him from the blow. He knew his sister loved Tishomingo, but would believe no ill of her. He talked his problem over with Thomas and the lawyer said, "Your sister's above reproach. Flournoy is an insanely jealous man. Think naught of it."

Donna told him the same thing. However, he finally went to Honoria.

"I've waited a long time," he said, "to talk to you of this thing. We've always been very close, Honoria. What is Tishomingo to you?"

"I love him," she said. "I've always loved him and always will, but I will not violate my marriage oath."

"Does Tishomingo know you love him?"

"I think he does," said Honoria. "But he loves you, Sam'l. And I love you. He'll do naught to hurt you and neither will I."

"Tishomingo hates Flournoy more than he loves me. Nothing would suit him better than to take the wife of

570

Lake Flournoy, even though she be my sister. He's an Indian, Honoria, and he does not think as we think."

"He's only half Indian, and even though I were weak enough to surrender, the English in him would cause him to respect my marriage and your friendship. I know there's talk. I'm used to talk, Sam'l. There was talk when I was a bound 'un in Georgia. My husband, I believe, no longer loves me. Of that I am glad, for I no longer love him. I really never did. But I've entered an agreement and I'll stick to it. We're both that way."

Sam was satisfied. Even if Tishomingo, or Donna, or anybody, had told him then that Honoria was lying he would not have believed them. She couldn't lie to him. They were old man Dabney's brats and they understood each other. Why should she lie to him, he thought. She knew he wouldn't condemn her, but would try to help her. He didn't condemn people for their weaknesses. People only lied when it was necessary and Honoria knew it wasn't necessary to lie to him.

Sam spent much time in the hamlet of Washington, the new capital of the territory. It was only a few miles from Natchez. Federal authorities had protested when Mississippi had named its capital Washington. It would be confused with the national capital. But Mississippi ignored the protest, and the people were determined to name the new land Washington when it became a state.

Sam was signing contracts with the planters when Thomas rode out with news that Robert Fulton's steamboat, the *Clermont*, had traveled up the Hudson from New York to Albany in thirty-two hours. One of Sam's riders had brought the intelligence down the Trace to Natchez and Thomas had ridden his horse into a lather to get the news to his friend. He was dumfounded at

Sam's reaction, for Dabney was calm when he heard the news.

"Great God!" muttered Thomas. "Do you know what this means?"

"Ay," Sam laughed. "That it takes thirty-two hours to travel in a boat between New York and Albany on a river that has a tide. And I know what you're thinking. That Fulton can put a steamboat on the Mississippi and ruin me. Have a drink, Thomas. You're excited."

The lawyer spluttered and ordered a drink. Sam said, "Use your head. It took that boat thirty-two hours to travel up the Hudson River with the tide in its favor some of the way. It cost a fortune to run the boat up there. There's lots of difference between the Mississippi and the Hudson. It would take weeks to run a steamboat upstream on the Mississippi and all the money in the world to pay for it. I can put goods into Nashville from New Orleans before a damned steamboat can clear Natchez. There's nothing to worry about there. It will take years to develop this thing; you and I will never live to see the day when man can haul goods upstream in a steamboat."

"I hope you're right," said Thomas doubtfully. "But why take a chance? You remember what the cotton gin did for this country. I told you what would happen and it did. All right, you pig-headed Irishman, these boats will be down here soon. Damme, Sam, this is a great thing. This will sew the United States together. Go easy on that cotton plan of yours. Put a little money in this steamboat business. Let me go to New York and see this man. Maybe we can get him down here to build a boat. Get in on the ground floor. Then you're safe."

"You're a loony. I won't put a dime in it. I made thirty thousand dollars last year on my wagon trains.

I'll make half a million on my cotton plans. I'm not worrying about steamboats. A steamboat on the Mississippi? Bucking that current to Louisville? It would take a thousand men between New Orleans and Louisville just to keep it in wood. Now forget it."

But Thomas couldn't forget it. Every merchant and planter in the new land laughed at him. That is, all except one. Lake Flournoy left *Maison Blanche* after announcing he was going to Louisville on business. He didn't stop in Louisville, however, but went on to Pittsburgh and there made arrangements for the building of a steamboat to operate on the Mississippi. He put up thirty-eight thousand dollars and promised that his slaves would stack wood along the river and load it on the new boat. He swore his associate to secrecy and no man in the new land knew that a keel had been laid and that a Watt and Boulton engine had been ordered from England. The engine was sent to New Orleans and one of Sam Dabney's wagon trains hauled it over the Trace. It took twelve mules to haul the engine. Sam's company charged double for the haul. Sam thought the engine was to be used in a saw-mill.

All summer Sam worked distributing contracts. He went to the planters' homes and bought their cotton as it stood in the fields, signing on the dotted line for delivery in the fall and for payment within ninety days. He paid as high as a cent a pound above the prevailing market in some cases. Frome sent word that he had tied up more than thirty percent of the Georgia cotton.

The English agents were in Boston. Frome and Sam sent them word that they would supply England all the cotton that England wanted, but that title must be taken in Savannah and New Orleans. Sam and Frome were taking no chances with Napoleon's Berlin decree, which sought to blockade England. Neither were they taking chances with England's Orders in Council which forbade neutrals to trade with France. England must come and get the cotton, pay for it cash on the barrel head, and take it away in her own ships.

It was late in October when Frome rode from Georgia to Mississippi to see Sam. There were lines about his face and his voice quavered when he spoke.

"Let's unload, Sam'l. My fortune is tied up in this cotton. We can sell now for a good price and pay off our contracts."

"Not I," said Sam grimly. "We can hold England up. Already I've been offered more than twenty cents a pound for my cotton. I'll demand thirty."

"But, man, haven't you heard?" Frome said. "This nation is on the brink of war with England. They're impressing our seamen and everybody in Tidewater is screaming for war."

"I've heard such prittle-prattle," Sam admitted, "but there'll be no war as long as Jefferson's our president. He'll let England and France cut each other's throats and we'll reap the rewards—West Florida, Canada, Mexico."

"But I don't like it," Frome persisted. "I'm selling."

"Then sell and be damned!" Sam roared. "I'm holding my cotton."

Sam stacked his cotton on the New Orleans wharves until the bales towered almost as high as the masts of the ships that were docked in the free port. Every dime he owned was in his cotton. He plunged recklessly, buying all day and drinking at night with the planters who swarmed around him, toasting him and flattering him.

Sam and Thomas were drinking the finest brandy in New Orleans when one of his riders brought the news. Congress had passed Jefferson's embargo! It prohibited

574

the departure for a foreign port of any merchant ship, except foreign vessels in ballast.

Sam stared at the rider. He had never believed the Embargo Act would be passed. He looked from one face to another and tossed his great head to clear it. The import of the news sank slowly into his brain. Nobody spoke. Sam thought first of Donna and Hoab. He stared at the floor for several seconds and his broad shoulders sagged. He straightened them and said slowly to Thomas, "I'm wiped out, Hosey!"

Thomas offered him a cigar and called for more drinks. The planters filed out, one by one, and Thomas put his hand on Sam's arm. "You're right back where you were when you came to the new land. You can't move that cotton. England can't buy it. And you've got about three weeks to pay your contracts."

Sam did not reply. Thomas watched him and tears came to his eyes. Sam seemed to grow old as he stood there. For the first time, Thomas noticed the gray hairs around his friend's temple. He noticed that Sam's eyes were tired. The thing that Thomas had feared had happened. Sam was a man who could scheme successfully for nine times running, but the tenth time . . . And this was the tenth time.

Sam looked into his empty brandy glass, then hurled it to the floor. "Pay for the drinks, Hosey. I was using my credit here and my credit has gone to hell!"

Sam got drunk that night. Perhaps if he hadn't got drunk he would never had gone to Lake Flournoy for the money he needed. He could have got the money from Frome if he hadn't been so proud. But he stayed drunk for weeks. He wouldn't listen to Donna or to Thomas or to Tishomingo. He went to Flournoy and borrowed enough money to pay for the cotton. He sold the cotton to New England and realized only about twenty cents on the dollar. He didn't curse Jefferson as most traders were doing. He didn't curse anybody except himself.

He would make it back. The Embargo might be a blessing. It would stimulate trade between the states and his wagon trains would still haul the business. He mortgaged Locha Poka to Flournoy.

"You needn't worry about payment of this mortgage," said Flournoy. "Your word is good. I'm taking a mortgage on your land and your slaves only because it is business. But there's something I must ask you to do."

"What is that?" asked Sam.

"Deliver to me at once those two slaves, Sukey and Dabby."

Sam could not argue. "You vow you'll not sell them to the Creeks?"

"It is a vow," said Flournoy.

"If you do," said Sam, "there will be trouble between you and me."

"I have vowed. I want those slaves for myself. They'll be part of the interest I'll charge you for the money. Now buck up and let's have a drink together!"

Sam drank himself into a stupor. Honoria could do nothing with him. Eventually, however, she smuggled word to Tishomingo and Chock came to *Maison Blanche* and got his friend and took him back to Locha Poka.

Donna did not scold Sam. "You have done what you thought best," she said gently.

He buried his face in her breast and sobbed for the first time in his life. "I'll make it back," he promised. "My wagon trains will make it back for me. I'll buy Sukey and Dabby back. I don't want to see them. I can't stand to tell them I have sold them. Jasper must tell them."

"No, Sam'l. You must do it."

Neither Sukey nor Dabby said a word when Sam told them that they now were Lake Flournoy's property. Dabby, sleek as an otter, went to her master and bowed her head. Sam patted her head and Dabby's heart rejoiced. It was a good omen if a master patted a slave's head. She looked up at Sam and smiled wanly. It hurt her to see her master unhappy. Sam tried to smile back at her. He loved Dabby and Jasper more than any other slaves he owned. Dabby was an alluring creature, trim and proud.

Sukey walked back to her cabin where Jasper awaited her. He helped her pack her few belongings—things that Donna had given her. She kissed the son that she had borne Jasper.

"Jasper'll take care of him," the Negro said. "Massa Sam and Jasper'll see that he grows up fittin'. Massa Sam is all upset. Don't you cry when you go away. It won't do you no good and it might make Massa Sam sad."

Dabby went to the big house to tell Donna and Hoab goodbye. Sam wouldn't see his son but hid himself in his study. He stayed there for hours until he knew that Sukey and Dabby were gone, but when he came out Hoab was waiting in the drawing room.

Sam did not look directly at Hoab. "I'll buy them back, son," he promised. "In a year or so I'll have them back. My wagon trains will buy them back."

Sam was too drunk the next day to understand what Thomas was talking about when the lawyer rode out with the news that a steamboat had been run successfully on the Ohio.

27

✶ ✶ ✶ ✶ ✶ ✶ ✶ ✶ ✶ ✶ ✶ ✶ ✶ ✶ ✶ ✶ ✶ ✶ ✶ ✶

HONORIA was bitter toward her brother because he had allowed himself to get into her husband's debt. It gave Flournoy a weapon he could use against her. He never missed an opportunity to remind her that Sam's well-being depended upon his generosity. It pleased his vanity to have his brother-in-law in debt to him. He didn't need the money and it would have served no purpose to have taken Sam's land. It was better to keep Sam in his debt.

Debt was sheer agony to Sam, and the fact that Flournoy never bothered him about the money only galled him the more. His pride and egotism were smashed by Flournoy's display of generosity. It was as though Flournoy were always saying, "I could ruin you if I wanted to, but I won't; I'll never let you forget, though, that you're my debtor."

It pleased Flournoy to tell his wife that her brother would have lost his home but for him. And Honoria blamed Sam. He should have gone to Frome. He should have sold his land and paid out. He should have done anything except borrow from her husband. Had he no feelings for her? He should have known that Flournoy would ridicule her.

Her bitterness toward Sam grew until it licked at the border line of hatred. Sam always had resembled their mother in some ways. He, too, was mealy-mouthed. He

578

had fallen in love with the first woman who had flattered his vanity. He was a fool. . . . The words turned over and over in her mind. He had failed. She had no confidence in him. Ay, but she had confidence in herself. She didn't need Sam. She didn't need anybody, except Tishomingo, and even he was weak in many ways. She would strike out alone. Her position was unassailable. She had wealth and prestige and she would keep it and would add Tishomingo to her possessions.

Only her husband saw through her and he seemed always to be laughing at her. Her hatred for Flournoy grew into a flame that obsessed her, but she would not leave him. It was something to be the wife of the richest man in the new land. She had paid dearly for the privilege and she would not surrender her position.

She wished Tishomingo would kill him, even though it would mean that her lover would have to flee his home or suffer death. Or would it? As Flournoy's widow she would have influence. Perhaps she would be able to save Tishomingo from the wrath of the law. She could have her husband's money and Tishomingo, too. However, she dared not suggest anything to Tishomingo. He was not a man to listen to the ideas of a scheming woman. But she would find a way.

Sometimes, as she lay awake at night, she tried to visualize the torture that Tishomingo would administer to her husband. She hoped Tishomingo would slap him first. The insult would bruise Flournoy's pride. Then Tishomingo must spit at him and kick him and scratch him. Then he must nick his ear with the tip of his whip, then slit his skin . . . peel his skin . . . cut his skin to bleeding ribbons. Sweat poured from her body as she thought about it and her breath came in gasps. She wanted Flournoy to cry out, to beg and scream for mercy. But he wouldn't. She knew he wouldn't. She knew what he would do. He would clamp his lips and stare into Tishomingo's eyes. A hundred times she lived the scene; then she always called a slave and had herself sponged and perfumed with lily of the valley. It drove away the smell of sweat. She hated sweat. Old man Dabney's brat hated sweat.

Lake Flournoy had told Sam the truth about Dabby and he made no effort to sell the girl and her mother to the Creeks. He bred Sukey to his best buck and cast around for a good mate for Dabby. The girl was coming in fresh, and was as sleek and trim as a pine sapling. She must be bred to a Krooman. The cross would be perfect—Creek, Gullah and Krooman. Flournoy's stock needed new blood and Dabby would furnish it.

Donna had taken much time with Dabby's training, and Honoria, at her husband's insistence, continued the education. She was instructing the slave to walk gracefully while serving guests, when an idea came to her. She couldn't help but admire Dabby's animal beauty. The girl walked on the balls of her feet as her Indian father had done. Honoria balanced a tray on Dabby's head and had her walk time and again across the dining-room floor. She taught her to hold her head high and to keep her shoulders back. She took off the girl's coarse dress and made her wear good calicut. Honoria actually was envious of Dabby's slender waist and high breasts.

Dabby was the most grateful slave she had ever seen. A woman in body but a child in spirit, she was the pet of the plantation. She was proud of her Creek blood and yet unashamed of her negro mother. She smiled often and her flashing teeth were like ivory set between her thin red lips. Her skin was light brown and smooth. She often sang snatches of Indian love songs, but sometimes when the weather was sultry and the moon was gone, she chanted the voodoo songs of the Gullahs.

Honoria told her husband that Dabby's training was progressing satisfactorily.

"You do well with slaves, my dear," Flournoy said pointedly.

"Thank you."

"You do very well for a girl who was reared without slaves and who was bound out as a child."

"You do very well with slaves, too," Honoria smiled at him. "Particularly with female slaves. Is that the reason you bought Dabby—so you could call her to your bed when you wearied of me?"

Flournoy had never thought of it, but the taunt enraged him. "You mean when my wife wearies of me," he said. "Thank you for the suggestion, my dear."

"You wouldn't dare," snapped Honoria. "My brother would kill you."

Flournoy laughed. "That's what Tishomingo said, but I'm still alive. Very much alive, in fact."

"But my brother isn't Tishomingo. If you insult me by taking up with a slave, he'll avenge me. You know it. That's why you haven't taken this girl before. I can see through you, Lake."

Honoria meant it as a dare and Flournoy took it as such.

She had scorned him and made him small in the eyes of his friends, but he couldn't divorce her without proof of her transgressions. He had not been able to trap her with Tishomingo and the defeat etched hatred in his heart. She hadn't seen Tishomingo for a long time. He knew that. Tishomingo had been away, to the Cherokees and to the Shawnees, attending to business for his uncle.

581

Tecumseh had organized his war party and the Shawnees had proclaimed a holy war. There was a report that Tecumseh was coming to the Southwest to plead with the great Indian nations there to join his confederation. Ay, Tecumseh was ready to strike. The signs were right. The United States and England were growling at each other and war was inevitable.

Flournoy was well aware of every move Tecumseh made, for he was a leader in the band of schemers who were stirring the Shawnees to arms against the United States. He was doing his duty to France. If he and the French party in America could convince the populace that England was supplying arms to the Shawnees, then the thin cord that bound Britain and America to peace could be broken. The West did not want to fight England. It would stand for almost anything. Let England impress sailors. Nobody in the West cared about sailors. But if England dared arm the Indians and set them on the settlers, then the West would fight. Flournoy had done his work well, as usual. He had acted not only as agent for the Indians but as agent for the stupid and blind British of the Northwest, and because of his efforts Tecumseh's war party carried British arms and he was able to tell the white men that England had launched an Indian war against the West. Josephine and Napoleon were proud of him.

In all the new land, there were only two men who could prevent the Choctaws from following Tecumseh. They were Pushmataha and Tishomingo. The time had come for Tishomingo to perform his great mission in life. He must, by any ruse, forestall a union of his nation with the Shawnees. He knew it would be suicide for the Choctaws. And because he was half English, the Indians listened to him when he told them that Tecumseh and the British were trying to trap them and lead them into certain defeat.

So Flournoy knew that his wife had not seen Tishomingo, for the mingo had been about his uncle's business. But he also knew that when Tishomingo came home Honoria would go to him and there was nothing he could do to prevent it.

Ay, she had made him ridiculous in the eyes of the world. He would pay her back in equal part. He would strike at her vanity. And, too, Dabby was luscious. Damme, he hadn't noticed her before. He had been too busy with his own affairs.

He had grown in wealth and power until his name carried influence even in Washington City. It was he who had arranged the sale of Choctaw lands in the United States. He had outwitted Tishomingo and Pushmataha on the deal. Pushmataha had advised against the sale, but at Flournoy's suggestion the white agents told the Choctaws that the sale would be evidence of their desire for peace and friendship.

"You talk much of friendship and peace," the white agents said, "but we want a sign. Sell us this land to prove that you mean what you say."

Jefferson's Embargo had ruined many men, but Flournoy had prospered. The Embargo had closed legal trade in fine wine and silks, so Flournoy smuggled them in, and a bottle of French wine became a badge of honor. Possession of such wine proved that a man could outwit the government, and a man who could outwit the government was honored. The law became a thing to break. Flournoy's agents often concealed their silks and small bottles in their boots and the people called them "bootleggers."

Flournoy was sorry when the Embargo was repealed.

Jefferson had tried every way he knew to make it a success. Even rowboats had been made subject to the law, and collectors of the ports had been given despotic powers over every ship that sailed. But the people scorned the laws and, with an election coming up, Jefferson gave in to the demands of public opinion and the Embargo Act was superseded by the Non-Intercourse Law. James Madison was elected president and a war party grew in power.

Flournoy used every ounce of his influence to line up the United States against England. The nation had almost as much cause for war against France as against England, but Napoleon was a better liar than the English and as Lawyer Thomas said, "That's going some, because neither side would recognize the truth if they met it in the road."

Sam was a leader of the war party in the Southwest. Anti-British, as always, he thought that the nation needed a war to offset the economic disasters of the Embargo. He realized that if the United States were to be consistent, it must fight France and England, for both nations had laughed at America's claim for freedom of the seas. The United States had nothing to gain from France, but by fighting England the country could snatch Canada from the British, and Mexico, Florida and Cuba from the Spanish. Spain was between hell and high water, for whichever way the United States jumped, his Catholic majesty was bound to suffer. Every man knew that once the United States took up arms, the people would grab all the Spanish land in sight, and that only the strength of England could save Spain one acre of land in the New World.

Flournoy flattered himself that he was responsible for Sam's anti-British opinions. He thought he held Sam in the palm of his hand, but he had misjudged his brother-in-law again.

Quietly, but with determination, Sam had begun to recoup his fortune and his prestige. For the first time in his life he took his wife's advice. It was Donna who had shown him the way out.

"The first thing to do," she counseled, "is to keep your mouth shut. Tell no man your business. Believe in the land. The land is good and the land will save you. Forget your pride. Forget that men will call you a failure or that they will laugh behind your back and say that you are old man Dabney's brat. No man should be ashamed of his birth."

Sam knew that it would take him years to get out of the hole into which his stupidity had plunged him and that Donna could not live to see his triumph. She knew it too.

"I know what you're thinking, Sam'l," she would say. "You're thinking, what's the use of trying to rebuild your dreams when I'll not be here to share them. Only a weak man would think so. There's always Hoab, but above all there's always Sam Dabney who is entitled to happiness."

Sam sold his wagon trains for a fair price before the first steamboat came down to New Orleans and doomed wagon travel along the Mississippi. Flournoy, as holder of mortgage against the trains, had given his consent to the deal. With the money he made, Sam lifted the mortgage on many of his slaves and sold them, applying the money on his debt.

He devoted much of his time to the land company's business and brought in settlers from as far away as Virginia and Kentucky. He made a special trip to Kentucky to line up prospects, and on one trip brought to Mississippi a poor family that he had found in a log cabin. The head of the family was not of much account but Sam had hopes that the settlers would be an asset to the new land. He especially had hopes for the baby, a boy named Jefferson Davis. So Sam brought them down the river, sold them their land and collected his commission. He argued all day with another family that lived in a log cabin about a hundred miles from the Davises. The head of that family was not of much account either, but the son, Abraham Lincoln, might make a good man. Old man Lincoln talked favorably of moving to Mississippi, but his wife wanted to go to the new land in the Northwest.

Sam took his commissions from the company in land. As much as he needed cash, he wanted land more. He acquired more than three thousand acres from the land company in payment for his work and mortgaged the land to Flournoy, thereby freeing much of his original grant from debt. But Locha Poka was still mortgaged.

Donna urged him to sell his five-thousand-dollar claim on the land in West Florida, but he refused. He had faith in the Kemper boys and was with them when they organized another filibuster in the Baton Rouge district.

The Kempers and Sam and about one hundred Americans crossed the boundary into Spanish territory and marched on the fort at Baton Rouge.

They had picked their time well. The Spanish commander was absent, and the fort was in charge of Lieutenant Grandpré, a mere youth who had only thirty men under his command.

The filibusterers commanded him to surrender but the boy drew his sword and stepped in front of his men.

"This fort is the property of the king of Spain and I will not surrender it without orders."

The lieutenant's bravery thrilled Sam. One of the Americans leveled his musket. Sam leaped to knock the musket down but he was too late and the lieutenant's head was blown from his shoulders. Cheering wildly over their exploit, the Americans poured into the fort and dragged down the Spanish banner. In its place they ran up the lone-star flag and proclaimed the independence of the commonwealth of West Florida. Fulwar Skipwith was elected president and a declaration of independence was drawn and signed.

It was Sam who pleaded with the leaders of the new nation to apply for membership in the union of the United States.

It was done. The United States hesitated to accept and then, defying the wrath of Spain, proclaimed West Florida to be a part of the Territory of Orleans.

But the Spaniards still held Mobile and Reuben Kemper recruited a force and attempted to subdue the city. The Americans got drunk, however, and the Spaniards dispersed the little army in a battle ten miles north of Mobile. The Americans also attempted again to wrest Texas from Spain and again were unsuccessful. Sam had a hand in all of it. He lent his prestige to the invasion of Texas and the attempted invasion of Mobile, and he lent his long rifle-gun to the revolution of West Florida, and his dream of seeing the Mississippi Gulf Coast as a part of the Mississippi Territory was realized.

The land he got for his part in the revolution was put under mortgage and he used the money further to retire his debts. By watching his pennies, he was able to reduce his indebtedness until Flournoy held only a mortgage on two thousand acres of land and on the buildings.

Flournoy had smiled at Sam's efforts. He thought he knew his brother-in-law. He thought Sam would stint himself to be free of debt and then plunge wildly into some flimsy speculation. He could trust his brother-in-law to do reckless things. Nay, Sam Dabney would never again be an adversary of Lake Flournoy. There were only two men that Flournoy must watch—Tishomingo and Lawyer Thomas.

Yes, he had been so busy with his own affairs that he hadn't noticed Dabby and now his wife was daring him to lay with the slave. It would be fitting punishment for his wife. Dabney would not dare avenge her. The Choctaw law protected him from Tishomingo and the white man's law would protect him from Dabney. Should Dabney attack him, the law would believe that Sam's debt was the cause of the assault. Flournoy smiled to himself as he thought about it. It was almost too good to be true. Even if Honoria went to her brother, Dabney would do naught and that would hurt her. Sam Dabney was no fool. And there would be Thomas to advise him. He knew what Thomas would say. He could almost hear him saying, "Don't be a loon, Sam'l; if your sister has been wronged let her divorce this man. If you kill Flournoy, you'll have to run away. You cannot run away and leave Donna. If you didn't run away, the law would hang you higher than Haman. Don't you see it, man? You're in debt to Flournoy. If he were killed, his money would go to your sister and your debt would be wiped out. No, you mustn't do anything. If your sister thinks no more of her honor than to live with this man, then you must not lose your head for her."

Honoria had thought on all of that, too. But she knew Sam. He wouldn't wait for Thomas. He wouldn't wait for any man. He would take his rifle-gun and his knife and kill Flournoy and think later. Then she would go to Thomas and Thomas could save him. No jury in Mississippi would hang a man because he had defended his sister's honor. She could marry Tishomingo and they could live in *Maison Blanche*. She would cancel her brother's debt. That would be her payment. She might even advance him money to get into a new business. Ay, she would give him an interest in Flournoy's steamboat. That was the thing.

She was well aware of the first night that Flournoy called Dabby to his room. Even if the bath slave had not reported the incident to her mistress, Honoria would have known. She would have known by the way Dabby looked at her the next morning, a frightened puzzled look. She would have known by the way the other slaves looked at her. Flournoy's actions gave him away, too. He was too proud of himself.

Honoria smiled at him over her breakfast coffee. "Did you sleep well?" she asked him.

"Ay, and did you sleep well?"

"Very well," she said. "I would like your leave, Lake, to visit my brother."

"It's quite all right for you to visit your brother, but have you any particular reason for doing so?"

"Donna is much worse."

"How did you know this? You haven't heard from Locha Poka. And, too, this is the first time I've ever known you to have any particular concern for Donna."

"Nevertheless, I want to see my brother. I'll leave next week."

"Are you sure it's your brother you want to see?" he asked softly. "Tishomingo has returned to the nation."

Honoria's voice was calm. "I hadn't heard of that. I hope he was successful."

"As a matter of fact, he was not. Tecumseh is certain to come to the Muscogees and the Muscogees will join him against the white man."

"The Choctaws, too?" asked Honoria.

"Yes, my dear, the Choctaws, too. You may be assured

that there soon will be war. The Choctaws and Creeks and Chickasaws will take up arms against the United States. The Indians will be vanquished. They'll be driven away, and because I have befriended the United States I'll have my choice of all the lands I want."

Honoria said, "It seems to me that you have an uncommon knowledge of these things. It could not be that my husband has added spying to his other accomplishments."

"Anything could be," Flournoy replied and smiled.

"I wonder what your life would be worth if I should report that you are aiding the cause of Tecumseh."

"You must not worry your head about my life," he said. "Nobody would believe you if you told such a story, because you're in love with Tishomingo."

"At least," said Honoria, "I've never betrayed my own people."

"Neither have I. I'm not an Indian. I'm a Frenchman."

Honoria said, "You may not have long to live, Lake. I suppose you realize that the only reason Tishomingo has spared you is because he wanted to be with his people to prevent them from fighting the United States. I know Tishomingo very well. When his task with his own people is done he'll turn to the task he relishes—the work of whipping you to death."

"Please allow me to worry about that. I know all about you and Tishomingo."

"You always were a wise man, Lake," Honoria mocked him. "Why don't you make that charge publicly and give my brother the pleasure of killing you?"

"I had thought about that, but frankly, my dear, I have no proof of what I know. You're a very crafty girl. Of course, being old man Dabney's brat, you're obviously well-trained in the art of living and loving in the bushes.

590

You've been most successful in concealing from me any proof of your very amusing but slightly nauseating affair with Tishomingo."

Honoria got slowly to her feet and curtsied. "You've not been successful in concealing your very nauseating affair with Dabby. I trust you feel at home with her. You should. I hope your presence isn't as revolting to her as it is to me." Then she laughed at him. Flournoy raised his hand to slap her but curtailed the impulse quickly. He was a proud man, literally too proud to slap his wife. It might leak out. The kinsman of Josephine must not slap his wife.

Before the month had passed every slave at Locha Poka knew that Dabby had taken her mistress' bed. The slaves spread the story. Some of them were even so bold as to treat Honoria haughtily. One day when Honoria called Sukey the slave took her time about answering the summons, and when Honoria scolded her, Sukey tossed her head and turned her back upon her mistress. No one blamed Flournoy. It was a man's privilege to lay with his slaves. The insult was on the man's wife. If she continued to live with her husband, she was scorned. Even the bath slave was amazed at Honoria's behavior and suggested that when Ta-lo-wah had been faced with the same problem she had gone away. Honoria would not go away, however. Let the slaves scorn her. Soon she would own them and she woud teach them a lesson in manners.

The day that Honoria left for Locha Poka, Flournoy sent word to Thomas concerning some business matters that affected Sam, knowing that the lawyer would go to Dabney for a conference and that he would be there when Honoria arrived.

His plan worked well. Thomas was with Sam in the drawing room when Honoria entered, her riding clothes rumpled and her cheeks flushed. She said "Oh!" when she saw Thomas, and suddenly her knees were weak. She had rehearsed her scene carefully. She would sweep into Sam's presence and announce dramatically that her husband had dishonored her. Then she would throw herself into her brother's arms and plead with him not to risk his own life by avenging her. She knew how Sam would react. He would not take time to think. She had gone over every detail of her act, but Thomas' presence upset her. He might see through her. He would restrain Sam. She forgot her lines when she saw Thomas and could merely say "Oh!"

Sam arose quickly and went to her and asked why she had come. "Is anything wrong?" he said sharply. A dread thought swept through his mind. Tishomingo and Honoria!

Honoria answered him. "Nothing is wrong. I came to see you." She tried to keep her eyes away from Thomas, but they would not obey her mind and when they looked at him he was staring at her, a quiet, knowing smile on his face. "I came to see Donna. I heard she was worse."

"No, she's about the same." Sam peered into her face but she avoided his gaze. She could feel Thomas' eyes on her. "Are you sure that there's nothing wrong with you, Hon?" Sam asked anxiously.

"There's nothing wrong." She said it quickly and hurried out of the room and up the stairs to see Donna.

Sam watched her and even continued to stare at Donna's door after Honoria had entered. He ran his fingers through his hair and frowned slightly. Then he faced Thomas. He wanted to confide in his friend, to beg advice. But that old fear haunted him—fear that men would think him weak if he asked help.

Thomas said slowly, "Some day, Sam'l, you're going to do what you want to do and ask advice of your friends."

"What do you mean?" Sam demanded harshly, surprised that Thomas had read his thoughts. He strode across the room and sat down and crossed his legs nervously. He tossed his head and uncrossed his legs and fidgeted, cocking his ear to hear any sound from Donna's room.

Thomas folded his hands across his belly, stared up at the ceiling and then eyed Sam. "Ay, you mule-headed bucko, you can't deceive me. There are many times when you want to talk to someone about your personal business but you never will. You'd rather let your own heart hurt. You're afraid men will think you weak. You fear that men will remember that you're old man Dabney's brat."

"You speak in riddles," Sam grumbled. "And now for this business. I don't understand why Flournoy sent you here."

Thomas had not understood either, but now he did. The message from Flournoy simply had asked him to call on Sam to arrange for interest payments on the loan. Flournoy must have known that Dabney always made his interest payments on time. So there was another reason, and now Thomas understood. It must be Tishomingo. Flournoy must have evidence against his wife. That was why she had hurried to Locha Poka. And she hadn't told Sam because he was there. Well, he would stay there as long as that dangerous minx was there. He wouldn't allow her to sweep her brother off his feet. Dabney was a fool about many things. But he was more than a fool about his sister. He was a stupid, addle-brained loon when it came to his sister. He would believe anything she said, Thomas thought. Or would he? Per-

593

haps Sam'l knew his sister better than anyone else. Well, he would take no chances. If there was to be any mischief, he would be there and ready to meet it.

Donna sensed trouble the minute she saw Honoria, and without ado demanded the reason for her unexpected visit.

"But there's nothing wrong, I tell you!" Honoria snapped. She scarcely glanced at Donna, but walked to a window and stared out, clenching her fists until her nails cut into her flesh. She knew Donna was watching her and she turned her head and flung her words over her shoulder. "Can't a sister visit her brother without causing such a commotion? I might have known that pot-bellied lawyer would be here!"

"You can't fool me." Donna sat up in bed. The effort tired her. A cough shook her frame and she held her hand over her mouth and closed her eyes as a dull pain spread through her body. When she opened her eyes, they were bright and challenging, and she pinned them upon Honoria. "Something has happened to you. I know it. And you've come running to Sam'l again. Can't you leave him alone? Can't we have a bit of peace? You have everything any woman would want. In God's name, can't you leave us alone?" A siege of coughing attacked her again, but she wouldn't lie down.

Honoria turned on her. "He's my brother. I have a right to come to him. He would have been all right if he hadn't married you!"

Donna laughed, a dry, crackling laugh. "Lily of the valley perfume will never hide the stench of your vileness. Hasn't Sam enough trouble without your adding to his burden? Has your husband caught up with you and Tishomingo?"

Honoria was too worried to be insulted. She dared not

594

tell Donna of Dabby. Donna would see through her, too. She couldn't fool Donna and Thomas. She couldn't fool Tishomingo or her own husband. She hadn't been able to fool Mrs. Frome or Anestasie. Sam was the only man she could fool. Everybody else knew her for what she was. Even Tishomingo.

She avoided Donna's eyes and tried to plot a course out of her dilemma. She knew well enough that if she waited very long to tell Sam her problem, her story would lose its sting. It was a thing she couldn't delay. A dishonored woman could not afford to think of expediency. Every moment that she waited was working against her. Perhaps she should return home and await a more opportune time.

She tried to be gay. She even helped in the sick room with Donna. She told Sam that she believed Donna was improving. She was determined to remain at Locha Poka for several days and then go back home and try again.

At the table that evening when Thomas told her brother than he would stay there several days to rest, she immediately approved his plans.

"It's nice of you to stay with my brother," she said. "It will cheer him up. I came here partly for the same reason, but if you are to remain here I'll return to my husband soon."

Thomas frowned at her. What was her game? Perhaps she was telling the truth.

She went to the drawing room with the men and saw to their drinks while they talked. Sam had his interest payment ready for Flournoy, so Thomas did not tell him of Flournoy's message. There were many business and political details to be discussed. The territory was clamoring for statehood. Its population had reached 42,000, including almost 20,000 slaves and about 200 negro free-men.

Sam and Thomas knew that war with England was inevitable. Both England and France impressed American seamen into their navies, but because England had the stronger navy her offenses were more numerous. All the old hatred for England which lingered in American minds from the days of the Revolution flared again.

England realized that the United States was rushing toward war with her. She was determined, nevertheless, to starve France, even if she had to fight the United States to do so. England's own people were suffering, however. Wheat was selling at almost four dollars a bushel and in London there was a cry that the Orders in Council be repealed to relieve a disastrous situation before the United States should be added to the enemies of England.

In the Southwest, it was not a question of *if* war would come, but only a question of *when*.

Honoria listened to their talk. She cared naught for the threat of war. Men would always fight wars. Wars were really rather exciting. She didn't understand much of the men's talk. Orders in Council, Non-Intercourse Act, impressments, peaceful coercion, the Chesapeake affair—re-fiddlesticks! It was too much for her. She wondered if she really could prove that her husband was betraying the Choctaws. They hanged traitors. She could understand that. But she very wisely kept her counsel and was sitting with the men and trying to appear interested when Tishomingo arrived.

The Choctaw wore the war dress of his nation, including two eagle feathers in his silver head band. One feather was white and the other was red. The white feather represented peace, the red feather war, and the fact that he wore both of them was evidence that his people had not decided between peace and war.

Sam got up quickly to welcome his friend and offered him a chair, but Tishomingo declined and stood very erect by the door to the drawing room. Honoria stared at him, hope and fear struggling for expression in her eyes. Tishomingo bowed slightly to her and to Thomas and said slowly, "Tecumseh has come. Before the moon wanes we'll know if there is to be war. We have need of you, Big Sam. You must go with me and my uncle to the war councils."

"What is this thing you say?" Sam asked. "Is there any danger of the Choctaws joining with Tecumseh?"

"There's much danger," said Tishomingo. "Tecumseh can perform magic with his words. He has proclaimed the holy war. We know that he is an envoy of England, but my nation may join his confederation."

Thomas lit a stogie and leaned back to hear all the evidence before expressing an opinion. Honoria sat very still, staring at the floor and thinking of her own problems.

"I can't go with you," Sam said. "I cannot leave my wife and my son and my land."

"If you love your wife, your son and your land you'll come with me. If the Choctaws join Tecumseh, they'll strike here first because they will be allies of the Creeks, and the Creeks hate you. For once in your life you must listen to the counsel of a friend. You must send your wife and son away."

"But my land! A war is coming. It's the thing I've been waiting for." He turned to Thomas and pointed his finger at his lawyer. "Mark my words, Thomas, I again will be master of the new land. War will mean that a large army must come to this land and I'll feed that army.

597

Locha Poka will become the bread-basket of Mississippi. I'll plant corn to my doorsteps. With my influence and your intelligence, we can get contracts to furnish this army with corn at our prices. It means a way out, Thomas!"

Thomas removed his stogie and spat upon Sam's rug. Then he rubbed the spittle with his boot and said, "If you will think of your own fortune before you think of the safety of your wife, then our association ends here and now, and I'll tell you that you are the God-damnedest rascal between the throne of England and the throne of hell."

Tishomingo put his hand on the stock of his bull whip. But the trouble he expected did not come. Sam smiled at Thomas and said, "And you'd be right. But I can protect my wife and son. I'll barricade this house."

"Hear me, please," pleaded Tishomingo. "Send your wife and child away and come with me. You have a duty to your nation, Big Sam. The Choctaws must not take up arms against you. Maybe we can prevent it. You'll have your war, for the Creeks surely will follow Tecumseh ——"

"Jim McQueen may be able to hold the Creeks in line too," said Sam.

"Jim McQueen is dead," Tishomingo replied solemnly.

"Great God Almighty!" Sam muttered.

Thomas whistled softly under his breath.

"Ay, he's gone." There was a cunning savage expression on Tishomingo's face again, and then it passed and his face was sad. "Jim McQueen was a good man. He died in his sleep. He died praying for peace between the red men and the white men. And the Creek chiefs already are fighting among themselves for power. The nation is torn by civil war. Tecumseh will be able to unite the nation against America. It's a sad day, my friends. The seeds have been sown and soon there'll be a harvest of hate."

Tishomingo's words echoed in the big room . . . against the suit of armor that Sam had bought and against his long rifle-gun. The men were silent for several seconds and then Sam said. "My wife may not be willing to leave her home."

"Your wife will do as you say," Tishomingo said. "She's an intelligent woman and intelligence often is at a premium in this house."

"But where can she go? She's sick. She couldn't survive a long stay in Natchez. She's too weak to travel to Georgia."

Thomas suggested, "We can send her down to old Sam Mims' place. Mims is a friend of mine. She'd be safe there."

"But Mims is an Indian," Sam said. "Can he be trusted?"

"Mims is an American. You remember he has held office in Washington County. You've been to his place."

Sam had. Mims' home was a mile from the Alabama River, several miles north of Mobile, and only a quarter of a mile from the Lake Tensaw boatyard. Mims was one of the richest men in the district and because he was an Indian, Thomas reasoned and Sam agreed, his property would be safe.

"It won't be a hard journey to Mims' place," Tishomingo added.

"I appreciate your advice," said Sam, "but this is a decision I'll make myself. You ask me to go with you to the councils. I'll go if you, as a mingo of the Choctaws, will send some of your men to Locha Poka to look after my interests. I'll keep most of my slaves here under

599

command of your men. They'll grow corn. Your nation will assume responsibility of my property. This is the price I'll charge your nation for attending your councils."

"It shall be done," promised Tishomingo. "My nation is willing to do anything to preserve the peace between your people and mine. Even if you're not willing to make a sacrifice, Big Sam, I am. You overlooked the fact that if my people join Tecumseh, you and your land will be destroyed anyway. I know and you should know that the United States will crumble before England and a confederation of Indians. But what you ask shall be done."

Sam excused himself and went to Donna's room to talk with her about the situation. He was not proud of himself for what he had done. He knew that Tishomingo had shown that he was a better Choctaw than he himself was an American. He had been bluffing in a way. Had there been no other way out of it, he would have forsaken Locha Poka. Of course he would send Donna to safety. Of course he would go to the councils. Of course he would do all he could to preserve the peace between his people and the Choctaws. But if in doing it he could drive a good bargain for himself, so much the better.

During the discussion Honoria had remained silent. She waited until she heard Sam close the door to his bedroom, then she glanced up at Tishomingo and he was looking at her. She could feel her thoughts going out to him. It was as though her heart was a book and Tishomingo read what he wanted to read and skipped over the pages he did not like.

They sat for several minutes in silence, Thomas watching Honoria as she twisted her handkerchief nervously. They could hear Sam talking to Donna, the mumble-mumble-mumble of his words. Every now and then his voice rose and they heard such words as "Sam Mims",

"Tecumseh", "corn for the army". Tishomingo, more to break the silence than for any other reason, said casually to Honoria, "I've seen your husband."

"Did you fight?" she asked quickly, hopefully.

"We did not fight. I called at *Maison Blanche* on business."

Honoria saw the opening and made the most of it. If Tishomingo had been to her home he must have heard the story of Dabby. Actually, Tishomingo knew nothing of the scandal, but Honoria suddenly saw a way out of her dilemma. She put her hands to her face as though to hide her blushes, but used the opportunity to rub her fingers in her eyes and make them red. The Choctaw was puzzled by her behavior, but Thomas only smiled. Something was going to happen and he would see it through.

She looked up at Tishomingo and, in a trembling voice, said, "Then you know. You know everything."

"I don't know what you're talking about," Tishomingo replied. "What's the matter with you?"

She jumped to her feet and ran to him. "You're having pity on me!" Her voice rose. She must speak so loudly that Sam would hear her upstairs. He *must* hear her. "I beg you, don't tell my brother!" Her voice was hysterical, a scream that carried as far as the slave quarters. "My brother mustn't know! He'd kill my husband!"

Tishomingo stepped back from her, bewilderment in his eyes. Had she gone mad? Thomas crossed his legs slowly, and calmly puffed his stogie, a cynical smile on his lips. By God, the woman was an actress!

Honoria heard Sam's door open quickly and heard his footsteps as he ran down the stairway. She bowed her head in her hands and her shoulders shook as she sobbed in mock anguish. "Don't tell my brother! Please . . ."

Sam strode into the room, his eyes blazing and his great fists clenched. He glanced at her, then at the two men. "Don't tell me what?" his voice boomed.

Honoria felt a chill sweep through her body. Sam was fighting mad. And she was afraid of him. She ran to him and put her head on his chest. Tishomingo and Thomas glanced at each other.

"Then you heard me, Sam'l?" She looked up at him, seeking pity in his face, but there was none there.

"Of course, I heard you," Sam snarled at her. "The dead must have heard you! You frightened Donna. Speak up, Honoria! Dammit, speak—or quit this damned nonsense!"

"But I didn't want to tell you!" She clung to him. "You have so many things to worry you."

Again Thomas and Tishomingo exchanged glances, and the lawyer smiled at the Indian. But Tishomingo was baffled.

"Enough of this slobbering!" Sam gripped her shoulders and shook her. "Out with it!"

Honoria's blood boiled and she wanted to slap him. Shake her, would he! But she forced herself to sob. "Tishomingo knows. Let him tell you. I'm ashamed to tell you."

Sam wheeled on Tishomingo, but the Indian shrugged his shoulders. "I know naught of the cause of this scene."

"But you do!" Honoria screamed and stamped her foot. "You said that you had seen my husband. You know that my husband has taken the slave Dabby to his bed! You won't say so because you fear Sam'l will kill my husband and rob you of that pleasure. I can't hide it any longer, Sam'l."

Sam's face drained slowly of color, and his lips parted as he took a deep breath. He buttoned his lips and his quick measured breathing was the only sound in the room. Tishomingo's face hardened, and then a doubt crossed his mind and he stared at Honoria, seeking to follow her reasoning. Thomas closed one eye and watched the drama. Sam's eyes caught Tishomingo's and he started to speak, to demand an explanation, but he changed his mind and towered over his sister.

"Is this true?" His voice was calmly ominous. "How long has it been going on?"

Honoria's tone also was smooth, almost a purr. Her eyes were no longer red. She dropped her mask. She could handle Sam now, as though he were tallow to be molded between her fingers. "I don't know how long it's been going on, Sam'l. I learned of it a month ago."

The muscles in Sam's neck suddenly grew taut and a look of disgust crept over his face. "A month ago!" He gripped her shoulders again. "Why didn't you tell me then? Have you lived in this man's house after learning this thing? Speak quickly, Honoria! And I want the truth!"

Honoria was speechless. Her heart sank. She had not expected her brother to reason so. Had Sam changed? He should have shouted for his horse! He should have ridden at once to kill Flournoy! Did he doubt her? Her mind framed a hundred questions before she found the answer. "I wanted to make sure," she blurted out. "I didn't want to accuse him falsely."

Thomas' eyes bulged and his mouth dropped open. God, what a woman! Quick as lightning in a crisis. Tishomingo was sick inside. He wished Sam would slap her. He wished he could slap her, slap her into a corner and leave her there whimpering. He hated her then. . . .

"Why didn't you tell me as soon as you arrived here?" Sam released her; he was sorry now he had shaken her.

"I wanted to," she said. She had felt a change come over Sam and she was confident again. "God knows I wanted to! But I didn't know how to tell you, Sam'l."

Thomas deliberately crossed his feet again, leaned back in the chair and rested his hands on his stomach. This thing had gone far enough. "Perhaps, Mrs. Flournoy," he drawled, "you didn't tell him before because I was here. In my business I meet many liars."

Honoria wheeled on him, ready to blister him with her tongue. Why didn't Sam strike him? Why didn't Tishomingo protect her? The Indian was watching the lawyer, trying to read his thoughts. However, there was no hate in Tishomingo's eyes. Sam took a deep breath again and stepped quickly in front of Thomas. "Careful, man," Sam said slowly. "Careful with your words."

Thomas' face did not change expression. "It's a lawyer's business to spot lies. She's lying. Make the most of it, Sam'l boy."

Sam hesitated and ran his hand over his forehead and looked from one to the other. Tishomingo turned his eyes from Thomas to Sam, folded his arms so his right hand was near his bull whip, and said, "Ay, your sister is lying."

Honoria's hand flew to her mouth and she stifled a scream. Sam threw his head back and glared at his friends. "Unless you can prove this charge, Chock, you'll answer to me—and you, too, Hosey."

"If you weren't blind," Tishomingo replied calmly, and his heart warmed under Thomas' friendly smile, "I'd not have to prove anything to you. Your sister said she learned a month ago. At that time Lake Flournoy was among the Shawnees. I saw him there."

"That's a lie!" Honoria cried desperately. She knew that she had been outwitted. She had expected Thomas to turn on her. But Tishomingo! The knowledge hurt her, but she felt sorry for herself for only a second. Then she was infuriated. "You're all against me! You ——"

No one had noticed Donna. Jasper was carrying her down the stairs in his arms. He brought her to the far side of the room and put her gently in a big chair. Honoria saw her first and gasped. Sam turned to rebuke Jasper for bringing her down but Donna spoke before he could open his mouth. "Thank you, Jasper. Now fetch me a pillow. One for my back and one to go under my feet." She arranged her dressing gown and ran her fingers through her thin, dry hair. "I didn't want to miss the performance," she said lightly. "I couldn't help but hear most of it."

Honoria fled from the room. Thomas looked admiringly at Donna. The tension in the room relaxed. Tishomingo leaned against the door. Jasper got drinks. Sam paced the floor for a minute. "I'm confused, Donna," he said. "I'm not ashamed to admit it."

"You shouldn't be confused. Your sister's all right. But she's getting older, Sam'l. She doesn't lie as well as she used to. A few years ago Honoria could have told a much better lie than that."

"Then you, too, think that she's lying?"

"I know she's lying. A dishonored woman would not have waited so long to tell her grievance."

"But why should she lie to me about such a matter?"

Donna did not look at Tishomingo. Neither did Thomas. "You had better ask her that, Sam'l," said Donna.

Sam left the room to find his sister. Donna waited until he was out of earshot and said, "Thank you, gentlemen. You've prevented my husband from doing a stupid thing. Perhaps we've been unfair to Honoria. I, for one, believe that she was telling the truth, but we've convinced my husband that she was lying. Lake Flournoy was not with the Shawnees a month ago, was he, Tishomingo?"

"Nay. He was at *Maison Blanche*. Honoria was telling the truth. I heard at *Maison Blanche* that Flournoy had freed Dabby and her mother. I thought nothing of it at the time because I was too worried about other matters."

"Why should he free her?" Donna said. "I can't believe that little Dabby loves him. If she's free, I wonder why she doesn't return to Locha Poka. Well, perhaps there's more to it than we know. Anyway, I'm grateful to you gentlemen. You're my husband's friends."

"That is so," said Thomas. "But he makes it rather difficult at times. We are your friends too."

Donna sipped the brandy that Jasper handed her. "Sam is blind about all matters concerning his sister. He wants to be blind. I believe he knows all about her. I'm convinced he knows of her affair with you, Tishomingo."

For one of the few times in his life the mingo bowed his head and was ashamed.

"I, too, now believe that Sam'l knows the truth," Thomas said. "I think I understand a side of Dabney I hadn't seen before."

"And what is that?" asked Tishomingo. "I know the man. If he knew what you know he would try to kill me."

"That's why he acts as though he is ignorant of a thing he knows," Thomas said. "He's your friend. He doesn't want to harm you. So long as the world thinks he is ignorant of his sister's behavior and the behavior of his best friend, he'll not have to avenge her. It's the easiest way out for him. It's very clear to me now. It is not a question of courage. If he admitted knowing the thing that we know, he'd have to fight you to save

606

his sister's honor and his own. So he elects to believe his sister. And she, without doubt, has sworn to him that the gossip of the frontier is that and nothing more."

Donna said, "He has never mentioned it to me. He has a strange loyalty toward his sister."

She paused to get her breath, and Thomas said, "I, too, believe that she's telling the truth about her husband taking up with this slave. But there's something behind it that I don't understand. I'll find out. In the meantime I could not afford to let Sam do anything silly. It would be suicide for him. That's why I accused his sister of lying."

"I lied about Flournoy for my own reasons," said Tishomingo. "I'm convinced he's guilty of this thing, but I'll never admit it to Big Sam. And now I know why Flournoy has freed Dabby."

"Ay?" Thomas arched his eyebrows. "And why?"

"Because she's with child. I'll wager that I'm right. Flournoy for all of his fine airs is still an Indian. An Indian will not allow his child to be born in bondage if he can prevent it."

Thomas turned his head away and muttered, "Damme! Then Sam'l will know and horses can't hold him."

"Flournoy won't be alive when the child is born," said Tishomingo evenly. "Big Sam won't have to avenge his sister."

In Honoria's room, Sam sat by his sister and they both were silent for a long time. He felt sorry for her suddenly and she could feel his sympathy. Finally he took her hand in his and said, "What is it, Hon? It matters not if you have lied. You and I made a pledge once and if you're in trouble I'll fight for you."

She kissed him full on the mouth and put her head on

607

his shoulder and sobbed. And this time there was no make-believe. She could never convince Sam that her husband had degraded her. He must find it out for himself. And when he found it out he would condemn himself for doubting her and would do anything to repay the wrong he had done her. Sam would believe her now if she told him what he wanted to hear. If she blamed herself he would believe her. "I lied to you, Sam'l," she said. "I came here to lie to you. I had thought it all out. I hate Lake Flournoy. I wanted to see him dead. If he were dead I'd inherit his property and you and I could do the things we've always dreamed of doing. I waited a long time for Tishomingo to kill him ——"

"There's a thing I must ask you now."

"About Tishomingo. I know what you're going to ask. I have not lied to you about that. I love Tishomingo but I have never violated my vows. I've been to see him, yes. I had hoped that I could persuade him to kill Flournoy. But Tishomingo loves his nation more than he hates Flournoy. I grew tired of waiting for him to make me a widow. So I lied to you, hoping you would do it. I knew the law would not molest you."

"I believe you," said Sam simply. "You must not go back to *Maison Blanche*. I'll send you away to safety."

"I'm going back to *Maison Blanche*."

"And live with the man you despise?"

"If I desert my husband he can divorce me."

"Is your honor not worth more than property?"

"I'll not surrender so easily what I've fought so hard to get."

Sam was stunned. He spoke deliberately. "I forbid you to return."

"Don't be a loon, Sam'l. Lake Flournoy can crush you.

608

He won't dare as long as 1 m his wife. I'll go back so 1 can be of help to you."

"I wish I could believe that. But there's no need for you to go back to help me. Flournoy can't crush me. I have a feeling that Flournoy will not live long. Tecumseh has come. There's something Tishomingo must do for his people and when he has done it he'll collect the debt that is long overdue."

"Then I know I'll go back," Honoria said. "I've suffered as Lake Flournoy's wife, but I'll enjoy being his widow. There's no need for me to try to deceive you. With my husband's wealth, perhaps I can save the man I love. I'm sure I can win him."

Sam said gently, "It's in my mind to tell you that if you go back to the home of this man—that if you go back to the bed of any man you hate as you do your husband—then you're a harlot. My mind tells me that. My mind tells me that if you go back I should forbid you my home and even the sight of your own child. But my heart will not let me say it. You're old man Dabney's brat, Honoria. Honor is a relative thing to you. You've set your hand to a plow and you'll not turn back. Come on, let us go back to the drawing room."

"I cannot face them," said Honoria. "I'm ashamed."

"You? Ashamed? You're ashamed only because your scheme failed. We'll go back down there and act as though nothing has happened. It's the only way."

Thomas got up and offered his seat to Honoria. Jasper fetched her a drink. Even Tishomingo took a chair and accepted the black drink. Donna said, "It's good to sit here for a while. What's the news of Natchez, Honoria?"

"I've had no news of Natchez in a long time," Honoria said. "It is good to see you sitting up, Donna. But you mustn't tire yourself. I'll see you to your room."

"My husband can carry me back to my room. Good night, Honoria. Tomorrow Hoab and I are going to Sam Mims' home. Lift me up, Sam'l, and take me to my bed."

Honoria, ignoring Thomas' presence, turned on Tishomingo when Sam and Donna were gone. "Why did you lie?"

"I won't allow you to rob me of my revenge."

"Why did *you* lie?" she demanded of Thomas.

"I won't see your brother make a fool of himself again," Thomas replied. "And as for you, Tishomingo, I want to congratulate you. You're a better man than I thought. You're a friend of Sam Dabney's. You showed it tonight. I'm not one to condemn a man and a woman because they fall in love."

Tishomingo started to speak but sealed his lips quickly, and Thomas continued, "You two are not deceiving anybody and you're in my debt. I could furnish Lake Flournoy with enough evidence to have the Choctaws kill both of you. He would give me half of his property for this evidence."

Tishomingo ignored the remark but Honoria said, "Why don't you? You hate me."

"Why should I?" Thomas asked. "Dabney has enough troubles without my adding to them. And, besides, Mrs. Flournoy, you and I are going to trade. Anestasie Duportail is sane. She was loony for a while. She even had a crazy idea that you were responsible for her troubles. But she very wisely has forgotten that. I'm sure she'll never think of it again. She's changed. She has become gentle and her hair is prematurely gray, but beautiful. She's a regal woman. You and your husband are responsible for her commitment. You and your husband will sign a paper requesting that she be given a sanity hearing."

610

Honoria's tongue clung to the roof of her mouth for a minute and then she said, "But she might go insane again and accuse me."

"She's too sane for that. She knows that if she ever gets out and accuses you of so absurd a thing she'll be sent back. You'll do this thing for me?"

Honoria felt Tishomingo's look. How much did he know? "Of course I'll do it," said Honoria. Her word meant nothing. She easily could say later that her husband had refused to sign the paper. For the time being she would promise anything to escape Thomas' piercing little eyes.

"That's fine," Thomas said. "I'll return to *Maison Blanche* with you."

Was there no avoiding the man? "I'll do all I can," she evaded. "But I can't promise for my husband."

"Your husband will sign, too. He wouldn't want me to make a public charge that he connived to keep a sane woman in the madhouse, particularly in as much as he got control of her property because she was declared insane at his behest."

Honoria said, "You've taken a tender interest in Anestasie. Is it because she's a beautiful woman?"

"Partly so. However, there's a thing called justice even in this land and it sometimes salves my conscience to be an instrument of justice. It makes me feel better to be a knight errant, a Lancelot with a pot-belly. And, too, Anestasie is the rightful owner of the key parcel of land on the proposed Mississippi-Georgia route. That land must not fall into the wrong hands. As your brother's lawyer, I must see that that land is protected, because his old dream of a great road from the river to the sea will never come to pass if that land isn't available when he wants it. Mrs. Duportail is a very beautiful woman. I like

611

to help beautiful women. That is, most of them." He smiled a compliment at Honoria when he said it.

"It's a noble thing," Honoria smiled back at him. "I hope your fee is fitting. Anestasie should be able to pay a fee that would satisfy even you. Or have you collected your fee in advance?"

"This has gone far enough!" Tishomingo rebuked Honoria angrily. "You're insulting this man! He won't slap you. If he should insult you, you'd expect me to protect you. That's what you want. I wonder sometimes if you're worth protecting."

Thomas shook with mirth. "Ay, Chock, she's worth it." He got up and waddled across the room and slapped the Indian on the back. "She's a filly for you. Hot on the hoof. All she needs is a check rein and a damned good whalebone whip!"

Chock smiled, too. The little lawyer could always put him in a good humor. He threw his arm around Thomas' shoulder and whispered loudly enough for Honoria to hear him, "And a branding iron, too—eh, Hosey?"

Thomas looked up quickly. "Only my best friends call me 'Hosey'. And if all my friends were worth only a dime each, the whole damned bunch wouldn't be worth a dollar."

"I'm your friend," said Tishomingo earnestly.

"There's *prima facie* evidence of that."

"How disgusting," said Honoria spitefully. "Grown men acting like boys."

"*You* wouldn't understand friendship," Tishomingo snapped.

Thomas laughed. "I don't mind her words. Really, I'm going to do her a favor. While at *Maison Blanche* I'll talk to her husband about his will. I'd like to draw his will. And I think the time has come for the noble kinsman of the noble Josephine to prepare his will."

Honoria and Thomas started for *Maison Blanche* that night. She had only a few minutes to see Tishomingo alone. She held him tightly and kissed his face and his neck. "I should hate you, but I can't. Please ride part of the way with us. Thomas knows about us and he'll leave us to ourselves. Just you and I. It's been such a long time."

Tishomingo pushed her away roughly. "It's never too late for a man to repent. You're a vile creature. I hope I never see you again."

"But you will," she said with assurance. "Everyone in this household has turned on me today except my brother. Be that as it may, you'll see me again. You and I can no more live apart from each other than the moon and the stars. I know it now. I've worried about it for a long time, but now I know it. You love me, Tishomingo. You, too, are human and weak. And you're mine and I'll never give you up." She put her arms around him again and her breath was hot on his face. His senses spun and he pulled her to him and kissed her.

"There!" she whispered triumphantly. "I told you."

Tishomingo did not reply but walked into the house to arrange with Sam the details of the next day's journey that would take them into the Chickasaw land where Tecumseh, like John the Baptist of old, was preaching in the wilderness and calling all the sons of the Great Spirit to repent and unite to drive the white man from the Promised Land with a sword of flame. He was preaching a gospel that his brother, the Great Prophet—The Open Door—was the Indian messiah. He was preaching that his brother had had a revelation from the Great Spirit and that the time had come for a revolution among the chosen people of Aba Inki, the one God of the Muscogees. It was a new gospel for the Indians and they were flocking to the standards of Tecumseh by the thousands.

28

FLOURNOY gave Dabby a gold chain for her neck and
a pair of golden earrings. The earrings were shaped like
raindrops. They had been the property of Flournoy's
mother. Once he had thought of giving them to Honoria;
now he was glad that he hadn't.

Dabby wept when he gave her the presents but she
didn't kiss him. She never kissed him unless he kissed her
first. She was so grateful to Flournoy and so overwhelmed by his attentions that she often would sit
silently at his feet and only look at him. Sometimes she
caressed the fine fabrics of his clothes. She enjoyed
fetching his pipes and his brandy. It made her happy to
do little things for him. But once, when she got on her
knees to help him with his boots, he put his hands on
her shoulders and lifted her up.

"I know you like to comfort me, Dabby," he said,
"but I don't like to see you on your knees."

Dabby did not understand what he meant, but she
understood the tender look in his eyes. Lake Flournoy
was almost happy for the first time in his life. He had
found a woman who loved him for himself alone. True,
she was scarcely more than a child. But she was old in
other ways, old and wise. And to the French-Indian half-
breed the little Indian-Negro half-breed was beautiful.
She was beautiful to look at, small-boned, trim—her eyes

614

seeing all and showing nothing, her teeth white as the ivory of Africa and her bearing as straight and as proud as the red war poles of the Creeks. And she was beautiful inside, too. She never hurt anything or anybody. She was kind to the slaves, to the sheep that cropped the lawn. Flournoy was not ashamed to admit to himself that he loved her. The melting pot had produced two strange creatures and a great affinity had brought them together. Flournoy cared nothing for the wagging tongues of the new land. He was holding life tightly and extracting the last drop of happiness. What cared he if people sneered because the kinsman of Josephine had bedded with a former slave!

Napoleon's divorce from Josephine was history in Europe before it was news in the backwoods of Mississippi. The frontiersmen cared naught for the goings-on of the French court and were interested only in the wars of the French emperor. As Lawyer Thomas said some years later, "A good bitch in heat was important to us, but the divorce of a Corsican son of a bitch from a Martinique bitch was not particularly impressive at that time."

The birth of a slave was news in the new land. It was news when a cow came in fresh, when a deed was transferred, when a farm was bounded. It was good news when a man took a wife and when the wife bore a son, when a calf was slipped and when new land was broken. It was sad news when a man died, or when his children caught the pox, or when his oxen sickened and his horse went blind. Such things were news, but the romances of Napoleon were things the people might hear about and forget. Why should they bother their heads about the love life of a philandering emperor when their own romances and the romances of their neighbors were far more interesting?

The French were not lusty lovers anyway. Napoleon had been known to lay with Josephine in a carriage while dictating a letter to his secretary. God's navel! Using a carriage seat for such a purpose. With all the woods in the world, that silly bantam would not take time even to copulate properly. No wonder she had never borne him a son. How could he expect her to conceive a son on a carriage seat? If she did, the son probably would have hair like a horse.

Josephine could not write Flournoy that she had been cast aside for a younger woman, and perhaps a fertile one. Her mail was watched but Flournoy got the intelligence from Martinique and his wrath knew no bounds. Bitterly he recalled all the services he had performed for Napoleon only because the emperor was the husband of Josephine. He had used his own money to promote an anti-British war party in the United States. He had spent his money recklessly to ally the British and Indians, knowing that such an alliance would cause every white man between Pittsburgh and New Orleans to spring to arms. He had hired outlaws to fire a few settlers' houses and had seen to it that the Indians were blamed. He had given much to the French emperor and now his family had been scorned.

His first impulse was to try to undo all the things he had done and to swing sentiment in the new land against Napoleon, but he had done his work too well. America was loping blindly down the trail to war with England and England was stumbling up the trail to meet her.

Flournoy wished Honoria were here. Damn her! She was at her brother's. She never was with him when he really wanted her or needed her. She was a cagy little hellcat and he needed her counsel. All night he pondered, unaware that Honoria and Thomas were riding leisurely to *Maison Blanche*.

His plan came to him early the next morning. He would strike back at Napoleon through Martinique. Rebellion! Ay, that was the thing! He would sponsor a revolution on the island where Josephine was born. It would be a fitting revenge for her. Maybe other French possessions would follow his lead. Once his mind was made up, he lost no time in launching his campaign. He wrote a letter to his wife and left it in her room. He wrote to his bankers in Nashville, Pittsburgh and Washington City. He told the bankers what to do and in his letter to Honoria he instructed her to manage the place. He knew she would come back. Honoria would not surrender the luxuries that she enjoyed as the wife of Lake Flournoy. He gave her no other orders. None were necessary. She could run *Maison Blanche*. Ay, with a rawhide whip!

He would take Dabby and Sukey with him. Sukey, because Dabby would want it that way. His child would be born in Martinique. For sure, Dabney would learn that he had cast aside his sister. Perhaps he already knew it. Maybe Honoria had told him. Well, to hell with him! Let the future take care of the future.

Dabby was anxious to go. Her child should be white, or at least cream-colored, and, born in a far-away place where the people were not so particular about blood strains, the child could be reared as a white child. And, too, she idolized Flournoy. He had given her freedom and she had given him everything that Honoria had denied him. She had a pillow for her head and often slept in the master's big bed. Any woman should love a man who gave her a pillow and shared his bed with her. White men were easier to love than Negroes. They did strange, tender little things. She had seen Negroes come to her mother and to the other female slaves. Flournoy was the first man who had taken her and she was glad. Negro men did not know how to love. They came and took what they wanted and grunted and groaned and laughed aloud in their ecstasy and then went away but always came back when it was raining or when the wind blew cold. Flournoy had spared her all of that and she loved him for it. She often thought of Sam and Donna and Hoab. Hoab would be a big boy now. Sam would always be the massa. She wondered if he would have given her a pillow had she come in fresh while in his service. No, he wouldn't. Something told her he wouldn't. Not Sam Dabney. He would not lay with his slaves. Of course, if he should ever offer her a pillow she gladly would take it. He had been good to her. He had saved her life. Willingly would she repay his goodness in the only way she understood. Lake Flournoy had been kind to her, too, and she would do anything to repay him. But his demands were so simple. Only that she bathe every day and wear a gown at night and lie close to him. Sometimes he thanked her. She wanted to thank him. Once her heart got so full that she wept and he asked her why she wept. She didn't know why. She just wanted to weep. She wept until her tears wet the fine pillow that her master had given her. He caressed her and the tears went away and she snuggled in his arms and slept like a child.

Flournoy's steamboat was beating down the river on its first voyage. He would have liked to have waited for it but he didn't have time, so he, Dabby, Sukey and a few servants hurried to New Orleans and took ship to Martinique. He would teach Napoleon a lesson. He would free Martinique. He would ask Josephine to return and rule her native land. Perhaps she would pass the crown to his child and the issue of Lake Flournoy and Dabby would be a monarch. By God! It wasn't impossible. *Maison Blanche* would furnish the money. He would furnish the brains. He could buy soldiers. He could buy them in Santo Domingo. They had made the French dance to a merry tune. The day before he sailed he dispatched a message to Honoria and instructed her to change the name of his place from *Maison Blanche* to *Malmaison* because he had heard that the unhappy Josephine had so named her home in France.

None of the overseers or slaves at *Malmaison* knew the master's plans and so could not answer Honoria's questions. She really didn't care where he had gone or that he had taken Dabby. She smiled triumphantly at Thomas. Thomas shook his head. Sam soon would know that his sister had told him the truth and Lake Flournoy was beyond his reach. Beyond the reach of Tishomingo, too. Honoria was jubilant. Oh, how her brother would suffer inside of himself when he realized how she had suffered. He would never forgive himself and never again would he doubt her. He would condemn Thomas and Donna. Ay, he would condemn Tishomingo, too. Maybe he would fight Tishomingo. Nay, not that. Sam and Tishomingo would not fight. She would see to it. Sam would ask her how he could make up for the wrong he had done her and she would tell him that he must forgive Tishomingo. Tishomingo would be in her debt, too. Hoity Toity, it was a good world. God bless Napoleon! He had done her a favor. She was glad her husband had run away with a half-caste wench. Now she was the mistress of *Malmaison*. Ay, she would name the place that. It was a pretty name and much easier to say than *Maison Blanche*. She wondered what it meant.

Without removing her riding clothes she called her overseers around her and told them to report to her every afternoon after the stock was put away. She remembered the slaves who had been disrespectful to her and ordered them whipped. So war was coming? Plant corn, she ordered. Clear more new ground. Put the new ground in cotton. Put the good bottom-land in corn. She went to her husband's office and studied his reports. She knew most of them already. She found the papers that proclaimed Dabby and Sukey free persons of color. She tapped the paper on her knee and smiled at Thomas.

"I suppose that wench deserves her freedom. She's earned it."

Thomas shrugged. "And I suppose you've earned the right to be mistress of this place. Under the law you have the right to exercise the power of attorney for your husband. His letter gives you that right. You can even destroy the mortgage against your brother's home. Why don't you?"

Honoria fumbled through the papers until she found the instrument that Sam had signed. Her brother owed Flournoy less than she thought. Only a part of his land and the buildings thereon, including Locha Poka, were under mortgage. She tapped the paper against her teeth.

"I'll not do it," she said. "My brother's a proud man. He would resent help from me."

She meant it. She also thought she knew Sam. It was good for him to be in debt. He would work harder. Debt made him conservative. It would cut his pride if she put him under obligations. It wouldn't hurt either to let Donna know that she, too, was under obligations to the girl she had mistreated.

Thomas had never seen such a worker as Honoria. She lined up the slaves and drove them past the snake pit, warning them that if they ran away the snakes would get them. She discharged two overseers, one because he did not bow to her and the other because a mule in his barn had an untreated sore. She ordered a double ration of rum for the slaves and told them to greet the sun from the fields and the moon from the furrows. She inspected the slave quarters and instructed that every house be white-washed. She found a child suffering with dysentery, and ordered him taken to the big house for treatment. She slapped the child's mother when the mother asked why. In another cabin she found an old man, paralyzed and dying of scurvy. There was no need to treat him. He was too old to work anyhow. She directed that he be taken away from his family and isolated. His wife wailed when the old Negro was taken away. Honoria would have slapped her too and cut her rations but the Negress was big'd. Honoria would not slap a pregnant slave; the child might be injured. She ordered the woman to come to the big house to live until her child was born and until her husband died.

Thomas marveled at Honoria's ability to organize and direct. He complimented her at dinner and her heart glowed. She loved compliments. Heaven knew she had had few of them. She ordered the best brandy for Thomas and told him, "We understand each other, Mr. Thomas. There's no reason for us to be enemies."

"None whatsoever, my dear," he said. "I admire you a great deal, but I don't trust you as far as I can heave a horse. Now sign a paper that you want Mrs. Anestasie

621

Duportail to have a sanity hearing and then I'll be on my way."

"I cannot sign without my husband."

"Your signature is enough for my purpose."

"But suppose I should refuse?" she asked coyly. "Anestasie is a very beautiful woman. You admire her. Perhaps I'm jealous of her."

"Damme," he said, "I cannot blame Tishomingo for losing his head over you. If I didn't know you so well I might lose mine too."

"I wonder if you know me at all," she said in a hurt tone.

Thomas downed his drink of brandy at one gulp. "Don't look at me that way. You make me forget that I have a pot-belly."

"Don't you like to forget it?" Honoria said.

Thomas looked at her a long time and shook his head and smiled. "My dear," he said, "I wish I were thirty years younger. I wish I didn't know the things that I know. I wish I could afford to be a fool and that I didn't love your brother, because you're the God-damnedest, most beautiful, most enticing, most luscious, most dangerous bit of flesh that has come down the pike since Eve smiled at another poor, damned fool and made this world a stinking, rotten place of delightful sin." He got to his feet and bowed and offered her his arm. He escorted her to her husband's study and drew up the paper. "Now sign it, Mrs. Flournoy."

"You can't make me sign it," she said defiantly.

Thomas put the pen down. "Very well, I'm going to New Orleans and I'll make you wish you had never heard of me or Anestasie Duportail." Honoria was frightened. She didn't know he was bluffing. She didn't know what he could do. She picked up the pen and signed. After all, she could afford to be generous. Anestasie could do her no harm. Thomas bowed again and called for his coat and left *Malmaison*. Outside in the fresh air, the little lawyer took a deep breath and muttered, "Damme, I wish I were younger. God, what a minx!" Then he thought of the paper he had in his pocket and of Anestasie and his heart and pulse quickened. He spurred his horse and galloped down the road whistling a few bars from "The Frozen Girl."

Sam hitched his best team to a light wagon and sent Donna and Hoab to old Sam Mims' place. He entrusted them to the care of Jasper. He told the slave, "Look after them."

Jasper said simply, "Yes, massa, Jasper will take care of 'em."

The slaves at Locha Poka wept when Donna and Hoab went away, but Donna did not weep. Hoab was too big a boy to weep and Donna's heart was too full. Sam put her gently on a bed of pine needles in the back of the wagon and kissed her goodbye. He didn't say anything except, "Goodbye, Donna. I'll call for you, soon."

Donna said, "Goodbye, Sam'l." There were no tears in her eyes; they were in her heart.

Jasper cracked his whip over the team and the wagon moved away, crunching the black earth of Locha Poka. Hoab sat by the driver and turned around and waved at his father. Donna raised her head and could see Sam and Tishomingo standing in front of the big house. She noticed a thousand details about the house in the few seconds that she looked back. She noticed that a curtain was blowing in the window of her room, that one blind was sagging.

Sam walked into his house before the wagon was ou~

of sight. He went to Donna's room and looked around quickly. Something was missing. The room seemed empty. Nothing seemed out of place but the room seemed just like any other room. Then suddenly he missed it. The conch shell! The conch shell was gone from the mantel. How like Donna to take it. Sam sat on the edge of the bed and stared at the place where it had been. He did not know how long he sat there, but, remembering he had much to do, he got slowly to his feet and went to his study to talk with Tishomingo.

He wrote letters to Harkins and Pierce and told all the news. He wrote to Frome at Walnut Hills (Vicksburg) and told him that an Indian uprising was imminent and he asked for goods. He wrote all the traders in the new land and told them to send goods to the Great Council Grounds of the Choctaws and Chickasaws, up the Tombigbee. He would give the goods to the Choctaws and try to buy peace. To hell with the Chickasaws and the Creeks and the Seminoles! Let them begin a war. The Choctaws must be pacified. And the Indian confederation would fail without the Choctaws.

He and Tishomingo made other plans and in midafternoon they mounted and rode rapidly northeastward toward the land through which Tecumseh was traveling with Seekaboo, a prophet almost as powerful as The Open Door.

They would make no attempt to check Tecumseh until they met him at the Great Council Grounds. They stopped at Pushmataha's lodge and found the chieftain in conference with his mingoes.

"Why aren't you in the Chickasaw Nation to meet the great Tecumseh?" Sam asked.

"The lesser always goes to the greater," said Push-

624

mataha. "Let The Crouching Panther, The Shooting Star, the one you call Tecumseh, come to me."

"Is the mighty chief afraid of the words of Tecumseh?"

Pushmataha said solemnly, "You're as a boy in the business of handling wise men. The Shooting Star is preaching now to my Chickasaw kinsmen, but his words are weak. He is puzzled. He wonders why I do not go forth to meet him and match my words with him. Let him ponder this thing. Let him go to the Great Council Grounds and speak to all the braves of the southern Muscogees. At the proper time, Pushmataha will arrive with a message from the one God."

"Why do you call him The Shooting Star, O Great Chief?"

"Because he has said that the will of the Great Spirit was revealed to him in a shooting star. He has said that a shooting star will be the sign from our god. He has told the Muscogees that when a shooting star flames through the heavens, it will be the sign for our people to unite and drive the white man from our land."

"And you do not believe him?" Sam asked.

"It is not put in the mouths of men to speak prophecies. A comet soon will appear. My American friends in Washington City told me about it just as Tecumseh's British friends told him. Tecumseh would have my people believe that the comet is his sign. But Pushmataha will outwit him. I will tip my dagger with rattlesnake poison. I will dip my arrows in the smoking waters of the Ouichitas. I will wear the hat that General Washington gave me. I will be strengthened by the spirits of my American friends. I will call my words from the sacred mound. I will clap my words over the head of Tecumseh as the thunder crashes over the saplings. I will shout my words and the wind will be hushed to hear me. The stars will listen and the moon will come close to the earth to hear the message of Pushmataha. Aba Inki will lean over from the battlements of heaven and hear my words, and his heart will be glad, for Pushmataha will speak for peace."

The old chief bowed to Sam, clasped his nephew on the shoulder and walked into his lodge. Sam was deeply moved by the old man's eloquence and, without a word, mounted his horse, and he and Tishomingo rode on, seeking the trail of The Shooting Star, traveling fast and light to prepare the way for the coming of Pushmataha.

The trail along the Tombigbee was strangely quiet. Nothing seemed to move except the dust that churned up from the horses' hooves and settled on the grass. The sun was like burnished copper and the moon had a circle around it. There was not a bird on the wing by day or a catamount to call at night. Sam was restless and uneasy. The world seemed to be standing still, holding its breath.

Neither man had much to say to the other. The first night they made their camp and ate cold food. Sam went out the next morning to get a squirrel for breakfast but came back empty-handed.

"What is it, Big Sam?" Tishomingo almost whispered the words. Whispers seemed appropriate. If he raised his voice he might awaken the world and the world seemed dead. The look on Sam's face frightened his friend. He was frightened because Sam looked frightened.

"Come with me," said Sam hoarsely.

"Did you get any game?"

"Nay, man, I haven't seen a thing move. Not a living thing. Not a lizard or a snake. Have you noticed that we haven't seen a bird since we left the lodge of your uncle?"

"Ay, I've noticed it."

"Come, let me show you something." He took his friend over a ridge and pointed to a valley below. Millions of birds lay upon the ground, their flesh rotting. A deer lay almost at their feet. Sam examined the animal. "Look, Chock, there's not a mark on this deer. Nothing killed it. It just died here. It was too young to die naturally."

"What could have killed it?"

"God knows. And those birds there. They've not been crushed to death. It is as though they just fell out of the sky, as though the sky had rained birds."

They left the haunted spot and rode up the trail. They found a bison in another valley. It, too, had died mysteriously. The air was filled with a stench and they passed the bodies of thousands of squirrels, huddled together as though the squirrels had met by appointment and killed themselves.

The horses would go no farther and Sam and Tishomingo had to dismount and lead them. The horses refused to drink water in the creeks, even to eat the grass.

Sam suddenly was glad that he believed in God. If he hadn't believed before, he would now. All morning they plodded along, neither speaking above a whisper. The land seemed to be covered with dead things. Dead things and dust. There was dust on the brown leaves that floated down the Tombigbee. The banks of the river were lined with carcasses. Sam counted catamounts and deer, squirrels and birds among the dead things. Suddenly he remembered that he had seen no dead beavers or otters. He had seen no dead fish or turtles.

All the dead animals he had seen had been animals that

627

lived entirely on land or in the air. He didn't mention the fact to Tishomingo. Every dead animal along the bank had its nose pointed toward the water. He motioned to Tishomingo to stop. He dared not speak loudly. The sound of his voice would reverberate around the world. It might awaken all of these dead things.

"Chock," he said almost under his breath, "have you noticed that every one of these animals has its nose pointed toward the river. Even the birds we saw and the bison—they were facing east. It means something."

"It means that they were trying to get to water when they died."

They almost stumbled over the doe before they saw her. She was standing on the crest of a ridge, her nose stretched out toward the river.

"She's alive." Tishomingo gripped Sam's arm.

They watched the doe. A dread feeling of foreboding gripped them. The doe was dying on her feet. Her eyes were blood-red and slobber oozed from her mouth. Her skin trembled and an expression of stark agony passed over her face. She tried to take a step toward the river but fell on one knee and rolled over on her side. Sam ran to her. He felt her muscles quivering.

"Some disease has struck this animal," Sam said. He ripped open her belly and examined her guts. He carved out her liver. It was a sickly green. He started to taste her blood but Tishomingo stopped him.

"If it's a disease you might catch it."

"That's the only answer," Sam said. "I don't believe in supernatural things. Some disease has swept this land, killing everything it touched. The animals and birds were trying to reach water. The water things were not stricken. Law! 'Tis a strange sight." He turned and looked at his friend and noticed that Tishomingo was

628

not listening to him. Sam opened his mouth to speak again but before a word could come he heard a hollow rush of air up the river and the ground trembled.

He and Tishomingo leaped together to reach their horses. They mounted and dashed to the crest of the ridge, then got down and looked around. The world was drunk. The trees reeled and crashed and lay upon the ground and trembled. Their roots quivered and their branches waved. Dust rose where the trees had fallen and settled in queer little heaps beside the trunks. The dust couldn't stay on the trunks, for the earth was having a spasm and the earth shook the trunks and the trunks shook off the dust and it formed in crazy little piles. That was the first thing Sam noticed.

Their horses stood very still and neighed. There was a growling in the earth's belly. The earth was sick. Its belly hurt. Sam thought of that, too. Gas pains in the belly of the earth. The new land was having a fit. The new land was sick, sick at its stomach. No wonder it was sick, Sam thought. Men made the earth sick. Maybe the world was coming to an end. He wondered if the world would come to an end everywhere at the same minute. Would it come to an end here and at old Sam Mims' place, too? Would Donna be frightened? Would Hoab suffer? Was Hoab ready to die? Did Hoab believe in God? He had never talked to him about God. He had been too busy. Too busy thinking about Sam Dabney to think about Hoab and God. Or should he say God and Hoab? God should come first. Of course, God should come first. God, I intended to put You first. You know I intended to put You first. You know everything. You know what I am thinking.

Even the little piles of dust by the tree trunks crumbled and were flat. Some of the trees rolled over on their

629

sides. Sam looked at Tishomingo. The Indian was standing very straight. He was facing the sacred mound of the Choctaws. That was the way for a man to die, facing home. Sam stood very straight too, and turned his face toward Locha Poka.

The earth seemed to yawn and to gulp. The rumblings in the guts of the earth grew louder. Ay, the new land was sick. It would vomit. Sam knew it would vomit. Things always vomited when they were sick. The earth would heave and cleanse itself. It would rid itself of its pains and of its corruptions. Maybe it would rid itself of men too.

Sam mumbled, "Lord, have mercy upon me and upon my people."

Was that old man Dabney mocking him? Or was that just the sigh of an old tree that fell on its side and kicked its roots up toward heaven?

The sky was dark, a moving blackness that swept from west to east. The passenger pigeons were moving again. Sam felt the wind as they roared over him. Then he had to gasp for breath, so great was the suction. Millions of other birds, geese and ducks, robins, sparrows, hawks—every kind of bird that Sam had ever seen—followed the pigeons. And when they had passed, the sky was bright again. It was the brightest sky Sam had ever seen.

The earth trembled again, once, twice, and then it wobbled. A crack appeared at the foot of the ridge and spread, cracking the earth in two, running along like a coach whip. The Tombigbee rose out of its banks and then seemed to turn inside out. Its black belly appeared and shook like soft tar. The river threw fish upon the banks. It threw up millions of tadpoles and pieces of rotten wood and bones. The river's belly came up and down like a sea serpent crawling. Suddenly, the river's bed disappeared and the water rushed back to the bed with a sickening sigh. The earth stopped trembling. The river rolled on. A few birds flew by, calling as they flew.

"Perhaps it is over," whispered Tishomingo. "I fear for my people. I heard my mother tell of another earthquake."

"Ay," said Sam, "it was an earthquake. My God! Chock, what strange things. Millions of dead animals and birds. The earth has a spasm. Millions of other birds fly away. The sparrow hawk flies with the sparrow, the robin with the owl, the dove with the eagle. What manner of things are these?"

"It is not for man to say," whispered Tishomingo. "It is the work of Aba Inki."

"I must go to Mims' place and see to my people."

"Don't be a loon, man. Let us go on to the Great Council Grounds. There will be runners there from all parts of the land and we can get news of your people."

Sam saw the wisdom of Tishomingo's suggestion. He looked around at the wasted, cracked earth again and they were ready to mount when Tishomingo said, "Look! The sun!"

The sun and the horizon seemed to race toward each other. The sun was blood-red and when it met the horizon it rushed beyond it, as though to get away from the awful sights it had seen. And then it was dark, so black that Sam could almost feel blackness.

The darkness felt slick and soft, like black silk. No, like black velvet. Sam could feel it brushing against his face as though the wind were blowing acres of black velvet across his face. He could not see Tishomingo, but he knew he was there because he could hear his breathing, a heavy, measured, steady breathing. Maybe Tishomingo's breath was blowing the black velvet across his face. The darkness was so gentle that it seemed that Tishomingo's breath could move it. Why didn't Tishomingo breathe heavier and blow the blackness away? Then the blackness got heavy. It felt like a blanket of tar creeping over the earth.

The flaming comet scattered the darkness. The comet leaped over the horizon and began crawling across the heavens, cutting a path in the darkness.

Sam could see Tishomingo in the light of the comet.

"Great God Almighty!" Sam gripped his friend's arm. "The shooting star! The sign of Tecumseh."

"Ay," said Tishomingo, "it will take much to hold the Choctaws in check after this. It is a comet all right. It will be visible for many nights and more earthquakes will follow it. Then will come storms and floods."

The moon broke through the darkness and billions of stars danced around the moon and darted around the comet, gamboling in its wake, bathing in the streak of light that followed it. The moon seemed as a shepherd herding the stars and calling them from their play with the stranger in the heavens. But the stars wouldn't heed. They leaped and darted and ran around the sky, leaving tiny streaks of silver. The whole sky looked as though a baby angel had dipped a quill into silver ink and had scrawled circles in the heavens. Then the stars seemed to stand still for a minute and to draw back from the comet as though the stranger had offended them, had shocked them, had hurt their sensibilities. The stars tried to run away from the comet but they stumbled and began falling.

"The stars are falling," Sam gasped.

"It is raining stars," said Tishomingo, awe in his voice.

632

The stars streaked out of the sky and melted into the darkness of the earth. The earth had a skin of blackness around it and the stars buried themselves in the skin and the earth was not hurt. The angels seemed no longer to draw circles in the sky with silver ink, but to draw straight lines. Sam would have sworn he heard the stars falling, but of course he didn't. But he almost convinced himself that he did. They seemed to come whistling out of the sky and then to explode with a dull thud. And their streaks seemed to sizzle while the comet moved across the heavens, majestic, magnificent. The moon seemed to step aside to let the comet by. The sky belonged to the stranger and the stranger was haughty.

For hours Tishomingo and Sam stood there on the ridge and watched the stars fall. They could see the trail in the light of the stars and the moon. Finally they mounted their horses and rode into the shower of stars to the Great Council Grounds of the chosen people of Aba Inki.

The shower of stars passed away some time near midnight. The moon began setting and the comet ran away, but the two men rode on, neither speaking. They rode all night and broke their fast the next morning at the Great Council Grounds, under a great oak not far from the lodge of Tecumseh.

Sam immediately sought news, but most of the Muscogees were too frightened to speak. Sam was a white man and they did not want to talk to him. The time was near to drive the white man away. Tecumseh had spoken and his arm had been seen in the sky. Many of the Muscogees had heard him deliver his harangues since the first day he had set foot upon Chickasaw ground. He had told them that he would stamp his foot and the earth would tremble, that his arm would stretch across the sky. Had not the things he promised come to pass?

Tishomingo circulated among them and gathered bits of news.

"Tecumseh is here with thirty warriors and Seekaboo. He has locked himself in his lodge. He will speak tonight."

All day long Indians gathered at the Council Grounds. There were Cherokees and Delawares, Seminoles and even a few Hurons. The western nations sent representatives. There had never been such a gathering of Indians. This day would Tecumseh strike a blow for freedom. This day would the Indians write their own declaration of independence and sign it with blood.

Runners poured in from all parts of the country. The earthquake had shaken Sam Mims' place but had done no damage. Locha Poka had not suffered. The Choctaws, with smoke signals, sent word to Tishomingo that all was well in the nation. The Choctaw overseers who were managing Sam's place sent words of good cheer.

The quake had shaken the entire Mississippi Valley. The great river had changed its course in many places. Only a few lives had been lost, however.

Sam and Tishomingo stood by the great oak and watched the crowds arrive. There came Frome and other merchants from as far away as Georgia. Virtually every trader in the Indian lands was there, and every agent. A lieutenant of the Mississippi Dragoons sprawled on the dusty earth near Tecumseh's lodge and appeared to be sleeping but his eyes never left the door behind which rested the man who might well hold the fate of the new land in his hand.

Frome saw Sam and approached him. "How does it look?"

634

"Bad," said Sam. "These devils will do anything Tecumseh says. That upheaval last night was enough to convince every Muscogee that The Open Door is the real prophet. Tecumseh is certain to tell them to go to war and they'll go."

"Pushmataha will defeat Tecumseh," said Tishomingo quietly.

Frome and Sam and several other traders distributed gifts among the Choctaws. They paid no attention to the other Indians. Sam passed by a group of Creeks while attending to his business and one of them spat at him.

Sam turned to strike the man but Tishomingo's bull whip encircled the man's wrist and the mingo jerked the Creek to his feet. Tishomingo's eyes pleaded with Sam not to strike the Creek. Sam folded his arms and Tishomingo held the Red Stick by his neck until his knees buckled.

"That was the Messenger of Death you spat at," Tishomingo said. "He is the man who scattered your people as the wind scatters grain. I am Tisku, a mingo of the Choctaws, and the friend of Big Sam Dabney. Beware of my presence hereafter. If ever you see me again turn from me and run, flee to your mother, for babes like you should still be at the breast."

He took Sam's arm and they passed on. "It is well that you did not strike him, Big Sam. They know who you are. It would have started a fight. We're here for peace. They will not bother me. There are five thousand Choctaw warriors here and they would die for me."

Tecumseh had not shown himself at noon. The Great Council Grounds were covered with a milling multitude. Sam and Tishomingo had done all they knew to promote the peace. They had circulated among the Choctaws, bribing them, threatening some, and pleading with others.

"Stand for peace," Sam said. "When the test is called, stand for peace."

They were eating lunch under the big tree when a Choctaw flathead appeared and whispered in Tishomingo's ear. Tishomingo arose and motioned for Sam to follow him. They disappeared into the woods and hurried toward the Tombigbee. Pushmataha was awaiting them. At his side was the old squaw who had befriended Tishomingo so often. She spoke to Tishomingo and Tishomingo patted her old cheeks.

Sam heard them speaking in Choctaw and smiled to himself. By God, that Pushmataha was a smart one. He couldn't give the old squaw instructions. It would have been beneath his dignity to have asked help of an old woman. But he could bring the old woman to Tishomingo and Tishomingo could instruct her. Pushmataha glanced at Sam, knowing that he had overheard the instructions.

"Ay, white man," said the old chief, "Pushmataha is a catamount in a night fight, a bear in a wrestling match, a deer in a race, a panther in a day fight, but he is as wily as the snake when he meets The Shooting Star. Think you that you saw things yesterday and last night? The Shooting Star has told my people that Aba Inki is on his side. But have faith in Pushmataha."

Sam and Tishomingo slipped back unnoticed to the Council Grounds and took their seats under the tree. All afternoon the Indians milled. The lieutenant of the Dragoons never left his spot. As the sun went down, the crowd became calm. A huge pile of logs was fired and the multitude formed into tribal groups and marched solemnly to their seats. They sat upon the ground, form-

626

ing huge circles around the fire. The chiefs and old warriors formed the inner circle closest to the fire. The middle-aged formed the next circle and so on to the outer circle which was composed of young warriors, thus carrying out the old Muscogee precept: "The old for council, the young for war." The pipes were passed around, but no man spoke. After each puff the smoker passed the pipe to his neighbor and then stared into the fire. It was the hour of meditation.

Sam and Tishomingo lingered on the outskirts of the crowd. Frome was near by and so were the other whites. Sam was ready. If the Indians got out of hand he could cover the retreat of the other whites. Tishomingo smiled at his preparations for a fight. "You really do not know Indians, Big Sam. In all the history of the Muscogees no man has ever drawn blood at a council."

"Just the same I'm taking no chances," said Sam.

A micco of the Chickasaws spoke first and welcomed the multitude. He said his nation was honored to be the host of Tecumseh. A Choctaw mingo arose and said, "We, too, welcome Tecumseh. We have come here to hear his message. Our great chief, Pushmataha, will answer him. Tecumseh wants war and alliance with the British. Pushmataha wants peace. We will hear them and decide the issue for ourselves."

The lieutenant of the Dragoons saw the door of Tecumseh's lodge open slowly and The Shooting Star and his warriors, accompanied by Seekaboo, stepped from the hut. They folded their arms and walked slowly to the council fire. Not a word was spoken. In his left hand Tecumseh carried his peace pipe; in his right his rifle.

Sam noticed that the great warrior limped slightly and that one of his front teeth was of a bluish color. Sam

637

was at least a head taller than Tecumseh, but the Shawnee seemed tall because of his erect carriage. When he closed his mouth and hid his teeth, he was the most handsome Indian Sam had ever seen, bronzed, muscular and confident. There were silver bands on his arms and a silver gorget was suspended from his neck. He wore a silver band around his head. A small red spot was painted on each temple and streaks of red paint extended outward to his cheek bones.

The Shawnee chief and his men were dressed and painted alike. They had tomahawks and scalping knives in their belts and they wore buckskin shirts and cloth flaps, short skirts that came to their knees. Their buckskin leggin's and moccasins were fringed and beaded. All wore garters below the knees. Their hair was plaited in a long queue of three plaits, hanging down between their shoulders. Their temples were closely shaven. The warriors' heads were adorned with hawk and eagle feathers but Tecumseh wore crane feathers, one white one for peace and one red one for war. Peace to the Muscogees, war to the Americans.

Tecumseh's warriors sat at his feet, but he stood, holding his arms and staring straight ahead.

He stood there for more than thirty minutes before a sign of nervousness appeared in his eyes. Where was Pushmataha? The delay upset Tecumseh and his eyes began darting around the crowd seeking the face of the Choctaw chief.

There was a murmur of voices beyond the shadow of the fire and the crowd parted to form a path. The bone picker of the Choctaws walked to the fireside and took a seat. Next came two flatheads, wearing only breechcloths and carrying only blow-guns. They looked contemptuously at the thirty Shawnee warriors and took their seats. Pushmataha did not need thirty warriors with rifles and tomahawks. Two flatheads with blow-guns were sufficient.

Pushmataha moved through the crowd, his peace pipe in his left hand, his rifle in his right. He paused near the fire to shake hands with the Choctaw mingo and handed him his rifle. He wore the hat that George Washington had given him. His short skirt was of white silk and his leggin's were doeskin embroidered with beads of gold. He was naked to his waist but there was no paint upon his chest, only a great scar. Pushmataha stood so the scar could be seen plainly.

He bowed to Tecumseh as though to apologize for keeping him waiting.

Tecumseh's voice was hollow and strained when he began speaking.

"In view of questions of vast importance, have we met in solemn council here tonight. Nor should we here debate whether we have been wronged and injured, but by what measures we should avenge ourselves. Our merciless oppressors, having long planned their proceedings, are not about to make, but are still making attacks upon those of our race who have as yet come to no resolution."

His voice warmed gradually as he spoke and his tones became resonant. The Shawnees said he was the greatest orator of all time. His magnetism electrified his hearers. He kept his arms crossed and his eyes roved over the vast crowd.

"The whites are already nearly a match for us, united and too strong for any one tribe alone to resist, so that unless we support one another with united forces, unless every tribe unanimously combines to give a check to the avarice of the whites, they will soon tear us apart and disunite us and we will be driven away from our native country and scattered as autumn leaves before the wind.

"Sleep no longer, O Choctaws and Chickasaws, in false security and delusive hopes. Our broad domains are fast escaping from our grasps. Every year the white intruders become more greedy, exacting and overbearing. Every year contentions spring up between them and our people, and when blood is shed we have to make atonements for the right or wrong, at the cost of lives of our greatest chiefs and large tracts of land. Are we not being stripped of the little that remains of our ancient liberty? Do they not even kick us as they do their black slaves? How long will it be before they tie us to a post and whip us and make us work in their corn fields?"

A muffled growl of indignation arose from the young warriors and several of them leaped to their feet and shouted their war cries. Tecumseh rebuked them for such undignified and premature display of feeling. Then he launched into the gospel of The Open Door. He urged the Muscogees to unite and return to the ways of their fathers, to shun the white man's whiskey and the white man's women and the white man's bed. Eloquently he pleaded for the Muscogees to abandon the practice of scalping women and children.

"It is not war to kill women and children," he said. "You cannot end wars by killing women and children. If you kill a man's wife and his child he will fight forever, and his grandsons will fight you. Kill the white man, ay, but spare their women.

"There must be war. We will not be driven from our homes and from the graves of our ancestors. The bones of our dead must not be plowed up. Let us by unity of action drive them back whence they came. War, or extermination, is our only chance. . . . I am now at the head of many warriors backed by a strong arm of British soldiers. Listen to the voice of duty, or of honor. Unite now and strike for home and for fireside. Follow me to victory or go your way to defeat. I warn you. Take your choice."

The Muscogees did not express their emotions, but as Tecumseh took his seat at the council fire he knew he had won, that he had accomplished his mission. A few of the miccos and mingoes arose and advanced to the fire and expressed their opinions of the speech. The majority of the leaders agreed with Tecumseh. The Shawnee was jubilant. Pushmataha waited until the murmurs died away; then he marched to the fire and faced the council. He removed his hat and laid it carefully upon the ground. He held out his arm and intoned:

"*O-mish-ke! A numpa tillofashi ish hakloh*. Attention! Listen you to my few brief remarks."

It was the ancient salutation of the Muscogees and every heart thrilled to hear it.

"It is not my design in coming here to enter into disputation with any man," Pushmataha began his speech slowly, "but I appear before you not to throw in my plea before the accusation of Tecumseh, but to prevent your forming rash resolutions upon things of highest importance, through the instigation of others."

He scarcely raised his voice, but spoke slowly, calmly. "Reflect before you act hastily in this matter. Remember the American people are friendly disposed toward us. You now have no just cause to declare war against the American people, or wreak your vengeance upon them. It is inconsistent with your national honor and glory to violate your solemn treaty; and a disgrace to the memories of your forefathers to wage war against the American people merely to gratify the malice of the English.

"A war against America will be the beginning of the end that terminates in the destruction of our race. You cannot defeat America. England cannot defeat America. England could not defeat the colonists, how then can she defeat the American nation?

"Reflect ere it is too late on what a war with the United States will mean. Tecumseh has England at his back. Ay, of what good is a comrade at your back. He should be beside you. England would have you fight her war. Will Englishmen be here to face the rifles of the Mississippians? Nay, you will face them for the glory of England.

"I implore you not to break the treaty with America. Do not violate your pledge of honor. But if you insist upon war ——"

Pushmataha drew himself very erect and ran his finger across the scar on his chest. "If you want war, you, O Shooting Star, you, O Seekaboo, if you author a war between my people and America, I here invoke the Great Spirit to bear me witness that I shall avenge myself upon you. We are not a people who have grown insolent with success, or become abject to adversity—but let those who invite us to those hazardous attempts by uttering our praise, also know that the pleasure of hearing such distinguished men as Tecumseh, speaking for the English, has never elevated our spirits above our judgment.

"There are many schemes to lead the Choctaws to war. I favor a confederation, but the confederation must rest upon a foundation of peace and justice, a pledge to respect treaties and the rights of all.

"In council we resolve, surrounded by security. In execution we faint, through the prevalence of fear. It is simple to utter brave words here in council, but face yon long rifle-gun of Big Sam Dabney. Sam Dabney is my friend. President Madison is my friend. I know the president and Sam Dabney is my neighbor. But if I invade his land and harm his people he will kill me or I will have to kill him. I will not fight my neighbor for English gold or take my commands from an English king. Listen to the voice of prudence, my countrymen, ere you act rashly. But do as you will. Know this truth that I speak: if war comes, the arms of Pushmataha will strike for the Americans. And now, O Muscogees, if you want war, cast your lot."

Tecumseh did not wait for Pushmataha to be seated, but sprang to his feet and shouted, "All who will follow me in this war lift your tomahawks into the air! I declare for the English!"

Thousands of warriors jumped up and screamed their war-cries, and waved their tomahawks. Sam eyed Tisho-mingo nervously and fingered his gun.

Pushmataha leaped to the center of the circle, drove his tomahawk into a tree and shouted, "All who follow me either to peace or to war against England show me your tomahawks."

The air seemed filled with weapons and war-cries. The division was even. Pushmataha was the first to realize the danger. He spoke to Tecumseh, "I have not bested you, and you have not bested me. Our people are di-vided. It might mean civil war. We must decide the issue tonight. You are a believer. We will let Aba Inki decide."

"Ay," Tecumseh answered. "I am willing that the Great Spirit decide. But how?"

Pushmataha said, "I will send for a Choctaw hopaii, a seer of my people. He will prepare the ancient sacrifice and will reveal to us the wishes of our god."

643

Some of the multitude heard and a chorus went up, "Send for the seer! Prepare the ancient sacrifice! The signs of Tecumseh are strong but the Great Spirit will reveal himself in the old sacrifice."

Tecumseh sensed a plot and demanded, "Who is the seer?"

"Of what matter is that?" Pushmataha asked. "He is a Choctaw hopaii and all of these warriors know him."

The Shawnee realized he was walking into a trap but there was naught he could do about it. If he refused to heed the seer, the Muscogees would desert him. He must abide by the wise man's decision. Pushmataha sent Tishomingo to fetch the seer and while Tishomingo was away the Choctaws built a scaffold under an oak and tied two red heifers to the scaffold.

The hopaii was dressed in feathers from head to foot. Tishomingo escorted him to a seat by the bone picker. The thousands were hushed as Tecumseh stated his case to the wise man. Then Pushmataha argued his opinion. The seer arose and tossed fresh brush on the fire and faced Tecumseh.

"Your powers are great. You say your arm has been seen in the sky. You say you have stamped your feet and the earth has shaken. You say the manifestations we saw yesterday and last night were signs from Aba Inki who answered your prayer. I call upon you to show us your sign again. When will The Shooting Star be seen again?"

Tecumseh scanned the sky for a sign of the comet. If the comet would appear, his cause would be won. But there was no comet. The British agents who had told him that the comet would appear had neglected to tell him the hour when it would be visible in Mississippi.

"Tecumseh is not one to haggle with Aba Inki," the

Shawnee said. "I have shown you my sign. Are you people of such little faith that you must have another sign?"

The hopaii scattered some gunpowder on the fire and spoke slowly. He had memorized the words that Tishomingo had taught him. "When the moon reaches the top of the tree under which I stand the shooting star shall appear again. Watch you."

The multitude stood. The silence was so heavy that Sam could feel it. There was no sound save the sputtering of the fire and the moaning of the wind. The moon reached the spot that the seer had designated. The wise man held up his hand and intoned, "Oh, Aba Inki, god of the Muscogees. Show us the sign." Every face was turned toward the hopaii. He pointed his hand to the sky and shouted, "Look!"

The comet appeared, its tail washing the horizon.

The Muscogees murmured, "Oh-h-h!" Aba Inki had answered the prayer of the hopaii. The great Tecumseh had not been able to show his sign again, but the hopaii of the Choctaws had asked and had received. Surely he was blessed of the Great Spirit.

The wise man ordered that the heifers be slain and their flesh cut into small pieces and put upon the scaffold. He set fire to the scaffold and ordered the multitude to stretch upon the ground, their faces against the earth. He prayed until the fire had consumed all the flesh on the scaffold, then he leaped to his feet and shouted, "*Osh Ho-che-to Shilup a-num-pul-ih*. The Great Spirit has spoken. He tells me to warn you against Tecumseh. The Great Spirit says the Americans are our friends and we must not take up arms against them."

The Choctaws and Chickasaws bowed their heads.

645

Aba Inki had spoken and must be obeyed. Tecumseh and his comet were not as powerful as the heifer sacrifice. The Shawnee chief grunted his disgust for he knew his mission had failed. He turned from the fire and re-entered his lodge.

The crowd moved away, each nation to camp on its own site. Sam patted Tishomingo's shoulder. "Come," he said, "we can rest now. The Choctaws and Chickasaws are our allies. Your wisdom is great, Chock. How did you know the exact minute the comet would appear?"

Tishomingo laughed. "It was predicted by wise men many years ago. I knew that if the night was clear the comet on this night could be seen when the moon reached a given position. I so told the hopaii."

"You've outwitted Tecumseh and saved your nation. The Choctaws will bless you and honor your name. Come, let's dig our bed."

"But first," said Tishomingo, "there's a duty to do."

He led Sam beyond the camp to the banks of the river where the old squaw was squatting over a tiny flame, warming her wrinkled hands.

Tishomingo smiled at her and touched her head. "Old woman, you have done a noble thing."

"Ay," said Sam, "the hopaii did as Tishomingo told you to have him do. My nation is in your debt. You deserve a reward. Name it."

The old woman looked up at him. "It is the law of the Choctaws that a son shall obey his mother. A dutiful son is any woman's reward. The hopaii has always been obedient to my wishes as a good son should be. That is reward enough."

29

THE mingoes of the Choctaws and the miccos of the Chickasaws met in conference the day after the great council and signed articles pledging their nations to support the United States in any war against England. Pushmataha gave the document to Tishomingo and told his nephew to deliver it to the Indian agent at Milledgeville, Georgia.

"Guard it with your life," directed Pushmataha. "It is our pledge of eternal friendship to the United States."

Tishomingo put the document inside his jacket and promised to fulfill his duty. He put his arm around his uncle and thanked him. "When this paper is delivered," Tishomingo said, "my duty to my nation will be done. Is that right, O Great Chief?"

"A man's duty to his nation is never done until he has given his life," Pushmataha replied. "There is an evil thought in your mind. You seek the blood of an enemy. With your whip you plan to wipe out a wrong. Blood has never righted a wrong. For years I have restrained you. I knew I would need you for this test in which we have triumphed. I will not restrain you further."

"Then I have your leave to seek my revenge?"

"You have my leave but not my blessing. I have kept from you a thing I have learned. Lake Flournoy has fled. I know not where."

647

"Did he go alone?" asked Tishomingo quickly.

"Nay, he took with him the girl who was his slave. I have a message from his wife for her brother."

He handed the letter to Tishomingo and Chock fingered it. "I have waited a long time to kill Flournoy and now he has fled. But I will find him."

"Do not seek him," counseled Pushmataha. "He will come back. He has too much at stake in this land to stay away. A wise man waits for his quarry. A wise hunter does not seek the deer but goes to the deer's watering place and waits for him. If you would trap Lake Flournoy, watch his home. He'll be in touch with his wife or his agents."

"They are wise words," Tishomingo said. "I'll do as you say. I'll stay here and wait for Flournoy."

He bade his uncle goodbye, and Pushmataha and his guard of flatheads moved away. Tishomingo took the letter to Sam. Handing it to him, he remarked, "I know what's in this letter. Lake Flournoy has run away with Dabby."

Sam read the letter slowly and lifted his eyes from the pages and looked at his friend. Then he tore the letter into bits and scattered it on the ground. "You lied to me, Chock," he said sadly. "Lake Flournoy dishonored my sister and you knew it. My sister told me the truth, but you lied."

"I lied," said Tishomingo.

"I'll not ask you why. My sister says you lied because you love me, because you did not want me to kill Flournoy and risk my neck in a hangman's noose. I believe you lied because you didn't want me to rob you of your revenge. Be that as it may, I'll not condemn you for the lie. My sister has been maltreated by all of us. Never can I make up for the hurt I have done her. But I can please her by heeding her plea that never again must I mention this thing to you. My sister asks it and I will do it. . . . We still are friends."

Tishomingo despised Honoria then. It was on his tongue to lash out at Sam and call him a fool. But he would not do it. His friend was hurt and he would not add to the hurt.

The white traders gathered around Sam and discussed the momentous events that had occurred. Frome did most of the talking. "We are in for evil days. Tecumseh isn't defeated yet. The Creeks surely will follow him. He has convinced them that the comet is his arm."

"I can understand the comet," said Sam. "It had been predicted. I also can understand the earthquake, but I cannot understand the plague that swept away so many animals and birds."

"And neither can I." Frome shook his head. "It's obvious to me that they were poisoned. Perhaps the earth had been rumbling inside for days, maybe weeks, before we heard it. Perhaps the earth brewed poison way down in its innards and spat it up through the salt licks."

"That's plausible," said Sam, "but I'm of a mind an epidemic of some sort struck the birds and animals and killed them like flies. Perhaps it struck the animals first and the birds, feeding upon the waste of animals, caught it and spread it. Strangely enough, the domestic animals weren't bothered. Only the wild things."

Tishomingo headed the delegation that called upon Tecumseh in his lodge. The Shawnee admitted them willingly and offered them food and drink. Tishomingo told him that the Choctaws and Chickasaws had allied themselves with the United States.

"So be it," said Tecumseh. "I had hoped for other things."

649

"We will furnish you an escort out of our nation."

"Am I in danger?" asked Tecumseh.

"You may well be," Tishomingo replied. "Should England and the United States begin war now, you'd be taken prisoner."

"I'm going to the Creeks," said Tecumseh, "and I will be grateful for an escort."

Tecumseh summoned his thirty warriors and he and Seekaboo waited under the great council tree until the escort was ready. Sam and Tishomingo selected five flatheads and five Chickasaws as guards, and the caravan moved to the west. They built rafts at the Tombigbee and ferried the river, swimming their horses behind the floats. Once inside the Creek Nation, Sam reminded Tishomingo that the presence of a white man might cause trouble.

"Nay," answered Tishomingo, "the Creeks will not attack us just because you're here. War has not been declared and the Creeks are too intelligent to start fighting until it has fairly begun."

Sam rode close to Tecumseh and talked earnestly with him. He was amazed at the man's knowledge and impressed with his honesty.

"What I cannot understand," said Sam, "is why you preach a war against my people and boast that you're an ally of England's. You say that all white men are enemies of the Indian. Are the English not white?"

"But the English don't threaten us. I don't hope to drive the Americans from this continent. We can live at peace with the Americans. Let the United States confine itself to the seaboard as was intended. Leave the Mississippi Valley and the Great Lakes to the Indians. Let the British have Canada and the Spaniards Mexico."

650

"If England defeats the United States, do you think she'll stay in Canada?"

"I don't know. The English agents have assured me that England covets no Indian land. However, the word of England is no better or worse than the word of the United States. I need a strong white ally. England has offered herself. That's all there is to it. My object isn't to crush the United States; I'm not a foolish man. I know I could not do that. My object is to preserve the Mississippi valley for the Indians, to form a United States of Indians."

"'Tis a great dream," said Sam. "I almost am sorry that you cannot succeed."

Tecumseh smiled sadly at him. "Ay, 'tis a great dream. You, too, are a dreamer. I have heard much of you. I regret that we must be enemies."

The first volley of musket fire came from a canebreak to the east of the caravan. One of the Choctaws fell from his saddle. Sam stood in his stirrups and aimed his rifle-gun at a clump of woods to the right. He knew the ambush lay on both sides of them. He saw only the scalp-lock of the Red Stick bobbing behind a stump and he blew a hole in the man's skull.

Tishomingo wheeled his horse and the party dismounted and formed a circle.

"Red Sticks!" said Sam. "They're after me."

Tecumseh saw to the priming in his rifle. "They have violated the rules of war. This was a peace party."

"We'll teach them a lesson," Sam shouted. "Chock, a company that will ambush a peace party deserves no sympathy. I'll walk ahead of our party. They may think I want to make talk. I know these Creeks. When they see me, every head in those woods will poke from behind a tree. Curiosity is a trait of the Creeks. They'll want to see what I'm going to do."

He called the flatheads and Chickasaws to him and instructed them to cover the cane-break. Tishomingo and Tecumseh would cover the rear. The other Shawnees would watch to the right. "Wait until I fire, then pick out your man and let him have it."

Sam walked deliberately in front of his company, holding his rifle carelessly in the crook of his arm. He saw a Creek directly ahead peer from behind a tree, but he continued walking. He glanced to the right and saw another face watching him. He waited until he saw the elbow of the Creek ahead move and expose itself. The man was cocking his gun. Sam knew the other Creeks were drawing a bead upon him. He discharged his own rifle into the air and dived forward, sprawling upon the ground. A blast of lead swept the place where he had been. But the Creeks exposed themselves to fire and the flatheads and Chickasaws blasted them out of their hiding. The Creeks fled and Sam rejoined his party.

"Now what think you of the Creeks?" he asked Tecumseh.

"I'm deeply grieved and shocked."

The Creeks vowed later that they did not know it was a peace party or that Tecumseh was with Sam Dabney. The Red Sticks obviously were telling the truth. They would not have fired upon Tecumseh had they known he was in the party. It was all a dreadful mistake. But the Creek bullet that killed a Choctaw flathead there by the Tombigbee was the first shot fired in the War of 1812. The Choctaws were allies of the United States and the Creeks soon would be allies of England. It mattered not to the frontiersmen that the Creeks had no connection with England when they ambushed the party. The frontiersmen didn't give a hang about that. The Creeks soon would be lined up with England. It was a British ball that killed the flathead. It was Spanish powder.

The British ball and Spanish powder that cut through sawgrass near the banks of the Tombigbee set fire to the Southwest. Now it would be war. For years the Mississippians had been waiting for war. There had been threats from France, from Spain, from the Indians. The Americans had threatened. There had been much talk and little action. But that shot from the gun of a Creek Red Stick set the woods on fire. Peter McQueen, kinsman of old Jim McQueen, claimed credit for the shot. Well, let him have credit. The voices from a thousand dead women and children were willing to give him the credit. The wail of the Red Sticks who saw their nation blown away was glad to give him the credit. It was an honor to start a war. Let the honor go to him who deserved it.

Tishomingo and Sam sent their flatheads and Chickasaws home soon after the skirmish and told Tecumseh that in as much as he was on friendly ground he and his party no longer were under their protection.

"But we'll ride not far behind you," said Sam.

"That is well," Tecumseh thanked him. "I am going to Took-a-batche on the Tallapoosa River, to the Council Grounds of the Creeks. There I will present my cause to the Creek Nation."

Tishomingo and Sam decided to attend the council. Sam borrowed a peace pipe from a Shawnee and carried it in his left hand. It was his immunity from attack. As strong as their hatred was, the Creeks would not attack him as long as he carried the sacred emblem of peace.

More than five thousand braves assembled at Took-a-batche. Sam saw many notables, including Big Warrior, a

653

great micco who was scheming and struggling to succeed old Jim McQueen. Sam and Tishomingo mingled with the Creeks and Sam learned, much to his amazement, that the nation did not want to fight the United States. The Creeks spoke often of war but they were referring to a civil war, a struggle within the nation between Big Warrior and other miccos. Sam learned that the Creeks were buying arms in Pensacola from the Spaniards, but they were not arms of war. The rifles were for hunting and the powder was inferior. Not more than one Creek out of twenty even had a rifle. God's navel, Sam thought, these people attack Mississippi! It was too absurd for consideration. He told Tishomingo so.

Tecumseh and his warriors did not mingle with the Creeks but were given a lodge of honor near the center of the Council Grounds and went into retirement. The next day Tecumseh spoke. It was the same speech he had delivered to the Muscogees, though this time it was delivered more forcefully. When he had finished, the Creeks seemed impressed, but they were not for war either. They were too involved in their own civil war and, moreover, they knew that the Americans were too strong for them.

"We're making a mountain out of a molehill," Sam told Tishomingo. "It's a pity that there are no other white men here to tell my people that the Creeks want peace with us. The Creeks aren't preparing for war against us; they're going to fight among themselves. The upper Creeks will fight the lower Creeks. Damme! After this council I'm going back to my home and bring my family back."

"Don't act hastily," Tishomingo cautioned.

"Nay, I shall bide my time. I'll not tell my countrymen to lay down their arms but rather to sleep upon them. I'll see that the people know the true state of affairs; that the Creeks as a nation will not go to war with Tecumseh. Perhaps there will be a few raids from time to time, but not organized warfare."

"I thought you wanted war, Big Sam," Tishomingo told him. "I thought you wanted war so you could feed the army."

"I did once. That was when I thought the Creeks were out to make war. But I'm not a man, Chock, to lie about my enemies."

"Have you a plan?"

"Ay, I'm riding to Natchez tomorrow. I know false reports will be in circulation there, for I know that many men will stop at nothing for an excuse to wipe out the Creeks."

"May the Great Spirit be with you in your task!" Tishomingo took his friend's arm and patted it affectionately. "I must go on to Milledgeville and deliver the document as my uncle instructed."

They parted before dawn, Tishomingo riding east and Sam riding west. Sam took the Three-Chop Way and upon reaching the Alabama River he discovered that the trail had been blazed—the old trail that he had wanted to blaze—the route between the Mississippi and the sea. He examined the markings on the trees. The notches were freshly made. Great God! Some surveyors already had violated the treaty with the Creeks. The whites had guaranteed that the Three-Chop Way would not be cut between the Alabama and the Tombigbee until the Creeks were paid for the land that must be condemned. Sam rode on and a few miles farther encountered the caravan he was expecting. He rode to the leader and reined his horse.

"I'm Sam Dabney. What know you of those notches on the trees? Who's blazing this trail?"

"I am, by God!" said the leader. "And I don't care if you are Sam Dabney or Jesus Christ, I don't like the way you talk."

"By whose right do you blaze this trail?" Sam's voice dropped and his eyes burned into the man.

"By my own right. We're heading for the new land. The trail was marked to the Alabama. When we crossed the Alabama we started marking."

"Your wagons are the first to ever roll through here," Sam said. "We have a treaty with the Creeks that our wagon road must end at the Alabama for the present and pick up again west of here at Duportail's ferry. We must do naught to provoke the Creeks."

"God damn the Creeks! Those bloody bastards are getting ready to jump us. Read this, you big bucko!" He shoved a piece of paper under Sam's nose.

It was a printed statement purporting to be Tecumseh's speech to the Creeks. Sam read it and his blood boiled. It was not Tecumseh's speech at all. Sam remembered Tecumseh's speech—this was a forgery. It made it appear that the great Shawnee chief had, with bloodthirsty epithets, attempted to incite the Creeks to murder every white person in the territory, men, women and children—even to dig the very corpses from the graves. Sam was horror-stricken when he realized that some group of rabble-rousing whites had already circulated this spurious document far and wide to incite the settlers to swoop down on the Creeks. It was the most diabolical plot he had ever heard of. It was the work of people who were absolutely determined that the Indians should fight the white men.

"Those aren't Tecumseh's words," said Sam. "I was there, I heard him."

"No white man was there."

Sam's hand clenched his whip. The knuckles stood out white. "You should measure your words before you doubt me. I have a mind to teach you a lesson, but you'll see enough blood. However, I ask you this: if no white man heard Tecumseh, who translated this speech into English and who wrote it?"

The traveler hadn't thought of that. He didn't want to think of it. Several of his men gathered around him and Sam spoke to them. "You're coming to the new land. We welcome you. Help us preserve the peace. If we must fight the Creeks, let them sound their war whoops before we prime our muskets. Never let it be said that we fought a people who wanted peace."

"I don't know who you are, stranger," said the caravan leader, "but you talk like a damned Injun-lover to me."

Sam stood in his stirrups and leaned over and jerked the man from his saddle. He hurled him to the ground. The other men gasped at his display of strength and were too surprised to draw a bead on him. Sam withdrew his pistol and dismounted quickly. He held his pistol in his left hand and uncoiled his whip with his right. He slashed the fringe off the leader's buckskins with his whip and then wrapped the rawhide gently around the man's waist and lifted him to his feet.

"My home is Locha Poka and the heart of the new land. If you consider yourself injured, stop there and leave your name and where you'll be, and when I have nothing else to do I'll look you up and break your God-damned head. Meanwhile, I'm in a hurry. If you mark another tree between here and the Tombigbee River, I'll send for my young son and have him beat hell out of you."

Sam remounted and hurried away.

He reached the Tombigbee at dusk and stared across the river at the house in which André Duportail had lived and died. He stood there for several minutes thinking of André and of the great things they had planned. And of Anestasie and her tragedy. He had always liked Anestasie. He wondered why she had turned against him in Natchez that day. Maybe it was because Honoria was there. She didn't like Honoria. Few people liked Honoria. That was because they didn't understand her. He understood her. Maybe Lake Flournoy had influenced Anestasie against him. She and Donna had been such good friends. He remembered the first time he had ever seen her. She had been dressed all frilly-like. She was a frilly woman. She loved flesh. Sam had thought so then. He had envied André such a vivacious bedmate. He wondered how Donna was. Great God! how long had she been sick? Forever it seemed.

He waited until his horse was cool and drove him into the river. He wouldn't wait for the ferry. On the other bank he dismounted and shook himself, checked his powder to be sure it was dry and then rode slowly up to the Duportail cabin. The place was well-tended. Trust Flournoy to see that his men kept the place in order. Flournoy knew how to treat good land. The slave cabins were white-washed. The Duportail barns were slate-gray and sturdy. There was a weather vane on one of the barns. His eyes roamed to the Duportail house and his heart pounded. It was a snug house, of a single story. It was not gaudy as Locha Poka was gaudy. It was put there to live in, not to be looked at. There was wisteria around the door and azaleas along the path that led from the road

658

to the house. He noticed patches of moss on the roof, and Spanish moss hung down from a tree and brushed against the roof. It was such a friendly place. And the land rolled away from it as though it were reluctant to leave. Much of the land lay fallow, but some of the land had been freshly turned and smelled good.

Sam got down from his horse and stood by the good land. He liked to smell it. He closed his eyes and inhaled deeply. The land smelled damp and musty. It smelled young and strong. He glanced at the furrows. They looked like small black waves, each piling up on the other. It was good land. It would give man all man wanted. It asked naught from man but understanding. It was willing to work. It would pour out its richness if man treated it gently. It was like a woman, Sam thought. It was just stretching there, ready to give. Waiting to be caressed. Anxious to produce. The rolling land looked like the black breast of Sukey. Perhaps of Dabby. He wondered if she had black breasts. Or were they brown. Brown and hard and round.

Donna's breasts had grown flabby and the blue veins showed in them. And her skin was dry and parched. He wondered again about Anestasie. This house was like she had been, snug, trim and friendly. He remembered a hundred little things about her—how her dress had swished when she walked, how her hips had moved, how her green eyes had laughed at him, mocked him, dared him. There had been a time when he might have had Anestasie. He was sorry now that he hadn't taken her. The thought made the blood surge through his veins and pound his brain, and there was a strange pain in his body as though his emotions had run together, as quicksilver runs together, and were crying and clawing to be let out. Then he rebuked himself. Why should he be thinking so suddenly about the things that he should not think? He and Donna had lain under a tree near here. Maybe that was the reason. He drove the thoughts away. He was proud that he was able to drive them away, proud that he had been loyal to Donna. Some day he would tell his son that he had been true to his pledge.

A slave took his horse near the front path and Sam knocked gently at the door. He would ask Flournoy's keeper to put him up for the night. He was tired. He wondered who was managing the place. Probably some Frenchman whom Flournoy had hired over in Louisiana.

He handed his hat to the slave who opened the door and asked, "Is your master or mistress here?"

The slave said, "Ay," and saw him to the small living room.

A lady stepped to the door of the room and stopped suddenly. Sam bowed. "I'm Sam Dabney, ma'am."

The lady smiled. "I'm glad to see you, Sam," she said.

He stared at her. "Anestasie," he said slowly as though he could not believe his own word, or his own eyes.

"You look like you're seeing a ghost."

"I am! What are you doing here? Where did you come from? What's happened to you?" His words tumbled out.

"One question at a time," she laughed. "Sit down and I'll send for brandy."

Sam backed to a chair and sat down, never taking his eyes from her. There was strength and understanding in her green eyes. And tenderness, too. He could see many things in her eyes—sympathy, loneliness, courage. Ay, she had changed. Sam didn't understand the metamorphosis, but there it was. Her hair was gray—youngish gray—but alive. He had never seen such hair. It swept back from her forehead and fell in rolls around her neck.

660

It wasn't silver, it was gray. Like the winter coat of the gray fox. Her eyes were bright. There was not a wrinkle in her face and her cheeks were daintily red. A natural red. Red cheeks were rare in the new land. Her hands were soft. He knew they were soft by looking at them. Her neck was full and her breasts still were high. He could see their outline through her bodice. There was an expression of infinite calm on her face.

She sat and looked at him, too—first at his eyes, and in them she saw the things that Sam saw in hers. Then she noticed the gray hairs around his temple. The gray hairs crinkled. His hair still fell to his shoulders like a great mane and he tossed his head with that old assurance and pride. He smelled of good leather and tobacco, a mannish smell. Ay, he had changed, too. There was no arrogance about him, only confidence. His waist still was thin and his great shoulders seemed to be bursting through his jacket. His teeth were fine and white, but not sparkling. She felt her breasts tingle as she looked at him and her heart seemed to be swelling inside of her and choking off her breath.

Finally she smiled at him, a slow smile that lighted her face. "Don't stare at me so. You embarrass me."

Sam didn't reply but continued to stare at her. Had Donna ever been so beautiful? Ay, surely. But when was that? Years and years and years ago. Donna had been tall and graceful then. She had smelled good, too. Anestasie must smell good. The last time he had seen her, she had smelled of lily of the valley. He had hated the odor. There was no such odor about her now. He took a deep breath, trying to smell her even across the room. She must smell of good clean soap, perhaps of suds lathered from ferns. No, she must smell like that good land outside, pungent. That was what good land smelled like. Good

661

land smelled like a beautiful woman. Worn old land smelled like dust. Great God! Donna smelled like dust. Dust . . . dry, crackling dust. Poor Donna, neither dead nor alive! He would always love her—but could a man love two women? If Donna should die could he ever love another woman? Would Donna's face always be before him when he lay with his second love? Would his second love do the things that Donna had done, and if she did, would he think of Donna then?

"How is Donna?" Anestasie's question startled him. Had she read his thoughts?

"She is at Mims' place. I haven't seen her for some time. I can only hope that she is well."

"Yes, Mr. Thomas told me she was there."

Thomas. He was the answer. Thomas had secured Anestasie's freedom.

"There are many things I must know, Anestasie," Sam said.

"There are many things to be told, Sam."

They sipped their drinks together and Anestasie told her story. She had been given a sanity hearing and had been pronounced well. Thomas had seen to everything. He had brought her back home and had left her alone, because it seemed to him that she wanted to be alone. Actually, she had regained her senses a few days after her terrible fright at Lake Flournoy's house and for years had lived with mad women. She didn't tell Sam about that. She didn't mention Honoria. Let the dead bury the dead.

"I wanted to come back here," she murmured. "Once I hated this land, but now I love it. I'm going to build a great plantation here. The land is mine and I'll hold it. I'll help you build your route to Georgia as you and André planned."

662

"The last time I saw you, Anestasie, you were of another mind."

"We squabbled that day, didn't we, Sam? I'm sorry. I can't explain why I squabbled with you, except that Flournoy egged me on. In those days I really was crazy, I guess. I had to live with insane people to become sane. I learned a lot in a mad-house. You may think it strange but I found a kind of solace there. Insane people usually are kind and gentle. Only the sane are brutal and heartless. Mr. Thomas came to see me often. Even Tishomingo came to see me and Donna often wrote to me. I heard great things about you. About your wagon trains and your triumphs. I'm proud for you, Sam."

"It does me good to hear you talk," said Sam. "Maybe I like to hear your flattery. All men like to hear women brag about them. My wagon trains failed. I was wiped out. But I'm coming back. We'll build that road from the river to the sea. But please go on—tell me more. Your voice is soothing, Anestasie. It used to be brittle, but now it is soft."

"Sam!" Anestasie laughed and blushed. "You talk more like a suitor than like an old friend."

"We *are* old friends, aren't we?"

"Yes," she said softly, "we're old friends."

They didn't mention Donna again. Sam was rather glad of that. There was no need to mention her. Her name would have been a sad note in a happy song. He and Anestasie could laugh together. They laughed at silly little things that had happened to them. It was good to sit there and talk about old times and to laugh at silly little things. They hadn't seemed important at the time, but now they seemed very important. It was funny, Sam thought, how a man forgot so many of the hardships

663

of life, so many of the dangers, and remembered the happy things, the silly things that had been amusing.

"I cannot get over how you've changed," Sam repeated.

"I'm glad I've changed."

"What are your plans?"

"I'm going to stay here. I'm going to work. Work is the greatest doctor in the world. Mr. Thomas says there may be a war and that an army may come this way. I'm going to do as you are doing and grow corn for the soldiers. I'm proud of this land. I love it. I like to sit on my porch and watch the river. I love rivers. I believe there is a river in heaven."

"I've often thought of that," Sam laughed. "I wouldn't like a heaven with streets of gold. I want a river. Not a fast, rushing river, but a slow, friendly river. A river that takes time to visit with the land it waters."

"A river like the old Tombigbee," Anestasie said dreamily. "And I hope there are fireflies there, and cicadas, and bullfrogs. Lots of bullfrogs. And I hope the mist rises from the river at night. I want heaven to have black land, too, miles of black land, always freshly turned, smelling good. There's no smell like the smell of good land, Sam'l."

Sam looked at her quickly. It was on his tongue to say that good land smelled like a beautiful woman. She caught his look and returned it. And a great affinity was born.

They talked for hours. A slave came and brought fresh candles.

Sam advised her to be ready to leave her home should the Creeks go on the war-path. He suggested that she go to Sam Mims, but she protested that it was too far from her land.

664

"But you can't stay here," Sam argued.

"I'll find a way."

Sam felt that she would. She would find a way out. She could take care of herself now. She had become strong and self-reliant, and if she needed help he would always be ready. He knew he would be ready. He knew that if he were at one end of the world and Anestasie at the other, if she called him he would go to her. He wanted to tell her so. But he didn't know how to express it.

"I'll be along this border if trouble comes," he said. "If you need me, send for me."

"If I need you, I'll send for you." She looked at him and dropped her eyes. Then she raised them again and looked him full in the face. She felt his thoughts and understood them. Her mind kept repeating his words "If you need me." God, how she needed him! She, too, was lonely. So this was love and it could happen so quickly. She wished he would walk to her and sit on the arm of her chair and take her hand and just hold it for a long time and say nothing. Then pull her head against his chest and she would let her head stay there forever and ever.

Sam said, "I feel better because I have seen you, Anestasie. I can't explain it."

"Don't try to explain it, Sam. You're a lonely man. You're a strong man. You've always been a strong man. Oh, I know you've done some things of which you're ashamed. And I know something else about you."

"Ay?"

"You used to talk much of your father. You spoke very seldom of your mother. You must be like your mother. Your mother, I understand, was a God-fearing woman, a tender person who dreamed great things for her children. Please don't interrupt me. Let me have my say. You have been drying up inside. Donna, heaven bless her, has been unable to give you the happiness and comfort you wanted. Don't look at me that way, Sam. Donna spoke to me about it. She was sick when you married. We are no longer children and we shouldn't think as children and act as children. There's been a great void in your life. You're a man who loves your land. You've always stayed close to your land. Your land, your home and Donna were all the same to you. You have never been able to separate Locha Poka from Donna. You have a strange conscience. Your conscience is your master. It's a rather narrow conscience, Sam, but it's a clean conscience. It makes me happy to have you say that if I need you, you'll come to me. If you need me, I'll go to you."

"There's a thing on my mind," said Sam awkwardly, "that I will not say. It's not right for me to think of you as I want to think of you."

Anestasie understood him. "Donna is my best friend," she said simply.

"I feel drunk." Sam's voice was soft. "Maybe I'm tired. I've been here only a few hours. It's the first time I've seen you in years. But it seems, Anestasie, that my heart has gone out to you and that you are holding it in your hands."

"In my heart, Sam—I'm holding your heart in my heart."

Sam gave a little gasp. His mouth, strong as a steel trap, suddenly was tender. He was unsteady on his feet, but he crossed the room and knelt before her and buried his head in her lap. She stroked his hair and when he looked up at her his face was streaked with tears.

"Is this wrong, Anestasie?"

"Only if you think it is wrong," she said.

666

"I don't think it is wrong. I love you."

"Say it again, Sam'l," she begged.

"I love you," he whispered.

He got slowly to his feet and stooped over and kissed her. She touched his face and kissed him. He sat on the side of her chair and pulled her head against his chest and they both cried. Then they laughed and cried again.

"What's the matter with us?" Sam asked and lifted her to her feet and whirled her around and caught her in his arms.

"I don't know," she whispered. "Whatever it is I hope it never passes."

She clung to him. He lifted her in his arms and took her to her room, lifting the candle from the mantelpiece as he passed by. He put her down on the bed and they laughed again and lay there on the bed in each other's arms. They were hysterical with happiness, drunk with emotion. Sam got to his feet and bowed elaborately to her. She put out one foot and he knelt and removed her shoes. He untied the ribbon at her throat.

She teased him as he fumbled with the ribbons on her chemise. "We're acting as children act when they first fall in love."

"Love makes children of everybody." He stepped back and looked at her and she stood very straight, her hands at her sides, her eyes closed. She was without shame and proud to be so. Sam took her by the hand and they walked together to her bed. . . .

A warm glow spread over her body and Sam kissed her again, her mouth, her neck and then her hair.

"Your hair is very lovely," he said.

She slept on his right arm. He wondered what time it was when he gently removed his arm, fearing she was uncomfortable.

"Don't go away," she begged. "Leave your arm there."

"I thought perhaps you were uncomfortable."

"In *your* arms? Never. Have you been asleep?"

"Nay. I've been thinking."

She didn't ask him his thoughts. She knew them. She simply said, "Do you still love me?"

"Yes," he said and caressed her. "I don't know how to explain it."

"Do you feel dirty inside? Are you ashamed?"

"Nay. And you?"

She snuggled close to him. "If I should die tonight I still would count this the happiest night of my life. But there's a thing I must tell you."

"Ay?"

"Mr. Thomas loves me."

"Are you betrothed to him?"

"No," she answered, stroking his face. "He has never mentioned it to me. But I know he loves me."

"Do you love him?" Sam asked.

"There's room in my heart for only one man. I have a big heart, Sam, but you're a big man. You've taken all of my heart. But Mr. Thomas has been my friend. I believe he'll ask me to marry him. I hate to hurt him."

"It's only natural that I should think of this," Sam whispered. "Donna has not long to live."

Anestasie answered softly, a catch in her voice, "I would be deceitful if I said I had not thought of that, too."

"Then you understand my meaning? You will wait?"

"Yes, Sam, I'll wait."

668

30

✰ ✰ ✰ ✰ ✰ ✰ ✰ ✰ ✰ ✰ ✰ ✰ ✰ ✰ ✰ ✰ ✰ ✰ ✰ ✰

HOSEA CINCINNATUS THOMAS drained his tumbler and stared at the bottom of the glass. Then he put the glass back on the bar and nodded quickly to the bartender to fill it again. He cocked his left eye at the men who had gathered around him in a Natchez tavern—planters and riff-raff.

"Did you ever hear the story, gentlemen, of the toad frog and the alligator?"

None of the men had, so Thomas continued.

"Well, one day an old 'gator that had been fighting a long time and was hungry crawled out of a creek to snatch a little toad frog that was sunning himself. The little toad hopped away. The alligator kept after him and the toad led him out of the swamp and on to a desert. The 'gator was too far from home to go back, so he just curled up and died. Ay, gentlemen, England is like that 'gator. She'll never learn. It looks like we're going to have to lure her over here again and stomp her guts out."

"That's right," said one of the men. "Hell is coming down the pike again, snorting and blazing. My father swore that he killed twenty Englishmen once. I may not be as good a liar as my father was, but I'm just as good a man. A little war with England will give me an excuse to get away from home for a little while. My wife has been powerful naggin' lately."

The United States, goaded to fatalistic desperation by England's high-handed and overbearing attitude, had declared an embargo against her as a preliminary step to war. It was a weapon England understood. A few weak voices in America still clamored for peace but could not be heard above the swelling chorus of Southerners and Westerners, demanding that England be brought to task and taught that she could not bully small nations.

Tecumseh had returned to the Ohio country without securing the Creeks as allies. During his absence, his brother had led the Shawnees into battle at Tippecanoe. Only four hundred Indians had attacked the American army and had killed and wounded one hundred and eighty-five. It was hailed as an American victory, however, because the Indians had retreated. William Henry Harrison, leader of the American forces, was proclaimed a hero, although he had very wisely waited until Tecumseh was absent before he had dared invade Indian land. The Shawnees had been armed by the British, and the United States chalked up another debt to be collected from the Redcoats.

England had no right to sell arms to the Indians. The United States said so. The United States had vowed that the Indian nations were recognized as independent states. But the independent states couldn't buy guns from England or Spain. The independent Indians could not even buy fowling-pieces. They couldn't buy English rum. New England rum was good enough for the Indians. They could either drink it or stay sober. Of course, some Americans sold guns to the Indians. But that was all right. The Americans had a license from their government to do so. Strangely enough, a musket ball fired from a licensed gun would blow out a white man's brain just as quickly as an English ball from an unlicensed gun. That wasn't the issue. The Indian belonged to America. He was America's burden. Americans could kick him and get him drunk and rob him, rape his wife, stuff Christianity down the mouths of his children and confuse his intellect with such petty platitudes as "all men are created equal." But England, keep your hands off! If you want to steal and rob and rape, go to India and China and Africa. But leave our Indians alone.

England, groggy from Napoleon's blows but still on her feet and giving better than she got, had a sudden change of heart toward the United States. Her purse was suffering and her purse-strings tugged at her heart. A hue and cry was raised for repeal of the obnoxious Orders in Council. Spencer Percival, the prime minister who stood stoutly for the Orders, was assassinated. Henry Brougham, a friend of the United States, pressed harder for repeal, and England at last listened to him. On June the 16th, 1812, the ministry announced that the Orders would be withdrawn on the 23rd.

It was too late. The war party had control of the Congress. Two days after England took the step that would have prevented war had the United States known of the action, the Congress voted a state of hostilities. The Senate voted nineteen to thirteen for war and the House's vote was seventy-nine to forty-nine. Only five senators from states north of the Delaware voted for the war and the struggle immediately became a sectional affair, the South and West against England and her American Indian allies. New England called it "Mr. Madison's war," and refused to support it.

The United States was unprepared for war as usual. Jefferson, hating war, had allowed the armed forces of the nation to go to pieces. He had ordered a few gunboats built but they were not even seaworthy. The officers of the Revolution were too old for service and West Point, recently authorized, had not had time to mould its material into serviceable goods. There was no money, and the nation refused to accept increased taxes. The moneyed class opposed the war. The money markets of Europe were closed. The army numbered six thousand and its officers were poppinjays, and the men called them such.

The navy consisted only of frigates, but the little ships were officered and manned by men with salt in their craws. Congress finally got through a bill to increase the regular army by twenty-five thousand and another bill authorizing the president to call out fifty thousand militia. The war party asked for a big increase in the navy but Congress refused. The war party asked for war taxes and was rebuffed. Finally the war party got a loan of $11,000,000. Eleven million dollars to fight England!

Thomas read of the declaration of war in the *Mississippi Herald* and was delighted.

"We'll strike through Canada," he said. "The Canadians will revolt and join us. If Spain opens her mouth we'll take all of Florida and even Mexico. Of course, England will blockade us, but, damme, we're used to that. England can't starve us."

The Northwest was itching for the Canadian campaign. The Southwest was hossing for the Florida expedition. General Hull moved out of Detroit against the British under General Brock. Brock's army was only half as large as Hull's and many of his fighters were Indians. Hull gave Brock time to concentrate his forces and then fell back, afraid to attack an army half the size of his own. Brock moved to Detroit and demanded its surrender. The Englishman was amazed when Hull accepted his terms. Hull was afraid to fight. His army almost revolted. Hang him! Shoot him! The yellow livered son of a bitch! Madison saved him after he was sentenced to be shot as a coward.

The Canadians shook their heads. Even had they been willing to join the Americans at the beginning of the war, they would never ally themselves with a nation whose soldiers fought as Hull fought. The British held Detroit. The frontier was wide open. Tecumseh rallied his Indians. Harrison began whipping an army into shape. He had to beg, borrow and steal supplies.

In Martinique, Flournoy heard the news and rejoiced. It was a blow against Napoleon. The United States, whether it admitted it or not, was lined up with France. Flournoy's cause was not going well. The islanders were too proud of their French allegiance to heed Flournoy's plea for a revolution. He sent for the Kemper boys to help him, but the Kempers were in Mexico brewing trouble against Spain. It was time for Mexico to free herself and the Kemper boys were on hand to help out.

Dabby's baby was a girl with cream-colored skin. They named her Josephine and Flournoy spent almost as much time with her as with the few men who were aiding his cause.

Tishomingo built a lodge near the Big Black and lived there where he could watch *Malmaison*. Honoria often visited him and promised she would report any plan of her husband to return to the United States. She was very happy, but Tishomingo was morose. He wouldn't admit to himself that he loved her. Perhaps he didn't love her. He often wondered. She had become a habit with him, a habit that he couldn't break.

Sam was at the territorial capital of Mississippi when

673

he got news of the war. He immediately wrote a letter to Anestasie and cautioned her to be on the alert.

He had ridden over most of the territory, talking with his friends and trying to convince them that the purported speech of Tecumseh was a forgery. The people wouldn't listen to him, however. They believed the Creeks wanted war. Sam pleaded that only a few of the Indians really wanted to fight.

"If we keep our heads," he said, "the feeling will die down. We must do naught to stir them up. We must build a string of forts along the border and be ready—but, in God's name, don't attack! If they're going to strike they'll strike soon. I have a feeling that maybe Peter McQueen and his boys will hit at us. But they're not the Creek Nation. Sleep on your knives and see what tomorrow will bring."

He visited Sam Mims' place and saw his family. Donna was in bed in the Mims' family home. The light of another world was in her eyes and Sam feared she would never see Locha Poka again. She was cheerful, however. He told her all the news. Donna was most interested in Anestasie's return. Sam talked much of Anestasie. Too much. Donna looked at him rather strangely as he talked, then closed her eyes and turned her face to the wall.

About ten families had gathered at Mims' place and Hoab was the leader of the boys. He took his father around the stockade and introduced him to his friends. Hoab reached to his father's shoulders and he laughed a lot and was a favorite of the place. As he and his father walked along, Hoab cut his eyes up at Sam and winked. "There's a man I want you to meet, papa. I told him a tale the other day and he won't believe me. But he'll believe you."

"You want me to vouch for your tale, eh?"

"You get the general drift, papa. You don't want these folks calling your son a liar, do you?"

"I'll back you up. But you better let me in on the tale first."

Hoab's face was very serious. "I was just telling that man about the time I caught that bob-cat by his tail, rammed my hand down his throat and turned him wrong side out. You remember that time, don't you?"

"Ay, son, I remember it. Leastwise I'll tell that man I do. The only trouble is that a bob-cat hasn't got any tail."

"Did I say bob-cat?" Hoab asked quickly. "I meant a catamount."

"A catamount and a bob-cat are just about the same thing," Sam grinned. "'You better make it an alligator, then you'll be safe."

Hoab put his hand upon Sam's shoulder and they both laughed until their sides shook. "You're a better liar than I am, papa. How could a man get his arm down an alligator's throat?"

"That's your worry, son. It's your tale."

Hoab often entertained the settlers with his music, and Sam joined in. "That Hoab is just like his father," one of the men said. "Always singing and cuttin' shines. Hope he's half the man his father is."

But several times Sam's tongue almost slipped, and he caught himself on the verge of calling the boy "Ab."

Sam was in Donna's room when Hoab came in, holding a little girl by the hand. She held back, but Hoab pulled her, begging her to come in and meet his father. The child was frightened, as a doe is frightened by a mastiff. Her red-gold hair hung in dirty curls to her shoulders and she often tossed her head to keep her hair out of her eyes. She was barefooted and wore a grease-spotted calicut dress. Her skin was fair; that is, it looked fair to Sam. He couldn't see much of it for the dirt. The child's eyes fascinated him. They reminded him of the big stars he had seen the night of the earthquake. Hoab introduced her as Shellie MacLeod. She bowed awkwardly to Sam and then fled from the room, Hoab at her heels.

"Who is she?" Sam asked Donna.

"She was here when we got here," Donna said. "Her father and mother were named MacLeod. They died of the pox up in the Creek Nation. The Creeks found her and brought her up. They never gave her a first name but called her 'MacLeod's girl.' The Creeks brought her here for safe-keeping."

"Who named her Shellie?"

"Hoab named her that. She was fascinated by my conch shell. The one you gave me, remember? She would hold it to her ear for hours and listen to the sea roar. . . . I used to do that when I was a little girl, Sam'l."

"And when you were a big girl, too, Donna."

"So you remember?" she said and smiled.

"Ay, of course I remember."

He leaned over the bed and kissed her cheek and she turned her face away again. There was a silence for several minutes and then Donna said, "Anyway, Hoab got to calling the girl Shellie. It's a pretty name. Hoab is very fond of her. They're almost the same age, I imagine. Of course, she doesn't know her exact age. She was like a little wild creature when we first came here. She would take off her dress and run through the woods and jump in the river. Hoab was shocked at first. She's like a fish in the water and a fox in the woods. Hoab was worried because she had no under clothes. I had the ladies here make her some out of some old sacks. But she won't wear them unless I see to it."

676

"She looked to me like she needed a good bath."

Donna laughed. "She probably went in swimming this morning and got clean. But it takes her only a minute to get dirty again. She eats with her fingers and plays in the dirt. When I am able to leave here I may take her to Locha Poka if it's all right with you."

"It will be all right," Sam said.

"I'd like to have a little girl around the place."

"Ay, so would I." Sam said it idly. He knew it would be years before Locha Poka would be safe. Donna would never see Locha Poka again. He gave her encouraging news about the times and said that if a Creek war came it would last only a few months.

He talked to the settlers who had brought their families to the Mims' place and counseled them to prepare the place for defense. "I don't believe there's any danger here," he said. "Sam Mims is an Indian and if some of the Creeks should strike, they probably would spare him. I believe they'll strike farther north and cut through and try to get to my place. But it's best to be on the safe side and prepare this place."

They erected a blockade, nearly square, enclosing about an acre. The Mims' family home was in the center of the square and there were about a dozen other buildings within the blockade, including the loom-house and the smoke-house. They built an east and a west gate and cut down all the trees for several hundred yards around the stockade to afford the settlers better vision.

"If you stay on the alert you can protect this place," Sam said. "Should war come, soldiers will be sent here. Keep guards posted and be ready."

In the Creek Nation, a new leader had arisen—Billy Weatherford, the Red Eagle. He had studied at the knees of old Jim McQueen and the patriarch of the

677

nation had nominated him for leadership. Weatherford had fought and schemed his way to the rank of micco. He had taken sides against Tecumseh. The most remarkable man in the history of the Creeks, Weatherford was only one-eighth Indian. When his brother, John Weatherford, cast his lot with the whites, Billy Weatherford went to the Creeks. He was small of stature and had chestnut hair, a white skin, and a soft voice. Only his eyes were Indian.

He wore an eagle feather in his silver head band and so they called him the Red Eagle.

Billy Weatherford pleaded for peace. Peter McQueen castigated him. The Red Eagle was seven-eighths white. His blood was white. He was not a warrior; he was a child. McQueen said as much. Weatherford did not fight McQueen but beseeched his people to be calm.

McQueen shouted, "The whites are going to attack us!"

The Red Eagle replied, "They'll not attack. There's no war between the Creeks and white men. The Americans are honorable men. They'll not attack without a declaration of war."

Up in Tennessee little Billy Phillips, a jockey, brought the news that the war with England was on. The president had sent him. Little Billy tucked the war proclamation into his jacket, mounted his horse in Washington, D. C., and nine days later galloped into Nashville. Eight hundred and sixty miles in nine days! Every Tennessean drank his health. The governor called for volunteers.

"Each volunteer, including company officers, is entitled to a powder-horn full of the best Eagle powder, one dozen new sharp flints, and lead enough to mould one hundred bullets," the governor's proclamation stated. "Avoid the use of smooth-bore muskets as much as possible. They do not carry straight. They may be good enough for regular soldiers but not for the citizen Volunteers of Tennessee."

Major General Andrew Jackson advised that the Volunteers wear dark blue or nut-brown homespun. Buckskins could be worn too, and if the men had them, they could wear white pantaloons upon parade. Tennessee raised two corps, one in the east and one in the west. The Southwest expected Spain to march. If Spain did not come to Natchez for the fight, then the western boys would go to Florida for one. The Tennesseans hied to Natchez to vanquish the foe. Jackson exhorted them to be brave. "There's not one individual among the Volunteers who would not prefer perishing on the field of battle rather than to return covered with shame and disgrace," the general declared.

There were no enemies at Natchez, however. America's most powerful enemy was the stupid war department. The Tennesseans had nobody to fight in Natchez and fought among themselves. Natchez was filled with drunken soldiers, whores and lazy Indians who were not classed exactly as enemies. The war department, listening to the scheming words of General Jim Wilkinson who feared Jackson's authority, ordered that the Tennesseans be disbanded. Jackson told the war department to go to hell and marched his soldiers back home. They had not perished on the field of battle but had returned home to the jeers of the multitude. Jackson fumed and fussed. His temper was short and the temper of his cohorts was shorter. Fist fights and feuds broke out all over Tennessee. His friend, Billy Carroll, was challenged to a duel by Jesse Benton. Jackson was Carroll's second. Benton fired first and suddenly doubled up and turned his behind to his enemy. Carroll's bullet plowed a furrow into the proud flesh of Mr. Benton's buttock and all Tennessee laughed. Even Mississippi laughed. It was the best joke of the war, but it was bound to lead to trouble. It did and in the fight that followed Tom Benton shot Andy Jackson from behind and almost blew away his shouder.

Lawyer Thomas was disgusted and told Sam, "If those damned Tennesseans would spill British blood as easily as they spill their own, we might win ourselves a victory."

Throughout the territory volunteers flocked to the army and got their quota of powder and went home again. They wearied of fighting whores and kicking lazy Indians in Natchez. There was much more fun to be had at home. Sam was offered a command of the Mississippi militia but refused it. He wanted to be a free agent.

"When I fight I don't want any damned officers giving me orders," he said. "Most of them haven't got sense enough to pour water out of a boot with directions on the heel."

He and other settlers built a chain of forts from Mims' place north along the border of the Creek and Choctaw nations. He was at Fort Madison, not far from the Duportails' ferry, when a runner brought word that Arthur Lott had been murdered by a band of marauding Creeks. Lott was the first white victim of the war and had died at Warrior's Stand. He and his family were en route to Mississippi, to a bluff* on the Halfway River which bore his name for many years. Sam sent for Tishomingo, left completion of the fort in his hands and went into the nation, carrying his peace pipe to insure immunity from attack. He saw Billy Weatherford, and told him, "The Creeks have killed a white man. It might mean war."

"Nay," said Weatherford, "it must not mean war. The

* Now Columbia, Miss.

680

white man was killed by Indian outlaws. When an Indian is killed by white outlaws, do we blame the United States?"

Weatherford and Sam called on Big Warrior and demanded that the outlaws be punished. A party of Red Sticks captured the guilty Indians and shot their leaders. Many of the Creeks grumbled but Big Warrior held them in check. A party of Otisees, drunk and in a mood for hell, then killed an old white man named Merideth. Big Warrior attempted to punish the Otisees but was killed. Up on the Creek-Chickasaw line a minor skirmish occurred. Pushmataha, angered at the turn of events, organized a party of flatheads and was commissioned an officer of the United States.

Sam and Weatherford, the sad Red Eagle, met for the last time near the holy grounds. They smoked a peace pipe and talked.

"It's beginning," Sam remarked wearily.

"Ay," declared Red Eagle. "It's beginning. The agents of Tecumseh are among my people. They have British gold and British rum. The war is beginning as a spring flood begins, as a forest fire begins."

"There's no cause for war between your people and my people," said Sam. "But as a tiny snowball starts rolling down a mountainside and grows into an avalanche, so is this war beginning."

"It's still not too late," the Red Eagle said, but his tone was one of hopelessness. "Those of us who stand for peace will punish the Red Sticks who want war."

"But you're no longer as strong as they. They're well-armed and organized."

"We'll arm ourselves against our own people. We'll fight them rather than fight you. Your nation will not sell us guns, but we can get guns in Pensacola."

"I wish you well," said Sam.

681

"My people hate you, Sam Dabney." The Red Eagle stood very straight. "But I do not. I'm your friend now because you're a good man. If war comes, however, I'll fight with my people."

Sam returned to Fort Madison and opened its gates to all the white settlers who wanted protection. About thirty families gathered there, panic-stricken. Rumors that the Indians were massing for an attack were rampant. A company of militia, one hundred and eighty strong, called at the fort and demanded provisions for an expedition into the Creek Nation. Sam almost bit his tongue in an effort to control his words.

"By whose orders are you going to the Creek Nation?" Sam demanded.

"By the right of self-protection," answered one of the officers. "A party of Red Sticks has gone to Pensacola for arms. We'll capture them."

"You damned fools!" Sam snarled. "Those arms are to be used against the Creek outlaws, not against you. If you cross into the nation you'll be guilty of invasion."

The officer spoke calmly. "We're going."

Because it was the code of the frontier Sam provisioned them and watched them march away. He called a small company of settlers around him and said, "There goes hell. There goes a line of Mississippi militiamen marching into the Creek Nation. Your children's children will look back on this day with regret and shame."

Leaving the post in the hands of a capable settler, he and Tishomingo rode rapidly into the nation, avoiding the soldiers. They must get to the Creeks and warn them. Perhaps it still was not too late. If the Creeks would retire, perhaps there would be no battle. But he and Chock were too late. The militia flushed a small band of Creeks at Burnt Corn Creek and attacked without warning.

The Indians had made camp, carefully stacking the

precious guns they had bought in Pensacola. They unloaded their horses and hobbled them and were eating tafula when the Americans opened fire. Jim Boy, a Creek leader, rallied his men and they grabbed their rifles and ran into a cane-brake. Shouting and laughing, the Americans poured into the abandoned camp and began looting. The Creeks fired from the cane-brake and the Americans suddenly were terror-stricken. They fired wildly and retreated. The Indians did not pursue them, fearing a trap.

Sam and Tishomingo found the militiamen resting not far from the camp, completely bewildered and sick with fear. They had had their bellyful of fighting. It would be better to go back to Natchez than to stay in these woods where the cane-brake spewed lead.

Sam did not laugh at the soldiers. Realizing they had enough of the fight he sought to teach them a lesson. "The Indians are in the cane-brake waiting for you to attack again," he said. "I'll go to them and ask for an armistice. You've lost several men and so have they. Call it a draw."

He handed his rifle to Tishomingo and walked toward the cane-brake. Billy Weatherford would recognize him. The Red Eagle would protect him. But Billy Weatherford wasn't there. Jim Boy glued his eyes upon Dabney and watched him stride down a ridge toward the creek, his head high, his right hand extended in a gesture of friendship. That was Sam Dabney. That was the man who had told the Red Eagle the white man wouldn't attack. He had been with the soldiers; then he must have been in the attack. Now he was trying to trick them—the Messenger of Death was trying to trick the Red Sticks.

Jim Boy fingered his rifle nervously. That man's scalp

683

would bring any Creek all the wealth he wanted, corn, women, wampum and rum. Honey and perfume, hides and bear grease, silver for arm-bands and gold for beads. That man's scalp represented a fortune. Jim Boy was thinking about it all when the young buck about twenty yards to his left drew a bead on Dabney and fired.

Sam pitched forward on his face, got to his knees and then rolled on his side. Tishomingo leaped from his hiding place and ran toward his friend. A handful of the soldiers followed him. A blast from the cane-brake drove all the men back except Chock and he put his hands under Sam's arms and dragged him to safety. The Americans exchanged shots with the Red Sticks until the Indians charged and drove them away.

Tishomingo cut Sam's jacket from him and studied the wound, a gaping hole in his left side. Sam stretched his neck and stared at the wound. "How does it look, Chock?"

"Not as bad as the first wound of yours I dressed. Remember?"

"Ay," gasped Sam. "You've been a good friend. Let's get away before the wound festers. I think I can ride if you can walk beside my horse and hold me. We must get to Fort Madison."

"I'll take you to Sam Mims."

"Take me to Fort Madison," Sam repeated stubbornly.

"But your family's at Mims'."

"Madison," said Sam again. "And send word for Anestasie to come and nurse me."

Tishomingo did not question the order but put Sam on a horse and they plodded back out of the nation, Sam thinking of the trouble ahead and of the joy Anestasie's presence would bring him. Tishomingo thought only of his friend and Anestasie. He was glad that Sam loved her.

684

Sam needed her and Tishomingo was happy because in his need his friend had found a person to help him.

The Red Eagle sent a messenger to Sam at Fort Madison that America must suffer the onus of the war. America had struck first. The Red Eagle would support his nation. His runner told Sam, "The Red Eagle says the war had not fairly broke out when your people attacked. The Red Sticks have buried their peace pipes and are dancing the war dance."

So the war was on. . . .

The Americans had occupied Mobile without firing a shot. The Spanish garrison had agreed to retire from the town but technically not to surrender it. The United States and Spain must settle the issue later. Spain couldn't protest. She was giving her life-blood to survive in Europe, so how could she protect her interest in the new world! The Americans simply moved into Mobile and said, "This town is ours. If Spain doesn't like it, then let her lump it."

The fiasco at Burnt Corn Creek caused alarm from Georgia to Natchez and a score of stockades were built along the Alabama River. General Ferdinand Leigh Claiborne, a brother of the governor, established headquarters at Mount Vernon, near the Mobile River, and distributed troops throughout the valley. He sent Major Daniel Beasley, a half-breed, to Mims' with one hundred and seventy-five volunteers. The militia, already on duty at Mims', numbered seventy and chose Dixon Bailey, another half-breed, to be their captain. The occupants of Mims' totaled five hundred and fifty-three persons.

Sam sent word to Donna not to worry about him. Anestasie stored her corn, closed her home and brought her slaves to Fort Madison. She did not attempt to explain her presence to Tishomingo. It was not necessary. She sat by Sam's bed every day and slept near his door at night. She read to him and cleansed his wound and nursed him as though he were a child.

Thomas, hearing of Sam's wound, came to the fort and, although surprised to discover Anestasie there, said naught about it. He, too, soon realized the situation and Anestasie knew that he was aware of her love for Sam. He had intended to stay there, but feeling that his presence was embarrassing to her and to his friend, he decided to go to Mims'.

He told Sam of his plan. "There's no danger of the Creeks striking there," he declared, "but I want to look the situation over. They've sent Major Dan Beasley to command Mims' place. They've built up quite a fort there. Beasley is a good man when he's sober but he drinks too much. I'm going down there and look around."

Sam agreed with him. "Send my son Hoab back up here. I may need him."

"Any other message, Sam'l boy?"

"Look after my wife, Hosey."

Anestasie went with the little lawyer to the stockade and opened the gate for him and watched him mount his horse. He took off his hat to tell her goodbye.

"I'm glad you understand," she smiled. "I'll always be in your debt."

"Dabney's a good man."

"It might have been otherwise," she said. "I wish I could make you as happy as you've made me. I don't know how it all happened. It just happened."

"I know, my dear," Thomas patted her head. "I wonder how his sister will feel when she hears. Well, that's not important. Goodbye, Anestasie, and God bless you."

"You should have lived many years ago," she said and

kissed his cheek. "Back when there were knights. You're a gallant man."

"A knight with Blackstone for his armor, eh? A gallant knight with a pot-belly and a bald spot. I'm a tolerant man, I hope. But there's one thing I cannot tolerate. That's stupidity. I was stupid even to think I could win you. And I once thought so, you know."

He didn't wait for her reply but wheeled his horse and jogged away, his pudgy little arms flapping as he rode and the long tail of his black coat waving in the breeze.

Hoab arrived at Madison a few days later. He reported that his mother was very sick but that she had sent word for Sam not to attempt to come to her. His duty was at Madison and, too, she knew he was too ill to make the trip.

Settlers began streaming in to the stockades and the whole countryside was alarmed. The Creek Nation was too still. Pack horses had been seen leaving Pensacola loaded with guns and powder. A red warpole stood in every Creek village. The miccos went into council and the minor prophets circulated among the people, exhorting them to drive the white man away, once and for all. The loyalties of the people were divided, for many of the Americans were half Creek and many of the Creeks half white. There was no enthusiasm for the war, but each side was determined to see it through, not because the fighters were angry or bitter but because there was nothing else to do except finish a task that stupid leadership had set for the people.

Despite Anestasie's protest, Sam left his bed to command the fort. He knew Claiborne would send them soldiers, but until they arrived he would defend the place. If the Creeks got through Madison then Anestasie's place and Locha Poka would be at their mercy.

His wound was healing slowly but satisfactorily. Tishomingo made him a couch of hides and pine straw and he often rested on it while he gave orders. He had every tree for two hundred yards around the fort cut down. He had trenches dug for garbage and to be used as privies. He slapped a child because the child drank unclean water and when the father protested Tishomingo knocked him down. Sam imprisoned a man because he did not cover his own urine with dirt.

"There'll be no disease here," Sam declared, "if I have to kill every one of you."

He drove cattle into the stockade. He had four wells dug. He stored corn and salted meat. He even saved the rats. He had them killed by the hundreds, dressed and put away. Nothing was wasted. The rats were as big as squirrels and Sam mixed them with the dressed squirrels. If they had to eat rat meat, the settlers would never know when they were eating rats and when they were eating squirrels.

Sam was dozing one night when he heard a sound that brought cold sweat to his forehead and left him bewildered and sick. Anestasie was sitting by his side, stroking his head. The sound came from the east, the long low cry of the catamount. Then another cry and another. He opened his eyes slowly and looked at Anestasie. "They've come," he muttered.

He did not tell her how worried he was. It was not like the Creeks to sound their cries unless they wanted the defenders of the fort to know of their presence. And why should they want Dabney to know they had arrived? It was a trick and Sam knew it. They would expect him to send to another fort for help and then they would attack the fort that had sent soldiers to Madison. It was a ruse all right, a smart trick of the Red Eagle's, an attempt to weaken some fort where the blow would fall.

Tishomingo reported that the fort was surrounded. "Our scouts have seen them," Chock said. "There are about three hundred of them in the woods around the fort."

A settler came to Sam and suggested, "Let me ride for help."

"Where would you go?" Sam asked.

"There are soldiers at Mims' and at many other stockades along this river. They will come to us."

"And as soon as the soldiers left the stockades, the Creeks would strike there," Sam said. "We'll defend this fort ourselves."

He called his company around him and instructed the women to dress like men. He armed the women with sticks that looked like guns from a distance. He drilled them. He made them march in single file past the smokehouse and as he marched his file by he had the first man or woman drop out of the line, duck behind the house and hook on at the end of the column. They practiced it for hours, then Sam had a huge fire built in the center of the stockade so that the Creek look-outs could see them. It appeared as though he had an army. He really had only sixty-three men and forty-five women.

He made them sing and laugh.

He strung rawhide and grapevine around the fort and tied up pine knots. He set fire to the torches, which lighted the ground for two hundred yards around the fort.

The settlers stood to their arms that night but the Indians did not attack. Tishomingo knew Sam was worried. Hoab knew it. But the others did not. Why should a Creek army appear at his fort and then not attack? He

sent Hoab and Tishomingo to scout and they reported
that only about thirty Indians were in the woods.

"It means something," Sam told Tishomingo. "God
damn it ——"

"Don't use God's name in vain," Anestasie rebuked
him. "We'll need God on our side."

"Right now I'd rather have a hundred more men,"
Sam said.

He went to a look-out on the south side of the fort
and studied the woods. For hours he stayed there, peering to the south toward Mims', then to the north toward
the neighboring forts.

The sun hit its peak and began slipping down toward
its bed. Heat waves danced across the bare ground
around the fort. A rabbit jumped from behind a stump
and scurried toward the woods, leaving a tiny cloud of
powdered dust. Sam watched the dust rise a few inches
and then fall. A field lark cried and darted out of the
woods. The cry alarmed a flock of doves that rose and
winged away, flying in reckless, disorganized formation.
Sam wiped the sweat from his face. A buzzard circled
over the river, wheeled and glided to the south. Not a
breath of air stirred. The leaves hung listless, waiting for
the sun to go away and take its torture with it. The night
would bring wind, a cool wind up from the Gulf. The
night would bring mosquitoes and fireflies and glow-
worms. And it might bring the Creeks too. If they carried the fort, he would trust Anestasie to Tishomingo's
keeping. Chock wouldn't want to leave. He would have
to make him leave. Get the hell out of here, Chock!
Take Anestasie. She wouldn't want to leave. Get the hell
out of here, Anestasie. Scatter! Into the woods. Run,
Hoab! Sam wouldn't leave. He was too weak to run. He
would get behind that smoke-house and pick off the red

690

'uns with his long rifle-gun. Then he would use his pistol, laying his gun carefully upon the ground. When they got close he would heave his tomahawk at them. Then his knife. Then he would pick up his gun and brain them. When they overpowered him he would smash his gun against the smoke-house. They couldn't have his gun. Hoab would get Locha Poka. If Hoab died, Honoria would get it. He wished Anestasie could have it. Tishomingo didn't want it. He would like to give it to Anestasie and Thomas if Hoab died. He knew it was senseless to think of Donna having it.

Poor Donna! She was lying down there in Sam Mims' house, her eyes closed, her breath rasping as one blade of saw grass rasps against another. Gnats were buzzing around her head, too, he knew. And flies. Jasper would be brushing them away. But when Jasper went to get water, the flies would come back, buzzing, crawling and occasionally biting. Maybe Donna could no longer feel the bites.

He shook his head to clear it and to banish his thoughts. He began humming, "Over the Hills . . ." He leaned on the rest of the look-out and stared toward the woods. Then he saw a figure dart out of the woods and race toward the gate.

A guard leveled his gun.

Hoab shouted, "Don't shoot! It's Shellie!"

"Cover the woods!" Sam ordered. "Don't let those bastards get a shot at her! Open the gate!"

The child, her hair streaming, sped across the cleared ground, darting among the stumps and never slackening her speed as she raced from shelter to shelter and worked her way to the gate. There was not a shot from the woods. The few Red Sticks who were there had seen her but had recognized her as the MacLeod girl and would not fire upon one who had been reared among them.

Sam did not wait for Tishomingo to help him to the gate, but limped there alone. Shellie ran into the fort and stood by the gate, her shoulders heaving, her flesh torn by briars and thorns.

"Fort Mims is gone! They're all dead!"

"My wife?" Sam was surprised at his own voice. It was calm and deliberate. Up there in the look-out he had had the premonition. He had felt that the Red Sticks were going to Mims'.

The girl looked from one face to the other, seeking Hoab. When she saw him she smiled and then faced Sam again.

"They're all dead. Your wife and the lawyer. Major Beasley, too. The Red Sticks jumped us. Seekaboo set the fort on fire. A lot of folks burned up. I could hear them yelling and smell them burning. They stank awful. Mr. Thomas fought like a little bear. And he cursed something awful."

Sam let her ramble. It was the best way to get the story. Let her tell it in her own words.

"He said words that your wife told me were bad. The Major cursed too. He let out one big curse and then they got him. They shot Hester—she's a slave, you know. They shot her in the stomach but she got away. Peggy Bailey got away, too. She grabbed a butcher knife and ran through the gate, waving the knife and yelling. The Red Eagle tried to make the Creeks stop, but they wouldn't pay any mind to him. They didn't take time to scalp good; they just hacked the scalps off. It was mighty poor scalping, worse than Choctaw scalping."

"How did *you* get away?" Sam asked.

"I ducked through a hole that Jasper cut. I swam the

Alabama and stole myself a horse, then cut up through the woods. The horse blowed just before I got here. I run him too hard, I reckon. He wasn't much horse anyhow."

Sam turned to Tishomingo and said softly, "Take five men and go there. I can't spare any more. They might strike here next. Bury the dead. Find Donna's body. Save her bones, Chock. I want to send them to Locha Poka. I want to bury her under the Big Tree. Donna really died many years ago and was buried under the Big Tree."

He looked at his son and Hoab looked away. "Your mother will not suffer any more, son. You and I knew she didn't have long to live. I wish God had spared her this. But, we'll avenge her."

Anestasie put her arm around the boy and led him into the house. Shellie walked a few paces behind them, rather reluctant to leave the crowd where she had been the center of attention. Anestasie cautioned Sam as she moved away, "You mustn't stay out here too long, Sam. You're still weak."

She said no more and Sam was glad. There was nothing else to be said. Donna was gone. Sam was glad that Anestasie didn't weep. She didn't weep for Donna and she didn't weep for Thomas. There was too much to be done for her to weep. It took time to weep, and Shellie's bruises had to be treated. Supper had to be cooked. The stock had to be fed and the cows milked. The fires had to be set. The guns had to be primed. It was woman's work.

Sam watched Tishomingo saddle his horse and when the Indian was ready to ride away Sam went over to him. "Look around, Chock, for an old conch shell. Bring it back to me if you can find it. Now, hurry, man. The buzzards will soon be there. Bury most of them in a common grave. But give Thomas a grave all his own. You know, a nice grave. Under a tree if you can find a tree. Give Jasper one, too. And bring Donna's bones to me."

The moon was waning when Tishomingo reached Mims'. He skirted Lake Tensaw, paused by the old boat-works and halted his men. A finger of white smoke spiraled up from the earth, flattened out and floated away. Some of the walls still stood, sagging and charred. The company dismounted, tied their horses and walked toward the ruins. Tishomingo scouted the grounds. A hundred Creeks must have died where he stood but he did not waste time looking for their bodies. The Creeks never left their dead.

He and his men cut torches and lit them and walked to the stockade, holding their torches high. Near the gate, they found Dan Beasley. His brass buttons had been cut off. The skin around his cheek bones sagged almost to his mouth and his mouth was black with ants. It had been a messy scalping job.

They moved among the dead, turning over the bodies, examining them. Many were simply black skeletons. Others were only half burned. Some he recognized, others he could not. There was no difference between white and black. Those who had any flesh on them at all were black, fire-black. Those who had no flesh had nothing but black bones, charred bones that crumbled at the touch.

He would recognize Donna's body. Maybe the Creeks had left her wedding ring on her finger. But even if they hadn't, he could find it. It would be where the big house had been, where her bed had been. He knew the spot well. Donna had the lung fever and the Creeks wouldn't take away the body of a person who had the lung fever.

694

They wouldn't scalp her. He was glad of that. Donna had had such beautiful hair before it had dried and had been burned by the fever. He knew her hair would be gone, burned away by the fire. But he would know her body. He thought that he would find Jasper's body by hers.

He found Thomas where the door to Donna's room had been. They had taken his scalp. His pudgy little face had one streak of flesh across it where he had thrown his arm and the flesh under his arm had not been burned away.

But where was Donna? Her body was not where it should have been. Great God! Had the Creeks carried her away? Because they hated Dabney so, had they taken the body of his wife into one of their villages where it could be seen? If they had, he would join Sam and Hoab and avenge her. His revenge on Flournoy suddenly became unimportant to him. He and Sam and Hoab would go into the nation and kill. He would tie a hundred scalps to his belt, scalps of women and children and Red Sticks. Every Creek he saw he would kill.

He searched for more than an hour for Donna's body. Then he remembered Jasper. He couldn't find Jasper's body either. The Creeks wouldn't take a Negro away. He did not tell his men that he could not find the bodies. The mystery would frighten them. They could understand death when they could see it. They were not afraid of the hundreds of bodies that sprawled on the ground. But had they known that two bodies had vanished they might have run away.

Tishomingo wept without shame as they gathered Thomas' body and the bits of flesh. He wished he had time to purify the body by burning it on a scaffold. He wished he had time to send for the bone-picker and to make a box of soft pine. He wrapped Thomas' remains in his own jacket and they dug the grave under a tree near the lake. Tishomingo scooped dirt in his hands and scattered it on the body and murmured, "Hosey Thomas, *Ta-fa-mah. Ah-hi-o-chubbee* . . . Hosey Thomas, the man who meets the great and lowly and is loved. I will find your killers and kill them."

There was nothing to mark his grave. There was no need to mark it.

They piled the other bodies in heaps near the gate and then began digging a common grave. They wouldn't bury them that night. People would come tomorrow and try to identify their dead so they could take them away. Tishomingo would wait until noon of the next day and then would bury all of the bodies that were not claimed. It was better to put them in the earth without names than to leave them for the buzzards.

They dug in silence. It was soft earth and turned easily. It was good earth to work a spade in. The moon went away and the world blackened quickly, enjoying a few minutes of cool still blackness before dawn.

Tishomingo heard the sound and laid aside his spade and reached for his rifle. It was a hollow sound, an echoing thud. It came from across the river. Someone was felling a tree. He counted the blows. It was a small tree because there were only a few blows. He motioned for his men to hide in the grave and walked alone toward the boatyard to get his horse and cross the river. His horse was gone. He stared at the lake for several minutes and then went back to his men and told them that all was well.

The company resumed its digging, but there was a great fear upon Tishomingo. He, too, was afraid of a thing he could not understand.

31

THOMAS had formed the habit of calling his bone-han-
dled pistols "Clotho" and "Atropos," two of the god-
desses of fate who drew out the threads of men's lives.
He slept with his pistols beside his bed in his tiny, stuffy
room at Fort Mims.

Frequently, during the hot nights, he woke up, always
feeling first for his weapons, for he feared that the day of
reckoning was coming at the fort. And he had no faith
in Major Dan'l Beasley. . . .

Major Beasley was drunk again today, even a bit
drunker than usual. His teeth felt like they were wearing
sweaters and his temper was much sharper than his wits.
He was hot, too. Hot and sweaty and dusty. The chair
on which he sat in his little headquarters at Fort Mims
was wet with the sweat that oozed from his flesh. It was
a horsehide chair. No wonder it was hot. Horsehide was
always hot. Even these damned addle-pated, mule-
headed, dirty-nosed folks in the Tensaw district should
have known that horsehide was hot. A horsehide chair
was all right in the winter time but was no good in the
summer time. A man sweated right through his breeches
and on to the hide. And when the hide got wet it stank.

The major drank his grog and then stretched out his
arms on the table so his aide would know that he wanted
another drink. The table was wet where his arm touched

697

it. Damme, this was a fine command for a first-class soldier, sweating his life away, nursing children, nursing
sick cows.

He wondered how Sam Dabney's wife was doing. Perhaps he had better go see about her. Sam Dabney was a
big man in the territory. He could repay favors. Dabney
would be grateful to him if he saw to all of Mrs. Dabney's needs. Perhaps Dabney could get him a command
in Jackson's army, or in New Orleans. New Orleans—
that was a place for a soldier. There was shade in New
Orleans—nice, cool shade—and women to sit in the shade
with a man.

It made him ill to look at Mrs. Dabney. He had seen
her the night before. She wasn't a fitting sight. And that
damned Thomas seemed to resent his presence. The
Negro resented him, too. Of course he had been a little
drunk when he called, but Donna Dabney had seen drunk
men before.

He had gone over to tell her about the excitement of
the day. Two Creek warriors had sent word to relatives
within the fort that an attack was imminent. The Creeks
had walked boldly up to Beasley and had warned him.
The major had laughed. A negro slave belonging to
John Randon had reported that he had seen twenty Red
Sticks in the brush. Beasley had had him tied up and
flogged for alarming the garrison. John Fletcher's slave
made the same report and Beasley would have flogged
him but Fletcher objected. The major had ordered
Fletcher and his family to leave the fort. Mrs. Dabney
had listened to his story without replying. Thomas had
scowled at him. The little lawyer had walked with him
back to headquarters and had requested that he bring no
more alarming reports to Donna. He had said that she

couldn't live more than two or three days and that she was entitled to a peaceful deathbed.

Beasley drank his grog at one gulp and ran his tongue around his parched lips. It was hard on Dabney having his wife down here while he was up there at Madison. Beasley wished he were at Madison. Maybe it was cooler there and he had heard that it was much cleaner. There was a stench at Mims' that even liquor could not hide. Some of the settlers went outside the fort to attend to their needs, but others just squatted on the ground. The cattle! Beasley did nothing about it, however. He ordered the gate left open and if the settlers had any modesty they could go through it and find privacy in the woods. Thomas had criticized him for leaving the gate open—but, what the hell!—he couldn't be ordering his guard to open the gate every time a settler wanted to get outside to get water or to get rid of it.

The well within the fort wasn't large enough for the people's needs and it was easier to let them go out to the lake or river than to dig new wells. The Indians were not going to attack. They might strike at Dabney at Madison, but they would never bother him. Hell, Sam Mims was an Indian. He had a hundred half-breed women in the fort. Some of them were cousins of the warriors in Red Eagle's army. Red Eagle wouldn't fight. After all, Red Eagle had only one drop of Indian blood in his veins. He wouldn't dare attack Dan Beasley, who was half Creek. The Red Sticks would rebel rather than fight against their own kith for a leader who was almost white.

Beasley saw Jasper come out of the big house and walk through the gate, heading toward the lake for cool water. He saw the slave return, walking rapidly, and watched him into the big house. A few minutes later Thomas and Jasper presented themselves and the lawyer said, "Major, Jasper here was just down to the lake. He saw some Indians."

"He's crazy with the heat," sneered Beasley.

"It seems to me," bridled Thomas, "that we should at least shut the gate."

The major laughed as though Thomas had told a very funny joke. "I started to shut it this morning but sand has washed against it and now it's propped open. I'll get some men to dig the sand away when the sun goes down and it gets cool." He glanced at Jasper. "Where do you think you saw those red 'uns?"

"Jasper saw them hiding in the gulley."

"You're lying. I whipped a slave yesterday for lying. You wouldn't know a Creek Red Stick if you saw one."

"Jasper knows Indians," the slave answered politely.

Major Beasley struggled to his feet, his face red with rage. "He's impudent! I have a cure for impudent slaves. Tie him up, men!"

Thomas stepped quickly to the door. He reached behind him and parted his coat tails and pulled out Clotho and Atropos. "The first man who touches that Negro will get a ball in his belly."

Beasley's mouth flew open and the soldiers stepped back. They were afraid of Thomas. They were afraid of him without guns, but when the little lawyer held pistols in his hands they were terrified.

Struggling to maintain his poise, Beasley thundered, "This is insubordination. I can have you court-martialed."

Thomas did not lower his pistols. "You know even less about law, Beasley, than you know about defending

700

women and children. This is mutiny. I'm guilty as hell. You have the right to court-martial me this minute and then line me up against the wall and shoot me. I'm going back to the big house. If you want me, come after me. Jasper and I are going to walk across the yard with our backs to you. If you decide to shoot me, for God's sake shoot me in the back of the head. And then go look up a preacher and get right with God. Sam Dabney might hear what you've done and he'd twist your head off. So if you want to kill me, be damned sure you're ready to die yourself. Good day, gentlemen. Come on, Jasper."

Thomas put his pistols back, turned around and walked away from the men. The soldiers looked at one another and then at their commander, but Beasley glanced away.

The major was playing cards when Jim Cornells returned from a scouting expedition up the river. He halted at the gate and shouted to the major, "Better get ready. The red 'uns are coming."

Beasley struggled to his feet and went to the look-out.

"Jim," he said, "are you loony, too? Good old Jim. Are you drunk?"

The scout did not laugh. "Pull yourself together, Beasley. Hell's a-coming."

"You just saw some red cattle," Beasley mocked, "and thought they were Indians."

"Those cattle are going to give you a hell of a kick before night."

Beasley ordered the scout's arrest. "I'll have you flogged," he thundered.

The soldiers around the gate agreed with the major. Cornells covered them with his rifle. "You're all drunk! You drunken bunch of sons of bitches! I'll stay here and fight if you want me to, but if you don't want me, I'm getting out of here."

The soldiers jeered him away.

Red Eagle stood in the ravine and watched a courier ride out of the fort. Peter McQueen watched him and so did Josiah Francis, a minor prophet.

Peter McQueen grinned. "The time has come."

"Nay," cautioned Red Eagle. "Let us wait until the cool of the evening." He watched the fort hoping to see the women and children march out. He had delayed the attack for days. He had sent warnings to the fort. His one thousand Red Sticks were mad for blood.

The drums rolled in Fort Mims, calling the people to dinner. It was exactly high noon. Josiah Francis crawled to the ledge of the ravine and faced the warriors. "Strike. Strike for The Open Door." The redskin force surged forward, taking Red Eagle with it. The braves were within thirty yards of the fort before a look-out saw them.

"Injuns!" the look-out screamed and fired into the ranks.

Beasley overturned his black coffee when he jumped to his feet and ran toward the gate. "Close the gate! Sound the alarm! Man the blockhouses!" He stumbled over his own feet as he ran. But he ran toward the enemy. Let that be said for Major Dan Beasley. He didn't even have a gun. He had only a sword, a sword that had been given him by the Territory of Mississippi. He didn't withdraw the sword. Dan Beasley was a good man with the rifle. He was a heller with a dirk, and a first-class fighting man with a tomahawk. But a sword and a sash! God's jaw bone! He never thought of his sword. He ran to the gate and tried to close it. He was alone there. Women and children were pouring out of the houses, shrieking and getting in one another's way. Drums rolled and the soldiers tried to assemble. The look-outs had to prime their guns.

Beasley put his great shoulders to the gate and shoved it, but it wouldn't budge. Sand was piled more than a foot around its base. He had his shoulder against the gate when a Red Stick cut him down, burying his tomahawk in his head. Fifty bullets ripped into his body. An Indian scalped him quickly, raised the bloody trophy and screamed his war-cry. A prophet, dressed entirely in feathers, rushed up and snatched the scalp away. Dixon Bailey hurried to the gate, shoved his pistol into the prophet's belly and blew him into the arms of Aba Inki. Bailey fell, his body slashed with knives.

Thomas ran out of the big house, his guns blazing. Jasper was right behind him, loading while Thomas fired. A handful of soldiers opened fire and the Indians fell back. Thomas kept advancing to the gate, cursing and shooting. He walked with a waddle, his little pot-belly shaking from side to side and his bald spot gleaming in the sun. The sun burned his tender skin and that irritated him. He had forgotten his hat. He hated to have the sun beam on his head. He hated sweat and dirt and blood. Hosey Thomas liked cool shade and good rum and good comrades. He loved a pistol and was the kind of man to handle one. He was awkward with a rifle but a pistol was small and pudgy and was a part of him. He blew down the barrel each time he finished shooting and then calmly handed the empty pistol back to Jasper and accepted a primed one.

The Indians retreated about fifty yards and went into council. The Americans scattered them with a withering but disorganized fire. The Red Sticks ran back to the woods and reassembled. Thomas stood by the gate, covering it to give the soldiers time to rally. He could see

Red Eagle standing in the center of the Indians, gesticulating as he talked.

"I won't do it," the Eagle was shouting. "I'll not kill women and children. That is not war. Heed Tecumseh. One of our prophets was killed. He died as any mortal man. You have been told by false leaders that the white man's bullets can't kill any of our prophets. Maybe Aba Inki is displeased with us."

The death of the prophet who fell under the pistol of Dixon Bailey was responsible for the Red Sticks' hesitation. They could have carried the fort easily, but a prophet had fallen and they had gone into council to discuss it. It might be an ill omen.

Seekaboo, fearing that Red Eagle would persuade the Indians to retire, sprang to his feet and yelled to the warriors. "The prophet who died wasn't a true prophet. I'm a true prophet. The bullets did not touch me."

"You were safe behind the bodies of the men," Red Eagle said. "Do as you will, but the Red Eagle will not lead you into that fort." He turned and walked away, praying that his men would follow him—but he walked alone. A few miles from the fort he met his half brother, David Tate, and told him what had happened.

"They'll attack again," Tate predicted. "And the white men will blame you. Because you are the accepted leader of the Creeks and the spokesman of the nation, you'll be blamed. Because you are mostly white, the white men will call you a renegade, a butcher, a savage."

"Before man, I'll take the blame," said Red Eagle sadly. "But before God, I'm innocent."

Back at the fort the soldiers milled around the yard and did not man their posts. They thought they had driven the Indians away. Thomas implored them, threatened them. The women and children gathered around

704

the soldiers and praised them as heroes. They had de-feated the Creeks with only a few shots.

While the Indians hesitated, Seekaboo, Peter McQueen and two Negroes slipped around to the boatyard. They hid there, tied rags to their arrows, set fire to the rags and shot the blazing arrows at the Mims' smoke-house. A tiny flame appeared and McQueen ran back to his men calling, "Follow me! The fort's on fire! The great prophet will bless you."

The Red Sticks surged forward again in a long col-umn that flanked the fort. Thomas measured their line with his eye. He estimated their number at eight hun-dred. He fired both his guns and fell back. Old Clotho was hot and smoking. He loaded and fired again, cocking his left eye as he fired. "Belch, madam!" he muttered, and held Atropos up and blew into the barrel. "Spit, you old hags! This day you and I are going to get a belly-ful of killing Indians. *Advokaten und Soldaten sind des Teufels Spielkameraden!* . . . Lawyers and soldiers are the devil's playmates!" Thomas smiled to himself as he repeated it. He wished he could sing. He picked off two more Indians and then tried to hum, "Over the Hills and Far Away." He laughed at his own efforts. He remem-bered the motto of his family and quoted it reverently. "*Dare fatis vela*—Sail where fate directs." Hosea Cin-cinnatus Thomas laughed again. At Harvard, his Latin and Greek had been the pride of his instructors. Now he gladly would trade all of his knowledge for just one cannon. Or for Sam Dabney.

The soldiers fired one volley as the Indians swarmed through the gate and over the walls, cutting down the few defenders who guarded the walls. They cleared the look-outs. The Mississippians were herded like cattle in the yard, and the Creeks butchered them as cattle are butchered. They rounded up their prey. Some of the Americans thought the Creeks were going to take them prisoners.

Seekaboo ran through the Indians, snatched a child from among the prisoners and severed its head with his scalping knife. The white people froze in horror. The prophet held the child's head by its hair, brandished his knife and shouted, "Kill!" He snatched for another child but before he could wield his knife Thomas shot the child through the head. Thomas couldn't get a bead on Seekaboo.

The Red Sticks hesitated for a minute. There were a few wild shots from the defenders and then the massacre began. . . .

The Creeks ripped and tore at the whites, clawing open their throats, hacking them. They smeared their own bodies with blood. The sun went behind a cloud as though to blot out the scene of horror.

The whites fought as best they could. Husbands ran to their wives and children, and stood before them, shooting down the Red Sticks until they themselves were overwhelmed. Many men shot their own families. One man cut his baby's throat. His wife went stark mad at the sight and he killed her, hurled his knife into the charging Creeks and died with twenty wounds in his body.

Thomas retreated to the big house, loaded a pistol carefully—it was not one of his two favorites—and handed it to Jasper. He put his hand on the Negro's shoulder. "Go to your mistress. She's already unconscious. The red 'uns mustn't take her. If they get to her room and she's still alive, shoot her."

Thomas was glad he was on the porch of the big house. It was cooler there and his vision was better. He watched the Indians dash around the yard chasing the children. It reminded him of a game he had often played with his kinsman, little Sam Houston. He used to chase Sam and tag him and then Sam would chase him. By God, Sam must be quite a man by now! Thomas picked the Indians off as they ran, shooting for their bellies. It was like shooting rabbits and deer. He always aimed just a fraction in front of his man. Damme! He didn't shoot the man; the man ran into the bullet. The Indians were killing themselves. Thomas removed his long black coat, folded it and laid it on the porch. Then he wiped his face with his big handkerchief and returned his handkerchief to his pocket. He talked to his guns as he killed—"Oh, you handmaidens of hell. Smoke, damn you! Pour out your spleen! *You* are the bloody sluts who make all men equal." He recited snatches of poetry to himself, verse after verse of Homer.

About fifty soldiers formed a band and rushed the Creeks. The Indians hacked them to bits. There were not many cries, only an occasional war-whoop, or a scream from a mother as she saw her children die. A few of the children shrieked, but most of them just whimpered. They didn't whimper for mercy, but for their mothers. If their mothers were with them the Indians could not bother them. Their mothers would protect them. Their mothers had always protected them against goblins and sickness.

Shellie MacLeod stood by a window in the big house and watched the carnage. When Jasper entered the house and left Thomas alone, she calmly went to the front porch and took up the task of loading the pistols. She saw many Indians whom she knew. There was Sanota, a handsome brave who used to cut willow whistles for her. His parents had been killed by the

707

whites and he had been adopted by Mrs. Vicey McGirth. Merciful God! Shellie thought, Mrs. McGirth was in the fort.

Thomas looked at the child and smiled as she handed him his pistol. He started to speak but changed his mind, leaned against the door to steady his aim and shot Indians until he retched at the sight of blood.

Flames from the smoke-house spread and the Red Sticks lighted other torches and kindled other fires. About sixty persons took refuge in the loom-house. The Creeks set it on fire and as the Mississippians ran out, the Indians grabbed them, slit their throats and ripped off their scalps.

A score gathered in the Steadham house near the big house, but the Indians battered the door down and killed them. Others gathered in the Randon house and were roasted alive. There were few shots. The soldiers were hopelessly scattered and fired occasionally. Most of them, however, used their guns as clubs. But the Creeks swarmed over their own dead, ripping and tearing the flesh of their comrades to get over them and reach the whites. A few women picked up guns and fired. Some used tomahawks and others used knives, slashing awkwardly as though they were cutting food. The children fought too, biting and kicking and clawing. Thomas kept blazing away, but his shots scarcely could be heard above the crackling roar of the flames that swept through the tents of the Volunteers and ate toward the big house.

The Indians used their knives and tomahawks. It was easy to kill with a tomahawk. The Creeks wrestled their victims to the ground, held them with one knee and shattered their skulls with one blow. Then they cut gashes in the scalps, inserted their fingers and ripped the scalps off.

708

A mile away at Pierce's Mill, Lieutenant Montgomery and a small company saw the smoke rising from the fort and heard the tumult. Perhaps the Creeks would strike there next. Lieutenant Montgomery assembled his men. Eagerly the Mississippi Volunteers fell into line. The lieutenant was going to take them over to Mims'. There was going to be a fight, boys! The lieutenant was going to lead them. Maybe they would die, too, but they would take some red hides with them. "Forward march!" the lieutenant commanded and marched his men away toward the river, abandoning his post. They marched in the opposite direction from Mims'. The lieutenant did not give them a chance to collect red hides, but he saved their own and his. He was a very cautious lieutenant.

Shellie saw Mrs. McGirth run from the kitchen, a log structure back of the big house. She was shouting in Creek. Sanota heard her and ran to her. He put his arm around her and led her and her children to safety. "I knew you were here," he said. "That is why I came. I came to save you, to repay a debt."

"Don't go back there!" Mrs. McGirth pleaded.

"I am a Creek Red Stick," the boy said. "I have done my duty to you and now I will avenge the death of my people."

Hester, a lithe slave wench, dashed from the kitchen and made a break for the gate. A Creek shot her in the side and leaped at her, his tomahawk raised. Thomas shot him in the belly with two slugs. The Red Stick dropped his tomahawk and ran around in circles for a few seconds, holding his entrails in his hands. Hester clasped her hand over her wound and kept running. She reached the Alabama River and found a big barge. She climbed aboard, poled the barge into the river and, while blood gushed from her side, she piloted the clumsy craft across the stream, a feat that would have given a strong man cause to boast. Once on the other side, the Negress ran through the woods toward Fort Easely to give the alarm to General Claiborne.

Peggy Bailey snatched a butcher knife from the table in the kitchen and ran across the yard, waving the blade and screaming. She cut down a warrior who sought to stop her and outran two others who gave chase. Reaching the big river, she turned and hurled her knife at her pursuers, then dived into the stream and swam across.

Two Spanish soldiers, deserters from Pensacola, threw down their guns and knelt by the well, imploring mercy from God and from the Indians. A big Red Stick put his arm under their chins, snapped their necks and tore off their scalps. A boy child ran by. An Indian reached out, grabbed him by the leg and battered his brains out against the well. He wiped the blood and brains off his hand when he completed the scalping and looked up. Thomas shot him through the neck.

Jasper came from Donna's room to see how the fight was going and Thomas spoke over his shoulder to the Negro. "Cut a hole in the north wall and let Shellie out. Maybe she can get to Madison. Maybe we can hold this house unless the fire gets us."

Jasper did as he was told and Shellie slipped through the opening, flattened herself against the wall and looked around. Then she dived for a stump and began working her way toward the river. Once in the water, she swam rapidly to the other side.

The Creeks stormed the Dyer cabin and then turned to the big house. There were eight men there, fourteen women and two children. The Americans beat back the first assault and the Creeks retired to the gate and waited.

They could afford to wait. The flames were leaping from the kitchen and were licking toward the big house.

Inside her room, Donna coughed fitfully and Jasper closed the windows and door to keep out the smoke. He wondered if she were unconscious, if she could feel pain. Blood formed on her lips when she coughed and a look of agony spread over her face. Jasper turned his face away. He couldn't look at her. But maybe she would want to speak. He must lean over her and watch her, so if she spoke he could hear her. Massa Sam might ask him about that. The smoke became so thick in the room that even he coughed. He prayed that the Lord would take her before the Indians attacked again.

"Lord," he begged, "take her."

It was right that he should pray to the Lord. She believed in the Lord and so did Massa Sam. He was a good Lord and a stout Lord. Then why didn't He take her? Maybe He was a stubborn Lord, or maybe He wasn't any Lord at all, but just another weak tobie. Jasper would take no chances. He prayed to Sam's Lord, but held his own tobie in his hand as he prayed. If Sam's Lord wouldn't hear him, the Big Tobie of the Congo would.

He saw the convulsion pass over Donna and he put the lobe of his ear near her mouth. Her breath was moist. He could feel her breath.

Back near the gate, the Indians amused themselves by cleaning the scalps they had taken. They milled around the yard, seeking wounded, and when they found a wounded person they clubbed him. Seekaboo watched the flames leap from the kitchen to the big house, and then commanded his warriors to advance. Thomas and the other men fired from the windows until the flames ate into the parlor where they had barricaded themselves. Thomas looked down his pistol barrel and blew into it and said calmly, "It's no use. Run!"

The Mississippians dashed out of the house and scattered. Mrs. Mims and three of her sons, David, Alexander and Joseph, got away. Sam Smith got away, too. The Indians took Mrs. Susan Hatterway and Elizabeth Randon as prisoners.

Thomas backed against the door that led to Donna's room and was crouching there when the Indians leaped into the parlor. He discharged both his pistols, then gripped their barrels and used them as clubs. A tomahawk crunched to the base of his skull, and Hosea Cincinnatus Thomas, Harvard *magna cum laude*, pitched on his face. The Creeks riddled his body with bullets and hacked it with knives. Seekaboo took his scalp, mumbling disapproval of the bald spot. The prophet took Clotho, too. Peter McQueen took Atropos.

Jasper heard the Indians try the door. Maybe they wouldn't know that Donna and he were in there. He breathed lightly, scarcely drawing in his breath and exhaling it quickly. The smoke hurt his lungs. The smoke was pouring in. It smelled like pine pitch and was black. The smoke also brought an odor of grease—burnt flesh!

The slave stood by Donna's bed and looked at her. She could not live more than a few hours. His first impulse was to lift her up and jump through the window and run for the gate. He knew if they were captured, they both would be scalped. Massa Sam would never forgive him if he allowed her to be scalped. However, there always was a chance that he might get away. He stooped over to lift her and a spasm of coughing passed through her body. The Indians lunged against the door, shrieking for one more scalp.

Jasper clearly heard an Indian shout, "Sam Dabney's wife is in there. Her scalp's worth almost as much as his." Jasper felt his way to the mantel and ran his hand

712

along it until he found the conch shell. He put it into his jacket. He pushed it around to his back so it would not press against him when he lifted her. Then he reached for the pistol Thomas had given him, watched a convulsion shake Donna for a second, pressed the pistol to her side, covered it with a pillow to muffle the sound, and jerked the trigger. He threw the pistol under the bed and lifted Donna, covering the wound with his right arm. He held her mouth close to his ear and could not feel her breath. He was standing there in the smoke when the Creeks broke in.

"There she is!" cried one of the Indians.

"She's dead," said Jasper calmly.

"We'll see," said the Indian. "It may be a trick."

"She's dead," Jasper repeated. "Massa Sam Dabney's wife died of the lung fever. Look at her mouth. See the blood there. She got to coughing when the smoke came in and then she died. Jasper's going to take her away. Let me through, Red Sticks."

The Creeks stepped back and bowed their heads. They would not touch a body that had died of the lung fever. They were rather weary of blood, anyway. Here in the presence of one that Aba Inki had taken they felt ashamed, and they were awed. There was nothing awesome about the bodies they had hacked and scalped. A man can understand his own work. A man can understand death when he causes it, but when Aba Inki kills, death becomes a mystery.

The slave walked out of the burning house and across the yard, stepping over some bodies, stumbling over others. He walked through the gate without seeing the body of Dan Beasley. Down to the river he went, and laid Donna on the bank. He went to the boatyard and collected lumber, nails and an ax and took them to the river. He found a canoe and put Donna and the supplies aboard and paddled across the Alabama.

Seekaboo and Peter McQueen ordered the Creeks to collect their dead, about one hundred and ten of them. Fifty more were dying of wounds. It was five o'clock when the Indians marched away and left Mims' in flames. The flames leveled the buildings and danced over the bodies of several hundred American dead. The Creeks did not count the persons they had slain. History would never know the toll. Some of the survivors said that about fifteen white persons got away. Others said that at least thirty-five survived. Some insisted that the Indians took a few whites and about three-score Negroes as slaves. But there was no record. The survivors scattered. The bodies could not be counted, for as soon as the Indians left, great packs of wild dogs and a few wolves raided the fort and dragged some bodies away and fought over them.

Twelve miles from Mims' the Red Eagle sat under a tree and planned his next move. The whites would really fight now. They would pour into the Creek country. Sam Dabney would come, Big Sam whose rifle roared like thunder and whose arms struck like the lightning. Andy Jackson might come, Old Jacksa Chula Harjo, Old Mad Jackson, as the Indians called him. The Red Eagle was ashamed of what his people had done. Ay, they would call him a renegade, the Red Eagle whose blood was purer than almost any man between the Ohio and the Gulf. In his veins was the blood of old Lachlan McGillivray, the wealthy Scotchman who made his fortune in the new land and returned to Scotland to die in peace, leaving behind his son, Alexander. The Red Eagle was Alexander McGillivray's nephew. He had

good French and good Scotch and good Spanish blood
in him, and his only Creek blood was a small strain of
the godlike Clan of the Wind. Ay, the whites would put
a price on his head and hunt him down. But he would
fight back. He would raise a good army and train it. He
would take British gold and buy supplies. In his heart he
knew what his Indian rabble had done at Mims', but he
would accept responsibility for its behavior. He was the
Red Eagle, the leader, and a brave leader always accepts
responsibility for the conduct of his men. He got slowly
to his feet and walked away, thinking of many things
and hoping that Sam Dabney's wife had died before the
Creeks reached her.

Jasper finished the coffin by the light of the moon and
put Donna into it. Massa Sam would never know how
she had died. He would tell the Massa that she hadn't
suffered, that she had just punied a bit and then died.

He heard men digging across the river where the fort
had been. He could see the finger of smoke spiraling up.
He thought he heard voices several times. The sound of
his ax, as he cut two strong saplings, startled him. He lay
the saplings upon the ground, braced them, and tied the
coffin across them. He wished he had a wagon, a light
Jersey wagon. It hurt him to think that Donna's body
would bounce in the box as the saplings were dragged
over the rough road and across the wilderness where
there was no road at all. He got in his canoe and crossed
the river and went to Pierce's Mill where he thought he
could steal a horse from the garrison. The mill was deserted. Jasper cut back near the boatyard and found the
horses tied there. He selected the strongest and led him
away. Swimming the horse across the river, he backed
him between the saplings. He lashed the saplings to the

saddle and picked up the ax and stuck it in his belt. He felt in his jacket to make sure the conch shell was safe. He would give it to Sam and would tell him, "She asked me to fetch it to you. That's all she said when she was dying." It would be a good lie. His Big Tobie would approve of such a good lie. Even Massa Sam's Lord would sanction such a lie.

Jasper took the horse's reins and they moved north toward Locha Poka, the horse dragging the saplings upon which rested the coffin. He would bury her under the Big Tree beside her baby. No one would ever see the body and no one would ever know that he had killed his mistress. Massa Sam wouldn't be at Locha Poka. He would be off fighting the red 'uns. If any of the slaves or Choctaws at Locha Poka demanded to see the body he would tell them that the lung fever was inside the coffin and that if he opened it, the fever would climb out and get them. No, nobody would see the body. Her body might be dust before they reached Locha Poka. Massa Sam didn't like dust. He was a funny man. Jasper wondered if Sam would get another woman. Would she be good to Jasper?

He would get the old spade that Massa Sam had fetched from Georgia and dig Mis' Donna's grave. He would put out a few flowers and have the grave ready for Massa Sam's return from killing red 'uns. He would get a stone to put there. That would please Massa Sam.

32

THE wild dogs and wolves returned to Fort Mims during the hours of sticky blackness. Tishomingo armed his men with clubs to beat off the scavengers, but the dogs slunk to the piles of dead and stole bones and flesh. The big rats came up from the river and feasted. The buzzards bivouacked in the trees. The spiral of smoke fell lower and lower, then rose slowly, then down again—a sobbing as a mournful symphony sobs to a close. The smoke exerted all of its energies and spiraled up again and spread out, writing an elegy in the sky. The white ashes fell apart and the wind lifted them and scattered them to enrich the earth.

A company of soldiers arrived soon after dawn and Tishomingo turned over to them the chore of burying the dead. He went to the boatworks and studied the ground. He found Jasper's trail and followed it to the river bank, and across the river he found the spot where the slave had made the coffin. He borrowed a horse and followed Jasper's trail toward Locha Poka.

He knew what he would find and he was not surprised when he overtook the slave.

Jasper apologized for taking the horse and nodded toward the coffin. "Jasper had to get her home," he said. "Mis' Dabney died while the red 'uns were fighting. The noise and all helped kill her. She didn't know what was happening."

Tishomingo patted the slave's shoulder. He was proud of Jasper. He was Jasper's master. The slave didn't know it. Only Sam and he knew it. He had never returned ownership of Jasper to his friend. Sam had never mentioned it again.

He took the conch shell from the Negro, bade him Godspeed, and that afternoon made his report to Sam at Fort Madison.

Anestasie stood by Sam while Tishomingo talked, and when Sam heard the story he stared at the floor for several minutes, then said, "You've done well, Chock. Jasper has done well, too."

Tishomingo left them and Sam put the conch shell safely away and faced Anestasie. She wanted to go to him, but he must come to her now. Sam hesitated for a moment and then embraced her. She stayed in his arms until she felt them relax and then she led him to a chair and put a pillow at his back.

"There's a thing you must know," he began.

"I know it now." She stroked his hair. "I really knew it before, Sam, but now I'm certain of myself. I know that you love me."

"There's never been a doubt of that, but there's another thing. You must become Hoab's mother. When the war's over, we'll go to Locha Poka and you must help me rear the boy. And Shellie, too. Donna wanted it that way."

"We're starting off with quite a family, aren't we?" She rubbed her nose playfully against his cheek. "Of course, I'll mother them. I'll be a good mother to Donna's son."

"Hoab isn't our son."

718

Anestasie straightened, caught her breath quickly and gasped, "No—no? You're teasing me ——"

"He's not my son, or Donna's." Sam's eyes looked old and his shoulders sagged.

"Whose son is he?" she demanded, but the words scarcely were out of her mouth before she knew the answer. "Ab? Ab's son! He's Ab's boy. He looks and acts like Ab ——"

"And Honoria," said Sam weakly.

"Merciful God!"

"Our baby died. Donna died at the same time, I think. Hoab doesn't know this."

Anestasie did not interrupt him, but a thousand thoughts whirled through her brain as Sam told her the story. Honoria had been willing, anxious, to give up her baby. The thought made Anestasie ill. Poor Donna. She prayed quickly that she might be as fine a woman and wife—ay, and mother—as Donna. For Donna *was* Hoab's mother. Never would Anestasie associate Hoab with Honoria. Perhaps with Ab. Thank God, he was more like his father than his mother. Poor Sam! She wanted to hold his head against her breast and stroke his face and comfort him. Rear Hoab and Shellie? Of course. She would love them. What a small thing Sam was asking her—merely to help take care of two persons she already loved. Sam had given her so much. She could never repay him. She took his hand and held it against her face.

"I'm glad that you've told me," she said. "You didn't have to, you know. Maybe I never would have found out. But if I had found out I might have doubted you. It's best that you have told me. To me, Hoab has always been the son of a woman I loved. Hoab will always be your son to me, and I will be his mother, even if we have children of our own. My love for you, Sam, is great enough to spill over and cover Hoab, too."

"It also gives you a weapon against Honoria," he added and watched to see the reaction of his words on her.

"I'll never wield it."

Sam kissed her again to seal the pledge and asked her to fetch Tishomingo. He told Chock, "The Creeks will be here soon. We must be ready for them. For every drop of blood spilled at Mims', my son and I will take a pint. See to it that no person leaves this stockade without my signed permission. If anyone tries to get out, flog him. If a woman tries to get out, lock her up. Man every look-out. Send out four scouts. We're going to teach the Creeks what it means to kill American women and children."

Up in Tennessee, Andy Jackson lay on a bed that was wet with the blood of his wound. They had said he couldn't live, that he couldn't survive Tom Benton's bullet. He heard of Fort Mims and said, "They must be avenged." He had a servant prop him up in bed and he wrote to his army that he would take command. The governor of Tennessee called for twenty-five hundred men and Old Mad Jackson vowed by the eternal that he would march within nine days. He scarcely could hold his quill to write. When he moved the blood gushed from his wound and soaked his mattress. But, by God, he could fight! He could sit a horse. It was better to spill blood on a saddle than on a mattress.

Old Mad Jackson was coming! The Red Eagle heard and rallied his Red Sticks. Young Sam Houston left his schoolroom and joined up. He pitched a silver dollar on to an army drum, the sign that he was volunteering.

He would avenge his kinsman, Lawyer Thomas. The Tennesseans poured out, fighting among themselves for the privilege of fighting the Red Sticks. It wasn't an army. It was a rabble. It knew only two commands, charge and fire. But its officers didn't say "Charge!" They said, "Go get the sons of bitches!" They didn't say "Fire!" as officers should, but told their men, "Lay a bead on the bloody bastards! If you don't shoot them in the left eye, it don't count!"

The war with England was going disastrously for the United States and the nation sorely needed a successful Indian campaign to strengthen its morale. The British had forsaken Detroit and in the battle that followed the retreat into Canada, Tecumseh had been killed. Red Eagle knew that his people no longer were fighting a holy war, but were fighting for the right to live. He dared not tell the people that Tecumseh was dead and so the Red Sticks went happily to their deaths for The Open Door and for Tecumseh who were already in the Indian paradise that was the reward of every brave who died for his nation.

As the Romans of old had thundered for the complete destruction of Carthage, so did the Southwest demand the destruction of the Creeks. The nation must be uprooted and scattered.

Couriers to Fort Madison kept Sam informed and he agreed with Jackson's plan to crush the Creeks first, then Florida and then England. British supplies had been seen in Pensacola and Sam knew that England was preparing a base there. The Creeks must be crushed before an English army arrived.

General Claiborne sent a relief to Sam at Fort Madison and instructed him to prepare to evacuate the place. Sam refused. He was threatened with arrest and court-martial, but he laughed at the captain who bore the orders from General Claiborne.

"I'll not do it, captain." Sam was adamant. "I'll not leave this fort. This fort is the key to the defense of Mississippi."

"But, sir!" the officer stammered, "I have orders."

"Stick your orders up your arse!" Sam thundered. "I've got women and children here. Do you think I'll send them to a fort where you yellow-bellies will leave them exposed to the Creeks as Beasley did at Mims'? We built this fort and we'll hold it. I'm a private citizen and I'll take no orders from you. Go tell your general I said so."

Baffled and enraged the officer reported to Claiborne and Claiborne smiled. "Sam Dabney was a mite upset, I'll warrant. But if he said he'll hold that fort, then he'll hold it."

Claiborne's army of Mississippi volunteers was ready to march against the Red Eagle from the southwest. A Georgia army was on the march from the east and Old Mad Jackson was coming down from the north. Old Andy had said he would march within nine days and he had.

Red Eagle faced armies on three fronts—north, east and south—and a string of American forts was to his west. And thousands of his own people were in arms against him. Sam reasoned that Red Eagle might try to break through the forts and strike for Natchez and the territorial capital, and he was not surprised when Tishomingo reported that the Red Sticks were massing in front of his fort.

He shook his head, however, when his scouts brought intelligence that the red army had concentrated all of its forces in the woods that faced Fort Madison's east wall.

722

"Red Eagle is not with them," Sam declared. "He'd never concentrate his whole army. He'd scatter and attack us from all sides. Only a fool would mass before our east wall, for it's our strongest wall. Nay, Red Eagle isn't with them and they'll be easy to defeat."

The assault on the fort came as a relief to the defenders. The days had become monotonous and life in the fort was a hardship. Sam Dabney was a hard leader and the settlers were glad when Tishomingo reported that the Creeks were coming up. Methodically the settlers went about the business of defending themselves. Sam assembled them and spoke slowly. He had told them so often what to do that it seemed useless to tell them again. "They'll strike first for the big gate. I'll be there. We'll let them get within fifty yards of the gate before we open fire. We'll stop them there. I'll announce my other plans later."

A prophet led the Creeks in the first attack and the charge fizzled before it got well under way. The settlers blew down the leaders and when the ranks formed again they blew gaping holes in the lines. Sam loaded an old blunderbuss with bits of chain and lead, and fired a charge into the Indians. They thought he had a cannon and retreated.

Sam gave his orders quickly. "Tishomingo, take twenty men. Slip out of the rear gate, cut through the woods and attack from the north. Yell when you attack. The Tennesseans always yell. Yell for Andy Jackson. Be back here within two hours."

He called another veteran to him and ordered, "Take some picked men, slip through the woods and attack from the south. Yell for Claiborne when you attack. Don't worry about the fort. We can hold it while you're away."

His plan worked. The Creeks thought Jackson's army was attacking from the north and Claiborne's men were attacking from the south. They fled into the woods and went into council. If only the Red Eagle had been there. But the Red Eagle would not attack Madison and he had jeered Josiah Francis for his plans.

"You're a fool," the Red Eagle had said. "You would waste time and blood on Madison because you hate Big Sam Dabney. While you're at Madison your country will be invaded. You cannot capture Big Sam. You're a child to him and he'll laugh at you."

The Red Eagle had headed his army toward the Holy Grounds. That was where the whites would strike first. It was the heart of the Creek Nation. The prophets had preached that no Indian could die on the Holy Grounds. Red Eagle wanted the Americans to attack there. He wanted some of his men to die so they could see that the prophets were false leaders. He must convince them that this was no holy war, but a war for life. It was not a struggle between Aba Inki and Jehovah. Aba Inki and Jehovah were the same God. He must teach his people to rely upon their brains and their arms and not upon the promises of prophets who assured them a place in paradise if they killed a white man.

Sam, confident that the Red Sticks had abandoned their effort to capture Madison, issued rum to the settlers and told them to celebrate. He allowed some of them to go beyond the stockade in search of fresh meat while he went to his room and locked himself in. He got quill and paper and drew a map of the Mississippi Territory, every trail and every river. He studied the map for hours and then went for Tishomingo and fetched him to his room.

"If you were the Red Eagle what would you do?"

Sam asked. "Size the situation up now, Chock, and think carefully. Remember Claiborne's army is down here near Mobile. The Georgians are pushing in from the east, and Jackson is coming down from the north. Remember, and this is important, that the Creeks are not a united nation. Keep in mind that every other Indian nation in the south is allied with the United States against them. The Red Eagle's chances are about a hundred to one. Now, what would you do?"

"I'd blow my brains out," Tishomingo laughed.

"I'm serious," Sam insisted.

"All right," said Chock. "The first thing I'd do would be to find out what my English allies were going to do."

Sam slapped his friend's shoulder. "Ay, you're wise. Pensacola is the logical place for the English to land and begin their invasion. That's the trouble, Chock. It's too damned logical. It's too close to Georgia. The Americans can get soldiers down from Virginia to meet an army that comes up from Pensacola."

"Mobile's the best place for the English to land," Tishomingo said.

"And that's what England will make us think she's going to do. That will hold Claiborne's army near Mobile. Don't you see it, man? They won't land at Pensacola or Mobile. New Orleans is the place."

"You're loony. The British wouldn't dare fight in those swamps."

"Who's to fight them?" Sam demanded. "They can take New Orleans and sweep up the valley."

"Where will Jackson be?"

"Fighting the Creeks. That's the plan, I believe. If Red Eagle can keep Jackson over here, then the game is up for us. I'm going to Jackson."

"And leave this fort?"

"This fort is one of the safest places in America. Red Eagle can't spare more than a handful of men to raid the border. They can't take this fort, but they can make the territory tremble with fright. I'll turn the fort over to a good officer. Then I'm going where the fighting is. Hoab will go with me."

"He's a good lad," Tishomingo agreed. "We can use him."

Sam threw his arms around his friend and chuckled. "I reckoned you'd want to go along. Hoab is a prime boy." His face sobered and he said, "Tell me, have you had any word from my sister?"

"Ay," replied Tishomingo. "I'll not lie to you again. She's well. She said that she would write you. She's very busy. She's bought a steamboat and is making huge profits by sending army supplies up and down the river. She's working many agents and has stored corn and rum at *Malmaison*."

Sam's eyes sparkled. "She's a sharp one, I tell you. Sharp as a saw tooth."

"She is that. She tried to buy into the steamboat business of a fellow named Nicholas Roosevelt—a Dutchman from New York. He's tied up with Chancellor Livingston and Robert Fulton and they've got a boat on the Mississippi. But they wouldn't let Honoria get a finger in their pie."

"I wonder why I haven't heard from her," Sam remarked gloomily.

Tishomingo evaded. "I do not know," he said.

"You told me you would not lie to me."

"It's a delicate thing."

"Is it about Anestasie? Then she has heard?"

"I suppose so, Big Sam. She wrote me that she had heard you were making a fool of yourself and asked me

726

to speak to you. I wrote her that if you were making a fool of yourself you were the happiest fool I had ever seen."

"Do you love my sister, Chock?"

"I don't know, Big Sam. I am not happy as you are happy."

"Have you heard of Flournoy?"

"He's still in Martinique."

"Does my sister write you about her husband? No, don't answer that. I'm sorry I asked it. If my sister is betraying her husband to the man who will kill him, I don't want to know it."

Tishomingo smoked his pipe for several minutes. "She has never mentioned him to me in her letters. Honoria would not betray him even though she hates him. She's your sister, Big Sam, and she will not betray her trust." The expression he saw on Sam's face made him glad that he had lied again.

"When she sees Anestasie," Sam said, "she'll love her. I know it. She cannot help but love Anestasie. Surely, there's no real grievance between them."

He and Tishomingo went to seek Hoab, to tell him their decision. They saw the boy, his back to them, sitting on a stump with a crowd of men around him.

"Yes, sir—sure as my name's Hoab Dabney," the boy's voice floated back to them. "I got a bead on that old coon. He was perched in a little tree over at our place, 'bout a four-hundred-foot sapling. He looked down and saw me and he held up his paw and said, 'Hoab Dabney, sure as I'm born. Hydee, Hoab. Don't shoot—I give up. If you're going to use my skin for a cap I don't want no hole in me.'"

Tears came to Tishomingo's eyes as he listened. Sam bit his lip. "There's not but one man who ever lived who would love that boy as much as we do," Chock said. "He was Ab."

Hoab's lean face lighted when Sam told him they were going to Jackson. "How many men has Red Eagle got, papa?"

"Oh, a thousand or so."

"Then you and Chock go on back home and make a crop. There's no use of us *picking* on the red 'uns. I haven't got anything else to do, and it would sort of be unbecoming for all three of us to jump 'em."

Sam was preparing for his trip to Jackson's army when the long-expected letter from his sister arrived. In justice to her, Sam told Tishomingo before he opened the letter that it had been delayed en route. It had hurt him deeply because Honoria had not written since Donna's death.

He went to his room to read the letter and as he read his temples throbbed and his blood felt cold and then hot. Honoria extended her sympathy and then delivered her ultimatum.

"You have always been a soft-hearted man, Sam'l [the letter read]. It is only natural that at this time you should be very susceptible to a woman's attention. It is my duty to warn you against Anestasie Duportail. I know this woman and I will not see my only brother involved with her. If you will not listen to reason I have other weapons and I will use them.

"Firstly, you're in debt to my husband whose business I am running. I had thought to free you of this obligation, but if you can afford such a luxury as Anestasie is certain to be, then I have the right to demand that you meet your moral and legal obligation to my husband. This debt has been dragging along for many years. There is no need to mince words with you. I can scarcely be-

728

lieve that you can be showing attention to this creature so soon after your darling and loyal wife's death. But I hear you are.

"It obviously is your plan to marry this woman. She is not fit to be your wife or my sister-in-law. If you marry her I will call the debt and pauperize you. I will do it for your own good. This woman will turn on you if you are poor. Maybe it will teach you a lesson.

"Secondly, this woman must not mother my son. If you have no pride for yourself or consideration for me, then you must have for Hoab. If you marry this woman I will go to court and take my son. I will tell everything.

"You perhaps are thinking that I dare not do this because of Tishomingo. But I *will* dare. You are thinking that my husband will divorce me and I dare not take that risk. You are wrong. I have made a fortune in my own name. I do not need Lake Flournoy any more. I do not need anybody any more. I will not allow Anestasie Duportail to triumph over me if it costs me your love, Tishomingo's love and my son's respect."

Sam held the letter to a candle and watched the flames eat it up. He lit his pipe and thought for a long time. He drank two glasses of brandy, the first brandy he had drunk in several years. The brandy would drive some of the bitterness out of his heart. He didn't want bitterness to be in his heart when he answered the letter. He actually smiled at his sister's conceit. How like their father she was. She thought she could rule other people's lives. But this time she had gone too far. Her remarks concerning Anestasie infuriated him, a smoldering fury. He would shun her. She had dirtied everything she had ever touched. Often, he had thought about it, but now it was clear to him that he and his sister had naught in common except the heritage of being old man Dabney's brats. And she had insulted the woman he loved. He reached for his quill and wrote slowly:

"I'm going to marry Anestasie when the war is over. We will live at Locha Poka. Four times a year you may come to see us and visit with our son. Anestasie is delighted over the prospects of helping me make a good man of Hoab, an honorable man. There is no reason why Hoab should not be a good man. Donna brought him this far and Anestasie will see him through. The association of two such splendid women will offset any characteristics that he may have inherited from his mother.

"Within three months I will repay my debt to you. You can never repay your debt to me. On second thought, you have repaid me, Honoria. You have repaid me with interest. My awakening is the payment.

"You should be whipped. If I were not busy, I would go to you and whip you.

"My first impulse upon receiving your letter was to show it to Anestasie and Tishomingo. But I will not do that. You will suffer enough. God will punish you and I will help Him. Tishomingo will cast you aside as I am doing. I will see to it.

"I encourage you to go to court and try to take Hoab. All of your money cannot overcome one handicap that you have. You are not a fit person to mother a son and I will brand you in court. It will shock Hoab. It will smear our name. Hoab and I are men and we can survive it. You can't. I await word from your lawyer.

"I am glad that our father and mother didn't live to see you as a woman. But I do wish Donna had lived longer. The only quarrels Donna and I ever had were about you. She was right. I wish she could have lived to have seen her opinions substantiated."

He called a courier and gave him the message. He went

to Anestasie's room and sat a long time with her, holding her hand and making plans.

"Now, do as I say, darling," he told her. "Have all the corn you own brought here. I will have my corn fetched here, too. And wagons and good mules. Get drivers and have them ready to travel the minute you receive word from me. We're going to make our fortune."

He left the fort in good hands and he and Tishomingo and Hoab struck north, traveling light and fast. They avoided the trails and Creek villages and had traveled only about fifty miles when Sam discovered that Red Eagle was systematically destroying every beef and ear of corn that might fall into the hands of Jackson's army. He got the information from a Creek deserter who was hiding in the wilderness. Red Eagle had burned every village in Jackson's path. The general, pushing south to find food, had found only smoking cabins and parched earth. Jackson's army was starving. Sam wrote a message to Anestasie and promised the deserter refuge if he delivered it. The Creek took the message and hurried toward Madison, while Sam and his party continued northward.

The Army of Tennessee was a starving, freezing, mutinous rabble that marched on partly because it loved Andrew Jackson, but largely because it feared him and the scorn of their kinsmen should they retreat.

The army had brushed with the Red Sticks, and Weatherford had raided and retreated, pulling Jackson farther and farther into a bleak wilderness where food was so scarce that the men shouted with glee when they found a fat worm in their acorn meal.

Sam and his companions looked with compassion upon the miserable soldiers, and Sam's heart hurt when the Tennesseans stopped his horse and begged him for food.

Sam asked of General Jackson and one of the Tennesseans replied, "You'll find him around somewhere. He's half dead, too. He's got dysentery so bad that sometimes he wraps his arms around a tree to hold himself up. Just yesterday one of the wounded boys asked him for food and old Andy shared his parched acorns. He's fightin' like we are and starving, too. But he won't go back."

Dabney found the general propped against a tree, his feet to a small fire and his hands tucked in his frayed coat. Sam thought he was seeing a ghost. He believed if he touched Andrew Jackson the old frizzled-haired Irishman would topple over. The man was dead and didn't know it. He was a dead man who wouldn't lie down.

Sam introduced himself. "I am Sam Dabney."

Jackson took him in and muttered, "We don't need more men. We need food. You look sleek." Then his eyes sparkled suddenly and he struggled to his feet, holding on to the tree for support. "Great God! Did you say 'Sam Dabney'? It's impossible!"

"I'm guilty of being Dabney."

"How did you get here?"

"I rode," Sam said. "And I didn't see a Red Stick warrior. I figured they would all be here, except for a few that are worrying the life out of the Georgians and the Mississippians."

Jackson smiled for the first time in weeks. "Sit down, man. I was thinking about you and up you rode. By the Eternal, it's uncanny! I was sitting here thinking to myself, 'If I just could get Sam Dabney, he could help us.' And here you are. It strengthens a man's faith in Providence. Have you got any food?"

"Ay," said Sam. "We have a bit."

"Enough for my wounded?"

"If you stretch it. And more is coming."

Jackson's voice was eager. "Say that again, man. Slowly. How did you know we were here? That we were starving?"

"I know Red Eagle. I figured what he would do and he has done it. He's destroying his own nation rather than let you take it. There are three armies against him. He'll harass each one and lure the white men from their bases and then strike one at a time. I reckoned your army was hungry so I sent word home that beeves and corn should be brought here."

Jackson gripped Sam's arm, but his fingers were weak. "How can they get through? I'll send an escort for them."

"Don't do that," said Sam. "The slave who is bringing it through can get gun powder through hell. The Creeks are watching you. If an escort goes out, it will be followed and the supplies will be lost. Let's sit tight, General."

From Jackson, Sam learned of the Battle of Talladega, where one thousand half-naked, poorly armed Creeks had made a stand against the Tennesseans. "We butchered them," Jackson muttered. "They lost three hundred men. We lost fifteen. Now my men want to drop back to Fort Strother where we have supplies. I'm going on. I'm going to catch Billy Weatherford and hang him!"

"You'll never catch the Red Eagle, and it would be a dishonorable act to hang such an honorable foe," Sam said, braving the general's wrath.

"He's a savage!" Jackson snarled. He glared at Sam from bleary deep-set eyes.

"He's a gentleman," Sam insisted.

"He's a traitor!"

"He's a patriot."

733

Jackson grumbled, but let the matter drop. Sam had the general's respect because he was not awed by Jackson's threats and blusterings. The commander even listened to Sam's suggestion that they fall back to Strother and venture out again with full bellies.

"Red Eagle expects you to stay here," Sam argued. "He didn't expect to fight you at Talladega. He came to Talladega to suppress the rebels in his own nation. We both know that Strother has been left defenseless. There are wounded there. If you push on into the Creek Nation, Red Eagle is certain to cut around you and attack Strother in your rear."

Jackson nodded. "You're right. We must return to Strother. I have eighty-seven wounded with me. There are two hundred sick at Strother and all of my supplies are there."

Without further argument, but in a low voice as though each word cut into his pride, the stubborn gaunt-faced Tennessean gave orders for his army of two thousand to retreat to Strother. The men cheered feebly. They straggled back to the fort and found it empty of rations. Jackson cursed until the veins in his forehead swelled. He had been assured that there were supplies at the fort. He called Sam to his headquarters and said, "I don't understand it."

"Who told you there were supplies here?" Sam asked.

"A scout. An Indian scout. He was a loyal man. He wore the deer tail in his cap. I have asked all Indians who are for us to wear deer tails."

"The Red Sticks are feasting now upon the supplies that you expected," Sam answered. "I will lay you odds, General, that Red Eagle sent one of his own men to you. You must not underestimate this man. He has outwitted

734

both of us. He has forced us to fall back. It will give him time to prepare his defenses."

"By God, I won't give him time!" Jackson thundered.

"You can't help yourself. If you order your army to advance now, it will mutiny. Red Eagle knows that. It will take you weeks to prepare your army for a march. In the meantime, Red Eagle will go south and take a whack at Claiborne. Then he'll go east and meet the Georgians. He'll force both of those armies into forts as he has forced you. Then he'll come back here and be ready to meet you. The man's a genius, General."

"I believe he has your sympathy, Mr. Dabney."

"He has, Mr. Jackson. Any man who can fight the United States, half of his own nation and the three most powerful Indian nations in the world, has my admiration."

Jackson snorted, but in his own heart he, too, admired Red Eagle. "When will your supplies arrive, Sam? They're our only hope."

"God knows! If you can hold this army together for a few more days, I believe my stuff will be here."

"It's difficult to hold starving men together."

He put Sam in charge of the meager supplies. Tishomingo and Hoab aided Sam and they rounded up every ounce of food available. They found a few pounds of biscuits and a few cattle to feed two thousand men. Sam butchered the cattle and he and Jackson and the staff officers ate the offal and gave the good flesh to the men. He organized squads of hunters, put them in charge of Davy Crockett, and sent them into the frozen wilderness to find game. He sent couriers to the ration contractors in Tennessee to hurry supplies. The first supply wagon that arrived was driven by a swarthy man with a bluish front tooth. Sam remembered Tecumseh's blue tooth

735

when he saw the man and if Tecumseh were not dead he would have sworn that the driver was the great Shawnee chief. The man even limped as Tecumseh had limped. But he had corn, good yellow corn. It looked like the corn of Locha Poka. Sam set a reasonable price for the supplies and the man laughed. He wanted ten times the corn's value and he wanted his money in cash.

Sam went to Jackson with his problem and while he was away the soldiers pressed around the stranger and bought his corn with their own money, fifty cents for one ear of corn. Money was no good to them. Those who did not have money traded with their valuables. They gave their watches, their rings, everything except their rifles. The man sold his supply before Sam returned with Jackson's permission to buy the corn at any price. The order would be payable in Nashville. Jackson had told Sam, "If he won't take this order and still demands cash, then knock him out of his wagon and take the corn."

Across the order Jackson had scrawled, "O. K."

The day after the trader arrived with his corn and collected a fortune, a swarm of profiteers descended upon the army, peddling acorns as though they were gold nuggets. Fat rats sold for two dollars each. Sam again went to Jackson for orders.

"These traders are all from the same place," he said. "I can do nothing with the men. They'll give their shirts for an ear of corn and their hope of heaven for a drink of whiskey."

"Take the supplies," Jackson ordered. "I know the politicians will curse me. But take them. These scoundrels will not take a fair price. I'm breaking the law, but you have your orders."

"Thank you, Andy." Sam rubbed his hands together and spat upon them. "This is a chore I relish."

"Don't hurt them," Jackson growled, then smiled. "At least, not while I'm looking."

"Look the other way then."

Sam and Tishomingo climbed aboard the wagons and threw the traders to the ground. Then they beat them, Sam with his fists. He smashed their noses, battered their bodies and broke two men's arms by snapping their wrists over his knee. The traders whimpered and pleaded, but Sam laughed at them. "You buzzards," he snarled. "Fattening on the hunger of American soldiers."

Tishomingo nipped off bits of flesh with his whip. He cut off one man's clothes and drove him naked into the woods, tearing his skin with the tip of his lash.

Sam heaved the man with the bluish tooth out of his wagon and into Hoab's arms. "Hold him, son, until I get through with the others. I have a special treatment for that one."

He held the man by the neck and knocked out all of his teeth on the left side, but spared the bluish tooth. The man fainted and Sam revived him. He slit the man's lip with his knife and notched his ears. "That's the way we notch hogs where I live."

"You—stole—our goods," the trader whined. "I'll—report this—to my employer."

"Who employs you?" Sam grasped the man's throat again, but when the trader either refused to reply or could not, Sam hurled him to the ground and kicked him. "All right, you blood-sucking bastard. Keep your secret. But tell your employer that if Sam Dabney ever learns his name, he'll kick his rump. That I swear by God."

The trader scrambled to his feet, wiped the blood from his face and glared his hatred at Sam. Then he ran into the woods before Sam could lay hands on him again.

The men feasted for days and their spirits revived.

There was no need to stint, for surely rations soon would come from the contractors, and, too, the Dabney wagons were coming. The days passed, however, and the food was gone again. The men blamed Jackson because he had not rationed the food more carefully. Jackson criticized Sam, and Sam threatened to leave the army to its own resources. He would take no criticism from the general, and when Jackson threatened his arrest Sam laughed at him.

"We're acting like boys," Sam said. "I can't say when my wagons will be here, but they're coming, I tell you."

"You're right, Sam," Jackson smiled. "We mustn't quarrel. It's bad for the men."

There was no discipline in the army. The men called their general by his first name. They weren't soldiers; they were hunters and traders from Tennessee. They were storekeepers and farmers and two-bit politicians. They were just as good as Andy Jackson. They didn't mind fighting, but it was damned foolishness to stay in the woods and starve to death when there was no fighting to be done.

The Tennessee militia was the first to demand permission to return home. There was no need to stay there and starve to death. They had come out to fight, not to shrivel up in a freezing fort. Of course, it was mutiny. The militia shouldered arms and marched out of the fort toward Tennessee and home. Jackson threw a detachment of volunteers in front of them with commands to fire unless the militia returned to the fort. The militia returned and then the volunteers mutinied and started home. Old Mad Jackson bluffed them with the militia and the volunteers went back to their posts. Jackson promised the men supplies and appealed to them not to forsake the wounded, but Hall's brigade of volunteers

738

voted to quit the campaign. Jackson was at his rope's end and published an order that if supplies did not arrive within two days the entire army would march back. Hall's brigade agreed to stick it out a while longer, but two days later the men called upon Jackson to honor his promise and lead them back.

He pleaded with them and exacted their pledge to remain two more days, and then he went into conference with Sam. "I despair of receiving supplies from you. I've held this army here in the hopes that your wagons would get through. I took your advice and did not send an escort out for them. I've played my last card."

"I'll go after them," Sam said. He walked from the general's presence and he and Tishomingo set off into the woods at a trot. Their horses had long since been slaughtered.

Jackson could hold his army no longer and led them out of the fort convinced that he was going back to Tennessee in disgrace and that his name would take its place alongside the names of Hull and other men who had been branded cowards. They were only twelve miles from the fort and had halted for rest when Tishomingo ran up with news that the Dabney wagons would arrive before sundown.

Andrew Jackson leaned against a tree and vomited; he might have collapsed if Tishomingo had not supported him.

"Walk with me to my tent," Jackson whispered. "The men mustn't see me faint. No—don't hold me. Just walk beside me."

Tishomingo looked down at the bitter little man with the long, sad face. His hair was matted, and now it frizzled out from under his hat. His shoulder was stained red, blood from his old wound. Tishomingo could smell

739

the rotten flesh. Jackson's face was deeply lined and his body quivered as pain darted through his frame. He looked as light as a feather—slight, bony. He looked dead, too, a dead man leading the doomed, a ghost leading ghosts. Only his eyes seemed alive; they burned with a fanatical hatred for some men and a tender love for others. Old Mad Jackson!

Anestasie drove the first wagon that rumbled over the hills and waddled to the valley where the men were camped. Jasper drove the second wagon and Sam was herding the beeves. Anestasie used both feet to brake the big wagon and her voice was cheerful as she shouted to her mules and guided them between the trees and stumps, making her own trail as she drove. Sometimes she spoke to the mules in French. Old Mad Jackson got to his feet and saluted her, helped her from the wagon and offered his arm to take her away from the prying eyes of his men. Anestasie curtsied and accepted his arm and helped hold Andrew Jackson up, but the men didn't know it.

The men were silent and ashamed. A woman had brought them food. They stifled their impulses to raid the wagons and sat on the ground and stared at their feet. Sam addressed them, "We'll mess within three hours."

He selected a company to slaughter the beeves and set Jasper to building fires, and then he went to General Jackson.

"This lady," Jackson said, "has saved my army. But she won't tell me how she got through. Perhaps she'll tell you."

"There are more wagons coming," said Sam. "We pushed on ahead with this food." Then he presented Anestasie.

740

"We've already met." The general bowed, sick though he was. "But I want to know how a lady handled a wagon train from the Halfway River to the northern part of the territory."

"We would have got here sooner," Anestasie laughed, "but for the floods. We lost two wagons and four men in fording the rivers. I came only because we could not get enough men drivers. They were afraid to come into the Creek country. I saw only one band of Creeks. We drove them off."

"How?" Jackson demanded. "How in the name of the Eternal could a woman with a company of slaves defeat Red Sticks?"

Anestasie explained, "We barricaded ourselves. We all sang songs and the Creeks thought we had more men than we had. They attacked only once and we beat them back. Then a few of us slipped out of the barricade and attacked from the north, shouting 'Hurray for Andy Jackson!' The Creeks ran away. Don't be surprised, General. I made the first trip to the new land with Mr. Dabney."

"Sam has told me about you. You must start back. I can't risk keeping you here. If anything should happen to you I fear Sam Dabney would strangle me."

Jackson bowed himself out of their presence and went to his men. Sam got a quill and paper, and he and Anestasie began making out their bill.

She frequently interrupted him to run her fingers through his hair and to kiss his ear playfully, but Sam did not scold her. He had rebuked her when he and Tishomingo had met the train on the trail. She shouldn't have taken such a chance. She should have let Jasper bring the train through. He had forgiven her, however, when she told him that she couldn't get enough men and

741

that rather than suffer delay she had ridden with the wagons.

The bill they had against the government would net them a neat profit and with contracts that Sam knew he could get he could redeem Locha Poka.

"Jackson will give us contracts to feed his army throughout the campaign," Sam told her. "Within three months we'll make enough to pay all my debts and when I take you to Locha Poka as my bride, I'll owe no man."

He seemed so happy that Anestasie could not tell him the thing that was in her heart. She didn't want to go to Locha Poka. Locha Poka was Donna's home. Everything she would see there would remind her of Donna. She wouldn't dare ask Sam to go to André's house, but he had no right to take her to Locha Poka. She would rather have a cabin, a tent, anything. To her, Locha Poka was not worth saving but she said naught of it.

"And after I redeem Locha Poka," Sam continued enthusiastically, "we'll build our road to Georgia."

Anestasie asked, "What of my property over on the Tombigbee?"

"We'll sell that."

"Sell it! No, not that. It will be yours, Sam, but don't sell it. I'd rather give it to Hoab or Shellie. Or maybe we'll have a son and we can save it for him. But we mustn't sell it."

Sam kissed her to humor her and closed the subject. He had hot fresh food brought to her, and while she ate he went to Jackson with his bill and contracts. It pained Jackson to write. His left arm still was in a sling and his right hand was so scratched and torn by briars that he scarcely could use it. He scanned the papers and wrote "O. K." on each of them.

"This army will buy supplies from you as long as it is

in the field," he promised. "This paper will be redeemable at any federal pay office."

Jackson was with Sam when he bade Anestasie goodbye. He sent an escort with her and she agreed to go due west to the Chickasaws before turning south to the new land. It was safer that way. When she and her company were gone, Jackson faced his men. "Your bellies are full," he said. "We'll return to Strother."

The army grumbled. Jackson called them to attention and commanded them to march to the fort. The men turned their backs on him and marched away toward Tennessee. The general rode rapidly around them and commanded them to halt. They kept marching, and Jackson commanded a handful of loyal cavalry to draw a bead on them.

"Go back," Andy Jackson bellowed, "or we'll blow you in two!"

The mutineers slunk back to camp. Jackson followed, and in camp he found an entire brigade preparing to desert. He made one last effort to control his men. Seizing Sam's rifle, Jackson rested it on his horse's neck and aimed it at the deserters.

"By the Eternal, I'll kill the first man who moves the wrong way! Now march!"

Sam Dabney reached for his pistol. Tishomingo fingered his whip. Two loyal officers took their places by the general's side. A company of loyal Tennesseans moved up behind the general and waited. The army hesitated for a minute and then began trudging back toward Fort Strother. Jackson returned the gun to Sam, and Sam leaned over and whispered, "It wasn't loaded, General."

"I know it," the general grinned, "but *they* didn't."

The mutiny had not subsided, however. The service

terms of many of the men were up and Jackson's threats and pleas no longer impressed them. Once he turned the cannon toward his men and kept them in line by sheer bluff. For days he cowed the mutineers, but the situation was hopeless when Tennessee sent fifteen hundred fresh troops to him. Jackson released the mutineers and read them out of camp. He could whip the Red Eagle with the new troops. His old army scarcely was out of sight before Jackson learned that his new troops had only ten more days to serve. His profanity rent the air. He ordered the new troops to get the hell and gone back to Tennessee. And Andy Jackson was left in the heart of the Creek Nation with no army. Had the Red Eagle struck then ——

Jackson could count less than two hundred effectives in the fort, and while he brooded over his plight, orders came from Tennessee for him to return. Jackson refused.

"I'll stay here as long as I have one man to stay with me," he threatened. "If I go back, we'll lose the friendship of the Choctaws, Chickasaws and Cherokees. They'll join the Red Eagle and the Southwest will become a slaughterhouse."

He called his handful of men before him and told them that they would stay and fight. He sent Sam out to scout and he put his fort in order. Red Eagle was only a few miles away with a thousand braves and some of the men began calling the fort "Fort Suicide."

Red Eagle would surely attack now and Jackson was ready, although outnumbered five to one. But again Old Mad Jackson underestimated the prowess of the Red Eagle. The Creek leader had seen the army march away, but he was too wise a man to attack Jackson's little band as long as they were behind the barricade. Jackson wasn't doing any harm in the fort and the Red Eagle left him there, cooling his heels and starving while the strongest

744

and fastest of the Red Sticks hurried south to the Holy Grounds to draw on Claiborne. Word that Red Eagle was at the Holy Grounds reached Claiborne and he marched immediately to do battle, ignoring winter weather and flooded streams. He attacked at the Holy Grounds and the Red Eagle retreated after losing only a few men. He gave his army orders to scatter and re-form against Andrew Jackson. He sent a few scouts to harass the forts around Madison, knowing full well that Claiborne would have to fall back to protect the forts. He stayed on the battleground until his last warrior had left and then, realizing he virtually was surrounded by Claiborne's men, he spurred his horse to a bluff that over-looked the Alabama River, paused for a minute on its brink and then disappeared from view. Claiborne's men thought he had leaped more than twenty-five feet into the river, and they marveled at the feat. Red Eagle, how-ever, had driven his horse down the steep bluff and had escaped through a ravine, passing within a few feet of the white men. The Mississippians took some tall tales back home of how Billy Weatherford, the Red Eagle, had ridden his horse over a twenty-five foot bluff into the river and how they had slaughtered hundreds of Creeks. Actually, they had killed only a few, just as many as the Red Eagle wanted them to kill to prove to his people that the prophets had lied in assuring them of protection from bullets. He also believed that an invasion of the sacred grounds would re-unite his nation, and he rode furiously back to the Coosa to tell the rebellious Creeks that the white men had violated their Holy Grounds.

The rebels were almost ready to join Red Eagle when eight hundred Tennessee volunteers suddenly appeared at Jackson's fort and offered their services. He had nine hundred and thirty men now and he wouldn't give them time to grow weary of the fort or to get hungry. He decided to attack.

Sam brought word that the Red Sticks were at Horseshoe Bend on the Tallapoosa River. Jackson marched that night and took his men seventy miles from the fort and only three from the Bend before he bivouacked. The Creeks struck him there, and Jackson drove them off. But he had to retreat. He was seventy miles from his base and Red Eagle could get to his rear and cut him to pieces. He fell back to Enotachopco Creek and the Indians struck again. Many of the Tennesseans threw down their guns and ran. Jackson cursed them until the air was blue. He ordered that the cowards be arrested and personally led a charge against the Creeks. The Creeks retreated and Jackson was satisfied to call the battle a draw. It was January the 22nd, 1814, when Jackson ordered his army to camp and began whipping his raw recruits into soldiers.

Every day he expected Red Eagle to attack, but the wily Red Stick calmly withdrew while Jackson was training his men, and five days later Red Eagle hurled a few hundred of his warriors against General Floyd and his sixteen hundred Georgia troops over on Callabee Creek, hard by Polecat Springs. The Georgians thought that every Indian between the Great Lakes and the Gulf had jumped them and they fell back to protect their border and await reënforcements. Red Eagle wheeled again and a few days later was back at the Horseshoe ready to meet Andy Jackson.

Within four weeks Red Eagle had met three American armies. Outnumbered but never outfought, the Creek leader had taught the Americans a few tricks in strategy and courage.

746

Jackson's army was beginning to take shape. "This army won't get away from me," he told Sam. "I'll teach them discipline if I have to break their skulls."

One of his officers spoke facetiously of the general's efforts to maintain discipline and Jackson sent the man back to Tennessee under arrest. A Tennessee boy defied a superior with a rifle and Jackson had him shot.

Recruits began pouring in and on March the 26th, Jackson counted three thousand three hundred effectives, including six hundred Indians. He had two cannon. The Red Eagle had eight hundred men, most of them armed only with bows. Jackson sat late that night and completed his plans. The Creeks had built their barricades around the Bend. Jackson would send his cavalry around the Bend to close the mouth of the Horseshoe and cut off any route of retreat. He would trap the Red Sticks in the Horseshoe and butcher them.

"So you think Red Eagle is smart?" Jackson said to Sam. "Look—he's in a trap. We can close him in and he can't retreat."

Sam did not agree and said so. "I cannot believe Red Eagle has trapped himself. And you're crazy, Andy, if you think the Creeks will think of retreating. That's holy ground, man, and the only way you can get those Indians off of there is to drag them off feet first."

The dawn of the 27th broke clear and crisp and Jackson formed his men and addressed them. "Any man who flees before the enemy without being compelled to do so shall suffer death."

The assault on the Horseshoe began at half past ten when two cannon opened fire and their balls sank into the soft logs of the Indian barricade. Creek sharpshooters picked off the gunners and the cannon was silenced. Sam returned from a scout and reported that women

747

and children were behind the barricade. The general withheld his assault until the Indians got their women and children to safety. Jackson ordered his cavalry to deploy around the Bend and block the rear. The Red Sticks were trapped in the Horseshoe and Tennessee was ready to avenge Fort Mims. At twelve-thirty, the Red Sticks signaled that they were ready for battle. Jackson ordered his drummers to sound a charge and his regulars gripped their guns and ran toward the ramparts. Some sang as they ran. Others bent forward and ran in silence. Others stumbled, grunted and lay where they fell. But they all ran. "Remember Fort Mims!"

Sam ran with them. Tishomingo and Hoab were at his side.

"This will be work for the knife," Sam said to his son as they ran. "Stay close to me." He began humming, "Over the Hills ——"

A few men were ahead of Sam and climbed up the ramparts. Major Lem Montgomery* was the first man over, and the Creeks shot him full of holes. The second man over stumbled as an arrow pierced his side. Sam glanced quickly at Hoab and the two went over together. Dabney fired both his barrels into the Creeks and then sprang among them with his knife. A platoon followed him. All along the wall the Tennesseans scrambled up, paused to fire, and then leaped among the Indians, hacking and screaming. The Indians fell back and Sam turned to help the man who had been wounded by the arrow.

"You're badly wounded," Sam told him. "You'd better go to the surgeon."

"Pull the arrow out," the wounded man muttered.

"I like guts," Sam said, "but I don't like foolishness.

* The capital of Alabama honors his memory.

748

This arrow is barbed. If I pull it out it'll take half of your side with it."

"Yank it out!" the man repeated, biting down on his lip.

"All right, you pup," Sam said, and pulled the arrow out. Then he stooped over the man to dress the wound. "You're a mite reckless, but a brave man. I'm Sam Dabney."

"I'm Sam Houston."

Sam Dabney swallowed hard and felt the tears well in his eyes. So this was Thomas' kinsman. He helped Houston to his feet, directed him to the surgeon and went off to find Hoab and Tishomingo and resume the fight.

The Red Sticks, their ramparts overrun, formed into little bands and retreated to the underbrush of the Horseshoe's one hundred acres. The whites sought them out and slaughtered them. More than a score of battles raged at once. There was little firing, only the snarls of the wounded and the curses of the dying. The men fought with knives and tomahawks. Sam hid his rifle and he and Tishomingo went into the underbrush with their knives. Hoab followed them, stopping often to retch. Dabney killed until blood coated his jacket and formed a crust. He and Chock cleaned out one nest of Creeks and ran for another.

"How many have you killed?" Sam asked his friend.

"Seven. And you?"

"Five. This is our answer to Fort Mims, eh, Chock?"

"Ay."

They both leaped for the Indian who appeared directly in front of them and charged. Sam gripped his throat and ripped his knife into his stomach. Tishomingo stabbed him in the side and Sanota, the boy who had saved the McGirths at Mims', sank to his knees. Sam hurled him aside and left him choking to death in his own blood.

"How's the boy doing?" Sam wiped his knife clean on the seat of his breeches and glanced around at Hoab.

Tishomingo said, "All right, but he hates this business of killing."

Sam called Hoab to him. "Hold your knife tighter, son." He might have been a teacher instructing a boy in mathematics. "Slash outwards, but don't lose the grip on your knife. Twist your knife as you cut. Go for their bellies, never their chests. There are bones in the chests."

"Yes, papa," the boy said weakly. He was pale. He wasn't afraid; he was ill. But he tilted his head and hummed Sam's war song.

"Aba Inki have mercy on you, Big Sam," Tishomingo muttered. "Teaching your son to kill."

"May God have mercy on me, and on him," Sam said reverently. "But he must know how to kill in this land. We have sown with blood and now we must gather our harvest of hate."

The Creeks taught the Tennesseans something of bravery that day. Not a Creek surrendered. Even the wounded would not surrender and many Indians were stabbed to death or their skulls bashed in as they lay prone, already dying but still fighting. Group after group was rushed and slain to the last man. A few tried to break through the cavalry at the mouth of the Horseshoe, but were driven back and went to their deaths chanting prayers to Aba Inki. Their prophets moved among them, preaching and praying. The tide would change, the prophets said. Aba Inki would send a black cloud and that would be the sign that he would fight with his people.

750

Jackson sickened of the carnage and sent orders that operations be suspended. Then he notified the Creeks that he would spare all who surrendered. A few of the Creeks wavered, but as they went into council a black cloud suddenly appeared.

"The sign! The sign from Aba Inki!" The prophets leaped to their feet and the Indians sent back word to Jackson that there would be no surrender. The Tennesseans were ordered to resume the slaughter. The sun went down on heaps of Indian dead and the Horseshoe was only a bloody, sloppy, trampled bend in the river. A monument of mud and blood to the proudest Indian nation of all time.

Only one company of Creeks was left. It was barricaded in a ravine. Jackson ordered that it be taken and Sam Houston, holding his hand over his wound, seized a sword and ran forward. A musket ball smashed his arm and another almost took away his shoulder. Sam Dabney shook his head as he ran by the wounded man. Sam Houston couldn't live, he thought. Well, he had avenged Lawyer Thomas. Big Sam and Tishomingo and a company of Tennesseans jumped into the ravine and cut the Indians to bits.

The Creek Nation had fallen. England's ally in the South was no more. The new land was safe from the tomahawk. Sam could build his road to Georgia. Andy Jackson had won a war by himself, but the Red Eagle had escaped. Jackson had lost forty-nine killed and one hundred and fifty wounded. The Creeks had lost seven hundred and fifty-seven dead. They had no wounded. A few others had been washed away in the river. There were no Creeks left to bury the Creek dead. A dozen or so prophets saved themselves by running away, but

751

every Creek warrior who faced Old Mad Jackson died before he would surrender.

After the battle, Jackson's men went among the dead seeking the Red Eagle, and when they reported that he could not be found the general said, "I have two regrets. Some women and children were killed by accident, and Weatherford has not been captured. I want the privilege of hanging him."

Jackson sent out notice that Red Eagle must be taken alive. He prepared to move farther into the Creek Nation, to continue the slaughter until he took Billy Weatherford. Sam slipped out of camp alone and went into the Creek country where he stopped at Indian lodges and left word that if the Red Eagle didn't surrender his people would be punished. Then he returned to camp. He was not surprised several days later when Billy Weatherford appeared. None of the other soldiers recognized him and Sam drew him aside quickly.

"I knew you would come, Red Eagle," Sam said with respect. "It may mean your life."

"If I had refused to come, many of my people would have been killed. Take me to Jackson."

Sam took his arm. "There are a few things I would know first. Why did you make a stand at the Horseshoe? Why didn't you fall back again? Why did you let us trap you?"

"I was not at the Horseshoe. I had ridden away to try and raise an army from among the Wind Clan. My men were poorly led."

"What happened to the leaders who escaped? Seekaboo? Josiah Francis?"

"They've fled to the Seminoles. Red Eagle would not go to the outlaws. Red Eagle has come to ask for peace for his people. Take me to your general."

General Jackson was leaving his headquarters when Red Eagle walked up to him and said, "I am Bill Weatherford."

Jackson sputtered and then regained his poise. "I am glad to see you, Mr. Weatherford." They went inside the tent.

"I have come," the Red Eagle said, "to give myself up. I can oppose you no longer. I have done you much injury. I would have done you more but my warriors were killed. I'm in your power. Dispose of me as you please."

Jackson could not help admiring the man. "You're not in my power. I had ordered you brought to me in chains. But you've come of your own accord. You see my camp, you see my army. You know my object. I would gladly save you and your nation, but you do not even ask to be saved. If you think you can contend against me in battle, then go and head your warriors."

"Ah, well may such language be addressed to me now. There was a time when I could have answered you. I could animate my warriors to battle, but I cannot animate the dead. I have nothing to request for myself, but I beg you to send for the women and children of the war party. They've been driven to the woods without food. They never did any harm. Then kill me if the white people want it done."

Jackson poured him a drink of brandy and told him he was a free man. He promised to save the women and children and the Red Eagle promised never again to take up arms against the United States. Jackson escorted him outside and bade him goodbye. He watched the Red Eagle walk away, scornful of the stares of the white soldiers.

Then Jackson went to his desk and wrote instruc-

tions for all the Creek leaders to come to him and make
peace talk. He received word that British marines had
landed at Pensacola and were inciting the Indians to
further hostilities. He sent word to the Creeks that unless they came to him their villages would be put to the
torch.

The leaders came, not begging mercy, but asking justice. They had not attacked the white man. The white
man had attacked them. Jackson watched the Creeks'
spokesmen, the captains and lieutenants of the Red
Eagle's army, file into his camp. They stopped often
to pick up and devour the grains of corn that fell from
the mouths of the white men's horses. They stirred in
the refuse from the animals until they found undigested
bits of corn and ate them. Jackson offered them food,
but they scorned it. They would not break bread with
the white man until the peace talk was made. The Red
Eagle had told them to surrender and they had come.

The terms of peace were read to them and the Red
Sticks looked from one face to the other, scarcely
believing their ears. Jackson demanded surrender of
twenty-three million acres, more than one half of all land
that the Creeks had ever held. Much of the land belonged
to the rebel clans that had fought as allies of the United
States. Jackson made no distinction between friend and
foe. The Creeks must be destroyed. They must be uprooted. Their land must be turned over first by the white
man's bayonet and their trees must be cut down by the
white man's cannon ball. Then the white man's plow
must turn the land, and the white man's ax must fell the
trees. The Creek was made of steel and he would not
bend. He must be broken. A few of the Creek leaders,
those who had fought with Jackson, pleaded for in-

754

dulgence, but Jackson turned his back. There were tears in his eyes when he heard their pleas.

Old Big Warrior faced Jackson and said that as a token of gratitude the Creeks would give the general three square miles of the very land he demanded.

Jackson said he would take the land if the President of the United States would approve, and that in payment for the land he would give clothing to the naked women and children of the people he had conquered.

Andy Jackson did not understand the subtlety of the Indians. They were saving their face, they were giving the general a present for the great things he had done for them. Old Big Warrior told the general, "We do not give to General Jackson land to be paid for in clothing. We want the general to live on it and when he is gone his family may have it, and it may always be known what the Creek Nation gave it to him for."

The Indians signed the treaty of peace and the history of the Creek Nation ended. Tishomingo watched the Red Sticks sign away their birthrights and said to Sam, "The Cherokees will go next. Then the Chickasaws. And then my people. The sun has gone down upon the Indian race, Big Sam. Tecumseh was right."

Red Eagle returned to Andrew Jackson a few days later. Jackson again offered him brandy and Red Eagle refused.

"Rome did to Carthage what you have done to us," Red Eagle said proudly. "I am seven-eighths white and I am sorry."

Old Mad Jackson bowed his head while Weatherford talked.

"You have crushed our nation," Weatherford continued. "You make loud noises and shout that all men are created equal, but you deny us the right to live. Oh, accursed be the white race! You have spilled our blood as a drunken man spills his wine. Ay, you have crushed us, but you cannot conquer us, for our blood will be in the blood of your grandchildren. And a hundred years from this day the MacIntoshes, the Weatherfords, the Baileys, the Wards, the McQueens, the McDonalds, the Pigeons, and a thousand other families who mated with my people will boast of their pure white blood and may never know that they inherited their strength from their Creek ancestors."

Billy Weatherford bowed stiffly to Jackson and walked away. The general watched him until he disappeared and then he sat down and wrote a letter in which he said: "Weatherford is the greatest of the barbarian world. He possesses all the manliness of sentiment, all of the heroism of soul, all the comprehension of intellect calculated to make an able commander."

It was a fitting tribute to a barbarian in whose veins coursed the finest free blood of old Scotia, France and Spain, a barbarian whose ancestors were civilized when the wild tribesmen forbears of Andrew Jackson were roaming the peat bogs of Ireland.

33

JACKSON next turned his eyes toward Florida, determined to punish the insolent Spanish at Pensacola for daring to harbor British marines. The British were manning the forts at Pensacola and their bayonets thrust like needles into the shanks of the United States. For sure, Andrew Jackson had no right to invade Pensacola. It belonged to his Catholic Majesty whose country had been saved by the English. But, by God, the Spaniards had no right to give haven to British soldiers, and Jackson decided to clean out the festering sore that threatened to spread throughout the Southeast. Two wrongs never make a right, but they are good arguments for war. Jackson wrote to the secretary of war that he was going to Pensacola. The secretary's reply was very formal and diplomatic, but it said exactly nothing. The secretary left himself in a position to cut Old Hickory's tough political neck if the Florida expedition failed. Jackson was to act on his own authority, but must not exceed his authority, whatever his authority was. It was as slick a letter as an English diplomat could have written, and almost slick enough to do justice to a Frenchman.

Jackson called Sam to his headquarters and told him he was bound for Florida. "I'm going to clean up Pensacola. If it means war with Spain, then let them have at it. I want you to scout for me."

757

"If that's a command I'll follow you," said Sam. "But I have other things I need to do. I must keep my supplies moving to you and I need money, Andy. I've got a pocketful of your O.K.'s. I must redeem some of them. I'll leave my son with you and my friend, Tishomingo. They're good scouts."

Jackson agreed and Sam took his leave, heading first for Anestasie's home. Thence he would go to Locha Poka.

The star of Napoleon had been blown down and England was ready to turn the full force of her wrath upon the United States. Ten thousand Peninsular veterans were landed in Canada and preparing to march into New York. Cochrane's fleet began harassing the seaboard and at Jamaica the greatest invading expedition of New World history gathered to crush the South. Maine was invaded, and Massachusetts, which owned the land, pleaded to the United States for help. It was the same Massachusetts which had refused to send her soldiers outside of her own borders. Now the United States refused to send help to Massachusetts and refused to pay that state's own militia with federal funds. She had refused to support the war, she had buried her gold rather than buy government bonds, she had flirted with England: now let her stew in her own spleen. Admiral Cochrane, a military pyromaniac whose proficiency with the torch would have shamed the Creeks, burned Eastport, looted Nantucket and laid tribute against Cape Cod. But in Boston, the anti-war leaders of New England celebrated England's victory over Napoleon, and in Hartford a convention met to discuss secession.

The British swept down from Canada and the navy checked them at Lake Champlain. The ten thousand veterans slunk back to Canada and Cochrane made for Washington. It was defended by three times his number. But the government fled, stumbling over American militiamen in a foot-race for safety. Cochrane burned the national capital. He shelled Baltimore while Francis Scott Key stood on one of his ships and wrote a poem that he put to the music of an old English drinking song. "Oh, Say Can You See —"

Yes, they could see! They could see Washington in ashes and the government scattered. They could see Dolly Madison with the Declaration of Independence tucked under her arm. They could see John McDonough's flag of victory flying at Champlain. They could see Andy Jackson marching into Pensacola, his band playing, "Hail to the Chief." They could see the British marines blowing up the fort at Pensacola and fleeing for their lives. They could see the Spanish governor surrendering and could hear Andy Jackson cursing. Ay, they could see. They could see Jackson marching back out of Pensacola after returning it to the Spaniards with the warning that if they got out of step again he would blow them to ribbons. They could see the British moving on New Orleans for one mighty thrust at the South. . . .

The Choctaw overseers and Sam's slaves had done a good job at Locha Poka and Sam was pleased. The fields were neatly tilled. He hesitated on the threshold of his home and dreaded to go upstairs. He went to his study and read all of the mail that had accumulated and even the newspapers. Then he went outside to the Big Tree and leaned against it and stared at the grave Jasper had dug. He was pleased with the little stone. He wondered where Jasper had got the stone. Perhaps it had come from the foundation of Locha Poka, a stone that had been brought over from Europe. He hoped it was from the foundation of Locha Poka. That would be fitting. Locha Poka was Donna's home. When he had mentioned Locha Poka he had always meant Donna. When he had said to his friends, "I'm going home to Locha Poka," he had meant, "I'm going home to Donna."

He hurried back to his study and got the conch shell that he had left there and brought it back to the grave and buried it near the stone. It was an impulsive thing to do. The idea had come upon him suddenly. Donna would like to have the conch shell by her headstone. He didn't need it. He could remember Donna without seeing the shell in which the sea roared. And it wouldn't be fair to Anestasie to have the conch shell where they both could see it. Then another impulse struck him and he called a slave and they went to Donna's room and got all of her clothes and burned them. He burned the sheets on her bed and then he had the bed burned. He would get a new bed, a new wife. He would have a new start. Donna would want it that way. She wouldn't want her things to be around when another woman took her place. He would close her room and lock it. No, he couldn't do that. Anestasie wouldn't understand. She would think he was trying to preserve his memory of Donna. And it wasn't that at all. He loved Anestasie, but he didn't want her to sleep where Donna had slept, for her clothes to hang where Donna's had hung. He opened the windows in Donna's room and let the air pour in. It had been a long time since the room had been aired. There was an odor of dust in the room. There had been an odor of dust in the room for a long time. There had been an odor of dust about Donna and now he was opening up the room and driving out the odor of Donna.

Sam lingered at Locha Poka for two days before he set out for *Malmaison* to confront his sister. He went by the way of Natchez and there he learned that French envoys were in the Southwest, seeking mercenaries for Napoleon's cause. They had fled France when Napoleon had been exiled and they had come to the United States to prepare a place for him. They would free him from Elba and bring him to America. Maybe Louisiana would leave the United States and make Napoleon its emperor. But better still, they would hire Mississippians and Tennesseans and send them to France. The Americans must take their own rifles and no European army could withstand the fire of American riflemen. Ay, that's what they would do. They would send the Americans to France and then liberate Napoleon. He would go back to Paris and an army of sharpshooters would be waiting for him.

Sam did not laugh at the plan. He knew soldiers. It is hard for soldiers to lay down arms that they have carried for years. Thousands of Mississippians and Tennesseans might answer Napoleon's promise of gold and fame. They hated England and Spain, and they would go anywhere to lay a bead on an Englishman or a Spaniard. There were men like Davy Crockett and the Kemper boys who would go anywhere to fight. Hundreds of them already were settling in Texas, half outlaws, drunks, debtors, riff-raff, gamblers, gentlemen—all with two things in common: a desire to fight and the ability to do so.

Sam journeyed slowly to *Malmaison*, thinking on the things he had heard. If Honoria was surprised at his visit she did not show it. She embraced him fondly and held him at arm's length and looked at him. "You've grown older, Sam'l. I see some gray hairs and there are wrinkles about your eyes."

"It is strange that I should appear older," he said coldly. "The things I've been through should not age a man at all. They should make him younger."

"You're being sarcastic," she said.

Sam could not help but smile at her. Damme, she had poise! She was more beautiful than he had ever seen her, trim as a sapling.

"I have come to talk business," he stated.

She took him to her office and sent for a drink, and when he had finished his drink she touched his hand and said, "A great hurt has been in my heart, Sam'l. I'm sorry that I wrote you as I did. I have a confession to make."

"I presume you've rehearsed it?"

"Do not be bitter. I'm your sister. I've always loved you. It is a strange kind of a love, Sam'l. I could never explain it even to myself."

"You've never loved anybody except yourself," Sam remarked bluntly.

"You're entitled to think that and I cannot blame you. But I was jealous of Donna because she took you away from me. I used to be jealous of our mother when you went to her for counsel. I wanted you to come to me. And when I heard you were going to marry Anestasie I lost my head and wrote you that letter. It is only natural that you should fall in love again. I ask you only one thing—to wait, for at least two years. When a man has suffered as you have suffered he's apt to run to the arms of the first woman who opens hers to him. Please wait and see if this love lasts."

"You've changed your tune, Honoria," Sam said.

"I have. Of course, I won't try to take Hoab away from you."

Sam stared at her but did not speak. She wondered if

he could read her thoughts. No, she didn't want Hoab. Tishomingo would scorn her if he knew the truth. And, too, she had met many elegant gentlemen in Louisville, in Pittsburgh. Proud nabobs from Washington City and from Boston had called upon her. They would never call again if they knew she had a son, a nameless son.

She might have been talking to an image for all the impression her words made on her brother. He seemed bored with her words, as though he did not care what her opinions were. Finally, she bluntly asked the question that was on her mind. "Does Anestasie know the truth about Hoab?"

"Ay. She knows."

Honoria's tone changed and she railed at him. "You fool! She'll tell. She'll lord it over me ——"

"Shut up!" Sam snapped. "Anestasie cares so little about you that she never bothers to think of you." That shocked Honoria's conceit. "What you'll never understand, Honoria, is that Anestasie loves Hoab. She'll never reveal the secret. It would hurt the boy."

Honoria sighed. Sam was right. Visibly relieved, she said, "Aren't you pleased that I'm willing to let Hoab remain with you forever?"

"Yes, I'm pleased," Sam said casually. "But I've never bothered about it. No court would give Hoab to you. And you don't want Hoab. You hope to make Tishomingo love you. You couldn't get him with Hoab. If Tishomingo ignores you, there are always other men to court the faithless wife of Lake Flournoy, or the widow of Lake Flournoy."

So Sam had turned on her! Even her own brother hated her. She could feel it. Her eyes narrowed as she looked at him, and she spoke softly without hesitation. "You say you came to talk business with me? I trust it's about the debt. My patience has been strained."

Sam reached into his jacket and produced the bills that Jackson had O.K.'d. He laid them upon her desk. "These are bills for supplies I sold the army. They have been approved by General Jackson. They're payable at any army pay office. There are enough here to pay my debts. Total them up and write me a receipt."

Honoria thumbed through the papers. "This isn't money."

"It's as good as money."

"I want American currency, Sam'l."

Sam folded the bills. "I had hoped you would be generous enough to accept these and to send one of your agents to have them cashed. Otherwise, I'll have to go to Nashville or New Orleans, or maybe to Georgia. I'm sorry I bothered you. I will have them cashed and send you the money." He returned the bills to his jacket and arose to go. "You haven't asked me, but I know you want to hear. Tishomingo is well. He's with Jackson. My son is well, too."

Honoria sent for more drinks and smiled at her brother. "Don't hasten; there are other things to talk about. Maybe we can strike a bargain."

"Ay?"

"If you marry Anestasie you'll get her property on the Tombigbee. If you'll sign a statement that you will give it to me I'll cancel our debt."

"You're cagey, Honoria. Of what good would a wagon road to Georgia be to me if you owned the Duportail ferry? You could control the road. Nay, I'll not sign any such statement."

Honoria mocked him with her cool laugh. "I cannot

764

say that I blame you. If you lose Locha Poka you can always go to your wife's house and live in a cabin that her first husband built. But I have another offer. You hold contracts to supply Jackson's army. If you'll give me those contracts, I'll free Locha Poka from all indebtedness."

Sam got up from his chair and walked to a window and stared out. He calculated rapidly. That was a good trade. An excellent trade! He turned quickly to his sister and said, "It's a deal. Draw up the papers. I'll give you my contracts in exchange for the mortgage."

"You draw the papers," she directed, "and I'll fetch witnesses to the transaction."

She left the room and Sam took a quill and wrote rapidly. For receipt of a cancelled mortgage against his home, he agreed to give Mrs. Lake Flournoy all contracts he held to supply the army of Andrew Jackson with corn, beef, rum and pork. He was busy finishing the document when Honoria returned. "I've fetched three of my agents to witness our signature," she said.

Sam glanced up and handed her the quill. Then his eyes fell on one of the witnesses—a man without teeth in the left side of his mouth but with a bluish stump in the right side. The man grinned at Sam: it was the trader who had sold food to Jackson's starving army at ten times its value!

Sam glared. So Honoria was the fellow's employer!

"I think you've met some of my men before," Honoria smiled. "They told me about it. You always were impetuous, Sam'l."

Sam got slowly to his feet and moved to the end of the desk, holding his hand near his pistol butt. The grin vanished from the trader's face and a look of fear took its place. Honoria glanced at her brother and her heart began pounding. Sam's eyes had narrowed to slits and his nostrils quivered. She had never seen him in such a rage. His voice was low and ominous.

"If that blue-toothed son of a bitch isn't out of here before I count five, I'll throw him out. . . . One— two——"

The trader turned to run, but Honoria stopped him. "You stay right here! This is my house! If my brother attacks you——"

"—four—five!" Sam grabbed the man by the throat, drove his fist into his mouth and shattered his remaining teeth. The two other men cowered in a corner. Sam lifted the trembling man, kicked open the door and hoisted him out. "I said I'd throw him out. I always keep my word."

The other men fled. Honoria screamed, then stifled the sound with her palm and stared at her brother, panic-stricken. Sam gripped her shoulders. "And I swore that if I ever met that man's employer, I'd kick his rump." He wheeled his sister around and kicked her with the broadside of his foot.

She would have fallen but he held her up. Fury and humiliation choked her.

Sam picked up the paper on which he had written and tore it to bits. "I'd rather lose my home than have anything to do with your scheme. I'll tell Andy Jackson that my sister was the one who profited when her agents sold rats to his starving soldiers."

"Get out!" Honoria found her voice and hissed the words. "You kicked me! You kicked me as though I were a slut! Get out! If your debt isn't paid within six months I'll take Locha Poka."

766

Sam walked out of his sister's house and, without looking back, mounted his horse and headed for Nashville.

Andrew Jackson's O.K. was not redeemable in Nashville. Oh, it was good, all right. The paymaster said so. He examined the papers and smiled. "That's Andy's handwriting, sure enough. The old heller never could spell. He always signs them O.K.'s when he means 'all correct.' But them papers have got to go to Congress. I couldn't pay any such amount even if I had the money."

"But there is no Congress," Sam argued. "Washington is burned."

"Then you got to wait till we get another Congress," the paymaster said. "A Congress ain't hard to get. The trouble is getting rid of it. Just keep your shirt on and Congress will get around to you."

Sam shrugged. He knew he could not get the money here. "Meanwhile, I won't have any shirt."

He could not cash the warrants in Louisville. In Pittsburgh a speculator offered him ten cents on the dollar. Sam traveled all the way to Philadelphia before he was convinced that he could not get his money. The government didn't have it and private business was not willing to gamble. Andrew Jackson's O.K. might be good, and then again it might not. Who was to say that there would be a United States within a year? The British were before New Orleans.

Sam's heart was heavy and his mind was confused when he turned south again. He must pass through Georgia on the way home. It would be good to see Georgia again. He knew that there was no hope of getting the money in Milledgeville, but he could stop and see Mr. Harkins and then go on and see Pierce. He might even drop down to the Chattahoochee to see if the old Dabney cabin was still there. And Frome. Frome was in Georgia. Ay, he had left his store in the territory in the hands of an assistant and had returned to his saddlery to fill army orders. By God! Frome was the man. Maybe Frome would buy his warrants.

He spent Christmas in his saddle and the coldest weather he had ever seen caught him on the road. It was colder than the dread winter that Ab used to talk about, the winter that had killed his parents, the winter when Ab and his sister had been saved by crawling into the carcass of a freshly killed ox. It was storming when Sam reached Milledgeville and the turn-in to the tavern was a sheet of ice. They had a fast post from Milledgeville to Frome's place, and Sam sent his old friend word to wait upon him. Frome came to Milledgeville the next day and when he saw Sam he embraced him and ordered drinks, hot rum for Sam and tea for himself.

He showered Sam with questions. Frome was rich. His store on the Mississippi was a big business. His factory in Georgia was netting him more than $50,000 a year. He no longer worked pauper labor and bound 'uns, but only free labor. "It's the only way to work," Frome said. "I pay my men two dollars a week and they're happy. Slaves? No, Sam'l boy, I own no slaves. I don't believe in slavery. It's bad business. Besides, I'm a Jew, and Jews are opposed to slavery. We've never been slaves. We've been thrown in bondage, but either death or God always delivered us."

He asked hundreds of questions about Sam's affairs and his family. He had heard of Donna's death. And he talked of the war.

"There's a report," he said, "that peace will come soon.

768

Already our envoys are meeting with the British envoys."*

"I heard something of that in the East," Sam nodded. "It would be an act of Providence if we got word to suspend hostilities before the British attacked in New Orleans. My son is there."

"Ay, it's possible, but not probable. And if we should get news here, it would be too late. I'm thinking that the British have already taken New Orleans."

"Not in this weather," Sam said. "I've never seen such cold weather."

"Nor I," agreed Frome. "My agents report that every creek between here and New Orleans is frozen and the big rivers are clogged with ice and flooding their banks. The Alabama is a mile wide. I hope Mrs. Duportail is all right."

"She's all right," Sam replied, glad to talk of Anestasie. "She can take care of herself. We're going to be married, you know."

Frome clapped Sam's shoulder and ordered him another drink. "I am glad, Sam'l boy. That's what you need. She's a fine lady, too. And you have a good head for business. If you marry her, you'll get that ferry and you'll build that road. Remember how we planned a road from the river to the sea? You would handle that end and I would handle this end. Maybe it will come to pass."

Sam saw his opportunity and presented his problem to Frome. Frome studied the papers and flipped them aside. "It's a lot of money, Sam."

"If you don't want to buy those warrants, then lend

* The treaty of peace had been signed at Ghent on December the 24th, 1814. America, of course, had no news of the signing. Technically, a state of war must exist until Congress ratified the treaty.

me money on Locha Poka. I'll take the money and pay off my debt and then I'll give you a first mortgage."

"I can't do it." Frome shook his head. "It's not good business. Who holds your mortgage now?"

"Lake Flournoy."

Frome muttered under his breath. "He'll show you no mercy. He needs money, too. Things are not going well with him down in Martinique. And, of course, your sister has no influence on him."

"No, she has none," Sam said. "She has tried to get him to be lenient with me, but he wants his money."

Frome fingered the warrants again. "I'll buy these. I'll take a chance on Andy Jackson. If we lose this war my business will be ruined, anyway. If we win the war, these will be good. I'll give you fifty cents on the dollar for them."

"That won't save me."

"But it's a good nest egg if you want to start over."

"Start over? Me?" Sam had not even considered it till now.

"Ay, if you have to. Don't be so high and mighty, Sam'l. I know you. You're too proud to marry Mrs. Duportail and live on her land. I can't blame you. But with this money you can start all over, if you should lose Locha Poka. But, better still, I know that Flournoy needs money. You offer him this money in hard cash and he'll snatch it up and extend your mortgage."

Sam drank his rum slowly. Frome's words were wise. Flournoy might return at any time and he could do business with Flournoy. And, too, half a loaf was better than none. So they made the deal and drank to it.

They bade each other good night and Sam went to his room and wrote Anestasie. He told her he would stay in Milledgeville for several days and rest. His horse had gone lame and he must trade him or wait until he healed. Besides, it was too cold to ride. He told her of his business transaction.

"It may be," he wrote, "that I cannot hold Locha Poka. But we'll cross that bridge when we reach it. Donna has been dead for sixteen months and I believe it would be proper for us to consider an immediate marriage. I weary of being without you."

In his room, Frome wrote a letter to Anestasie, too. He congratulated her upon her engagement to Sam and then added, "I will not mince words. You know Dabney's financial status. It is entirely likely that he will lose Locha Poka. He is too proud a man to accept help from you. He will never consent to live on your land. I have always wanted the property you own. If Dabney loses Locha Poka he will never build the road. Somebody else will have to build it. I would like to build that road. I will never allow Lake Flournoy to control the Mississippi-Georgia route if I can help it. I will buy your property for enough money to enable you and Dabney, with the money he has already collected, to pay his home out. You will not have to give this money to Dabney. Just give me your word and I will lend him enough money to see him through, and this deal will be a thing between us."

The express rider took the two letters the next day and Anestasie dispatched a reply to Frome that she must give the matter careful consideration, knowing full well she wouldn't sell.

Even as as she wrote, the legislature of the Mississippi Territory met in extraordinary session to consider war measures, including the transportation of troops from Georgia to the valley. The legislature exercised the right of eminent domain against Mrs. André Duportail and passed an act providing that the ferry across the Tom-bigbee River was a public necessity and convenience. No tolls could ever again be collected. The bill had been written by Lawyer Thomas many years before when he feared that Lake Flournoy might get the property. The legislature resurrected the bill and passed it. Honoria's agents bought many rounds of drinks for the lawmakers the day the territory made a ferry of Anestasie's little barge. Honoria was triumphant. It had not taken much of her money or time to locate the dead bill and have life put into it. Ay, her brother would rue the day he had kicked her.

The legislature voted Anestasie five hundred dollars compensation and a fee of five hundred dollars a year to operate the ferry. The value of her property dropped tenfold and without consulting Sam she sold her slaves so she would have a dowry. A French lady must have a dowry. Sam wouldn't understand, so she didn't wait to discuss it with him. But she wouldn't sell her land. It was her land and it was good land and she would keep it. Her frugal French soul hurt at the idea of selling her land.

Although his horse was not entirely sound, Sam decided to leave Milledgeville Christmas week. He and Frome sat in the tap room of the tavern and drank and ate together.

Andrew Jackson sat in his headquarters at 106 Royal Street in New Orleans and contemplated the job he had cut out for himself. He was about five hundred miles, as the crow flies, from the capital of Georgia. He was in bad repute with the government nabobs, for not only had he violated Spain's neutrality by invading Pensacola, but he had left Mobile and New Orleans unprotected.

772

The armchair generals didn't believe that Jackson could clean out Pensacola and then march back to New Orleans in time to save the city, but he did it. The general was so ill that he often had to rest on his sofa and give orders while his body trembled in pain. He counted noses for the hundredth time—1,000 regulars and 2,000 militiamen. Three thousand men to defend New Orleans against the greatest invading force that any nation had sent across the Atlantic. The British could count 10,000 seamen, 1,500 marines, and 9,600 troops, the troops that had conquered Napoleon.

The British officers had brought their wives with them, and the women had brought their best frocks. They had heard that New Orleans was a lively place.

A man less stubborn than Andrew Jackson perhaps would have deserted New Orleans and fallen back to the bluffs to make a stand. There were six routes to the city and Jackson didn't have enough men to defend one route. He was a hill fighter, but he remembered one thing that all other men had forgotten. His Tennesseans had never fought in swamps such as those that stretched before New Orleans. But neither had the British! A hundred armies had bogged down in the mud of Flanders, and the mud of Flanders was mild and gentle compared to the mud of Louisiana. So Andy Jackson would make a stand at New Orleans. He had the best riflemen in the world in his little army, and mud and swamps were his allies. He had the routes from the coast blocked by fallen trees. He dug canals. He made ready to do what everybody said he couldn't do, hold an exposed city against the greatest army then under arms.

And he had no support from the government. Virtually every bank west of the Hudson had suspended specie payment. New England Federalists were begging for peace. The governor of Massachusetts reviled America's peace commissioners at Ghent because they would not accept England's terms and surrender the Northwest.

The British had cleared the path to the Louisiana coast and the Armada was ready for its windfall. It was on Louisiana's soil. It was at Villere's plantation! It was a magnificent army, a brigade of Wellington's men, the kilted Ninety-third Highlanders, two West India regiments, a regiment fresh from fighting at the Cape of Good Hope, and four regiments of other veterans.

Recruits began coming to Jackson. There were black Santo Domingo soldiers who carried their big tobies to worship, and their big knives to kill. There were the Mississippi Dragoons who boasted that they could outdrink any soldiers in the world. There were Kentuckians and Tennesseans. There were Louisiana Frenchmen and Carolina Scotchmen. Mulattoes with their *gris-gris* and Georgians with dried potatoes in their pockets, a sure preventive of dysentery. There were a few Ohioans with buckeyes in their pockets to ward off rheumatism. The streets of New Orleans rang with a medley of songs— "Ca Ira," "The Frozen Girl," "The Marseillaise," "Yankee Doodle," "Le Chant du Depart," and "Over the Hills and Far Away." Some of Jean Lafitte's men were there. There were Choctaws and Chickasaws, Cherokees and Creeks. There were black men, brown men, red men, white men and men whose blood was so mixed that they spoke Spanish and looked like Vikings. It wasn't an army. Each class hated every other class and each man had only one thing in common with his neighbor. Each man loved liberty. The melting pot of the Southwest had conceived and had spewed out a mongrel force that was ready to die for the right to live in the melting pot.

So the British had landed. Well, let the British beware.

"By the Eternal, they shall not sleep on our soil!"

Old Mad Jackson sprang from his couch and pounded his table. He told his officers, "Gentlemen, the British are below! We must fight them tonight!"

"Vivé Jackson!"

"Hurray for Old Mad Jackson!"

"God bless Old Andy!"

New Orleans rang with his praise, even while Sam and Frome sat together in Milledgeville and wondered how things were going in New Orleans.

Frome asked Sam, "What do you think of the British peace proposals?"

"I do not know what they are."

"They want the Northwest and half of Maine."

Sam laughed. "Is that all? As for me, I won't give them anything but hell, but they can have clear title to that. They're a funny people. Weeks ago their spies posted notices in Louisiana guaranteeing the people there protection against the United States."

"Is Jackson getting any supplies?"

"I hear he's getting some. Tennessee has sent down fifty thousand cartridges. They are superfine cartridges and each contains a musket ball and three buckshots. Mr. Harkins tells me, however, that Jackson has not received word from the war department in sixty days. Jackson wants national conscription but he can't have it. The nation is broke."

Sam heard the hooves of the express rider's horse pounding on the frozen ground and he glanced up quickly at Frome and walked to the door of the tavern. Any man who rode a horse that fast on such a cold day was in a God-awful hurry. The express rider reined in at

775

the turn-in and tried to dismount. He was frozen to the saddle. Sam cut the belly bands and lifted the man gently to the ground and then carried him, saddle and all, into the tavern. The man's face was matted with ice and he was too frozen to speak. A crowd gathered around and Sam cut away the saddle. Eager hands poured brandy down the rider's throat and the man fumbled in his jacket and found a pouch of dispatches addressed to General Jackson. The pouch was marked "Urgent" and was from the war department.

Sam examined the pouch and spoke quickly to the tavern-keeper, "Get Harkins!"

Then he devoted his attention to the rider. The man's buttocks were a mass of bleeding flesh and his hands were swollen and stank of gangrene. A doctor was called and he examined the courier. "This man is dying. His hands froze and then gangrene set in. He has pneumonia."

They took him to a room and Sam returned to the barroom to meet Harkins. Harkins was tapping the pouch against the table and staring into space.

"What do you think of it?" Sam asked.

"I do not know. These dispatches may mean anything. They may mean peace, or at least an armistice until the peace is settled. Then again, they may mean nothing. But they've got to get to Jackson."

"I can leave in a few hours," Sam said.

"Why should it take you so long?"

"I must get a new horse."

"Pick out a good Morgan," suggested Harkins.

"I don't want a Morgan," Sam said. "I want an Indian pony."

"Get the best. The government will pay for it."

776

"Like hell it will!" Sam snapped. "It hasn't even paid me for supplies."

Frome smiled at Sam and patted his arm affectionately. "I'll pay for the horse. If Sam'l is willing to ride from here to New Orleans in such weather, it's the least I can do. You can't make it, Sam'l. Every creek is frozen and every river is flooding."

"I can make it. I'll head for Duportail's ferry and then cut south to the wilderness."

He ordered the inn-keeper to prepare a bag of tafula for him and a sack of Indian corn for his horse, and then he went outside the town to an Indian camp and began trading for his horse. He selected a pony with a long mane. Harkins protested. "That pony's no good."

But the Indians looked at Sam admiringly, and the owner of the pony said, "He's a good pony. His name is Paddy. Big Sam knows horses."

Back at the tavern Dabney slipped into his bearskin vest and his doeskin jacket. He borrowed the best pair of deerskin breeches he could find. He put on woolen stockings and moccasins. He left his rifle-gun in Frome's care. It was too heavy to carry. He armed himself with a light pistol, his knife and a tomahawk. Slipping the pouch under his jacket, he shook hands with Harkins. Then he shook hands with Frome. "Ay, Ben, I hope you soon will come to Locha Poka for my wedding. And bring my gun when you come. Goodbye, gentlemen." He waved and mounted Paddy at the turn-in and headed into the biting wind.

A few Creeks who loitered around the tavern saw him ride away and they mounted and rode rapidly into the Creek country. Big Sam was going alone to the Creek lands. The Creeks had a debt to collect.

Sam pulled his neck into his shoulders and hunched

over as he rode, turning his head away from the wind. He set his horse at a steady gallop and held him on it. He leaned over and watched the horse's nostrils and when Paddy began breathing heavily, Sam slowed him to a walk. The dawn of January the 1st, 1815, overtook Sam Dabney as he was riding through the village where he first had seen Donna. He rode by Pierce's house. A sentinel was on duty there and Sam waved to him. The sentinel blinked his sleepy eyes and waved back. There was a light in the kitchen of the Chadbourne mansion and a light in Pierce's room.

The Chattahoochee was frozen. The old ferryman did not want to brave the ice.

"I'll help you pole," offered Sam. "We can get through. I'm Sam Dabney."

"Ay?" the old ferryman peered at him. "I knew your father. I was with him at King's Mountain. We'll get across."

On the journey across the river Sam learned that the old Dabney homestead had been burned by the Creeks.

"Ain't nothin' there now," said the ferryman.

"Did you ever see a grave around there?" Sam asked. "We buried our mother and father there."

"I never saw no grave. The weeds have taken it long before now." He waved Sam Godspeed as he shoved the ferry against the bank and Sam clattered off the boat and into the Creek Nation. The Three-Chop Way was well-marked. Ice had formed in the wagon ruts. He saw trees that he had marked. He ate in the saddle. He poured a handful of tafula into his left hand and ate it raw. He paused long enough to feed his horse and rubbed him furiously while he ate his corn. Sam let him cool off a bit and broke ice in a creek to let the horse drink.

Then he rubbed him again and walked him down the road.

He felt ice forming in his nose and around his mouth. His ankles got cold first, and he lifted one foot out of the stirrup and rubbed his ankle as he rode and then rubbed the other ankle. The sweat of his horse dampened his tafula and it froze, and Sam had to bite it. He reckoned he was making at least fifty miles a day and was far into the Creek country when he had to make camp and seek food. His tafula could no longer be eaten and his fodder was gone. He must go to an Indian village and try to buy food, but would the Creeks sell food to Big Sam Dabney? If not, he would have to steal it. He huddled close to his small fire and studied his problem. The catamount cry of the Creeks sounded to the north and another to the east. Sam put out his fire quickly and led Paddy into the woods beside the road. He examined his pistol. He took out his tomahawk and drove it into a tree where it would be handy. Then he waited.

The hoofbeats thundered on the frozen ground and Sam scowled. The Creeks wouldn't attack him on horses. They would know that he could hear hoofbeats. Only a friend would make his approach so apparent. Sam went back to his camp site, rekindled his fire and stepped back into the shadows. The Red Eagle paused as he rode into the camp light and looked around and called, "Big Sam, it is I. Bill Weatherford. Show yourself, man."

Sam stepped from behind a tree and the two men shook hands solemnly. "I have brought you food," said the Red Eagle. "I have food for your horse, too."

Without another word he began roasting fresh meat over the fire and while the meat cooked he put a bag of Indian corn on Sam's horse and a bag of tafula.

"How did you know I was here?" Sam asked.

"Creek scouts from Milledgeville came and said that you were riding to Old Mad Jackson. They wanted to kill you."

"I'm grateful to you," said Sam.

"I'll see you through the Creek Nation. That is, what is left of the nation. And tell General Jackson that I saw you through. It is part of my payment for the Christian compassion he showed my people. Tell him that Bill Weatherford gave his word that he would never take up arms against the United States and that the word of a Creek is good."

Red Eagle rode with Sam until they reached the Tombigbee and then bade him goodbye. Not a hostile Creek had been seen. But many a Creek warrior had seen Sam Dabney. None dared attack, however, as long as Big Sam rode with the Red Eagle.

It took Anestasie's ferryman more than an hour to get his barge across the Tombigbee, through the ice. Sam stayed with Anestasie only long enough to eat hot food and get a drink of hot rum. They didn't have time to discuss their plans, but as Sam kissed her goodbye, he said, "I'll be back soon and we'll be married."

He left the Three-Chop Way at Anestasie's house and cut south for the wilderness, an untracked territory in the southern part of the new land. Sam rode many miles before he noticed the difference. But the winter was gone and the earth was lush. He had never seen such a land. There was not a trail. It was a complete wilderness, untouched by white men. There were no signs of Indians. Sam wondered if any man had ever lived in this land. It was a land of deep, dark water, with black earth along the rivers. Pines stood at attention on the ridges, scarcely swaying in the gentle wind that blew up from the Gulf. The birds were friendly. They flew in front of Sam, chattering and scolding him. Bobwhites called from the saw-grass and blue jays roughhoused. Squirrels scurried in the hickories and the pine needles were so thick that Paddy seemed to be walking on down. Sam dismounted by a river and let Paddy drink the cool, clean water. Sam lay down on the ground for a minute to rest. He turned on his side and scooped up a handful of the dirt and let it pour through his fingers, feeling it. It was good dirt. Soft and warm. There were little red particles of clay in the black loam. Ay, that was good dirt. It was virgin earth. They were virgin trees and this was a virgin river. He forgot his mission and sprawled there and watched the sun go down. The river turned a deep red as the dying rays of the sun caught it. A red river. It wasn't as big as the Tombigbee or the Pearl. It was a small friendly river that took its time about moving, as though it had nowhere to go and was in no hurry to get there. It was scarcely big enough to be called a river, Sam thought. It was more of a big creek. A big red creek. Bogue Homa, red creek. He would name it that. Some day he would come back and explore it. Maybe he and Anestasie could camp here and sleep on the virgin earth. Sleep where no white man had ever slept before and hunt and fish where no white man had ever been.

He left the place with regret, but Paddy was rested and so was he. He felt almost young again. The strength of the land seemed to come up through his feet and give him strength. When he mounted Paddy and rode away he was singing. No particular song. Just singing snatches of songs. And then he whistled. The blue jays scolded him. The squirrels ran into the hickory trees and peeped at him, cocking their heads at the strange sound. The mockingbirds tried to whistle, too, and the woodpeckers ceased drumming and stared at him, unafraid but curious.

Two days later Sam reined his horse at Lake Pontchartrain. He was seven days out of Milledgeville and he gave a fisherman his pistol to take him across the lake. The morning of January the 8th he galloped along the levee of New Orleans and then into Royal Street, to Jackson's headquarters. An echo of thunder from the river rolled into the city. The crackle of small arms startled him. Jackson was fighting. He was not at his headquarters. He was before the city, cursing and commanding 6,000 men of every race and creed who were making a stand against 15,000 of the best-trained troops of Europe.

Unable to reach Jackson, Sam rode down to Chalmette and found the Mississippi Dragoons, commanded by General Hinds. Sam inquired of Jackson, and Hinds shrugged. "Great God, man, you can't see him now! He called us out at one o'clock this morning. There's going to be hell to pay this day."

"All right, General." Sam handed him the pouch. "If Sam Dabney can't see God Almighty Jackson after riding from Milledgeville, Georgia, in seven days, then *you* deliver this. It might mean peace."

Sam turned from Hinds and hurried along the line of Dragoons until he found Tishomingo and Hoab crouching behind breastworks of logs and mud. Hoab threw his arms around his father and Tishomingo patted Sam on the shoulder and welcomed him.

"How long have you been fighting?" Sam peered over the breastworks into the spreading dawn.

"For more than a week," Tishomingo answered. "I don't know exactly how long. The days all seem alike. We have skirmished almost every day and there have

782

been two pretty fair fights. We have licked them at every turn."

Hoab ran to fetch a rifle for his father and Sam studied the battle field. A canal was directly in front of the American line and to the right and west was the Mississippi. The Americans had a battery on the other side of the river that could sweep the field. A swamp was to the Americans' left and east, and the canal ran from the river to the swamp. A heavy fog rolled over the Plain of Chalmette. Sam whistled softly. "Damme, the British picked a hell of a place to fight."

"They didn't pick it," Tishomingo winked. "Jackson picked it."

"They haven't got a chance," Sam said. "We can hem them in between the river and the swamp, and they'll never in God's world get to us. It's suicide. They've got to cross that field and expose themselves. If they get across that, they've got to cross that canal and storm these breastworks."

"They've assaulted us before. Not here, but in a place almost as bad. Some damned fool American had the idea of making barricades out of cotton bales. The British blew them up and set them on fire. Then Old Andy fortified this place. He turned us all out with shovels and we deepened that canal and got ready. The British are loons to attack here. They think we have about 15,000 men, too. Some of their prisoners told them that story and stuck to it. The prisoners got away and came back and reported to us."

"Who's commanding them?" Sam wanted to know. "The damned fool has got more guts than sense."

"Ned Pakenham. Major General Sir Edward Pakenham, brother-in-law of Wellington, hero of Spain, and a young heller."

783

"An Irishman, God!" Sam marveled. "Trust an Irishman to pick a bog to fight in. It's a coincidence, Chock. Pakenham was born in a castle in County Antrim. Jackson's folks came from the same county."

The British detachment tried to cross the river to get at the American battery, but the strong current swept them downstream. Young Ned Pakenham didn't know that. Gibbs' Forty-fourth Regiment was ordered to take facines for crossing the canal and scaling ladders to use on the ramparts. The regiment neglected to carry out the orders and three hundred men had to run back from the British line to get the equipment. Pakenham hesitated before he ordered the attack. He must have known it was suicide, but he dared not go back and face Admiral Cochrane with the suggestion that the assault be postponed. He waited for a signal that the American river battery had been captured, but there was no signal. He had wanted to attack before the sun came up. His men were perfect targets in sunlight. Most of his plans, however, misfired. At six o'clock when the fog was thickest, Ned Pakenham ordered that a signal rocket be discharged. It burst in a shower of blue. Another rocket answered.

"That's the signal to attack," said Sam. "Get ready. Here comes hell." He glanced at his son. The boy was priming his rifle. Sam whispered, "Point your gun toward the British when you prime it, son. Then if it misfires it won't hurt anybody."

Tishomingo also spoke softly, "They are somebody, Big Sam. They're men like we are."

"I didn't mean my remark to sound like it did," Sam answered. "I know they're men. May the Lord help them and us, too." He didn't know why he spoke so softly. Men do strange things before battle. Some of them laugh, usually a crackling, forced laugh. Others pray. Some don't do anything except look at their guns and then glance up at the enemy and back at their guns, judging the distance. The kidneys of some men flush in the excitement and they stand on one foot and then on the other, shaking their legs, the butt of jeers from their comrades.

The fog rolled away and the British were in plain view. Pakenham's last chance to surprise the Americans was blown away by a gust of wind that swept over the Mississippi. The British were about six hundred yards in front of the barricade, marching in perfect order. The dry grass on the plain was dressed in frost and the sun struck the frost and reflected on the brass buckles of the British soldiers.

"Merciful God!" Sam exclaimed. "Look at them! Do they think they're parading before their king? Look at their officers up front. They're about five hundred yards away. Hold up, Hoab, until they get within two hundred yards. See that man on the horse to the left? He's a captain. He's yours."

The boy cringed at the words. This wasn't war, this was murder. Hoab ran the back of his hand over his nose and sniffled. He didn't want his father to know that he was sniffling. Sam turned his eyes sharply and saw that the boy was crying and then he looked straight ahead quickly. "This powder gets in a man's eyes, ay, Chock?"

"Ay," said Chock. "It brings tears to the eyes."

The word was handed down the line, "Fire for the cross-plates."

A twelve-pounder opened the battle. It resounded with a deep *b-l-ooo-m*. The other American guns opened at five hundred yards. The British cannon aimed at the flashes of the American guns. The soldiers sent word to

Jackson that the smoke from the cannon would spoil their aim. Jackson ordered the cannon to cease firing and the word was passed along, "Ready!" The rabble raised their guns.

"*Aim!*" The Americans drew their bead. Hoab laid his rifle-sight on the breast of the British captain.

"*Fire!*"

A solid sheet of yellow and orange burst from the American ranks. The first line of redcoats fell to its knees and the men pitched on their faces. The captain gripped his belly and slid from his horse. Hoab loaded again. He stepped down from the parapet to load and his father stepped up to the parapet and drew his bead and fired. Sam didn't wait to see his man fall, but stepped down again and gave his place to Hoab. Sam began humming and Hoab tried to hum, too. The British ranks were blown down as brittle saplings fall before a hurricane. Gibbs tried to urge the men forward with his sword. The blundering, bewildered Forty-fourth Regiment still was without its ladders and facines. Its fore ranks wheeled toward the rear and the column was thrown into confusion. Gibbs went down. Pakenham hurried up to take command and was blown from his horse. The Ninety-third Highlanders ran to the aid of their comrades and were ordered to lead the second assault. Colonel Dale, their commander, handed his valuables to a surgeon and said, "Give these to my wife." Then he led his Scots across Chalmette and the Americans slaughtered them. The Scots hesitated only a moment before the fire, and then panic seized the British army. The officers struck their men with their swords, but they wouldn't go on. They huddled in desolate little groups. They threw away their knapsacks and tried to scatter, but the Americans picked them off as though they were rabbits. Major Wilkinson of the Twenty-first North British Fusiliers rallied one hundred men and ran to the parapets. Twenty men got across the canal and charged the Americans. Wilkinson scrambled over the parapets and fell dead.

Pakenham was dead. Gibbs was dead. Dale was dead. The British army was in flight. The battle had lasted scarcely two hours and the charge about twenty minutes. The Americans silenced their guns and gazed in awe at the field. From among the dead, more than five hundred Britons got to their feet and walked toward the Americans. They had fallen and had pretended that they were dead to avoid charging. They were sent back with the other prisoners, among whom was Major Mitchell, the man who had applied the torch to Washington.

The leadership of the British army fell upon the wounded shoulders of Major General Keane and he asked for a truce to bury his dead. More than two thousand Britons lay upon the field. The Americans had lost seven dead and six wounded. Outnumbered two to one, the Americans had won a victory that prompted Napoleon to say, "If I had some of those men and their rifles I could sweep Europe."

The British put Pakenham's body in a cask of rum to preserve it. Keane wrote Jackson a prideless letter begging for the return of his sword. Jackson sent it to him. Jackson remembered that when he was thirteen, an English officer had slashed him with a sword because he wouldn't shine boots. But Andy didn't mention that when he returned the sword to Keane with a very formal letter that he hoped the general would recover quickly from his wound.

Sam blew down his rifle barrel and propped his gun against the parapet. He stretched his tired, aching mus-

787

cles and left his son and Tishomingo, to go in search of Jackson. He found the general in his headquarters, resting on his couch. Jackson struggled to his feet and offered Sam his hand. The general had been living for days on nothing but rice, and was so weak that he scarcely could stand.

"It was a great victory, Andy," Sam congratulated him, his face beaming.

"We would have destroyed them if Morgan's Kentuckians had held fast."

"Did you get the dispatch that I gave to General Hinds?"

"Yes."

Sam said, "I had hoped it might be news of the peace."

Jackson did not reply for several seconds and then he said sadly, "If I had had the message a few days ago, I might have prevented this battle."

"Then it was news of the peace?"

"Nay. But it might have meant an armistice. The war department reports that there soon will be peace and hinted that I should seek an armistice. They passed the whole load to me as they always do." He rested his head on his hands and returned to his couch. "I don't know if the British would have given me an armistice—or if I would have asked one."

"This victory will make you the hero of our nation. In a way, I'm glad the message was late."

"Being a hero, Sam, isn't worth the candle. However, if I had received the message, I might have saved those poor devils. But the war department is always too late. Where did you get the dispatches?"

"In Milledgeville. A rider killed himself getting them there. I picked them up on December the 31st."

788

The general ran his hand through his frizzled hair and gawked at Sam. "From Milledgeville to Louisiana in seven and a half days? In this weather? Through the Creeks? It takes my post eight days to ride from Mobile. You're drunk, Dabney!"

"Your friend, Billy Weatherford, got me through the Creeks. I made it in a bit more than seven and a half days."

"By God! It's about five hundred miles as the crow flies! You must have ridden 'way more than that."

"I don't know how far I rode. I cut through the wilderness after I left the Duportail ferry. God, what beautiful country! New land ——"

"But how did you do it?" Jackson cut in.

"Traveling light, Andy. No saddle bags and an empty belly."

"I want you to go back to take news of our victory."

"I can leave within an hour. Paddy will be all right then."

Jackson demanded, "Who's Paddy?"

"My horse."

Jackson sat up and shook his head. "You rode one horse all the way?" The general visibly was skeptical.

"That's right. The horse is like I am, a bit tough, Andy."

"I'll get you the best horse in New Orleans," Jackson said. "Be ready to leave within an hour."

"I'll be ready. So will Paddy."

Sam went back to find Hoab and Tishomingo, but his son had marched away with the Dragoons. While he was seeking Tishomingo, a French officer, dressed in gold and white, approached him. "You are Sam Dabney?"

"That's right."

The Frenchman introduced himself. He was an exile from France, having fled when Napoleon was sent to Elba. He had fought with General Jean Humbert, another Napoleonic exile, during the day's battle.

"You're a leader in this part of the country," the Frenchman continued, "and I'm prepared to offer you a good proposition. The United States has defeated England. We're trying to raise at least one regiment of American riflemen to go to France. The emperor will not stay at Elba. He'll return and lead you. What is your price?"

"My rifle-gun is not for sale," Sam said. "I am a planter and a trader, not a soldier."

The Frenchman made no effort to persuade him, but bowed politely and took his leave. Sam searched the field for Tishomingo and found him near Hinds' headquarters, packing his gear.

"What's up?" Sam asked. "Have you permission to leave the army?"

Tishomingo did not look up. "Lake Flournoy has returned. I'm going home."

"Where have you learned this? Did my sister write you?"

"No. Some soldiers from Santo Domingo told me. Flournoy has heard that Napoleon is trying to raise an American army and he's come back to try to prevent it. He was seen in New Orleans a week ago."

"Did he come back alone?"

Tishomingo tightened his horse's belly band. "Dabby came back with him. Their baby is dead. The pox. Sukey is dead, too. A fer-de-lance struck her while she was roaming in the woods where Flournoy was hiding from loyal French troops. Dabby caught the pox, too. She's marked badly, but she's alive."

"Did Flournoy take his mistress to *Malmaison?*"

"Ay," said Tishomingo and put his hand on Sam's arm.

"It's a gross insult to my sister. I should kill Flournoy!"

"I once said that nothing could break the bond between us." The look of cunning and savagery returned to Tishomingo's face. "But if you should rob me of my revenge . . ."

"You've waited a long time, haven't you?"

"Years." Tishomingo fingered his bull whip.

"Then go on, man! And strike one blow for me."

Tishomingo swung into his saddle and leaned over and gripped Sam's shoulder. "When I do this thing, I may have to flee the country. Goodbye, Big Sam."

Sam clasped his hand over Tishomingo's and smiled up at him. "Goodbye, Chock."

Sam slapped the horse's rump. Tishomingo dug his heels into the horse's flanks and Sam watched him disappear to the north.

Sam turned away sadly and stared at the frozen ground as he walked toward Jackson's headquarters. An express rider, bound for Nashville, brushed passed him and Sam waved him on. It was little Billy Phillips, the jockey who had ridden from Washington to Nashville in nine days. He carried several dispatches from Jackson, and as a favor to Tishomingo, he was carrying two letters to Mrs. Lake Flournoy. One letter instructed Honoria to leave the second letter where her husband would see it. The second letter was also addressed to Honoria and was signed by Tishomingo. It asked her to meet him for a tryst near the Big Black River.

34

* * * * * * * * * * * * * * * * * * *

Tishomingo's letters reached Honoria before Flournoy and Dabby arrived at *Malmaison*. Flournoy escorted Dabby into his house through the front door, and Honoria bit her lips in anger while the slaves gulped and tittered. Her husband stood before her in the drawing room and bowed stiffly. Dabby went to the kitchen to see her friends.

Flournoy was as bronzed as his Indian kinsmen and his sensitive face showed several wrinkles. The wrinkles were becoming to him. He had grown a mustache and the mustache was jet black, in sharp contrast to his prematurely gray hair. He wore good linen and his thin lips smiled at his wife.

"The bad penny has returned," he said.

"You weren't as successful with your revolution as you were with your mistress," Honoria mocked him. "I hear she bore you a child."

Flournoy's face was hard. "If ever again you mention my child I'll thrash your very charming rear with my riding crop."

Honoria laughed at him. "You're a brave man to come back here, but a fool. When my brother hears you've returned he'll wait upon you."

"I'm at his service." He bowed again to his wife and

said, "You look well, Honoria. You're very beautiful, as an icicle is beautiful."

"I'm well, thank you. You look well, too, Lake, but Dabby looks misused. The pock marks on her face are rather repulsive to me."

Flournoy frowned. "You're not jealous, are you?"

"No, not in the least bit. I've enjoyed your absence. That's why I look well. I hold no grudge against you. It's quite natural for one half-breed to bed with another."

"Why didn't you divorce me?"

"There'll be no divorce until you have made a settlement upon me. What are your plans?"

Flournoy took a seat and stretched his legs and relaxed. He ordered a drink and sent word for Dabby to go to a guest room and rest. Then he faced his wife. "I have much to say, so please hear me out. I'll give you a divorce. I'll have the legislature grant it. And I'll make a settlement."

"How large a settlement?" Honoria demanded quickly.

"Large enough. Pardon me." He called a house slave and said, "See that Dabby rests. Take food and wine to her and bathe her. She's to be treated as a guest in my house." He turned back to his wife. Honoria's hand was trembling and her anger had driven all the color from her cheeks.

"Could it be possible, Lake, that you love this woman?"

"I do. You'll never understand it, Honoria. Dabby is loyal and good. She's the only woman who has ever loved me for my own sake. I could call her now and she would go with me without questioning where. It wouldn't matter to her if I were poor. . . . But back to the business at hand. I'm leaving the United States

793

I'm going to England. England is the only civilized country in the world."

"England is too civilized to accept a man whose mistress was his slave," Honoria said.

"Dabby is my housekeeper. I'll give *Malmaison* to you. But you must help me."

"Yes. Go on."

Flournoy lit a cheroot and spoke slowly. "Napoleon's envoys are trying to raise an army in the new land. I must prevent it. I have engaged men in New Orleans and Natchez to help me."

"I've heard of Napoleon's plan. But how can you stop it?"

"Most of the men who are considering going to France are poor farmers. My agents have offered them a very high price for all the cotton and corn they'll raise this year. Many of them will go back to their farms instead of going to France."

"But what of the others?" she asked.

"When Napoleon was married to my kinswoman he lay with her in a carriage while dictating to his secretary. It's one of the favorite stories of Europe. I don't know if it's true or not. That isn't important. But my agents are spreading the story in the new land. And no American will dare go to France and fight for a man who was so dishonorable. Their womenfolk won't let them go. Their preachers won't let them go. Americans have a strange idea of morals. When that story is spread to the four winds, Napoleon won't be able to raise a corporal's guard in this country."*

"I must admire you for your scheme," Honoria admitted. "But what would you have me do?"

"Help keep the story alive. Help me liquidate all of

* Flournoy was right. The army never materialized.

our assets except *Malmaison*. You know the business. I'm in a hurry."

He got up and started toward the office. Honoria ran to him and said frantically, "Where are you going?"

"To the office," he said. "What's the matter? Are you hiding something from me?"

Honoria looked into his eyes for several seconds before she spoke. "I think we understand each other, Lake. You arrived home unexpectedly. I have some personal mail in the office. I know that you are too honorable to read it."

"Thank you, my dear. That is the first compliment you have paid me in a long time. I'm not interested in your mail. I'm rather proud that you have told me and that you weren't childish enough to try to slip the mail away."

"I didn't have time to slip it out," she said. "Of course, I trust you, but I ask you to let me get my mail before you go to the office."

"Of course," he said, and sat down while Honoria went into the office and made as though she was running through her papers. She had destroyed Tishomingo's letters. Tishomingo was foolish to think that he could trap Flournoy so easily. She knew her husband. She returned to the drawing room and thanked him and he went into the office and began examining the books.

Damme, Honoria was a business woman. Every detail was in order. Flournoy smiled to himself. She was much better at business than her brother was, he thought. He ran through the papers until he found the mortgage against Sam. The interest was several days overdue. He would give the paper to Honoria. She could have the pleasure of returning the mortgage to Sam. She had earned that privilege. Some of the letters that she had taken must have been from Dabney. And from Tishomingo. Tishomingo had probably been there often, in his room. He probably had drunk his wine and eaten his food and enjoyed his wife. The Frenchman in Lake Flournoy was rathed amused, but his Indian blood surged to his brain and commanded him to avenge his honor. He felt the scar on his face that Tishomingo's whip had left. He was Tishomingo's equal with a pistol. A pistol made all men equal. All men are equal in the sight of a pistol. He had never attempted to kill the mingo, for he would have had to run away to avoid punishment of the law. But now he was going away, anyway. He searched frantically through the papers, seeking one line from Tishomingo. But he found none.

He put the thought out of his mind and went back to the books. He stayed in the office until late afternoon, and was very busy when Honoria entered.

"Is all in order?" she asked.

"In excellent order."

He noticed that she was nervous, that she couldn't sit still. He didn't know how fine an actress his wife was.

"How long will you be here, Lake?" she demanded. "I want to have the servants prepare your favorite dishes if you're to be here for several days."

Flournoy said quickly, "I'm riding for Natchez this afternoon. I'll be there a day or so and then I'll return and make our final arrangements here."

"Why don't you wait until tomorrow to go to Natchez?" she said. "You're tired and the rest will do you good."

"I might consider that," he smiled, "if I could go to your room tonight."

Honoria laughed. "It's very tempting, Lake, but I'm afraid Dabby would object if you went to your wife's bed. You'll forgive me if I decline the honor."

"Then I must ride for Natchez. After all, there's business in Natchez and only pleasure here. The rather dubious pleasure of your company. So if you'll be so kind, please have one of the slaves saddle a horse."

"Are you going to leave that woman here with me?"

"No. I'm taking her with me. She wants to see your brother before she goes to England. I'm going to send her to Locha Poka."

Honoria cried, "You fool! My brother will beat her."

"It is possible that I know your brother better than you do. Sam Dabney won't strike a woman, even a woman who has been a slave. He's too just a man to condemn her. He'll condemn me, yes. But he'll not vent his wrath upon her. She loves your brother and your brother's son. She wants to go to see them and I'll let her go."

Honoria went to have a horse saddled. She dared not smile but she wanted to. Lake Flournoy armed himself with two pistols. Then he sent for a slave he could trust and asked, "When your mistress rides away, which route does she take?"

"She rides the pike to the Big Black."

"When was the last time she went away?"

"Many months ago. But she asked yesterday ir the Big Black was flooded and if the ferry was running."

Honoria did not watch her husband and Dabby depart. She could not bring herself to face Dabby. She went into the study and locked herself in while Dabby told the house slaves goodbye and gave them presents. They wept when she went away.

Beyond sight of *Malmaison*, Flournoy checked his

horse and instructed his escort to take Dabby to Locha
Poka. "I'll meet you in Natchez within a week," he told
her and patted her arm tenderly. The little party disappeared from view and Flournoy concealed himself beside the pike and waited.

He primed his pistols carefully. He loaded each with
a ball and two buckshots. It was cold there in the woods
but Flournoy's smoldering anger and determination
warmed him. He saw Honoria ride by in the moonlight
and fell in behind her—about a hundred yards behind
her—keeping his horse at the edge of the woods where
the soft snow deadened the hoofbeats.

When Tishomingo's whip wrapped around his arms,
Flournoy's first thought was that a vine had trapped
him. The jerk that pulled him from his horse was his
first realization that Tishomingo had come to collect his
revenge. Flournoy did not speak when Tishomingo dis-
armed him. Neither did Tishomingo. Flournoy's first
words came when Tishomingo wrapped a rawhide
thong around his wrists and pulled him toward a tree.

"So a mingo of the Choctaws uses a woman for a
decoy?" Flournoy sneered.

Tishomingo ignored the remark and pushed Flournoy
against the tree and tied him.

Flournoy's Indian blood prevented him from crying
out. He turned his head, for his belly was against the
tree, and said, "I'm not begging for mercy, but if you'll
let me go I'll give you a fortune and I'll give you my
wife."

"I don't want your fortune, and your wife is already
mine." Tishomingo gripped the stock of his whip and
stepped back about ten feet.

"Then I ask you to see that Dabby is protected. Honoria will deal harshly with her."

Tishomingo relaxed his grip on his whip and asked, "You love Dabby?"

"I do."

"Did you love Ta-lo-wah?"

"No."

Tishomingo said, "If I had done to you the things you have done to me, what would you do?"

Flournoy answered calmly; his voice did not quaver. "I would kill you."

The man's courage impressed Tishomingo and he hesitated a moment before he struck. Flournoy's shoulders were squared and his head was held high. He bit his lips and pressed his face against the tree and waited. . . .

Tishomingo stared at his back, at his fine clothes, at his proud head. "The quality of mercy . . ."—the words rang in his head. But he quickly blotted out the thought, and his mind flashed back to Ta-lo-wah and then to Ab. He had vowed to Aba Inki that he would skin this man alive! He flicked his whip behind him and cracked the tip against Flournoy's back. It cut through the fine cloth and a trickle of blood ran down his enemy's back. Tishomingo struck again. Flournoy's legs buckled, but he straightened himself. He made no sound, only a heavy measured breathing as he forced his breath through clenched lips.

The whip cut his back to shreds, raw bloody shreds. His fine linen was beaten into his flesh. He feared consciousness would leave him, so he turned his head and taunted Tishomingo, "The arm of the mingo is weak."

The whip lash cut across his face, gashed his mouth and his words were choked in blood.

Tishomingo deliberately removed the frayed tip of his whip and substituted a new one. His right arm was tired. His muscles ached. He had not counted the strokes. He transferred the whip to his left hand and lashed Flournoy from his buttocks to his neck. Flournoy bit into the tree to stifle the moans. His fingers clawed at the bark. His head sank to one side and he collapsed, but the rawhide thongs still held him up.

Tishomingo went to him and jerked back his head. Blood poured from his mouth. There was no skin on his back, but he still was alive. Tishomingo untied him and laid him on his back and gripped his whip again. The lash sang and then cracked and chewed into the unconscious man's chest. Tishomingo raised his whip to strike again, but a feeling of revulsion gripped him. He couldn't flog an unconscious man, a brave man. He was nauseated. His revenge suddenly seemed sour, bitter. Wormwood and gall. He knelt over Flournoy and closed the man's eyes. He heard the death rattle in his enemy's throat. Flournoy was mocking him! He glanced up quickly. Were the spirits mocking him, too? Or was that the wind? Was it Ta-lo-wah begging for mercy for the man who had despoiled her? Was it Ab pleading with him to kill the man and be done with it? Or was it Lawyer Thomas rolling his words like claps of thunder, " 'Hate shuts her soul when mercy pleads.' "

Tishomingo was awed and there was no triumph in his heart. Impulsively, he gripped his whip handle, and struck Flournoy across the base of the skull, crushing it. He stared at Flournoy until death stilled the quivering flesh. Then he covered the man's face with a remnant of his fine shirt and mounted his horse and rode toward the Big Black, where Honoria was waiting for him.

She ran to him but he didn't hold her. He didn't want to. He didn't even want to look at her.

800

"Did he suffer?" Honoria asked eagerly. "Did he cry out?"

"He did not cry out, but he suffered. He suffered more than a man should suffer. . . ."

"He made me suffer," she cried. Then she realized that Tishomingo was shocked at the brutality of her words and she added quickly, "But I'm glad you did not torture him."

"I'll dispatch a Choctaw to get his body and have it taken to the bone picker. Perhaps I should send it to Dabby, but I won't do that. Lake Flournoy was a Choctaw. He will be buried near the Sacred Mound. He was a Choctaw when he died. Only a Choctaw could have faced death so calmly."

"Let us go to *Malmaison*," Honoria suggested. "We'll never have to hide in the woods again."

"*Malmaison!* Do you think I could go into the home of a man I have killed and eat his food? We must make ready to leave. My life will not be worth the rope it will take to hang me if I am caught in the new land I'm ready to travel. You go home and get the things you need. We can leave tonight. By morning we'll be in Louisiana and in a few days we'll be in Texas. I will be safe there."

"Texas?" Honoria toyed with the fringe on his jacket, twining the fringe around her right fore finger. "Trust me, darling. My plan to lure my husband here worked perfectly. And I have other plans. I am the widow of Lake Flournoy and I am rich. I can protect you from the law. There is no need for us to go away. Besides, if we run away, we'll have to begin all over again. And Dabby would inherit my husband's property."

"You're wasting words," he snapped. "We must leave in a few hours."

"And leave all this? Leave Flournoy's fortune to that slave wench?"

Tishomingo looked at her for only a moment. He suddenly felt unclean inside, and ill. He had heard the old squaws tell stories of vampires and of evil spirits that came back to earth and abided in women's bodies. Tishomingo was an Indian at that moment, and the culture that he had inherited from his white father, and the meaningless civilization that the white man had taught him, vanished. Suddenly he believed as his people believed: there really were vampires and witches. This woman must be a witch. She had sapped his strength. Flournoy was a braver man than he, for Flournoy had known how to die. And Flournoy had experienced at least one good clean love in his life. Even though she had been a slave, Flournoy had loved Dabby. But he, Tisku, mingo of the Muscogees, had succumbed to the temptations of Na-lusa-chi-to, the Soul Eater, the evil one who lived upon the souls of men. This woman was Na-lusa-chi-to.

He stepped back from her quickly. There were words on his tongue, but he did not utter them. Honoria smiled at him and held out her arms, but Tishomingo mounted his horse and, without looking back, galloped away to the west, toward the river beyond which lay Louisiana and Texas.

Honoria could not speak for several seconds, then she called to him, "Tishomingo! Wait!" Her words were drowned out in the clatter of his horse's hooves and the wind picked up the echo and carried it away. She didn't call but once. He would come back. He always had.

Frome and Pierce drove to Locha Poka for the wedding of Sam and Anestasie. It had been Anestasie's suggestion that they invite Pierce, and Sam had agreed eagerly. She had presented him her dowry, the money she had received for the slaves, but Sam still did not have enough money to lift the debt from his home. Realizing that Sam could not be happy if his sister owned Locha Poka, Anestasie agreed that Sam trade her land to Honoria. With her land and the money they had, Locha Poka could be redeemed.

Sam did not invite Honoria to the wedding. He would go to her soon and settle with her and then banish her from his life.

It was a simple wedding because Anestasie wanted it so. Little Shellie, uncomfortable in the yellow silk dress that Anestasie had made for her, ran out of the room when the ceremony was over, and Hoab ran after her. She was sobbing when he found her and she said, "They didn't do it right. They ain't really married. Anestasie didn't give him any present."

Hoab laughed at her and tried to explain that Christian ceremonies were not like Indian ceremonies.

"I like the Indian way best," Shellie said timidly. "Will you give me a present?"

Hoab crossed his heart and vowed he would, and they held hands as they walked back toward the big house.

Frome and Pierce left Locha Poka soon after the wedding supper, and Sam and Anestasie had retired when the soldiers aroused the house. Sam demanded an explanation and the officer said, "Tishomingo has killed Lake Flournoy. We're seeking the mingo. We thought he was here."

"How is my sister?" Sam demanded.

"She's all right. She said the mingo was last seen heading up the Trace toward Nashville."

"I'm not surprised that this has come to pass," Sam remarked thoughtfully. "I hope he gets away." He wondered why Honoria had not gone with him. And then, suddenly, he knew why. She would never sacrifice her comforts. She must have lied about seeing him go up the Trace.

The officer said, "But he will not get away. You'll help us find him. You're the only man in the Territory who can catch him."

"I will not do it. He's my friend."

"He killed your brother-in-law. It's your duty. I have orders that make you a deputy marshal. I can administer the oath. If you refuse, it will mean that every white man in the new land will shun you. And I can arrest you for neglect of duty. It is the government's privilege to conscript any citizen in time of emergency."

Sam ordered drinks for the officer and his men. Anestasie dressed and came to the room. Sam paced the floor for several minutes, thinking rapidly. "It's an unpleasant duty, but I will do it."

Within an hour he was on the trail, riding west, but across the Halfway River he turned north, circled, and reached the grave of Ta-lo-wah the next afternoon. Tishomingo's old lodge was still there and Sam made himself comfortable and took up his vigil. He was cooking food, enough for two, when Tishomingo entered the lodge and stood by the door.

"Supper will be ready in a minute, Chock," Sam welcomed him.

"You're still the fox," Tishomingo laughed. "I knew someone was here. At first I was frightened, but then I realized it must be you."

"Ay, I knew my friend wouldn't go away without taking the bones of his beloved. You're still an Indian,

Chock. I knew you'd come back here. I've been ordered to arrest you."

Tishomingo accepted some of the food that Sam had cooked, but before he ate he said calmly, "I will not be arrested."

Sam cut a piece of meat with his knife. "You talk like a child. I'm not going to arrest you. The only reason I took those damned orders was to help you. That soldier who gave me the orders thought I didn't know any better. But my government can't conscript a private citizen in time of peace. A soldier can't make me a United States marshal. But I took the task, because I wanted to get to you before you reached Texas. Texas is too damned big for me to go out there and hunt for you."

"How did you know I was going to Texas?"

"Texas is wild and Texas is a foreign country. But look, Chock, you don't have to go out there. I've found a new land—a greener land." Tishomingo's face lighted. "Tall trees . . . good land. A quiet land."

The sadness seemed to disappear from Tishomingo's eyes. His face was calm, peaceful, and he breathed softly, alert to catch every word.

"Even the birds are friendly." Sam continued, and put his hands on Chock's knees. "The land is warm and lush. And Great God, what trees! They just stand there and look way down at you. Ay, Chock, that's the Promised Land. *This* isn't the Promised Land. This is the land that we sowed in blood and sin and where the harvest was hate. And, too, this land is getting crowded."

"Are you going to the new land?" Tishomingo asked softly.

"Nay," Sam said sadly. "I've taken roots here. I have a family. But you must go there. It's down on the Bogue Homa. I named it myself. There's no settler there. The law will never find you. And you'll still be in the land of your people. You can take the bones of Ta-lo-wah. Texas is far away. The shadow of Nanih Waiya doesn't reach to Texas, but it reaches to the Bogue Homa, for the Bogue Homa is within the ancient domain of your nation. Go there, Chock. And sometimes I can visit with you."

"It sounds like a fine land. . . ."

"Ay, and you'll be safe there. I'll report that you have crossed the river. I'll see the hopaii and tell him to verify my story. The white people will believe him."

Tishomingo walked to the door of his lodge and stared out into the night, first toward the trees under which Ta-lo-wah and Ab slept, then in the direction of the great Sacred Mound. He let his hands drop to his sides, tilted his head, stared into the heavens and prayed softly. "O Nanih Waiya, your top is above the trees and your black shadow lies upon the ground. Forgive me my transgressions. Send your spirit with me as I go away from your protective shadows."

He lowered his head to his chest and stood quiet for a moment, his eyes closed. Then he turned to Sam and said simply, "I will leave tonight for the Bogue Homa. Bring Hoab to see me sometimes. Let me teach him some of the ways of my people. I will always be in your debt."

"I'm only repaying my debts to you. And now I want to ask you one question. Please tell me the truth. What of my sister?"

"She had naught to do with Flournoy's death." It was an easy lie. "I asked her to go away with me, but she wouldn't give up *Malmaison*. I'm glad, Big Sam. I had wandered far from the paths of my people. I was becoming a white man. I'm glad that she made her choice. Now

I can take the bones of Ta-lo-wah and go away as a Choctaw mingo should."

"What of Jasper?" Sam asked. "I had hoped you would give him back to me."

"I do."

Sam held the torch while Tishomingo dug into Ta-lo-wah's grave. The torch attracted the night things and they crept into the shadows, but none cried out. Even the catamounts were still, and the owls. Only the wind moaned, murmuring sadly to the trees and the trees nodded in understanding.

Tishomingo found the bones of Ta-lo-wah and wrapped them in a deerskin and tied the skin to his saddle.

"What of Ab?" Sam whispered.

"I will not take him away. I'll leave him here so his spirit can guard this place."

"I am glad. I'll have a stone fetched here for his grave."

Tishomingo embraced his friend and rode slowly away. Sam saw the night swallow him up, then he filled the grave and stomped the earth. He went into the lodge and put out the fire and destroyed all evidence of having been there. There was a great loneliness in his heart, but when he thought of Anestasie and Hoab, the loneliness was gone.

35

* *

ANESTASIE ran down the path to meet Sam when he returned to Locha Poka and told him that Dabby was there. There were tears in Anestasie's eyes. "She's just a girl, Sam. Please do not deal harshly with her."

Sam patted his wife's cheek and strode up to the house. Dabby was standing beside Hoab. She wore a dress of calicut and her lips trembled when she saw him. She smelled like the Dabby he had known before she had gone to Flournoy—sweaty and animalish. It was a good smell to Sam, a clean rough smell. There was no lily of the valley about Dabby. She hesitated until Hoab gave her a gentle push, and then she walked slowly to Sam and bowed her head. Sam smiled at her. "Hold up your head, Dabby." He examined the pock marks. "I have some oil that will help those. Have you had food? Good. Then go to the kitchen and I'll have the oil sent to you."

The negro half-breed fell at his feet and gripped his knees. "Massa Flournoy is dead."

Sam reached down and took her arm and lifted her to her feet. "I know he's dead. You may stay with us if you want to. You're a free woman, but you'll be a servant in this household. Flournoy was a fool to set you free. There's no place in this land for a free Negress. There never will be. You're too good for your own people and not good enough for mine. God has punished you enough. It's not for me to add to that punishment. You're welcome here and you'll never want."

Anestasie was very proud of Sam. She told him so as she helped him pack his saddle bag in preparation for his trip to *Malmaison*. Dabby helped, too, and finally mustered enough courage to say, "Massa Sam, I've got some things for the slaves at Massa Flournoy's place. Please take them. The slaves were good to me. And make Miss Honoria buy a tombstone for Massa Flournoy. The Choctaws buried him, but he needs a tombstone."

Sam nodded, then frowned as he heard a horse clatter up the front path. He hurried to the door and stood speechless. It was Honoria. She leaped from the saddle and ran into the room, shrieking as she ran. She raised her riding crop when she saw Dabby and the Negress screamed, and cowered beside Sam. Jasper, without a word, snatched the whip from Honoria's hand. It was a bold, impudent thing to do. Anestasie stood at Hoab's side and Hoab put his arm around her to protect her. Sam pushed Dabby behind him and faced his sister, waiting for her to speak. Honoria's hair was disheveled and her eyes were not pleasant to look at. She glanced at all the faces in the room and then took a deep breath to control her fury.

"You let him go!" Her voice was almost a purr. "You helped him get away! You knew he was mine!"

Sam suddenly thought of a catamount he once had cornered. Honoria seemed almost ready to spring on him. Sam's voice was bitter and cutting. "He never was yours. And he didn't need any help to get away! He wanted to go, just to be away from you."

Hoab patted Anestasie's shoulder. Dabby crouched

behind Sam. Jasper folded his arms and stood by the door.

Honoria took two steps toward her brother. Her eyes were blazing. "You didn't try to stop him! You knew he was going to Texas, and you could have caught him. I could have saved him. But you didn't want me to have him!"

Sam spoke slowly. He wanted each word to sear its way into Honoria's brain. "If I had ever thought he would go to you, I would have killed him."

Honoria no longer made any attempt to control her rage. "You mealy-mouthed fool! You disgraced me. You weren't satisfied with sheltering that pock-marked wench who bore my husband a bastard, were you? You had to marry a mad woman, a woman who tried to take my husband, a damned French harlot ——"

She sprang at Sam and clawed his face, spitting and kicking at him. Dabby screamed and fled to a corner of the room. Anestasie tried to go to Sam's side, but Hoab restrained her.

Sam stood very still while his sister clawed and scratched and spat. A look of disgust spread slowly over his face and then the expression was gone, and cold fury took its place. He tossed back his head and gripped both of Honoria's hands in his left hand and slapped her. She reeled across the room, but Sam caught her before she fell and slapped her again. Hoab cried out for Sam to stop, but Sam ignored him. Anestasie screamed and clutched her husband's arm, but he shook her off.

Honoria did not cry, but lashed out at her brother. She snatched a candlestick and hurled it at him. It opened a small gash in his head. He held her with one hand and beat her with his open palm until she fell prostrate upon the floor and lay there whimpering in pain and anger.

810

Sam stared down at her, then looked around wildly at his family. Hoab ran to him, stepping over Honoria's inert body, and wiped the blood from Sam's face. Anestasie looked at the wound and when she realized it was not serious, she stooped and lifted Honoria to a chair. "You shouldn't strike a woman, Sam," she said, but there was no reproach in her voice.

"I'm sorry that I lost my temper in front of you, Anestasie," Sam whispered. He wiped Honoria's mouth where the blood trickled from his blows. She opened her eyes. "Now get out of my house, Honoria!"

"*Your* house!" Honoria laughed hysterically. "This is *my* house!" She lashed the words at Sam. "But I won't throw you out. You may always stay here—you and that woman and even Dabby. You should all get along well together. You can even pretend that it's your house. I'll never come this way again, but every time you see this house, you'll remember that it's yours only because I let you have it." She laughed at him again. She knew Sam's pride. She would crush his pride.

Sam's face was ashen white. "Your goodness overwhelms us, Honoria. But I won't give you the joy of salving your conscience with such a gesture. I can pay my debt here and now. Anestasie has given me her property. I have some money. The property and money are enough to satisfy your claim against me."

Honoria laughed coldly. "I don't want the Duportail property. And even if you had the cash, it wouldn't do you any good. Your last interest payment is more than a week overdue. You were too busy getting married to remember the interest date, and the title to Locha Poka has already reverted to me as the widow of Lake Flournoy."

No one said a word, but all eyes were fastened upon

Sam. His shoulders sagged and his eyes clouded. He started to speak, to ask her to reconsider, even to beg her not to let her hatred spoil her judgment. But his tongue was tied. Beg Honoria for mercy? He would rather enlist as a scout in Texas, or bound out Hoab and Shellie. He would rather leave Locha Poka to its ghost and go away. He turned his back on his sister and walked to a window and stared out at his ferry and his factory and his land. He looked at the trees down by the river. They once had seemed such big, friendly trees. But now they were small trees. There were big trees on the Bogue Homa. Tishomingo was there. O Locha Poka—the place for many to rest. But there had never been any rest here. He squared his shoulders and turned and smiled at Anestasie. "I suddenly am weary of this land. Let's go away. To Texas. It's a big land."

Anestasie uttered a cry of delight and ran to him, laughing. She threw her arms around him. "Will you do that, Sam? I want to so badly. I want to go away where we can build our own home. This is Donna's."

Honoria watched the scene, mockery in her eyes. Old Jasper walked to his master and said humbly, "Le's go, Massa Sam. There's a heap we ain't seen. This land is wore out. So is old Jasper."

Sam stroked Anestasie's head and his heart danced. He forgot momentarily that Honoria was there. . . . The Promised Land. He would go to the Promised Land. "I've really been thinking about it for several months. I thought I couldn't pull up and move away. But why can't I? I'm in my prime. We can lease your property, Anestasie. Frome will want it. We'll let him build the road to Georgia. It was his dream, too, you know."

Honoria laughed. "Go away and starve?" she jeered them. "You're no fool, Sam'l. You're middle-aged. You can't go away and begin again. It'll take money ——"

"We're not going to Texas. We're going to a new land down on the Bogue Homa. I said Texas to fool Honoria. This is the *real* Promised Land we're going to. Tishomingo's already there."

She laughed gayly, proudly. "The Promised Land is always the land on the other side of the river. When you're an old man, Sam, you'll still be seeking the real Locha Poka, the real Promised Land, the real place of rest. And I'll be with you."

Shellie and Dabby rode with Anestasie. Hoab walked before the mules. Jasper walked beside them. Sam followed in the rear, tasting the dust and breathing the odors of his mules, of his wagon. He rested his long rifle-gun in the crook of his left arm, cracked his bull whip over the heads of the mules and they moved away toward the Promised Land.

Hoab's clear voice floated back to him. The boy was singing "Lord Lovel." He heard Anestasie, Shellie, Jasper and Dabby join in, and he sang, too:

"He rode and he rode on his milk white steed,
  'Til he reached fair London town,
  And there he heard St. Varney's bell
  And the people all mourning around."

Sam tossed his head and felt his mane fall on his shoulders. He tilted his head and sniffed the air. There was no smell of dust, only the smell of green trees and black earth. . . .

They crossed the river and Sam could no longer see Locha Poka. Then he remembered. He instructed Hoab to halt the caravan and turned and hurried back to the big house, running easily as he went, running as an

Indian runs. He went to the Big Tree and dug under the headstone and got the conch shell. Then he ran back to his caravan, pausing before he reached it, to catch his breath.

He waved a greeting to Hoab and Anestasie and shouted for them to move on. Around the bend, at the base of the ridge, he made camp. The ridge was between his family and Locha Poka. Sam picked the spot carefully so they could not see Locha Poka, but must look ahead toward the Promised Land.